Introductio

Remember Me by Kimberley Com[...]
North suffers an injury, loses his memory, and believes he is a Scottish pastor. Helen hopes he just might fall in love with her, if he isn't bound by his social standings as a duke.

Shirley, Goodness, and Mercy by Kristy Dykes
Shirley feels like she's never known anything of life beyond her little country church. She wants more out life. Then she meets Forrest Townsend, the new parson—who just might change her mind.

Miss Bliss and the Bear by Darlene Franklin
Annie knits hats and mittens for soldiers. But chaplain Jeremiah Arnold isn't sure he wants a woman hanging around the fort—even one as beautiful and well meaning as Miss Bliss. . . .

A Bride for the Preacher by Sally Laity
It's Emma's dream to doctor the needy, and she hopes there might be a place for her in new territory out west. She isn't interested in marriage—until she nurses a certain preacher's fever.

Renegade Husband by DiAnn Mills
Audra moves to frontier Colorado to marry the local pastor and is assured a life of adventure. She never realizes how much adventure until her stagecoach is robbed and her future husband seems to be the culprit. . . .

Silence in the Sage by Colleen L. Reece
Ever dutiful and just, Reverend Gideon Scott takes a bride in name only. But soon the reverend abandons both family and church in search of truth that will clear his tarnished name.

Six Old-Fashioned Romances
Built on Faith and Love

The
Preacher's
BRIDE
COLLECTION

DiAnn Mills, Colleen L. Reece,
Kimberley Comeaux, Kristy Dykes,
Darlene Franklin, Sally Laity

BARBOUR BOOKS
An Imprint of Barbour Publishing, Inc.

Remember Me © 2005 by Kimberley Comeaux
Shirley, Goodness, and Mercy © 2003 by Kristy Dykes
Miss Bliss and the Bear © 2013 by Darlene Franklin
A Bride for the Preacher © 2003 by Sally Laity
Renegade Husband © 2005 by DiAnn Mills
Silence in the Sage © 2004 by Colleen L. Reece

Print ISBN 978-1-68322-881-3

eBook Editions:
Adobe Digital Edition (.epub) 978-1-64352-121-3
Kindle and MobiPocket Edition (.prc) 978-1-64352-122-0

All rights reserved. No part of this publication may be reproduced or transmitted for commercial purposes, except for brief quotations in printed reviews, without written permission of the publisher.

Scripture quotations marked KJV are taken from the King James Version of the Bible.

This book is a work of fiction. Names, characters, places, and incidents are either products of the author's imagination or used fictitiously. Any similarity to actual people, organizations, and/or events is purely coincidental.

Published by Barbour Books, an imprint of Barbour Publishing, Inc., 1810 Barbour Drive, Uhrichsville, Ohio 44683, www.barbourbooks.com

Our mission is to inspire the world with the life-changing message of the Bible.

ECPA Member of the
Evangelical Christian
Publishers Association

Printed in the United States of America.

Contents

Remember Me

by Kimberley Comeaux

Dedication

To Josie Delonie Kennedy, my grandmother. And special thanks
to Julie Rice and Melissa Alphonso for coming to my
rescue and helping me with this project.

Chapter 1

1815

Trevor "North" Kent, the Duke of Northingshire, breathed in the fresh sea air as he relaxed against the smooth railing of the ship that was carrying him to America. His blond, wavy hair, which he'd allowed to grow longer during the voyage, was blowing about his face, tickling his nose as he focused on enjoying his last day aboard ship. They would be pulling into port in the morning; and although the voyage had been a long one, it had been one of much-needed peace and relaxation, something North hadn't even realized he required until he was away from England.

For four years, he'd been planning to make the trip, where he was to join his cousins on the sugar plantation that he'd invested in with them. But because of the war with England, travel had been made impossible. Then there had been a personal matter that had caused him to want to reschedule his trip, also, but it had since been settled to his satisfaction.

The delay had also let him go to the aid of his two best friends: Nicholas, the Earl of Kenswick, and his brother, Lord Thomas Thornton.

The two brothers had been through war, the death of their father, a shipwreck, and, through all that, raising Thomas's motherless son. North had been there for both of them, giving them advice or just being a friend when they needed it. But now both of them were happily married to two wonderful women, and North was glad to leave the men in their capable hands.

All North wanted was to spend time on the plantation and be free from any-one's problems, except maybe his own. His two cousins were married and hope-fully didn't need his advice or support with anything dealing with the state of one's mind or happiness.

Now his own happiness was another kettle of fish altogether, and North had high hopes that he, too, would be able to find love and happiness in his future.

But at the moment, his only concern was how he was to travel and find the plantation, which was located some forty-five miles southwest of New Orleans. He'd sent a message to his cousins telling them of his impending arrival, but the captain had told him that because of the war, mail was slow. It had to be routed through ships going to other countries since there was no travel directly from England. His own journey had been made longer when he'd had to travel to France to board one of their ships.

"The captain has just informed me a storm is headed our way." A Scottish-accented voice spoke beside him, stirring North from his thoughts.

North turned to Hamish Campbell, the minister who was traveling to Louisiana to be the new pastor of a church there. They'd become friends during the long voyage, and North wondered at the troubled look in the older man's eyes. "Well, it is too early in the season to be a hurricane, so I would imagine that it'll pass over us quickly. We are very close to the port, so I don't think there is cause for too much worry," North tried to assure him.

Hamish gripped the railing in front of him as though it were a lifeline. "I know you might think me daft for saying this, but I'm not sure I'll make it to Louisiana."

North stifled a sigh as he felt the need to comfort yet another friend. He knew God was the compelling force in his life that urged him to reach out to people, but he sent up a quick prayer that the Almighty would see fit to give him a little break during his stay in Louisiana.

"Hamish, my dear fellow, these ships are built to withstand storms. Are you sure you are not just experiencing a case of nerves about your new post?"

"Not at all," Hamish insisted as he reached into his plain, brown coat and pulled out a small, worn Bible. He held it against the rail in both hands, his thumbs stroking the leather cover reverently. "It's. . .it's more of a feeling, I suppose. I've been sensing for some time that my time on earth is almost at an end."

Hamish's words put a chill in North's heart as he struggled to understand. "You are not so old that you will soon die," North reasoned. "And, too, why would God send you all the way over here if He did not mean for you to become the pastor of the church at Golden Bay?"

Hamish didn't answer for a moment. The slightly balding man, who was near North's size and height, just stared off into the now choppy sea as if contemplating his next words. Finally he muttered something that North couldn't decipher and turned to him, his eyes serious. "I think it has something to do with you."

North raised a dark blond brow. "I beg your pardon?"

Hamish nodded his head. "Yes, that must be it! I have felt compelled to befriend you ever since I boarded the ship." He held up his Bible in a strange moment of contemplation and then thrust it toward North, hitting him in the chest. "Take it, please!"

North's hand automatically caught the Bible, but he immediately tried to give it back to Hamish. "What do you mean, 'Take it'? Will you not need this to construct your sermons and what have you?"

Hamish ignored North's attempt to return the small book and turned back toward the railing. "I will not be needing it, I fear. I beg you to take it and—"

Hamish's plea was interrupted when one of the ship's crew ran over to them and gave a brief nod to North. "Your grace! The captain's askin' all to clear the deck." He pointed out to the increasingly rough waters. "We're lookin' at some rough weather ahead. You could be washed overboard."

North agreed with the young sailor, but when he motioned for Hamish to begin walking toward their cabins, his friend shook his head and pointed to one of the chairs a few feet away from them. "I must retrieve my spectacles. I left them lying on the chair," he insisted as he began to head toward the chair and away from shelter.

The wind was picking up, and North could hear large waves hitting against the ship's hull. It seemed as though the noonday sky had gone from sunny to almost dark in just a matter of minutes. North knew he could not leave Hamish alone, so he tucked the Bible inside his coat and began to walk quickly to him, although the swaying of the ship was making the task very difficult. The ship jolted sharply, and Hamish stumbled and then fell. North was able to grab hold of a deck chair and steady himself before moving to where his friend had fallen.

"Are you all right?" he called loudly over the wind.

Hamish nodded as North helped him stand back up. "I didn't realize the weather could change so fast," he commented as they again steadied themselves against the swaying deck.

North focused on getting them to the chair to retrieve the small wire-framed spectacles. Once they were finally in Hamish's possession, North led him to the railing. "Use the railing to steady yourself and follow me," he yelled as he looked back to make sure the older man was holding on. Together they began the trek back to their cabin.

A large wave slapped hard against the ship, spraying them both with water. North found it hard to hold on with the chilling wetness making both the railing and the deck slippery. Finally, they were mere steps away from the door that led to their cabins. North glanced back to see how Hamish was faring, but his attention was caught by the vast wave that was several feet above the ship and heading straight toward them.

He tried to yell for Hamish to hold on, but there was no time. The water hit both men with more force than either could withstand. As the water swept over the ship, North could feel his body being picked up. Panicked, he tried to keep his head above the water while at the same time looking for his friend. But then pain exploded in the back of North's head. Though he tried to fight unconsciousness, the pain was too great.

His last thought was a prayer that Hamish had somehow managed to keep from being washed overboard.

⌒

Two Weeks Later in Golden Bay, Louisiana

The large and rather bored-looking alligator barely glanced in Helen's direction, despite her yelling and waving a broom about like a madwoman to shoo him away from the house. After about five minutes of this, Helen finally gave up; plopped herself down on the grass, not even giving a care of her dress as she would have months ago; and glared at the huge reptilian beast.

Before coming to America three months earlier, Helen Nichols had not even heard of an alligator, much less thought that she might stand so close to one.

No, Helen, a gentleman farmer's daughter, had been gently brought up in her native England with no more cares than what pretty ribbon she'd wear for the day. It had sounded like such a grand adventure when Claudia Baumgartner, granddaughter and heir to the Marquis of Moreland, approached her with the offer of paid companion to her little sister, Josie, in America. Claudia had explained her parents wanted an English girl to provide not only companionship to the lonely girl who lived on her parents' plantation, but also to instruct her in the proper ways of a lady.

But adventure was not the only thing that compelled Helen to leave her family and friends behind. It was the same reason she ventured often to her best friend Christina's home when she heard a certain person had arrived. It was the reason she allowed Christina, who was also the Countess of Kenswick, to provide her a whole new wardrobe for the London season, even though she was mostly snubbed by those who were of much higher class. It was the first thing she thought of in the morning and what she dreamed of at night.

Helen Nichols was in love with North, the Duke of Northingshire.

And the duke was traveling to America, just twenty or so miles from where she was living in Golden Bay.

Helen knew it was foolish to believe that she would even see North while he was staying at his plantation. Yet she knew the Baumgartners, her employers, were acquainted with North's relatives and held out a small hope they would at some point socialize with one another.

She didn't even know if North had arrived in Louisiana. So day after day, she'd kept a keen ear out to hear any news about the Kent plantation. So far, though, she'd heard nothing.

"What are you doing?" a young voice sounded behind her. Josie Baumgartner, Helen's precocious thirteen-year-old charge, skipped around and plopped down in front of her. With wildly curly brown hair, freckles, and a mischievous gleam constantly glowing in her hazel eyes, Josie looked just like the wild child that she was. In fact, Helen despaired ever turning the young girl into anything remotely resembling a proper lady. She liked to ride astride horses, fish while wading in the swamp, and climb trees. Those were the semi-normal things she did. The other activities consisted of playing practical jokes, collecting every creepy-crawly thing she could find, and voicing her opinion about every subject her father and mother would bring up at the dinner table, usually expressing an opposing view.

But despite her incorrigible behavior that would likely leave most of English society agog, she was an extremely likeable girl with a personality that made it hard to reprimand or be angry with her for long.

Helen sighed as she answered Josie's question. "I am trying to get this big lizard to move away from the front door so I can go into the house." She pointed at the ugly beast. "But it seems he is determined to ignore my commands."

Josie giggled. "We have five other doors, you know. Why don't you just go through one of those?" she reasoned in her drawn-out American accent.

Helen sniffed. "It's the principle of the thing, my dear. I will not be ruled by a slimy green creature!"

Josie jumped up and crept closer to the alligator, though still at a safe distance. "Did you know they eat small animals? Dorie LeBeau said one ate her cat once."

Helen shivered with disgust. "Well, that's just uncivilized, isn't it?"

Josie turned back to Helen with a look of long-suffering. "You think *everything* is uncivilized if it's not from England."

Helen stood and brushed off the skirt of her gown. "Well, of course I do," she stated matter-of-factly. "We're the most civilized people in the world!" She had a brief recollection of Christina and her running about the countryside with dirty dresses and faces. They were forever rolling about with puppies and kittens and trespassing on others' property to climb their trees. Not a very civilized way to behave for a couple of young ladies.

Helen wisely kept the memory to herself.

"Well, we can go get Sam to come over here and kill it. They make for pretty good eating, you know," Josie said, interrupting Helen's thoughts. Sam Youngblood was a Choctaw Indian who lived on property adjoining the plantation. He also fancied himself in love with Helen and was forever trying to barter horses or cows with Mr. Baumgartner for her. He said it was the Choctaw way.

Helen told him the practice of bartering for a woman was just plain barbaric!

Helen shivered again as she got back to Josie's comment. "*Ladies* do not *eat*—"

"I know, I know," Josie interjected. "Ladies do not eat *anything* that *crawls* around on its belly. It's *quite* uncivilized!" she mocked, using Helen's higher-pitched English accent.

"Scoff if you must, but you will do well to—"

"Miss Helen! Miss Josie!" a male voice called out from behind them. They turned to see George, the Baumgartners' house servant who usually ran their errands in town, running up the dusty drive.

Though the Baumgartners owned many slaves to run the vast plantation that consisted of thousands of acres, a sugar mill, the slave and servant quarters, not to mention the huge three-story white mansion, they had freed many of those who worked in the house and the higher-ranking field hands. The Baumgartners were good people who treated every worker and slave fairly, but Helen secretly felt the whole slave system was unjust and inhumane.

"What is it, George?" Josie asked as he stopped before them and tried to catch his breath.

"The preacher. . ." His voice cracked as he took another deep breath. "They found him. He ain't dead like they thought."

Helen and Josie exchanged a disbelieving look. "You mean he did not drown as we were all told?" Helen attempted to comprehend. Just over a week ago, the people of Golden Bay had been informed that the preacher for whom they'd been waiting had fallen overboard with another man and had drowned. The Baumgartners, LeBeaus, and Whitakers were all distressed and saddened, since it was these neighboring families who had gotten together to build a church and then pay for his voyage from Scotland.

If this news were true, they wouldn't have to go to the trouble of searching for another minister!

"A couple of fishermen fished him out of the gulf and took 'im back to they cabins 'bout thirty or so miles from here," George explained. "They sez that he didn't wake up fer about fo' days, but they found a Bible on him that had his name on it. They sez he didn't know who he was when he finally woke up, but after they told 'im his name and that he was a preacher headed for our town, he seemed to remember."

Josie clasped her hands together. "Why, that sounds like a bona fide miracle!" she exclaimed. "Is he in town? Can we go see him?"

"Yes'm, Miss Josie, you sho' can. That's why I ran back lickety-split." He ran the back of his sleeve across his beaded brow. "They's wantin' the mastah to come out and give 'im a proper welcome with any food or house gifts to help 'im get settled."

"Oh, this is exciting, isn't it?" Helen whispered eagerly as she looked from George to Josie. "It will be so refreshing going to a proper service again instead of waiting for the circuit preacher to pass by. It will be just like it was in—"

"England! We know, we know," Josie finished for her with exasperation. "Let's just hurry up and tell my parents so we can meet him!"

It didn't take long for the family to assemble the goods they had set aside for the new preacher and to load their wagon and carriage. Ten or so minutes later, they pulled into the small town that consisted of the blacksmith, a general store, and the newly built church. The town was actually owned by three plantations, unlike many others along the river that were self-contained. The three families signed an agreement that they would share the profits from the businesses as well as the labor to keep them running.

There was already a small crowd in the tiny yard of the church, with its small parsonage on the side. Mr. and Mrs. Baumgartner stepped out of the carriage first, followed by Josie and Helen.

As they drew nearer, Josie walked on her tiptoes, trying to see over everyone's heads. Helen, herself, tried to see around them but could only see the top of a man's head. In fact, the hair was such a pretty golden blond, a person couldn't help but notice through all of the dark heads gathered around him.

Helen was finally close enough to see better, and as the crowd parted, she was disappointed to see the man's back was turned as he spoke with Mr. Baumgartner. She studied his longish, wavy hair then the width of his broad shoulders for a moment. He seemed almost familiar to Helen, as if she had met the gentleman before, yet she was sure she had never heard of a Hamish Campbell until she had arrived in Louisiana.

"Oh, I wish Papa would turn him around so we could see him! I had imagined he would be an older man, but he appears to be younger than I thought," Josie whispered as their neighbors chatted excitedly around them.

"Indeed," Helen murmured as she tried to inch her way closer to him. She noticed he was quite tall. Though they seemed to be a little ragged and faded, his clothes were very well made, cut like those worn by the nobility.

When she finally was able to hear him speak, Helen suddenly realized who the preacher reminded her of.

He was the same height and build and sounded just like. . .North, the Duke of Northingshire.

Helen briefly rubbed her brow, thinking that of course she must be mistaken and perhaps had been in the sun too long. The preacher was supposed to be a Scottishman, and the accent she thought she heard was clearly a cultured English one.

"Ah! Here are my wife and daughter," Mr. Baumgartner said, motioning toward Helen's direction. "Let me introduce you."

As she began to turn, Josie bumped her as she scrambled to go to her father, and then Mrs. Baumgartner stepped in front of her, again blocking her view. She heard the man speak to her employer and daughter and again was struck by his rich voice.

I just miss North. I am clearly hallucina—

"And this is Josie's companion, Miss Helen Nichols, who has come from England and been with us for two months now," she heard Mrs. Baumgartner say as she stepped back. For the first time, Helen got a view of the tall man's face.

For a moment Helen said nothing, frozen by the sheer shock of seeing the man before her.

It *was* North!

And he was smiling pleasantly at her without so much as a gleam of recognition shining in his light blue gaze.

"Pleased to make your acquaintance, Miss Nichols," he responded smoothly with a nod.

Helen was horrified that he did not recognize her. She had spent many hours in his presence in the past and thought it humiliating that she didn't seem familiar to him at all. But then she had a second thought: Why was he pretending to be a preacher?

Confused, she found herself blurting, "North? Do you not remember me?"

Chapter 2

An immediate hush fell over the group as every eye turned to stare at Helen, including North. Helen focused only on him as she watched the strange expressions move across his handsome, strong face.

At first he appeared to be afraid, but then it went to what looked like confusion, and then it was as though a mask fell across his face, shielding her from his thoughts entirely. He seemed to compose himself as he nervously glanced around the group and then turned his gaze back to Helen.

His eyes were unreadable as he smiled at her and finally responded. "Of course I do. It's just. . .I suppose it has been quite awhile, hasn't it?" Helen wasn't sure if he was telling or asking. Neither would make a bit of sense to Helen since she'd only seen him four months ago. "It is good to have a friend nearby," he finished cryptically, perplexing her even more.

She was about to ask him what he was doing here, but he turned from her suddenly, stopping any further communication between them.

Doubts assailed her as she thought maybe the man wasn't North after all. Perhaps he had a cousin that looked like him.

But then, she amended her thoughts, why did he pretend to know her?

Oh, it was very vexing on her nerves to reason his behavior all out in her mind.

"You know him?" Josie exclaimed, startling Helen back to the present. "Why didn't you tell us you knew the preacher?"

Helen shook her head absently as her eyes stayed on who she was sure was the Duke of Northingshire. "I didn't know his Christian name. I've always called him North," she lied, since she knew very well that his name was Trevor Kent and certainly *not* Hamish Campbell!

Josie frowned. "You addressed a preacher by calling him North? That's strange and not at all the civilized thing for a lady to do." She paused for effect. "According to you."

Helen licked her lips nervously as she tried to answer without too much lying involved. "I knew him when he wasn't a minister." She finally dragged her eyes away from the confusing man and tried to appear nonchalant. "I don't suppose I knew him as well as I thought." That was an understatement!

"Well, you shall have plenty of time to get to know him in the future," Josie reasoned as she took Helen's hand and pulled her toward the nice lawn beside the church. "Let's sit over there and wait for my parents."

Helen agreed and allowed Josie to pull her to the white wooden benches, which were placed under a great oak shade tree.

As soon as they sat down, Josie immediately brought their conversation back to the preacher. "Don't you think he is the most handsome man you've ever seen?

And to think you know him!" she expressed in a lovelorn tone. She sat up and looked at Helen as if she were suddenly hit with an idea. "He is unmarried, and you are unmarried! You would make a great match!"

If only it could be so, Helen thought longingly. But until she figured out why North was pretending to be someone else, she could not even wish for it. "Josie, he did not even recognize me. How could you think he would want to marry a lady that has made no lasting impression in his mind?" She sighed. "Besides, I am here to work and teach you to be a lady. Wishing that I would fall in love with North just so you will not have to learn your lessons on etiquette will only bring you a headache."

Josie sat back on the bench and groaned. "Why does being a lady seem so *boring*?"

Helen hid a grin. "One day when you become interested in a young man, he'll expect you to act like a lady and then you will thank God I bored you so!"

"I will never be interested in boys!" she declared.

"That is too bad, for I have a feeling you will grow up to be quite a lovely woman one day," a man's voice spoke beside them.

Startled, Helen turned and looked up to find North standing over her. "North!" she exclaimed automatically but then quickly amended, "I'm sorry. I mean *Reverend*."

He seemed preoccupied as he presented her a small smile. North quickly stepped closer, whispering in an urgent voice, "I must speak to you alone, Miss Nichols." He nervously glanced around as if to see if anyone was watching him and then looked briefly at Josie. "There is some very important information I need, and I'm positive that only you can help me."

Helen felt butterflies of excitement fluttering about in her chest, just as she always did when North spoke to her. It didn't matter if he was acting like the craziest man alive or that he was pretending to be a minister, which Helen imagined was a big faux pas in God's book! All that mattered was North, the love of her life, had asked to talk to her. Alone!

She jumped up with more enthusiasm than was warranted, for she startled both Josie and North. "Of course, you can speak with me!" she said brightly as she reached down to pull Josie up from the bench. "Please be a dear and excuse us, will you, Josie?" she threw to her charge without so much as a glance and then latched her arm around North's elbow. "Let's walk, shall we?"

North looked a little dazed but gave her a tentative smile. "Not too far. I would not want to bring suspicion on your character or mine. I may not remember much, but I do know that talking alone with a young woman out in the open public is considered a social blunder if she is not accompanied by a chaperone."

Helen stopped suddenly upon hearing his words, let go of his arm, and turned to stand in front of him. "Did you just say that you might not remember much?" She shook her head. "What does that mean?"

North stood there, staring down at her, looking more handsome than ever before. His countenance, however, was not the easy-going and self-assured gentleman she'd known in England. Instead he looked tired, confused, and not at all the confident man he should be.

He took a deep breath as he stared off to his left for a moment then slowly brought his gaze back to her. "I do not remember who I am." Helen gasped, but North held out his hand so that he might continue. "I apparently fell off the ship that I had been on during a storm. Two fishermen dragged me out of the water and brought me to shore, where I finally came to my senses. But that is where every one of my memories begins. I wouldn't even know my name except I had a Bible inside my coat that had the name Hamish Campbell etched into the leather."

Helen could not even speak for being so dumbfounded by his story. She had never heard of a person forgetting his own name and past. "So you don't remember anything? Not your family, friends, or any sort of past memory?"

He shook his head as he walked past her to lean against the oak.

"And no one knows you've lost your memory?" she asked as she walked over to him.

"No, I didn't want to make everyone think I'd lost my mind or had become crazed." He took a minute to rub the back of his head then continued. "To tell you the truth, when the fisherman that I was staying with finally told me he'd found out where I was heading and that I was to be the vicar of a church in Louisiana, I felt even more confused. I pretended, however, that I suddenly remembered." He looked back to Helen. "That is why I am so anxious to talk to you. You know who I am. You and you alone can tell me about myself, what kind of family background I have or anything that might possibly help me to remember. . .*something*!" His eyes bore into hers as if he were trying to read her thoughts. "You can also confirm I am indeed who they say I am or if it is some sort of mistake." He paused and seemed to try to calm himself with a deep breath. "Helen, am I the Reverend Hamish Campbell?"

Helen opened her mouth to inform him that he definitely was *not* the good reverend but stopped before any words could escape. A thought suddenly seized her—a truly wicked thought.

If North knew he was a duke, a nobleman, sixth in line to the throne of England, then Helen could never hope to win his affections for he would be socially far above her station.

But as a reverend. . .

Oh, surely she could not consider it, much less go through with such a deed! But she could not help it. If North believed he was a reverend, then he would be in the same class as she. The barrier of position and means would no longer be an obstacle, and the brotherly affection North always showed toward her could change into something more if he believed he was Hamish Campbell.

"Miss Nichols? Were you indeed telling the truth when you said you knew me? You suddenly seem confused about. . ."

"You are!" she blurted out before she could think twice about it. "I. . .I mean. . .you are. . .the reverend. . .Hamish Campbell," she stammered as she began to already feel the weight of the lie she had just told.

He let out a breath as he ran a hand through his shimmering blond curls. "I was hoping. . ." He paused and began again. "I don't know what I was hoping. It's just that I do not feel like a Hamish Campbell. I cannot imagine choosing to be a vicar, either. I do have a sense I am a follower of God and have attended church in my past, but. . .being a vicar does not seem to. . .*fit!*" He threw his hand in the air with frustration.

If he only knew! Helen thought guiltily. "What sort of man did you imagine yourself to be?"

North seemed to think a minute before he answered. "I really don't know, except I look at my clothes, and though they are faded and worn from being wet and then dried in the sun, I somehow know they are very finely made and that the fabrics are not something a poor man would wear." He held up his long, lean hands. "I look at my palms and see no evidence of calluses from hard work."

"Perhaps you spent your time in studying and contemplation," Helen inserted.

"I suppose you could be right, but it doesn't explain the clothes."

All the lies were making Helen very nervous, and she wasn't finished telling them yet. "Perhaps your family is somewhat wealthy, but as you were the youngest son, you chose the church as your occupation," she improvised.

He raised a dark blond brow. "Perhaps? You mean you don't know?"

"Uh. . ." Helen scrambled to answer him without telling another lie. "We were introduced through a mutual acquaintance and saw each other only a few times after that," she answered truthfully.

His expression fell to a frown. "Then you don't know me well enough to tell me anything significant?"

Helen breathed a sigh of relief, hoping that this revelation would stop his questions. "I am sorry, but no." She looked toward the crowd and noticed the Baumgartners were looking her way. "I'd better go. My employers are about to leave."

She started to walk off, but he stopped her by touching her arm. "Wait! May I ask you one more question?"

Seeing the confusion in his beautiful blue eyes, Helen could not turn down his request. "Of course you may."

"Everyone keeps telling me I have journeyed here from Scotland, yet I clearly do not have a Scottish accent. Do you know anything about this?"

This question she could answer truthfully. "Actually, I do. You were raised in England, but later your family bought an estate in Scotland, and you would spend summers there. I suppose you've moved back there recently." She felt compelled to put her hand over his. "Good-bye, Nor. . .er. . .I mean Reverend. I'm sorry I was not more helpful."

He gave her a small, preoccupied smile, nodded, then stepped away from her.

Helen took one last look back before she ran to where her employers were waiting for her. As she suspected, they were full of questions.

"You must tell us how you know our new preacher, Helen!" Mrs. Baumgartner ordered immediately as they settled in the carriage. Imogene Baumgartner looked much younger than her forty years. Though she didn't have the style the ladies in England had in the way of clothes or hairstyles, she was always very prettily dressed in her flowered cotton and linen gowns that she so preferred, her dark brown hair knotted low on her neck.

Robert Baumgartner, on the other hand, sat quietly, as he usually did whenever his wife was going on about something, preferring the solitude of his thoughts as he looked out of the carriage window. Helen often wondered if he regretted his choice of marrying the daughter of his father's butler. After all, it caused him to be disinherited from his father and, in turn, to renounce his claim to the title of Marquis of Moreland. Josie had told Helen they'd taken his small inheritance from his mother and moved to America soon after.

It seemed like such a grand love story, and since Helen was also in love with a man above her station, it gave her a small hope her own life could have a happy ending with North by her side.

"Helen, dear?" Mrs. Baumgartner prompted, shaking Helen from her thoughts.

After remembering her employer had asked how she knew North, Helen answered, "I knew him briefly through a friend." She wished Mrs. Baumgartner would take the hint that she did not want to talk about it, but the woman was very persistent when she wanted to know something.

Imogene stared at her as if waiting for more, but when Helen remained silent, she tried again. "He certainly was wearing a very fine suit of clothes to be a poor vicar. I almost had the feeling when studying his bearing and regal pose that he might be a nobleman!" She leaned closer to Helen from across the carriage. "Do you know if he is indeed from a noble family?"

Helen could feel sweat beading on her forehead, and it wasn't just because of the humidity. "I know he is from a wealthy family."

That answer seemed to be enough for Imogene. She leaned back and folded her arms as if pleased with herself. "Of course he is. I am quite good at spotting a gentleman of means." She paused and frowned. "Although he must be quite a younger son and not entitled to the wealth if he has chosen to be a clergyman."

"Must he?" Helen answered, trying desperately not to lie.

"Well, of course he must!" Imogene declared. "But his misfortune is our good luck. I had not looked forward to trying to find another vicar to take his place."

The questions seemed to be at an end as they rode the rest of the way in silence. But Helen's reprieve was only a brief one.

"Helen, it just occurred to me he might be a good match for you!" Imogene exclaimed as they exited the carriage.

Josie piped up, "I had told her the same thing!"

Imogene clasped her hands together as if thrilled with her idea. "You are a gentleman's daughter, Helen, and he is a gentleman! If you married him, you could stay right here in Golden Bay with us. Wouldn't that be just the thing?"

Just thinking about living in the rugged, swampy lands of Louisiana forever made Helen shiver with horror. But on the other hand, if she could spend her life with North by her side. . .perhaps it might not be so bad.

"I barely know him. . . ," she prevaricated, but Imogene was not one to let anything distract her.

"We have all the time in the world for that!" she declared. "Leave it to me, dear, and you shall see yourself wed by fall!"

As Helen followed Imogene and Josie into the house, she wished her employer's words could be true; but if North remembered who he was before he could fall in love with her, her hopes of even being his friend would be permanently dashed.

Chapter 3

The more North learned of his life, the more confused he became. Many days and long hours since he was rescued, he tried to find just the tiniest of memories, just the smallest tidbit to help him feel less lost, less bewildered.

The only information he'd heard that felt as though it belonged to him was when Helen Nichols had called him North. The more he said it to himself, the more the name seemed to fit him, as though he'd finally had one little piece of his missing life back.

But saying it did not bring any more memories or any other sense of familiarity like he hoped and prayed it would. There was nothing in his mind other than a few memories since he'd awakened. The rest was this large, gaping black hole that refused to give up any answers.

Now as he sat in the tiny house the church leaders had shown him to, with its two rooms divided only by a large piece of cloth, he felt more out of his element than ever.

Since he had nothing but his deep-down gut feeling to rely on, North assumed he had never lived in such a small, barren house, nor had he ever known anyone who had. Before they had left him, he'd been shown the barn behind the house, where a cow and a few chickens were kept. He trusted the feeling of dismay that washed over him when they told him that the animals would give him all the milk, eggs, and poultry he could eat.

They actually expected him to *milk* the cow and somehow get eggs out from *under* the chickens. Then, if he actually wanted to *eat* chicken, he would have to *kill* one to have it?

Appalling!

He almost told them so, but when they said that North should be familiar with the animals since he had been raised on a farm, North bit back any retort he had been about to make.

Helen Nichols had left out that little piece of news. If his family had been wealthy, why would he be milking his own cows?

Confusion crowded his mind as he thought about it. Perhaps they'd lost their money, he tried to reason, which is why he never tried to pursue a deeper acquaintance with Helen Nichols.

Oh, yes, those thoughts had run through his mind when she'd informed him they barely knew one another. The very first thing that popped in his head was he must have been a blind fool to let such a beautiful, delightful woman slip in and out of his life so easily.

And she *was* beautiful, with her inky black curls that fell about her rosy cheeks and those dark blue eyes that seemed to look right though him straight to his heart.

When he realized he was contemplating pursuing a woman instead of focusing on his immediate problem, he jumped up from his hard, wooden seat and stomped out of the cottage.

As he breathed in the cooling air that the darkening sky had blown in from the gulf, North strove to find some sort of peace, anything to take the uncertainty from plaguing his heart and mind. Spying the church that was in front of his cottage, he began to walk toward it. The church leaders had told him the building had been used seldom, only when a traveling preacher was in the area.

North thought it looked as lonely as he was, standing there empty with its freshly painted walls and its dark, gleaming windowpanes. Again North tried to look inside himself, to find some sort of connection with the church, to feel the calling he must have had—but he came up empty.

God must surely have some reason for taking away his memory, North tried to rationalize. Perhaps in his forgotten past he needed to learn a valuable lesson, or perhaps someone's life would benefit from his dilemma. Of course, he couldn't think of one thing that would benefit anyone, but he was only a man, and God was all-knowing, so there must be a reason.

Briefly, North reached out and braced both hands on the smoothed planks of the church. "Help me, dear Lord, to remember. If I have been called by You to serve as Your minister, then I want to know that certainty once again. I am frightened by what lies ahead of me, Lord, and I have an idea that I don't feel this way normally. But most of all, dear God, please do not let me fail these people." He stopped as he once again felt the enormity of his situation bearing down on him. "In Jesus' name, amen," he finished quickly and backed away from the church.

He was about to walk back to his cottage when the sound of horse hooves broke the calm silence of the night.

North immediately recognized the two-wheeled, small curricle as being one of excellent quality, though he wished he knew *how* he knew this! Instead of focusing on the frustration that was boiling up within him, he watched as a tall, slim, brown man climbed down from the conveyance and walked toward him. The man was dressed in a black suit with a fluffy white cravat tied at his neck. North noticed there was an air of self-confidence about him in his walk and posture, and he wondered, not for the first time, about the class system within the slave and nonslave community.

"Rev. Campbell," the man's deep voice sounded as he gave him a brief bow. North returned the gesture, and the man continued, "I've been sent by Mr. and Mrs. Baumgartner, sir, of the Golden Bay plantation. They would like to extend to you an invitation to dine with them this evening."

Food! It was the only thing that stood out in North's nutrition-starved mind. He was invited to eat food he wouldn't have to cook, milk, or kill.

⤡

"Oh, this dress is wrong!" Helen wailed as she stood in front of her mirror, critically surveying the light blue taffeta. "The ribbon is wrinkled, and the material just droops in this heat!" She dramatically grabbed two handfuls of hair on either side of her head. "And just look at my hair! It will do nothing but curl! I look like a ragamuffin."

Millie, the young slave woman who served both Helen and Josie, propped her hands on her slim hips and made a *tsk*-ing noise as she shook her head. "Miss Helen, I don't know what's wrong with yo' eyes, honey chil', but there ain't nothin' wrong with that dress or yo' hair." Millie took Helen's arm, pulled her away from the mirror, and directed her to sit at her dressing table. "Now yo' jus' got yo'self all in a lather 'cause o' that young man who's comin' to dinnah, tha's all! Now sit still and let me fix yo' hair up real pretty."

Josie took that particular moment to let herself in the room without so much as a knock. "I knew it! I knew she was sweet on the preacher!" she crowed with delight.

Millie stopped brushing Helen's hair to shake the brush in Josie's direction. "Miss Josie, I done tol' ya and tol' ya. You gonna listen at the wrong do' one day, and it's gonna get yo' in a mess o' trouble!" She pointed the brush to the chair next to Helen. "Now sit yo'self down, and I'll get to yo' hair next."

Josie did as she was told because Millie, slave or no, just had the kind of voice you obeyed. It was then Helen noticed the dress the younger girl was wearing.

"Josie, you can't wear that old dress to dinner!" she blurted with horror.

Josie frowned as she looked down at the plain beige dress made of slightly wrinkled cotton. "What's wrong with it? I've worn this to dinner lots of times, and you've never said anything about it."

Helen took a deep breath to calm her nerves, and then in her best teacher's voice, she instructed, "When guests are dining with your family, you must dress in a more formal manner." She noticed Millie looking for a hairpin and opened her drawer to find one for her. She then continued, "Especially when you have a guest like the d—" She stumbled over the word *duke* and quickly corrected herself. "—er, North."

Josie let out a breath to show her frustration with the whole conversation. "He's just the preacher. It's not like he's the president of the United States."

No. More like the Duke of Northingshire. If Helen's nerves were this frazzled with trying to keep her story straight and not saying the wrong thing, how was it going to be in front of North?

What a mess she'd gotten herself into!

In the end, Josie kept her plain dress on, and with her hair done up "pretty" by Millie, Helen decided, droopy or not, her dress would have to do, also. She noticed as she approached the three adults that the Baumgartners wore their usual casual attire; and when she saw North, she was glad they did.

Of course he would have no other clothes! How silly of her not to remember that all his belongings had not been brought from the ship. And even when they were, would he realize the garments belonged to someone else? Would he remember that his own trunks contained the finest clothes England had to offer and not those of a poor vicar?

She had to remind herself not to get into a mental tizzy as she walked up and greeted him.

"Hello, Reverend," she greeted as she tried to ignore the guilt she felt over calling him that false title. "Are you getting settled in?"

The smile he gave her was lacking in confidence, and his words were those of someone putting on a brave front. . .and failing at it. "Uh, yes, I think so. I'll just need time to adjust to the. . .uh. . .culture change."

The Baumgartners all laughed at that, and though Helen joined them, it was only out of politeness. Since she, too, was still experiencing quite a culture shock, it was difficult to joke about it just yet.

They were all seated in the dining room, which boasted a long table that could easily seat sixteen people. Helen was not accustomed to such extravagance, since her own family manor was of modest means. Neither was she accustomed to all the house servants that worked around the clock to make sure the family had all they needed.

No, she wasn't accustomed to such a lifestyle, but she knew North was. This was apparent only to her as she watched him walk into the room without so much as blinking at the expensively carved furnishings or the heavy blue brocade and satin drapes framing the ten large windows in the room. The only thing that caused him to pause was when he noticed the large cloth-covered fan above the table that was framed in the same carvings as the table and chairs. Attached to the fan was a blue satin cord that ran along the high ceiling all the way to the corner, where a small child was pulling it, causing the fan to swoosh back and forth, creating a breeze.

"Remarkable," was the only comment North made as he seated himself by Mrs. Baumgartner and across from Helen. There was a smattering of small talk as they were served their first course, and Helen noticed North was clever enough to keep the conversation off himself by inquiring about the plantation and Mr. Baumgartner's plans for it. Under normal circumstances, it might have been enough, however North had never dealt with Imogene Baumgartner.

"Oh, enough about business! You must tell us about yourself, Reverend. I quite expected you to have a Scottish dialect and am curious as to why you do not," she voiced, interrupting the gentlemen's conversation.

Helen could actually see the nervous sweat start to bead on North's brow as he paused before answering. "I was raised in England but spent summers with my family in Scotland. I later moved there, but my accent was already established," he answered, parroting the explanation she'd given him earlier.

"And what town were you from in England?" she persisted.

North glanced briefly her way, and Helen could see the rising panic in his eyes. He had no idea where he was from, and Helen scrambled for a way to answer for him. Her only problem was that by saying the name of Northingshire, it might make him remember suddenly who he was. So she thought of the town next to it.

"Lanchester, isn't it? In County Durham? I believe you mentioned that town when we last saw one another," she blurted out; and from the odd looks by the Baumgartners, she knew her answering for him in such a forceful manner seemed quite odd.

But North adeptly smoothed the awkward moment, as would anyone used to handling all manner of social affairs. "Yes, I used to call Lanchester home. Excellent memory, Miss Nichols," he answered easily; and Helen was amazed that, though he couldn't remember his own name, he still acted like the nobleman he actually was.

Helen prayed his answers would satisfy Mrs. Baumgartner, but to no avail. "And your parents, are they still living?" Imogene asked.

Once again, his panicked gaze flew to Helen, and once again, she intervened. "Oh, I meant to tell you how sorry I am that I was not able to attend your father's funeral." Helen looked at Mrs. Baumgartner, whom she noticed was looking a little put out by her interruptions, and added, "It was influenza. His mother, however, still lives in Scotland."

North seemed to be digesting what she'd just said, and Helen had to add one more lie she would have to beg forgiveness for later. In truth, she didn't know how his father had died. She only knew he'd become duke at the age of ten.

North's panic was now curiosity as he looked in her direction, and she could tell he was trying to remember what she'd told him.

"Really, Helen!" Mrs. Baumgartner scolded, causing both of them to look to her. "I really think that the Reverend Campbell can answer my questions himself."

"I'm sorry, ma'am," Helen apologized as she forced herself to look contrite. In truth, she was just plain stressed by the position she'd put both North and herself in. But it was too late to fix it now! What was she to do? Quickly, she scrambled to find a reasonable, believable explanation for her behavior. "I suppose I am just excited about seeing a familiar face from England."

Helen couldn't have come up with a more perfect excuse. Immediately, Imogene's face changed into one who thought she knew a secret as she slid her gaze from North to Helen and back again. "Of course you are, dear!" she crooned as she put a hand to her chest and sighed. "I forgot you haven't had a chance to reacquaint yourselves."

"So do you holler when you preach?" Josie piped up in her usual straightforward fashion.

"Well, my word, Josie! What a thing to ask!" her mother reprimanded her.

The thirteen-year-old shrugged. "Well, the preacher at Joseph's church down the bayou hollers. Joseph says it is because the preacher wants to make sure the devil knows they won't fall for his tricks."

Helen quickly covered her mouth with her napkin to conceal her laughter, and when she looked across the table, she noticed North was having a hard time containing his own.

"Maybe it is because sometimes the preacher believes his *congregation* is hard of hearing when he sees them doing something that isn't right," North suggested when he had his laughter under control.

Josie nodded sagely, unaware she was entertaining them all. "You could be right, Reverend. So *do* you holler, too?"

North appeared to think about it and then answered, "I don't believe I have ever hollered in church."

Helen had to cover her mouth again when she pictured North "hollering" at all. He was much too dignified. Again, North slid his gaze Helen's way and shared a smile with her.

Their look apparently did not go unnoticed, although it may have been misread. Surprising them all, the usually silent Mr. Baumgartner spoke up. "Why don't you walk him out to the bayou, Helen, and show him our newly built pier? It is a full moon tonight, so there should be plenty of light. It will give you two a chance to get reacquainted." He took a drink of water and then continued, "I'll have Joseph follow you at a distance to act as a chaperone."

Helen stared at her usually quiet employer, and she was further surprised when he gave her a brief wink that only she could see. "All right," she murmured, looking back at North. "Would you like to see the bayou?"

A look of pure relief relaxed North's strong, manly face, and a smile curved his lips. "Only if you tell me what a bayou is."

They all laughed at his comment, and Helen stood from her chair. "It will be better if I show you."

In a matter of moments, Helen and North were walking the path that led out to the pier.

"I want to apologize for putting you in the position of having to answer for me," North told her as he looked over to her, admiring how the moon illuminated her soft features. "But I thought you said you didn't know much about me." He hoped she knew more than she let on, not only for the sake of getting his memory back, but because it might mean that she'd been interested enough in him to find out.

She didn't answer right away, and when she did, there was regret on her face as she gave him a quick glance. "I'm afraid I told a small lie in there just now." She blew out a breath and stepped in front of him to stop him from walking. "I lied about your father."

He had trouble focusing on what she was saying, so drawn was he by her beauty and the soft tones of her voice. But when he did realize what she'd said, he frowned in confusion. "What are you saying? That he is alive?"

She seemed horrified by his question as she put her hands on either side of her face. "Oh no! I didn't mean that. . .I mean. . .he is deceased." She shook her head. "Oh, dear! I meant he didn't die of the flu like I said. I hope I did not give you false hope."

North reached out and took her hands from her face, squeezed them, and let them go. "You didn't injure me, Miss Nichols. When you said my father had died, I instinctively knew you were right. I can't explain how I know this, but it was the same when you called me 'North.'" He thought for a moment. "Do you know my mother?"

Helen looked regretful when she shook her head. "I'm sorry, but no. I never met her, nor do I know anything about her."

He sighed. "It seems a shame not to remember one's own mother." He smiled at her wistfully. "It seems a shame not to remember you, either."

Helen looked up at him for a moment, making North wish even more for his memories back, if only the ones he had of this lovely, enchanting woman who was gazing into his eyes. Then she seemed to grow uncomfortable with the intimacy of their situation. The moment was over when she turned to resume their walk to the pier.

When they arrived at the pier, she announced to him that the stream of water that looked like a small river was the bayou they had spoken of. From there, she explained that smaller ships and barges could move their sugarcane out to the gulf.

They discussed the merits of such a waterway awhile longer but soon fell silent. Helen and North stood there a moment, letting cool air off the bayou's water stream over them as they breathed in the sweet smell of the magnolia blossoms on the nearby trees.

"Did you know my house has only two rooms?" he commented, finally breaking the silence with an odd subject.

She looked up at him and laughed. "I beg your pardon?"

He held up two fingers to her but kept his gaze looking over the water. "Only two. A bedroom and a living room that has a large fireplace from which I am supposed to cook my meals."

From the corner of his eye, he saw her cover her mouth to hide her smile. "Oh, dear. I didn't realize it was so small," she said in a muffled voice from behind her fingers.

"Can you tell me, Miss Nichols, have I ever lived in such a small house before?"

"Uh. . .no," she answered with certainty. This time a giggle escaped.

"No, no. Go ahead and laugh. I expect I shall get used to it. At least that is my goal."

She laughed, and he joined in with her. It went a long way in releasing the stress he'd felt ever since arriving at Golden Bay.

"I must have been prepared for such a life of imposed poverty. Why else would I have journeyed to such a primitive part of the United States to be their pastor?" he said after their laughter had subsided.

He watched as apprehension seemed to cloud her eyes for a moment. She looked away quickly but then looked back up to him. "North. . .I mean. . .Reverend. . ."

"Please call me North," he insisted, since it was the only thing that made his life seem real.

"North," she said his name softly. "There is something I need to tell you—"

"Can you tell me something?" he interrupted, barely hearing her words. He knew he had to ask his next question because it had burned constantly in his heart since the moment he laid eyes on her. "Did I ever call on you or ever do anything to make you think I wanted to see you more?"

"No, but you really must hear what I—"

"You see, that is what I cannot figure out," he continued, as if she hadn't spoken. "Why didn't I call on you? Did you have a beau, or for that matter, *do* you have one?"

She stood there frozen, as if shocked by what he was asking. "I've never had a beau."

Elation swept over North as she spoke those precious words. It suddenly didn't matter why he had not pursued her in the past. There was nothing stopping him now.

"Excellent!" he exclaimed with a wide grin. He held out his arm to her. "Shall we go back to the house?"

She did as he asked, but he could tell she didn't understand his response or his delight. That didn't matter.

It wouldn't be long until she realized he was determined to be her first and *only* beau.

Chapter 4

When North awoke the next morning, he was disappointed to find his memory had not improved. He didn't even feel as though he was close to remembering anything. He tried to recall if he'd dreamed of anything, and yet he knew his dreams had only consisted of one thing...Helen.

In his dreams, she was smiling and gazing into his eyes; but North was fairly sure it wasn't a dream of his past with her, but a dream of what he wished would happen.

Slowly North pulled himself from his bed and once again found himself shocked by the bareness of his surroundings. *Would Helen want to live in such conditions?* He obviously was not, nor would ever be, a man of great means if he continued on his current course as a minister; so would such a life be acceptable to her?

He had not even thought about that, possibly because this life seemed so unreal to him, as if he were walking in someone else's shoes. It would seem more reasonable for him to believe he was a wealthy man instead of someone who was used to doing without.

He realized he never fully discussed his background with Helen. Perhaps she could fill in the missing information and provide insight on his exact status in life. If he had money, where was it and how was he to get it? He thought about writing his mother about it, but then he would have to explain about his lapse in memory.

There seemed to be no solutions in sight.

The strange foreign feelings he'd been experiencing all morning only increased when he pulled on the plain cotton shirt and britches he'd been given by one of the church members. They were slightly tight around his broad shoulders and a tad long in the leg, but it was the quality of it that made it seem so odd. If he lived and helped out on a farm, wouldn't he be used to dressing like this?

How he wished he could find just one answer.

He walked through the cloth that divided his room from the living area. There was a basket of food items set on the table; and the only thing he could manage to eat, since it required no cooking skills, were the plums. The rest of the bag contained rice, potatoes, dried beans, and a few jars of figs, which North instinctively knew he did not like.

Since his stomach was growling, he knew that he was left with only one choice: He would have to go out and gather some eggs and get milk from the cow. Then, of course, he'd have to figure out how to actually cook the eggs.

Taking a deep breath for fortitude, North stepped out of the house, walked across his front porch, down the steps, then behind the house to the small barn.

The first thing that greeted him was the cow. She had such a baleful look on her face as though she were afraid he was about to have her butchered. North decided right then and there the cow would be called Queen Mary, after Mary, Queen of Scots, because he had an idea that was what the martyred queen's face must have looked like when she was being led to her execution!

"Look here," he spoke to the wary cow. "I don't have the slightest idea what I'm about, so if you'll be patient with me and let me take some of your milk, I'll let you have all the grass you can eat. Do we have a deal?"

Queen Mary continued to stare at him without so much as a blink. "Come on, give over, old girl," he urged as he patted the coarse hair on her back. This time the cow just turned her massive head away from him and let out a long breath. "Hmmm, not very trusting, I see."

"Are you expecting her to just hand over her milk in a bucket?" a young voice asked from the doorway. Embarrassed, North jerked around to find Josie and Helen standing there smiling at him.

"How long have you two been standing there?" he asked carefully.

"Long enough to see you know nothing about farm animals," Josie answered, only to receive a nudge from Helen.

"Josie, don't be indelicate," Helen scolded.

North held out his hand. "No, don't correct her, for she is right. I fear that I will starve for my lack of animal husbandry knowledge."

Helen and Josie giggled at his pitiful expression. "You won't this morning!" Helen told him, holding up a cloth-covered basket that smelled delightful. "We have brought fresh muffins and milk, so your. . .uh. . .Queen Mary, is it? Your Queen Mary will not have to be bothered this morning."

Hunger overcame any embarrassment North might have been feeling. He quickly led them to the benches under his oak tree. It wasn't until he had finished off two of the muffins that he was able to talk.

"These are quite delicious!" he complimented with a satisfied sigh as he reached over to take another.

"I knew you would like them. Christina told me you once ate a whole plate of them," Helen told him as she brushed the crumbs from her light pink skirt. Today she was clad in a short-sleeved cotton day dress, and her hair was tied back with a matching pink ribbon. It was a simple gown, but one suited for the hot, humid weather, and one that suited Helen's beautiful creamy skin, with her black lash-framed eyes and pink lips.

His ears perked up at hearing a name she had not mentioned before. "Christina? Who is she?"

There was a stillness that came over Helen that North did not understand. It was as though she had said something she shouldn't, yet it didn't make sense. How did Christina fit into both their lives?

"She is a girl I grew up with," she answered vaguely and quickly. She then jumped up from her seat and said in an edgy tone, "I have an idea! Since I grew up on a farm, I could show you how to milk the cow." She started walking toward the barn. "There is no time like the present," she yelled over her shoulder.

North didn't know what to think of her behavior. Confused, he looked at Josie, and the young girl just shrugged. "She only becomes nervous and does crazy things when you're around, you know," she explained in a conspiratorial whisper. "The rest of the time she is extremely proper and concerned at all times about being a lady."

Hmm. Interesting. Perhaps Helen liked him as much as he liked her.

That didn't explain the evasiveness about her friend Christina, though.

"Let's go learn to milk a cow, shall we?" he asked Josie as he extended his hand to her.

Josie, clearly not thrilled by that prospect, rolled her eyes and sighed, "Oh, all right. But I'm almost sure this is not on the list of ladylike duties I have to learn."

North laughed as he led her to the barn. "No, probably not."

How could I be so careless? Helen lamented as she paced back and forth in the barn. The more information she offered, the more he was going to want to know, and the more lies she would have to tell.

Oh, this was truly the most awful idea she had ever schemed! Once North found out how much she deceived him and concealed from him, he would never want to see her again! Last night she had tried to tell him the truth, but he wouldn't listen. And she couldn't tell him now because Josie was with her.

Helen was caught in a web of her own making, one that was created for the cause of love but was truly selfish at its very core. All because she wanted something she couldn't have.

"We're here for our lesson!" North announced cheerfully as he and Josie dashed through the barn door, startling the cow and upsetting the three chickens sitting over in the corner.

Helen looked at the cow and wished she hadn't been so hasty in her suggestion. Though she'd seen cows being milked a dozen or so times by her father's servants, she'd never actually milked one herself. "Well. . .," she sounded, stretching the word out as she thought of what to do. "We need a bucket, but I don't see one."

Josie snatched a bucket that was hanging by a nail on the wall beside her. "I found one!"

"Wonderful," she replied, trying to sound confident as she took the bucket from her charge. "Well, now we need a stool."

"Like the one there beside the cow?" North asked. Helen looked keenly at him to see if he was on to her, but she couldn't tell whether he was teasing her or not.

"Uh, yes. There it is." She slowly edged her way to the side of the cow, praying the animal would not be difficult. She carefully sat down and stared with much apprehension at the cow's underparts in front of her.

She was going to have to touch the animal for this to work, and she didn't want to touch it at all. She remembered petting a cow once, but that was the extent of it. She had never touched the underbelly of one.

She glanced back at North, who had come to stand behind her, and once again, he seemed truly interested in what she was doing. "Are you all right?" he asked when she looked back at the cow and then to him once more.

"Oh, yes. . .yes. . .I am fine. I just wanted to make sure you were paying attention," she answered.

"You have my full concentration," North assured.

"Capital, just capital!" she murmured between gritted teeth. Taking a deep breath, she slowly reached out and took hold of the cow. The cow stirred a little, but that was all.

She tried to pull like she had seen the servant do, but no milk came out.

"Trouble?" North asked.

Helen ignored him as she pulled again, and still nothing. Three, four, then five times she tried but only succeeded in making the cow become irritable.

Finally, she couldn't take it anymore. Helen jumped up from her seat, causing the stool to fall back, the cow to move around, and the chickens to be once again upset.

"I don't think she's in the mood to be milked," Helen said quickly as she brushed at her skirt then tried to push a few stray hairs away from her face.

North folded his arms and appeared to study the cow. "I wasn't aware that cows needed to be in the mood."

"Yeah, I've never heard that, either," Josie added. "Are you sure you've milked a cow before?"

Putting her hands on her hips, Helen held her chin up with as much bravado as she could muster. "Actually, no. But I've seen it done plenty of times." She tapped her fingertip on her hips. "Enough to know when a cow is in the mood to be milked or not!"

North narrowed his gaze at her, but she could see the humorous gleam shining in his eyes. "So how do I know when she's in the mood?"

Helen suddenly realized he'd known all along she was faking it. She pointed her finger at him and charged, "Why didn't you tell me you were on to me? You actually let me touch that. . .that. . .thing!"

Both Josie and North were doubled over laughing by this point. "I can't wait. . .to see how. . .you do. . .with the chickens!" he said between laughs.

Helen smiled confidently as she marched over to one of the hens and deftly slipped her hand under the chicken and quickly withdrew it, holding an egg triumphantly in the air. "Now let's see you try," she challenged, knowing what the outcome would be to a novice.

Just as she thought would happen, North walked over to the hen, poked and prodded through its feathers, and instead of an egg, got a painful peck on the wrist for his efforts.

"Oh, dear," she said with mock innocence. "I fear you did not do that correctly."

North frowned as he rubbed his hand. "I take it you've done this before?"

"Many times."

North grinned at her, and her heart did a flip-flop. To finally have all his attention directed at her, after all the months of having him be merely polite to her while she pined away for him every time she saw him, was a heady experience indeed. The sight of him being so natural and at ease, standing in a barn surrounded by chicken feathers and a smelly cow, made her wish he were truly who he thought he was—a simple preacher.

While it was true that North was always a very nice man, despite his exalted position in society, he always seemed to be aware and took care of everything he did—every move he made. He seemed bound by the dictates of his society and the boundaries of the English society, or the *ton*, as they were called.

Now he didn't have those restrictions on him. There was no one watching how he dressed or with whom he kept company. There were no responsibilities on him since he didn't realize that he had the burden of taking care of four estates and watching after his many investments, not to mention the people who depended on him for their livelihood.

He thought he was simply a country preacher whose only worry at the moment was probably the sermon he would have to preach on Sunday and how to get his cow to give milk.

Despite his confusion, he seemed relaxed and content.

Because of his confusion, there was nothing keeping him from hiding his interest in her. There was nothing keeping him from smiling at her and looking at her as though she was the most important person to him.

But that doesn't make it right, said a tiny voice, which she knew was the conviction of God nudging at her heart. He deserved to know who he was. His cousins deserved to know that their family member was still alive and well.

"Shall we begin again?" he asked, breaking her from her musings. "Perhaps if we three put our heads together, we can figure out how to milk this cow."

Laughing, Helen agreed, and so did Josie. Of course the younger girl was up for anything that kept her from her lessons.

For about an hour, they worked on the poor cow. They finally got some milk out of her, but Helen had a strong suspicion that it was because the animal got tired of their pulling and prodding!

The difficult part, however, was dodging North's probing questions and her trying to answer without actually lying.

"So Christina is married to a man named Nicholas who is a former soldier?" He repeated what she'd just told him, and Helen could tell that he was trying to see if the names were familiar to him.

"Nicholas and Christina are the Earl and Countess of Kenswick, you know," Josie informed him, much to Helen's dismay. She'd forgotten all about telling her of them. She quickly looked at North to see if he recognized any of these names.

North's brow furrowed as he stood up from his seat by the cow. "They're nobility?" he asked curiously, and Helen couldn't help but breathe a sigh of relief that his thoughts had taken a different direction from what she imagined he was thinking.

"Yes," Helen affirmed as she walked over to the chickens and finished gathering their eggs. "Christina is only a vicar's daughter, but Nicholas fell in love with her despite the *ton's* objections."

"Ah, you tell the story with a wistful sound in your voice," he said with a grin. "I gather you thought the whole affair was sentimental and romantic."

She handed the eggs over to Josie, who ran out of the barn to take them to the house. "As a matter of fact, I did," she answered with a raised brow, challenging him to say something against her romanticism.

"I'll bet when the censure came from England's society and his family, it did not feel quite as romantic as they dreamed it would be. Marrying against one's own class can cause a great deal of heartache for all involved." He stopped and blinked. "Well, I say! I don't know where that little insight came from!" he retorted with a chuckle.

Helen laughed in return, but it was a hollow gesture. If he felt that way now, he'd still hold to those convictions once he got his memory back, she realized. Perhaps North, as a duke, didn't want to shake up his life unnecessarily whether it was for love or not.

"I don't think that particular thing is something we have to worry about, do you?" he teased, but she could see the interest for her burning in his gaze as he looked at her. How she wished things could always be as they were now.

"We'd better get this milk stored to keep it cold," she said instead of answering his question.

If she thought North would not notice her evasiveness, she was wrong. As he picked up the bucket of milk, he gave her a long look that let her know she would not be able to avoid his questions forever.

Chapter 5

A loud knock awoke North the next morning, and with a jolt, he was sitting up in his bed, scrambling to get his bearings. His bleary eyes scanned the room, and he noticed that it wasn't even light outside yet.

Who in the world would be out at this early hour? Where were his servants, and why weren't they doing something about the loud noise?

Bit by bit, the fog of sleepiness lifted, and he remembered where he was. He remembered *who* he was. . .at least he remembered who everyone *told* him he was.

"Hamish Campbell. I am Hamish Campbell, the vicar of this hot, muggy spot of America." He recited this to himself to try to lift the odd confusion that had come over him since he'd awakened. For a moment. . .he felt different somehow. Not at all like Hamish Campbell, the humble, poor preacher of Golden Bay.

He remembered thinking that his servants would answer the door. He wondered why he would automatically think he had servants to see after him. Did he once have them in England and Scotland?

Once again several loud raps sounded on his door. North grudgingly pulled himself out of bed and quickly donned his plain, wrinkled clothes.

When he finally opened the door, he was surprised to find a tall, slim, black man dressed in a fine brown suit with a darker brown-and-black-striped vest over a snow-white shirt and expertly tied cravat.

"*Bonjour, Monsieur* Campbell," the man greeted in a crisp, confident tone as he bent in a short bow. "I am Pierre LeMonde, a freedman from New Orleans and currently in the employ of Mr. Robert Baumgartner. I am versed in all manner of household chores and have been at Golden Bay to teach their household staff the correct methods in which to carry out their duties. I not only speak excellent English but also French, which is my first language."

Slightly bemused by the lengthy, confusing speech, North automatically responded to his last statement without any thought. "*Bonjour, monsieur. Heureaux pour vous rencontrer,*" he replied in French, telling him he was pleased to make his acquaintance.

"*Et vous aussi,*" Pierre answered, and North understood him to say that he was pleased to meet him, too.

But he didn't know *how* he knew this.

Would a simple preacher know this? Was this something one learned at seminary or university?

"I'm sorry, monsieur, but are you all right?" Pierre asked, bringing North's attention back to the present.

"I think I am a little unclear as to why you are here," he told him bluntly, still shaken from discovering yet another odd piece of the puzzle that didn't seem to fit in what he knew of his life.

"Miss Helen Nichols informed her employers you were in need of. . .how shall I say. . .domestic help."

North grinned at the man's effort at being tactful. "She told you about the fiasco with the cow and chickens, did she not?"

Pierre put his hand against his mouth and let out a little cough. "Uh hum. Well yes, monsieur, she did."

North laughed as he stepped back and motioned for the man to come into his small house. "I will take help any way I can get it, even if I have to promote my embarrassing moments to get it."

Pierre smiled broadly as he entered the house. He inspected the room and then quickly turned to look at North with the same critical eye. "You are not what I imagined you'd be," he said finally, his deep tone thoughtful.

Intrigued, North cocked his head to one side as he asked, "Why do you say that?"

Pierre shook his head as he shrugged his slim shoulders. "I have been in the employ of some of the richest families of south Louisiana. English, Spanish, and French—it does not matter. They all had the same quality about them, the same air. They spoke differently—they walked differently than the average man or woman." He motioned his hand in a sweeping gesture toward North. "You possess these same qualities."

North scampered to remember what Helen had told him. Did she say his family was or had been wealthy? Oh, yes. She had been very vague as to the exactness of his financial status. So instead he went with his intuition—what he felt deep in his heart. "I am from a wealthy family," he answered, praying it was not a lie.

Pierre lifted an eyebrow as he nodded his head slowly. "Then that explains it. And you gave up your comfortable life for God's calling," he reflected aloud. "Very noble."

If only he could feel the calling, North thought sadly. He must have felt the zeal that had caused missionaries and preachers through the centuries to leave their friends and family to do the work of God. All he felt was scared and uncertain about his ability to minister effectively to these American people.

"I'm just doing the will of God," he said to Pierre, and as he said it, he knew that statement to be true. Somehow, some way, God had a plan, and North was a big part of it.

"Then you are fortunate," Pierre told him, his face solemn. "There are many of my people here in this country who cannot be free to do work such as yours but are bound by the dictates of their masters."

North nodded. "It is indeed a travesty. I would think, however, you are not sitting idly by," he guessed, sensing Pierre would be one who worked behind the scenes, trying to help those slaves whom he could.

Pierre pretended to straighten the cuffs of his sleeves and nonchalantly answered, "I have no idea what you mean, monsieur."

At that moment, North heard his stomach growl, reminding him of his hunger. He started to ask Pierre if his talents extended to knowing how to cook when another knock sounded at the door. Shaking his head, North lamented, "Americans are certainly early risers!"

Pierre smiled as he breezed past North, heading for the door. "Allow me, monsieur."

This time there were two men at the door, and both were holding either end of a large trunk. Pierre spoke to them briefly then turned back to North to inform him that these were men from the New Orleans port.

"Excellent!" North exclaimed. "Just put it on the table there." The men did as asked, and Pierre gave them water for the journey home.

After the men had gone, Pierre helped North bring the trunk into his small room and then, much to North's eternal thankfulness, left him to make breakfast.

North didn't open the trunk right away. For a moment, he stood there contemplating what the old, beat-up trunk might hold. Would there be mementos inside to help him remember? Would the smell of the clothes or the sound of the trunk's creaking hinges unlock the closed doors of his mind?

He put his hands on the scuffed metal that framed the lid and slid them over until they reached the latch. Carefully, he lifted the lid and waited for something familiar to wash over him.

It never came.

It was a trunk filled with clothes that seemed as though they belonged to a stranger. There was nothing vaguely familiar about them. Not even the smell of them gave him the tiniest twinge of remembrance.

Disappointment struck North to his very soul as he slumped down on the bed, his shoulders bent in defeat. He wiped his hands down his face then through his hair as he tried to assure himself it did not mean anything, that his mind just hadn't healed sufficiently to get his memory back.

 Curiosity, however, soon overpowered his disappointment. North stood again and started sifting through the contents of the chest. Perhaps if he could not remember, he could at least try to piece together certain aspects of his life.

Underneath a small stack of neatly pressed white shirts, North found four very worn books. But when he saw the titles and the authors, he was more confused than ever. The first three were religion-based writings by Jonathan Edwards, an evangelist from the Great Awakening period of America, and John Wesley, the man responsible for starting the Methodist movement in England. Curious, North just stared at the books as he tried to comprehend the greater meaning behind his apparent choices in literature.

Was he a Methodist or part of the Church of England? North could not remember how he obtained the information, but he knew the Methodists in England were a religious people only just tolerated by society. The Church of England would not accept their teaching in their chapels and abbeys, so they would meet elsewhere, building their own buildings and oftentimes moving to America, where they could worship without censure.

North understood their ministers spoke passionately when they preached, which caused many to call them radical, or religious zealots. North was aware, however, he didn't feel this way about them but only felt a curiosity when he thought about it.

He truly wished he could remember what denomination he was! What if he taught something that this particular congregation did not agree with?

It was just one more thing he'd have to ask Helen about and pray that she knew something about it.

Setting those books aside, he then noticed the title of the fourth book, and he immediately smiled. Daniel Defoe's *Robinson Crusoe*, he intuitively knew, was one of his favorite stories. Perhaps it may have been the catalyst to bringing him to America.

A shimmer of shining metal caught the corner of his eye, and he looked down to notice a gold frame peeking out from under a folded pair of britches. North set the Defoe book aside and reached for the frame.

As he got a better look at it, he saw it was a double-oval frame that contained two miniatures of a man and a woman. North concentrated all his energies into the study of the small portraits as he moved his gaze from the brown-haired man's eyes and smile to the pretty woman's red curls and delicate features.

It struck North right away that neither of them had blond hair. As a matter of fact, neither even looked like him.

North didn't know why this upset him, but it did. In fact, he was more affected by the miniatures than by any of the other disappointments he'd yet encountered.

Agitated, he gripped the frame and began to pace the room. Closing his eyes and gritting his teeth, he focused hard, trying to make his mind remember something. . .anything!

Absolutely nothing was achieved except perhaps a headache from the pressure of trying.

Walking to his window, he pushed the light blue cotton curtain aside. His eyes focused on the church, which was situated in his direct line of view, and then he did the only thing he knew to do.

Pray.

"God, I cannot understand why I can't remember. I cannot understand why I become more confused looking at my own belongings. Most of all, I cannot understand why I don't feel like Hamish Campbell." He took a breath and lifted the miniature up to the sunlight. Thoughtfully, he rubbed his thumb along the edges of the frame. "I can only conclude that You have a purpose, Lord, and need me to fulfill it. I will endeavor to feel honored You have chosen me for Your task, and please forgive me when I have felt otherwise since I arrived in Golden Bay. I will strive to do my best for You, dear God. Please help my faith to stay strong." He ended the prayer and stayed a minute more, gazing out the window, letting the heat of the sunlight bathe his face and rejuvenate his spirits.

In fact, he felt so much contentment in his heart that he wasn't even fazed when he tried on his clothes from the trunk and found the shoulders were just a little tight and the arms just slightly too long.

Apparently, I had an atrocious tailor in Scotland, was his only thought as he made his way to the kitchen and to the delicious food Pierre already had spread on the table.

"Josie, a lady never grabs the body of her teacup with both hands!" Helen stressed as she was unsuccessfully trying to tutor the young girl on the correct way to take tea.

Josie looked at Helen with a typically bored expression on her features. "Which would you prefer: my picking the cup up by the handle and dropping it, getting tea everywhere, or would you rather see me using both hands to make sure that doesn't happen?"

Considering the cost of the teacups they were using, the young lady had a point. But Helen couldn't tell her that.

"Josie, if you practice, you will be able to hold on to your cup without dropping it and look elegant at the same time," she instructed patiently, knowing Josie was barely paying attention. The younger girl kept looking out the window with a longing expression. She cleared her throat to get Josie's attention. "Shall we begin again?"

Josie sighed with vexation. "Why don't we go visit the reverend and see how he's getting along? It's been over a week since we've seen him," she said, suddenly perking up.

Helen wanted more than anything to go but knew it was wiser to stay away. It was getting more and more difficult to live with the lie she had told him. Seeing him only compounded her guilt. "Josie, please...," she began only to be cut short.

"Can't we go fishing instead? Sam is going to be there, and he was going to show me how to use crickets for bait."

Helen shuddered at her words. "Your fascination with that Indian is beyond the pale! Young ladies do not go traipsing around alone with young men who are not in one's family!"

Josie's chin rose, and Helen knew she wasn't going to back down. "You just don't like Sam because he keeps wanting to trade horses for you."

"Exactly! He is a barbarian!" In truth, Helen was a little fascinated with Sam, the tall, red-skinned man who dressed in his leather-fringed britches and only covered his upper torso with a closed vest, leaving his arms bare. It was even a little flattering he seemed so taken with her.

Josie slumped in her chair and folded her arms defiantly. "I should have been born an Indian, then I wouldn't have to learn all these dumb rules."

Helen smiled. "I'm sure there are a whole different set of rules you would have to learn as an Indian girl."

Josie's rebuttal was stopped short when her mother breezed into the room at that moment. "I just received a note from Pierre that all is going well at the Reverend Campbell's house," she informed them as she waved a small piece of paper in her hand.

Helen stood and looked at her employer gratefully. "Thank you so much for sending help," she told her earnestly. "I saw he was unfamiliar with animals and even how to prepare his own meals, so I feared he would starve without immediate assistance."

Imogene raised an eyebrow as she studied Helen with a critical eye. She made

Helen feel like the woman could see straight inside her mind. "I see I was right in my assumptions."

Helen could feel her heart beating with nervousness. "I beg your pardon?" she said, hoping she was misreading the direction of Mrs. Baumgartner's thoughts.

"You have feelings for Hamish Campbell!" she declared with certainty. "Your eyes light up when you speak of him, and an inner joy exudes from your heart and into your words. I would even be so bold as to say that you were in love with the reverend even before you came to Louisiana. Am I right?"

Helen tried to swallow the lump in her throat, but she was so frozen by what she should say next, she was unable to accomplish the task. She said the first thing she thought of, hoping her words would defuse Imogene's assumptions. "I can honestly say that I am not in love with Hamish Campbell." She was only in love with Trevor "North" Kent.

She must have sounded convincing because Imogene frowned with confusion. "Are you absolutely sure?" she asked but then continued without an answer. "Perhaps you have not realized your feelings for him yet! Of course!" She clapped her hands together. "You need time to sort them out!"

Did a girl really need time to realize that she had found her true love? The moment Helen had laid eyes on North, she knew he was the only man she wanted to be her husband, the only man she could love.

"You can only be sure of your feelings if you spend time with him!" She patted Helen on the cheek and spun around to walk toward the door. "Don't worry, dear! Leave it to me. You'll realize he is your one true love in no time!" she exclaimed over her shoulder as she left the room.

Bemused by Mrs. Baumgartner's words, Helen could only liken the feeling to being run over by a runaway buggy.

"You may be good with manners and such, but you are wretched at handling my mother," Josie spoke from behind her as Helen still stood staring at the door.

Blinking, Helen finally turned and looked at the younger girl. "I don't suppose you can give me any pointers on how I should do that, can you?"

Josie's smile was one of pure cunning. "Only if I can go fishing with Sam today."

Plopping back down in her chair, Helen waved her hand toward the door. "Just go," she told her in a tired voice, and in just a matter of seconds, the girl had flown out of the room and down the stairs.

Helen thought about all that had transpired since she had arrived in Louisiana and wondered if things could become any stranger. Here she was in love with a man who had no memory and whom everyone believed was someone else. She was trying to hide the fact that she was in love with him, but now Imogene Baumgartner was determined to see them together.

Why am I fighting this? Helen thought, but deep down she knew the answer. Guilt was holding her back. Guilt over lying to poor North about who he really was. The whole purpose of making him think he was Hamish Campbell was to have a chance at winning his heart. But even if he never got his memory back, could she live with such a lie hanging over her head? Could she even keep up the charade without anyone finding out?

She imagined telling the vicar from her village, the Reverend Wakelin, about her deceptive deeds and wondered what he would say. Helen knew he would be very disappointed in her because she was growing more and more ashamed of herself.

Chapter 6

"Pierre!" North called out as he entered his house, holding a basket of eggs. He'd been in Golden Bay nearly two weeks now, and dealing with the animals was still a daily challenge. "I got out every single egg without damaging myself in the process!" he announced proudly as he put the basket on the table.

Pierre peered over his shoulder as he knelt in front of the fireplace, where he was adjusting the metal rack mounted inside. "Very good, monsieur. Perhaps tomorrow you will be able to get a little more than half a cup of milk from the cow."

North laughed at Pierre's droll tone. "Could you let me savor my small victory before criticizing my failures?"

"I am just helping you to strive for more, monsieur," Pierre countered with laughter in his deep voice.

"Well, I am about to strive to write my first sermon, so if you'll excuse me, I'll go and get my Bible."

"It is Saturday!" Pierre exclaimed with disbelief. "You are only now preparing your sermon?"

North stopped in his tracks and looked to Pierre with concern. "That's not the way it's done?" he asked cautiously, not thinking about his words.

Pierre blinked at him and paused a minute before asking, "You don't know?"

North felt like a fraud. Here he was pretending to be the person he really was. . .except he couldn't remember being that person. And if everyone knew he couldn't remember, then they would either think he was crazy or doubt his ability to lead them.

Which would be a proper assumption in his case because he had no idea how to be a vicar and no inkling as to whether he was even good at public speaking. Maybe the reason he came all the way to America was because everyone back in Scotland thought he was a terrible preacher.

"Uh. . .my experience has been somewhat. . .limited," he finally answered with the biggest understatement of the decade.

Pierre's right eyebrow rose in query. "How limited?"

"Practically nonexistent."

Pierre just stared at him for a moment, making North wonder what he was thinking. Would he go tell the Baumgartners that he was a fraud? A novice who had no business pretending he knew *anything*?

Then Pierre suddenly turned from him, and his shoulders began to shake. North peered closely at him, and when he'd walked to face Pierre once again, he realized the man was laughing!

"I'm sorry, monsieur, but you English are very funny," he said as tears started to run down his dark cheeks. "I wish I could be in that church tomorrow. It would be more" —he interrupted his own sentence as he tried desperately to hold on to his usual dignified disposition— "more entertaining than watching you milk that poor. . .cow!"

North sighed as he watched Pierre sit down at the table and completely cover his face as his whole body shook.

North wished he could see the humor of the whole situation. He could use a good laugh.

Leaving the still-laughing servant in the kitchen, North dragged his feet into his bedroom and took the Bible from his night table. He opened the book at random, praying for divine intervention, and landed in the book of Exodus. He read the story about how Moses led the children of Israel out of Egypt and how their disobedience kept them in the desert, which should have taken them a short time to go through, for forty years.

He sat there for a moment and thought about how that story could be used in a sermon, but then he had a horrible thought. What if he had done some incredibly bad thing or had been disobedient to God before he came to America? Perhaps God was punishing him for this.

Perhaps he would be stuck in a wilderness of forgetfulness for forty years like the children of Israel!

Looking back down at the faded pages of the Bible, North quickly flipped the pages away from that particular book. He decided it would be best to look for something else.

He looked through several passages, and none seemed to be right for his first sermon until he found the book of Job. Here was a man who had lost everything but still would not blame God for any of his misfortunes. And in time God restored him above and beyond his former glory because Job stayed faithful to God.

North rubbed his chin as he thought about how Job's life was similar to his own. Everything had been stripped from him, so if he continued to keep his faith in God, perhaps He would restore to North what he had lost.

He determined he would build his sermon around the story of Job. North felt that since he was so affected by the story, he would have the passion to convey the lesson to others.

Encouraged that he had a theme for his message, he took several sheets of paper from his trunk and went to the kitchen with pen and ink in hand.

"You look pleased with yourself," Pierre observed. "I will assume it is because you have found a theme for your sermon?"

"Yes, you may assume," North said with a relieved smile. "I am speaking about the life of Job and how we should keep our faith in God when things go wrong in our lives."

Pierre looked impressed. "An excellent topic. How will you begin?"

North thought a moment. "I will open by reading the scriptures." He opened his bottle of ink, situated his papers just so, and dipped the tip of the pen into the bottle.

"And then?"

North looked up as Pierre sat across from him. He had on the same suit as yesterday, and North couldn't help but notice his own servant dressed better than he did.

"Then. . .I will put the story into my own words—explain it, if you will."

He began to write down the scripture reference in his bold, yet expertly done, script.

"Ah. . ." Pierre sounded thoughtful. "And where shall you go from there?"

North smudged his paper when his hand jerked at Pierre's words. "I should have more?" Suddenly the process seemed complicated again.

"*Oui*, monsieur. What you've described will take less than seven to ten minutes. It will need to be a great deal longer than that."

North looked from the near-empty paper to Pierre with dismay radiating from every pore of his being. "I don't suppose you could. . ."

Pierre made a *tsk*-ing sound. "I write very poorly, monsieur. And besides, if I do it for you, it would not be from your heart but mine."

North sighed and ran a hand through his wavy blond hair. "Yes, I suppose you're right," he conceded, although he wished he knew what to do.

Helen suddenly came to mind, and he wondered if she could help him. Of course she had been to church before, so perhaps she could give him an idea of what to do. And besides, she was the only person who would understand *why* he didn't know what to do.

He quickly gathered his papers and put the top back on his ink. "May I borrow your barouche, Pierre?"

Pierre seemed taken aback by his sudden change. "Of course, but why?"

"Because I'm going to see Helen. She'll be able to help me."

Pierre helped him don his coat and put his things in a leather satchel, which North had found near the bottom of the trunk. "Perhaps there are other reasons you want to see the pretty lady?"

"Mind your own affairs, Pierre," he ordered as he walked briskly to the door.

He heard Pierre shout as he closed the door, "But yours are so much more interesting than my own!"

⚜

North's heart was beating excitedly as he knocked on the Baumgartners' door. Just the prospect of seeing Helen once again seemed to reduce him to a nervous schoolboy with his first crush.

Of course, since he couldn't remember even going to school, she would actually be the first.

A tall black man dressed in fine black attire greeted North with a solemn nod and asked him the reason for his visit.

Before he could answer, Imogene Baumgartner came hurriedly down the staircase to greet him. "Rev. Campbell! How wonderful you have come to visit us."

They both nodded to each other in lieu of a curtsy or bow. "Good morning, Mrs. Baumgartner. I came by to see if I might have a word with Helen."

North was surprised to see the older woman's eyes light up. "Of course you did!" she exclaimed as she put a hand against her throat and looked at him as if she knew a secret. "Our Helen is a very special lady, if I might be so bold as to say." She leaned forward and whispered, "But I think you are already aware of that."

North was well aware Imogene Baumgartner was not a lady of high society. Pierre had told him about her being the daughter of a servant in England and that Robert Baumgartner had given up everything to marry her. But despite her obvious lack of ladylike behavior, she was a very engaging woman who quickly endeared herself to all those she would meet.

Again, North had no idea how he understood the differences of society and their behaviors. He couldn't even remember if he'd been considered a gentleman or simply a rich commoner. And there was a difference. Whereas a gentleman was born to his distinction whether he was wealthy or poor, a commoner, no matter how rich, could never hope to be recognized on the gentleman's level.

In America, however, it seemed that whoever had the most money or the drive to better themselves could achieve anything they wanted.

So North supposed it didn't really matter what he was, as long as he worked hard to establish himself and proved himself worthy to be called a minister to the Golden Bay people.

North smiled at Imogene, leaned forward, and whispered back to her, answering her assumption. "You are correct. I think Helen Nichols is a very lovely girl."

Imogene giggled with girlish delight, and North smiled with her, enjoying the merriment dancing in her light hazel eyes. "Why don't you wait right here in the library while I go and tell her you are here." She directed him to a small room off their grand foyer, just beyond the staircase.

North remained standing after she had left and looked with startled interest about the room. It was indeed a library with shelves made of what looked like heavy oak, but there were no more than twenty books spread about them as they circled the room. The rest of the space was taken up by potted plants, figurines, and a few miniatures.

"It seems sort of an atrocity to call this room the library, doesn't it?"

North turned toward the female voice that he was coming to recognize so well. He took a moment to admire how Helen had left her dark curls to flow around her shoulders, complementing the light violet of her morning dress. "Indeed, it is," he agreed. "It seems to be nothing but old books of poetry, scientific works, and. . ." His voice drifted to a pause when he noticed a stack of books in one far corner that seemed to be newer than the rest. "What are those over there?"

Helen smiled. "Those are mine. I'm afraid I wasted a lot of time in England reading and not applying myself to other studies as I should have."

Suddenly a thought popped in his head, and North spoke it without realizing what he was saying. "Of course! I remember you like to read gothic romance novels, am I correct?"

The moment those words were out, they both froze—staring at one another in unbelief.

"How do you know that?" she finally asked, her voice sounding almost fearful.

North shook his head in wonderment. "I don't know. The information just appeared in my mind like a memory normally does."

"Well, do you remember anything else?"

North closed his eyes and tried to concentrate on the memory he just had but could remember nothing else. He opened his eyes and sighed. "Absolutely nothing."

Helen looked at him with sympathy. "I'm sorry, North. I'm sure more memories will come to you. Perhaps if you try not to think about it so much, you will one day remember everything."

"I suppose you're right," he readily agreed. It just felt so good for that tiny moment to have a true memory of something. It was like God giving him a small gift to get him through the day.

"What's that in your hand?" Helen prompted as she spied the satchel he had taken from his shoulder.

"Ah, yes." He'd almost forgotten his reason for being here. "I've come to ask for your help with my sermon." He dipped his hand into the satchel and brought out his papers. "Since I can't remember preaching or even hearing a sermon, I don't have the first idea how to go about constructing one."

He watched as Helen smiled prettily and crossed her arms in front of her in a motion of confidence. "Well, Reverend, you've come to the right person!"

∽∽

Helen was still a little jittery after North told her about his memory. Sure, it was a tiny memory, but who knew what he would remember next?

This was bad—very, very bad. *She* was bad for even creating this situation. But what could she do? If she told him now, it would not only confuse him but also upset the whole town!

She was trying to calm her nerves when he asked her the one thing that would help take her mind off her problem.

He needed help with his sermon. She could do that!

Helen motioned for North to sit at the desk on the far wall, and she pulled a chair beside him. "Can I assume you have a little knowledge in the area of sermon writing?" North asked as he reached over to take a Bible down from the shelf behind him.

"My best friend's father is a vicar. Every Saturday Christina and I would take his notes in his very sloppy script and rewrite it so that he could better see it from the pulpit," she explained. "I know exactly the structure in which he wrote all his sermons. They would have one major scripture reference and at least three points. At the end he would bring it all together and bring out one last nugget of truth, maybe other scriptures in the Bible that might tie in with his first one. He was a very respected and widely known vicar in our parish."

North seemed surprised by her information. "You don't know how relieved I am that you seem confident in how to do this." He paused for a moment. "Uh. . .Helen, this congregation here in Golden Bay. . . Are they a Methodist congregation? That is to say. . .am I a Methodist?"

Helen shrugged her shoulders. "Actually, it is a sort of blended church. There are a few Methodists, Baptists, and members of the Church of England, as the Baumgartners and I are. I'm almost certain you are, as well." Actually, she was *very* certain he was, but she'd already told him that she knew little about his personal life.

For over an hour, they labored side-by-side, working with his passage from Job and choosing points that best brought out the lesson he wanted to be most understood.

When they had finished, he leaned back in his chair and stretched his arms forward. "I think I could use some fresh air," he said with a yawn.

Helen thought about how humid it had been outdoors earlier when she'd stepped out for a moment, and smiled. "I don't know if *fresh* is the appropriate description of the Louisiana air, but I do concede that it would be nice to walk around a bit."

Together they stepped out onto the porch, which wrapped around the house, and made their way down the ten or so steps, following the path to the pier.

"So what caused you to leave England and journey to this place?" North asked as he picked up a long, thick stick from the path and then used it as a walking cane.

There was no way Helen could tell him the truth—that she'd come to America because she had hoped to see him. "Well, I suppose it sounded adventurous," she answered, giving him only half of the truth. "My best friend had gotten married, and I suppose I just wanted a change of setting. My parents were hinting around for me to marry a young farmer in my village, and I just didn't want to settle for someone I didn't love." She shrugged her shoulders. "When Lady Claudia told me about the position of being a companion for her little sister, I felt God was opening a door for me. So here I am."

"Well, might I be so bold as to say I am eternally grateful that you did not settle for the farmer or else I might have never seen you again," he said in a teasing tone as he looked down at her with appreciation.

Helen could feel her cheeks reddening, and she quickly looked away before he could read her true feelings. She knew he liked her, but it would be hard to explain the feelings of love she carried for him so soon.

North, however, was adept at stemming the awkwardness as he changed the subject to her earlier comment about Lady Claudia. She was trying to explain that Claudia, Robert Baumgartner's eldest child, had been accepted by her grandfather to inherit the title of marchioness after his death, when something large moved in their path, blocking the sun.

Helen knew, before she lifted her gaze, who it was.

Standing before them with all the confidence a chief of his tribe would possess—wearing his usual buckskins and vest—was the Choctaw Indian, Sam Youngblood. In his hand were three ropes that led to the horses situated behind him.

Helen could sense the moment North noticed him, and after a period of stunned silence, he barked out, *"What is that?"*

Chapter 7

Helen glanced back and forth between the two men nervously; and if she were pressed to describe their first reaction to one another, it would most definitely be *hostile*.

Even *that* would be an understatement.

As soon as the words had left North's mouth, Helen feared Sam would surely take offense. And if his flaring nostrils and narrowed, angry eyes were any indication, Helen knew she was right in her assumption.

Realizing she would have to try and unruffle the Indian's feathers, so to speak, she began to walk toward him. Helen had only taken two steps when she was suddenly jerked back by North and pulled to his side.

"What are you doing? That is a savage!" North barked, sounding as though he were horrified at even being in Sam's presence.

Knowing how Sam usually liked to play up to people's stereotypical thinking that all Indians were uneducated, barbaric, and dangerous, Helen knew he was probably already thinking of what to do to shock North even more.

"But, North, he's. . ."

"They've been known to scalp a fellow before he could even let out a scream," he stressed in a low voice, all the while keeping his eye on Sam. "They also like to take white women back to their camps and use them as their slaves."

Helen stopped short of rolling her eyes. "You know this, but you can't remember your own name," she whispered back with exasperation. Then in a louder voice, "North, if you'll just let me intro—"

"Why don't we start walking toward the house very slowly? Perhaps he'll leave us alone." He started to pull her to walk around Sam when the Indian suddenly pulled out the long knife that had been strapped to his hip.

As Sam made a show of examining his blade, flashing the metal against the sunlight, Helen noticed North appeared to be growing more apprehensive by the minute.

"All right, you've had your fun, Sam. Now put the knife away," she called out.

Sam scowled at her. "But I haven't even shown him my frightening war cry," he complained.

North looked at her with disbelief. "You *know* him?"

Helen's arm was starting to hurt as North unconsciously kept tightening his grip. "If I vow with all sincerity that he will not scalp us, will you let go of my arm?"

North immediately let go, his face matching the apology he offered her. "Please accept my forgiveness, I did not realize. . ."

"Are you hurting my woman?" Sam roared angrily as he stomped over to where they were standing.

Helen groaned, holding out a hand to stop the tall man. "Will you cease calling me your woman?" she lamented. "I've told you time and time again that—"

"I demand to know what he means by the words *my woman*," North interjected, his question directed to Helen but his eyes steady on Sam.

Helen put her hands on either side of her face and shook her head. "Oh, dear! This is getting dreadfully out of hand. If you both would stop and listen—"

"I have tried three times to barter a trade between myself and Baumgartner for Helen," Sam started to explain in his blunt way.

"You've done *what*?" North interrupted, but Sam, unfazed, continued.

"He has rejected all my offers, but this time I don't think he will." He waved a hand back toward the black horses. "This time I have brought not two, but three of the finest horses around this area. I do not think he will refuse."

"Trade. . ." North choked as he listened to Sam. "That is the most preposterous thing I have ever heard. You can't be serious," he barked and turned to Helen. "Tell me he isn't serious."

"Sam, I told you our people do not trade women or even men for horses or anything else! It's just simply not civilized."

Sam scoffed at her words, which he'd heard many times before. "I have seen white men barter for the black men and women," he countered. "I see no difference!"

How can I argue with that? Helen stared at Sam, disconcerted. "Sam, I am not for sale, and there is no more I can say about it. Mr. Baumgartner, even if he wanted to, could not trade me to you. He doesn't own me."

"I can't even believe I am hearing this conversation. Why are you trying to reason with him?" North said, exasperation threaded in his tone.

"This is none of your business, white man!" Sam barked, his eyes glaring at North.

Helen quickly jumped in, in an attempt to diffuse whatever was happening between the two mistrustful men. "I haven't introduced you two, have I?" she asked brightly as she stepped between them, causing them both to back up. "This is Sam Youngblood, Rev. Campbell. He lives just across the bayou. Sam, this is my friend, North. He is the new preacher in town."

Suddenly the hostility left Sam's face, and he smiled broadly. "You are a preacher?"

North seemed unsure of how to react to the Indian's sudden change of attitude. "Yes," he answered after a brief pause.

Sam nodded as he zeroed his focus on Helen, his interest in her shining in his dark, mysterious eyes. "That's good. Because if I can't barter for Helen, then I suppose I'll have to get her another way," he stated.

North tried to move around Helen, but she kept sidestepping him. Finally he just pointed to Sam over her shoulder. "And what other way would that be?"

Helen moaned, "Oh, dear!" She looked over her shoulder and saw Sam was actually enjoying the fact he was upsetting North.

Sam shrugged, and with a sigh that sounded as though he was quite put out, he answered, "I'll have to woo her into marrying me, I guess."

"Mar—" North choked on his words again. "Did you hear what he just said?" he practically shouted at her.

Oh yes, she'd heard, and she was just a little perturbed at his seeming reluctance to try to court her. It didn't matter that she didn't want him to!

"You don't have to seem as though it would be a great hardship to woo me!" she scolded Sam. "You were certainly willing to give up your best three horses for me, so what is the difference?"

North, standing behind her now, tapped her on the shoulder and whispered forcibly in her ear, "Helen, do you hear what you are saying?"

"It's a lot less work!" Sam answered over North's whisper.

"Well, I never!" Helen huffed, insulted by his words.

"So can you marry us?" Sam asked over her shoulder to North, ignoring Helen's outrage.

"Absolutely not!" North stated with a steely resolve.

"I never said I would marry you!"

"Why not?" Sam said, his question not directed at her but at North again.

"I am not marrying anyone, so please stop discussing a wedding that will never happen!" she yelled at them both as she backed away and glared with hands on hips.

"Do you always yell like this? I'm not sure I want a wife who is so loud," Sam observed with a sudden frown.

Helen tapped her fingers on her hips. "Then I shall make sure to yell at you every time we meet!"

Sam scowled at that answer. North smiled at her with admiration.

Both men were driving her crazy.

Without so much as another word, she whirled around, tossing her dark curls behind her, and marched to the house.

⌒⌒

North watched Helen flounce away, and he couldn't help but admire her spunk and the way she had stood up to Sam. She would indeed make a fine wife, but not to the Indian. No, she would make a very fine wife for a man like himself.

At least the man he imagined he was, he amended, as he thought about how his own past was still a mystery.

"So I have competition for Helen Nichols," Sam commented, as though he already knew the answer.

North answered anyway. "No, because you have no chance in winning her heart." It was an overconfident statement for which he had nothing to back it up except his own hopes for Helen.

Sam stared at him as if he were trying to decipher the truth. "You believe you do?"

North smiled a confident smile filled with determination. "I know I do."

North returned the Indian man's stare measure for measure. Finally, Sam answered with equal conviction, "We shall see, preacher man." And with that he nodded his head and turned to gather his horses.

As North began to walk back toward the path that Helen had taken, he realized he actually liked Sam, despite his fondness for the woman of North's choice. He found he looked forward to learning more about Sam's culture and way of life.

Did Indians of his tribe actually scalp people?

It wasn't hard to locate Helen after he'd reached the plantation house because she was sitting on the front porch with Josie sipping tea. The first thing he noticed was that she'd tied back her beautiful black hair with a ribbon.

Pity.

"I was wondering if you two brutes had killed one another," she told him as he walked up the many steps to where they were seated.

"Let's just say we had a few things to talk over," he prevaricated.

"Did he show you his big knife? I once saw him cut a snake clean in two with one swipe!" Josie threw in, apparently not wanting to be left out of the conversation.

"Never mind about that!" Helen waved toward the younger girl as if dismissing her words. "What possible things would you have to discuss with Sam?" she demanded to know.

North had to try hard not to smile at her curiosity. "I believe the subject revolved around"—he paused for effect—"your marriage."

"My *marriage*!" she gasped, coming out of her chair and nearly spilling the tea on the wooden floor.

"You're getting married?" Josie queried in an exciting voice. "Who are you getting married to?"

"Nobody!"

"Wait and see."

They spoke at the same time, and Josie clapped her hands with delight. "I'll bet it's Sam! He's been in love with Helen since she got here!"

"But she's not in love with *him*," North answered without thinking, only realizing until after he spoke how self-assured he sounded.

One should never, ever presume to tell a woman what her feelings are, he remembered too late.

She gasped with incredulity at his words. North couldn't help but admire how beautiful she looked even when she was angry. "Perhaps I want to marry Sam!" she stated, emphasizing each word.

North knew good and well she didn't, but it didn't stop him from feeling irritated that she'd said it. "You've turned him down three times!" he countered with a snap of his fingers, remembering his earlier conversation with Sam.

Helen looked less angry, as if she thought she had the upper hand in the conversation. Almost deliberately she began to study her nails. "Maybe I was holding out for four horses."

The whole conversation seemed so silly that North began to laugh. A quick glance at Helen told him that she, too, found the whole exchange ridiculous. Soon they were both laughing.

"I don't know what is so funny," Josie huffed as she stood from her chair. "If you don't want the horses, I'll take them!"

That just made them laugh harder.

Chapter 8

It was with great excitement that Helen and the Baumgartner family dressed for church the next morning. In fact, the whole area was abuzz with anticipation of finally having church services and their very own pastor. Weddings would not have to be delayed, and funerals could finally be done properly, with a minister presiding over them instead of someone just reading scriptures. There had been no one for spiritual guidance and no one qualified to go to for clarification on certain scriptures.

Among the females in the area, however, their excitement was not focused so much on the spiritual benefits but rather on the fact that he was young, single, and extremely handsome. Helen didn't really want to listen to that particular rumor from Imogene as they walked into the church, but there was plenty of evidence to support it when they entered and saw every female in the church dressed fancier than Helen had ever seen them.

Helen was amazed at the elaborately decorated bonnets that all seemed to match their frocks perfectly. It was almost like being transported back to London, so stylish they all looked. She glanced down at her own gown, which was nice with its pink flowers at the bodice and flowing cream taffeta below the high waist, yet it wasn't as stylish and well made as most of the dresses in the room. Even her bonnet, though one of her finest, seemed dowdy in comparison.

These were like all the society ladies whom North was used to being around in England. Would the sight of them jog his memory?

As she thought of North, she looked around but was unable to see him among the twenty or so people there in attendance. Helen took her seat beside the Baumgartners on one of the middle rows. It was then that she saw North enter the church from the side door by the pulpit.

She was only able to partially see his face as he took a seat in the front pew, and she wondered why he didn't look about the room at all. In fact, he seemed a little tense as he faced forward, not speaking to anyone.

Helen glanced to her side, and Josie, too, seemed to be studying North's strange behavior. But before Helen could whisper anything to her young friend, Ollie Rhymes, the self-appointed hymn leader from the Hill plantation, called for everyone to stand and turn to hymn number twenty-three. It was then that Helen noticed the handmade booklet with words to songs written out in plain script and tied together with a heavy string. Since she was sitting on the end and there was only one booklet per pew, she was unable to sing the words to the unfamiliar song. It really didn't matter because poor Miss Ollie sang like an injured housecat; and since she was hard of hearing, her volume was one of gargantuan proportions.

Though Josie was all but holding her ears as she grimaced with mock pain, Helen barely gave Miss Ollie a glance, her gaze still fixed on North.

What is wrong with him?

"What's wrong with him?" Josie echoed her thoughts, talking louder than a whisper as she tried to make herself heard over the caterwauling.

Helen noticed the disapproving frown from Imogene directed at her daughter, so she just shook her head in lieu of an answer.

Finally, Miss Ollie ended the song, and Helen could almost hear the audible prayer of thanks from everyone in the small church as the petite, elderly woman stepped down from the pulpit.

Miss Ollie smiled and nodded toward North, giving him his cue that it was his turn.

Apparently he didn't know the cue.

North just sat there, and after a few seconds, the congregation started whispering and moving around.

What *was* wrong with North?

Finally Miss Ollie apparently got tired of standing there and smiling at him. She went over to him, slapped him on top of his shoulder, and said, "It's your turn, sonny."

This time North responded with a jerk as if he had awakened from a dream. He quickly stood and looked around nervously. Stiffly, he walked to the pulpit and put down his Bible and notes.

It seemed like an eternity passed as he slowly flipped through his Bible, adjusted his papers, then cleared his throat at least four times.

"Has he ever done this before?" Josie whispered, still too loud. A smattering of laughter trickled from the people sitting around them as they heard her comment.

"Shh!" Helen sounded sharply as she prayed North would be able to calm down and begin his message.

Finally he read the scripture passage they'd chosen together. His voice sounded steady and strong as he read expertly from his Bible, and Helen started to relax.

He was doing fine. Of course, he could do this! He was, after all, a duke!

Unfortunately, poor North didn't have any idea who he was or what he was capable of. For after he read the scripture, he looked up at the crowd, looked back down at his Bible, and. . .

Nothing! He seemed unable to speak another word.

<hr />

North was so seized with self-doubt that he couldn't seem to get another word out! He just couldn't seem to fathom why he had chosen the occupation of clergyman when he was so obviously afraid of speaking in public.

Wouldn't it be something that comes naturally? he wondered hurriedly as he struggled to get hold of his panic. But then nothing else had come naturally. Not taking care of animals, providing for himself without the help of a servant, and certainly not writing sermons. Why should he believe this would be any different?

Nothing felt right. His collar was too tight, his shoes were actually a little too big, and he thought he might have gotten a splinter in his hand when he stepped up to the pulpit and ran his palm on the top of the wooden surface.

Read! Just read your message. It is all written out for you, he told himself so sternly that he feared he'd spoken it aloud. But when he looked at the congregation, they merely seemed curious and puzzled as to why he was just standing there not saying anything.

He didn't want to tell them of his memory loss because they would believe him to be crazy. If he didn't control his fear, they were going to come to that conclusion anyway!

Taking a deep breath, he prayed he would find a peace and be able to proceed. And miraculously, God must have heard because he was able to take a deep breath, his heartbeat slowing down so he could focus.

He lifted his gaze and saw Helen's concerned eyes fastened on him. A feeling like North knew he'd never felt before seemed to hit him square in the chest and straight to his heart. But it didn't make him more nervous; instead, it gave him a greater peace, knowing she was there supporting him.

He smiled at her but quickly moved his gaze about the room so as not to let everyone think he was flirting with a woman in church and in sight of everyone. When he briefly looked back at her, she was returning his smile, looking quite relieved that he seemed to be all right.

He looked back down at his notes and began to read. He kept trying to stop and make comments on what he was reading without having to look directly from his notes, but he couldn't seem to think of anything. So he read. And read.

And read.

He didn't *once* look up.

He finished the sermon in what he was sure was record time for a clergyman. In fact, the whole thing including the scripture reading could not have lasted more than ten minutes.

When he finally spoke the last words on his page, he looked up to find everyone staring at him with sort of a dazed expression on their faces. Not knowing what else to do, he quickly bowed his head and said a closing prayer, which sounded amateurish at best.

The members of his congregation were as polite as they could be as they filed out of the building, shaking his hand as they passed him. Every once in a while someone would actually tell him that his sermon was good, and North had to wonder if God wouldn't mind the lie so much since they were only trying to be nice.

Finally Helen was standing before him, giving him a smile that could only be described as one borne out of pity. Splendid, he thought grimly. The woman for whom he carried great affection felt sorry for him.

"You did it!" she whispered with encouragement. "It can only get easier from here."

North didn't feel quite so optimistic, but he did manage to murmur, "Thank you."

"You read really fast," Josie offered. She was wearing the same expression as Helen.

Helen nudged the younger girl and scolded, "Don't say that, Josie. He read quite nicely."

"I was trying to compliment him!"

North stemmed whatever Helen was about to say by stepping up and putting his hand on Josie's shoulder. "Thank you, Josie. You are very sweet," he told her, touched that she, too, was trying to help him feel better.

The sermon *really* must have been appalling.

"Rev. Campbell! Will you join us for our noonday meal?" Imogene asked, coming up behind Helen and Josie. "We have invited the whole church to come and picnic with us on our plantation."

There was nothing North wanted to do less than be around the congregation, but he saw no way to bow out graciously. "Of course I'll join you."

"Excellent!" Imogene exclaimed with a smile. "Then would you mind taking the barouche with Josie and Helen? I'll ride with my husband in our carriage."

He told her he would, and when everyone had exited the church, he closed it up and headed for the carriage, where Helen and Josie sat waiting for him.

Helen's face blossomed into a breathtaking smile when she saw him. North suddenly didn't care that he had embarrassed himself or that he would still have to face his congregation once again.

He was about to spend another day with Helen.

Nothing else mattered.

All through North's sermon, Helen couldn't help feeling responsible for putting him through the whole tedious ordeal. She felt such admiration for him because, even though he didn't know what he was doing, he was willing to give it his best efforts.

In fact, Helen realized now that she hadn't really known North at all back in England. She had only been taken by his good looks and charming ways. She had never seen the giving, caring person who was nervous about public speaking and so determined to do what he thought was right—to be the man everybody thought he was even though he didn't feel like Hamish Campbell.

He was truly a good, decent man. A wonderful Christian man.

She didn't deserve him, but she couldn't tell him that. She couldn't tell him any of the truths she, and only she, knew to be true, because it would not only hurt him but everyone she respected in Golden Bay.

Helen felt terrible she had let things go this far. When she first thought of lying to him, she never stopped to consider the consequences. All of her reasoning was based on herself.

Now all she thought of was North. Every night she prayed not that God would forgive her but that He'd help her find a way of helping North get his memory back without hurting him too much in the process.

Unfortunately, it sounded like an insurmountable task.

"All right, ladies. You are being too quiet, and Josie keeps smiling politely at me as if she's been instructed to do so," North said suddenly, breaking the long silence as they rode toward Golden Bay plantation. "Why don't you just give me your honest opinions? Trust me, it could be no worse than what I have already thought of myself."

"Well. . ." She hesitated, desperately trying to think of something positive to say. "You have a very nice voice for speaking. It's deep and very pleasant to listen to."

North threw her a look that told her he knew she was evading the question. "Wonderful! I read swiftly and I have a pleasant voice. Anything else?"

"You could use some practice," Josie told him bluntly, making Helen groan with embarrassment. "Well, it is the truth, and that is what he asked for, isn't it?" she tried to reason after Helen glared at her.

"Josie, don't you remember our lesson on tact?" Helen stressed while throwing North an apologetic smile. "A lady does not voice every thought that pops in her mind!"

"Please don't scold, Helen," North interjected. "She is quite right. I do need practice."

Helen thought a minute about how the Reverend Wakelin prepared for his sermons. "If you start writing it tomorrow, perhaps by the time the week rolls by, it will become familiar to you. Perhaps it will help take away your nervousness and give you more confidence."

"Yes! And then you can practice your sermon on us!" Josie added excitedly. "We shall be your congregation, preparing you for the real one on Sunday."

North looked over to Helen, and she found herself moved by the appreciation that was radiating from his beautiful blue eyes. Her heart ached with all the love and affection that seemed to grow each time she was in his presence. There was a hope inside her that still refused to die.

A hope he really could love her and desire to marry her.

"Would you mind doing as Josie has suggested?" he asked, still holding her gaze as if he, too, could not look away. "I wouldn't want to bring a conflict between you and your employers."

"Oh, don't worry about that," Josie answered before Helen could speak. "Mama has been hinting around to Helen that you would make her a good husband." Josie ignored Helen's horrified gasp. "I know she will agree to let us visit you."

With a face she knew was flaming red, Helen watched North's expression to gauge his reaction. She was relieved when he appeared to be happy with that news.

Helen's gaze slowly lowered to Josie, and she saw the young girl looking at her with a sheepish expression. "I'm in quite a lot of trouble, aren't I?" she whispered in an apologetic voice.

"You can be assured of it," she whispered back as they entered the main yard of the plantation.

Helen scanned the lawn and noticed for the second time just how many young women were in attendance. Most of them she'd never seen before this day.

And when the sound of the carriage drew everyone's attention, every single female smiled and began to walk straight for the barouche.

There was only one word running through Helen's mind, and it wasn't a nice one.

Competition!

Chapter 9

Hello, Rev. Campbell!" said the one with the huge blue bonnet decorated with lighter blue flowers.

"Yoo-hoo! Over here, Reverend," said the brunette in the bright yellow dress.

"I truly enjoyed your sermon this morning," said the one with the light blond hair as she fluttered her eyelids.

What a liar! Helen thought mean-spiritedly, her mood darkening with each little shrill giggle. He had barely handed Josie and Helen down from the barouche before the ladies surrounded him, all giving North one simpering compliment after the other.

North looked a little dazed, as he appeared to be trying to make sense of their words, since they were talking all at once.

Helen and Josie were both wearing frowns as they watched him being led from them over to where the table of food was set.

"It's like watching a bunch of crabs all trying to grab hold of a baited string at one time," Josie commented; and since Helen had no idea what she was talking about, she would have to take the younger girl's word for it.

"He's certainly not fighting off their attentions," she observed but then felt petty for voicing it aloud.

"I think he's just overwhelmed!"

"Hmm," Helen sounded skeptical as she continued to watch North. They were actually preparing him a plate of food, each one adding to it. They were creating a small mountain not even three men could possibly eat.

"Girls! You've lost him!" Imogene cried for their ears only as she came running hurriedly up to them. "Helen, you must do something!"

She had to be joking! "Mrs. Baumgartner, what can I possibly do? He doesn't seem to mind the attention," Helen told her, and again she heard the jealousy in her tone.

Imogene waved her hand as if to refute her words. "Of course he doesn't." She sucked in a loud breath. "Did you see that?" she asked excitedly as she pointed in North's direction. "He's looking around. . . . See! He looks like he needs rescue! So *go!*"

All Helen saw was North looking at the pile of food on his plate with something akin to horror and then peering around for a place to sit. That was quickly resolved for him when the blue bonnet girl led him to an empty table.

"I'm going to get something to eat," Helen said instead of responding to Imogene's urgings. Determinedly, she began to walk toward the table of food.

"But, Helen!" Imogene pleaded after her. Still, Helen doggedly kept walking. It took a lot of willpower not to look at North when she passed his table, which was now occupied by all the ladies.

"Helen!" she thought she heard him call, but it could have only been her wishful thinking.

These women were ridiculous in their behavior, Helen observed as she heard them giggle and chatter. In England, never would a girl go up to a man she hadn't been introduced to and speak to him.

It was too bad North couldn't remember that!

Or maybe he did, she amended her thoughts as she plopped the food on her plate without really paying attention to what she was getting.

She found a table on the other side of the lawn from where North sat with his admirers.

When she realized she had scooped a large amount of collard greens on her plate, a vegetable that was her least favorite food, she sighed and pushed her plate away. She really wasn't hungry anyway.

She was jealous, and it was silly to feel that way, really. Everyone believed North to be their clergyman and wanted to know him better. And since there was quite a shortage of young, marriageable men in the area, they probably all had higher hopes they could know him *much* better.

" 'It isn't ladylike to pout,' " Josie quoted as she sat beside her while placing her plate of food on the table. Helen could tell Josie had managed to fill her plate without her mother looking on, for it was filled with slices of cake and pie. " 'It puts one's face in an unattractive position and causes tiny lines to form between one's eyes. . . .' " She paused from her speech, in which she used an exaggerated English accent, and thought a moment. "Or was the lines between the eyes thing for when one is jealous *and* angry?"

Helen sighed. "I suppose I have become a bit fond of North." She nibbled on a piece of bread and then noticed the boiled crawfish on her plate. *How did that nasty little creature get there?* She could never understand how civilized people could get so much enjoyment out of cracking open the outer shells and biting the meat out of the tail with their teeth.

She knew ladies of London's society who would faint dead away at the sight of such a spectacle.

"I may be only thirteen, but I am not blind, Helen. I could tell you were in love with him the moment you realized who he was on that first day. Even Mother agrees."

She spoke like a woman of twenty! "You are too young to know what love is," Helen countered as she carefully picked up the crawfish by one of its pinchers and tossed it on Josie's plate.

"Oh, thank you!" Josie automatically responded. And just as Helen knew she would, she cracked and peeled the shellfish in no time at all.

Helen shuddered.

"I do know about love." Josie picked up the conversation after she had wiped her hands on her cloth napkin. "My father left behind a title and his father's riches because he loved my mother. One day I'll find love like that." She sighed dreamily as she said this, and Helen didn't remind her of her earlier statement about not even liking boys.

Helen also didn't mention the fact that Josie's father wasn't exactly poor after he was disinherited, either. She wondered if he'd have married Imogene if there had been no inheritance from his mother and if they'd had to start from nothing. She looked across the lawn and saw Robert walk by his wife at that moment. Before continuing to where his friends were standing, he put a hand on her shoulder and squeezed it. A sweet gesture. Perhaps he would have married her no matter what.

"I hope you will find true love, Josie," Helen said instead as she finally allowed her gaze to settle on North. She was startled to see him staring straight at her. She glanced around him and noticed there were other people besides the young women around him now.

North smiled at her then looked back to the man on his right, who appeared to be speaking to him.

Helen sighed dreamily, already forgetting her earlier jealousy. That smile from North had undone all the hurt she'd felt over being pushed out of the way by the other girls.

It was then she became aware that the blond girl with the fluttery eyes was still sitting next to him. North was looking at her, and she seemed to be telling him something.

Suddenly Helen was struck by a horrible thought. What if North fell in love with someone else? Not only would it make Helen terribly sad, but it could also spell disaster if North got his memory back!

If he fell in love with any of these young ladies and even married one of them, he could wake up one day and realize his whole life was a lie. He and his future wife would be devastated. It would be more disastrous than if he married Helen.

Steps had to be taken to insure this did not happen!

She was going to have to embarrass herself. There was just no other way about it!

"I'll be right back!" she told Josie as she jumped up from her chair and all but ran over to where North was sitting. . .still talking to *Blondie*!

What do I say? What do I do? she asked herself over and over as she drew nearer to him. It had to be some reasonable excuse to pull him away from his table and from *her*!

"Uh. . .Reverend. . .uh. . .Campbell!" she stuttered as she tried to catch her breath and remember what to call him.

"I. . .uh. . ."

She drew a complete blank. She glanced about the table and noticed every eye was on her, curious as to what she was going to say.

"Uh. . ." Nothing. She wondered if this was how North felt this morning when he was trying to deliver his sermon. Her eyes strayed to the blond, and there was a certain smirk about her rosy lips that suggested she knew what Helen was up to.

"What's wrong, Miss Nichols?" North asked, his tone more questioning than concerned.

"Uh. . ." She stalled again. She glanced at the blond again and noticed she was back fluttering her eyes at North, trying to get his attention.

It was the eye-fluttering thing that inspired her.

She began to bat only one of her eyes. "My eye!" Batting one eye was not an easy thing to do. "I believe there is something in it."

North looked at her with a somewhat bemused expression. "It looked fine just a moment ago."

"It comes and goes," she answered quickly, realizing how ridiculous she sounded. But since she had begun the ruse, she might as well finish it. "Would you mind stepping over there in the sunlight and looking at it for me?" She pointed to a spot far from the shaded area they were seated in.

"Pardon me, but might I be of some help?" the man beside North questioned, finally bringing all the attention off of Helen and onto him. "I am Dr. Giles. I have a practice in New Orleans, but I come through Golden Bay every month to check on everyone here. Why don't I take a look at it?"

"Oh. . ." Helen sounded like a deflating balloon. Just like her bright ideas! "I suppose that would be all right," she relented after coming up with no reasonable excuse to turn down his offer of help.

"I'll walk with you," North chimed in, and Helen could have kissed him. Did he know what she'd been up to? "I will hold your hand while the doctor performs the surgery," he added teasingly. One quick glance at his eyes told her she hadn't fooled him one bit.

"Never take the eyes lightly, Reverend," the doctor cautioned, unaware of Helen's subterfuge. "One tiny shard of wood or glass can cause a world of damage."

"Of course, Doctor," North answered contritely as they followed the older man, who was dressed rather more like the dandies of the English *ton* than the usual American mode of dress she'd seen thus far. His coat was a rich gold color with red trim at the sleeves and lapel. The vest underneath matched the ruby color of the trim and was made of shiny brocade. Considering every other man at the picnic wore more somber colors in shades of black, gray, and brown, he quite stood out.

Helen felt ridiculous as Dr. Giles examined her eye. He kept making the sound "mm-hmm," and she wondered if he actually saw anything.

He didn't. "I'm afraid I cannot tell you the source of your irritation," he finally told her, looking perplexed.

Helen could have told him her source of irritation had blond hair and was flirting with the man she loved. Instead she thanked him for at least going to the trouble of examining her. "Perhaps the wind blew it out," she offered.

He accepted that it could have happened, and both she and North walked him back to the table.

Blondie was still there. Waiting. She was already smiling at him, and the fluttering eyelids would certainly be next! "Nor. . .uh. . .Reverend! Would you walk me back to my table? I just wanted to have a word with you for a minute."

North didn't even look surprised by her request. "Of course. Will you excuse me?" he asked to the table at large, and Helen was glad to notice he didn't so much as glance at the blond.

"If you wanted to talk to me, Helen, there was no need to go to such theatrics. Next time, just ask," he told her in a low voice as he smiled at her, flashing his even, white teeth.

Helen's face felt heated with embarrassment. "I noticed the blond girl was so ill-manneredly monopolizing all your time, and so I thought that since you might not know how to extricate yourself without hurting her feelings, I tried to do it for you," she offered, the lengthy explanation hardly making sense even to her!

But North agreed. "Aye, I was feeling quite uncomfortable. I might not remember much, but I do know the young ladies here are not skilled in the art of ladylike manner or etiquette. These are some of the finest families in the area, and yet I do not understand why this facet of their children's upbringing is overlooked."

"Many of the English families are not former nobility such as Robert Baumgartner is but have come from little or nothing and become wealthy with hard work. I've heard the Creole plantations are a little different because more of them are from aristocratic families hailing from mostly France and Spain." Helen shrugged. "That is why I am here. The Baumgartners wanted to make sure their youngest daughter was taught those things."

They both looked to see Josie still sitting at the table stuffing cake in her mouth. Helen noticed there was white frosting smudged on both cheeks, and she, along with North, began to laugh. "Whether she will follow your teachings is quite another thing altogether."

Helen laughed more. "I'm afraid you are right. Even her sister was having a tough time adjusting to all the rules of society when last I saw her." Helen thought about the beautiful and friendly Claudia Baumgartner whom she'd met while visiting London with Christina. "Claudia is determined to be the lady that her grandfather, the Marquis of Moreland, wants her to be, yet I can't help feeling she's very unhappy. It's like seeing a caged tiger at a circus that you know just longs to be free."

"Did I ever meet her?" North asked, and Helen remembered that indeed she had seen him talking to her once.

"I believe you had been introduced," she answered truthfully for she had no idea if he was better acquainted with her or not.

North and Helen sat down at the table, and Josie chose that moment to get up, announcing she was going for another round.

North laughed. "She is going to be sick."

"Not if Mrs. Baumgartner sees her!" Helen peered over her shoulder to where Josie had just reached the dessert table. Just as she knew she would, her mother was there to intercept and lead her over to the regular food.

They chatted for a moment, topics ranging all the way from the weather to the people they'd met in Golden Bay. Finally, their words drifted away; and for a sweet moment, they sat looking into one another's eyes, neither looking away. Helen was surprised to have no feeling of awkwardness, and she got the impression he felt the same.

"Helen, if I may be so bold to ask this, what is there between you and me?" he suddenly came out with, surprising them both. He sat back, rubbing a hand over his face. "I am sorry to have spoken so forcibly out of turn," he began to apologize.

"No, it is all right," Helen expressed, her heart pounding with fear and expectation all at one time. "You cannot remember anything, so—"

"But you see, it is not that reason for which I am speaking." He looked around as if to see if anyone had heard his impassioned statement and then let out a breath. "I am experiencing feelings for you I feel did not just begin when I first saw you two weeks ago. It's as though my heart remembers even though my mind cannot. I know we did not act upon them, but was there a mutual attraction between us?"

Helen could only be confused by his words. North had never given her any indication he felt anything but friendship for her when they were in England. He thought her pretty—this much she knew from Christina—but wouldn't she have sensed anything deeper from him? When he looked at her with his dazzling, friendly smile, wouldn't she have read something more in the depths of his blue gaze?

She had certainly looked hard enough for any sign, any shred of love or deep affection.

She had lied to this man and misled him on so many things. And even though she had the golden opportunity to make him believe there was more between them so that he would feel more confident to pursue her, she just couldn't tell another lie.

"I will tell you honestly, North, that I never knew you thought of me as anything but a friend. If you felt more, then I was not aware of it," she told him, careful not to mention her own feelings.

North shook his head. "I know I must have, Helen. The question is why did I not act upon it? Why did I not call upon you and pursue what I know I must have been feeling in my heart?"

Helen tried to comprehend what he was telling her, but she couldn't believe it. Surely he had to be wrong! North had feelings for her when he knew he was a duke?

Helen thought back on the times she last saw him and realized that he started to avoid her at the balls she would attend. He would say no more than a few words before he'd excuse himself to go talk to a friend and such. Could it have been because he liked her more than he should yet saw no hope in it?

Helen looked at North, with his lock of golden hair falling in a wave over his brow and the stylish yet simply made suit, which was tight about his shoulders. His handsome looks and elegance did not fit the image everyone had put him in. They thought he was a clergyman, so they did not look past that title to grasp that this was no ordinary, common man.

"Perhaps your family would not have approved of me. I am, after all, just a gentleman farmer's daughter. They could have been pressuring you to settle on a woman of means," she offered truthfully.

"Hmm," North sounded, rubbing his chin thoughtfully. "I had not thought of that. It would seem like, judging from my attire, my family may have been in a financial quandary. Perhaps they were pressuring me to find an heiress," he murmured more to himself than to her as if he were trying to reason it all out.

Abruptly, he raised his head and smiled like a man who knew all the answers. "I have it all figured out!" he declared.

Helen felt as though her heart had fallen to the pit of her belly. "You remember everything?" she asked, trying not to sound dismayed by that prospect.

North, however, shook his head. "Unfortunately no, but I have been struck with insight! I know the reason I came to America!"

Helen blinked, trying to adjust to the path their conversation had taken. With North, she felt like she was often riding on a wild carriage ride, not knowing where they were heading or what sudden turns they might take. "It wasn't to be their preacher?" she offered, interested to know what scenario his mind had conjured up.

"Helen, I chose Louisiana because I knew you were going to be here!"

Chapter 10

One week then two passed, yet Helen could not stop thinking about North's words at the picnic. Though she tried to dissuade him from his reasoning, he would not be influenced. To him, everything made perfect sense, and he treated his "epiphany," as he called it, almost like it was a true memory.

Helen frankly did not know what to do or say when North wanted to talk about it. Which he did—quite a lot. He wanted to know about each meeting they had, what they said, and how they treated one another.

It was so taxing on her poor nerves that Helen began to make excuses to stay away from his house. But that didn't work because he would just come down to the plantation to see her. It was an easy thing to do since he had an ally in the house, namely Imogene Baumgartner.

One good thing that happened was that North's preaching, thanks to Josie and Helen's helping him prepare, was greatly improved on the next Sunday and one might say even inspiring on the third one. He seemed to be acclimating himself within the community as he visited families and prayed for their sick. As odd as it was, he seemed to be thriving in the occupation he was never meant to perform.

Helen would give herself headaches at night just thinking about the what-ifs. What if he never got his memory back? Would he be happy and content as Hamish Campbell? What if he didn't remember until he was fifty? Would he want to rush back to England and try to acclimate himself into his old life, or would he decide to continue as a preacher?

Helen was certainly no philosopher about life's mysteries, but it sure opened her mind to possibilities outside what she'd always known. She even raised the question to herself as to whether God had, indeed, meant for North to take poor Hamish Campbell's place.

But He didn't mean for you to lie and break one of His commandments, a voice would always remind her whenever she began to justify herself and her actions.

A knock sounded at her door, pulling Helen from her pondering. It was Monday morning, and she was supposed to have been brushing her hair but had, as usual, gotten lost in her thoughts.

After Helen called out for her visitor to come in, Imogene Baumgartner walked into the room, her face clearly upset. "Helen, I have just heard the most devastating news," she stated right away, her voice full of sorrow as she pulled a chair up so she could sit beside Helen.

Helen immediately thought of North. "Has something happened to Rev. Campbell?" she cried, not even realizing how easily his false name just rolled off her tongue.

Imogene quickly assured her that wasn't it. She placed her hand over Helen's and told her, "It concerns Lord Trevor Kent, the Duke of Northingshire, who is related to our friends at the Kent plantation."

Uh-oh, Helen thought with mounting dread. In the few weeks North had been in Golden Bay, not once had she considered that if North were here, everyone else in the world would presume he was dead. How incredibly selfish and single-minded she had been!

"I'm afraid he has been declared missing and assumed to be dead," Imogene said gently, speaking the words Helen had already assumed would be the news. "I believe Josie said you knew him?"

Helen glanced at her and then quickly lowered her eyes, hoping to give her employer the notion that she was shocked by the news. "Yes, but I knew him only as an acquaintance while I was in England," she said softly and carefully, trying not to lie yet not wanting Imogene to know of her feelings for the duke.

"Oh, then I am truly sorry," she offered in condolence as she patted Helen's hand again. "I have often heard from the Kents of what a fine man he'd been and how generous he was to his friends and loved ones. I had been hoping to meet him."

Helen listened to Imogene and heard her sigh sadly. "He was very nice to me when I first met him," Helen said, feeling like she needed to say something. In truth, she felt sick inside as she thought of his poor relatives and what they must be going through. Then she asked, trying to keep the worry from her voice, "Have they notified his family in England?"

She was relieved when Imogene shook her head. "No, they said they would search a little longer before they sent word. They are hoping against all odds that he still lives."

Helen wanted to cry. What was she to do now? Again the situation had grown more complicated.

"Well, I'll leave you to your grooming," the older lady said as she got up from her seat and straightened the bow on the high waist of her fawn-colored morning dress. She was almost at the door, when she seemed to suddenly remember something. "Oh! I also wanted to ask a favor of you."

Helen, still overwhelmed by this latest obstacle, nodded absently.

"Pierre, poor dear, is sick this morning with what appears to be some sort of stomach ailment. Is there any way you and Josie could take the barouche and make sure Rev. Campbell has all he needs today? Pierre tells me he still burns everything he tries to cook, and I know you have some knowledge in this area. . . ?" She let her voice drift off in a question.

Helen managed to curve her lips into a smile that she truly did not feel. "Of course I'll go."

"Excellent! I normally would have one of the house servants go, but since I know you like to spend time with him, I didn't think you would mind," she told her in a gentle, teasing tone and then left the room.

Yes, Helen loved spending time with North; but the more she was in his presence, despite their growing feelings for one another, the more she got the feeling that a future between them could never be.

There was a great deal of self-pity in North's thoughts and even in his walk as he practically dragged himself from his little house out to the barn. He'd sat in his house an hour after he'd received word that Pierre wouldn't arrive, hoping someone would be sent as a replacement.

No one came.

So he came to terms with the fact that if he didn't go out and retrieve the milk and eggs himself, plus get a slab of bacon from the underground ceramic urns that served as a way to keep his food cool, he was going to starve.

Well, he amended to himself, he would certainly be very hungry. That would lead to his being cranky, and he would be unable to begin to study his new sermon for the upcoming Sunday.

Since he was actually beginning to enjoy his studies of the Bible and finding just the right message to share with his congregation, he decided to search for nourishment.

So here he was, about to enter his least favorite place in this world. . .his barn.

He had to admit, he was getting better at milking the cow, although he managed to connive Pierre into doing it most days.

Thankfully, this morning Queen Mary must have "been in the mood" because she gave over her milk without a lot of fuss. The chickens were another matter altogether, however. They seemed not at all like themselves; instead, they were restless, jittery, and unwilling to part with their eggs as usual.

He finally managed to grab a few but not without war wounds to show for his struggle.

He'd no sooner swung open his heavy barn door when he spotted the source of his chickens' anxieties. There, stretched out straight with his mouth wide open toward North, was the most ferocious, ugly beast he'd ever encountered.

Alligator!

What had he heard about them? His mind raced. Did they attack? Did they eat humans? The creature chose that moment to snap his jaw shut and crawl forward a couple of inches as if showing North what he was capable of.

North didn't doubt him one little bit!

The wise course of action at this moment, he knew, would be to get away from the alligator as quickly as possible. The problem was that when the reptile moved forward, he blocked the door from being shut, and there was no other door in the barn.

Except. . .

North glanced around to gauge the distance between himself and the ladder to the loft. From there he could try to jump out of the hayloft door.

Hopefully, he would not break a leg and arm in the process!

As he turned and sprinted toward the ladder, he held tight to his bucket of milk and basket of eggs. Climbing was a lot more difficult with them, but there was no way he was letting that beast take what he'd worked so hard to get!

Once he was out of harm's way, North watched the alligator to see if it would go away.

It didn't.

For what seemed like hours but actually was only minutes, the creature just lay there, not moving one muscle, despite the fact that his animals were all restless and moving about noisily.

Even *they* recognized danger.

After a few more minutes, North concluded he was going to have to try to jump from the loft. For all he knew, it might be days before the creature would decide to leave.

It took him a moment to locate a rope to lower his items. He was in the process of tying them together when he heard a movement from below. Quickly, North scrambled to the loft door leading to the outside and peered down.

He nearly toppled out of the small door when he spotted Sam cradling the now-dead alligator in his arms as he walked out of his barn.

"What are you doing here?" he barked brusquely. He suddenly felt ridiculous hiding up in his hayloft while the Indian had taken no more than a few seconds to take care of the problem.

Sam didn't so much as glance up as he tied the reptile to the back of his horse. The black gelding stirred in protest because of the weight of his new passenger. "Rescuing you from an alligator, preacher man," he answered sardonically as he checked then double-checked his knots.

North, feeling less than a man, backed away from the small door and, with his milk and eggs, made his way back down the ladder. He placed his goods down on a table and then walked out to meet Sam. North noticed him examining his small garden.

"I have something to put on the soil of these carrots that will help them grow," Sam offered. Again he hadn't even looked up to see North walking toward him, and North was sure he hadn't made a sound while walking on the soft grass.

"Thank you, but I have my own way of gardening," he answered, knowing it was childish but finding it hard not to show his irritation where the swaggering Indian was concerned.

North heard Sam make a snorting sound, which just made him more irate.

"How many gardens have you planted?" Sam asked, this time standing up and looking straight at North. The Indian had an unnerving stare.

North couldn't know for sure, but he was almost certain he'd never even *walked* around a vegetable garden in his entire life. "Is there a reason for this visit?"

Sam smirked at him, still giving him that odd stare. It made North, for the first time, wonder if he'd been a violent man in his past because he truly wanted to hit him.

The truth was, however, that North felt strangely inferior to the Choctaw. He seemed to be a man of the earth, capable of defending, feeding, and protecting himself and anyone he cared about. He appeared comfortable with this wild, untamed land, whereas North constantly felt like an outsider.

North was smart enough to know he shouldn't compare himself to the Indian because they were raised in two different worlds and taught very different things, but he found he did anyway.

He hated not to be able to do simple things for himself. He even had trouble dressing himself and was almost certain he'd had a servant to do it for him in Scotland.

He didn't want to be pampered and waited on. He didn't want the kind of life he saw the plantation owners leading, where servants or slaves did everything for them and they did nothing for themselves.

"In your country, what do you do when another man wants the lady that you want?" Sam asked, bringing North's attention back to the smirk he was still sporting.

North had a feeling this was the reason why Sam had come. "The lady chooses the one she loves," he stated with confidence, knowing with all his heart that Helen was falling in love with him. It was in every glance, every smile she gave him. As far as he was concerned, Sam wasn't a rival for her affections.

Sam surprised him by bursting out with a loud, mocking sort of laugh—the kind that really set North's teeth on edge. "You let your women decide? Your people do things peculiarly!"

"And just how do *your people* do things?" North countered. "Throw the women over your horses and whisk them off to your caves until they relent?"

"Since we don't have caves in Louisiana," Sam began, his voice slow and deliberate as though he were talking to a child, "we issue a challenge to our opponent."

North didn't like the sound of that. With a disapproving frown, he told him, "Are we talking about a duel? Because I am most certain they are illegal."

Sam sighed and looked skyward as if trying to hold on to his patience. "This is another thing that irritates me with *your* people. You jump right away to the worst conclusion." He turned and walked back to his horse and withdrew a bow. "This is what I am talking about. A challenge. A contest to see who the better man is."

North eyed the bow and made every effort to pretend to be unfamiliar with one. He knew instinctively that he was familiar with how to handle the weapon. "You want to challenge me to an archery contest?" North asked to make sure he understood that they weren't going to be shooting it at each other. "And if I don't know how to handle a bow...?"

Sam shrugged, his overconfident smirk back on his face. "There are always guns or knives."

North wanted so badly to accept the Indian's offer and show him that he was just as much of a man as Sam was. But he had the distinct feeling Helen would not be pleased and neither would his congregation, once they found out their preacher was in a contest to win a girl's affections!

"Well, Sam, as interesting as that sounds, I will have to turn your offer of challenge down," he told him and watched the Indian's face turn to disappointment.

North couldn't help but wonder if the Indian was trying to befriend him in his own odd little way. "But I would love to join you for target practice sometime. Maybe even try my hand at hunting," North impulsively offered, just to see if he would accept.

Sam appeared interested but only after he studied North a moment, unsure of the preacher's motives. "I will come by in two days, then," he told him and then pointed toward the alligator. "I'll bring you half of the meat I get from the alligator tail, too."

Alligator tail? North didn't say a word. He didn't want Sam thinking he was less of a man because he'd never eaten any. He'd eat every bite if it killed him!

Sam gathered the horse's reins and began to walk off when he unexpectedly stopped and turned for one last comment. "I am still determined to marry Helen Nichols, preacher man," he stated, wanting that particular point understood.

"So am I," North countered, knowing he truly did want nothing more than to marry Helen.

They exchanged a measuring look, and then without another word, Sam grinned and turned to walk away.

Both were surprised to see Helen come from around the house with Josie. "Sam!" she exclaimed, clearly shocked to see him. "What are you doing here?"

"Alligator hunting," was all Sam said as he walked past her, tugging his horse behind him.

Helen opened her mouth as if to say something as she turned to watch him walk away, but no words seemed to come out.

"Did you really go alligator hunting, Rev. North?" Josie asked, using her own version of his name, as she ran up to him, her long, bound hair bouncing as she went.

North reached out and gave her hair a playful yank that made her giggle. There was absolutely no way he was going to tell them what really happened. A man had to maintain some sort of dignity. "Something like that."

"You weren't fighting with him, were you?" Helen asked as she, too, walked up to meet him. "Sam can be a little overbearing, but I wouldn't let him aggravate you. He lives by a whole different set of rules than any man I know."

North reached out and pulled a ladybug off of Helen's shoulder. It was interesting to note that she didn't flinch or jerk away from his touch. Instead she looked at his hand and smiled as the red bug flew away. "Sam *is* very different from most white men," he noted, watching to see what her reaction would be to his next words. "Some women like the outdoorsy, rough and tough type that he is."

He almost laughed when Helen actually shuddered. "I don't know of any woman who enjoys polite society and gently bred manners that would want Sam as a husband!" she stated emphatically.

"I would!" Josie piped up, causing both of the adults to gape at her with astonishment. "He wouldn't care if I had any manners at all!"

Helen shook her head disapprovingly. "You will not get out of learning your lessons on the art of curtsying today, so stop trying."

Josie made a *humph* sound and folded her arms defiantly at her chest. "Why do I need to learn that? I'm an American! We don't bow down to anyone!"

North exchanged a long-suffering glance with Helen, then she looked back down and answered, "Your sister will one day be the Marchioness of Moreland. She will have to bow before the king, and you and your parents will have to do the same thing."

Josie rolled her eyes and made a growling noise. "I'm going to go talk to the chickens. At least there I don't have to be polite or remember my manners."

Helen and North laughed softly as the young girl stomped into the barn.

"You know, if Sam can wait a bit, Josie just might be the perfect match for him," North observed. "But you can't always choose the person you fall in love with. And if he is truly in love with you, he might not want anyone else."

North saw a sadness fall over Helen's face as she murmured wistfully, "That's true."

He bent his head toward her and brought her chin up so she was looking directly into his eyes. "Helen," he began, almost afraid to ask the question. "Were you once in love with someone?"

She just stared at him for a moment, and North wasn't altogether sure she was going to answer him. But finally she did, and the answer hit him squarely in the heart. "Yes, once. A few years ago."

His hand was still on her chin, and she didn't seem to mind when his thumb began to softly caress the skin along her jawline. "What happened?"

"Nothing. He was not a man of my station. In fact, he was way above it." She paused as if she were gauging his reaction. "He was a nobleman, and though I knew he was attracted to me, he chose not to pursue any relationship outside of friendship."

A fire lit within North's heart, and indignation for her hurt flowed from his lips. "That is preposterous!" he articulated passionately. "To throw away a chance at love that may only come once in one's lifetime, just because of one's birth, is an injustice to God and all He created us to be."

He spoke it with such fervor and with such vehemence that North had the feeling he'd grappled with this very situation before, only it had been he who'd faced such a decision.

He realized then that Helen was looking at him as if she didn't believe a word he said.

Chapter 11

Helen could only stare at North with marked disbelief as he moved his hand from her chin to run through his hair in a gesture of perplexity. It wasn't so much what he said but *how* he said it. It was like someone trying to make a case for himself.

What *did* that mean? Did he once grapple with the same feelings—go through the same situation?

Helen could barely think it but couldn't help but hope for it.

Had he been in love with her after all?

But another thought followed directly after that one—if he *had* been in love, he hadn't acted on his feelings. In fact, he'd even started seeking her out less and less at gatherings.

What did *that* mean?

Finally she voiced part of her musings. "You speak as though you have struggled with this dilemma yourself. Did you remember something?"

She held her breath until she saw him shake his head no. "It's odd, really. I feel as though I've made the same argument before, but where? Had you once told me this? Is that what I'm remembering?"

Helen shook her head. "No, I've never told anyone except my best friend, Christina." And she always tried to discourage Helen from letting her attraction to North grow for she feared Helen would be hurt.

North looked so confused and seemed to be trying hard to remember something that would make sense to him. It compelled Helen to reach out spontaneously to hold his hand. The gesture seemed to freeze North for a moment, as his eyes focused on their hands.

Uh-oh. She was being too familiar. Too forward. "I'm sorry, I didn't mean...," she began to ramble as she tried to pull her hand away, but he held fast and interrupted her.

"No! Please...," he cried softly as he looked directly into her eyes, his own searching as if trying to decipher her thoughts. "I like it that you feel so comfortable with me."

She smiled shyly, aware of the change of mood between them—of how important this particular moment seemed to be. Her feelings were so overwhelming to her that she had to remind herself even to breathe.

"I just need to ask you one thing," he said softly, pulling her closer to him. "Are you still in love with the nobleman?"

Now that is a tricky question, Helen thought, panicking for a brief instant. But as she thought of the man she knew in England versus the man she knew him to be here in America, she knew she could answer truthfully. "No, my feelings are not what they were."

North emitted a breath of relief as he looked down for a moment and took her other hand, bringing both of them to his lips. "Helen, you must know of the growing feelings I have for you." She nodded jerkily, still having a hard time comprehending she was standing so close to North. "I would like to openly begin calling on you," he explained. "That would mean everyone would know you and I have an affection for one another, and that includes the congregation. You might come under some scrutiny, so I wanted to warn you beforeha—"

Helen stopped him by putting her fingers over his lips. "Yes," she gushed excitedly, unable to contain her joy.

He took hold of her hand again. "Are you sure?"

She nodded, and they stared into one another's eyes again. Helen forgot that almost everything about their relationship was built on a lie. She forgot the guilt she'd been under and the fear of what might happen in the future. For this one moment, she was going to revel in the love she had carried for so long for this man and remember it when she was old and alone with nothing but memories to get her through.

North leaned forward to brush a stray hair that had blown across her cheek, and when Helen turned to see what he was doing, they found themselves nose to nose.

North paused and looked at her searchingly. And whatever he'd been looking for, he must have found, for he gently pressed a kiss to her lips.

Helen held tight to his hand as his mouth gently caressed hers. Her heart was beating madly, and her mind was swirling, trying to reconcile her old emotions with the brand-new feelings she was experiencing. All the romance and gothic books she had ever read had not even been close to describing the feeling of being in his arms and being kissed by him.

Perhaps God felt sorry for her a little bit, and since He knew she would probably never live down the scandal of what she'd done to North and therefore never find a man who would want to marry her, He was giving her this little bit of bliss to live the rest of her life on.

Helen almost protested when he finally drew his head back and smiled at her. But the wonder in his eyes filled her heart with gladness as he gazed at her one last time before stepping away.

Helen suspected that North must have kissed a half dozen or more women in his lifetime. But he didn't remember any of them, and kissing her was like his first time.

"I can't wait to tell Mama you kissed him!" Josie exclaimed, causing them to jump farther apart and guiltily look at the young girl.

Helen swallowed and threw North a nervous glance. "Uh, Josie, it might not be a good idea to tell your mother about this."

Josie frowned. "Oh, why not? I have to tell somebody!" She smiled, apparently coming up with a better idea. "I know! I'll tell Sam!"

"No!" both Helen and North yelled out to her at the same time.

"You don't want to hurt his feelings, do you?" Helen tried to reason in a softer tone.

"Well, what good is it for me to know if I can't brag about knowing something that no one else knows?"

Helen sighed, rubbing her temples, wondering if the child could ever be tamed. "Josie, later we shall discuss the merits of guarding our tongues."

"Why don't the two of you get the milk and eggs from the barn, and I'll get the bacon from the urns," North suggested, as he must have known Helen was growing weary of dealing with the younger girl.

He knew her so well. "Yes, let's do that!" she agreed, eager to take everyone's mind off the kiss they had just shared.

Well, maybe not everyone should forget. Helen certainly could never forget it, and she had a feeling North wouldn't, either. Now if only Josie *would*!

The two of them took North's food into the kitchen, and she began to prepare the skillet over the fire. A knock sounded at the door.

Josie ran to open it. "Hi, Mrs. Chauvin!" she greeted, and Helen could hear a female voice telling her something from outside.

Helen got up and walked to the door to find Marie Chauvin standing there, holding what looked to be a letter.

"Oh! Hello, Helen," Marie greeted, surprised at finding Helen in the preacher's house. "Is the reverend here?"

Helen wondered what Marie was thinking. The middle-aged French woman, who was petite in stature and a little plump, was the wife of the area blacksmith and one of the nicest ladies Helen had met in the area. She was the perfect person to handle everyone's mail because she was not a gossip or nosy by any means. She knew the woman would not draw false conclusions and think the worst. However, Helen wanted to make it clear why she was here at North's house.

"He is around back, I believe. Josie and I were sent by Mrs. Baumgartner to make sure Rev. Campbell had breakfast. Pierre is sick and unable to help him today."

Marie smiled at the explanation, seeming to accept it at face value. "Ah yes. I know my husband would not be able to do one thing for himself if I were not there to do it for him. He'd probably starve."

Helen chuckled. "It was the same with my father," she told her. She looked down at the paper Marie was holding. "Did you need to tell him something? I know that he should be back any minute."

Marie smiled and waved the note in front of her face. "No, no. I'll just leave this with you, and you can pass it on to the reverend. I believe it's a letter from his sister, judging by the name and the postmark from Scotland. I remember my husband telling me he'd mentioned living with his sister in some of the correspondence we had with him."

It took everything in Helen to hide the dismay she was feeling as she reached out and took the letter.

She and Marie exchanged a little more small talk, which she could barely remember later, then Marie left.

For a moment she found herself just staring down at the letter with the scratchy penmanship addressed to Hamish Campbell. She couldn't help but feel sorrow for his sister and the fact that somehow she had to be told her brother was missing or most probably dead.

But how could Helen do that without North trying to write her back?

The web of deceit and the problems it was causing were growing thicker and more intricate every single day. When she got one thing under control, something else would pop up that made the situation worse.

"How come he never mentions his sister?" Josie asked. Helen could tell she was dying to read it.

So was Helen.

"Perhaps it makes him sad to talk about her since she is so far away," Helen prevaricated. She noticed how easily false excuses just rolled off her tongue.

That definitely wasn't a talent to be proud of.

She then realized she had to give the letter to North when they were alone so he didn't make a slip and say he didn't know he had a sister or something equally as telling. Helen truly wished she could just hide the letter from him and write one back to the woman, giving her the bad news.

But Marie might ask him about receiving it. Then Helen would be in even more trouble.

What a calamity!

"Josie, would you see to the fire while I go and show this to North?"

In typical fashion, Josie made a face of protest but did as she was asked. The younger girl was obedient for the most part, even though she was extremely vocal about her opinions.

North was just coming up the side steps of the porch when Helen met him. He smiled at her in a way that let Helen know he was still thinking about their kiss and the new commitment they'd made to one another.

It was such a thrilling feeling to know he liked her so much.

It was just too bad their relationship was built on nothing but deceit.

"North, Marie Chauvin came by to give you this. I wanted to make sure Josie wasn't around so you wouldn't be surprised to know that it is probably from your sister."

North looked at the letter she was holding out without even trying to take it from her. In fact, he looked at it as if he didn't want to open it at all.

His eyes flew back to hers, questioning. "I have a sister?"

Helen scrambled to find the right thing to say. "I didn't know," she explained, going with the truth. "I've never heard you mention a sister."

North looked back down at the letter, a frown of concentration on his face as he was trying to remember something. . .anything!

Slowly he reached out and took it from her. He read the name Fiona Campbell written above the seal. For a moment he seemed as though he wasn't going to open it.

Finally he lifted the seal and quickly read through the brief letter. "It is from my sister," he told her, his eyes still focused on the paper. "She writes that all is well in Melrose and for me not to worry about her. She says she has recently been called upon by a local sheep farmer that she knows I would approve of." North looked up at Helen with troubled eyes. "She urges me to write back as soon as possible, Helen, but how can I when I can't even remember her?"

Helen's heart broke at the misery pouring from his voice and the despair in his eyes. Reaching out, she put her hand on his arm in a comforting gesture. "I will help you write it. There is no reason to tell her you've lost your memory. Just tell her about your church and the people living here."

He smiled at her and placed his hand atop hers. "I will tell her about you, too," he said low and tender.

Helen thought that was the sweetest thing she'd ever been told. Unfortunately, Helen would have to find a way to make sure any letter that was written would never make it to Fiona Campbell's door.

She smiled at him, trying not to show how unsettled she was by this latest problem in her life. "Why don't I come by tomorrow and help you write it?"

He grinned broadly at her. "Why not today? Or are you just trying to come up with an excuse to see me tomorrow, also?" He tucked her hand in his arm and began to lead her to the door.

Actually, she needed time to come up with a plan. She did, however, like being with him any time she could. "I don't think I'll answer that, for I fear you are becoming too sure of yourself!"

North laughed as he opened the door and allowed her to enter first. "Ah! So that is the reason for the delay!"

She pretended to sniff at his comment as she stuck her chin up and looked down her nose at him. "Nonsense! Josie and I have lessons to finish, that is all."

"Ugh!" Josie sounded with more than a little disgust. "She never forgets!" she exclaimed with marked disbelief as she set the skillet down noisily on the metal rack of the fireplace.

Helen exchanged a look with North, and her heart skipped a beat when he teasingly winked at her. "Perhaps tomorrow I can talk her into a picnic that would take up most of the afternoon and therefore most of your lesson time," North suggested to Josie but kept his gaze on Helen.

Helen pretended not to like that idea. "I don't know. . . ."

"Oh, please say yes, Helen. A picnic sounds like such fun!" Josie pleaded, practically jumping up and down with excitement.

Helen thought a moment and then smiled at Josie. "I know! I can teach you how a lady makes polite conversation during a picnic or some other sort of gathering. I have so many—"

"Do you see what I mean, Reverend? She never lets me take a day off from my studies!"

North bent down to Josie and whispered in her ear, though it was plenty loud enough for Helen to hear. "Perhaps I can distract her tomorrow so you can play or go fishing."

He straightened and looked back at Helen. She hadn't even realized how much time passed as they stared into one another's eyes until Josie pulled on North's coat and motioned with her finger for him to bend down to her.

With an equally loud whisper, she told him, "If you could just keep staring at her like that for a few more hours, I might be able to miss today's lessons, too!"

North laughed, and Helen felt her face heat up with embarrassment. With determination, she grabbed the basket of eggs and made her way to the skillet, ignoring North when he asked her if she knew what she was doing.

Chapter 12

The next morning, North woke to the wonderful smell of bacon frying and the sound of a French song being badly sung, bringing him to the conclusion that Pierre was in his house.

"Good morning, monsieur!" The smiling black man greeted North as he walked into the room. Pierre had just placed the freshly fried eggs on the table.

"Good morning, Pierre," he greeted as he looked at his friend carefully. "Are you quite sure you are well enough to be here?"

"Of course," he assured him. He set a glass of milk beside North's plate. "It was only one of those maladies that lasts about three-fourths of the day. By the time the sun had started setting, I was feeling better."

"Well, I said many prayers for you, and I'm ashamed to say some of them were very selfish ones on my part," he admitted honestly with a sheepish grin. "I hate to admit it, but I am not a man who is used to taking care of himself."

Pierre sat across from him and sipped on a cup of coffee he was often fond of drinking. "You are not telling me anything I do not know, monsieur."

North frowned. "Am I so obviously inept?"

Pierre held up his hand and shook his head. "No, no, monsieur!" he assured. "But I see what no one else sees since I am here all day." He seemed to study him through the coffee's steam. "You seek to change, monsieur?"

North leaned forward, eager to talk to someone about what he'd been thinking over. "I do, Pierre. I suppose I've had things done for me all my life, and now that I'm here"—he threw his arms wide—"I see men who are well respected who do things for themselves. They are not waited on hand and foot!" he finished in an impassioned voice. He was discomfited to realize his voice had risen, and he was practically shouting.

But it didn't seem to faze Pierre. "If you are determined to change, then you can change, but it will take dedication," he stated firmly. "The important matter here is that you show a desire. Most men are satisfied to stay where they are and settle for what life has brought them."

Pierre was truly an amazing person. If all men were as passionate about what they believed and what they wanted out of life as he was, the world would be a greater place to live. Every day he and North talked about everything from the war to slavery and politics and even debating the merits of Cajun French cuisine versus true French. Pierre had an opinion for everything and profound insights about things North was sure he'd never even thought about.

They even discussed God and the Bible, and even then, he loved to hear Pierre's convictions about certain matters and how he was so careful to live his life the way he felt God was leading him, taking advantage of every open door.

That was the way North so wanted to be. He wanted to be a man God could look down upon and say, "He is a man after My own heart!"

The two of them chatted a bit more, and then Pierre remembered something. "Oh yes! I forgot to tell you I received good news yesterday. My sister, who lives in New Orleans, had a fine baby boy. It is her first boy after giving birth to four girls, so everyone is happy about the *le petit garçon*," he told North proudly and went on to tell what else his sister had written in a letter. North barely heard him.

A baby. North suddenly had a flash of a genuine memory of holding a baby. Afraid to even move lest he do something to make the memory disappear, North slowly closed his eyes and concentrated on what he was seeing in his mind.

He was in a garden filled with brightly colored flowers, and he was dressed in a very fine navy suit. A baby in a linen dressing gown was in his hands, and he was holding the infant up, talking nonsense to him, causing the dark-headed child to laugh.

He wasn't alone in the garden! With him were a man and two ladies. The man with dark brown curly hair was chatting with a lovely redhead. He knew instinctively they were in love with one another.

Suddenly the other woman, a beauty with wisps of black curls falling about her rosy cheeks, sat beside him. He looked over to her and felt a tugging at his heart like it always did whenever she was around. She reached for the baby, and he gave him to her. He watched her lovingly kiss the infant on the head.

"North?" she looked up at him, and he noticed it was his Helen.

"North? Monsieur Campbell?" Pierre called out again, causing the memory to suddenly come to an abrupt halt. "Sir, are you all—"

"Wait a moment, Pierre," he said urgently as he put his fingers at his temples and tried desperately to bring the memory back.

"If you are ill with a headache, I—" the servant tried again, but North interrupted by a shake of his head.

"No, no, it's not that," he said, sounding defeated. He knew the memory was lost for the time being. "I was remembering. . ." He stopped when he realized what he was about to confess then quickly thought of something else to say. "I was remembering something I told Helen," he said instead. He got up quickly from the table, not even noticing he'd barely touched his breakfast.

"Where are you going?" Pierre asked, also coming to his feet.

"Pierre, I'm sorry, but I need to ride over to the Golden Bay plantation. There is something I need to ask Helen about," he called out as he ran to his room to find his coat. He knew he wasn't making any sense, but he couldn't explain, either.

He dashed back out and found Pierre just leaning against the table, watching him—and looking at North as if he'd lost all his senses. "You have to go. . .right now?"

North smiled apologetically as he glanced at the table and saw his uneaten meal. "I'm sorry, but it's important."

"You're not asking her to marry you, are you?" he asked suddenly, his voice wary.

North opened the door and turned to grin at his friend. "Not today," he answered mischievously. "Oh! Is there any way you can prepare a food basket for three? I've invited Helen and Josie for a picnic today."

Pierre barely got a nod in before North was out the door and running to the buggy in which Pierre drove over every day. He'd been told he could use it any time he needed.

He was so eager to see Helen and ask her about his memory that the usually short trip seemed to take longer. It did, however, give him time to dwell on the images for a bit longer, to study them and try to figure out what he saw and how he felt. The main question that burned in his mind was the obvious one. It was the one thing he wanted to know before he asked anything else about Helen being in his memory.

Whose baby was he holding?

Finally when he had arrived, North jumped from the buggy and threw the reins to the stable boy who had come running up to meet him.

Luckily, Mr. and Mrs. Baumgartner were either out of the house or busy with other things, so he was able to instruct the servant to fetch Helen right away for him without having to make small talk with her employers.

He was pacing back and forth in the library when she breezed into the room, her expression indicating her surprise. "North! What are you doing here so early?" He swung around to see her and noticed her hair was totally unbound and flowing around her face and shoulders. She had always had at least the sides of it pulled back before, so it fairly took his breath away to see it in its natural state.

"Your hair. . . ," he murmured, feeling a little dazed and momentarily forgetting what he'd come for.

Immediately her hands flew up to her head, and she began pulling it back. "Oh no! I ran out of the room so fast, I forgot about my hair!"

"No!" he cried, putting out his hand to stop her. "It's. . .it's fine, I assure you."

She gave him a look that said she didn't really believe him, but she decided to let it drop. "Well," she said as if not really knowing what else to say. "Would you like to sit down?" She motioned toward cushioned chairs that faced one another.

North spied a sofa on the other side of the room that was more to his liking. "How about there? We have a view of the window."

They both walked and sat close together. North turned slightly askew so he could better see her then took one of her hands. "Helen, I remembered something this morning and I need to ask you about it."

North felt Helen stiffen at his words, and he assumed it was due to the excitement that he could actually be getting his memory back.

"Oh?" she said, and North got the feeling she was a little nervous about what he was going to say.

⌇⌇⌇

Helen had never been more nervous in her entire life. What had he remembered? How *much* had he remembered?

"Did you remember. . .everything?" she asked carefully

She was a little relieved when he shook his head. "No, actually it was only a small segment, but it really brought a lot of questions to my mind."

Helen swallowed, knowing this was not going to be easy. "All right. Suppose you tell me about it."

North explained what he'd seen about the three people being there and the baby. Helen knew exactly what he was talking about.

"First, I guess my biggest question is: Whose baby was I holding? I think I was calling him Ty?" He shook his head as if the details were a little sketchy.

Helen nodded, feeling safe to answer that one. "Yes, that was Tyler Douglas Thornton, Nicholas and Christina's nephew. They were raising him for a while when everyone had thought Nicholas's brother had been lost at sea," she explained, hoping she wasn't giving him too much information.

But North only nodded thoughtfully and looked a little relieved. "I'll admit the baby had me worried. I'd wondered if you'd been married before and had a child or if I had. But then, of course, that is silly. You would have told me anything important such as that," he stated assuredly.

If he only knew what I've been keeping from him, she thought shamefully.

"I was friends with Nicholas, wasn't I?" he asked as he seemed to be figuring things out.

"You were best friends," she affirmed. "Are you remembering anything else about him?"

He shook his head. "No, but when I think about him, I feel a strong bond between us." He smiled. "And I think you can guess who else I saw in that memory."

Helen could still remember the day like it was yesterday. It was probably the second time she'd ever talked to North, and she'd been so excited. "You saw me," she said with a wistful smile.

North rested his arm along the top of the sofa and touched the back of his hand to her smooth cheek. "I saw you," he confirmed, his voice husky with emotion. "I remember what I felt, too, when I looked at you. You had taken the baby from me and were holding him in your arms, and it made something in my heart yearn for things I'd never really thought of before."

Helen could hardly believe what she was hearing. This was a memory from North the nobleman, not North the commoner. "What was that?" she asked breathlessly, so anxious for his answer.

His hand reached back to cup behind her ear, sending goose bumps down her spine. "I wanted a family. A wife, a child." He frowned, as he appeared to be analyzing his memory again. "You know, it's so strange. There are so many pieces missing, but I'll just tell you what I remember feeling." He took a breath. "I remember looking at you and feeling such a strong attraction, but coupled with that was a sort of regret or. . .or maybe it was indecision. I just don't know. But it was like I felt feelings that I believed could not be realized or shared."

"You've spoken of this before," Helen broke in, unable to stop herself as she remembered an earlier conversation.

"I know! But this time I felt it even stronger than before," he stressed, seeming so desperate for answers. "Why did I feel this way? I know we've been over this, but what was keeping me from pursuing a relationship with you?"

Tears began to sting the backs of Helen's eyes, and she quickly looked down so that he wouldn't see them. This was the frustration she had always felt when she was in his presence, and, too, here was the answer she'd always looked for.

And maybe she knew it deep inside all along.

He had wanted her but was not willing to defy society to have her.

"I can't tell you that," she answered finally as she looked up at him. The sudden anger she felt over his inability to take a chance had dried up all her tears. "I had no idea you felt that way, North. You never, ever let me believe you wanted anything more than friendship."

He turned more so he was almost fully facing her. Cupping both hands on either side of her face, he asked urgently, "What was the obstacle? Was it my family? Was it because I knew you loved someone else?"

Tears came to the surface again, and this time she could do nothing but let them fall. "I can't tell you that. Only you can know the answer," she said softly, her voice small and broken.

He stared deeply and intensely into her eyes, and she noticed his own seemed a little misty. "I don't know what it was," he said, his voice husky with emotion that she'd never heard before. "However, I will promise you this. When my memory returns and I find out what the barrier was that kept me away from you, I vow to you now that I will never let it come between us again."

Guilt and shame ate at her soul as she tried to shake her head, yet he held fast to her. "You can't make that promise," she cried, trying to speak sense to him. "Perhaps it was insurmountable."

She nearly started crying again when he smiled at her with wonder and love shining so brightly in his eyes. "Helen, I promise," he stated emphatically. Then as if to seal his word, he pressed his lips to hers in a solid, strong kiss that lasted only a few seconds but spoke more than words could ever say.

North reached into his coat pocket and produced a white handkerchief, and he proceeded to gently wipe the remaining wetness from her cheeks. "You're even beautiful when you cry," he teased.

"No, I'm not," she said as she sniffed and tried to look down.

North took her chin and brought her face back up. He appeared to study her skin carefully. "Well, there is the matter of the red nose." He nodded in mock seriousness. "Yes, the red nose definitely brings the compliment from beautiful down to merely lovely."

She laughed and slapped his hand away. "You're horrid," she laughingly charged.

He laughed and tucked his handkerchief back into his pocket. "Why don't we get a little fresh air while the temperature is still cool outside?"

Helen nodded, eager to take her mind off North's troubling vow. "I'll dart upstairs and get my shawl."

❦

North followed Helen out of the room and watched her as she disappeared up the staircase.

He leaned on the railing, daydreaming about the poignant moment they'd just shared when a stern voice spoke behind him.

"That was quite a display back there," Imogene Baumgartner said crisply. North turned to see her looking every bit an irate guardian, with her lips stretched in a thin line and her blazing eyes narrowed on him with more than a little distrust.

"I beg your pardon?" he asked, although he knew she had seen the kiss. But had she heard what they'd said?

"Let's not play games, Hamish." He noticed she'd dropped the "reverend." Not a good indication. "I saw you kissing her, and as I am Helen's guardian, I have a right to demand what your intentions are toward her."

Well, that was an easy question. "I love Helen and intend to marry her."

That took the wind right out of Imogene's sails. "Oh," she said, sounding quite deflated.

North stepped closer to her, his face set in a sincere, heartfelt expression. "Mrs. Baumgartner, what you saw in there was me reassuring Helen that my feelings for her are real and my intentions are true. I do intend to court her in a proper fashion before I ask for her hand, but there is no doubt in my mind Helen Nichols will become my wife."

Imogene just stared at him unblinkingly for a moment with her hand at her throat. Suddenly tears were pouring from her eyes. "I haven't heard such a romantic speech since Robert proposed to me even though he knew his father would disown him!" she blubbered. "I knew. . .I just knew you were the right man for our Helen!" She was crying so much that North felt compelled to reach back into his pocket and bring out his slightly soiled handkerchief again.

He gave it a wary examination, shrugged his shoulders, and handed it over to her.

Imogene never noticed.

Chapter 13

Helen, North, and Josie spent most of the morning down by the pier. After a spirited lesson in archery, which Josie was already pretty adept at, thanks to Sam, North sent for the basket of food from his house so they could have their picnic by the water.

"This chicken is delicious!" Josie said enthusiastically as she bit into a chicken leg, not caring that the juice was running down her chin.

Helen had a brief, uneasy moment while she wondered which one of North's chickens they were actually eating, but it truly was so delicious that she soon forgot to worry about it.

She did chide Josie for her unseemly manners. "Josie, please use your napkin. You are about to stain that dress, and you know how Millie fusses," Helen warned.

Hearing Millie's name mentioned did what Helen hoped it would do. Josie immediately wiped her mouth and started being more careful with her food.

North exchanged a smile with her, and though they'd exchanged pleasantries and small talk, she could tell he very much wanted to ask her more questions about his memory. It was difficult to do so with Josie around, however.

Finally, he seemed to think of something he could ask in Josie's presence. "Oh yes! I meant to tell you I started the letter to my sister last night."

Helen took a sip of water and hoped she didn't look as though she were dreading the topic at hand. "You did? What did you say?"

North leaned down on the blanket, propping himself up with his elbow. "I confess I didn't get very far into it. I still need your help with it."

"Please tell me about your sister!" Josie insisted with interest. Helen knew that the girl missed her own sister dreadfully. "What is she like? Is she younger or older?"

Helen didn't have a clue, so she was powerless to help him. She watched as a glimpse of panic flashed on his face but was quickly masked. "Uh, let's see. . ." He stalled as he threw a pleading look to Helen. "She is younger. Yes, I have a younger sister," he stated as if he were trying to convince himself. "And. . .she's nice! Really and truly nice."

Josie looked at him with a scowl, clearly not pleased with the lack of details. "Well, what else? What does she like to do for hobbies or entertainment?"

North thought again and suddenly smiled. "She likes to knit! She is knitting me a sweater and plans to send it to me as soon as she finishes it."

"Oh," Josie responded with lackluster. Abruptly she brightened and asked another question. "Does she like puppies?" Helen knew exactly where this line of questioning was heading. Josie's friend Sarah had received a puppy for her birthday, and now Josie wanted one, too.

Imogene was scared to death of anything with four legs, except maybe a horse.

"Uh. . ." North hedged. "I suppose so." When Josie turned her head to grab another plum from the basket, North mouthed "*Help me*" to Helen.

What was she supposed to do? She didn't know the woman, either!

"Josie!" Helen exclaimed quickly, as she saw the younger girl's mouth open, ready to ask another question. "Didn't you want to go fishing today? I believe Joseph said he would take you out in the pirogue."

Those were the magic words. Josie loved nothing better than to paddle down the bayou in the small boat where she might get to see an alligator or snake. "He did?" she gushed as she jumped up, throwing crumbs all over them. "I'm going to go pull on some britches!"

Helen knew she should say something about dressing like a boy, but she decided to let it be. Being able to talk to North alone was more important than what the little girl wore. "Just don't let your mother see you dressed that way."

"I'll sneak out the back way," she yelled over her shoulder as she raced to the house.

"I hate to disillusion you, but it's not going to be easy to turn her into a lady. I wouldn't be surprised if she deliberately sought to marry an Indian or even a more common man to avoid any sort of etiquette altogether," North commented as they watched Josie disappear from sight. He sat up and began to put the uneaten food back into the large wicker basket.

Helen sighed and reluctantly agreed. "She's already threatened it, but I just keep hoping something will change her mind."

North chuckled. "Like what? Holding out for a miracle, are we?"

Helen shook her head and with a secret smile answered, "No, just a man." North raised his brows in question, and she explained, "All it will take, once she's a little older, is for a young man to totally captivate her. She'll strive to do everything she can, including remembering all the proper behaviors that I have taught her, just to show him she's worthy of his attentions."

North just stared at her as if he'd never heard of such a thing. "Is that what you did? When you wanted to attract the nobleman you've spoken of?"

Oh, dear! She hadn't meant for the conversation to take this turn. "I've always wanted to better myself," she replied truthfully. Christina was forever teasing about how Helen loved to know about the aristocracy—how they dressed and the way they conducted themselves and spoke.

It was ironic that for all those years she'd wished to marry a nobleman so she could live in the society she so admired, and she now wished North would remain a simple country preacher so they could continue to live their lives uncomplicated by titles and riches.

A disturbed look fell across North's face as he looked back down at the basket and started moving things around. "You will not be 'bettering yourself' if we marry," he said gruffly. "I do not want to be the person you settle for because you have no one else."

Helen couldn't help but notice how ironic his words were, considering who he really was. "Oh, North." She whispered his name softly as she stalled him by putting her hand atop his. "Every day that I am in your presence, I feel like a better person. You are the kindest, most thoughtful, gentlest man I have ever known. You make me laugh, you listen to me, and I can feel you truly care for me, as much as I do you. That is more important than riches or what place you hold in society."

A wide smile stretched across North's handsome face as he peered at her with teasing, narrowed eyes. "You've never told me you care for me. I could see it sometimes when you would look at me, but I like hearing you speak it."

She knew she was blushing, but inside she also felt another pang of shame. The more serious their relationship became, the worse it would hurt when he got his memory back. "Why don't we finish your letter?" she quickly asked, trying to change the subject.

North shook his head at her as if letting her know he knew what she was about. "All right, we'll leave that discussion for another day," he conceded, but she knew he would not be put off for long.

They worked on the letter and finally were able to construct one to North's liking. Thankfully, he didn't seemed to mind, either, when Helen offered to mail the letter herself. She'd hold on to it for a while before writing another one telling Miss Campbell that her brother was missing at sea.

They were just gathering their picnic supplies when a pebble suddenly dropped in Helen's lap, startling them both. "Where did that come from?" Helen exclaimed as she began to look about.

Sam Youngblood stepped out from behind a tree, and he didn't seem happy as he took in the scene before him.

Helen quickly sat back, snatching her hand away from North and receiving a frown from him by doing so.

Excellent. Now both men were unhappy with her.

She was about to ask Sam what he was doing skulking about when he tossed another pebble in her lap.

"Sam, is there a reason for you throwing rocks at Helen? I have to tell you, in our culture, it is not considered polite," North told him as he stood then reached down to give Helen a hand up.

Once again Sam eyed their briefly clasped hands with suspicion. "It is my observation that your people consider many things impolite," he countered.

North murmured, "So we're back to the 'your people' issue, are we?"

Helen wondered what that meant as she looked back and forth at the two men. At first she thought North was a little angry at Sam's presence, but now both men seemed to be just bantering with one another as if they enjoyed it.

How much time did these two spend together? Helen wondered, perplexed.

"In our Choctaw culture, throwing pebbles at a woman's feet means you are declaring your intention to marry her," Sam explained as he looked over to Helen and smiled.

Helen had to acknowledge that Sam was actually quite a handsome man, with his dark, golden skin and his straight, black hair that fell to his shoulders. He was quite muscular, too, she easily observed since his attire was minimal, at best. All her life she'd been around men who wore several layers including a shirt vest and sometimes two coats. The American Indians certainly liked to keep things simpler. . .and cooler, it would seem.

"And just what is the woman supposed to do? Throw them back if she doesn't want you?" North asked. He seemed more curious than offended by the fact that Sam was still pursuing her. Didn't he care?

Sam shrugged his shoulders to North's question. "If she agrees to engage herself to the man, she looks at him and acknowledges his presence. If not, she simply ignores him and walks away." He pointed at Helen and smiled. "Since she is looking at me, I'll assume we will soon be wed."

Helen gasped, just a little embarrassed at being caught staring. "I didn't know the rules!" she cried defensively as she threw up her arms. "It doesn't count if I'm not aware of such a custom!"

"Why not?" Sam asked.

Helen gasped and for a moment was unable to speak from being so flabbergasted by the whole thing.

It got worse when North started laughing.

"What is so funny?" she demanded, exasperated.

"You have to admit that throwing rocks at a woman as a way to propose marriage is exceedingly amusing."

"No more than some of the silly customs of your people. I've heard you organize a whole party of people and dogs just to hunt down one little fox. And then you don't eat it!" Sam expressed, clearly disgusted by the waste.

North's laughter turned to interest. "Speaking of hunting animals and such. . . You know, I've thought about the alligator you killed, and I was wondering exactly how you went about doing it."

"Well, I—"

"Pardon me, but could we please get back to the subject at hand?" Helen asked loudly, feeling a little left out. Wasn't she usually the center of both their attentions? What was happening here?

Both men looked at her blankly. It was North who replied, "I'm sorry, Helen. What were we talking about?"

She glared at both men. "It doesn't matter. Please continue with your manly talk of hunting and killing. I'll just gather the picnic supplies and be out of your way!" She let out a dramatic sigh as she whirled around and began to stack the soiled plates, not caring that she was close to cracking them from the force she was using.

As she moved on to the silverware, she realized she no longer heard them talking. Helen wanted so desperately to turn and find out what they were doing, but she was determined to ignore them.

She couldn't believe it when she felt another pebble hitting her back. She whirled around to fuss at Sam and demand he stop doing that, when she saw it wasn't the Indian at all but North who was standing there, tossing a pebble back and forth in his hands and smiling at her. Astonished, she couldn't hold back the giggle that bubbled from her throat.

North grinned as he slowly tossed his last pebble at her feet. Helen looked to see if Sam was still around but noticed he had already disappeared, leaving them alone.

Her eyes returned to North's, and she sauntered over to him. "Are you acknowledging my presence?" North asked teasingly, repeating Sam's words.

"Yes, but throw any more rocks at me, and I just may throw some back."

North laughed again as together they gathered all their picnic supplies and then headed back to the plantation.

⌇

Two days later, North was told to go to the bedside of John Paul Hughes, a young man who was a member of his church and the son-in-law of Silas Hill of the Hill plantation. He'd been accidentally shot while hunting, and the doctor was unsure whether he would live or die.

For those two days, North did nothing but stay by that young man's bedside, read his Bible, and pray. It was a true test of his faith, as the time seemed to stretch endlessly for himself as well as the young man's family. He prayed he was saying the right things to them and doing all he needed to do in comforting them.

Finally John Paul's fever broke, and he awoke at the end of the second day. Once the doctor told everyone that his wound had no infection and it seemed he would live, North made his way home with Dr. Giles.

On the way there, North broached the subject of memory loss and asked if the doctor knew anything about it, mostly how long it usually lasted. The doctor, however, told him he knew very little but had known one man who never regained his memory after falling off his roof.

It was not the encouraging news North wanted. He chose to believe instead that God would bring his memory back in His time.

Once he arrived home, he was turning the corner at the church, and the first thing he noticed was Helen sitting on his front porch with Josie and Pierre. It was the most welcoming sight in North's recent memory, and probably in his life, he'd ever witnessed.

Helen waiting for him to come home.

He didn't even think as he began to jog toward his house. He leaped up the steps, taking them two and three at a time, and walked right up to Helen. North pulled her up from the chair and enveloped her in an embrace.

He felt her hesitate, but only for a second. Her arms were quick to circle his waist and begin patting his back in a comforting gesture.

They stood there for a moment as he slowly let all his tension and anxiety drain away and allowed himself to be rejuvenated by her embrace.

It overwhelmed North sometimes to realize how much he actually loved Helen and how he needed her in his life. He wanted to spend the rest of his days making her happy and showing her how much he loved and adored her.

Josie's giggle, then Pierre's discreet cough, brought him back to the reality that there were other people around them. He, too, began to become conscious of just how inappropriate his actions were.

He backed away from Helen, giving her and the others a sheepish half grin.

"Uh, I'm sorry, but I feel I'm not myself this afternoon. I've not had any sleep since Wednesday."

They may not have totally believed his excuse, but they were willing to give him the benefit of the doubt. Helen quickly took his arm and directed him in the house. "You poor dear! Come and sit down, and Pierre will get you a bowl of soup."

"Yes, of course!" Pierre responded quickly, going to the fireplace, where a huge black pot was slowly boiling over a low fire. "You will eat and go right to bed," he instructed North sternly.

North grinned tiredly as he sat down. "You'll get no arguments from me."

Josie slid in the chair beside him and put a comforting hand on his arm. "Shall I go and fluff your pillows and turn back your bed?" she offered, concern clearly written on her small features.

"That would be nice, Josie," he answered, leaning forward to give her a kiss on the forehead.

The younger girl giggled and jumped up to go do the task.

He couldn't help but reach for Helen's hand as she sat by him, looking at him with concern brimming in her eyes. "Have you been here all day?"

She squeezed his hand gently. She began searching his face as if making sure he was all right. "Yes," she answered. "Josie and I wanted to help Pierre clean your house and do some of your chores before you got home. How is John Paul faring?"

"The doctor said he should be fine. But a few times they weren't sure he'd pull through." He stared at her a moment, hoping to convey the feelings he'd felt the last few days. "For the first time, Helen, I finally experienced being comfortable with my occupation. The family needed my strength to lean on and my prayers. I wish I could tell you what peace I felt, as if I were doing something I'd done many times before, performing the deed that God had made me for—ministering to the hurting."

He was about to say more, but Pierre chose that moment to set the bowl of soup in front of him. "We'll talk more about this tomorrow," he whispered as he exchanged a smile with her. He squeezed her hand once more before letting it go to take hold of his spoon.

"Oh, let me get you a slice of bread to eat with that," Helen told him as she got up from her seat to walk over to the counter.

"Just cut a small slice. I'm too tired to eat a lot tonight," he mentioned then took a bit of the soup, closing his eyes from the warmth and the tantalizing taste of it.

"Yes, your grace."

North's eyes widened at Helen's words, and he noticed she, too, seemed frozen, no longer cutting at the bread.

Your grace. . . What did that mean? Why was it familiar, and why in the world did Helen say it?

Perhaps he hadn't heard just right. "I'm sorry, did you say—?"

Helen whirled around from the counter, and North was perplexed to see panic flashing in her wide eyes. "Yes! Yes, I was about to quote my favorite verse in the Bible!" she said just a little too brightly.

She is quoting a verse? Now?

" 'Your grace is sufficient for me,' " she misquoted, North noted.

"Uh, I believe it is a part of a scripture that actually reads, 'My grace is sufficient for thee,' he corrected, still unable to get rid of the feeling there was something important connected with the words, and Helen knew it.

"You know, I believe you're right!" she said, her smile just a little off kilter and forced. She placed the bread in front of him on a small dish.

"You know, I just realized how late the hour has grown!" Helen exclaimed unnaturally loudly. "We'd better get Pierre to drive us home and let you get some rest."

"Helen, are you all right?" North asked, but his question was ignored as she flew to his bedroom to get Josie.

North rubbed his eyes wearily as the words *your grace* kept ringing in his head, only it was different voices than Helen's saying it.

"Perhaps you should get into bed, monsieur. I'll be back in a moment to finish cleaning the kitchen," Pierre told him, and North wearily agreed as he watched Helen fly out of his bedroom, towing a reluctant and confused Josie behind her.

"Maybe I do need some sleep," he murmured, thinking that possibly everything would make sense in the morning.

Chapter 14

Indeed, everything did make sense the next morning when North opened his eyes from a restful sleep. The sun appeared to be shining brightly as beams of light pushed through the openings of his curtains. He listened and thought to himself that even the birds seemed a little more cheerful as they whistled and chirped like never before.

In fact, the whole world seemed to be a much brighter and certainly a much clearer place to live on that particular morning.

And it was all due to the fact that North woke up knowing *exactly* who he was. And it wasn't Hamish Campbell.

Every last memory North had ever collected and remembered was there for him to pull up at will. Suddenly everything made sense, from his ill-fitting clothes and his being unfamiliar with simple chores, to his feeling at odds with his profession and not being comfortable with public speaking.

The only thing that made no sense at all was why Helen played along with everyone's wrong assumption that he was their long-lost preacher.

Propping his hands behind his head, North thought back to their first encounter in Golden Bay and how shocked she'd been when he hadn't remembered her. Suddenly all the guilty expressions that had flashed in her pretty face and the reluctance she exhibited for telling him any information about his life made complete sense.

The little minx! She actually allowed and even encouraged him to believe he was someone else!

Suddenly he laughed as he realized the length at which she'd gone to keep the truth from him.

Was it done so that she might have a chance with him?

It made him smile even more. Of course she would have thought that way. Helen had no idea he'd spent night after night thinking of some way to convince his family to allow him to marry someone several classes beneath him. He'd never been the sort of person to rebel against his position or want to cause dissension in any way; so when he realized he had feelings for Helen Nichols, a poor farmer's daughter, he didn't know how to tell his mother, friends, or peers.

He'd even tried to tell Nicholas, who had himself married a woman who had been a vicar's daughter, but Nicholas had laughed off his feelings, telling him he'd get over his infatuation.

But he hadn't. In fact, North had grown more in love with Helen each time he was with her, and he was sure she felt the same way.

He'd made excuses to postpone his voyage to America and had been glad when the war helped to delay the trip. He just hadn't wanted to be away from Helen that long.

Finally he had found a way to go to America *and* make a way to ask Helen to marry him while being away from his peers and immediate family. After speaking with Claudia Baumgartner, Josie's older sister, about her search for a companion for Josie, he persuaded her to seek out Helen for the position.

He reasoned that once he arrived at the Kent plantation, he would make contact with her and convince her to marry him.

He had a feeling that Helen took the position because she knew *he* was coming to Louisiana.

How sad it was they'd both gone to such great lengths to be together. Especially Helen, since she had had no idea how he felt about her.

North sat up in his bed as he thought a moment about all Helen had told him. She'd said she had always wanted to better herself. Even Christina, her best friend, had told him that Helen knew everything about the aristocracy and longed to be a part of that world.

He still loved Helen, no matter how much she had tried to deceive him into thinking he was someone else. She had done it because she loved him. That he had no doubts about.

But he wondered if she would love him without all the riches and the titles in front of his name. What if he truly were Hamish Campbell? Could she live the life of a poor minister's wife?

As North slowly got out of bed, he found it hard to concentrate on anything, much less reason out Helen's feelings for him. He found it a bit difficult to merge his old memories with the new ones because he felt like such a different person than he used to be.

In all honesty, he could remain Hamish Campbell for the rest of his life and be completely happy with that choice.

But he had other people to consider beside himself. He had four large estates that depended on him. If his cousin Wilfred, his next of kin, got hold of them, they would be run to ruins because of his excessive gambling habits.

Then there was his mother, who was the epitome of the proper noblewoman and embraced all of what the *ton* stood for in style and behavior. But although she could be an extreme snob and terribly bossy, he loved her—even if she did urge him constantly to marry and to marry well.

She would not be happy once he brought Helen home as his wife. But hopefully, after they gave her a grandchild or two, she would forgive him.

As he thought of his family, he tried to imagine what his cousins at the Kent plantation must have been going through. They had probably gotten word he was missing or even dead.

He wondered again if the real Hamish had somehow made it ashore. The man had seemed so calmly resolute in his belief that he would soon die. Perhaps God had prepared him and given him peace. North truly hoped so.

But somebody had to tell his sister! He realized that since Helen had taken the letter they had written to her, it probably would never be mailed. She must have taken it because she had planned to write a new one, telling Hamish's sister that her brother had been lost at sea.

Poor Helen. The more North thought of the situation that Helen had created and how she must have felt when it grew to be more and more complicated, he really felt sorry for her. But it also made him feel humbled she'd done it all for him. If she'd only known he had planned to court her anyway and to declare his love to her, she wouldn't have had to go to so much trouble.

He began to dress himself, pulling on his simply made clothes, and he realized he would actually miss dressing in the simple garments. His usual suit consisted of so many layers and had to be buttoned, tied, and ironed just so or a person might find his name gossiped about all over London for not knowing how to properly dress. He did hope his own trunks, bearing his fine garments, had been taken to the Kent plantation. Once he told everyone who he really was, he'd be expected to dress appropriately.

Pulling on Hamish's brown coat, he walked to the window and pulled back the curtain. As he looked out to the little white church in his view, he had a moment of regret that he would not get to enjoy being the town's pastor for very long. He knew it wasn't his calling, but he felt the work so much more worthwhile than anything he'd done before.

He stayed at the window a little longer as he tried to decide his next course of action. The one thing that kept ringing in his head was that he didn't want everything to come to an end just yet. Once Helen knew his memory had returned, she might start treating him differently, and so would everyone else. They would have to become adjusted to his being a duke again, and that would take all the fun and excitement out of their fresh, new relationship.

One more week or two as Hamish Campbell surely wouldn't hurt anyone, would it? he wondered, already liking the idea. He could find a way to sneak off to the Kent plantation to assure his relatives that he was all right, but other than that, he could enjoy being at Golden Bay awhile longer.

≈

Helen woke up the next morning, still a bundle of nerves over what happened with North the night before. He seemed to react to her slip of the tongue so oddly that she feared she had shaken loose some of his memories.

Did he remember he was a duke?

In fact, she had worried so much about it, her head ached. Imogene suggested that she sit out under the cypress trees in the swing and let the cool morning air soothe her head.

So far, it hadn't helped. Sitting so close to the bayou, all she could hear were the crickets and frogs making such a loud noise together in a sort of a fast rhythm that it seemed to go along with the pounding of her head. When a woodpecker joined in the chorus, she finally decided a cold cloth in a nice dark room might be a better choice.

Helen walked back to the house, and when she was almost to the yard, she heard the distinct sound of a carriage coming up the drive. Squinting through the haze of pain, she finally focused on the driver of the barouche.

It was North, she realized in a panic, making the pain in her head worsen.

But as he jumped from the vehicle and ran to where she was, she noticed he was smiling at her and. . .he was holding a bouquet of flowers!

"Helen!" he called as he waved to her. The closer he got, the less her head hurt. It was amazing, really.

Slightly winded but still smiling, North trotted to a stop before her as he held out the bouquet of wildflowers. "I'm so glad I caught you outside. I didn't really want to disturb anyone else," he explained as he looked at her with love shining in his gaze.

Helen was relieved he seemed not to remember her odd behavior from the night before. Perhaps he was too tired to remember anything! "You're here early," she commented, hoping he'd reveal the reason for his visit.

"Yes," he answered cryptically, without explanation. "Is there somewhere we can go to be alone? I know it is an improper thing to ask, but I just had to see you and talk to you this morning."

Hmmm. What does this mean? "We can go out on the bayou in Joseph's pirogue," she suggested. In the last few days, Sam seemed to be watching for her at the pier as he kept trying to "woo" her, as he called it, by serenading her with his flute.

"Is that anything like a rowboat?" North asked warily.

Helen laughed and tucked her arm into his. "If you're asking if you have to use a little bit of muscle to make it go, then the answer is yes!"

Minutes later, they were paddling down the bayou, searching for a nice shaded spot to stop for a while.

"Oh, look! There are several large oaks over there and an old root sticking out of the bank to tie the boat to," Helen told him as she pointed over his shoulder to show him exactly where it was.

North almost upended the boat as he moved about the shaky vessel to grab hold of the root and then wrap the rope around it. He looked at her and joked, "I'd better be careful! Last time I fell out of a boat, I lost my memory. I'd hate to see what would happen if I did it again."

Helen looked over the boat and could only imagine what was beneath the murky water. "You'd probably be eaten," she quipped with a shiver.

North chuckled as he climbed out of the boat and then helped her up the slightly steep embankment.

As they walked to the base of the huge, sprawling oak, Helen knew she couldn't have picked a more perfect place for them to sit and talk. It was peaceful and cool under the shading leaves with only small rays of sunlight able to peek through.

North dragged a log over so they would have an elevated place to sit and lean against the tree.

At first North and Helen didn't speak a word—they only sat there enjoying just being next to each other.

"I did a lot of thinking last night and this morning," North finally said in a low voice, as if he didn't want to spoil the mood of their special place.

Helen didn't know what to make of that statement. Did he remember something, after all? Her stomach began to twist in knots with worry. "What were you thinking upon?" she asked, even though she wished only to change the subject.

North sat up and turned so that he could look at her. "I thought about you and the feelings I have for you."

Helen's stomach eased a little as he looked at her with such love and gentleness shining in his eyes. "You did?" she asked, unable to say anything else. She wished she could remember some of the clever things her favorite heroines would say during such intimate situations as this.

North nodded and reached to take her hand. As he caressed her palm with his thumb, he seemed to be weighing what he wanted to say next. "And I thought about what your feelings were for me," he continued, watching her cautiously. "Do you love me, Helen?"

Helen's breath caught at the straightforward question. She wasn't expecting such directness from him on such a delicate topic. She felt so conflicted as she looked up at his handsome face. Like a fly caught in the web of a spider, she felt like any move she made would only make things worse. Even saying nothing or even confessing would accomplish the same thing.

The truth of the matter was that she did indeed love him with all her heart. There was no way she was going to make him believe otherwise.

"I do love you, North."

A look of pure joy spread in the form of a smile across his face as he let go of her hand and placed both hands on either side of her cheeks. "And I love you, my sweet Helen. You have wound yourself so deeply into my heart, I can't imagine my life without you," he expressed wholeheartedly then bent forward and kissed her.

Tears borne more of sorrow than happiness stung her eyes, and she returned his kiss, finally letting free all the pent-up feelings she'd kept locked away since she'd first met him. After a moment he moved his lips from hers to string tiny kisses across her cheeks and up to her brow. Then leaning his forehead against hers, he appeared to be slightly winded. "Marry me, Helen," he said suddenly, startling her so much, she nearly fell off the log.

"What?" she gasped as she pulled back from his embrace. "But you only just asked to court me and—"

He shook his head and interrupted her words. "I know what I feel, and nothing is going to change that!"

He had no idea what he was saying, she thought, growing panicky. "You don't know that for sure, North. Perhaps if we just wait—"

North put his hand over her mouth, a loving smile curving his lips. "I said nothing," he stated firmly and resolutely. "God brought you into my life, Helen. He took a situation that could have been disastrous with my memory loss and then sent you to help me get through it. We were made to live together, raise children, grow old with one another."

Helen looked away in order to try to stop herself from crying again. Once he found out it was she and not God orchestrating this whole situation, he would change his mind about wanting to marry her.

This is such an impossible dilemma, she cried silently as her panic only grew. If only she had someone to talk to. If only Christina wasn't an ocean away to help her know what to do.

"Helen, I'm sorry," he said gently as he brought her face around with his hand. "I've gotten carried away, haven't I? I've had all morning to think about this, and you haven't had time to let it all sink in."

She shook her head, and a tear escaped despite her best efforts at keeping them at bay. "I'm sorry, North, I guess I am a little overwhelmed."

"And of course I haven't thought about you needing to inform your parents, also," he thought aloud, his hand still caressing her cheek.

Helen smiled as she placed her hand over North's hand. She couldn't help but be amazed at his impromptu proposal and his childlike excitement at the prospect of them marrying. Whenever she had daydreamed about North proposing to her, it was a very dignified and proper picture of North bending down on one knee and placing the family betrothal ring on her finger.

This was so much better than her dreams.

It was just too bad she couldn't enjoy it.

"North, I would like nothing better than to marry you tonight. I want you to know that. It's just that I do have so many things to consider and plan for before we take that step," she finally said, hoping it would stall him long enough for her to come up with a way to tell him the truth.

North gave her a quick kiss on the cheek and then grinned happily at her. "Just hearing you want to marry me is enough for now. I can be patient until you're ready to set a date." He chuckled. "At least I'll strive to be."

As he stood and gave her a hand up, Helen prayed he'd not only be patient but understanding once all was revealed and the truth finally made known.

Chapter 15

Sunday arrived, and North found himself actually looking forward to delivering his message. He had begun studying when he sat with John Paul and decided then to speak about Paul's conversion and how God had used miraculous means to get his attention. He wanted to make the point that God had a plan for everyone, and when we weren't truly listening to what He wanted to tell us or we were going our own way instead of the way He would have us go, He'd use all sorts of ways to get our attention.

He'd had no idea just how much that applied to his life until the day before. God had wanted North to learn something, and apparently it wasn't going to be discovered living as he had been, surrounded by wealth and having everything done for him at just a snap of his fingers. North was ashamed to admit it, but though he went to church and always strove to live right, he had really never talked to God—never really prayed and studied the Bible.

His life had been too busy with social events, his estates, and friends. He had even been caught up in the dilemma of what to do about his feelings for Helen. Instead, he should have prayed and asked for guidance about it. God would have led him to the same conclusion that he'd come to himself: They were simply meant for each other. It didn't matter if they stripped him of his title and he had to live out his days as a poor man. His love for Helen was so much more important.

But of course they couldn't strip him of his title. He was already the Duke of Northingshire, and the worst that could happen would be they'd spend a few years being cut by the *ton* and passed over when invitations for the season were written. He just prayed Helen could bear up to the snobbery she would face once they returned to England.

England, he thought with a sigh and was surprised to realize he felt reluctant to return. He truly liked Louisiana, even though he stayed sweaty all the time and was constantly battling mosquitoes. The people were truly nice and were more apt to cross social borders than those in his homeland. The only thing that bothered him was slavery. Pierre had made him aware of so many atrocities that most white people just turned their heads to, pretending it was a normal part of life.

Today North dressed in his usual black suit, the nicest one that had been in Hamish's trunk. After running a comb through his thick locks (and making a mental note that he really needed to get a trim), he made his way to the church.

Because the weather was so pleasant and unusually cool for late May, there were more people gathered outside the building. Several people walked up to greet him when he was noticed, including a couple of young ladies who never failed to make their presence known to him. He could now remember other young ladies flirting with him back in England, but he was never sure if it was him or the title they sought. So it was a little flattering that these ladies hoped to catch his attention, even though they knew him to be practically penniless.

Helen obviously was not flattered or amused by the women's attention. He noticed quite a determined glint in her eye as she marched over to him and placed herself directly in front of his admirers. "Good morning, North," she said informally, knowing it would cause speculation from the onlookers, with such a familiar address.

North managed to stifle his chuckle over her territorial behavior but did smile broadly at her. "Hello, Helen," he returned the greeting, playing along with her plan. "I trust you are doing well this morning?"

He was rewarded with a radiant smile. "Indeed," Helen answered, probably not even aware she was looking at him with all the feelings showing clearly on her face.

Of course the same could probably be said of him, too. Their declaration of love was so new and fresh to North, it was hard not to think about it when he looked at her.

"Shall we go inside?" he said quickly before he could find himself doing something stupid like reaching for her hand or kissing her cheek just to be nearer to her.

"I think we might hear wedding bells soon," someone whispered, and he heard a few others agree. Then he thought he might have heard a cry of protest from some of the young ladies walking behind him but thought again that perhaps it was just a bird.

A few moments later, much to the congregation's obvious relief, Miss Ollie sang the last stanza of her hymn and sat down in her pew on the front row. North walked up to the pulpit after that.

As he scanned the room, looking at the faces of those he considered his friends, he felt a real sadness that he wouldn't be with them much longer. Part of him even wished he could continue the work of a minister. It was true, he wasn't the best at delivering a message, but he mostly liked just being a regular person, not revered for a title or riches, but counted and respected as one of a small community.

North began his sermon. Because of his renewed confidence from the return of his memory and the fact that he believed in his message so strongly, he was able to preach like never before. In fact, there was a sort of surprised look on the faces of most of the congregation as they stared and listened intently to what he was saying.

Had I been that bad?

When he had finished with a closing prayer, he glanced over to where Helen sat with Josie and the Baumgartners, and he was pleased to see her face beaming with pride.

"That was wonderful!" she whispered to him afterward, when almost everyone had gone.

"Yes, you're like a real preacher now," Josie commented, having heard what Helen had said. She had her bonnet in her hand, holding it by the ties and twirling it around.

"Josie! I do wish you would learn to hold that tongue of yours!" Imogene scolded with exasperation. "And would you put your bonnet back on?"

Josie scowled, still swinging it. "But it's too hot!"

Imogene gave her a narrowed look of warning, which made the little girl quickly plop it back on her head.

"You will dine with us today, will you not?" Imogene queried North. "I would love to discuss some of the points of your sermon I felt were particularly inspiring."

With her comments, as well as most of the congregation's, North felt a little overwhelmed by all of the sincere praise, whereas before it had been halfhearted, at best. "I was hoping for an invitation. There is also something I would like to discuss with Mr. Baumgartner."

"Excellent!" Imogene crowed, clasping her hands together at her chest. "You can ride in the carriage with Josie, and I will ride in the barouche with Robert."

North was able to steal a few moments alone with Helen before Josie joined them. "Helen." He called her name softly as he reached across and held both her hands. "I am going to speak with Mr. Baumgartner today about my intentions toward you and that I've asked you to marry me. I know you have not given me a definitive answer, but I feel we should make him aware of our feelings for one another."

North watched the warring emotions play across her lovely features, and he felt a little guilty himself for not telling her he knew the truth.

"But shouldn't we wait until your memory returns?" she fretted.

"What if it never returns? Could you be happy living here with me even though I can barely remember ever knowing you before?"

"Oh, North, I could be happy with you in any place or any circumstance," she declared so passionately, he couldn't help but feel she was sincere.

"And I, you," he responded softly, wishing he was able to kiss her once again.

They heard a sound outside the carriage and quickly sprang apart, sitting back in their seats. Josie stuck her head in the doorway, laughing. "You were holding hands!" she charged merrily as she hopped aboard the vehicle, stumbling over their knees to her seat beside Helen.

Helen lowered her head to shield a blush as she busily straightened her blue dress. "Whatever do you mean?" she hedged.

Josie looked back and forth between them. "I mean I was peeking at you through the window and saw you holding hands." She then turned all her attention to North, her head bent in a quizzical stance. "And whatever did you mean about remembering something or other? Did you ever remember that you once knew Helen before, when you were in England?"

North sent an alarmed glance Helen's way as he searched his mind for a feasible answer.

"A lady does not skulk about listening at doors and spying on her elders!" Helen scolded in the meantime, obviously trying to change the subject from what Josie had heard. "And I see you've removed your bonnet once again! Whatever did you do with it?"

Josie blushed this time. "I...uh...tied it on Boudreaux's head," she confessed, speaking of Miss Ollie's mule that pulled her tiny wagon. The old mule was famous for getting loose from his fence and trampling the neighborhood's gardens.

Although North was relieved to find the younger girl had completely forgotten their previous conversation, he looked forward to the day when there were no more secrets to conceal.

⁓

"What's he saying now?" Imogene whispered as the three females squeezed together in a small closet that connected the library and dining room. The dividing panels were easily removed so they could move forward to peer through the cracks of the closet door. Helen was bent trying to peek through the keyhole, Josie managed to kneel down below her trying to get a better view, and Imogene kept pushing against Helen's back, nearly toppling her over as the older woman tried to peer over her shoulder.

The thing they were all agog to witness was the meeting between Mr. Baumgartner and North.

"I don't know. I can barely hear them," Josie complained as she wiggled around trying to get comfortable and leaned on her mother's foot in the process.

"Oww!" Imogene hissed. "Do take care, Josie!" They all moved around a bit to try to get more comfortable. "How did you know the boards were removable, anyway?"

"I just discovered it one day," Josie answered easily, and Helen could only guess who she was trying to spy on when she made that discovery.

"He just declared he loves Helen and has asked her to marry him," Josie whispered a little louder than she should.

"Shh!" Helen warned. "They will hear you!" She peered again through the crack. "Uh-oh! Mr. Baumgartner is frowning."

"What?" Imogene questioned as she tried to take a look for herself. "What's wrong with him? Has he forgotten what it's like to be young and in love?"

"Oh, wait!" Josie cried, this time in a softer voice. "He just asked him if he is able to afford a wife. They're quite expensive, Father says."

"How dare he say that!" Imogene gasped, and Helen was thinking it might not have been the best idea to invite her employer along.

"Hmm. . . This is interesting. North just told him he has recently found out that he has an inheritance coming to him," Helen told them as she wondered where this news had come from. She'd only read part of the letter Hamish's sister had written. Perhaps he'd learned of it from there.

But why didn't he tell her about it?

"Oh, look. Papa is smiling!"

Helen squinted to see the men shaking hands. "It appears they've reached some sort of an agreement."

"Oh, I wish I could see!" Imogene complained, pushing even more against Helen. To balance herself, she tried to brace her arms on the frame of the door.

"If you truly love her, then you have my blessing, Reverend. I would imagine that, as you are a man of God, you are being guided by Him, so I can do nothing less than to approve of the match, also," Helen heard Mr. Baumgartner say to North.

"Thank you, sir!" North replied, a wide smile on his face. "God has indeed brought us together. In Helen He has given me more than I could ever have hoped for in a mate."

"Oh, that's so romantic!" Josie expressed with a dreamy sigh.

Helen brushed at the tears on her cheeks. "He is so sweet, isn't he?"

"That is wonderful, and I'm sure Helen appreciates hearing the sentiment, as well."

Helen watched with trepidation as Mr. Baumgartner looked straight at the closet they were hiding in. "Don't you Helen, dear?"

Imogene, still trying to see a little better, chose that moment to lean forward and, in the process, caused Helen to lose her grip on the door frame and fall directly into the door.

All three of them tumbled out of the closet and landed in an embarrassing heap at the men's feet.

Since she was on top of the pile, Imogene was the first to pull herself to her feet. "Well, I must say this is very embarrassing!" she murmured as she smoothed back the curls that had come loose from her hairpins.

Helen and Josie managed to scramble to their feet, both ignoring the men's offer to help them up. "We were just. . .uh. . . ," Josie began, trying to excuse her behavior, as usual.

"Eavesdropping, dear. I believe that's what they call it," her father supplied for her in a droll voice.

"Why don't I call for a pot of tea?" Imogene mentioned brightly, obviously hoping to diffuse the awkwardness of the situation. "Better yet—I'll go make some myself!" She began to walk quickly from the room, and Josie hurriedly followed her.

Helen watched helplessly as they left her to face them all alone.

"You know, I really should take my leave," North said as he looked to Helen. "Would you like to walk me out to the stables?"

Helen looked over at her employer, who smiled at her and nodded. "Have a good night, Reverend," he directed toward North.

"I am so embarrassed," Helen groaned as soon as they walked outdoors. "It *seemed* like a good idea when Josie mentioned the closet."

North laughed. "Well, at least you know we have Mr. Baumgartner's approval. We only need to try to send a letter to inform your parents now."

"Speaking of letters," Helen began as she was reminded about something he'd told Mr. Baumgartner. "You mentioned an inheritance in the meeting."

"Yes, so you don't have to worry about my being able to support you," he said confidently.

He didn't however explain *how* he knew it. "Oh, I know you will, but. . . umm. . .did your. . .uh. . .sister write in her letter about it?" she persisted.

"No, I actually remembered something about it."

Helen's heart started beating faster. "Oh? You've had more memories?"

He looked down at her, the full moon reflecting a soft glow on his face. "A few," he said as if it were nothing of great concern.

She tried to read his expression to get some idea of what he knew exactly, but it was just too dark to tell. "Well, that's good," she commented lamely, unable to think of anything else to say.

"Oh, I also wanted to tell you that I may be going to the Kent plantation soon."

His words caused Helen to stumble, so horrified was she by what he'd just said. "Why?" she asked, her voice noticeably shaky.

"I heard they are the relatives of the other fellow who was thrown from the ship. I thought I would go there to convey my sympathies and offer them any comfort I can."

This is bad. Terribly, terribly bad.

She turned her head away from him to take a few breaths, trying to calm herself. "When will you go?"

"Tomorrow."

All Helen could think of was running away and finding a good place to cry her eyes out. It wouldn't solve anything, but it might help her feel a little better. Then she thought of another solution that could very well help. She needed to pray! Only God could help her find a solution to the dilemma she'd caused for herself and North—not to mention the entire area of Golden Bay.

Complaining of a sudden headache, Helen left him standing at the stable door. When she reached the porch, she realized that she hadn't even told him good-bye.

Chapter 16

Helen spent a restless night tossing and turning as she grappled with what she should do. She had tried to pray, but the guilt she felt was so great. How could God forgive her when she would never be able to forgive herself?

The more Helen weighed her options, the more she realized there was only one course of action she could take. It was the cowardly solution, but she just couldn't witness the hurt and betrayal in North's eyes when he realized what she had done.

Darkness still filled the early morning as Helen quietly pulled a small bag from under her bed and stuffed as many of her clothes and belongings as she could manage into it. Then, opening the drawer to her night table, she untied a handkerchief that contained all the money she'd earned since coming to Golden Bay. It wasn't a large sum, by any means, but she prayed it would be enough to purchase a passage back to England.

Helen then tiptoed into Josie's room and gently shook the girl awake.

"What. . . ?" she mumbled sleepily as she tried to open her eyes and adjust to the lamp that Helen had lit beside her bed.

"Shh!" she sounded as she put her fingers over Josie's mouth. "It's me. I need to talk to you."

Josie sat up, rubbing her eyes. She seemed so young in her ruffled sleeping cap and high-necked cotton gown. "What's wrong?" she asked with a yawn.

Helen patted her on the shoulder and regretted she might not see her little friend again. "I have to leave, and I need you to explain to your parents for me."

Quickly she told her the truth of what she'd done and about North not knowing that he was really Trevor Kent. "Everyone will hate me once they find out, so I have to leave," she explained.

"Please don't leave, Helen. Everyone will understand. I won't even complain about my lessons anymore if you'll please stay!" Josie pleaded, tightly grabbing hold of Helen's hand.

Helen shook her head as tears filled her eyes. "I just can't, Josie. I'm so sorry, but I can't," she sobbed as she got up and pulled her hand away.

Josie began to cry, too. "Will you come back?"

"I hope so," Helen whispered as she quickly bent down and pressed a kiss to the little girl's cheek. "Good-bye."

"But Helen. . . !" Helen heard her call out as she ran out of the room and closed the door behind her.

Helen managed to get out of the house without being noticed, but once she'd run a few steps, she realized she had no idea where to go.

Then she thought of the only person who would help her.

Sam!

Although she'd never been there, Helen knew Sam lived down the bayou, so she quickly began to make the trek down to the pier, hoping that she'd be far enough from the house before it became too light.

It was already getting easier to see, as the dark sky began to show streaks of dark pink and orange on the horizon. Helen scurried as fast as she could along the embankment. As she went deeper into the area where the cyprus trees were thick along the border of the property, she could only pray that she wouldn't meet up with an alligator or even a water moccasin snake. Frankly, there were just too many creepy-crawly things to worry about, so if they were around her, she tried not to notice them.

Her running slowed to a breathless stride as the minutes seem to drag by and her bag grew heavier with each step. She felt as though she was now a ways from the house, but there was no sign of any dwelling or camp where Sam might live.

She honestly didn't know what kind of place the Indian would live in. Would it be like the teepees she'd read about? Sam seemed so primitive at times, yet he spoke very well, and Helen always had the impression he was probably more educated and informed on the customs of the white race than he let on.

As the sky began to brighten her path, Helen grew so weary that she plopped down tiredly on a log to rest a bit. Three times she slapped at the same mosquito as she considered she should have come up with a better plan than just running away. If only North hadn't decided to go to his cousins' plantation, then she might have done better; but as it was, there was simply no time to think much less plan.

"Does this mean you've changed your mind?" a voice spoke behind her, startling Helen so much she screamed.

Whirling around, she saw Sam standing there, laughing at her reaction, and that made her mad. "It's impolite to sneak up on someone like that! You nearly scared me to death!" she charged as she placed a hand on her chest as if to steady her beating heart.

Sam raised a black brow as he pretended to check her over. "You look alive enough to me," he teased. With his calm expression, it was quite hard to tell. "So does this mean you want to marry me?" he tried again, this time his expression changing to a hopeful smile.

Helen sighed. "Sam, you know I can't marry you. I don't love you, and I'll bet you don't love me, either."

Sam looked at her as if she were crazy. "A man doesn't choose a wife because of some silly emotion like love! If she's a good woman, hard worker, and likes children as you do, that's all I need." He shrugged. "It's hard to find a good wife with those qualities, you know."

Helen shook her head, needing to get to the point of why she had come looking for him. "Sam, enough about that. I came because I need your help."

He immediately became concerned. "What has happened? Are the Baumgartners all right? That preacher hasn't done anything to hurt you, has he?"

"No!" she quickly assured him. "It's me, Sam. I've done something very bad, and I need your help to get away from here before everyone finds out."

Sam clearly did not believe her. "Helen Nichols, what could you have possibly done that was so bad? You're a good woman."

She quickly blurted out her story, giving him the basic facts and not painting herself as anything but a deceiver and liar. "So you see, Sam, once North arrives at the Kent plantation, he'll know the truth and then he'll hate me for what I've done not only to him, but the church! The people will be crushed to find out he's not really their preacher."

Sam threw up his hands. "So marry me, and it won't matter if they are upset with you. In time they will forget, and we can have a happy life together."

Helen covered her ears with frustration. "Sam, will you please stop with the proposals! I cannot marry you for I love North!"

Sam shook his head as if he didn't understand her words. "But since he won't marry you after this, why not me? I may be your only chance to marry once everyone finds out."

She glowered at him. "You're not making me feel better, Sam. Will you help me get back home or not? I'm not even sure I have enough money to get home."

Sam let out a resigning sigh. "I'll help you, Helen Nichols. My cousin is captain of a merchant ship that makes regular trips to France. He doesn't sail, however, until tomorrow. You might as well come home and stay with us until then."

Helen looked at him, confused. "Us?"

"My elder sister, Leah, has a house next to mine. You can stay with her."

"You have a sister?" she asked, a little too surprised, for Sam scowled at her.

"Yes, and I have a mother, father, and two brothers. Did you think I was raised by wolves?"

Helen thankfully didn't have to answer that question, but Sam bent down and grabbed her bag. "Follow me," he said gruffly.

By the time they reached Sam and Leah's houses, she'd apologized for everything from turning Sam down to thinking he was so barbaric. He finally accepted her apology, but she could tell he was still miffed that he had been unable to talk her into marrying him.

The cleared area where the two very English-looking cottages were set was surprisingly beautiful and unlike any of the homes she'd seen in the area. They were placed side by side and faced the bayou. There was even a path that led down to a large pier and a swing hanging from a large, shady oak. The houses were painted yellow and blue with white trim and shutters. Rosebushes surrounded both residences, along with various other flowers that Helen knew must be tended to every day for they were so perfectly groomed.

"What a lovely place you have," Helen complimented as he walked her to the yellow cottage. Before knocking at the door, Sam threw her a glance that said that all this could have been hers, too.

A tall, very beautiful woman with golden skin and long, black, shiny hair answered the door. She might have looked like any number of Indians in the area except for her startling blue eyes. "Hello," she said hesitantly as she looked from her brother to Helen with a quizzical expression.

"Leah, this is Helen, the woman I've been telling you about," Sam told her in his straightforward way.

Helen, so fascinated by the woman's eyes and the fact she was wearing a pretty morning dress instead of leather, blurted out, "You are not completely Indian!" As soon as the words left her mouth, she started to apologize, but Sam interrupted her.

"I never told you, but my father is an Englishman. He and my mother live in Brighton, England. So you see, I'm not a complete barbarian," he told her wryly.

Helen was trying to digest that startling piece of news when Leah said with excitement, "You are to marry my brother then?"

"No!" Helen said a little forcibly. When she saw Leah's smile turn to a confused frown, she quickly added, "I mean, I've come to ask Sam to help me get back to England," she told her briefly.

"Why don't you brew us some tea, Leah? We will fill you in on the predicament Helen Nichols has made for herself."

Sam certainly has a way with words, Helen thought morosely as she stepped into the charming cottage and began to tell her story once again.

⌒

When North rode from the reunion with his cousins the next morning, he couldn't help humming a happy tune as his borrowed barouche rolled steadily back toward the Golden Bay plantation and back to Helen. The Kents had been so relieved to see he was alive and had tried hard to get him to stay a few more days with them, but he told them that he must get back to settle his affairs and to make the truth known of who he really was.

He was ready to tell Helen that he knew the truth. They'd played games with one another long enough, and he so wanted everything to finally be in the open with no more secrets between them.

When he finally pulled into the front of the plantation, however, North knew right away that something was wrong. Several neighbors were gathered on horses around Mr. Baumgartner, and he seemed to be instructing them to do something for him.

He looked to the front porch and noticed Mrs. Baumgartner hugging Josie, and both seemed to be very worried about something.

And where was Helen? Why wasn't she outside with them?

As he climbed down from his vehicle, Josie spotted him and ran down from the porch, with Imogene following closely behind her. "Rev. North!" Josie cried as she ran straight into his arms. She mumbled something about Helen into his coat, but she was talking too fast for him to understand.

As his arms came around her to try to comfort the hysterical little girl, he looked worriedly at Imogene. "Where's Helen? Has something happened to her?"

"She's gone, North," Imogene told him, using the nickname she'd probably heard Helen speak so often. "She told Josie about your memory loss, but she also told her something else that might come as a big shock to you." She paused, seemingly having a hard time getting the words out.

"I know, Imogene. I know I'm not Hamish Campbell," he supplied for her, and he watched her let go a breath of relief.

"Then you know that you're. . .uh. . ."

"Trevor Kent, the Duke of Northingshire. Yes, I do know that."

"Helen's really sorry she lied to you, Reverend. . . ." She was cut off when her mother whispered something in her ear. "I mean. . .your grace?" she called him, wrinkling up her nose in question as if it didn't sound right. "Anyway, she was crying and saying you would hate her after you found out, so she's decided to go away," Josie explained in one breath.

North's heart felt as though it had dropped to his toes. "Gone? Where could she have gone?"

Imogene shook her head. "She told Josie she was going to sail back to England. I suppose she's found a way to get to the port. We're about to send some men down to look there for her."

"You don't hate her, do you? She didn't mean for all this to happen. She was just trying to get you to like her," Josie pleaded, grabbing hold of his coat.

North took the time to comfort the young girl by putting his hands over hers. "I don't hate her, Josie. I know she loves me, and I still love her. But I need to go look for her." He looked at Imogene. "Tell your husband to keep looking around the area just in case she's lost in the swamps or forest. I'll ride down and see if she was able to get aboard a vessel."

"Take a horse from the stables," Imogene offered, pointing to where one of their stable boys was standing. "Tell him to saddle one for you."

In a matter of minutes, North was on a horse and riding as fast as he could toward the port. He prayed he could remember the directions that had been given to him as the horse darted along the unfamiliar wooded path.

He could hardly believe his eyes when a man suddenly stepped into the path of his horse. He barely had time to recognize the man as being Sam, when his horse reared up in fear and promptly knocked him on his back.

Chapter 17

After he finally got his wits *and* his breath back from the hard fall, North pulled himself from the dirt and glared at the Indian, who just stood there staring at him with narrowed eyes. North had been under the impression they had become friends. They'd gotten along famously during their target practice, which had turned into a competitive yet enjoyable archery match.

"What is wrong with you, man?" North yelled at him as he tried to shake the dirt off his coat and britches. "You could have been trampled!"

"I just wanted to save you the trouble of looking for Helen," Sam answered calmly.

North was surprised when Sam mentioned her. "What do mean? Do you know where she is?"

"She's decided to accept my offer of marriage, and I even get to keep my horses." He spoke again with the same even voice. He could have been talking about the weather, he seemed so nonchalant. Didn't he know North was insane with worry?

"You're lying! What have you done with her?"

Sam's eyes flared at the implied accusation. "If you're asking if I'm holding her against her will, well, think again. She came to me, white man!"

North didn't know what to believe. Surely he wasn't telling the truth, he thought, starting to doubt. Surely she couldn't decide to marry Sam just because she thought North would be upset with her?

"Listen, Sam. I am out of my mind with worry for her. If you can drum up any compassion within your heart at all, you'll take me to her. I have to see her," he told him, trying a different approach with the Indian.

Sam seemed to take an exceptionally long time to study him, as if looking for the truth. "You're not going to hurt her, are you? She seems to think that you hate her now."

North shook his head, growing irritated by the long wait. "I love her! And when I find her, *I'm* going to be the one who marries her," he stressed. "Now, please, take me to where she is!"

Sam had the audacity to laugh. "You were a lot calmer before you remembered you were a duke," he told him then turned his head toward the woods and whistled. One of his prized black stallions he'd been trying to trade for Helen came trotting out to him. Sam hopped into the saddle, motioned for North to follow, and took off in a run.

North snapped his reins and rode with the Indian until they arrived at two pretty cottages in a clearing. North didn't wait for Sam to show him which one Helen was in. He jumped off the horse and began to call her name.

He stopped short when a beautiful Indian woman walked out of the yellow cottage, her brilliant blue eyes studying him curiously.

North found himself just standing there for a moment looking at her. She had the face and hair of an Indian and the eyes and dress of an Englishwoman. *Very odd and yet very striking, indeed!*

"You are North? The English duke?" she asked in a soft American accent.

He nodded. "Yes. Can you tell me where I may find Helen?" He got to his point right away.

She didn't answer him at first but leaned her head to the side in a thoughtful, contemplative sort of manner. "You won't hurt her, will you? Helen said you would be very upset with her."

North frowned with incredulity. "Why does everyone suppose I am a violent man? I just want to take her back to the plantation."

"I've told him that I'm to marry Helen," Sam said loudly as he walked to stand by his sister. North saw the twinkle of laughter in his eyes, but he was in no mood to play games with the Indian.

The striking woman merely sighed at Sam's words and told North, "My name is Leah, North. . .or should I call you Lord Kent?" She shook her head. "Anyway, wait right here and I'll call for Helen."

North saw her open her door and stick her head in as if to talk to someone. The door opened wider, and Helen reluctantly walked out. Her face was a mask of guilt, and she only glanced once at him before looking back to the ground.

Was it guilt for what she'd done, or had she truly agreed to marry Sam instead of him? He didn't wait to find out! He stormed right up to Helen and grabbed her by the shoulders. Her eyes flashed at him with surprise.

"Tell me that you are not marrying Sam," he demanded, not caring that he might sound like a lunatic.

Confusion creased Helen's brow as she shook her head. "Is this why you are here? You are upset because you believe that I am marrying someone else? Aren't you even upset that I lied to you and made you think you were Hamish Campbell?"

North moved his hands down her arms to link his fingers with hers. "I already knew that, Helen." He brushed her concerns aside, not noticing Helen's fiery reaction to that statement. "Are you or are you not marrying Sam?" he asked again.

It shocked him when Helen let out a cry of outrage and shook off his hands. "You knew!" she cried. "How long did you know?"

North realized his mistake right away. "Uh. . .I got my memory back the morning after you called me 'your grace,'" he explained carefully.

Helen just stared at him a moment, hurt and anger swimming in her eyes. "And you knew I would be feeling horrible with guilt over it, and yet you said nothing!" He tried to touch her arm once again, but she promptly slapped it away.

"Wait just a minute," North countered, getting a little irritated himself. "*You* are the one who lied to *me*, remember? I was just trying to figure out your motives for deceiving me. *That's* why I said nothing."

"My motives!" she echoed, pointing at herself. "I've been in love with you for two years! I thought you wouldn't consider me for a wife because I'm not of your class, so I simply just made you think you were of *mine*!"

"Are you understanding any of this?" North heard Sam ask aloud to his sister, but Leah told him to shush and kept her eyes glued to them.

Wonderful. In all his born days, he'd never even come close to making a public spectacle of himself.

Until today.

Then North was suddenly struck by something that Helen had told him before. "I am the nobleman you were in love with, aren't I?"

Helen pursed her lips as if she were loathe to admit it. "Yes, but as I said, you did not feel the same for me."

"Helen," North said softly as he tried again to touch her arm. He was encouraged that this time she allowed it. "I have been in love with you from the very moment I saw you at Kenswick Hall."

Her eyes widened with surprise and a little unbelief. "But why—?"

North caressed her shoulders as he shook his head shamefully. "I didn't know what to do about you, Helen. I've always done what my family expected me to do. So when I knew I wanted you for my wife, I tried to find a way to make that happen in a place where our every move wouldn't be scrutinized or judged too harshly."

"I don't understand," she began to say, and then her eyes widened with comprehension. "You knew I was coming to America! But how?"

He quickly explained how he talked to Claudia Baumgartner about offering Helen the job of companion for her sister.

"I planned to court you once I had arrived and marry you here. We would have had time to get to know one another and be stronger as a couple to face the criticism of my family and the *ton*."

Tears filled Helen's eyes as she looked at him with dismay. "You mean I caused all this for nothing? You were intending to marry me anyway?"

North folded Helen into his arms to comfort her. As he glanced over her shoulder, he saw Leah and Sam still standing there watching and listening to everything. Leah was even crying a little, dabbing her eyes with a lacy white handkerchief.

"I've had the time of my life, Helen," he assured her, pulling his attention back to their conversation. "God used this to get my attention and to make me aware of how much I need Him in my life." He leaned back a little and framed her face with his large hands. "It's made me realize, too, I should have never wavered in acting on my love for you."

"Oh, North!" she sighed.

"Oh, my!" Leah sighed with another sniff.

"Oh, brother!" Sam groaned, putting his hands to either side of his head as if the whole thing were giving him a headache. "This is getting embarrassing."

Leah elbowed him. "You're just jealous that you didn't win her."

"No," Sam insisted. "I'm just irritated that I have to start this whole courting business all over with another woman!" With that he threw up his arms and stomped off to his cottage.

"I'll go get your bag," Leah told them, leaving them alone.

North took advantage of their absence. He pressed a kiss to her lips and felt his heart leap when she threw her arms around his neck and kissed him back.

After a moment, he looked down at her and smiled. "Does this mean you are not marrying Sam?"

Helen shook her head, smiling dreamily. "No, I think I will marry you."

"Wise decision."

"I think so."

✎

Two Weeks Later

"You look like an angel!" Imogene sighed as she peered over Helen's shoulder into the mirror. They were admiring the beautiful ivory lace gown that Millie had made for Helen, with its pearl-lined neck and stylish empire waist. Millie came up behind her and placed a crown of pink roses and baby's breath on her dark curls and adjusted the lace veil sewn onto it.

"She sho' nuf is, missus. Sho' nuf!" Millie said as she joined the ladies at the mirror.

"I don't see why I have to have all these flowers stuck in my hair," Josie complained from behind them, causing them all to turn and look at her. She was dressed in pink satin with a circlet of roses in her hair, just like Helen. "I'm not the one getting married, so what does it matter?"

Helen reached for the younger girl's hands and couldn't help but notice how lovely and grown-up Josie appeared in her pretty dress. "But you're my maid of honor! And for that you get the privilege of wearing roses like me."

Josie let go of her hands and rolled her eyes, letting Helen know the "privilege" wasn't appreciated.

Imogene stepped up to adjust the string of pearls that she'd lent Helen for her special day. "We are going to miss you once you've gone back to England," she said as her eyes grew misty, just as they always did when the subject of Helen's leaving was broached. "It will be quite dull in this big house without you around to cheer us up."

"Yeah," Josie seconded as she sat down on the window seat. "I won't miss the lessons, but I truly will miss having you to talk to."

Helen blinked back the tears as she rushed to comfort her young friend. "We are to stay for three more months, Josie. We have lots of time to finish your lessons," she teased to brighten everyone's mood.

Josie pretended to be put out by that news, but Helen could see that she was in better spirits.

"We must hurry if we're to get to the church on time!" Imogene said as she looked at the clock on Helen's mantel. "We can't keep Lord Kent waiting!"

Lord Kent. It seemed so strange to Helen to think of North as a duke anymore. Because he'd offered to stay on for three months as the church council searched for another minister, he still seemed like an ordinary person to her.

But he wasn't. And soon, when Helen became his wife, she wouldn't be, either.

Lady Helen Kent, Duchess of Northingshire. Just thinking of the title made Helen anxious—anxious she would have a hard time adjusting to her new life once they arrived back in England. Could she cope with the censure and the coldness she would receive at marrying so far above her station? She prayed every night that God would help her to do so.

That was one of the reasons she and North decided to marry in Louisiana. Their day would not be ruined by gossip and speculation but could be shared with the people they had grown to love in Golden Bay. Helen did feel a little remorse that her mother and father would not be able to see her marry, but she'd promised them in a letter she'd write down every detail to share with them after it was over.

Of course, there was one other reason they were not waiting to marry in England—North simply told her he would not wait that long to make her his wife.

North had teased he was afraid that Sam would talk her into marrying him instead, but she knew that he was just as eager as Helen to start their lives together.

"Well, I think we are finished here!" Imogene announced as she looked Helen over once more. "Are you ready to go meet your future husband?" she asked with a happy twinkle in her eyes.

"I've been ready for two years!" Helen stressed as she took Imogene and Josie by the hands and laughingly pulled them toward the door.

<hr />

"Are you sure you want to go through with this, monsieur?" Pierre asked as he helped North don his dark gray overcoat.

North smiled at him, purposely misunderstanding his question. "Of course I want to marry Helen. I'm practically giddy with anticipation!"

Pierre narrowed his eyes and wagged his finger back and forth. "No, no. You know what I'm talking about," he corrected, his face quite serious. "You should reconsider having me stand up with you as your groomsman. It will cause some to walk away and not stay for the ceremony."

North shook his head. "That is why we are holding the wedding outdoors under the oaks. I want everyone who I consider to be my friends to attend, and that includes Sam, the servants and slaves at Golden Bay, and *you*. If someone is offended, then they can leave without causing a commotion," North stated firmly as he checked his hair in the mirror of his dressing table. The fancy piece of furniture as well as the tall four-poster bed looked out of place in the small room, but North had wanted it to be more comfortable for the three months he and Helen were to live there. Once his cousins realized that they could not talk him into living at the Kent plantation, they had generously lent him all the furniture that he needed for his brief stay.

"I don't believe I have ever seen such a crowd of people, monsieur," Pierre observed as he peered out the window. "And I see that Helen has just arrived with the Baumgartners."

North's heart skipped a beat at the mention of her name. He hadn't seen

Helen in three days because of all the preparations for the wedding, and he missed her dreadfully.

He vowed to make certain that after today, they would never have to be apart.

After one last inspection, North and Pierre walked out of his house and made the short trek to where everyone had gathered. He greeted the minister who had driven from New Orleans and then faced his friends and family, waiting for his bride.

There was a momentary silence as everyone acknowledged Pierre would be standing up with him, but everyone stayed where they were. He glanced around and saw Sam and Leah standing by his cousins; and standing away from the crowd but close enough to see and hear the ceremony were all the servants and slaves from the Baumgartners' plantation.

A violin began to play a sweet tune just as Helen and Josie stepped between their guests and started walking toward him.

North's eyes met Helen's as she drew closer to him, and he felt his heart swell with love and thankfulness. God had given him so much, and that included his heart's desire—Helen Nichols.

When she'd reached him, he eagerly took her hand and tucked it in his arm. He smiled down at her, not really hearing what the preacher was saying until he got to the part about anyone objecting to the marriage.

When they heard someone clear their throat as if they were about to say something, North whispered a name the same time as Helen, "Sam!"

Horrified, they glanced back to look at the Indian, only to see him smiling benignly at them with a look of mock innocence. Leah had her face covered and was shaking her head in obvious embarrassment.

North quickly turned around and found the young preacher frowning at him. "May I continue?" he asked, apparently perturbed that North seemed to not be paying attention.

North glimpsed at Helen and found her trying to hold back a giggle. "Yes, please do," he stressed, relieved that Sam had behaved himself.

Except for the fact that North heard someone whisper that, as a duke, he *could* have provided benches or chairs for his guests, the rest of the day went off without a problem.

⁂

Five Months Later—London, England

"The Duke and Duchess of Northingshire!" the wiry butler announced to the ballroom at large, causing every person in attendance to stop what they were doing and stare at the couple standing at the top of the stairs.

"Oh dear, they're all looking as if they've received the shock of their lives. Wasn't it posted in the *Times* some while back?" Helen whispered nervously, gripping her husband's arm as if her life depended on it. Even though they were in the familiar surroundings of Kenswick Hall, she still felt like an outsider.

She looked up to see North smiling as if he had no cares in the world. "Of course they know. It's been the talk of the town if not the entire country. Smile and pretend you don't notice them."

"That will be a little difficult," she said between a clenched-teeth smile.

Carefully they walked down the stairway, and Helen prayed she wouldn't fall, giving them something more to gossip about! They'd spent a wonderful week in North's Bronwyn Castle in Scotland, and though Helen knew that attending her best friend's ball was important, she would have rather stayed up in the Scottish hills with North.

They had just cleared the last of the steps when Christina, her best friend and the Countess of Kenswick, appeared through the crowd with her husband, Nicholas, in tow.

"Helen!" she cried and threw her arms around Helen. "I am so glad to have you back home!"

"I am glad to see you, as well," Helen told her as she returned the hug and stepped back to look at Christina with surprise. "You're expecting another. . ." She didn't finish her sentence but looked wide-eyed at Christina's slightly rounded tummy.

"Yes!" she nodded happily.

She turned then to greet Nicholas, while Christina warmly welcomed North. Out of the corner of her eye, Helen noticed most of the people had pretended to lose interest in them, but she could see by their glances over their fans and between their gloved fingers that they had not.

"Oh, don't be bothered by them," Christina said, waving a dismissive hand toward the crowd. "You will only be of interest to them until someone else within the *ton* does something to shock them even more. Then you'll be yesterday's news and merely tolerated."

"I hope so," Helen answered, only to find out later that it was better than even Christina had hoped. Perhaps they had underestimated the power that the Duke of Northingshire wielded or perhaps it was another sign that God was looking after them.

As the couples walked about the room greeting other people, Helen was surprised to find most were, if not friendly, at least forbearing of her presence.

The one person that she was excited to see was Claudia Baumgartner. The pretty American girl was truly excited for her marriage and wanted to know all about how her family was faring in Golden Bay.

Finally North whispered into her ear, asking if she would like to step out to the terrace, and she quickly agreed, so tired was she from the stress of anticipating the evening.

"Are you glad to be back?" North asked her softly once they had walked outside and found a nice private part of the terrace. He placed himself behind her as she leaned on the railing and linked his arms about her middle, hugging her to himself.

"I am, but I am surprised to find I miss Louisiana, too. I would love to go back one day," she sighed, as she thought of how sad everyone had been on that last Sunday there.

"Of course we'll go back. The Kent plantation is partly mine, too, so I'll want to check its progress every so often." He paused a moment, and Helen could sense he was hesitant to ask her something. "Do you regret we married in Louisiana?"

Helen smiled and glanced up at him. "Not at all. Under the oaks with all our friends around us was perfect."

Helen had never felt such love as she walked toward North as he waited for her by Pierre, wearing a proud smile. He'd looked so handsome in his dark gray suit and white cravat, and so regal, since it was from his own collection of fine apparel.

While it was true the congregation had been saddened by the fact that North couldn't remain as their pastor, they were thankful that they'd stayed for three months while they located a new pastor.

If only the members of the ton *could have seen how North and I lived those months after we were married*, Helen thought fondly. They had continued to live in the little house behind the church, milking the cow and taking care of the house alone, except for the occasional help from Pierre.

It had been the perfect honeymoon, living so simply and happily together.

There, of course, had been sad moments along their way. The body of the real Hamish Campbell had been discovered by fishermen, and North had the unhappy duty of writing his sister and telling her the bad news.

All in all, Helen believed North had enjoyed his time away from the some-times stressful job of being the Duke of Northingshire, yet she had worried he would somehow change when he returned to that position.

But she should have known he wouldn't. Even though they were back in England and living in luxury and style, North remained the same as he had been when he thought he was a simple preacher.

"What are you thinking about?" North asked as a breeze blew by, cooling their faces and ruffling their hair.

"I'm trying to picture how your mother would look if she saw you milking our cow."

North chuckled and then placed a kiss on her ear. "I miss Queen Mary. We were just beginning to get along," he teased. "Now my mother is another story." North's mother had still not come around to accepting Helen for a daughter-in-law. But Helen had faith that one day she would.

In fact, Helen's faith had grown tremendously in all aspects as she and North studied the Bible and prayed together. It united and strengthened them so much that Helen knew God could help them overcome anything.

Even the English *ton*.

Even North's mother, the dowager Duchess of Northingshire!

Helen turned her head slightly to smile up at North and to possibly steal a kiss, but she became distracted when she saw a woman walk to the other side of the terrace and look up into the sky. As the moon caught the curves of her delicate features, Helen could see sadness in her expression and the slump of her shoulders.

The woman was Claudia Baumgartner.

"Now what are you thinking?" North asked as he often did when she became quiet and introspective. He never wanted to be left out of anything. . .even her mind.

"I'm just thinking about a friend who might need my help." Already her mind was whirling with ideas about what she could do to lift Claudia's spirits and help her feel more comfortable with life in England. She'd just finished reading a novel called *Emma*, about a matchmaker who found love herself. Perhaps that's what she could do for Claudia.

North brushed her lips, bringing her thoughts back to him. "You are a very thoughtful friend," he complimented her, smiling into her eyes.

As North looked at her, all previous thoughts jumped out of her head as she reflected again on just how much she loved him. She turned in his arms and placed her arms around his neck. "Now what are *you* thinking about?" she asked, teasingly.

"You," he whispered huskily, as he slowly lowered his head to prove his answer true.

Shirley, Goodness, and Mercy

by Kristy Dykes

Dedication

To my hero husband, Milton,
who is my collaborator in the deepest sense of the word—
he's believed in me, supported me, and cheered me on
in my calling to inspirational writing.

The eyes of your understanding being enlightened;
that ye may know what is the hope of his calling.
EPHESIANS 1:18

Chapter 1

Hickory Hollow, Missouri, 1894

Sitting on a grassy knoll overlooking her grandfather's church in the verdant valley below, Shirley Campbell smoothed her serviceable brown skirts and replaced a hairpin in the chignon high atop her head.

This was something she never did—sit and while away time. But her beloved grandmother's burial that morning prompted her mother to give her some time away from the never-ending farm work.

"Oh, Grandmother," she whispered as her eyes misted over, "I loved you so. You were the only one who truly understood me. We were like knitted souls, you and I." A tear trickled down her cheek followed by a deluge, and she wiped her face with her hanky and kept it at the ready instead of tucking it back in her waistband. "Such good times we had together. How will I make it without you?"

Holding her well-worn copy of *Little Women*, she stroked its cover as reverently as if it were the family Bible that held a prominent place in the Campbells' farmhouse.

"How you used to enjoy it when I would read to you from these pages."

When her grandmother came down with the heart ailment, she asked for Shirley—of all the grandchildren—to come and help her one afternoon a week. Shirley soon found out that her grandmother didn't want help with dishes and sweeping. As the preacher's wife, her grandmother was besieged with offers of help from the saintly ranks. No, what Grandmother really wanted was for Shirley to read to her from the pages of *Little Women*, of all things.

Where Grandmother got the book, Shirley never knew, or why she wanted Shirley to read to her at all, she never could fathom. But from the very first, Shirley devoured the heartwarming tale of the four charming young ladies and their doting mother in prim and proper New England—a world away from Hickory Hollow, Missouri, both in distance and in deportment. She had read *Little Women* so often in the past year, she knew certain passages by heart.

Shirley envisioned the plucky heroine, Jo March, and quickly found the description of her in the opening pages of the book:

> *Jo was very tall, thin, and brown, and reminded one of a colt. . . . She had a decided mouth, a comical nose, and sharp gray eyes which appeared to see everything, and were by turns fierce, funny, or thoughtful. Her long, thick hair was her one beauty.*

"Sounds like me." Shirley smiled as she thought of Jo, the fledgling writer who every few weeks would don her scribbling suit and "fall into a vortex."

"Does genius burn?" Jo's sisters would ask when they popped their heads in the door of her attic writing room.

Shirley flipped to the passage about Jo's literary endeavors and read aloud:

When the writing fit came on, she gave herself up to it with entire abandon. . .while she sat safe and happy in an imaginary world, full of friends almost as real and dear to her as any in the flesh.

Shirley found the entry she loved about the girls' devoted mother. Marmee, they called her:

She was not elegantly dressed, but a noble-looking woman, and the girls thought the gray cloak and unfashionable bonnet covered the most splendid mother in the world. . . . The first sound in the morning was her voice as she went about the house singing like a lark, and the last song at night was the same cheery sound.

She could see Marmee in her big armchair surrounded by her adoring daughters, encouraging them in their pursuits: Meg in her role as little mother to the younger girls; Jo in her writing ambitions; Beth in her piano playing; and Amy in her artistic leanings. Marmee was their comrade, but more than that, she was their encourager, their champion in the relentless quest of their goals and aspirations.

"Oh, to have a mother like Marmee March." Immediately, Shirley felt ashamed for voicing such an errant thought. Her mother was a good mother, a wonderful mother, but she was. . .she was. . .what was Mama? How best to describe her?

"Ah, Mama." Pictures of her mother appeared before her eyes as if they'd popped out of the picture book she treasured as a tyke, the only book she ever owned as a child, the book that was torn up long ago by her sister Gladly, though Shirley now had a few books she could call her own such as *Webster's Dictionary* and *Shakespeare's Plays*.

Thinking of Mama—Mama at the washtub on Mondays, scrubbing clothes and bed linens and white curtains, getting the dirt out with a vengeance, then starching and ironing each item, then folding and putting them away, week in and week out with never a letup in her strict regimen.

Mama at the woodstove morning, noon, and night, turning out mouthwatering meals and cakes and pies and other delectable dishes.

"Be sure and get Amanda Campbell to bring her strawberry pie," folks were known to say. Or her pecan pie or her cinnamon peach cobbler or a host of other sweets she could whip up in the blink of an eye.

Back to the mental pictures. Mama beating the rugs. Mama tending the garden. Mama sewing the family's clothing. Mama getting her brood to Grandfather Hodges's little stone church in the wildwood and, before Shirley took over the children's Sunday school class, Mama herself teaching it, making sure the Campbell children as well as the other youngsters hid the Holy Scriptures in their hearts. Mama visiting the poor of the community and the infirm in the congregation, sometimes bringing them good things from her kitchen.

Mama, Mama, Mama. . .always working, always going, always doing, a constant buzz of activity, like a honeybee on a hyacinth, never just being. . .or feeling. . .or dreaming. . .like Shirley often did.

Oh, it wasn't that Shirley shirked her work. She could turn out a meal almost as fast as her mother, and her fancy stitchwork was praised all over Hickory Hollow by friends and family alike. After all the chores were done that a farm demanded, she helped Grandfather Hodges nearly as much as Mama did with what he called divine service. Besides comforting the sick and bruised of heart, Shirley corralled all the children under the hickory trees every Sunday afternoon in the warm months and taught them Sunday school lessons, and they couldn't wait to get there every week to hear her.

"Shirley makes them Bible stories come alive right before our eyes," the tykes told their parents.

Most certainly, she always did her part wherever and whatever the workload required, but as she toiled every day, she thought and she dreamed and she saw and she felt. . . . "You've got your head in the clouds, Shirley," Mama was prone to say. "That won't stand you well in life."

Shirley had tried to talk to her mother once, a few months back. She confided in her about how she saw and felt things so deeply, how she dreamed and aspired and longed for—what, she knew not. But she was hoping her mother would know and could help her.

"Mama, at times it seems my musings and longings are otherworldly," she told her, "so far away, something distant and unattainable, yet so yearned for. Oh, what does it all mean?"

She even gathered the courage to tell her mother about the stories that bubbled up inside her and ached to be shared with the world.

Mama only said, "Fiddle-faddle, Shirley Campbell. Such as that won't find you a good man. You'd best forget about that froth and frippery and put your head to getting yourself a husband. After all, you're eighteen now, soon to be nineteen."

Shirley rolled her sleeves a mite higher and unfastened the top button of her high collar to let in some air. Oh, if only she had the time to get those stories down on paper. Paper? Well, not the fancy, store-bought kind. They could never afford that. But she'd be willing to write them on plain brown wrappers and old envelopes, if only she had the time.

Maybe she could get up earlier and write before breakfast. But she was already getting up at dawn, like Mama and Papa did. And if she got up before break of day, there would be no light. And her mother would never allow her to waste lamp oil for. . .for froth and frippery. She winced, thinking of those hateful words Mama used to describe her. . .her dreams.

No, getting up before dawn wasn't the answer. And neither was writing on Sunday, the day of rest. She let out a little snort. By the time she got back from morning service, ate dinner, then headed back to teach her Sunday school class, the day was over. The last moments on Sunday evenings were consumed with helping Mama tend the children. Always the children were clamoring for Shirley's attention in the everyday busyness of life—her little brothers and sister washed, dressed, and fed, over and over again, and sewed for and cooked for and readied for school.

Perhaps she could find a few minutes every now and then and get her musings recorded. She knew with a surety that she would never find large blocks of time to devote to her writing endeavors. It would have to be in bits and snippets. Yes, that was the answer. And when a sufficient number of days passed, she would have whole stories fleshed out.

So happy did she feel, so grateful she was for a resolve to her dilemma, she laughed as she hugged her knees to her, almost like it was Grandmother she was embracing, and her heart beat hard in its perch in her chest. For if she could get her stories written down—it was a long shot, yes, but perhaps—she could become an authoress.

Like Jo March!

The thought was so strong and so weighty with all its implications, for a moment she almost couldn't breathe. Somehow, some way, certainly so, she could become an authoress.

Like Louisa Mae Alcott!

With childlike abandonment, she leapt to her feet. Hugging the book to her, she dashed through the wild spring daisies. So hard and so fast did she run, she panted like Papa's hunting dog on a chase, hurting from the stitch in her side.

But she kept on running with not a care in the world, and she called out to Jo March and to Louisa Mae Alcott and told them that one day, she, too, would be joining their elite ranks, and it seemed they answered her back.

Determination and diligence are the pathway, my dear, and if you possess those, you will succeed in your quest.

Their advice thrilled her, for indeed, she had a goodly portion of both.

When she came to a tall stand of hickories and pines and beeches with a magnolia or two among them, she halted to catch her breath. With wonderment, she noted that the singing of the birds was almost as loud as the singing in her soul.

For a long eon she stood there, drinking in the serenity of the sight, robins and jays zipping between the towering hickory trees and lush chortleberry bushes, the hummingbirds buzzing in profusion about the honeysuckle vines, and she reveled in all that was being birthed in her heart and soul, thanking the heavenly Father for this revelation.

Presently, still clutching *Little Women*, she came to the meandering brook that bordered Grandfather's church far downstream. She stopped for a moment and read Miss Alcott's short biography in the front of the book:

Louisa Alcott's first story was published when she was twenty. When she was twenty-three, things began to improve. A book of hers sold well. She went to Europe a few years later, and then came her great success: the publication of Little Women *in 1868.* Good Wives, Little Men, *and* Jo's Boys *followed.*

These four books made her name and her fortune.

In awe, Shirley took up her trek beside the gently flowing, crystal-clear, gurgling brook, visions of grandeur appearing before her eyes. . . .

Miss Shirley Campbell, authoress, being feted at a tea among society's cream of the crop.

Miss Shirley Campbell, authoress, autographing her books at a book signing in a large city.

"Shirley," someone called from a far place.

Miss Shirley Campbell, authoress, speaking before a distinguished crowd at a university.

"Mama's needing you, Shirley," came the voice again, this time with a whine. "Why'd you stay gone so long?"

Miss Shirley Campbell, authoress, hobnobbing in the North and the South and the East and the West with the literary greats of the United States—no, the world.

"Mama said to come right now. There's a horde of people eating at Grandmother's house, and we've used every plate in her cupboard, as well as our plates from home—not to mention all of Aunt Charmaine's. Mama said you and I are to do the dishes and to be quick about it."

Shirley looked over and was startled to see her sixteen-year-old sister, Gladly, on the other side of the brook. It was as if she had dropped down from the sky. Only Gladly was no angel.

"Gladly?" Shirley said blankly, taking a deep breath, trying desperately to climb down from the dais at the university where she was standing, trying to disengage herself from the places she had soared.

"If you don't come right now, Shirley Campbell," Gladly yelled, "I'll tell Mama your wits have gone a-woolgathering again."

Suddenly, Shirley was disengaged. . .

from the high-society tea. . .

from the big-city book signing. . .

from the university. . .

and from hobnobbing with the literary greats.

She was also disengaged from her dreams of becoming an authoress.

They were dashed to the ground. For after all, she was only Shirley Campbell, a plain-looking, little-educated farm girl from Hickory Hollow, Missouri, with nothing but a life of drudgery ahead of her.

"Just like Mama's," she said under her breath. With an audible groan, she turned and crossed the brook pell-mell over the large, flat stones Grandfather had positioned decades ago when he was building his church. Now she used them to make her way to. . .to. . .the work that awaited her.

Chapter 2

The Reverend Forrest Townsend drove his horse and buggy down the street to the social for the young people of his congregation, thinking about the letter he had received in the mail from the Reverend Hodges in Hickory Hollow. He planned to answer it first thing tomorrow—a firm no.

What the Reverend Hodges requested—as well as how he requested it—was far off the beaten path. Why, pastoral changes were simply not carried out in the manner he suggested. Forrest's late father, a bishop in the church, would highly question the reverend's tactics. There were procedures and protocol to follow.

As Prancer *clip-clopped* down the road, Forrest envisioned the Reverend Hodges's unusual letter, the missive that seemed to be branded in his mind:

Dear Rev. Townsend,

I've come to know of you and your ministry through the church conference. I reside in a little place called Hickory Hollow. I have highly admired you—and your father before he passed on—and I've heard nothing but the very best about you.

Twenty-four years ago, we built and dedicated our little church in the wildwood to the glory of God. Now I am old. My wife passed away, and I can no longer shoulder the burden of pastoring. I know this town is not as big as the one you are now living in, but Hickory Hollow has a host of good people with big hearts.

I am writing to ask if you will accept the pastorate of my church. I believe you will find ministry here rewarding and fulfilling. Because I started this church, my heart is tied up in it, and I want the very best for it. I feel that with your fine qualities and capabilities, you are the man who should fill my shoes.

Of course, I want God's will in the matter. As I prayed, I felt strongly impressed that you could be the one—if God deals with your heart. Will you seek the Lord about this matter and then let me know your answer? I would deeply appreciate this.

One last thing. Please do not share this matter abroad. No one in Hickory Hollow knows of my intentions.

Sincerely,

Preacher Anson Hodges

Riding down the road, Forrest looked at the lovely brick homes that lined the street. Why would he want to leave First Church of Harrisonburg? He had been here two years, and he didn't see any need to change pastorates. The congregation had grown, and besides, it was situated prominently on Main Street.

The Reverend Hodges's place of ministry was a church in a wildwood. Why move down and take a little country congregation when he could continue serving this fine city parish?

He thought of the ramifications if he were to accept the Reverend Hodges's offer. In their church conference, the bigger one's congregation was, the higher one could climb on the ladder of ministerial success. There were positions of prestige available in the conference such as becoming a bishop, a leader of ministers as his late father had been, and there were certain steps one took to achieve a role such as that. Perhaps a lofty position was in his future. Frankly, he hoped so. Pastoring people got tiresome at times, whereas pastoring pastors was an enticing thought. The size of the congregation he served definitely had bearing on his future, so why leave his city church?

He turned down another street and continued on his way, thinking about his swelling membership and the finances that accompanied it. Perhaps he would send an offering from his church fund to help the Reverend Hodges's church. That was how he could assist the church in Hickory Hollow. He wouldn't have to move there to help them. Sending money would suffice. Perhaps one of the burdens the Reverend Hodges was facing was a lack of funds. Perhaps that played a role in his intended resignation.

"If I send him some money," Forrest mused aloud, "maybe that will buoy him up and help him continue in his pastoral ministry until a future date."

Forrest had it all figured out. He was a man of action, who put foresight and forethought into things. He knew how to run ministries and programs in churches. He prided himself on that. Of a certainty, his plan to send funds to the little church in the wildwood was the answer to this situation.

"Giddyap," he said gingerly, realizing he'd let Prancer slow to a walk. "Let's go, girl. Miss Euphemia Devine is waiting." As his horse set off at a clipped pace, Forrest wondered what Miss Devine would think of the Reverend Hodges's request.

If things were to develop between him and Miss Devine, how would she take to moving to a country town when she was a city girl? She was born with a silver spoon in her mouth and had never lacked for anything, especially the fashionable things of life. Her parents doted on her and kept her steeped to the lips in finery.

From the moment Forrest had first met Miss Devine, he had admired her. She was an intelligent, well-bred young woman, and besides that, she was a feast for the eyes with her delicate blond beauty and piercing blue eyes. A regular snow maiden, she was.

Lately, he'd allowed time for serious matrimonial musings. He would make sure he married a woman who could contribute to his ministry. That was important to him—at the top of the list even. He smiled. Miss Devine would be a fine asset to his pastoral ministry.

Long ago he'd made up his mind that whatever woman he chose must have a keen appreciation for the Lord's business. That was the main requirement he was looking for, and Miss Devine fit the bill admirably. She was a chaperone for the young people's group and had given of her time untiringly in this endeavor.

He smiled again. Things were well on their way to turning out splendidly for him in the matrimonial department, namely with Miss Devine.

That was another reason he would never accept the Reverend Hodges's offer. He could not envision Miss Euphemia Devine as a country parson's wife. She would miss her china-painting lessons and her charcoal portraiture club and her gracious entertaining of society women. No, he would not ask that of her.

And the last reason he would not consider the Reverend Hodges's request was because he didn't care to live in Hickory Hollow. It was a rough sector of the state—or at least it used to be. Everyone knew that, years ago, outlaw gangs had holed up around Hickory Hollow and caused a lot of trouble. Their evil influence was probably still lurking, and he certainly didn't want to take on any more trouble than was necessary.

He would not give the offer another thought. But what he would think about was Miss Devine—with pleasure. Within a quarter hour, she would be sitting beside him on the buckboard, wearing her frip and finery that always made him proud. They would ride in the moonlight to the young people's social, enjoying genteel conversation and occasional covert glances between them.

When the time was right, he would ask for her hand in matrimony.

He smiled as he thought about Webster's definition of "divine," a word that so closely matched Miss Euphemia's surname, "Devine." He had looked it up last night on a whim to get an exact definition.

"Superb. Heavenly. Proceeding directly from God."

He smiled again. "Most apropos, Miss Devine. Divinely inspired? Giddyap, Prancer," he called with gusto. He thought about the verb "divine." Webster's said it meant to perceive intuitively. "I divine that a divine girl is in the future for me. I wonder if she'll be a Devine girl?"

With that welcome prospect in mind, he threw back his head and chuckled heartily.

Chapter 3

Y ou're doing what, Pa?" Shirley's mother exclaimed, her rocker suddenly motionless.

Shirley could only watch the interchange between her grandfather and her mother on the porch, where all three of them were sitting on Saturday afternoon, her and Mama shelling pecans. Well, her anyway. Mama's hands were momentarily stilled from their busyness, rigid in tight fists, and words were flying too fast for Shirley to get one in edgewise.

"You can't mean this," her mother said, provocation in her voice. She put her bowl of pecans on the floor with a plunk.

"Yes, I do mean it. I'm resigning." Grandfather had that unwavering look to his eyes, and his jaw was firmly set.

"But Pa, you're a strong man yet, even with the years on you. There's no need to do this—"

"I don't have the will or the inclination to continue pastoring." None of them was rocking now. It was as quiet as a schoolhouse on a summer day.

"But we all help out at the church, Pa. You know that. Shirley, Matthew, Edmund, me, all the others—"

"This church needs more than piecemeal parcels. And it needs more than Hodgeses and Campbells and Randalls. If it's going to grow, it's got to have fresh ideas and a new young preacher to lead it."

"But you started this church. You gave it your heart and soul—"

"And it won't be easy leaving it—as its preacher, that is. I'll always live in Hickory Hollow. I'm moving out of the parsonage and in with Edmund and his family, but I'll still attend church every time the door's opened."

"Who could possibly take your place?" Mama's eyebrows were upside-down Us.

"His name is the Reverend Forrest Townsend." Grandfather paused, amusement written in his eyes. "That's what city folks call preachers. 'The Reverend.' Remember that, you hear?"

"You've already secured a replacement?"

"When will the new preacher arrive?" Shirley managed to interject. "I mean, the new reverend?"

"On Thursday of next week. I plan to resign to the congregation in the morning. I figure on having my things out of the parsonage by Monday afternoon, and you womenfolk can clean it Tuesday and Wednesday. He can move in on Thursday—"

"Maybe you can get the Randall women to help you," Mama said, sounding a little angry.

Shirley thought about her mother's peculiar comment regarding the Randalls, and her mind wandered to the feud that started years ago when Mama and

Papa began courting. Zeke Randall, Mama's former suitor—or at least he thought he was—hadn't liked it one bit when Papa came along. Not long after, Zeke left town. Later, after Mama and Papa married, Zeke came back with his uppity new wife, and through the years there'd been contention between the two families, all of it instigated by the Randalls. Thankfully, Zeke's sister, Ivy, who lived in the East, had continued to be Mama's best friend.

"It'll take a leap of faith to make things right between the Campbells and the Randalls," Mama said when the feud would flare up occasionally.

"A new preacher in Hickory Hollow. . ." Mama's words trailed off, jarring Shirley from her musings.

Grandfather let out a long sigh. "Ah, Amanda, the apple of my eye. Did you think I'd keep preaching until my toes turned up?"

"I suppose I did." A sob shook Mama's voice. "It never crossed my mind that any other preacher would stand behind the pulpit you built with your own hands in the church you and Matthew carved out of the woods. And then, with Ma dying and all. . ." Tears trickled down her cheeks, but she made no move to wipe them away.

He reached over and patted her hands, which were limp now, then handed her his handkerchief, and she dabbed at her tears. "This is for the best. You'll see. The town is growing. And the church needs to grow, too. I believe the key will be a new young preacher. And this one is known across the Missouri conference for his innovative ways."

"Grandfather's right, Mama," Shirley chimed in. "This new preacher—what's his name, Grandfather?"

"The Reverend Forrest Townsend."

"The Reverend Forrest Townsend will probably institute new programs and attract new people," Shirley went on. "And then he'll generate more workers for divine service."

"And after the Reverend Townsend builds up the congregation," Grandfather said, "maybe he'll add wings onto the church for more space."

Shirley's mother picked up her bowl of pecans and began to rock, and Shirley and her grandfather began rocking, too. "Perhaps you're right, Pa."

"That's my girl."

The rockers shifted back and forth, and Grandfather hummed "Blessed Assurance," and the pecans came loose from their shells under nimble fingers, and the perfume of flowers borne on a gentle spring breeze filled the air.

"As I said earlier," Grandfather said, "this is the best thing that's happened to our church in a long while—getting a new young preacher. . .I mean a reverend." He paused. "And it might be the best thing that ever happened to you, Shirley."

"What do you mean, Grandfather?"

"The Reverend Townsend's not married."

"He's not?" Her mother's face was as bright as a ray of sunshine.

"What does that have to do with me?" Shirley spouted, fighting the consternation she felt rising inside of her. She had to be respectful, she reminded herself. That was her raising. But it was hard. Why was everyone trying to get her married off? Then her conscience assailed her. Well, not everyone. But certainly Mama was. And now Grandfather. "Where is Rev. Townsend from?" Shirley asked sweetly, trying to distract them.

"Harrisonburg. Listen well, Shirley. You couldn't find a finer husband in all the world than the Reverend Townsend."

I'm not looking for a husband, Grandfather, especially not a preacher-husband. I'm looking for. . .oh, what am I looking for? The authoress visions were back, parading before her mind's eye.

"You're a whole year older than I was when Matthew Campbell came to Hickory Hollow," her mother said, a sentimental look in her light green eyes. "And it didn't take me long to find out he was the man for me."

"Shirley?" Grandfather asked, a gentleness in his tone.

"Yes, sir?" Shirley studied the black veins on the brown hull of a pecan.

"Rev. Townsend couldn't find a finer wife in all the world than you, girl. You'd make a fine preacher's wife, just like your dear departed grandmother. Saint and sinner alike loved her to pieces."

"If Shirley'll mind her p's and q's," her mother said, "I believe she can lasso this new preacher—"

"I don't want to lasso the. . .the reverend." Shirley jumped up and set her bowl on the floor with a thud, a few pecans jumping over the rim and landing on the porch. "I don't want to lasso anybody. I want. . .I want. . ." She dashed across the floorboards and jerked open the door. "I. . .oh, never mind. You wouldn't understand. Neither one of you."

The door slammed behind her.

≈

That evening, as Shirley lay abed beside Gladly, with little Milcah snuggled in the trundle to her side, she made a firm resolve. *I'm staying as far away as possible from the Reverend Townsend. I want nothing to do with him.*

Being a preacher's wife was the ultimate life of drudgery, worse than farmwork even, and she wanted better things for herself—and for her family. Besides that, even if being a preacher's wife somehow fell to be her lot in life, she couldn't do it. She was simply unequipped. For sure, she would steer clear of the Reverend Townsend. She would resign her afternoon Sunday school class immediately. That way, she would only see him at Sunday morning services. That would suit her just fine.

Why, I wouldn't marry a preacher if he was the last man in the world.

Chapter 4

So this is the girl I've heard so much about," Forrest said of the young woman standing beside the elderly Reverend Hodges. Forrest was in the doorway, greeting his new parishioners in Hickory Hollow as they filed by. He smiled—broadly. "Let's see, Rev. Hodges," he said, "didn't you tell me your granddaughter's name is Shirley?"

"That's right. This is my granddaughter Shirley Campbell. Shirley, this is the Reverend Forrest Townsend." He nudged Forrest in the ribs. "You'll have to get her to tell you how her mother came to name her Shirley."

Forrest thrust out his hand for a shake, but for some reason the young woman didn't respond in like fashion. "It's a pleasure to meet you, Miss Campbell. Your grandfather's given me a glowing report of you and your dedication to the Lord's business." This was a woman he wanted to get to know—and know well.

With hesitation, the young woman finally shook his proffered hand, then released it as if she had touched a hot coal. "Thank you, Preach—" She stopped abruptly. "Reverend." Her look was polite but unfriendly, and her tone was definitely clipped.

Forrest fiddled with his tie. What was wrong with Miss Campbell? Her grandfather had raved about her, going on and on about her duty and her devotion and her distinction, that she was of noble character, honorable. Yet she was indifferent and most decidedly inelegant—and without proper decorum it seemed.

"I'm delighted to make your acquaintance," Forrest said, forcing cheer into his voice, trying with all his might to dispel the sudden dampening of the pleasant spring air.

Rev. Hodges slipped his arm around the young woman. "Shirley, I told Forrest the day he was moving into the parsonage that you were sure to be along any time. I told him, 'If there's a church activity going on, Shirley'll be there if nobody else shows up.' Only, you didn't show up."

She looked at her plain brown shoes that peeked from beneath her plain blue skirts. "I–I. . ."

Forrest felt the need to put the young woman at ease. "Well, Miss Campbell, as I said earlier, it's a pleasure to meet you. Your grandfather has my curiosity piqued. One of these days, you'll have to tell me whom you were named after."

"Not named after," the young woman spoke up, almost in rebuke. "How I came to be named Shirley."

"It's a unique story that'll bring you a chuckle or two," Rev. Hodges said.

"I see." Forrest rocked up and down on his feet, toe to heel, heel to toe. He was indeed seeing a number of things. First, he was seeing that for some reason Miss Campbell had no use for him. That was all right. He had no use for her, either. Second, he was seeing a drab young woman. Oh, she wasn't drab in her looks so much. In fact, she was quite attractive with her thick swath of dark hair and her exquisite features and her piercing gray eyes that seemed to read your thoughts. But in dress and deportment, she was as countrified and unpolished a woman as ever he'd come across, a woman who would never be of interest to him.

His mind flitted to Miss Euphemia Devine and her winsome, charming ways. She could come up with witty sayings at the drop of a hanky. The belle of the ball was a good way to describe her. But it was no use thinking about her. She let him know in no uncertain terms that she thought his move to Hickory Hollow was folly.

"There you are, Reverend," called the Widow Ford from the bottom of the steps. She was adjusting her hatstrings under her double chin, which jiggled every time she talked. She dabbed behind her ears with her handkerchief, then moved it around to the back of her neck and rubbed hard like a waterfall was back there. Forrest had to squelch a smile as he pictured a Niagara Falls of perspiration gushing over her.

"Are you almost ready, Reverend? I'm about to wilt in this heat, April though it is. Wonder what August will bring us?" Mrs. Ford touched her rotund midsection. "I hope my gall bladder doesn't get to acting up on me again." She shook her head from side to side, and her double chin jiggled all the more. "My baking hen will be baked clean off the bones if we don't get home soon. Are you finished talking yet?"

"Have a good day, Reverend." Miss Campbell whisked down the steps and in moments was out of view, and Forrest could only wonder.

"I asked, are you coming now?" the Widow Ford piped up.

"Why, yes, Mrs. Ford," he said distractedly, still thinking about Miss Campbell. "I'll be right along."

"Then I'll be on my way and get my baking hen out of the oven. You'll be there directly, Reverend?"

He nodded. "And thank you for your gracious invitation to join you for Sunday dinner. I'm looking forward to spending time with you."

"Same here, Reverend." She turned, her voluminous, out-of-date skirts swishing, and made her way down the walk.

The elderly Reverend Hodges nudged Forrest in the ribs, twinkles dancing in his eyes. It was a mannerism Forrest was quickly growing familiar with. Why, if Rev. Hodges continued this practice, Forrest would have sore ribs at every turn.

"That's the last time you'll be able to say you're looking forward to spending time with the Widow Ford," Rev. Hodges said, the twinkles still in his eyes.

"I don't catch your drift." Forrest had to force his thoughts back to the Widow Ford and to what the Reverend Hodges was saying. He was still brooding over Miss Campbell's abrupt departure.

"The Widow Ford's known for her organ recitals."

"She plays the organ?" Forrest came alive. "That's wonderful! Why didn't she play this morning? Singing to organ accompaniment is much better than a cappella."

Rev. Hodges nudged him yet again. "Organ recitals, Forrest. Liver. Heart.

Spleen. Gall bladder."

Forrest threw his head back and laughed, finally catching on. "Every church is blessed with at least one of those."

Rev. Hodges winked at Forrest. "The Widow Ford is a kind old soul, but oh, the pains she bears—and she recites every last one of them."

In a jovial mood, Forrest clasped his hands together and looked heavenward. "Lord, give me patience." In his heart, he meant every word.

⁂

Forrest thought about his new pastorate in Hickory Hollow as he drove toward the Widow Ford's house. The church was small, but it was growing on him. When he'd first read Rev. Hodges's letter of invitation, he thought to answer with a firm no. But he finally decided that taking a small church and helping it grow into a big one would be an excellent entry on his list of ministerial accomplishments.

The parishioners were growing on him, too. All except one—namely, Miss Campbell, who thought she was Miss Panjandrum when she was nothing but a country mouse. He recalled their conversation—or rather, lack of one—on the church steps a half hour ago. Why had she acted that way? It was a snubbing if ever he'd seen one.

"Hmmmph," he snorted. "Miss Campbell is playing that age-old game of Hard to Get. I can play it, too. Only my game won't have the same goal Miss Campbell's obviously does. Why, I wouldn't have her on a silver platter."

Chapter 5

Standing in front of the discolored mirror that hung over the bureau in the cubbyhole of a room she and her two sisters shared, Shirley drew her long dark hair into its usual chignon and pushed her combs firmly into the sides.

"My one beauty," she said, peering closely at herself. "Just like Jo March's hair." She fluffed the front part, silently thanking the curl papers that they had done their job. She endured the torture devices every Saturday night and for special occasions. Today was one of those—the Sunday school picnic.

"If only I'd been born with beauty." She put down her brush and tidied up the top of the bureau. "But when the Good Lord was passing out looks, I thought He said, 'Books,' and I said, 'Give me plenty of those.' "

She smiled at her little joke. As she looked down, she saw a smudge on one of her cuffs and brushed it away, grateful to see the dirt disappear so easily. She was wearing her second-best shirtwaist, and she had nothing else presentable to change into except her best, which she had to save for Sunday.

She wondered why Mama wanted her to go to the Sunday school picnic. She had quit teaching her class right before Rev. Townsend came and had no connection with Sunday school now. Mama could've told her to take the children and come back home. The corn was in, had been all week, and Mama needed her. They had worked like Trojans, the lot of them—even little Milcah. Mama had set the tyke to shucking ear after ear so she could can some of it to use next winter. The rest would go to market. So why was Mama wanting her to go today?

Rev. Townsend, of course.

Shirley thought about their new preacher's looksome ways. His hair was as dark as hers, and his eyes were about the same shade of gray. But that was where the likeness stopped. Where she was plain, he was perfect with his handsome features, his fine chiseled jaw, and his even, white teeth. Besides that, he was tall and robust and cut a dashing figure in his expensive suits and ties—sometimes string, sometimes cravat-style.

She pondered over their differences again. In the looks arena, she was a wren. He was a cardinal. In the brains arena, she was a simpleton. He had the knowledge of the world. In the deportment arena, she was raw, green, a slow coach. He was a brilliant-cut diamond.

Her mother must be intending to thrust them together at every opportunity. Matchmaking Mama. That was what she should be called. Shirley didn't even feel a smile coming on at that thought. It only conjured up a frown.

"If you don't hurry up, Shirley Campbell, we'll be late for the picnic," her sister Gladly whined through the wall. A sharp rap sounded on the door.

"Hold your horses, Gladly. There's plenty of time." Shirley put on her frumpy-looking hat, lamenting her lack of a new one. But it was not to be. There were simply too many mouths to feed in the Campbell household for such things as that. Perhaps she could replace the ribbons come fall, when the crops were in and accounted for. That was what she had done for two years in a row without complaint, though her mother had detected her desire for a new one.

"I never cared much for fripperies," Mama whispered to her when they were purchasing new ribbons last year, "but when you get married, maybe your husband can buy you a new hat—or two or three—if that's what you think will truly make you happy."

In the last year or so, there had been a reference to marriage in nearly every conversation between them. Not that Shirley didn't want to get married someday. Of course she did. She wanted love and marriage and children, what all women wanted. But the key word was "someday." Before the inevitable someday came around for her, she wanted to see her goals and aspirations fulfilled. Her thoughts drifted to the high-society tea, and the book signings, and the university dais, and the literary greats.

"Shirley!"

"I'm coming." She grabbed her frayed reticule from the hook on the wall, resolving to keep it turned toward her skirts so no one would see the worn spots.

"Yes, I'm coming," she whispered to the dreams of her heart as she dashed out the door.

❧

Forrest made his way out of the sanctuary and into the churchyard, greeting his parishioners who milled about the grounds. Children's voices called out to each other from both sides of the church, and the smell of good things to eat wafted through the air. He noted that even old Mr. Wilbur, a vet from the War Between the States, was there. Sunday school picnics were always well attended. Too bad Sunday school wasn't. But he would soon change that.

In the distance, he saw Miss Campbell alight from her wagon, her brothers and sisters clambering down almost before she got it stopped. When she approached with a basket on her arm, he took a step toward her.

"I'm surprised to see you here, Miss Campbell," he said. He prided himself that he kept the acrimony out of his voice. He had been teaching her class for each of the six weeks since he became pastor. The thought filled him with chagrin—he, the parson, having to contend with twenty-seven wriggly, writhing, hot, and sweaty children—with no help. Didn't country churches know that pastors didn't teach children's classes? That there were more important things for pastors to do? Apparently not.

"Since you gave up your Sunday school class, I assumed you wouldn't be attending today," he added.

"I had to bring my brothers and my sisters," she said, her tone clipped as usual. "Mama and Papa—neither one could bring them. The corn is in."

"I see, Miss Campbell." This time, the acrimony was evident. *Forrest, you're the pastor. "Be ye kind, one to another, tenderhearted, forgiving each other,"* he quoted silently. He forced a smile. "We welcome you."

She touched the basket at her arm. "Where shall I put this?"

He pointed to sawhorse tables on the side of the church, under a canopy of hickories. "Over there."

She made her way to a table, delivered her basket to three young matrons from the congregation, and came back to the front of the church. "Rev. Townsend?" She held her reticule in front of her, her fingers working furiously, squeezing each fringed knot at the bottom.

He noticed spots that were badly frayed on her small bag and couldn't help but compare it to Miss Devine's showy accoutrements. She had the good fortune to be born on the sunny side of the hedge. Obviously, Miss Campbell didn't.

"I was wondering. Do you need any help. . .with the games?"

"I hadn't planned on games."

"No games at a Sunday school picnic?" Her eyebrows shot up above her light gray eyes.

He tried not to stare. Was she criticizing him? He'd been to plenty of Sunday school picnics, and he knew very well that there were games of all sorts and sometimes wagon rides. But those were picnics he didn't have to plan. This picnic, he decided, would be just that—a picnic. They would eat and visit, and then they would go home.

"May I organize some games?"

Conscience pricking you, Miss Campbell? he thought but didn't say.

"I was thinking of Blind Man's Bluff and Mother, May I? And maybe a few more," she persisted.

"Certainly. I welcome your participation." *In more ways than one. Why don't you take your class back and relieve me of this burden?*

"Thank you, Reverend. I'll get a game started, then." She looked at him as if waiting for his permission.

"Yes. Meantime, I'll ask the ladies to prepare the food for serving. After we eat, you can have one more game, and then we'll dismiss." *Thank the Lord.*

⌗

All afternoon, Shirley led the children in games and frolics to their hearts' content. She even let them wade in the creek, hovering over them like a hen over her chicks, making sure not a one suffered an injury. That was how it was when she taught their Sunday school class, watching them as intently as if they were her brothers and sisters.

Though she hated to admit it, she admired Rev. Townsend for taking on the challenge of teaching her class. He loved children as much as she did.

"Let's have a play party," shouted a snaggletoothed, redheaded little boy. "Let's do Skip to My Lou."

"Yes, my favorite," called out a flaxen-haired young miss.

"All right, children," Shirley said. "One last game. A play party, it is. Form two lines, please." She touched the snaggletoothed boy on the shoulders. "Timothy is first in this line." She pointed to a spot six feet away. "Millie will be the first in the other line. Everyone else, get behind them."

The children scurried to form two lines, and on a lark, Shirley joined the first one.

"You're playing, Miss Shirley?" a little girl said from behind, delight in her eyes.

"Yes, I thought to. Now, children. Settle down. I need to get a head count." That done, she realized the second line was a person short. This was a partner game.

From out of nowhere it seemed, Rev. Townsend stepped up and joined in. "I'll make it an even number."

Shirley was surprised. "You will?"

"Yes."

"But we skip."

"I understand."

"And we sing."

He nodded.

"You know how to play Skip to My Lou?"

"Of course. I've seen it done many times."

She swept her gaze away from him, wondering. Why would he want to participate in a children's game? Ah, because he taught their class. He was trying to build camaraderie with them, and that made her admire him all the more. A city preacher who would skip with country children? Why, he was ten feet tall in her eyes.

"It's time to begin, children," she announced. "You know what to do."

She led them in the song, and as they sang lustily, a child from each line formed a partnership with a child from the other line and skipped down the center aisle, holding hands. When their turn was finished, two more formed a partnership and took their turn skipping and holding hands down the center aisle.

Flies in the buttermilk, shoo, shoo, shoo!
Flies in the buttermilk, shoo, shoo, shoo!
Flies in the buttermilk, shoo, shoo, shoo!
Skip to my Lou, my darling.

On and on the play party went, the children singing at the top of their voices.

Little red wagon, painted blue,
Little red wagon, painted blue,
Little red wagon, painted blue,
Skip to my Lou, my darling.

The singing and skipping grew more frenzied.

Skip, skip, skip to my Lou,
Skip, skip, skip to my Lou,
Skip, skip, skip to my Lou,

Skip to my Lou, my darling.

When the line moved on and Shirley was the next person up, she was startled to see that Rev. Townsend was going to be her partner. How could that be? He'd been at the end of the line when they started.

The children yelled for them to go on with the play party, and she and the reverend came together, locked hands, and began skipping down the aisle. Suddenly, the words of the song stung her ears.

Bart's come a-courtin, yes, yes, yes!
Bart's come a-courtin, yes, yes, yes!
Bart's come a-courtin, yes, yes, yes!
Skip to my Lou, my darling.

Panting, she and the reverend came to a halt at the proper place but said not a word. When Shirley looked up at him, he was peering at her, his chest heaving up and down from the strenuous activity. For a moment, their gazes were locked, and she could think of nothing to say. A tingly feeling took hold of her heart.

To her side, she felt more than saw the children dispersing, running this way and that, calling out cheery good-byes, and in the distance, she knew that wagons were pulling out. But her attention was fixed on the reverend, and his on her.

"Preacher, looks like we have a prophecy being fulfilled right before our eyes," old Mr. Wilbur said from behind them, laughing like a hyena.

Neither responded.

"I said, 'Looks like we have a prophecy being fulfilled right before our eyes.' You know—the song."

A little gasp gurgled up in Shirley's throat as she caught his meaning. The song talked about courting.

"A prophecy, Mr. Wilbur?" Rev. Townsend said at last, breaking their intense stare.

"That's right, Preacher. A prophecy. It means, 'a prediction of something to come.' "

"Every minister knows what the word 'prophecy' means," Rev. Townsend snapped. But his brows drew together as if he were perplexed.

Shirley was convinced her face had turned scarlet, as surely as if she were looking in a mirror. Courting?

"Isn't your first name Bart, Preacher?" Mr. Wilbur stroked his white waist-length beard, amusement lurking in his gaze. "Like in the song?" He belted out, "Bart's come a-courtin, yes, yes, yes!"

"No, it's Forrest," Shirley blurted, then felt flustered. She should've let Rev. Townsend answer for himself.

Mr. Wilbur chuckled. "Forrest is your middle name, right, Preacher?"

Rev. Townsend's expression grew sheepish, and he gave a boyish grin. "As right as rain. My full name is Bartholomew Forrest Townsend."

"Well, well, well," Mr. Wilbur said, stroking his beard again, smile twinkles in his eyes. "That's a deep subject."

Shirley blushed once more, could feel the intense heat in her face, and said a hurried good-bye to the reverend. As she walked toward the wagon, she smiled. She wouldn't have told Mr. Wilbur that her middle name was Louise for all the tea in China.

Chapter 6

Hurry, Milcah," Shirley crooned to her little sister. "It's almost time to leave for church. Put your socks on, and I'll button up your shoes for you."

"Yeth, Thirley," came the little girl's lisping reply.

Shirley continued dressing. She pulled her shirtwaist over her head and fastened the tiny buttons up the front, then put her lace collar around her shoulders.

For nearly four months now, ever since last April, when the Reverend Townsend had come to Hickory Hollow, their paths had crossed over and over, though inadvertently. It started with her taking her class back after the Sunday school picnic. Her conscience had simply gotten the best of her—she would never forget the hurt look on Grandfather Hodges's face when she withdrew from it. Teaching Sunday school again had brought about several conversations between her and the Reverend Townsend. She recalled one in particular. . . .

She arrived on the church grounds one Sunday afternoon, and as she alighted from the wagon, she saw him coming out the church door.

"You certainly handle Deacon Hunter's children well," he said. "Something I could never seem to accomplish when I was teaching your class."

"Thank you," she replied shyly, taking a quilt and a basket from the wagon and walking toward the hickories. "I keep them busy mostly." Under the canopy of trees, she grasped hold of the quilt by two ends, and in a flash he was at her side, grasping the quilt by the other ends, and they shook it out and spread it on the ground.

"I tried that, too," he said, "keeping them busy. But it didn't work for me. Those Hunter children are as rambunctious as ever I've seen." He rolled his eyes.

Shirley gave a shrug and smiled as she smoothed one end of the quilt. "I've been known to send the two older ones for a pail of drinking water two and three times in an afternoon, and the next three children I use as play actors for my Bible stories. The two little Hunter kiddies give me very little trouble if they know I've brought cookies."

He rolled his eyes again. "I never thought of that. Imagine. Seven children underfoot. And every one of them going in different directions. I don't know how Mrs. Hunter manages."

Shirley didn't say anything. She knew only too well how Mrs. Hunter managed. The same way she did. And Mama did. There were seven children in the Campbell family, too, six still living at home. Shirley let out a little sigh. One simply did what one was expected to do. And one did the best job possible. It was as plain as that.

"I don't think it's the assignments you give the Hunter children that keep them corralled. I think you have a keen knack for handling kids, Miss Campbell, and I commend you."

Now, as Shirley stood in front of her bureau smoothing her collar, she recalled the warm feeling that had seeped over her that day as Rev. Townsend complimented her. It was affirmation she rarely received, and it felt like water to a dying plant.

Another duty she had taken up was cleaning the church. She was surprised when her mother suggested it and was willing to release her from house and farm work for three hours every Saturday afternoon. That as well had prompted occasional conversations with the reverend in regards to special cleaning needs for certain events.

Then, at the box supper last week, he'd purchased her dinner, his bid the highest. That was when he asked her to tell him the story of how she came to be named Shirley. . . .

"When my mother was a little girl," she told him as they sat side by side at a sawhorse table under the hickories in the churchyard, "she heard my grandfather reading the last verse of Psalm 23 one Sunday morning."

He paused from eating, his fork in midair. "The one that says, 'Surely, goodness and mercy shall follow me all the days of my life: and I will dwell in the house of the Lord forever?' "

"That's the one. My mother mistakenly thought the verse said, 'Shirley,' not 'surely.' "

He threw back his head and laughed heartily.

"When they got home from church that day, she announced to my grandparents that someday she was going to name her little girl Shirley. When they asked why, she told them it was straight from the Bible, that Grandfather had read it that morning. Grandfather put two and two together, and he and my grandmother got a big chuckle out of it."

"And that's how you came to be named Shirley." He swung his head from side to side, smiling. "How intriguing."

"The other children in our family have equally unusual names, and they're all biblical."

"Oh? And what are they?"

"Peesultree's the oldest—"

"That is unusual."

She could feel smile twinkles dancing in her eyes. "It's from the book of Psalms. Grandfather used to pronounce the word 'psaltery' as 'peesultree.' It wasn't until a visiting minister heard him say it that he had any inkling he was mispronouncing it."

The reverend let out a belly chuckle.

"Mama was taken with the sound of Peesultree, and that's how he got his name. He's two years older than I am and works in Springfield. I come next. Then there's Gladly, which is biblical, too."

"It's found throughout the Psalms."

"Yes. Mama said it sounded lyrical. Then there's Moses, Mordecai, and Malachi, all boys of course. And then there's little Milcah, our baby sister."

Now, as Shirley put the finishing touches to her chignon, she continued thinking about Rev. Townsend. Every time their paths had crossed—inadvertently, she reminded herself—they found common interests and even laughed together.

She remembered the children's midsummer program they worked on in tandem, choosing the songs to be sung and the Scriptures to be quoted, even collaborating on the writing of the play, which was deemed a success by all who saw it.

That last thing brought joy to her heart—the writing of the play. As she'd promised herself on the day of her grandmother's funeral, she had carved out bits and pieces of time to write. So far, she had completed four stories.

Just as it was said of Jo March in *Little Women*, so it could be said of her, and she quoted the lines:

> *When the writing fit came on, she gave herself up to it with entire abandon. . .while she sat safe and happy in an imaginary world, full of friends almost as real and dear to her as any in the flesh.*

She smiled, her mind back on the new friend who had become real and dear to her in the flesh—the Reverend Townsend.

Her face grew warm, recalling old Mr. Wilbur on the day of the Sunday school picnic, talking about prophecies being fulfilled when she and Rev. Townsend skipped-to-my-Lou while the children sang, "Bart's come a-courting, yes, yes, yes."

Perhaps Mr. Wilbur's words were prophetic after all. There had been no formal courting, but she and Rev. Townsend had enjoyed a lot of fellowship these last four months. Her heart had grown tender toward him, and she sensed the same thing had happened in him.

A hard tremble shook her. *You've been silly to dally with a man so terribly wrong for you.*

"Thirley, I've got my thockth on," little Milcah said. "And my thewth. I'm ready for you to button them up."

Still tremulous, Shirley strode over to where her sister was sitting on a rag rug in front of the bed. She knelt before her and pulled Milcah's shoe buttons through the loops with the button hook, one by one, noting the fraying across the toes and the worn spots in the soles.

"Is the preacher thweet on you, Thirley?" little Milcah asked.

Shirley felt a lump rise in her throat. "Why do you ask that, dearie?"

"Becauth I heard the Widow Ford thay it."

The lump grew to boulder size, and she took a deep draught of the morning air flooding through the curtains. "I–I. . ."

"I heard Mama thay it, too."

Shirley started working on the second shoe. One button. Two. Three. Four. Up Milcah's ankle she went. So everyone was talking about her? About the two of them? That there was something going on between them?

Jumbled thoughts rose in her mind. Of course she was flattered by Forrest's attentions. She corrected herself—Rev. Townsend's attentions. She had no claim on him and therefore no right to use his given name, even in her thinking. But it rolled off her tongue with. . .enjoyment? "Forrest," she said distractedly.

"Ithn't that Preacher Townthend' name?" little Milcah asked.

Enjoyment? Yes, that was what she felt when she was with him, she admitted to herself. And affection? Her hands shook as she continued buttoning little Milcah's shoe.

"Thirley, did you hear me? Ithn't the preacher'th name Forretht?"

The shoe buttons fastened, Shirley sprang up, little Milcah's questions sinking into her befuddled mind. "I think so. Now hop up, dearie. It's time to go."

⟨⟨⟨∞⟩⟩⟩

All the way to church, Shirley's heart beat in time with the horse's hooves and just as loudly it seemed, and her breath came in short spurts.

Affection? she questioned herself earlier, when she was thinking of Rev. Townsend. Her heartbeat speeded up. *Affection? Most decidedly.*

But it can't stay, she told herself sternly as she remembered the vow she once made. *I wouldn't marry a preacher if he was the last man in the world.*

Marriage to a preacher—reverend, she corrected herself—meant a life of drudgery, like her grandmother had led. Shirley had her dreams and goals and aspirations. She wanted a life surrounded by interesting people in stimulating settings. And she wanted material comforts for her beloved family. Living totally immersed in divine service—as a preacher's wife—offered nothing of the sort.

Sorrow filled her heart at the forthcoming loss of her real-and-dear-in-the-flesh friend. But nevertheless, she resolved to keep her vow.

I will not marry a. . .a reverend.

Chapter 7

As Forrest looked out over his congregation, waiting for the service to begin, his heart skipped a beat when his eyes came to rest on Miss Campbell. They had been in each other's company numerous times over the past months, and long ago he had given up his mistaken notion that she was a drab country mouse.

On the contrary, she was full of vim and vigor and amusing thoughts and feelings that he had become aware of in his tender discovery of her.

He tapped on his bottom lip. She had blossomed before his very eyes, like a flower budding forth. But then perhaps she hadn't. Perhaps she had always been in full bloom, but he had only recently come to see it. Yes, that was definitely the case. She was a magnolia and always had been, like the ones that dotted the church grounds under sprawling limbs, and her fragrance was just as sweet. Sweeter, in fact. He drew in a deep, throaty breath, thinking about Miss Campbell and the luscious scent of a magnolia.

He once thought Miss Devine was a snow maiden, but Shirley was the real snow maiden. She was the perfect example of the Proverbs 31 woman, and he was as smitten with her as ever a man could be. It wasn't because she would be an asset to his ministry. It was because she was a woman uniquely created for him.

That last thought warmed his heart. God had been watching out for him, as an earthly father cared for his son, when He sent him to Hickory Hollow, Missouri. God knew that there was one Miss Shirley Campbell, whom He was preparing for one Forrest Townsend. Shirley was the one in a thousand for him and for him alone.

He smiled, recalling pleasant times spent in her company. He thought about the day she told him the amusing story of how she acquired her name, as well as how her brothers and sisters acquired theirs.

"Pssst, Reverend," whispered a voice from the choir loft behind him. "It's time to start the service."

Forrest was so startled, he dropped his Bible. "Thank you," he whispered as he swooped down to pick up the holy book, then stood and strode across the platform, his long legs carrying him quickly.

"Shall we bow our heads in prayer?" he intoned from behind the oaken pulpit.

❧

This is going to be painful, grievous even, coming to church every Sunday and seeing him. Shirley's hands were perspiring so profusely, there were wet marks on the hymnal where she was grasping it.

My heart is his, she admitted to herself. *But my will is my own. And what am I going to do when I see him at afternoon Sunday school every week? And what about when I clean the church on Saturdays? Oh, Lord, help me.*

All through the sermon, she managed to keep her mind on the latest story she was developing. If she concentrated on him and his sermon, she might. . .what might she do? She didn't know. She only knew that she had to keep her thoughts clear of him.

As she filed out the church door after the service was over, she gave him the perfunctory handshake and smile but avoided his eyes and whisked a few steps beyond him, hoping he would be too busy with the church people to take note.

"Preacher Townsend," bellowed old Mr. Wilbur from behind her. "The Bible says, 'Surely, goodness and mercy shall follow me all the days of my life.' You already have goodness and mercy. When are you going to get Shirley? When are you two going to get hitched, Bart?"

Shirley was mortified. Should she turn and greet the old gentleman in politeness and try to change the subject? Or should she keep going and act as if she hadn't heard?

It was decided for her.

"You make an excellent point, Mr. Wilbur," he said, enthusiasm dripping from his voice.

Had Shirley been looking at him, she knew she would see his face aglow with affection, his eyes warm with the tenderness she had become familiar with.

"Perhaps we need to talk to the lady to find out," he said softly.

Shirley rushed down the steps and crossed the churchyard lickety-split. She was glad Papa had the wagon at the ready. She climbed on board, and all the way home, her heart was in the same state it had been in on the way there—beating in time with the horse's hooves and just as loudly.

Chapter 8

The next Saturday, Shirley rode toward the church faster than she should've, but it couldn't be helped. "Giddyap, girl," she said to Old Glory, and the wagon surged forward.

She didn't want to run the risk of seeing him when she went to clean the church today. Most Saturday afternoons, he made visits in homes, so she felt relatively sure that she wouldn't see him. But one never knew. Perhaps he would get back earlier than usual. If that happened, she must be done cleaning and out of there. But to accomplish that, she had to hurry.

She pulled up in the churchyard. In her quick perusal of the parsonage across the way, she was relieved to see that his buggy was gone. Good. Out of sight, out of mind, as the old saying went. That would be her discipline from now on. The stirrings in her heart were simply too strong to be trusted. She must stay away from him as much as possible. Then, when sufficient time passed, her heart would calm down.

Perhaps the Widow Ford would keep him inordinately long this afternoon, rehearsing her gall bladder attack of last week. She smiled, knowing the elderly lady was lonely and just needed a caring ear.

Perhaps Mr. Wilbur would detain him. But that thought dismayed her. Mr. Wilbur liked to talk about courting and prophecies and matrimonial things.

Perhaps Deacon Hunter's wife would invite him to stay for supper. For sure, there would be plenty of time to clean the church if that happened.

As she climbed down from the wagon, Shirley laughed, envisioning Deacon Hunter's wriggly, writhing, screeching children around the reverend as he sat at their large plankboard table, forks a-flying and spoons a-pinging, giggles and chatters accompanying a number of knocked-over glasses with milk a-flowing. At least that's the way it was the last time she'd supped with them. In light of the remarks he made about the rambunctious Hunter children when she came to know him better, she laughed even harder.

For two hours, she worked her heart out cleaning the church, polishing the altars and pulpit, sweeping the floors, dusting the benches, and spic-and-spanning the windows.

In the hot August weather, beads of perspiration formed on her forehead, so hard and fast did she toil. All the while, she formulated a new story in her head. She had found a nifty little literary device—that of utilizing her work time by tooling out her stories. Then, when she found a minute to herself, she wrote them down.

She dashed outside, poured out her cleaning water, then rushed back inside the church and gathered her cloths and bucket and broom, making ready to put them in their closet and be on her way pell-mell.

"Miss Campbell, I've been wanting to get a word with you."

Startled, she dropped the items in her hand, and they clanked on the hard wooden floor.

"Miss Campbell?"

Her back to him, she froze like a statue. He was the last person she wanted to see. Why was he here, anyway? He was visiting church members, wasn't he?

"I didn't mean to frighten you. Please forgive me."

She knew by his voice that he was directly behind her where she stood near the altar. Evidently he had come in the front door of the church and walked up the aisle. She felt hot and cold all at once and knew not what to do. Turn around and greet him? Greet him as she picked up the items so she wouldn't have to make eye contact with him?

Instinct kicked in. She dipped to the floor and gathered the bucket and the broom. "I wasn't expecting you, that's all, Reverend."

In his gentlemanly way, he dipped, too, and swooped up the cloths. They arose together, and when they faced each other, he tucked the cloths into the bucket on her arm. "I got back a little early from my pastoral rounds. The Widow Ford is fit as a fiddle today." He chuckled. "So I arrived back sooner than I thought. I've been wanting to see you all week, Miss Campbell. But woe is me, our paths perchance did not cross. Ah, the misery."

Keeping her eyes on the floor, Shirley toyed with the bucket handle. Was he making fun of her? He knew her literary pursuits. He knew the words he was speaking were Shakespearean and not used in everyday vernacular. She had confided her dreams and hopes and aspirations to him. Now, she felt naked in his presence.

"Art thou in Grub Street? Thou wast so engrossed when I came upon thee."

She glanced his way. Yes, he was making fun of her. Every writer knew that Grub Street was the London abode of literary hacks in the seventeenth and eighteenth centuries. Why, the nerve of him.

He chuckled. "Let's see. You were writing—in your head. I've seen you like this many times. You're present in body, but your mind is far from here, spirited away to other worlds. Isn't that true, Miss Campbell? Does genius burn?" He leaned against the pew behind him, his arms folded across his chest, his smile still lurking, his eyes twinkling.

"I–I. . ." She felt silly for stammering and even sillier for not being able to give him a quick comeback. Oh, to have the pluck of her sister Gladly, a speed-of-lightning thinker who could deliver a retort that burned the ears.

"Please don't think I'm making light of your giftings. For that's what your writing is, you know. Giftings. From God Himself." He paused as if he were deep in contemplation. "God has equipped you with something unique, Shirley," he said, his voice exuding tenderness as he spoke her given name. "The rare talent of writing. Many people seek to write, and some foolishly think they have the gift. But few ever accomplish anything. You are going places in the literary world, mark my words, all for the glory of God."

She swallowed hard. *Not if I marry a. . .a reverend.* The lump in her throat grew bigger, and she willed herself not to let the tears in her eyes escape down her cheek. But what kind words, what affirming words. Why, no one had ever said anything of the sort to her about her writing. Suddenly, without warning, the stirrings in her heart for him grew to tidal wave proportions. *Oh, Forrest...*

"Will you sit down? I have something of great import to ask you."

She looked into his eyes but quickly averted them. Her heart was too telltale. He might read what it was saying.

"Please? Surely you can spare a few minutes." He sat down on a nearby bench and patted the spot beside him.

She hesitated, dreading this tête-à-tête. If only...

She smoothed the sides of her hair and took a seat behind him on a bench all to herself. She couldn't chance closeness right now.

He turned around to face her and propped his arm across the back of the bench. A puzzled look filled his eyes, but then he brightened. For nearly a quarter hour, they talked, him mostly, about the two new Sunday school classes that were recently formed due to church growth. The Lord's business, he called it. He told her the Sunday night sing-along he was planning would attract a large crowd and that he intended to have more special events, a strategy he used with success in Harrisonburg.

She smiled and showed interest at appropriate times and even added to the conversation when she could muster her courage. But for the most part, she sat there, her heart hurting beyond words.

Affection? she'd questioned herself earlier. *Is that what I feel for him? No,* she answered now. *Love. I feel love for him.* She blinked hard to keep her eyes from misting over. *But,* she told herself sternly, *I must purge it from my heart.*

"From what your grandfather says, the Hickory Hollow church has never had a sing-along service before."

She tried to force her mind to think of high-society teas and book signings and the university dais—and all that this would bring to her family, but it refused to obey. *Forrest, Forrest, Forrest!* her heart shouted.

"Did you hear me? Are you back on Grub Street?" He smiled a boyish grin, and she thought her heart would melt and slide down the seat. "That's all right with me," he continued, his heart-melting smile seeming to radiate from the very sinews of his soul. "I'm proud of your pursuits—and accomplishments. That's just one of many reasons why I came to love you...."

Love? She nearly bolted out of her seat. She wished she could be translated like Phillip in the Bible. But instead of getting up, she willed herself to stay still. Her heart was beating so hard, her lightweight cotton shirtwaist was vibrating at the movement, and her breath was coming so short, she felt faint.

"Miss Campbell...Shirley..." In a flash, he was sitting on her bench, a space between them, his long, Bible-thumping fingers an inch away from her shoulder. "I'll say this in language you adore." He let out a long sigh.

A love sigh, she fleetingly thought.

He cleared his throat and recited:

"If I could write the beauty of your eyes

And in fresh numbers, number all your graces,
The age to come would say, 'This poet lies;
Such heavenly touches ne'er touch'd earthly faces.' "

For sure, she was going to swoon. His sweet, rhythmic words were straight from a sonnet of Shakespeare's.

"From the moment I laid eyes on you, I knew you were a part of my destiny."

She resisted the urge to grab the cardboard fan in the hymnal rack and fan her face. Rather, she clasped her hands rigidly together and kept staring straight ahead, as she had been doing all along.

"When your grandfather introduced us on the church steps, something leapt within me, and though I resisted at first, I came to know you and love you. Let me hasten to add that the reason I resisted you was because I thought you were resisting me. I thought that your quiet ways signified you weren't interested. I didn't know the real you back then, the you down inside that sees and feels and knows things so deeply. And so tenderly. . ."

He trailed his finger across the top of her hand, and she felt as if she had died and gone to heaven.

His hand properly back on the bench again, he leaned in a little closer.

"She's beautiful, and therefore to be woo'd;
She is a woman, therefore to be won."

Another tear threatened at his beautiful Shakespearean language, but she kept it in check.

"Shirley, 'come live with me and be my love. . . .' "

Marlowe verses? She smiled despite her pain. This man was simply sent down. What an apropos analogy. He really was sent from above to Hickory Hollow, to do the Lord's business. And to woo her? She resisted the thought.

In another flash—he could certainly do things swiftly—he was on his knees in front of her, and she squelched a smile at his big hulking stature bent up like a screw jack in the narrow space between the benches.

Her breath was coming in short snatches again. She knew what a man on bended knee meant. This couldn't be happening. Here. Today. Right now.

"I'm asking for your hand in marriage, Shirley. I'm proclaiming my love for you, oh Beautiful Eyes with numbers of graces. Wilt thou have me as thy wedded husband? Wilt thou be my wedded wife?" He took her hand in his and kissed the back of it, then gently released it.

This time she bolted up out of her seat on the hard wooden bench—couldn't help doing so—and rammed right into him, where he knelt in the narrow space.

"I–I'm s–sorry," she stammered, feeling like Joey in the Harlequinade. "I didn't mean to. . ."

He bolted up beside her, brushing at his knees.

She felt like a cornered fox on a hunt and looked every which way. She would never be able to look him in the eyes again, not after today, not after this.

He backed out of the narrow space and came to stand in the aisle. "Apparently, I caught you off guard."

Holding on to the back of the bench, she edged away and came to stand in the aisle several feet from him.

"You obviously don't share my sentiments," he said.

She looked down at the floorboards she had swept only three-quarters of an hour ago. She wanted to speak. She wanted to proclaim her love like he had done—in the same fanciful, heartwarming language he used. She would never forget his sweet words for her entire life. But she couldn't say a thing. It was as if her mouth was sewn shut as tightly as the lace collar she had placed stitches in last evening.

"Please. Let me spare you further embarrassment, Miss Campbell." A hard steeliness gripped his voice. "I wish to make a pact with you."

She looked at him, wide-eyed.

"At last, you've looked at me. I should feel privileged, I suppose. All these months, as I came to know you and fall in love with you, I thought of you as a snow maiden. You know as well as I do that that's the epitome of womanly perfection." The disgust in his tone grew intense. "Well, you're no snow maiden, Miss Campbell. You're an ice maiden."

She let out a little gasp, couldn't help it. *Dear Lord, please help me to keep my resolve. Please help me to be strong in the greatest trial of my life.* But the Lord wasn't helping her, or so it seemed. She was withering inside, dying a thousand deaths.

"Here's what we'll do, Miss Campbell." His jaw was rigidly set, his eyes narrow slits—almost menacingly so. "We'll go about our lives as if none of this transpired today. We'll be pastor and parishioner and nothing more. We'll be polite in passing, Christlike in demeanor. I think we both have that down to a science. But underneath, we'll both know the truth. You abhor me." He swallowed hard, still staring intently into her eyes. His look said it all. *And I abhor you.*

She turned on her heel and fled out the door in such deep despair, she didn't know if she would live another day.

Chapter 9

S hirley shivered in the crisp autumn air and pulled the covers up to her chin, being careful not to disturb Gladly at her side. Night after night, she was given to lying awake, unable to sleep, wallowing in her misery.

Her heart was as bleak and barren as Missouri's winter weather that would soon be upon them—cold, frigid even. Her writing was the same way. Or lack of writing, she should say. Ever since the day of the proposal, she hadn't written a word on paper—or in her head. It was as if the day her heart died, her aspirations did, too. Oh, that was a fine turn of events. She had refused him in order to pursue her dreams. Now, she had neither him nor her writing. Why did life have to be so hard?

"Forrest, Forrest, Forrest," she whispered under her breath. "How my heart longs for you."

She contemplated her dilemma. Maybe she should give in and marry him. He was dashing, almost debonair so to speak, and gentle and courteous. He was suave even, with his love of Shakespeare and literature. But could she marry someone who, because of his chosen profession, would force her to live a life of burdensome servitude to lackluster people? Marrying him would mean living in Hickory Hollow right on, her dreams dashed, the grandeur in her head gone, divine service claiming her every waking, breathing minute the livelong day.

She had eyes. She knew how Grandmother had lived, a preacher's wife at the beck and call of the congregation. Could she do that? What was the answer to her dilemma?

A chill ran up her backbone. *Forrest would never have me now.* On that fateful day when she'd refused him—more by action than answer—he made it quite clear to her—more by tone than words—that he wanted nothing further to do with her. Like Pontius Pilate when he washed his hands of Jesus, so Forrest washed his hands of her. He would just as likely take to her now as to Deacon Hunter's seven wriggly, writhing, screeching youngsters. He disdained them, she knew, just as he now disdained her, and that was how things stood between them.

She must never contemplate her dilemma again—whether to marry him or whether to cling to her dreams. There was no dilemma.

There's only oblivion, tortuous oblivion, she thought as she finally drifted off to sleep.

Chapter 10

Forrest rode down the lane, his first thoughts about Miss Campbell hitting him with full force. "I wouldn't have her on a silver platter," he said.

He remembered saying that when he assumed she was playing the age-old game of Hard to Get. But at the Sunday school picnic, he assured himself he had been mistaken, and that's when the tenderness for her took root in his heart.

After that, she resumed teaching her Sunday school class and asked his advice on everything from the location of the class to the midsummer social. When she started cleaning the church, that brought about more conversations between them. It seemed everywhere he turned during those months, she was at his elbow, her face all sunshine and smiles, her talk dotted with Shakespeare and lexicon language.

He shook his head from side to side. All that time, she had indeed been playing Hard to Get, and he didn't have sense enough to see it. Now he knew her for what she was, an ice maiden, what he'd called her to her face.

He winced, lamenting his harshness and remembering that he was a gentleman who should have shown better manners—and besides that a minister. But it simply couldn't be helped. He'd bared his heart to her, and she'd squashed it in the ground as if it were a weed to stamp out.

Well, he would take care of that. He had learned his lesson and learned it well. He would raise up a shield over his heart and never lower it for one Miss Campbell, even if she came begging at his feet.

He smiled, envisioning that very scene. He knew there were few unattached men in these parts. He knew he was clamored for. After all, he had fair looks and a pleasing personality, and beyond that he was a minister, a man everyone looked up to, especially maiden ladies and young widow women. When Miss Campbell experienced a dearth of suitors, a drought of Cupids, a dry spell of troth plighters, she would look his way again. And it would give him distinct pleasure to refuse her.

Absently, he yanked on the reins, and Prancer jerked back. "I'm sorry, Prancer. Didn't mean to give you a toothache or most certainly a neck ache. I'll be more careful, I promise."

On Prancer trotted, toward town. Today, Forrest was to meet with the editor of the newspaper. He was going to convince him to write an article about the city pastor who had willingly taken a little country parish and, because of his expertise, had seen attendance mushroom in only six months.

"While I'm at the newspaper office, I think I'll take out an ad that says, 'Beware of Miss Campbell. She steals your heart and stomps it in the ground.'"

He snorted like Prancer often did. Miss Campbell was flighty, frivolous, and farcical. Of all the young women in Hickory Hollow, why did he have to be drawn to her? Why didn't he have the wisdom to steer clear of her? Why, she had no substance, no depth of character.

He heard a clap of thunder and looked up, but the sky was cloudless, with not a hint of rain on the horizon or a whisper of wind in the air, despite it being a cool fall day.

Forrest...

He looked around. Had someone called his name? But there was no one on this deserted country road. He was a good quarter mile from the nearest house.

Forrest...

He heard his name again. What was the meaning of this? Into his mind popped two references in the Bible where men's names had been called out of the blue. One instance was Samuel, when God called him to be a prophet. The other was the apostle Paul, only he was known as sinful Saul. What was going on?

Forrest, you've been flighty, flimsy, and farcical.

"What do you mean, Lord?" Immediately he knew it was the Lord speaking to him, just as it had been with Samuel and Saul.

You have no substance, no depth of character.

Forrest was in anguish. "Haven't I given my all to You, God, and dedicated myself to Your business?"

For what reasons? For what gain?

"Lord..."

Like a parade, things appeared before his mind, a long string of incidents....

Forrest, at first refusing to pastor the Hickory Hollow church because he thought it was beneath him...

Forrest, finally accepting it—only because he thought it would help him climb the ladder of success...

Forrest, looking for a wife more for how she could enhance his ministry than for herself...

Forrest, enduring people instead of enjoying them—because he thought it would bring benefit to him and his career.

"Father, forgive me," he cried out.

Suddenly, rain began to fall, a driving one with force, and he pulled his muffler more tightly about his throat. What to do? He saw that he was passing the Widow Ford's house.

"What a thrilling proposition," he said as he turned into her yard. "I guess I'll have to wait out the storm hearing the details of her recent stomach ailment." Guilt assailed him. "Oh, Lord, will I never change? Have mercy on me."

In minutes, he was standing on the Widow Ford's porch, rapping on her door, the rain falling in sheets. No one came. He rapped harder. Still no answer. "Mrs. Ford," he called. Then louder. "Mrs. Ford." He saw a note pinned to a cushion on a rocker:

Bertha,

Please leave the jars of applesauce and the layer cake you promised me on the porch. Doc Brewster said part of what ails me is that I don't get out much, though I can't imagine why he would have such silly surmisings. Staying in bundled up against the weather in winter and away from people's germs in the summer is the best way to prevent illness. But when I looked out this morning and saw sunshine, I decided to try his advice. 'Course you're always saying the same thing. I've gone to see my sister. I'll be gone all day.

Obligingly,
Gloramae Ford

Forrest didn't know whether to laugh or cry, figuratively speaking, of course. Mrs. Ford wasn't here, so he wouldn't have to endure her litany of maladies. But because she wasn't here, he would have to proceed on and brave the rainstorm. When he got to town, he would be a cold, wet mess, in no condition to talk to the editor of the newspaper.

He looked around the minuscule porch. Surely she wouldn't mind if he stayed here and waited out the rain. He wouldn't go inside, despite the chill in the air. He would wait on the porch, even if the rain set in for the entire afternoon.

And during that time, he would make his peace with the Lord.

His heart contrite, Forrest fell to his knees in front of Mrs. Ford's rocker, his elbows on the caned bottom, his hands clasped together.

"Lord, I'm a sorry excuse for a minister. I've been accusing Shirley of being hollow, and yet I'm the real culprit. I saw a mote in her eye, and there's a beam in mine. She has a speck of pomposity, and I have a wagonload. Oh, Lord, wash me clean. Change me."

A sob caught at his throat. "Make my heart and motives pure. I–I've been a baseless fabric of a vision when I needed to be a bedrock. How could I expect to lead a congregation when I'm nothing but a brass farthing—a tinkling cymbal, as Thy Word says?"

Tears misted his eyes, something that hadn't happened to him in a long time, perhaps since childhood. "Lord, I ask Thee to take away my sins of pride and arrogance and vainglory. Forgive me, Father. Let me take on the humility of Christ and be clothed in His righteousness."

In his mind's eye, he envisioned himself in a white robe, pure and clean before the Father, and into his soul came a joy, full and real and powerful—like the gushing of a geyser. He laughed and laughed, a peace as sweet as honey flooding over him, seemingly from his hairline all the way down to his shoes.

"Thank You, Lord." He paused, enjoying the quiet stillness, the rain long stopped. Out of the corner of his eye, he saw a rainbow. "I've been newborn," he fairly shouted as he arose and dusted the knees of his trousers.

"What's that you say, Reverend?" came a woman's voice from out of nowhere it seemed. "Who's got a newborn? Surely you didn't find one of those at the Widow Ford's house?" She cackled.

Forrest was startled as he turned to face the road. Miss Bertha Brown, an elderly spinster in the church, was making her way up the front walk, her arms laden, a black parasol tucked under one armpit.

He ran down the steps and took the cake plate from her. "Good afternoon, Miss Brown."

"Afternoon, Reverend. I told Gloramae I'd bring her some things to cheer her up." She held out the sack she was carrying, and jars clanked inside. "I've told her a thousand times if she'd take exercise like I do, even in cool weather, she'd do a heap better."

"You walked all the way from your house? Two miles?" No wonder he hadn't heard a wagon.

"That's mighty right. These legs were made for walking, Reverend, even through the puddles." She patted the sides of her skirts. "Now, what's that you said about a newborn?"

A quarter hour later, Forrest was on his way to town—after hearing all about Miss Bertha Brown's daily exercise regimen, and her apple-a-day routine that she claimed kept her in good health, and her morning prunes that she insisted kept her skin unwrinkled—and he hadn't minded one bit.

On this leg of his journey, he was a changed man.

Chapter 11

S hirley sat on the settee in the parlor, ready for church earlier than any of her family, lamenting about losing the two great loves of her life.

"Matthew, my darling," came her mother's gentle voice from her bedroom nearby. "Will you button me up the back?"

Her father's deep musical laughter wafted down the hall, and Shirley could see him in her mind's eye, his blue-gray eyes and his still-dark hair and his endearing limp. "I can think of nothing I'd rather do, Amanda, my dear," he said.

A girlish giggle was her mother's only response.

"On second thought, there is one thing that would please me more," he said, his voice husky.

Another giggle. Another laugh. The sound of lips meeting lips in a tender kiss. "This is what I was talking about." Lips met lips again.

Shirley jumped to her feet and shut the parlor door, envisioning her mother and father locked in a warm embrace, what she'd seen many times during her growing-up years. But she didn't want to think about that now—it was too painful.

"I'll never have the joy of experiencing that," she whispered, tears coming to her eyes. "They say there's only one great love of your life, and I rejected mine."

Later as Papa pulled the wagon into the churchyard, she wondered how it would be to see him. As time had passed, she'd thought it would grow easier. But she was wrong. Her heart was bleeding this morning.

As she dawdled toward the church, taking her time in her dread, she saw a group of people clustered around the left corner of the building. Some were pointing at something while others were engrossed in animated conversation.

"Shirley," called her grandfather, his face lit up with enthusiasm. "Come." He was waving at her, beckoning her to proceed his way.

"Yes, Grandfather?" she asked as she approached.

He pointed to the cornerstone. "Jeb told me Rev. Townsend wants to have a dinner-on-the-grounds to celebrate the twenty-fifth anniversary of our church. He says we're going to have it the first Sunday of November. Look at the cornerstone." He pointed downward.

Silently, she read the words on the smooth square of limestone set in the jagged-edged stones all around it:

On this eighth day of November, in the eighteen hundredth and sixty-ninth year of our Lord, this church is hereby dedicated to God's glory, consecrated for His service, for all generations to come.

"Will you write a history of the church?" her grandfather asked.

"That'd be a right nice thing to have," Jeb Hunter chimed in. "We could keep it in the permanent records, so's nobody would ever forget the hard work that went into the building of it. And since I'm on the board of the church—"

"Who would've ever thought that Jeb here"—her grandfather smiled and gestured at Deacon Hunter—"would grow up to be a deacon?" He punched Jeb in the ribs.

Jeb grinned. "The Lord works in mysterious ways, His wonders to perform. Anyway, as I was saying, I believe I could get the church treasury to kick in some money for a writing tablet for Shirley to work on and some fancy paper to copy it on when she's done."

"Will you, Shirley?" her grandfather asked. "I know you don't have much time, and it's only two weeks away. But I'll speak to your mother about it."

Shirley silently reread the poignant words on the cornerstone. Write? She hadn't picked up a pen for eons. She hadn't been able to. Her wellspring was simply dried up. But maybe this was the priming it needed. In fact, she had been praying that the Lord would give her a rebirth in her writing.

"Will you, Shirley? I can tell you the details. And you could talk to some others in these parts. You could make it like a story, kinda like one of them you're writing all the time, only this one would be true. Will you do it, girl?"

A story? Her breath came in short snatches as she relished the thought.

"If you'll write it, I'll ask Rev. Townsend if I can read it that Sunday. What a day of rejoicing that will be, to think back on the founding of our church. The people'll be pleased with a written church history, I'm certain. And so will Rev. Townsend." Her grandfather paused and lowered his voice, a knowing look in his eyes. "It might take a leap of faith for you, Shirley, but the Lord'll help you."

She brightened. Leap of faith? She'd heard her grandfather preach about a leap of faith all her life. It meant that a person needed to leap over their chasm of troubles while holding fast to God's promises. Leap of faith? That's what she sorely needed.

"Yes, Grandfather," she eagerly said. "I'll write the church history. Or at least try." She turned and made her way pell-mell toward the sanctuary, her mind awhirl with facts and dates, determined to write to the best of her ability. Suddenly, she stopped dead in her tracks.

I hope a broken heart doesn't impede my flow.

⁓

"Here's the Bible, Shirley," her grandfather said Tuesday morning. "Your grandmother's and mine." He pushed the large, leather-bound volume across the kitchen table where they were sitting.

"It'll be a help, I know." Shirley was already opening the thin, finger-smudged pages, being careful not to tear them.

He nodded. "Like I told you, your grandmother wrote down some important dates in there." He dipped his head toward the Bible. "Anything else you need to know before I go?" He shifted in his chair.

"No, sir. While you talked, I took enough notes to write a book, I believe." She smiled as she looked at her sheaf of scribbles, hastily jotted down as he told the story of the building of the church. "But if I need clarification, I'll let you know."

"What mighty big words you use, girl." He arose and reached to hug her.

"I like to read Webster's." She not only read Webster's, she studied the words and their definitions diligently.

"Your mother used to read the lexicon, too. When she was young."

"I never knew that." All she knew about her mother was that her middle name was work.

"Speaking of your mother, she assured me that you can take as much time as you need with your writing."

Shirley nodded. "Yesterday, I drove all over Hickory Hollow talking to church members and taking notes." She got to her feet and slid her chair under the table.

"Well, I'd best be going. I'll be praying for you, that the Lord'll quicken your mind and anoint your words. Did you know the Good Book says, 'my tongue is the pen of a ready writer'?"

She marveled. "I've never read that verse before, Grandfather."

"Psalm 45:1."

As she followed him to the front door, she wasn't thinking about the verse in Psalms, wonderful though it was. She was thinking about Mama and why she used to read the lexicon.

❦

For two hours, Shirley sat at the kitchen table, poring over the Hodgeses' family Bible and the copious notes she had taken as her grandfather talked. In the Bible, in her grandmother's handwriting, were dates of when and how the land was acquired, notations of when the work began, who worked on the building, how Mr. Randall tried to take back the land, and how long the actual building of the church took.

There was even a detailed account of the dedication day and the very first dinner-on-the-grounds, complete with the naming of every singer and every dessert on the long sawhorse tables. That account was in a different handwriting than the other items.

"Who wrote this, I wonder?" Shirley said under her breath, gazing intently at the storylike notes, so well written she felt like she was there observing it. Yet it had occurred two-and-a-half decades ago.

"Did you say something, Shirley?" Her mother was at her side, peering over her shoulder, a knife in one hand, a potato in the other, a long brown peel dangling in a spiral floorward.

Shirley pointed to the account. "I was reading about the church dedication day—"

"I wrote that. . . ." Her mother's voice trailed off, and she had a faraway look to her eyes.

"I didn't know you liked to write, Mama."

"I never was any good—"

"But you were. Your story made me feel like I was there. I could almost hear the Blackstone brothers singing, and I could almost taste Grandmother's cinnamon-peach cobbler swimming in heavy cream."

"Fiddle-faddle." Her mother walked briskly back to the tin sink on the drainboard and resumed her potato peeling. "You'd best be getting through with your writing this morning. Your father will be in directly for dinner, and we need to get the table set."

"May I have another quarter hour?"

"All right, then."

⸎

Shirley's eyes watered and her breath came in staccato puffs as she read the words on the last page of her grandparents' Bible. It wasn't about the church. It had nothing to do with it, in fact. It was a journal-like entry in her grandmother's handwriting, sort of her treatise on being a preacher's wife:

> In many ways, Anson and I have been wealthy. We've been surrounded by a great cloud of witnesses, God's dear people who have brought us joy and enriched our lives. I thank God every day that He chose me to be a preacher's wife. What a privilege! What an honor!
>
> I was unworthy, unequipped, and frankly, unwilling. Then the Lord showed me this verse: "The eyes of your understanding being enlightened; that ye may know what is the hope of his calling," in Ephesians 1:18.
>
> Suddenly, it was as if my eyes were opened, and I embraced this high calling with all my heart, and that's when the joy came. I soon found out that whom God appoints, He anoints, because He equipped me with all that I needed. After living a lifetime in divine service, I can confidently say that I wouldn't trade my life for all the riches and fame in the world.

"Have you ever read this, Mama?" Shirley asked, a tear slipping down her cheek. "What Grandmother wrote on the last page of her Bible?"

Her mother was pulling a pan of biscuits out of the oven with a stove cloth. "About a thousand times—like everything else in there." Her face was red from the heat, and she set the pan down and wiped her forehead with the corner of her apron.

"This is astounding." Shirley ran her hand over her grandmother's words. How could her mother have read this that many times and been so unaffected? This was the most earth-shaking thing Shirley had ever read, and she felt like dancing a jig at the liberating sensation that enveloped her.

Her mother looked over at her, as if she were studying her. The otherworldly musings that often enveloped Shirley seemed to envelop Mama, too. After a long moment, she finally broke the silence. "Shirley, honey, can you clear the table? And sometime today I'd like to talk with you. I have a lot of things to tell you."

"Yes, Mama." Shirley scooped up the Bible and her writing materials and dashed out the door, wondering what Mama would say to her. "I'll be back in a few minutes to set the table."

In the quiet of her bedroom, Shirley dropped to her knees in front of the bed, thankful that Gladly was spending the day with their cousins. Otherwise, she might be afoot.

"Lord, I submit my will and my way to Thee." Her tears fell thick, and she didn't bother wiping them, just kept her hands clasped and her gaze heavenward.

"My eyes are opened at last. It was really You I was fighting against, not the ministry and being a preacher's wife. Please forgive my stubbornness." Joy tears replaced the tears of contrition, and gladness bubbled within her.

"Dear Lord, I embrace what I know is before me. . .being a preacher's wife in divine service. I promise to serve Thee and Thy people with all my might and being, as Thou givest me the strength and power. In Jesus' name. Amen."

She swiped at her eyes with her hanky and arose from her knees, as happy as she'd ever been, happier than when the love tingles were developing for Forrest.

"Forrest!" she shrieked. She reeled, feeling like a load of limestone had hit her. She fell to her knees once more.

"Dear Lord, Forrest doesn't want me anymore." The tears were back, and she writhed inside. "He detests me. I can feel it every time I'm around him. Oh, what a mess I've made of things."

Daughter, be not afraid.

"Lord? Is it truly Thee speaking?" She was in awe.

It is I. Be not afraid.

She felt the comfort of the Lord. But then her doubts returned. "He'll never have me." A sob gurgled up her throat. "I love him, Lord. What am I going to do?"

Daughter! I will work it out. Trust Me.

The Lord, the King of the universe, had spoken to her? "Thy will be done," she said softly.

Her grandmother's Scripture verse filled her mind, her heart, her being: " 'The eyes of your understanding being enlightened; that ye may know what is the hope of his calling,' " she quoted, then smiled, feeling as if she could conquer the world.

"Shirley!" came her mother's voice.

"Thank You, Lord, for Thy peace so sweet. I can hear the joybells ringing in my soul." Then loudly, she replied, "I'm coming, Mama."

Chapter 12

That evening, Shirley sat at the kitchen table writing, the lamplight shining on her tablet. The tablet was nice. Deacon Hunter had said she could keep it when she finished this project—a pleasant thought. The church even threw in some extra money to pay for lamp oil in case she needed to work after dark—a kind gesture.

She glanced down, pleased to see five pages filled, with not one line blank. She was nearly done with the story of the history of the church.

She pondered the experience that had happened in her bedroom that morning. She was so overcome by the magnitude of it, she had walked on clouds all day, the story formulating and building in her head. Perhaps that was what made it especially fine, even if she did say so herself.

"About through?" her mother asked over her shoulder. She was ready for bed, her heavy wool wrapper around her, her hair in a long braid.

"Yes, Mama. What I've not finished tonight, I can do tomorrow or the next day."

Her mother sat down at the table and pulled her chair close. "I've been wanting to talk with you. I–I'm proud of you, Shirley." A smile lit her face so caressing, it was a hug itself. "For writing like that." She touched the tablet. "And for all the other writing you do. I'm right pleased for you."

"You are, Mama? Proud of me?" Shirley was aghast and thrilled at the same time. Her mother had never said anything like this to her.

"I am, dear."

"That means more to me than you can know." She paused and drew in a breath. "May I ask you a question?"

Her mother shrugged, but she smiled again. "I suppose."

Shirley contemplated her words as she stared down at the tablet. "Mama, when you were a girl, did you have a deep desire to write? Like I do now?"

Her mother sat, not saying a word. Long moments passed.

Shirley looked over at her, wondering, knowing her mother had heard her. She was less than three inches away. "Mama?"

"Yes, I did."

Shirley was trying to digest this astounding news. Why had Mama never shared this with her?

"I used to read the lexicon—"

"Grandfather told me."

"I wanted to write. Stories came to me, especially when I would lie down at night. Sometimes they were so vivid, I couldn't sleep."

Shirley nodded in understanding. "Why didn't you keep on writing?"

"Life never led me that way."

"But couldn't you have done something about that?"

"Shirley, every person who loves God is called to walk a certain path." A romantic look filled her eyes. "For me, that path was to be the wife of Matthew Campbell and the mother of Peesultree, Shirley, Gladly, Moses, Mordecai, Malachi, and Milcah." She laughed softly in the dim lamplight. "That was my calling."

"Why didn't you ever encourage me in my writing endeavors?"

"Because I've had such a good life with your pa that I wanted the same thing for you. I was afraid if you pursued writing, you couldn't have the love of a good husband like I enjoy. But now I see that I'm wrong. A moment ago, I said God has a path for each of us to walk. Shirley, your path is twofold."

"Twofold, Mama?"

Her mother nodded. "Writing and being a wife—a preacher's wife at that." She smiled broadly. "The Reverend Forrest Townsend's wife."

Shirley felt that familiar tingly feeling on the inside.

"Somehow, Jesus will fix things. He will bring all of this to fruition in your life."

"You know that, Mama? Why didn't you talk to me about this sooner?"

"It only came to me this week, the surety of it." She touched the family Bible with Grandmother Hodges's entry in it, and a knowing look filled her eyes, a wise look.

Shirley was a chatterbox all of a sudden, asking her mother things she'd never dared, about writing and about men, Forrest in particular, and Mama answered with God-given wisdom.

Her mother slipped her arm around Shirley's shoulders. "The book you used to read to Ma before she passed on—"

"*Little Women?*"

Her mother nodded. "That was mine when I was a girl."

Shirley couldn't believe her ears.

"Ma somehow scraped together some money and purchased it for me. She knew I longed to write. I think she discerned that in you, too."

"So that's why. . ." Shirley's voice trailed off.

"Strangely enough, a passage of Louisa Mae Alcott's writing pointed me in the right direction, much as a passage of Ma's clarified things for you."

"Oh, Mama, this is rapturous to hear." If Shirley had been looking in a mirror, she was sure stars would be in her eyes, so joyful did she feel, and she reached over and hugged her mother. "Show me this passage. I'll go get *Little Women* for you." She made a move to get up, but her mother touched her arm.

"No need to get it. I can quote it. It's a saying of Marmee's."

"Marmee's?" Shirley fairly shrieked. She was in a transport of delight.

Her mother nodded, a guilty look crossing her face. "I wish I could've been the mother she was. My own ma was a lot like her—"

"Oh, but Mama, you've been a good mother, a fine mother." A tear rolled down Shirley's cheek and landed on the tablet, blurring the words it fell upon. "I've always felt your love in so many ways. You kept us clean and clothed and fed, and you made sure we memorized the Scriptures like King David did, and you always had such a kind heart. I know that's where I got my compassion for people.

That'll stand me in good stead when I'm a preacher's wife. . .Forrest's wife." The tingles were back, dancing down her spine.

Her mother smiled. "That saying of Marmee's—she was talking to Meg and Jo and Beth and Amy. She said, 'I want my daughters to be beautiful, accomplished, and good; to be admired, loved, and respected; to have a happy youth, to be well and wisely married, and to lead useful, pleasant lives, with as little care and sorrow to try them as God sees fit to send. To be loved and chosen by a good man is the best and sweetest thing which can happen to a woman; and I sincerely hope my girls know this beautiful experience.' "

It was so quiet, Shirley could hear every breath her mother took, a steady sucking in and out. But she couldn't hear her own. She had forgotten to breathe.

Shirley sighed and yawned at the same time, her chest expelling and taking in a great gulp of air, and she jumped to her feet and her mother did, too, and they hugged each other. Embracing, they wriggled back and forth like a fish on a hook. Then they laughed together, the mirthful sounds filling the quiet kitchen.

"Mama?" Shirley finally said, still in her mother's warm embrace.

"What, dear?"

"You have a beautiful experience with Papa."

"I know." A pause and a giggle. "Shirley?"

"Yes, Mama?"

"You'll soon have a beautiful experience with Forrest."

In response, Shirley only smiled, feeling as radiant as a bride on her wedding day.

Chapter 13

Y ou want me to do what, Lord?" Forrest exclaimed in response to the Lord's voice He had grown familiar with. He was just finishing his last parishioner call late Saturday afternoon and was headed toward the parsonage. In this nippy November weather, he was looking forward to taking his boots off before a fire and eating the chicken pie the Widow Ford insisted he take home. "Surely You can't mean that, Lord."

That is precisely what I mean, Forrest.

"To go see Miss Campbell?" Forrest let out a snort. "Why would I want to go see her?"

You'll know when you get there.

"She's the last person I want to talk to."

Do you want to be a tinkling cymbal or an instrument of My love?

He swallowed deeply. "An instrument of Thy love, Father." He slowed Prancer and at a wide place in the road made a complete turnaround in his buggy and then headed toward the Campbell home.

"Lord, self is hard to bring under subjection, but I submit my will to Thee yet again. I'm trusting Thee to give me strength and wisdom."

My grace is sufficient for thee.

"Hallelujah!"

༺༺

Shirley stood at the drainboard, slicing the huge ham she had just pulled out of the oven. Most evenings, they ate light suppers, but today her father smoked fresh ham meat, and so this meal would be like a feast. Tomorrow, at the dinner-on-the-grounds when the church celebrated its twenty-fifth anniversary, the Campbell family would bring more of the sliced ham plus the trimmings—mashed potatoes with red-eye gravy, buttered creamed corn, green beans, and Mama's delectable desserts.

"The preacher just pulled up in the yard," Mrs. Campbell whispered to Shirley. "Why don't you go freshen up? I'll finish slicing the ham."

Startled, Shirley turned, questions in her eyes. Had he come to read the story she wrote about the church history?

Her mother seemed to discern her questions. She patted her arm. "Jesus is fixing things, Shirley."

Shirley nodded, feeling the peace that passed understanding flooding her soul. She pecked her mother on the cheek, thankful for the new bond that had grown between them in the last weeks, then crossed the kitchen on her way to her room.

"Be sure and get my bottle of rosewater off the bureau in my bedroom and use it liberally," her mother called.

"Thank you, Mama."

A quarter hour later, Shirley was washed and dressed in her second-best outfit, her hair freshly done up, the prized rosewater generously dabbed behind her ears and on her wrists. She entered the kitchen to resume her supper chores, as if this were the way she did things every day of the week.

"Here she is, Preacher," Mama announced, smiling broadly. "He was asking for you, Shirley. I invited him to stay for supper."

Shirley floated toward him. She didn't say a thing when she reached him. His eyes seemed to be reading hers, and the look that passed between them was sweeter than words.

"Shirley," he said softly, peering intently at her, his eyes searching her face and caressing her features. "After supper, may I speak with you?" He paused. "Privately?" he whispered.

She nodded shyly. "It would be my pleasure." She swallowed. "Forrest."

"Supper's ready," her mother announced. "Will everyone please gather at the table?"

After supper, Forrest followed Mr. and Mrs. Campbell and Shirley into the parlor, and all four settled comfortably into the chairs and settee.

A quarter hour of conversation ensued, mostly about church and farm work. Then Mr. and Mrs. Campbell took their leave, Mrs. Campbell saying she had to see to the children, Mr. Campbell mentioning something about a chore in the barn.

Forrest watched in amazement as Shirley got up from her chair and came to sit beside him on the small settee. His breath caught in his throat. He thought he would have to ask her to move closer, but she had taken the action on her own. "Shirley. . ."

"Forrest. . ."

He took her hand in his and kissed it softly.

She trembled in response, and her face lit up.

He didn't say anything. He was enjoying the look passing between them, like what they shared briefly before supper. He studied her face and her luxuriant hair, and he thought about her loveliness and her sweetness and her diligence and the other attributes that endeared her to him. He pondered the love he had for her and the love she had for him.

" 'Let him kiss me with the kisses of his mouth,' " she whispered, smiling up at him, like she was baiting him in the tenderest of ways.

His heart raced. He was surprised—and thrilled—at what she said.

"That's from Song of Solomon." Her voice was as gentle as the cooing of a mourning dove.

"I know." He smiled—broadly—enjoying her tender bantering. Then he did what she asked. He gathered her in his arms and brushed her lips with his.

"Forrest," she murmured as she eagerly kissed him back.

" 'Thou hast ravished my heart. That's from Song of Solomon, too.' "

"I know." She smiled.

In a flash, he was on his knees before her. "I love you, Shirley, with every breath I breathe."

"I love you, Forrest, with every breath I breathe."

"Will you be my wife, to have and to hold from this day forward?"

"I will be your wife, to have and to hold from this day forward."

He was delighted at her boldness. It thrilled him through and through. "My darling. . ."

She made a gesture for him to get up, and he sat down beside her. She snuggled into his embrace and told him how and when she came to love him, and how her repugnance for the role of preacher's wife had kept her from his arms. She related the journal-like entry in her grandmother's Bible and the impact it had on her. She shared about her experience with God in her bedroom, and she told him of the wise counsel her mother gave her.

In turn, he told her about his talk with the Lord on the Widow Ford's porch and how he had a heart change.

"I relish the idea of being in divine service as the wife of the Reverend Forrest Townsend," she said with confidence.

"Divine service?"

"What Grandfather calls the ministry."

I divine that a divine girl is in the future for me, he had once said. At the time, he'd wondered if it would be Miss Devine.

He drew in a deep, heady breath of rosewater as he looked down at the divine Miss Shirley Campbell, memorizing every nuance of her countenance. He took both of her hands in his and held them fast. "A divine girl for divine service."

"How sweet," she whispered.

"And a divine girl for me. Superb. Heavenly. Proceeding directly from God."

"Oh, Forrest. . ."

" 'Shall I compare thee to a summer's day? Thou art more lovely and more temperate.' That's Shakespeare."

"I know."

"I treasure you, my beautiful one. How I thank God for you."

She dipped her chin and smiled. "You make me feel beautiful. You make me feel like a princess."

"You are. You're a King's daughter." He pointed upward.

Long moments of pleasant togetherness passed. Then Forrest broke the silence. "Pending approval from your parents, is it agreeable with you if we announce our betrothal tomorrow at church?"

" 'So smile the heavens upon this holy act.' " She winked at him coquettishly. "That's Shakespeare, too."

"Ah, what a delight you are." Once more, he kissed her, was loathe to release her, but he did. "The first thing I need to do at church tomorrow morning is look up Mr. Wilbur."

"Mr. Wilbur?"

He chuckled. "I need to tell him I finally have Shirley."

She peered up at him, amusement lurking in her eyes. "Along with goodness and mercy?"

He nodded. "All the days of my life."

Miss Bliss and the Bear

by Darlene Franklin

A soft answer turneth away wrath:
but grievous words stir up anger.
PROVERBS 15:1

Chapter 1

Annie Bliss hesitated as Fort Blunt, located about five miles from the town of Calico, came into view. Reaching behind her, she touched the bundle of socks, scarves, and mittens she had knitted for the soldiers stationed there. The idea shimmered like a leaf after the rain when it first occurred to her, but now each clop of her horse's hooves on the hard ground brought a smidgeon of doubt. *Lord, please let them accept this offering in Your name.*

Gladys Polson rode with her. After their sewing circle decided to take on local mission projects, Gladys acted first. Her bravery in reaching out to the town's curmudgeonly rich hermit encouraged Annie to think of young men serving their country far from home.

"They're just boys like my brothers. Nothing to it." Annie spoke the words as if hearing them out loud would bolster her courage.

Gladys darted a glance in Annie's direction before returning her attention to the road ahead. "You'll be fine."

A man's voice boomed through the thick fortress wall, loud enough for them to catch words here and there. "Poorly laundered. . .wouldn't pass inspection by a blind general. . ."

Annie took a deep breath. Although the man's anger frightened her, it also gave her impetus to go ahead. Perhaps God would use her gifts to remind angry soldiers like this one of His goodness.

The stockade gate swung open and a petite woman came out, her shoulders hunched over with more than the basket full of uniforms. She glanced at the two women on horseback with a wan smile. "Good day."

A burly figure lumbered away from the gate, each footfall echoing his words to the trembling woman in front of them.

Even if the woman was a poor laundress, she didn't deserve the soldier's anger. Annie said, "Maybe he just woke up on the wrong side of the bed this morning."

"I don't think his bed has a right side, at least when it comes to women." The laundress shifted the basket to her other hip. "I hope your visit doesn't involve the Bear."

"Bear" described the man's gait perfectly, and Annie smothered a giggle. "Thanks for the warning. Can we help you carry that laundry somewhere?"

"It's just around the corner, but thanks for the offer." Nodding her farewell, the laundress headed in the direction of a stand of trees on the south side of the fort.

"Ready?" Gladys asked.

For answer, Annie urged her horse through the open gate. Around the flagpole, a platoon drilled under the careful watch of their lieutenant. The cantankerous man had disappeared.

The lieutenant called one of the soldiers to take over the drill and walked through the ranks toward the women. Young and handsome, his features suggested someone who didn't take life too seriously. "Lieutenant Chaswell at your service." He swept his cap from his head and bowed. "How can I assist two such fair ladies today?"

Annie smiled at the flattery. "We're hoping to speak with Captain Peate, or if he is unavailable, with his wife."

"Certainly." Chaswell lifted his arms, and Gladys accepted his help in dismounting from her horse. Annie followed suit, her hand brushing against the bundle of knitted items, reminding her of her purpose. Any chance to slip in and take care of their business unnoticed disappeared with the men drilling. As they walked to the captain's lodgings, every pair of eyes tracked their progress. Out of the corner of her eye, Annie spotted the Bear making his way to a building with a cross on top, probably the fort's chapel. At least he was heading in the right direction for a man with a troubled spirit.

Jeremiah Arnold hadn't missed the arrival of the two women, nor the way Chaswell had jumped at the opportunity to greet them. Although he kept his gaze averted, he hadn't missed the way the sunshine bounced off golden hair cascading below a green cap, and it disturbed him more than the laundress ever had with the poor quality of her work. Had he been too hard on her? *No.* Women had to be as tough as men to survive in this harsh environment, perhaps even more so.

The visitors reminded him of his reasons for joining the army. He shook his head to dislodge the memories that threatened to pour over him like molten lava if awakened. No wonder the soldiers called him Bear. Years of trying to make restitution for past sins often left him as grumpy as a bear awakened out of hibernation.

In the absence of assigned duties, he headed to the chapel. Once he crossed the threshold, peace welcomed him. The chapel wasn't much, a wooden structure that barely rose above freezing in the winter and baked them in the summer. But on this fair day in late April, spring had arrived and the atmosphere was perfect, the temperature matching the uniform like a glove on a lady's hand.

Thinking about women again, are you? With a growl worthy of his nickname, Jeremiah jumped to his feet and walked the perimeter of the pews. The captain sat in the first row week by week unless away on business, his wife at his side. Jeremiah hurried through his prayers on their behalf, not wanting to dwell on Mrs. Peate's visit with the two guests.

On to the second row. Chaswell attended every week, along with a handful of young recruits who struggled more than most with army life. Although Jeremiah hoped to have a similar impact on the men placed under his care as Chaswell seemed to have, very few of the younger men sought him out during their free time. Fighting against jealousy, Jeremiah thanked God for Chaswell's faith.

Jeremiah continued down the rows, lifting up specific prayers as he passed each man's usual seat. Seats in the pews were tightly regimented, by the men's own choice.

At last he arrived at the back row, the refuge of the five men who drifted in and out of the services. Their names were branded on Jeremiah's brain. Who needed military discipline the most often? Any one of these five. Which recruits might desert their post? One of them already had, his replacement arriving with the same rebellious attitude.

Which men spent their paydays at the saloon in town, taking advantage of all the entertainment the place had to offer?

The thought confirmed Jeremiah's sermon topic for tomorrow: a warning against strange women, drawn from several passages in Proverbs. Sometimes Captain Peate chided Jeremiah for preaching too often on the same subject, but each and every time he felt God's leading.

The front door squeaked open, and Jeremiah opened his eyes. The young man in front of him snapped a salute. "Lieutenant Arnold, sir!"

"At ease, soldier."

The lad dropped the salute. "Mrs. Peate wishes to see you in her quarters, sir."

"I will be there promptly." Jeremiah remained behind while the private left, breathing in the quiet before heading outside. A light breeze stirred the air, heady with gentle rains and thunderstorms, new tree leaves and blooming flowers. A perfect day for a ride if he had time later.

With a longing glance at the stables, Jeremiah headed for the captain's quarters. Whatever Mrs. Peate wanted with the chaplain involved the morning's visitors—unwelcome, intruding females.

⁂

"I think it's a marvelous idea. Even the roughest of the men will welcome the homey touch." Mrs. Peate filled the coffee cups.

After a single sip, Annie reached for cream and sugar. Even so, she could barely swallow the strong brew. Gladys set down her cup after a single taste.

"Over the years I've become fond of army coffee." Mrs. Peate lifted her shoulders in apology. "But I know it's not to everyone's taste. I have cool water if you prefer."

At nods from both guests, she bustled into the kitchen. She reappeared a few minutes later carrying a tray with a pitcher, glasses, and a plate of cookies. "Please help me eat these. The cook doesn't like me baking for the men, and I can't eat them all myself." A wistful look raced across her face, replaced by her pleasant smile. "I apologize for keeping you waiting. Lieutenant Arnold should be here shortly. As chaplain, he is in the best position to know who will appreciate the scarf sets the most."

Gladys patted Annie's hand in silent support. Ever since Haydn Keller, the grandson of Calico's richest citizen, had asked for Gladys's hand in marriage, she believed anything was possible. If only God had led Annie to assist a family instead of a fort filled with strange men.

Not men, she reminded herself, but lads like her brother. A touch of home might keep them on the straight and narrow. Her thoughts strayed to the grumpy man she had observed yelling at the laundress. Now that man could benefit from kindness.

Someone knocked on the door, and Annie straightened her back. Why waste energy worrying? The chaplain would make an excellent ally.

"Here he is." Mrs. Peate walked to the door and opened it. "Thank you for coming so quickly, Lieutenant. We have guests who are eager to meet you."

A booted foot with a heavy gait. . .stocky body and scowling expression. Surely God wouldn't expect her to. . .

The Bear was the chaplain?

Chapter 2

Annie's knees shook a teensy bit as she stood and faced the chaplain while Mrs. Peate introduced them. Lieutenant Jeremiah Arnold looked ordinary enough, average height, with a build more like a boxer than a man of the cloth. His resemblance to a bear came mostly from his attitude, exuding a barely controlled strength. Gray streaked a thick, reddish-brown beard, and dust coated his blue uniform. Annie thought she could sense him struggling to hide his impatience.

He bent at the waist. "Pleased to make your acquaintance, Miss Bliss. Miss Polson." His deep tones came out as a growl.

Annie opened her mouth to respond but didn't know what to say. Before the silence stretched too long, he said, "I'm at your service. Can I assist you in some way?"

In contrast to his appearance, not to mention the anger he had directed at the laundress, a hint of interest flickered in his dark brown eyes. Was it interest. . .or a challenge to give him a reason for him to help her?

Have not I commanded thee? Be strong and of a good courage; be not afraid, neither be thou dismayed: for the Lord thy God is with thee whithersoever thou goest. The verse Annie and her friends had chosen as their motto came to mind. If David could kill a real bear in battle, she could face down her Bear as well. Annie might wield knitting needles and yarn instead of a slingshot, and she certainly wasn't looking to kill anyone. But she *was* battling for the souls of young men. "My brother is stationed at Fort Laramie. Sometimes he gets lonely and longs for a reminder of home. His letters gave me an idea for a mission project, and Fort Blunt came to mind."

⌬

She's pretty when she blushes.

Where did that thought come from? Jeremiah had eschewed the comforts of hearth and home after his personal dance with the devil years ago. He hadn't allowed anyone or anything to come between him and his vow of chastity in all the years since. Flattening his features, he kept his voice level. "Mission? Are you handing out free Bibles? We already take care of that."

"Nothing like that." Miss Bliss opened a burlap sack and dumped the contents on the table for his inspection.

Bliss. . .what an appropriate name for such a stunning example of prairie beauty, with her halo of golden hair and rosy cheeks. Jeremiah had expected the young woman to have a chocolate cake or maybe dried apple pie in her sack. Instead, she presented him with a woolen cap, mittens, and scarf, all of a durable navy blue that matched his uniform. Next she handed him a pair of thick brown woolen socks. Every soldier could use such practical items. "I could also knit sweaters if they would be of any use."

Jeremiah picked up the socks and examined the stitches while Mrs. Peate did the same thing with a mitten. A brief nod informed him of her approval. But Jeremiah had other concerns. "Where did this 'mission project' idea come from?" *Are we going to be inundated by a lot of do-gooders hoping for a glimpse of the soldiers?*

Miss Bliss opened her mouth, but Mrs. Peate spoke first. "I'm sure you have a lot to talk over. Lieutenant, why don't you escort our guests back to Calico and discuss your questions along the way? My husband mentioned you had no official duties today."

Although Mrs. Peate phrased it as a suggestion, Jeremiah knew better than to disagree. If he felt responsible for the souls of the men at the fort, the captain's wife felt the same way about Jeremiah.

He swallowed a chuckle as he remembered his earlier desire for a ride in the open. God's sense of humor was at work once again, answering Jeremiah's unspoken request with the unwelcome company of two women. Accepting the inevitable, he brought his heels together and bowed slightly. "Certainly, Mrs. Peate. Miss Bliss, Miss Polson, I will return in a few moments with my horse."

Jeremiah considered the two women as he fetched his horse. Why did he find himself drawn to Miss Bliss? *Stay away. Focus on things more important than a pretty face, like country and duty and family.* The advice he doled out to straying men did little to change the direction of his thoughts. Staying away was easier said than done, since Mrs. Peate had practically ordered him to accompany the women. He prayed for an extra helping of the self-control he had needed since his fiancée's death.

When he returned, the sack in Miss Bliss's hands was empty, and she was prepared to leave. He nodded his appreciation at her readiness.

"I look forward to seeing you again, Annie. And Gladys, feel free to return as well. I'm thrilled to hear how God is working through your projects." Mrs. Peate hugged each of them in turn.

Jeremiah dismounted to help both ladies into their saddles. Mrs. Peate waved good-bye as they headed toward the gate. She would expect a report on what he learned when he returned.

"Let's go. The men won't see you if we leave now, since they're heading for the mess hall."

The women simply nodded, and he was thankful for their sensible response. After the gate shut behind them, the sun came out from behind a cloud and poured its glory into Jeremiah's soul.

Stick to business, Lieutenant. Don't let a pretty face lead you astray.

⸻

The ride back to town stretched out. Gladys was probably thinking about her beau, Haydn Keller. Of course he knew all about the sewing circle's mission projects—he had to, since his grandfather was the first person to benefit from the love shown in Christ's name. Annie hoped Gladys wouldn't reveal her secret project to help the soldiers to anyone else.

Lieutenant Arnold relaxed in his saddle, looking slightly more human on horseback, but he didn't speak. If she mentioned her plans to him, she suspected he would scowl at her. Even so, she wanted to communicate her mission to the man tasked with the soldiers' spiritual well-being. She spurred her horse to come alongside the lieutenant.

"Lieutenant Arnold."

"Miss Bliss." He didn't offer any indication that he wished to speak to her.

Annie chewed her lip while considering what to do next. She decided on a risky move. "My prayer that God will comfort young men so far from home will only succeed with your help. I want us to be friends." She drew a deep breath. "So please, call me Annie. My friend's name is Gladys." Out of the corner of her eye, she saw Gladys's nod. "And what may I call you?"

"Bear" ran through her mind. She couldn't guess which of them would be more embarrassed if she used it.

His back straightened and the muscles around his eyes tightened, as if trying to recall his Christian name. "You may call me Jeremiah."

If he was named after the weeping prophet, they shared more than the vocation of preaching. The lieutenant seemed to carry a heavy weight. But she would make the syllables sing on her tongue. "Thank you, Jeremiah. What would you like to know about my project?"

He slowed his horse down. "I only saw a few knit items. Well executed, no doubt."

The compliment brought a faint smile to Annie's lips.

"What kind of help do you need? Why do you need my help?" He stopped, as if realizing how rude he sounded. "Start at the beginning."

"Gladys came up with the idea in the first place."

Gladys took over the explanation. "Last Christmas, a missionary to China came to speak at our church. The Ladies Sewing Circle decided to support them." She gestured for Annie to continue.

"I've always done better when I can see what I'm doing." Heat tickled Annie's cheeks. "They sent us a picture of the children in their orphanage. They were all so skinny. The first thing that came out of my mouth was—"

"—they look like the Smith children." The two women spoke as one, and Annie laughed. A grin flickered around the Bear's—*Jeremiah's*—mouth. He looked much nicer when he smiled.

Gladys picked up the story thread. "Then Ruth—the schoolteacher, Miss Fairfield—mentioned that every year there's always at least one family that's dirt poor. So we decided we wanted to help them, too. When we got to thinking about it, we knew there were several people in town who needed a demonstration of God's love. So all four of us prayed about what God wanted us to do."

Jeremiah pounced on the mention of a fourth woman. "And who is the last member of your quartet?"

Annie schooled her features not to show the inward wince. How to explain Birdie's inclusion in the group?

Gladys came to her rescue. "It's our local seamstress, Birdie Landry. She does exquisite work."

Jeremiah narrowed his eyes, as if he knew of Birdie's reputation. Annie rushed in before he could make the connection. "Gladys knew what she wanted to do right away—it's a lovely story. . ."

A scowl reappeared on Jeremiah's face, and Annie hastened on. "But that's a story for another time. I couldn't make up my mind on my project until I received a letter from my brother. He doesn't ever complain, but this time he mentioned how much he missed us at Christmastime. Then I read an article about Fort Blunt in the newspaper"—a wide grin lit up Gladys's face at the mention of Calico's first newspaper—"and I knew what I wanted to do. Everyone at the fort is someone's brother or son or sweetheart, and many of them would welcome a touch of home." She shrugged. "I'm good with knitting needles."

"And so she came up with this marvelous idea." Gladys beamed.

"I had a sweetheart once." Jeremiah seemed surprised that he had spoken aloud. His horse stopped moving altogether at the lack of direction, and the man's torso twisted, as if he was surprised.

Annie reached out a tentative hand then pulled it back, biting her lower lip. "What happened?"

"She died—in a gunfight." He clamped his mouth shut and offered no further explanation.

"How awful," Annie said. The thought that Jeremiah Arnold's bear persona owed its existence to such a sad occasion made him seem almost human.

Maybe God intended for Annie to tame the Bear.

She'd rather face down a firing squad.

Chapter 3

A silent Jeremiah wrestled his memories back into the lockbox where he stored them. The women kept quiet while he brooded, a minor miracle. One of the playful memories of his father surfaced. *I have it on good authority that there will be no women in heaven.*

And why is that, Mr. Arnold? Mother knew the answer, of course, but she played along.

Because the apostle John says after the seventh seal was opened, "There was silence in heaven about half an hour." And I never knew a woman who could keep quiet that long.

Jeremiah didn't blame men for wanting the kind of marriage his parents had had. But women like his mother were as rare as a snowstorm in July. His one foray into romance had proved that. Fannie might have died in the gunfight, but their relationship was doomed long before that happened.

The magnetism in Annie's face drew his eyes. Curiosity played across her features, maybe wondering what caused his smile a moment ago.

But she didn't say a word, not until they passed the nearest farm to the center of town. "Mrs. Peate said you could provide me with information about the number of men in your regiment, but I need pencil and paper ready when you tell me. Why don't you come ahead to my house? You can rest while I write it all down before you go back to the fort."

But I'm not tired. Jeremiah didn't say the words aloud. Instead, he said, "I don't want to create additional work for your mother."

A smile played around Annie's lips. "Between my mother and Aunt Kate—she's not actually my aunt, but we all call her auntie anyhow—they would feed the whole state every day if people would only come by. We always have plenty."

"As long as I'm back before taps." Mrs. Peate would expect him to stay a bit, but also a part of him—a small part, but something he recognized nonetheless—wanted to spend more time with Miss Bliss. *Annie.*

They rode into the town proper and passed a large house with baskets of ferns and flowers dangling from the eaves of the porch. The two women grinned like children with a lollipop.

Annie slowed down the pace of her horse. "Gladys is too modest to tell you herself, but she's the one who hung all those flowers on Mr. Keller's house. God surprised us all by sending her to the richest man in town." She sighed. "I hope God blesses my endeavors with the soldiers as much as He blessed Gladys's with Mr. Keller."

A story lay behind those short sentences. Jeremiah started to ask for more information, like what could a rich man need from this young woman? But before he could voice his curiosity, they reached a corner and Gladys paused her horse.

"My house lies down this street. It's been my pleasure to meet you, Lieutenant Arnold. I'm praying for God to bring revival to the fort." She said good-bye to Annie and turned her horse down the crossroad.

Jeremiah found himself alone on the street with Annie, subject to scrutiny by any passersby. They had reached the main street. At any moment, someone might appear and start rumors about him or, even worse, about Annie. "Is your house nearby?"

Annie pointed across Main Street. "Straight ahead a couple of blocks." She flicked a glance down the street before urging her horse forward. Her horse picked up the pace as if he knew home was only a short distance away. Jeremiah's mount followed. On the way back to the fort, he would give her free rein to stretch her legs in a long, loping gait. He did some of his best thinking while on horseback, and he had plenty to talk over with the Lord after the events of this day.

They came to a stop in front of a house painted a cheerful yellow that reminded him of Annie's hair as well as her personality. Even the tulips blooming around the front of the house were yellow. Yeasty aromas floated through the open window, teasing his taste buds. Jeremiah followed Annie to the barn, where they settled their horses. Back outside, he hurried forward to open the door for her.

Annie flashed a grin at him and called through the doorway. "Mama, I'm home, and I brought company."

"Come on in."

Jeremiah followed Annie through the door and spotted a woman who must be her mother. Aside from the silver mixed in among her golden strands, they shared the same wide smile and merry blue eyes. Her gaze took in his uniform. "Lieutenant, welcome to our house."

At her word, his shoulders straightened and his back stiffened as if at attention. His one vanity was the success he had made in the army. It was one of the reasons he kept reenlisting, although that decision was looming again before the end of the summer. He was impressed that Mrs. Bliss could differentiate the various ranks in the cavalry. Maybe her son's service had prompted her recognition of his insignia.

"Mrs. Bliss, it is my pleasure."

Annie bustled around the kitchen. Without any verbal communication, he found himself at the table with two thick slabs of bread and butter and fresh-brewed coffee. Better than anything Shorty the cook had served in the canteen anytime recently. Mrs. Bliss added both sugar and milk to her coffee, took a sip, then turned her pleasant face in his direction. "So what do you think of Annie's idea? Do the men need socks and mittens and such?"

Jeremiah wished he could say no. That would alleviate the problems presented by Annie and her winsome ways. Half the young men in the regiment would vie for her attention, and the other half would wish they could.

But every winter he heard grumbling among the men about the bone-crunching cold of Kansas winters. More than that, Jeremiah saw God's hand in Annie's mission. He wouldn't say no to God, not even when a woman was involved. "The men will welcome the knitted items. Even now, in April, we get an occasional cold spell. My greatest concern is for your daughter's safety."

"I can't think of a safer place for my daughter than among the men sworn to protect our country." Mrs. Bliss smiled.

As if wondering where the food had gone, he stared at the empty plate before him. Annie whisked it away and returned with a slice of dried apple pie with a wedge of cheese, as well as the coffeepot. She topped off his cup before sitting again, this time with paper and pencil in hand. She looked at him expectantly. "How many soldiers are at the fort?"

Jeremiah calculated the answer. The number varied on a monthly, if not weekly, basis. "The number of officers is fairly stable. In addition to Captain Peate and myself, there's one more lieutenant and eight sergeants. A couple of them are married." If he could limit her mission to the officers, perhaps no harm would result from her interference.

"I discussed that with Mrs. Peate. She suggested I make sets for everyone— maybe even for the wives themselves. I need an exact number of the soldiers and their wives."

Cornered, Jeremiah gave her the total.

Annie jotted the numbers down. "Mr. Finnegan—the owner of the mercantile—has ordered extra yarn." She turned her hand over, palm up, and studied it. "The men's hands will be larger than mine, of course. Is anyone an unusual size? Any six-fingered hands?" She grinned at her own joke.

The conversation continued in much the same vein, her questions stretching Jeremiah's knowledge of the men under his care. By the time the interview ended, Mrs. Bliss had refilled his plate twice more, once with a ham sandwich, and again with a bowl of bacon-flavored green beans. When she gave him corn bread fresh from the oven, he raised his hand in protest. He was already full enough that he would battle drowsiness during his evening duties.

Annie frowned at her notepaper. She made a few more calculations and set the pencil down. "I have all the information I need. I should have a good start within ten days. When would you like for me to return to the fort?"

"That's not wise." Jeremiah knew his refusal sounded harsh, but he would not tempt his men, nor would he put Annie in harm's way. "It would be best if someone from the fort comes here to get them." Like the next time Mrs. Peate came to town for her shopping.

"Lovely." Mrs. Bliss answered instead of Annie. "Plan on taking your lunch with us on Tuesday next."

Not me again. But to refuse the invitation would be rude. "I, uh, will of course let you know if anything comes up to prevent my return." He would prefer a gunfight to facing down two such charming ladies. History had proven his weakness when it came to women.

⁓

From her spot at the window, Annie watched Jeremiah's back until horse and rider disappeared from view. He confused her more than any man she had ever met. At times he was as grouchy as a bear intent on finding food. Other times she glimpsed a cuddly cub that was hurting and wanted his mother.

Children ran and skipped down the street. Where had the day fled that school had already dismissed? With a sigh, she turned back in her mother's direction. "Do you need help with supper?"

"No, go ahead and get started on your knitting." Her mother shooed her out of the kitchen.

Annie took a skein of navy blue yarn and cast stitches onto the needles. Three rows later she realized she had miscounted the first row, and she unraveled everything back to the first knot.

Her mother joined her in the parlor and pinned her with one of those looks. "So. . .tell me."

Annie tucked her tongue in her cheek while she finished counting the row. Once again she had miscalculated the number of stitches. She pulled them off the needle with a savage yank. The story about the conversation between the laundress and the "Bear" poured out of her. "I can't decide whether he's a bear waking up from his winter's nap or a bear cub that's, well. . ." Heat rushed to her face.

"As cute as a baby kitten?" Mama's voice held a hint of laughter. "He's probably both. No one is all good or bad all the time."

"Not even Pa?" Annie dared to ask.

A faraway look swept across her mother's face. "You wouldn't know it to see him now, but he was as rough as a man can be who has spent most of his life only among other men." Mama picked up one of the boys' trousers for mending. "And we've both heard how grouchy Norman Keller was the first time Gladys visited. Now he's showing up at Aunt Kate's diner several times a week." She winked. "There are a few of us who would love to see the two of them find love the second time around."

Annie harrumphed. Perhaps some woman could picture Lieutenant Bear Arnold as a nice man, but not her. "He's helping me only because Mrs. Peate asked him to. How can my plan work if he opposes it?"

Mama stuck her needle in the trouser leg. "Annie Abigail Bliss, you're giving one man too much power. If God is for it. . ."

". . .who can be against it?" Annie rubbed her forehead. "You're right, of course." She forced a smile. "But you have to admit it would be easier if he was as excited about it as I am." She cut off the end of the yarn that she had twisted too much to use. She shifted to green, to remind her of spring, and dug in her basket for larger knitting needles. This time her first row came out evenly spaced and with the right number of stitches. "Thanks for reminding me."

"Easier, perhaps—but not as much fun." Mama's laughter resounded in Annie's ears, and she made short work of the mitten's cuff.

Chapter 4

A loud cry awoke Jeremiah in the night. He battled his blankets and sat up straight in bed, his Colt in his right hand. His head swung around, but no one moved in the shadows. Chaswell, the only other officer in the bachelor's quarters, snored, his sleep uninterrupted.

No enemy threatened Jeremiah or the regiment's safety; only his own painful nightmares troubled him, the same ones he'd suffered after Fannie's death followed on the heels of his parents' deaths. Those dreams had ended years ago until Annie Bliss and her knitting project had disturbed his peace.

The women Jeremiah had dealings with as chaplain fell into two categories. He offered officers' wives the same respect he afforded their husbands. As far as camp followers and other such women in every station and town in the west, he warned his soldiers to keep out of their way and took care to follow his own advice.

He had minimized his contact with pretty young things like Annie Bliss. Chaswell likened his behavior to a horse with blinders. But Annie had burst on the scene, tearing the blinders from his eyes and forcing him to see the spirited, godly young woman with a mission from God.

The sky had lightened to a predawn gray, and he saw no point in seeking slumber again, "perchance to dream," as Hamlet despaired. After he scrubbed his face, he grabbed his Bible and headed for the stable. He had enough time to ride to his favorite place to greet dawn, about a five-minute ride from the fort.

He had spent more time on horseback in the past ten days than he had in the past ten months, and today he would add more miles to that total. He had to ride into town for his second meeting with the self-proclaimed missionary to the military.

Inside the stable, familiar odors greeted Jeremiah, and his horse's soft nicker welcomed him. He rubbed her nose while feeding her a bit of carrot. "I'm spoiling you." She stood quietly while he saddled up and led her outside before closing the door and climbing on her back.

The guard at the gate called, "Morning, Chaplain." Waving back, Jeremiah headed into the cool spring Kansas morning. Winter snow had disappeared only a week ago. God knew Jeremiah needed a place to escape and think things over.

Once he reached his spot and settled his mare, he reached for a blade of new spring grass. He tried whistling down the shaft, without success, before he stuck it between his teeth. David might have done the same thing when he was a shepherd. The habit lingered from Jeremiah's boyhood.

The mare matched Jeremiah well, but she was getting up in years. If he chose to reenlist, he would need a new horse. She deserved to end her years in peace, but where could he find her a home?

Annie's horse was well cared for, as was everything he noticed about her home.

Annie, again. Jeremiah jerked at the blade of grass and spat it on the ground. What did it take to get the girl out of his mind? This spot near the fort had become sacred ground as he spent time here, bringing the faces of his departed loved ones to mind. Over this past winter, their faces had lost focus, smudged by a mental eraser. The lack of fidelity to their memories, not to mention his disastrous dalliance with a saloon girl, made him feel unclean, unworthy. He had dreamed of being Hosea to her Gomer, only she dragged him down to her level and then died in a drunken gunfight at the saloon. He had fled into the army for escape six years ago next month.

Had all his years ministering to the men under his care counted for nothing? Sunshine rippled over his open Bible. "Lord, You promised me perfect peace if I keep my mind stayed on You. I'm trying, Lord. But I'm not at peace. I want to head in the direction You're leading me, whether to remain in the army or leave it for something new."

No answer came, at least not one he could hear. Today he would cling to the promise of God's abiding presence when he came face-to-face with Miss Annie Bliss for their second meeting.

His mare nuzzled his neck, bringing him a small measure of comfort. He stood and scratched her nose. "If God gave you the gift of speech like Balaam's donkey, what would you say?" After he climbed on her back, he urged her to a gallop, one that cooled his skin and cleared the fuzziness of his brain for the morning ahead. If he couldn't resolve his feelings, he could at least ignore them for a few hours and complete his duties out of force of habit.

Upon his return to the fort, the young guard saluted him. "Lieutenant Arnold, Mrs. Peate has asked to see you after breakfast."

Jeremiah bit his lip. He wouldn't get the expected reprieve after all.

❧

"Are you sure you don't need my help?" Annie hovered in the kitchen.

Her mother chuckled. "If you keep this up, I'll bring out my damask tablecloth and china."

Annie could just about imagine the horror on the Bear's face if they went to such lengths. "Don't do that!"

Mama laughed. "I have everything under control. Why don't you bring your basket in here to finish that last mitten, and we can visit while we work?"

Annie tilted her head sideways while she considered. She usually kept her projects away from the kitchen, where flour or water could destroy hours of needlework with a single fling of a spoon. But she could tuck the mitten and skein into a small sack that would protect them from most spills. "I'll do that."

In the living room, she glanced at the basket full of completed sets. She was working on the final pair. God Himself had sped her hands, and even the additional yarn had arrived at Finnegan's Mercantile two days earlier than expected.

She sat down at the table and cast the first row with blue yarn, which she would mix with bright yellow stripes. Like the last one she'd finished, she'd make it large, a good match for the strong, sturdy hands she had seen as the Bear handled the reins on his horse.

She shook her head, hoping to clear away renegade thoughts of the chaplain. "It's a good thing I finished these early."

Mama looked up briefly from the pudding she was stirring. "I confess, I was hoping for more opportunities to invite Lieutenant Arnold for a visit. He seemed so sad. You mentioned he lost his fiancée, but that was a long time ago."

Annie didn't know how to respond to that. The most serious romance in her short eighteen years consisted of a stolen kiss from Abe Pettigrew on the occasion of their graduation. He had wed Hannah Swenson last November, and Annie rejoiced.

"You feel sorry for *him*?" Annie doubted the laundress at the fort would agree. She had felt the scrape of the Bear's teeth first hand. She finished the cuff of the mitten and began work on the hand.

Her mother tested the pudding and took it off the fire. "Annie girl, don't you know that grumpy people usually have been hurt in some way? Don't you remember Mr. Keller's reputation as a scary hermit before Gladys braved him in his house and discovered a lonely old man?"

Were Mr. Keller and the Bear alike? "I guess if the Samaritan could love the man on the Jericho road, I can find a way to get along with the—" She stopped herself from saying "Bear" just in time. "Lieutenant."

"That's the spirit." Mama dished pudding into individual bowls and began whipping cream.

A short while later, Annie finished the last stitches before tying off the yarn inside the thumb. Outside the window a chestnut-colored mare appeared. Annie's heart sped and her dry mouth forced a cough from her throat. She tucked the finished mitten into the sack and stood.

"Why don't you go ahead and greet our guest while I set the table?" Mama grinned as if she knew every one of Annie's thoughts and desires.

Draping a shawl over her shoulders, Annie headed out the door. The lieutenant looked less like a bear today, more human, the way he was rubbing the mare's nose and talking to her.

"Good morning, Jeremiah."

He jumped at her words, the wary look returning to his face. "Annie."

She noticed the absence of any kind of gloves or mittens on his hands and hoped he would find her blue-and-gold creations useful.

Mama opened the back window. "Dinner is ready."

"We'd better hurry." Nervous laughter bubbled from Annie's mouth. "She's been cooking enough food to serve an army." A genuine chuckle followed that comment. "I mean. . ."

He smiled, and his features lightened, making him look like someone closer to her brother's age rather than an aging officer. Someone—almost attractive. She couldn't help noticing the shine of his boots, the crisp creases of his uniform.

With two steps, he reached the door first and opened it for her. He bowed and gestured her inside. "It smells heavenly in here."

"We're serving you breakfast. I hope you don't mind."

He looked at her, a question in his eyes. "I don't mind. I hope your mother didn't go to any extra trouble for me, though."

"She loves it. My brother—the one in the army, up in Wyoming, you know—he says he never gets a decent fried egg."

"Eggs scrambled with every ingredient on hand, but not fried, no."

The sadness sliding through his eyes reminded her that he had no one to cook his eggs to order for him. She wondered about his family. Mama's words about hidden hurt made a little more sense, especially as long as this softer, kinder bear cub stayed in charge.

They arrived in the kitchen before they could engage in further conversation. Mama pulled a pan with toast from the oven and slid two slices onto Jeremiah's plate. "Lovely to see you again, Lieutenant. Tell me, how do you like your eggs?"

"Over easy." He settled into the indicated chair and studied the array of available jams.

Annie fixed Jeremiah's coffee the way he liked it. Mama filled the frying pan with four eggs, and Annie hid a smile. When Mama joined them at the table, she invited Jeremiah to say the blessing.

Jeremiah folded his hands into a tent and bowed his head. "Thank You, Lord, for Your bounty and these kind folks who have served it. Please lead us to do Your will. In Jesus' name, amen."

The simple prayer caught Annie by surprise. He spoke like someone who talked with God like a friend, who used everyday language to battle everyday problems in the arena of prayer. Another layer she hadn't expected from the Bear. She breathed her own silent prayer. *Lord, let me see the lieutenant as You see him.*

When she opened her eyes, steady brown eyes studied her. He smiled as if he had heard her internal prayer then turned his attention to the food in front of him. Mama replaced his toast as soon as he finished his two slices. He ate every bite with relish before pushing back from the table. "Thank you for the delicious meal, Mrs. Bliss." His eyes sought out Annie, questioning whether she had helped.

"It wasn't anything hard. Annie's been working night and day on the hat and scarf sets."

Jeremiah lifted his eyebrows. Annie rose and reached for Mama's plate, but Mama shooed her away. "You go into the other room to discuss your project with the lieutenant. I'll take care of the dishes."

Jeremiah appeared behind Annie's chair in a second and then escorted her to the front room, treating her with all the courtliness of a born gentleman. So far today he had been politeness personified.

"From what your mother said, you've been working hard." Jeremiah gestured to the sack with bright colors peeking out of the top.

She nodded. "I finished the last set this morning. I wanted everyone to receive his at the same time. This sack here"—she handed the bag at her feet over to Jeremiah—"holds the special sizes. The rest are back in my room."

"Do you need any help?" Jeremiah asked.

She started to say no, but she had too many bags for a single trip. His suggestion only made common sense. She nodded and led him to the back room. While he gathered the bags, she reached for his special set. Her breath quickened, and she made herself count to five. After a deep breath, she straightened her shoulders and returned to the living room a step behind Jeremiah.

"Is there anything I should know before we distribute the scarf sets?"

His question kindled a fire in her stomach that spread up her neck and cheeks. Swallowing to moisten her dry throat, she held out the small paper sack. "I made these especially for you."

Chapter 5

*A*nnie *made a set especially for me.* Jeremiah reached down from his mare's back and touched the bulging saddlebag to reassure himself of the reality. Vivid blues and almost-gold stripes. As smart as a dress uniform during a parade march. She had even added the correct insignia appropriate to his rank. As far as he knew, none of the other sets had anything so unique. The sky overhead and the bracing wind both predicted the same weather: a late-season cold snap, one that could range from hailstones to tornadoes or even a snowstorm. Jeremiah might have a use for Annie's gift sooner than expected.

The men might talk about the special touches added to Jeremiah's set, but he couldn't refuse Annie's gift any more than he could tell Mrs. Peate he had neglected to offer her invitation to tea. The gift had rattled him, and he escaped soon after that, forgetting the message from the captain's wife. He'd have to go back.

If he turned around now, he had time to offer the invitation before the dinner bell sounded at the fort and before bad weather set in. The hope of avoiding future trips to town exceeded his embarrassment about his oversight. Maybe this would be their last meeting and he wouldn't have to return after today. He turned around and headed back into town.

On the way back into town, he spotted Annie's friend Gladys with a young man. Funny, he hadn't lost a moment's sleep because of her. She had already completed her mission; Mrs. Peate would worm the entire story from Gladys the next time they met.

This young woman didn't frighten him nearly as much as Miss Annie Bliss. Jeremiah reined in his mare and approached the couple. The horse snorted, and they turned in his direction.

"Why, Lieutenant Arnold, how pleasant to see you again." Gladys looked up at him with a welcoming smile.

The man with her bowed in Jeremiah's direction. "Haydn Keller, at your service, Lieutenant."

"Pleased to make your acquaintance." Jeremiah nodded at young Keller. "Mrs. Peate asked me to extend an invitation for the four young ladies involved in your mission project to join her for tea on Saturday afternoon." He handed Gladys an official invitation.

Gladys held the letter where Keller could see while they both read it. "I would be delighted to accept. How thoughtful of her to have the tea at a time when Miss Fairfield can come. Please thank her for us." Her eyes swept over the sacks attached to the back of the mare. "I see you've already been to Annie's house. I trust she said yes, too?"

"No, actually"—the words came hesitantly to Jeremiah's mouth—"I forgot to ask her." He considered asking Gladys to deliver Annie's invitation, but Mrs.

Peate would not approve. Before Gladys could ask another question, he said good-bye and headed toward Main Street and beyond, to the house with the pretty yellow paint.

This time when he rode up to the house, no one poked her nose outside. He tied his mare to the stair rail leading to the front porch. After retrieving the remaining invitations from his saddlebag, he knocked on the front door. When Annie opened to his knock a minute later, her hair was messed, her eyes sparkled, and she looked as relaxed as Jeremiah had felt as long as he was riding in the direction of the fort.

"Why, Jeremiah, I didn't expect to see you again so soon. Please, come in." She opened the door to invite him in.

Jeremiah stepped inside the door. "Mrs. Peate asked me to deliver these invitations to you when I saw you, but I forgot. She is inviting everyone involved with your special mission projects to tea on Saturday." He cleared his throat. "I ran into Miss Polson with Mr. Keller on my way back. She has already accepted."

Annie clasped the envelope that Mrs. Peate had penned with such care close to her chest without opening it. "I shall of course come, and I will get the invitations to Miss Landry and Miss Fairfield as soon as possible. Tell her thank you for us." He remained in place one awkward moment too long, and Annie smiled. "Would you like some tea before you return to the fort? The air is getting nippy."

A warm drink, a cheerful kitchen, and a young lady's smile. . . He forced himself to remember such things were forbidden to the likes of him. "I am sorry, but I have already tarried too long." On impulse, he added, "I truly appreciate the items you made for me."

He clapped his hat on his head and skedaddled, her surprised face etching itself on his mind.

⤝⤞

"Mrs. Peate is very nice. I don't think I could have finished my project without her support." Annie dangled the sleeve for the sweater she had started in front of her. A couple more inches for length, she decided. She changed the colors of the stripes with every sweater to individualize them.

Birdie pinned together material for a dart. A skilled seamstress, she dressed perfectly modest yet managed to look the most stylish of the four of them. The dresses she made for herself could have been taken from the pages of *Godey's Lady's Book*. "I don't know if I should go." She kept her eyes focused on the sewing in her lap.

Ruth turned the invitation she had received over and examined it again. "Mrs. Peate invited all of us." She looped thread around her needle for a French knot and finished the stitch before looking up again. "Did you have any. . .business. . .with the soldiers in your former occupation?"

A pale pink spread across Birdie's face. "Yes." The word came out as a whisper.

All sewing ceased for the moment. Tears formed in Birdie's eyes. Annie handed her the handkerchief she had tucked into her sleeve.

Ruth, ever the pastor's daughter, revived first. "God has forgiven your past.

You no longer have a reason to be ashamed."

Birdie shook her head, raising her wet face to the others. "But just seeing me might lead some of them to sin."

"You comport yourself very differently now. Besides, we'll be going straight to the captain's quarters, so we may not run into any soldiers." Annie scrambled for words to assuage Birdie's worries. "And you look so different now, they might not recognize you in any case."

Ruth nodded. "Your sunbonnet will hide your features."

"Please say you'll come." A frown formed on Annie's face. "You don't want to miss a chance to meet the Bear. If Mrs. Peate invited him." Even as Annie said the words, guilt assaulted her. Even though he had softened the last time they had met, he might condemn Birdie if he ever learned about her past. He was the kind of man who wouldn't tolerate less than perfection, or any immoral behavior. Or maybe he was one of the soldiers who. . . No. Even her worst suspicions about him hadn't entertained that picture. "Then again. . ." Annie almost regretted repeating the invitation.

Resolution animated Birdie's face once again. "Mrs. Fairfield keeps telling me I should venture more into the community and live the new life Jesus died to give me. I will go to the tea."

"That's the spirit." Gladys smiled. "Let's pray that yesterday's snowfall will melt before Saturday."

"I wonder if they distributed the scarf sets before the storm." Annie changed green yarn for blue. "I'm not wishing for more winter, but I'd like it if the soldiers can use them before next November."

The others laughed, and Ruth patted her hand. "They can at least use socks year-round."

On Saturday they met for an early lunch, and then Annie drove them out to the fort in her father's wagon. Once they left town, they could see the new grass carpeting the countryside.

Annie flicked the reins over the horse's back, and he picked up speed. A figure on horseback flew down the road toward them, fast enough to deliver the message that Paul Revere carried on his important ride. The pace was so fast, in fact, that she didn't recognize Lieutenant Arnold until he slowed down to greet them.

The cool air dried the cobwebs from Annie's throat as she drew a deep breath. "Lieutenant, I wasn't expecting you to accompany us."

The Bear straightened in the saddle, transformed from a Pony Express rider back into a soldier. "We received word of a small renegade Indian band roaming the next county over. We wanted to ensure your safety on the road." In spite of his wooden appearance, his voice carried urgency.

Gasps came from behind Annie in the wagon. Gladys asked, "Is Calico threatened, then?"

"Not so long as you stay in town, Miss Polson. But the commander has expressed concern about travelers headed east."

"Thank you for joining us today." Annie brought her hand to her throat. She glanced at the horizon, empty except for the new grass and a stand of trees in the distance. "Shall we get moving?"

The lieutenant altered his speed to match the pace of the wagon, traveling at their side and swiveling his head every few moments to spot any potential dangers. When they arrived at the fort, the gate was barred and every guard post manned with two soldiers.

So much for an unobtrusive entrance. Annie glanced back at Birdie, who was looking away from the fort and had bent her head and folded her hands as if in prayer. There had to be another way. "Lieutenant, we don't want to disturb the men on duty. Is there a back way to reach the captain's quarters?"

Jeremiah nodded as if in approval. "Of course. After we get through the gate, we'll take a sharp turn to the left."

In spite of their plan, the wagon trundled through the gate at the same moment a barked order of "about face" turned all the men in the regiment in their direction. Birdie's head dropped even lower.

Military discipline reigned, and the men remained at attention. However, Annie was certain the men would comment on their visit. According to her brother, any alteration to a soldier's schedule provided fodder for speculation. The arrival of visitors would be the centerpiece of dinner discussion in the mess hall.

"I apologize for the timing." Jeremiah didn't look at her, but the stubborn jut of his chin suggested how much the apology cost him.

"There is no need. Of course the men are training for the potential Indian threat." She trusted she was speaking for all of them. They arrived at the captain's quarters without further commotion.

His touch as he helped her off the driver's seat felt soft as he brushed her arms, at odds with his posture. This close, she felt his strength and the urge to provide and protect radiating from him. Qualities that made him a fine soldier also testified to his character, in spite of her initial impression.

Solid husband material. Annie rocked on her feet as the thought crashed into her mind.

Chapter 6

Jeremiah glanced over his shoulder as he followed the ladies to the door. No one had followed them, but he was sure he would be teased, by Chaswell if no one else, about the bevy of women he accompanied that day.

For now, he focused on the task in front of him. Mrs. Peate insisted he remain with them for tea in case something regarding Annie's project came up. During the minutes he had spent taking care of the horses, the five women in the small parlor had seemed to multiply, the air filled with high voices, soft laughter, and a rainbow of colors rarely seen outside of flowers in a field. Mrs. Peate had promised her husband's attendance, but accompanied by two squads, he had left early in the morning to scout out the Indian threat. Jeremiah was on his own with the quintet of women. Shooting a glance at the ceiling, he sent a pleading look in God's direction. *Is this Your sense of humor at work? Because it doesn't make any sense to me.*

Visible evidence of Annie's mission hung on the coatrack—Mrs. Peate's scarf and mittens. They had already proven their worth during the late winter storm. Both personal and practical, the gifts had earned a big thank-you on behalf of the company.

Why did God continue to arrange meetings with the first woman to catch his interest since his fiancée's death? After today he hoped to put her behind him. The course Jeremiah had chosen since his fall from grace hadn't changed even if he was less and less satisfied with the prospect of spending the rest of his life alone. Any one of these young women would turn the heads of every soldier in the fort; some of the men might even make good husbands.

"Come in, Lieutenant. Thank you for escorting our guests safely to the fort." Mrs. Peate motioned him forward. "Captain Peate is convinced the rumor is nothing more than that, a rumor. If he believed there was any substance to it, he would have insisted I cancel the tea."

Jeremiah nodded. He hadn't been sure if he preferred a postponement over getting the occasion done with. Keeping her voice low, Mrs. Peate admonished, "Come now, Lieutenant. Relax. You never know what will happen."

Jeremiah relaxed his shoulders and shook his hands by his side to release some of the tension from his body so he wouldn't crush a hand in a handshake. The four guests had taken spots around the parlor. He guessed that the one with her dark hair up in a bun must be Ruth Fairfield, the pastor's daughter and teacher. Gladys's hair was an ordinary brown. The other two crowns of hair sparkled in spite of the fading light outside the window—Annie's hair was pure gold, and the last woman had hair the shade of a rich cinnamon, almost red. Had Annie told him her name? If so, he had forgotten it.

Mrs. Peate introduced them to him, repeating each one's name as if she had known them for weeks instead of a few minutes. He had correctly pegged the dark-haired lady as Ruth Fairfield, the schoolteacher. The redhead, Birdie Landry, made her living as a seamstress. Something about her stirred a memory, but he couldn't place it. "Of course you have already met Miss Polson, who helps out at Aunt Kate's diner, and Miss Bliss, who has worked so hard on behalf of the men here at the fort."

Annie's smile widened, implying a long acquaintance instead of their brief encounters. "Mrs. Peate was telling us that you have distributed all the sets I sent. The men who have them were grateful for them when the storm hit, and the rest are looking forward to receiving theirs."

Jeremiah thought of his own mittens and scarf, hidden beneath his great coat on the coat tree. After all her work, Miss Bliss deserved a better thanks. "I know I made good use of them myself. The men kept so warm, they had enough energy left over for a snowball fight when they were off duty."

The thankful smile on Annie's face gladdened his heart.

❦

Annie clapped her hands and laughed. "Wonderful!"

"In fact. . ." Mrs. Peate poured tea into a cup and handed it to Jeremiah before she addressed Annie. "Your gift went over so well that I wondered if you would be willing to expand on your original idea."

Annie clapped her hands together again then tented her fingers under her chin. Ruth laid a hand on her shoulder.

"I already started working on sweaters for the men, although I don't know if they can use them before next fall. Here's the first one." Annie reached into the bag at her feet and pulled out her finished product, done in forest greens and sky blues. Form dictated she should give the first sample to the captain, even though she had pictured Jeremiah while she made it. "This one is for the captain." She handed it to Mrs. Peate.

Jeremiah followed the exchange with a flicker of interest in his eyes. Mrs. Peate ran her fingers over the yarn, making appreciative noises as she did so. "You do amazing work."

"It's nothing."

Ruth clucked her disapproval at Annie's less than gracious response. Annie hastened to add, "I enjoy working knitting needles more than a hook and eye. With three older brothers, I've had a lot of practice darning socks and making mittens."

Their hostess passed the sweater to Jeremiah, and he took up the conversation thread. He held up the sweater against his chest, and Annie pictured how he would look wearing it. "As long as it's this weight, it will fit under our uniforms." He nodded his approval, and a ridiculous happiness grew in Annie's heart.

Mrs. Peate refilled their cups of tea then took a sip of hers before leaning forward as if imparting a secret. "The sweaters are a good idea, but I was thinking of something more imminent. My husband and I feel that our young men would benefit from socializing with lovely young ladies such as yourselves."

Annie glanced at Jeremiah. His eyes were fixed on the fire, unreadable.

Mrs. Peate continued. "Are there any upcoming events that our men could attend? A parade, a barn dance, a box social?" Her smile seemed to dare him to disagree in spite of the scowl on his face.

Annie looked to Gladys and Ruth, the three of them communicating in silence the way they always did when a question arose. Birdie kept her eyes fastened on her lap. She might not welcome the arrival of a bunch of rowdy soldiers in town, especially if any of them might recognize her.

Then Birdie glanced up. "I think that's a good idea." She returned her gaze to her lap.

"I can think of a couple of events coming up where our soldier boys would be welcome. Gladys, perhaps Haydn knows of others." Annie looked at her friend.

"I can ask him if he's heard anything," Gladys said.

"Perhaps we could do more. I know several people in town who have family members in the army. Maybe they would like to adopt the young men so they can enjoy a taste of home." Annie's eyes misted as she thought of her brother. "And of course, the visits might ease the longing the families feel for their boys."

Mrs. Peate's nod revealed her enthusiasm about the idea. "What a lovely idea. Don't you agree, Lieutenant?"

He agreed more readily than Annie expected, although she spotted a gleam of amusement akin to her brothers' before they planned a practical joke on their unsuspecting mother. Or maybe Mama only pretended she didn't suspect anything. What had she said? *Behind every grown man lurked a small boy who wanted to come out and play.*

Jeremiah looked every bit the grown man when he said, "Of course we don't want to expose the fort or the town to danger as long as the Indians remain at large."

Indians. Annie repulsed a shudder at the thought. Calico had been peaceful for all the years she had lived there.

"Naturally we will wait until this threat is settled. Lieutenant Arnold, you are the logical person to serve as a liaison with the community. And Miss Bliss, will you represent the community?"

Ruth normally took the lead in situations like this, but the men at the fort were Annie's project, not Ruth's. Annie extended her hand to the man who resembled a bear less and less every time they met and more like an ordinary—perhaps even extraordinary—man.

～

For the first time in his life, Jeremiah almost hoped the soldiers might encounter signs of Indian activity. If the men were involved chasing a phantom enemy, they could delay exposure to womanly wiles.

Not every woman was like Fannie, of course. But his distaste for the task only increased after the women left and Mrs. Peate relayed a bit of essential information, gleaned in a few quick seconds from the woman herself. Redheaded Birdie

Landry worked at the Betwixt 'n' Between Saloon before she came to know the Lord last year. Mrs. Peate promised Birdie was a new person in Christ, and he could trust her. But in case any of the soldiers had strayed with her. . .

Jeremiah ground his teeth at the thought. In principle, even prostitutes could be redeemed—consider Rahab and Mary Magdalene—but he found the account of Hosea's wife more believable.

Jeremiah brought his attention back to Mrs. Peate, who was still talking. "I know you think you are hard on the men, that they'd rather go to Sergeant Chaswell about their problems, but when it comes to serious questions, they come to you." She leaned forward. "That's why my husband recommended you as chaplain at this fort. He saw that men seek you out when they need someone to talk with. He only made it official by getting you assigned here."

Jeremiah had no response to that, but only stared down at his hands. Guilty hands, ones that had failed the woman he claimed to love twice. First, he used her in the same way other men had. And then he deserted her when she needed him, and she had paid with her life. Ever since then he had been unable to turn away anyone who came to him for help. He'd taken a vow of chastity—and sworn to keep others from repeating his mistakes. "I just listen, that's all. And pass on a few words of advice."

"And now you'll advise them about taking part in the community activities." Mrs. Peate patted his hand. "I'm trusting God for a quick and safe solution to the Indian problem. But you will hear of that before I will."

Her prayer must have flown to heaven on wings, because the captain returned the next evening and sought out his officers. He and the scouts had found a few Kaw Indians, doing nothing worse than trying to hunt the long-gone buffalo before returning to Indian territory. After determining they posed no threat to white settlements, the scouts escorted them to the border before returning to the fort with good news.

The captain kept Jeremiah back when the others left. "I see that Miss Bliss has been busy with her knitting needles again. That sweater she made for me is a work of art."

"Yes sir."

"I understand my wife has suggested the soldiers join the folks of Calico for community events."

Jeremiah nodded.

"And that since you and Miss Bliss have established such a good working relationship, that the pair of you should partner on this project as well."

"Yes." Jeremiah kept his answer as simple as possible, hoping his brevity might convey his distaste for the task.

"Perhaps you and Miss Bliss will partner in other ways as well, hmm, Lieutenant?"

Jeremiah's face pulled in a frown before he could stop it. The captain waited him out, forcing him to make some response. "I doubt that, sir."

"Lieutenant." The captain hesitated before he said, "Jeremiah. I have known you these many years. Perhaps the time has come for you to set aside the fears from the past and march into the future that the Lord has for you. God sent Miss Bliss to our fort to do more than distribute hats and scarves."

Jeremiah couldn't get the captain's words out of his mind as he went to bed that night.

Is it possible, Lord?

Chapter 7

I sn't God wonderful?" Annie knew she was carrying on like a schoolgirl, but she couldn't stop herself. Jeremiah was escorting her back home after making arrangements for "adopting" the soldiers. "You identified six young men who could benefit from a homey touch, and we found exactly that number of families willing to spend time with them."

"In that case, He supplied in excess of the need. I thought you intended to assign someone to your own family, because of your brother."

Annie stopped in midstride. Did the man not realize. . . ? "He supplied exactly the right amount. My mother and father believe God arranged for my family to take *you* in. As the spiritual leader of the others, you need a place you can cast those worries aside."

Annie had tried to convince Ruth to ask her father to take the chaplain under his wing. Ruth declined. "Why would God want that when He sent the lieutenant to you?"

Jeremiah drew in a deep breath. "Shall we walk a ways farther?" Instead of heading left toward her house, he pointed in the opposite direction, toward the Keller mansion and the Polson home. Annie could only agree.

They strolled—far from the lieutenant's normal pace, which was so fast Annie felt like she was drilling with the army—down the street without exchanging a word. Annie's senses expanded, taking in the smell of the new leaves forming on cedar trees, the beauty of sunflowers dancing in the breeze, the song of a sparrow, even the warming temperatures that defied comfort in either wool or cotton.

At the Keller mansion, Jeremiah paused to look at the baskets of flowers cascading across the fresh wood of the porch. Annie knew that the difference Gladys had made in the Keller family went far beyond house repairs. Mr. Keller hadn't missed church a Sunday since Easter, and he had even shown up at Aunt Kate's diner on a regular basis. Such a positive outcome for Annie's project remained unclear.

Annie opened her mouth, but God's still, small voice told her to hush.

"The more I've worked with you, the more I've seen God at work. So I will accept your invitation to join your family." He shrugged his shoulders, as if getting rid of a heavy weight.

"It's our pleasure." *It's my pleasure.* A warm feeling washed over Annie. The Bear was turning more and more into a cuddly cub every day, one who still mourned the loss of his fiancée. But she feared any mention of that would bring stony silence. She rushed to the next topic on her mind, to rid herself of the unexpected emotions flooding over her. "The first community event will be a box social, a week from Saturday. The money raised will go toward the charity the entire women's missionary society supports." She smiled at him. "The society has been very kind and supportive about our individual mission projects. It's time we returned the favor."

The bemused expression on the lieutenant's face suggested she should hurry. Mr. Keller came out to the porch and waved, reminding Annie how long they had lingered on the street. The lieutenant offered her his arm. "Shall we go back?"

Strong fingers cupped her elbow. Annie didn't know what to make of his touch, so she continued with the discussion of the box social. "We are hoping that the majority of soldiers at the fort can take part. Or we could bring the social to the fort—" She hurried on at the frown that crossed his face. "Or we could hold two box socials, so that everyone can attend one or the other."

Jeremiah blew out his breath. "Two separate days sounds like a good idea."

≈

"And the basket goes to Mack Jackson."

Annie stepped forward, a warm smile beckoning Private Jackson forward.

Jeremiah released a breath he didn't realize he was holding, fighting the feelings that swirled in him. When Mrs. Peate echoed Annie's request for Jeremiah to attend both socials, he hadn't anticipated this situation. Surely he couldn't—it was impossible—jealousy?

No. He pushed the thought away. In light of the speculation circulating about him and Annie, he should be happy that someone else had won her box. After he unknowingly bid on her box last week, he had made private arrangements with Pastor Fairfield to donate money this time instead of bidding.

But of all the men in the company who could have won Annie's basket, Jeremiah would have listed Jackson as the least desirable. He had spent time in the stockade more than once. He resisted even Chaswell's attempts to get to know him.

Jeremiah realized he was still scowling in Jackson's direction and hoped no one had seen him. All manner of good-natured ribbing would follow if they had.

Chaswell won the next box, and Jeremiah smiled as Ruth Fairfield stood. Haydn Keller had bid on Gladys's contribution—that must have been prearranged. Mrs. Peate approached him. "This next box should prove interesting." She smiled at the larger-than-usual box.

Jeremiah raised his eyebrows. "Why is that?"

"Kate, the lady from the diner, decided to contribute. She told me she had the right because she was unmarried, and some of the soldiers might prefer a more mature woman."

Jeremiah wondered how Mrs. Peate knew all this. He was amazed at the way women communicated—information reached the most remote home even faster than the Pony Express.

Ned Finnegan, the storekeeper acting as auctioneer, peered inside the box. "Lots of good food in here. Ham sandwiches thicker than a man's fist. Crispy fried chicken. Beans and potato salad, two pies, a wedge of watermelon. . ." He smiled. "I can't tell you the name of the lady who fixed this box, but we can all make a guess." He winked at the men remaining in the audience.

An older gentleman stood, leaning on a cane. Even before Gladys appeared at his side, Jeremiah guessed he was Mr. Keller. His surprisingly strong voice called out, "Is the auction open only to our soldier boys, or can anyone in the community bid?"

Finnegan glanced at Annie, whose eyes sought Jeremiah out, questioning him. He nodded his approval, and she whispered in Finnegan's ear.

Finnegan banged his gavel. "We have no objection. Let the bidding begin."

A couple of soldiers—one thinner than a stick no matter how much he ate and the other an older, stocky man with a hearty appetite and a body shape to prove it—combined their resources to bid on the box, but they couldn't keep up. When the bid reached fifty dollars, they dropped out. The entire group broke out in applause when a blushing Miss Kate accepted Mr. Keller's arm and retreated to a quiet spot on the church lawn. Jeremiah looked back at Annie. She was clapping, bouncing up and down, her skirt lifting enough to show an intriguing patch of stockinged leg. Jeremiah looked away. He was too old to be distracted by the glimpse of a lady's limb.

All around Jeremiah, couples separated from the group gathered in front of the auctioneer. Five soldiers remained, not counting himself or the captain, and five baskets remained for auction. Annie must have arranged that. Interesting to see that the fourth member of the younger women's circle hadn't sent a basket. At least he assumed she hadn't; he hadn't seen her at today's festivities at all. For someone with her background, she showed great discretion. From what he had observed of Birdie's involvement with Annie's group, she was proving her new life in Christ over and over again; but how could he say anything to her without causing offense? Instead, he offered thanks to God and revised his long-held opinions.

But one woman's change didn't mean every one would follow her example, any more than most prostitutes followed the example of Mary Magdalene in the Gospels, Jeremiah reminded himself. He was still right to warn the men under his care against the dangers of women, especially those who fell into sin.

When Mrs. Peate learned that Jeremiah didn't intend to bid on a box this week, she had insisted that he join her and the captain for the meal. As the auctioneer called "sold!" on the last basket—coupling a shy young lass with an equally shy soldier—he crossed the lawn to the spot near the front steps where the captain had spread their quilt. Jeremiah appreciated the central location, which allowed him to keep an eye on most of the young couples.

He surveyed the groupings, probing for potential trouble spots. Mrs. Peate leaned over and poked him gently in the arm. "At ease, Lieutenant. This is a social event, and the captain has commanded that everyone have fun."

"Even you, Jeremiah." The captain was one of the few people who called Jeremiah by his given name.

"Especially you," his wife added.

Jeremiah listened with half an ear while he sought for the one couple he cared about the most. Annie spread a quilt under a tree even as Mack gestured toward a spot farther back. She shook her head and continued working. When she turned her back to unpack the box, Jackson withdrew a flask from his coat pocket and poured something into the jar of lemonade Annie had already set out on the quilt.

Jeremiah sprang to his feet, Mrs. Peate looking up in alarm. "Come, now, you must relax and enjoy yourself today."

Jeremiah directed his response to the captain. "You may wish to join me." He stalked across the grass, soldiers and townsfolk alike looking up in alarm as he strode past.

❧

Annie busied herself smoothing out the wrinkles in the quilt as best she could. Even after Ruth informed her that the lieutenant wouldn't bid today, she knew she must set an example and entertain one of the soldiers. Now she prayed for grace to endure the meal. So far, Private Mack Jackson had set her teeth on edge with his abrasive actions and his attempts to lead her farther and farther away from the main group.

When she could avoid him no longer, she prayed for one last measure of grace and turned around with a smile on her face. He offered her a glass of lemonade. That was thoughtful of him. She told herself to give the young man a chance.

As she reached to accept the glass, someone knocked it out of Jackson's hand. Before she turned, she suspected who she would find. The Bear had returned.

Chapter 8

Jeremiah grabbed Private Jackson by his uniform collar, lifting him until his toes dragged the ground. They filled her view, two figures shadowed against the noon sun, locked in fight. If it could be called a fight—the private's arms flailed wildly without reaching their target.

Annie heard rather than saw people gathering around them. Mrs. Peate appeared silently and took Annie's arm, edging her away from the two men. Slowly, she tuned out Jeremiah's heavy breathing and the private's indignant protests.

Voices crowded in. She couldn't identify the speakers.

"Maybe he was getting fresh with her."

"I hear she's the one who made us the mittens."

Others chimed in, all talking over each other, too many to make out more than a word here or there. Mrs. Peate eased her backward through a sea of blue uniforms, and they reached the ring of watching townsfolk. At the opposite side of the circle, Annie saw Ruth talking quietly with Pastor Fairfield. As he shouldered his way to the center of the circle, Annie sent up a prayer for a peaceful resolution. Had all their prayers and hopes led to this? Why had Jeremiah attacked Private Jackson?

The pastor stood between Jeremiah and the private, arms extended to keep them apart. Other men from the town joined the circle, but Annie couldn't distinguish their voices from those of the soldiers to know what they were saying. Captain Peate joined the preacher at the center, and Annie breathed a sigh of relief.

Pastor Fairfield dropped the hand holding Jackson back. The private lunged forward, swinging a right hook at Jeremiah. His fist connected with the lieutenant's nose with a bone-shattering thud.

A lad young enough to still be in school landed a punch on a soldier's arm. Three, four, five punches followed, as the ladies backed away in fright. Mrs. Peate tugged Annie in the direction of Ruth and her mother, who were part of a group of women who stood at a safe distance from the brawling men. "You are the pastor's wife?"

Mrs. Fairfield nodded.

"I am Mrs. Peate, the captain's wife. Let's gather the women together and pray." At Mrs. Fairfield's agreement, they called to the others, gathered in a circle, and Mrs. Fairfield voiced a quiet prayer.

In spite of the men's shouts, Annie was aware when more women joined the circle. A hand clasped hers, and she opened her eyes briefly to catch sight of Aunt Kate standing next to her. Annie then reached on her other side for Ruth.

As each woman added her prayers, the sounds of the fight intruded less and less. Gladys was pouring out her heart when the pastor's voice broke into their prayer meeting. "It's over, ladies."

Annie opened her eyes. At the spot where she had begun her lunch, Captain Peate had gathered the soldiers in rows. The men of the town circled the lawn, collecting baskets and quilts.

A grim-faced lieutenant marched toward the women. He kept his eyes trained on Mrs. Peate and Annie as he addressed the group. "I apologize for the disturbance today. I have the captain's word that everyone responsible for starting the fight will be sent to the stockade." He paused, and Annie noticed the swelling forming around his nose and left eye. "Including me." He looked at the ground then straightened his shoulders in determination. Thrusting his shoulders back, he looked determined to face the worst. "I saw the private adding liquor to Miss Bliss's pitcher of lemonade. Several other men brought liquor with them, against the captain's orders. They also will be punished."

Private Jackson had added liquor to her lemonade? Annie shivered at how close she had come to drinking alcohol. In that case, she was glad for the way the lieutenant had barged in and knocked it away. She nodded her understanding and appreciation.

The women disbanded, joining their husbands to clean the lawn. At the captain's command, the soldiers ran in formation around the perimeter of the lawn behind the church. Jeremiah nodded at the men running in rank. "He'll keep them at it until they're exhausted, and then he'll make them march double time all the way to the fort."

"Does your nose hurt?" The question blurted out of Annie's mouth instead the words of reproach she had imagined earlier or the words of thanksgiving he had earned.

Touching the offending feature, he winced. "It's not broken. I've suffered worse." He dropped his hand back to his side, and he stared at the ground as if looking for encouragement. When at last he lifted his face, pain that had nothing to do with his nose showed in the lines wrinkling his forehead and tugging his mouth into a frown. "An apology can't begin to express my regret about what happened here today. Miss Bliss—Annie—we have failed you. I have failed you."

The man I've called the Bear just apologized? It was time to return that nickname to the cave where it belonged.

Jeremiah looked to the back, where the men began to slow their pace. He belonged back there, accepting the discipline he deserved for starting the fight, for not preventing trouble in the first place. Instead, he stayed rooted to the spot, imprisoned by the kindness of the woman before him.

A soft hand floated against his nose, tracing the path of the broken skin. "Look at me."

He lifted his face and looked into her bluebell-colored eyes, tears rimming the bottom of her irises. "It is I who must offer thanks to you. If you hadn't knocked the glass down, I would have. . ." He followed the path of the swallow pushing down her throat. "I would have drunk it."

He opened his mouth to apologize again. If he had done his job, no one would have brought whiskey to the social.

Her feathery fingers fell against his lips. "Don't apologize. I am thankful that you protected me, as well as anyone else at risk."

Jeremiah didn't agree. If he hadn't agreed to the risky idea of the soldiers mingling with townsfolk, she wouldn't have been in danger. But her faith, her passion, convinced him to try. Hadn't his experience taught him anything at all? Six years ago he thought he could change a woman's heart, and instead, she died in her sin. Perhaps he should be thanking the Lord that no one was seriously hurt today; but there was danger, and some promising young soldiers might lose heart for the military life. He took a step back, the spot where her fingers had touched his lips burning at the separation.

He forced backbone into his words. "Given what happened today, I need to reconsider whether we should continue with the planned activities or not." He turned on his heels before she could protest and crossed the grass to the ranks of soldiers at a pace as fast as their run.

A week later, life at the fort had returned to normal. Jackson spent three nights in the stockade for his role in throwing the first punch; the other culprits spent a single night. The captain had questioned Jeremiah for his side of the events. When he explained about the whiskey flask, the captain relaxed.

The captain called him back today. Jeremiah remained at rigid attention. Although Captain Peate had not sent him to the stockade, Jeremiah still felt responsible for every man who ended up there. Against all his vows to avoid entanglements, he had allowed Miss Bliss—Annie—through his defenses. And look what had happened. He kept his chin up and his back straight, ready to absorb whatever reprimand the captain threw his way.

"At ease, Lieutenant—Jeremiah." The captain sat down and motioned for Jeremiah to do the same. "You have my decision on the incident at the box social. I do not hold you responsible for the brawl. Sit down—I hate looking up at you." Jeremiah accepted the invitation but kept his back straight, only touching the chair at his shoulders.

"Now, concerning the continuing relationship with the community. That is a thornier issue." He glanced at the sheet of paper in front of him, lifted it between thumb and forefinger, and gestured with it to Jeremiah. "Pastor Fairfield has written a letter to me. He suggests postponing the planned events to give both parties a couple of weeks to simmer down. The folks of his church have graciously agreed to give our men a second chance, and I have promised him that the men responsible for the problem will be restricted to the fort. Miss Fairfield and Miss Bliss will be here shortly to discuss the details."

Jeremiah headed for the stable to put his horse away. He rubbed the mare's nose, trying to lasso his thoughts. Although he knew what he must do, he feared his best intentions would disappear the instant he caught a whiff of the smell of white jasmine in Annie's hair.

He was adding extra oats to his horse's feedbag when he heard the stable door open. Mack Jackson stood in the doorway. "Chaplain?"

Love your enemy. . . . This is hard, Lord. "Yes, Private?"

"I know Miss Bliss is here from the church."

Jeremiah stiffened, not wanting to hear whatever he had to say. "You'd best not go near her."

"Oh no, sir. I only wanted you to tell her how sorry I am for the way I behaved. I don't expect her to forgive me. I don't deserve that. But. . ." His voice trailed off, and he shrugged.

Jeremiah narrowed his eyes and stared at the young man through slits. "I will convey your words to Miss Bliss."

Jackson didn't move.

"You are dismissed, soldier!"

Jackson saluted and left.

Jeremiah slowly followed. No use wishing the women wouldn't come. One last look heavenward, and he walked with purpose to the captain's quarters.

The door opened as soon as his knuckles rapped on the door. Annie—Miss Bliss, he reminded himself—hovered in front of him, her face echoing his own uncertainty. Tears spilled out of her eyes, when she hadn't even cried on the day of the box social.

"Oh Lieutenant." She sniffed and dabbed at her eyes with a handkerchief. "How good of you to come."

At the signs of her distress, he wanted nothing more than to comfort her. He settled for holding the back of the chair for her.

On her right, Ruth tipped her teacup in his direction.

A burlap sack lay open at their feet, hues of dark blues and greens peeking at him. Annie had been busy with her knitting needles again. Catching the direction of his glance, she handed him the garment. "This is for you. I wanted you to have it, even if. . .I don't see you again." Her face crumpled, and she began crying again.

Had someone demanded the soldiers no longer go to town? Why hadn't he been informed? "What has happened, Annie?" Her name slipped out of his mouth.

"My brother—Samuel, the one in the army—has been in an accident. His captain contacted us, telling us that his wound is serious. Mama took the next train out. We haven't heard anything since then."

Jeremiah's memory flew back almost seven years, to the day he had arrived home to a house that reeked of death. He leaned forward until he was nose to nose with Annie and the other women faded into the background. "Oh Annie." His hand reached of its own accord, his thumb brushing away the tear hovering beneath her left eyelid.

At his touch, she shuddered briefly. She opened eyes so blue that the whole of the Atlantic Ocean could flow in tears to express her sorrow. "The person who wrote the letter said my brother might die. Lieutenant—Jeremiah—I'm so scared."

When she reached for him, it felt like the most natural thing in the world to take her in his arms and rest her head against his shoulder while her tears drenched his uniform. He wanted to keep her there forever.

Chapter 9

As soon as Gladys reached for the last cookie, Annie grabbed the empty plate and headed for the sink. Footsteps followed her into the kitchen. Annie busied herself with refilling the plate before turning around. Ruth, as she'd expected. Ruth, who had witnessed the humiliating display she had made at Mrs. Peate's home. Annie drew a deep breath and steadied herself to face whatever her friend had to say.

"You can't avoid me forever." The smile that accompanied Ruth's words held no reproach. "Gladys tells us everything that happens with Haydn."

"But that's different." Annie bit her lip.

"How?" Ruth broke one of the ginger cookies in two and handed half to Annie. "Eat this. Maybe the sugar will help you calm down."

Obediently Annie bit into the sweetness, but her insides still churned. "Gladys always said how charming and kind Haydn was. And all I've done is worry about working with the Bear. I made a terrible mistake."

A rustle of skirts alerted Annie to the presence of the others. "Do you mind if we join you?" Gladys asked.

Ruth motioned them in, and Gladys gestured for Birdie to join them. Soon the four women were sitting around the kitchen table, their sewing projects abandoned in favor of a good visit.

"You can trust us, Annie." Birdie spoke first. Annie didn't doubt her. She spoke so little that she wouldn't give away any secrets. "Have you told your mother?"

Annie shook her head. "Not everything." In spite of the low mutter, her friends heard. Heat racing into her face, she met their concerned gazes one by one. "I should have known better. I'm not the right person to do missions. I'm too selfish, too flighty. . ."

"And I'm good enough?" Soft pink tinged Birdie's cheeks. "You all keep telling me I'm a new woman in Christ. I am not the person I used to be." Lifting her chin high, she looked pointedly at Annie. "It's time you listen to yourself. You don't have to be perfect, only forgiven." She hurried on before anyone else could barge in. "And the same is true for your Bear. You've never doubted his faith, only his abrupt ways."

"Have you ever considered that maybe he's the person God wanted you to help all along?" Ruth smiled at Birdie.

Annie dropped her head into her hands so she could hide her face. No one spoke until she looked up again, somewhat composed.

"Even if all of that is true—and you're right—I threw myself at him. No better than a. . ." With an apologetic glance at Birdie, she said, "Well, you know what I mean."

"I was there." Ruth spoke in even tones. "He initiated the intimacy. And if there was anything inappropriate about it, Mrs. Peate would have put an end to it right away. You know that."

Gladys grinned. "From what Ruth has told us, he sounds like a man in love."

"Then why hasn't he contacted me?" Annie shut her eyes against fresh tears. "I'm afraid he's disgusted with me and never wants to see me again."

"You're not done with each other." Ruth grinned. "My father met with the church elders, and they are ready to plan the next social. We need you and the lieutenant to help us plan."

"Oh no, not again." Annie groaned.

"I can do all things. . . ." Birdie quoted Paul's words to the Philippians. "Stop worrying and let God work through you."

Annie looked at her friends, letting her gaze linger on each dear face. "You're not going to give up until I agree, are you?"

"No," Gladys said cheerfully.

"Then I'd better get back to knitting sweaters." She stood, and the others followed.

A week later, Annie kept reminding herself of all the reasons why she had agreed to meet with Mrs. Peate and the lieutenant again. This time Gladys rode with her.

"You're quiet today." Gladys bounced on her horse. Annie knew she would have preferred a sturdy walk, but the fort was too far away. "You have a lot on your mind, between your brother's injury and the lieutenant."

Annie nodded. "I can't do anything for my brother, and I wonder if I'm doing the right thing with the soldiers. All I wanted to do was to make things for young men who were cold and lonely so far from home."

"If it matters, Mr. Keller and Haydn both like the idea very much." Gladys's face softened as it always did when she mentioned her beau. "Haydn says his mother would like to start a similar project at the closest fort. And my mother wonders why the ladies didn't think about doing it long ago. In spite of what happened." Gladys added the last under her breath.

Annie brought her thoughts back to the present. Gladys remained pleasantly quiet while they passed cottonwood trees, their leaves now green instead of white, the rush of winter runoff sounding over the stones in the brook. *He washed me white as snow.* Even here in the open fields green with new wheat, God reminded her of the gift of new life in Christ, the clean slate He gave those who believed.

A meadowlark swooped overhead, its cry raising praise to God, at peace in doing exactly what God had created it to do. After a week's soul searching, Annie knew what God wanted her to do. She just didn't know if she could do it. Even if she wanted to. *Lord, fix my "wants." I will obey You; make me a vessel of Your love.*

The yellow-bellied bird glided through the air and landed on a tree branch. Cocking its head, it chirped at Annie. Such a simple act reminded her of God's promise to love her more than the sparrows of the field.

"It will be all right." Gladys interrupted her thoughts. "You'll see. 'All things work together for good to them who love God.' You know what Paul says. Even when you work with a bear of a man." She chuckled. "Come to think of it, at the beginning Mr. Keller was a bit like a bear waking up from hibernation, hungry and growling."

That almost made Annie laugh. In the distance, she spotted the gates to the fort. "Good. We're almost there." She urged her horse to a slightly faster pace, and they arrived at the fort not much later. The guard was one she had met several times before. What was his name? Ruth would remember, along with a number of pertinent details. He tipped his cap at the two women. "Good morning, Miss Bliss. Lieutenant Arnold informed me you would be visiting Mrs. Peate today with a guest." He swung the gate open.

"Thank you, Private." She gave him her bravest smile and rode in.

"Thank *you*, ma'am, for the socks. They've been most welcome."

His kind words and the beam Gladys directed at Annie helped sugarcoat the fears rumbling through her stomach. This shouldn't be so hard. *I can do all things through Christ which strengtheneth me.*

Jeremiah appeared on the lawn in front of the captain's quarters as they neared. Annie knew the moment he spotted them. A smile spread across his face. He had shaved his chin so that he sported a goatee instead of a beard.

Jeremiah felt the smile forming on his lips. He wanted to call it back when he saw the answering look on Annie's face. Stricken, afraid—of him? His heart constricted in ways he hadn't felt since his fiancée's death.

Annie glanced at her friend and said something Jeremiah couldn't hear before she dismounted and walked with her horse in his direction. "Good afternoon, Lieutenant."

A small smile had taken the place of the frown.

Lieutenant again. How Jeremiah wanted to invite her to call him by his given name again, but he didn't dare ask. Not here, not like this. Instead, he nodded, removing his cap. "Miss Bliss."

Her mouth twisted, but she edged closer to him by a few inches. Her horse snorted, blowing warm air over Jeremiah's suddenly cold hands. He reached in his pocket for a bite of carrot he had set aside for his mare and held out his hand with the treat. While the horse munched, he faced Annie. "How are you today? Any news about your brother?"

"Nothing about Samuel yet." Annie sighed. "But I'm fine. I'm glad I met you out here."

Jeremiah's heart double-timed in his chest. "Is everything all right?" What a ridiculous question to put to the woman he had held in his arms. The hard shell that he had put so much effort into erecting around his heart had shattered, and every question pierced him like a fresh arrow.

Mrs. Peate stood in the doorway. After waving to her, Jeremiah offered Annie his elbow and led her away from the Captain's quarters, granting them as much privacy as was available at the fort. "What's troubling you? Have you changed your mind about helping with the outreach between the fort and the town?" He held his breath. "The men who acted inappropriately the last time will be confined to the fort."

She shook her head. "That's not it at all. I believe. . ." She kept her face toward the ground, where he couldn't read her expression. When at last she looked up, resolution shone in her eyes. "I believe God wants me to speak with Private Jackson. With a chaperone, of course." Her voice sped up. "God wants me to forgive him as He has forgiven me."

Jeremiah blinked against the sense of unreality flooding him. "You wish to speak with Private Jackson?" He repeated her question foolishly, as if he was slow of understanding.

Annie nodded. "And I would like you there as well."

Jeremiah had no answer to Annie's convictions. Not when God was prodding him to do the same. "You shame me, Miss Bliss. When do you want to see him?"

Annie's clear blue eyes searched his face. "Now, if he's available. I don't feel free to make further plans until I have settled this matter."

Jeremiah nodded. "He should be nearby. I'll let Mrs. Peate know we'll be back soon so she won't worry." He pressed her hand, spoke briefly to their hostess, and rejoined Annie. "Come with me." After they took care of the horses, he led Annie to the chapel. "I'll be back with Private Jackson. You should be safe enough here." He smiled ruefully. "Aside from Sundays, I'm almost always alone in our house of worship."

Annie's gaze swept across the room, and she chose a seat on the front row. "I'll be praying."

On the way to find Jackson, Jeremiah wanted to slow his pace. Instead, the Holy Spirit urged him to speed. He spotted Jackson striding away from the barracks. "Private!" Jeremiah shrank at the edge in his voice.

Jackson stopped in his tracks, turned smartly on one heel, and faced Jeremiah. "I was coming to see you, Lieutenant."

That solved one problem, how to explain his sudden reason for seeking out the private. "Come with me to the chapel."

Jackson took a couple of steps away from the open windows of the barracks, where they could speak without fear of being overheard. "I know that Miss Bliss is here again today. I wish to speak with her." Before Jeremiah could form an answer, he rushed on. "To apologize for my behavior the last time we met."

Jeremiah nodded. "That's good, because she wants to see you as well. She is waiting for us in the chapel."

Chapter 10

When Jeremiah opened the door to the chapel, he saw no sign of Annie. Then, with a rustle of skirts, she stood to her feet by the front pew, a serene expression having overtaken the fear etched there earlier. She nodded her thanks to Jeremiah, but she looked directly at Private Jackson.

Rather than walking to the front, Jeremiah remained near the door, where he could see and hear what happened. "Go ahead." He nudged Jackson's back, praying that he was making the right decision.

Jackson walked the aisle with military precision. The uniform he wore today was clean; he had spent as much time on his appearance as he had back on that fateful Saturday. He cleared his throat. "My mama says ladies should go first, but I'm the one who did you wrong, so I figure I better speak up. The captain told us no alcohol would be allowed, but some of the boys. . ." He glanced back at Jeremiah and shrugged his shoulders. "Mainly me, I admit. I didn't see the harm in a small drink or two, and I thought it would help when I was speaking with a woman I never met before. We'd both be more relaxed, see. . ." His voice trailed off.

"If we were both drunk?" Annie's voice held a strong hint of vinegar.

Jackson hung his head. With shoulders hunched over, he lifted it again. "I'm sorry. I did wrong, and maybe I encouraged some of the others to do the same thing. You don't have any reason to forgive me, but I wanted to speak my piece."

At that, Annie smiled, a sweeter smile than anything she had ever sent Jeremiah's way, and jealousy tickled his nerves. Then she smiled at him as well, and his world turned right side up again. "That's why I wanted to speak with you, Private. God reminded me that I need to forgive you. I've already talked with God about it, but I needed to tell you in person. I have already forgiven you."

Jeremiah had shifted his place so that he could see both their faces. The enthusiastic nod of Jackson's head resonated like a great huzzah.

Annie lifted a finger. "But there is one more person you need to apologize to."

Confusion crossed Jackson's face. He nodded at Jeremiah. "The chaplain?"

Annie looked confused for a moment, then her expression cleared. "Perhaps. But I was speaking of God. Have you asked His forgiveness? For what you did at the picnic?" She drew a Bible from the back of the pew on her right. "Have you ever asked Him to forgive you for all the bad things you've done in your life?"

The wooden floor squeaked as Jackson shifted his feet. "Not exactly."

"Do you want to?"

When he nodded, Annie turned a pleading look to Jeremiah. "We have the right man here to help you do that.

I can share what I know, but. . ."

"I guess that's all right."

Annie returned to the first row of seats and knelt. Jackson bent his knees and joined her on her left. Jeremiah joined them on the other side. "You don't need any fancy words, Mack." Calling him by rank or surname seemed inappropriate for a man seeking a relationship with the personal God. "You've already done the hardest part, admitting what you did was wrong. With God, you admit you have done wrong things—sins—many things." He went on, talking about Jesus' death on the cross and the forgiveness God offers to everyone who believes in Him.

Annie joined the conversation. "Do you have any questions?"

"No." Jackson shook his head. "I mean, I've heard you preach about this lots of times. I just never thought I needed to worry about it." He looked a long second into Jeremiah's eyes. "Until now."

"So is this something you want to do?" Jeremiah paused. He always felt he had to add this last bit. "I'm not asking you as Lieutenant Arnold. If you only say the prayer because your superior officer says it's a good idea, it won't go any higher than the ceiling. I'm asking you as your fellow man, another sinner who needs God's grace as much as any other man."

"Yes sir. I know this is what I want to do." Jackson looked between Annie and Jeremiah. "So is this when I pray?"

Annie and Jeremiah nodded as one, and Jackson prayed a sinner's prayer, one more man brought into the family of God.

Tears tumbled from Annie's eyes, and only strict discipline kept Jeremiah's from brimming as well. All of his calling and Annie's mission to befriend soldiers had led to this moment in time.

❧

The soldiers marched into Calico to cheering crowds in honor of Decoration Day. Annie scanned their ranks. Young Private Jackson wasn't among them, even though they had decided the wrongdoers could attend if they wanted to. If the rest of those soldiers were like Mack Jackson, they needed the reminder of God and family more than the others.

Children ran in circles behind the soldiers, boys on bicycles, girls waving streamers. Men who had served in the Civil War, regardless of which side they fought for, carried the stars and stripes. One of the youngest veterans, who would have been only a boy during the fighting, beat a slow drum as they marched, each man's face a study in hidden memories.

Their expressions reminded Annie of Jeremiah. She spotted him, his uniform emphasizing his broad shoulders, at the back of the line. Most of the soldiers under his care were too young to have fought during the civil conflict, but she imagined that chasing rampaging Indians and hunting for criminals also caused a measure of pain. Of course he would reenlist. He must. His calling didn't allow for the same things that other men enjoyed, things like family and a permanent home. A shadow fell across her heart.

Jeremiah had promised Annie two surprises today. She hoped he didn't plan on announcing his reenlistment plans. He had kept himself aloof from her today.

She had no idea what his surprises would bring.

The parade reached the end of Main Street and halted at the town square. A few booths had been set up on the grass. Wanting to keep to their original purpose—to raise money for schoolbooks as well as to reach out to the soldiers—businesses around town had proposed several moneymaking schemes while leaving other things free of charge. Aunt Kate offered free weekly dinners for three months and one of her best lemon custard pies to the highest bidders, while serving free ham and beans to everyone at the fair.

The fort supplied the beverages. Annie joined the line in front of the booth and scanned the square for Jeremiah without success.

"What would you like to drink? Lemonade? Sweet tea? Water?"

Annie studied the sign on the booth. The first glass cost five cents, but the refills were free. "I'll take a glass of sweet tea, please." She dug a nickel out of her reticule and turned to hand it to the soldier behind the table.

She stared at Mack Jackson's face, eyes stone-cold sober. He was dressed in his heavy woolen uniform, and looking unbelievably happy in spite of a slight sheen of sweat on his forehead. "Miss Bliss!"

Annie felt herself answering his wide smile. "It's good to see you again. You look like you're doing well."

"I am, thanks to you and the Lord. And Lieutenant Arnold of course." He glanced behind Annie. "I'd better take care of our guests."

"I'm happy for you." Annie leaned close for one last question. "Do you know where Lieutenant Arnold is? I didn't see where he headed after the parade."

Mack shook his head. "I'll tell him you're looking for him if he comes by here."

Annie thanked him and slipped through the crowd. An equally full crowd gathered in front of Aunt Kate's booth—where she knew Gladys was helping—so she decided to wait. A brief stop at each booth did not produce Jeremiah. His absence surprised her.

She crossed the square, mingling with the crowd, in the direction of the church. People spilled over into the street, and she thought she caught sight of Jeremiah's distinctive form heading toward her from the north, on the road leading out of town. She moved toward him, sliding through gaps in the crowd, until at last she reached the edge. She had a surprise in store for him as well.

Two people accompanied Jeremiah, a man and a woman. She recognized the woman instantly. *Mama. What is she doing back in Calico? With Jeremiah?*

The other man came out of Jeremiah's shadow. Walking with the aid of a crutch, the man dragged his left leg. His gaunt face haunted her memories. He looked like—it couldn't be—her brother Samuel.

She broke into an unladylike run and raced down the nearly empty street, into his waiting arms.

❧

In the past, Jeremiah had done his share of informing relatives of the death of a loved one.

This was the first time he'd taken part in reuniting a wounded soldier with his family. That must account for the warm feeling spreading through his limbs. No, that wasn't the reason. Not if he was honest with himself. If he had learned anything in the last few days and weeks, he couldn't hide behind assumptions and half-truths. Happiness had sped his steps home, but he didn't start smiling until he saw Annie.

If only he could be certain she returned his feelings. She had marched into his life, challenging his faith and his ministry and turning his world upside down. Whether she saw him as a man worthy of love—her love—he didn't know.

Samuel stopped his forward progress and braced himself. Mrs. Bliss stood by his left side, offering her support. Jeremiah retreated behind them. Whatever Annie's feelings toward him, this moment belonged to the Bliss family.

Tears streamed freely from Annie's face as she flung herself into Samuel's arms.

Samuel's face twisted, and he blinked. Jeremiah guessed he was ready to cry, but that would embarrass a young man who already had lost so much. He stepped into the gap. "Captain Peate corresponded with your brother's commanding officer. I received word earlier this week that it was time for him to muster out, and Captain Peate agreed I could escort him and your mother home. So—here we are."

Mrs. Bliss placed her hand on Jeremiah's shoulder, embracing him as part of her family. "The lieutenant has been wonderful. We would have had a hard time making it back without his help." The look she directed in Samuel's direction spoke volumes of love and family. Love Jeremiah had once experienced and had doubted he would ever enjoy again this side of heaven, until he met Annie.

Annie glanced at Samuel's leg but immediately looked up at her brother's face again. "You can tell me about that later." She laid her head on her brother's chest. "I'm so happy you're home. I want to run home with you, but I'm responsible for the dance in the town square." She stepped back. "Everyone would love to see you, but I'm sure you're tired."

"We have a lot of time to catch up with each other. Go ahead and have fun." Samuel smiled at his sister. Annie took a reluctant step in the direction of the square.

"I'll see him safely home," Jeremiah promised.

"After that, promise me you'll come to the social." Annie sounded worried that he wouldn't make it. If only she knew. "I saw Private Jackson at the beverage booth, so I believe I have discovered both your surprises, but I have one of my own."

Jeremiah would have marched double time for a full day to receive another one of her dazzling smiles. "I'll come as soon as I can."

As they neared the Bliss home, Samuel's speed increased to a jagged run, his left leg dragging behind him. He collapsed into the chair in the parlor that Mrs. Bliss readied for him. "Go ahead, Lieutenant. You have business to attend to with my sister."

Jeremiah resisted the temptation to study his reflection in the store window.

Nothing he could do would make him worthy of Annie's beauty. In a deep blue calico dress, a red, white, and blue ribbon attached to her collar, she shone with a patriotic brilliance. He hurried his steps to join the jostling crowds, fiddle music replacing the chatter of the crowd.

However, first he had to attend to his duties as chaplain. He sought out Mack at the beverage stall, which was doing a brisk business. "Lieutenant!" The private grinned. "What would you like? It's on the house." Mack dropped a nickel into the coin jar.

"Lemonade, please. I'm glad to see you doing so well." Jeremiah scanned the crowd, not spotting Annie.

"Miss Bliss was here earlier, looking for you. But I haven't seen her since the dancing started."

"I'll look for her there, then."

He found her at the edge of the dance floor, her dress swaying slightly in time to the music. When she saw Jeremiah, she whispered in the fiddler's ear and walked in Jeremiah's direction.

Annie reached Jeremiah when the music ended. The fiddler addressed the crowd. "This next dance is lady's choice. Gentlemen, await your ladies."

A shy smile skipped across her face. "May I have this dance, Jeremiah?" She extended her hands toward his, inviting him to swing her around in his embrace.

She picked me. "It would be my pleasure." Gathering her close, he led her onto the dance floor. Thanks to long-ago lessons, he slipped into the rhythm easily, and Annie felt natural in his arms. The music ended all too soon. "Can you escape for a moment, or do you have to stay here?"

"I can get away for a few minutes." She accepted his arm as he led her to the only semiprivate spot within reach, near the library. He wanted to pick one of the tulips planted there but left them for others to enjoy. All he had to offer Annie was himself. That would have to be enough.

"Miss Bliss. Annie." He had practiced what he would say at this moment, but now that the time had arrived, he couldn't find the words.

"Yes, Jeremiah?" Her blue eyes invited intimacy.

"The first day you showed up at the fort, you set an earthquake in motion in my life. I know I'm just a used-up soldier, ready to leave the army and see what God has next for me. But you've opened my eyes to what God can do with a willing heart. Do you have room in your heart for someone like me? I promise I will spend my life trying to honor you and love you in the way you deserve, every day, for the rest of your life."

Fresh tears glistened in her eyes. "Jeremiah. People told me you were a bear, but you're a cuddly cub, one who wants to be loved. I would be honored to be that woman—whether you stay in the army or whether God leads you somewhere else." She stepped into his embrace, raising her face to his.

Jeremiah slowly savored the taste of her lips. With God ahead of him and this woman beside him, he could move into the future, free of his past.

A Bride for
the Preacher

by Sally Laity

Dedication

To the valiant souls who braved the hardships
of the Oregon Trail and found love along the way.

Chapter 1

Is that Oregon, sissy?" Eight-year-old Susan pointed ahead. Emma Harris kept pace with their family's wagon as it rumbled and creaked over the bumpy trail in the vast green valley surrounding Chimney Rock. "No, I'm afraid not. We still have a long way to go." She gazed up at the distant vista, then at the aperture that had loomed on the horizon all day like a beckoning finger.

"How long? More than a week? My feet are tired."

Mine, too, Emma wanted to say, but held her tongue. "We'll be making camp here in this valley. Perhaps Papa will let you ride on the seat till we stop."

Her sister's impish face brightened, and she skipped ahead, her blond pigtails bouncing. "Papa. Papa. Can I ride with you?"

"Sure, Pumpkin. You can sit by your pretty mama. She's resting her feet, too."

Emma watched her dad bend down to help his youngest daughter aboard before grasping the traces again.

"I don't think we'll ever, ever get to Oregon," twelve-year-old Deborah muttered, her high-top shoes clomping step for step with Emma's. "And even if we do, I won't have a single friend there. I wish we'd have stayed home in Philadelphia."

"I know," Emma commiserated. "But we'll make new friends once we're settled."

"Think so?" Shaded by the brim of her sunbonnet, eyes the same deep brown as her hair softened with hope.

"Well, we've made new friends already on the train, haven't we? And they'll all be there." Even as she spoke, her gaze focused on Jesse Brewster's wagon, directly in front of their own. He was already making the turn to form the night circle in the green meadow dotted liberally with black-eyed Susans and other late wildflowers. She couldn't spot him from this angle, but the young pastor's poignantly boyish face had been imprinted on her mind since the before-trip assembly in Independence.

Almost as quickly, she began to recognize, without a glance, that commanding voice, which held folks' attention during the rousing Sunday sermons, yet could turn amazingly gentle when singing hymns around late-night campfires or when comforting a whiny child. The tawny hair atop his head curled with wild abandon, and he had the most amazing eyes. . .eyes a deep indigo blue that seemed to see right inside a person's soul. For all his lofty idealism, the parson seemed akin to the romantic heroes Emma had read about in novels.

"At least we'll be camping in a pretty place," Deborah said, her girlish voice drawing Emma out of her musings. "I'll pick Mama a bouquet for the supper table."

Nodding, Emma concentrated once more on the surroundings, admiring the tall limestone landmark that dominated the view. It was the first of several rock formations in a misty semicircle stretching to the west. The morning sun had made them appear ever so grand in the distance; and now, closer up, with the slanting sun behind them, their starkness softened into a breathtaking magenta hue.

One thing she could not deny was the abundance of beautiful scenery since the company had embarked on what her father termed their "Great Adventure." Mama had been far less enthusiastic about leaving their successful city pharmacy and uprooting the family on a whim to go to the unknown. Nevertheless, she dredged up the optimism she'd possessed in her younger years and determined to support the husband she loved. Emma hoped and prayed it wasn't to everyone's folly.

As always, wagon master Rawhide Rawson made the rounds to make sure the prairie schooners were in position. Men, used to the routine, quickly unhitched the oxen teams and saw to the stock, while the women and girls got busy with supper fires.

Emma barely squelched a smile as she noticed Jesse Brewster hard at work tending to his rig, and she wondered which family had invited the handsome minister to share their evening meal this night. As always, the big yellow dog, Barnabas, stayed near his master.

A stone's throw away, newlyweds Dr. Josh Rogers and his wife, Bethany, fussed about their wagon. It seemed they hadn't stopped smiling since Parson Brewster pronounced them husband and wife at the onset of the trip.

"Emma, dear, do quit dawdling," her mother scolded. "Your papa will be hungry when he gets back from looking after the animals."

"Yes, Mama." Dutifully, she removed her bonnet and got out the crates they'd use for chairs during the meal, then retrieved the sturdy tin plates purchased especially for the journey. The fancy china dishes remained packed in a barrel beneath the wagon's bowed canvas cover, along with Papa's medicinal supplies, books, equipment he'd kept from the apothecary, and the trunks filled with lovely dresses they wouldn't wear until they reached their destination. Emma yearned for the day when they would arrive at the journey's end and life would return to normal, with the family settled in a nice house filled with her mother's pretty things. With the miles passing by so slowly, though, she had to agree with Deborah. They'd never get to Oregon.

Gradually, various cooking smells drifted from individual wagons and mingled in a delectable mix that made stomachs growl. Muffled voices carried on the night air as folks gathered to partake of their supper fare, sometimes sharing with other families.

"We must've made a good fifteen miles today," Papa said, taking a healthy bite of fried rabbit leg from the creature he'd shot just before they'd started down into the valley. "Nary a mishap in the company since sunup yesterday. That must be a good sign."

"I hope so, Ambrose," Mama said, "for all our sakes. I fear the worst part of the journey is yet to come."

He gave her knee a comforting pat. "We'll just have to trust the Lord, Nettie, like young Pastor Brewster says. Trust the Lord and help each other along the way. Can't go wrong with that kind of advice. And if trouble happens, we'll deal with it the best we can."

Emma's ears perked up at the mention of the minister.

"Will we get to Oregon next week?" Susan asked, scraping the last bit of beans on her plate onto her spoon.

"No, Pumpkin. Not quite. We all have to be patient awhile longer."

She sighed, then gave an unconcerned shrug, and drained the remains of the water in her cup.

From across the grassy circle came the sound of Mr. Green's fiddle, and as a flute and a guitar joined in with the lively tune, folks began clearing away supper things and preparing for the evening's festivities.

"I'll wash the dishes," Emma offered.

"Wouldn't you and Deborah rather join the other young people?" her mother asked. "They seem to have such a grand time singing and dancing."

"Deborah can go if she wants, but I was hoping to read for a while before it gets too dark."

"As you wish, dear," Mama said, a dubious frown knitting the fine brows beneath her light brown hair. "But I do think you'd enjoy the trip better if you'd join in a little more. Oh, there's Idabelle. She's been wanting my recipe for camp bread." She waved to the other ladies, who were gravitating toward the cluster of people already enjoying the music. Then, she turned and headed toward them, her proper posture making her slight figure look too thin.

Papa settled back to watch after her. "Always was a pretty little thing, your mama. I love the way those hazel eyes of hers turn colors with whatever dress she has on. She's been a good helpmeet, too. I hope I'm not doing wrong, dragging the lot of you out West."

"I hear it's beautiful there," Emma said consolingly, rinsing each of their plates. "I'm sure you'll have a fine new business going in no time."

"Hope so. Well"—he clapped his palms on his knees and stood—"guess I'll go get in on the singing. Sure you won't tag along?"

She shook her head. "I'd rather not. Next time, perhaps." But as he ambled away, Emma couldn't help wishing he'd have pressured her to go. She did like the songs. . .she just didn't feel at ease going over there and entering a crowd that had already gathered. She'd always felt more at home with books. Still, without forethought, her gaze scanned the gathering, trying to pick out Jesse Brewster. And trying to see which of the other girls was sidling up to him.

⌇

Jesse stroked Barney's golden fur as they sat on the grass near the center of the camp, listening to the fiddle's cheerful tune. Small cooking fires slowly died out on the perimeter of the circle while womenfolk tidied up after the meal. Some were already laying out bedrolls under their wagons.

Must be nice, he surmised, *having a wife to look after life's little comforts*. But since his plans in that direction had met such a doleful end, it was obvious that

God wanted him to concentrate on his mission. Probably wouldn't be much of a life for a woman anyway, saddled with the kids at home while her husband was off evangelizing sparsely settled Oregon for who knew how long at a time. Certainly none of the young women in this company seemed suited to such an existence. His gaze meandered to Miss Lavinia Millberg, who sat, as always, attired in enough frills to drown a body. She seemed strangely out of place in this company, and she likely would have been happier if she had remained back in the comfort of the home she and her family had left. The other gals might be a bit more adventurous; but so far, they all stayed pretty much together in cheery calico clusters, giggling, chatting, and passing a dime novel around.

That is, all but one...

"A right purty night," wiry Frank Barnes commented as he eased himself down beside Jesse, a whittling stick in hand.

"Sure is."

"Thought I'd find me a quiet spot while the wife gets the baby settled for the night. Picked a fine time for cuttin' teeth, that young'un. Spent most of the day fussin' and frettin'."

"This, too, shall pass," Jesse quipped with a mischievous smile.

"And soon, I hope. It gets to wearin' a body out, and that's a fact."

"Maybe Doc Rogers has something to ease her through it."

"Could be. I'll ask him later." The farmer began making short strokes with his whittling knife. "That was a fine sermon you preached at us yesterday, Parson. Fine, fine sermon."

"Thanks. I'm glad you enjoyed it. I'm thinking of continuing on with the same theme this coming Sunday. We can all learn a lot from the life of King David."

"That's a fact. A pity he made such a mess of a good thing, though, with that wanderin' eye of his."

"I couldn't agree more. The Bible says that he who finds a wife finds a good thing...but I know the Lord didn't mean for us to look in the wrong places to do it."

"I expect you'll be lookin' for a gal of your own. Mebbe right here on this train."

"Maybe. I'm not in a hurry, though." Even as he spoke, Jesse's thoughts insisted on straying across the way to Emma Harris. Strange, how she avoided so many of the evening gatherings. She didn't give an impression of unfriendliness, but rather shyness. She did attend the Sunday services with her family and sometimes walked with some of the other gals her age along the trek. But more often than not, she kept to herself or stayed near her mother and younger sisters, usually with her nose buried in what must be some of her pharmacist father's big, heavy-looking books.

Jesse saw no reason to divulge to Mr. Barnes how often his thoughts revolved around the dark-haired Emma with her serious nature and deep brown eyes. Or how often he took a backward glance toward her family's wagon just to make sure she was still there. Jesse didn't understand it himself, since the young woman never showed a spark of interest or encouragement. But she did make it hard for him to rein in his mental ramblings and concentrate on the subject of his next sermon. Even as he chided himself for being distracted yet again, he saw Emma hop down from the family wagon and roll out the bedding she'd held in her arm. Beside him, Barnabas yawned and settled his muzzle down on his forepaws. "I'm with you, old boy," Jesse muttered. "It's been a long day. Time to turn in." Rising, he gave a parting wave to Mr. Barnes and the others nearby and headed for his rig, where no one else had to be looked after, and the sleeping mat remained in readiness. Barney stretched and slowly got up, then pattered after his master, who cast one last questioning look at the Harris wagon before climbing into his own.

Bright and early after breakfast the next morning, the prairie schooners resumed the westward journey, holding to a trail along the gently sloping land rising from the marshy meadow. Emma watched the ever-changing sunlight splay delectable shades of ochre and soft pink across the ridge of knobby outcroppings beyond Chimney Rock, and she wondered where this night would find them.

When she tired of the view, she opened a book of poetry from Papa's library and pondered the lovely phrases and thoughts as she walked. Beside her, Susan and Deborah skipped along, unmindful of the dust stirred up by the wagons ahead. They gathered wildflowers for Mama, who walked with one of the other women today.

"Oh, look, sissy," Susan called out. "A cross of stones."

Glancing up from her book, Emma saw the small but distinct grave marker mostly hidden by the tall grasses alongside the path. "Yes, well, leave it be." Normally a person who died along the way was buried right in the trail itself, leaving no mark to be discovered by scavenging Indians or marauding wolves. She saw no sense in alarming her younger sisters over what was obviously a small child's resting place. Expelling a sad breath, Emma tried to concentrate on reading again, but a vision of some young mother grieving over an unspeakable loss kept getting in the way. She swallowed and slipped the book into her skirt pocket.

The nooning stop seemed far too short, but Rawhide wanted to press on quickly, hoping to make Scott's Bluff by nightfall.

After the long, hard day of steady travel, the company did just that. From a distance of four or five miles away, what had appeared to be nothing more than a huge blue mound in the wide open country began to resemble a medieval castle. And as they came closer, its contortion of weathered towers, parapets, and gulches gradually defined themselves, rising up majestically from the beautiful valley floor.

Papa's grip on the traces tightened as his rig crawled single file after the others through knoll-filled Mitchell Pass. Deep ruts carved by prior westbound wagons added to the roughness of the route closest to the North Platte. "According to Rawhide, we're about a third of the way to Oregon, at this point," Papa called cheerfully over his shoulder when they'd finished navigating the pass.

Emma's heart sank. She'd been hoping they'd gone much farther by now.

Deborah put words to that thought. "You mean, we have to go as far as we've traveled now two more whole times?"

"Yes, sweetie, we do. But we'll get there. You'll see."

"Then I hope you and Mama brought lots more shoes for us."

He chuckled and gave her a wink.

By the time the wagons reached a cold spring and circled for the night, barely any daylight remained. The two younger girls could scarcely hold their heads up to eat. Emma herself struggled to stay awake long enough to help clean up after the meal. The whole camp seemed more subdued. No one ventured out to sing and make music.

Just as well, Emma decided. Another long day like this one, and she'd be dead on her feet.

The trail boss rode up as the bedrolls were being unfurled. "How're you folks doin'?"

"Just fine," Papa said. "A mite weary, though."

"Just like I figured," Rawhide replied. "Thought we'd rest a day here, do some repairs, and the like."

"That's the best news we've had all day," Papa said.

"Well, just passin' the word, is all. There's a harder pull comin' up." The wiry man nodded, touched the brim of his hat, and nudged his mount forward.

Feeling considerably cheered, Emma watched him ride toward the remaining wagons, then climbed aboard the rig to change into her sleeping clothes. A whole day to rest. . .and not even a Sunday.

She glanced to the pastor's wagon, wondering if it would be improper to offer to do his laundry tomorrow. It would be a proper exchange, considering all the sermons he'd prepared on the train's behalf. . .the Christian thing to do.

Chapter 2

Put the bedding out to dry, will you, dear?" Mama asked after breakfast. "It's still damp from last night's shower."

"Yes, Mama." Emma hefted the bundle of blankets and pillows they had brought into the wagon at the onset of rain. After placing it near the seat, she hopped down and reached up to retrieve it.

A shadow fell across her arm...one that strongly resembled the curly-haired pastor. "Need any help, Miss Emma?" he asked in that pleasant, manly voice.

Hoping her skirts had kept her modest when she'd jumped to the ground in such unladylike fashion, she struggled to catch her breath. "I–I think I can manage. Thank you."

"Just seems neighborly to ask, is all." Jesse Brewster's indigo eyes warmed as a smile spread across his lips. "I reckon lots of folks had their sleep rudely interrupted when that storm blew over us."

"Indeed." Having rarely been in such close proximity to the handsome minister without the benefit of her parents' presence, Emma found herself staring at his strong features and noting how much bluer his eyes looked against the cobalt shirt he had on. And how the green and tan stripes in his vest didn't quite go with the brown-and-black-checked pattern of his brown trousers. Why, the poor man needed a wife to help him coordinate his wardrobe, if nothing else!

A warm flush enveloped her face, and she redirected her gaze elsewhere. After all, though he was handsome enough to turn a girl's head and possessive of a compelling personality, the last thing on her mind was getting married. Particularly to a minister. She had far grander aspirations for herself.

All around the camp, other folks who'd been sleeping beneath their wagons when the sudden shower hit also set about drying bedding. Blankets in a rainbow of hues lay strewn across the brush like patches in a crazy quilt. A few adorned wagon wheels and hitches, any place that would catch the breeze.

"We missed you at the evening gathering last night," Reverend Brewster said casually, drawing her attention back to him.

"I...was busy. Reading." With no idea why she'd elaborated, Emma shook out two of the heavier coverlets and draped each over a wheel, then unfolded the lighter blankets to spread out over desert sage.

"I've often noticed you reading a book," he remarked. "Even when the train is in motion. Is it something you find particularly interesting? Or do you just read to pass the time?" Moving nearer as she struggled to untangle one of the sheets, he peeled off two of the corners and helped her lay it out over a boulder, then did the same with the last one as well.

"Thank you," she murmured. As she straightened to her full height, her hands suddenly seemed far too empty. She rested one on her hip to occupy it. "Mostly I read my father's books, on medications and herbs and things."

"A lot of folks would find that pretty dull reading."

The mischievous twinkle in his eyes put Emma on the defensive. "It isn't to me. I find it fascinating, learning about plants or concoctions that can help heal sickness. God put a lot of thought into creating this world."

"I quite agree, Miss Emma. I meant no disrespect," he said gently. "It's just that most of the other young women in the company who enjoy books choose lighter fare. Novels and the like."

His explanation smoothed her ruffled feathers. "I read novels sometimes," she confessed. "James Fenimore Cooper is my favorite."

"Ah. The adventuresome type."

"And I also enjoy studying the Scriptures," she added, lest he think she sought only worldly pursuits. For some reason, that seemed important.

He gave an amused nod. "Always a wise choice."

Neither spoke for a moment. Emma, never accomplished at making small conversation, racked her brain trying to think of something to say.

Barnabas ambled over to them just then, saving her the trouble. The minister smiled and bent to stroke him behind the ears. "What have you been up to, Barney, old fella?"

"He's a really nice dog," Emma said, cringing at her lack of brilliance. "Nice and quiet."

"Yeah, he's a pretty good boy," Reverend Brewster returned. "Lots of company." He glanced at her as he spoke, and the warmth in his eyes—along with something she could not define—made her heart skip a beat.

"Would you like—I mean, Mama and I will be doing some laundry while we're stopped here today. Is there anything we might wash for you?"

"Mighty kind of you to offer," he said, dazzling her with an incredible smile that deepened the laugh creases alongside his mouth. "But I pretty much took care of it at our last stop."

"Well, I'd best get to the chores," she blurted, turning to join her mother aboard the wagon.

"Will we see you at the evening gathering?" he asked.

Emma paused, one hand grasping the edge of the wagon frame. "Perhaps."

He touched the brim of his hat with his thumb and forefinger. "Miss Emma."

"Reverend." With a small smile, she climbed up into the rig.

Her mother, however, was nowhere to be seen. No wonder she hadn't come out to take part in the conversation. And to think the minister had actually come over and helped put the bedding out to dry! Emma placed a hand over her heart to calm its erratic beating. . .though why he should affect her so eluded her.

An hour later found her knee-deep in the river with some of the other young women of the company washing clothes. She and her sisters each had two sturdy cotton dresses for travel. . .one to wear, the other to wash; and despite the aprons and pinafores worn to protect them, constant travel amid dust and dirt took its toll on the hems. Particularly Susan's. The girl was forever stooping to pick flowers or examine something curious along the way. Emma gave particular attention to her youngest sister's dress, soaping each section of the bottom edge and rubbing it between the knuckles of both hands to get out the grime.

"I declare," Bethany Rogers said as she and her sister-in-law, Penny, labored at the same task a few feet from Emma. "Keeping Josh in white shirts is going to occupy a lot of my time." She brushed a lock of damp brown hair from her eyes with her wrist, then continued working soapsuds through the garment.

"I suppose doctors are a lot like ministers," Emma replied, "always feeling they must dress properly when they perform their duties."

The young bride paused with a dreamy smile. "And I do want him to look the part. Truly I do. But I fear we're fighting a losing battle, what with the constant dust along the trail."

"I wouldn't worry overmuch about that," blue-eyed Penny chimed in, tucking stray blond hairs behind an ear. "I'm sure my brother understands." She rinsed several pairs of sturdy stockings in the steady current, then squeezed them out.

Straightening her spine to ease a kink, Emma spied Reverend Brewster strolling along the river with snooty Lavinia Millberg. Though Emma had no designs on the man herself, she believed he at least deserved a woman who'd be an asset in his vocation. It peeved her to watch the way plump Lavinia fawned over him, batting those silly eyelashes and giggling after some of his remarks. The girl never had to soil her lily-white hands with something as mundane as laundry, since the family's Irish maid got stuck with all the drudgery.

Emma wrung excess water from the last of the dresses and underthings with more force than necessary, then looped them over an arm. "Looks like I'm finished. See you all after a while."

"Yes, the celebration feast this evening should be great fun," golden-haired Megan Crawford chimed in. "The men shot some antelope today. When I left the wagon, my sister-in-law was already baking a cake."

Hearing the other girls embark on a new, livelier topic as she left, Emma couldn't help but wonder if her presence had dampened their spirits. Then again, she reminded herself, Bethany and Penny had been friends even before Bethany's marriage to Penny's brother made them sisters-in-law. It was probably natural she felt the outsider. Small comfort, but it helped a little as Emma hung the clean dresses on a clothesline strung between the wagon wheels. Still, she couldn't help casting a curious glance back at the river and the girls who chatted so amiably.

She had observed Bethany and Doc Rogers growing closer since their wedding in Independence, noting the way their shared smiles would bring a faint blush to Bethany's cheeks. Emma wondered what it must be like to spend one's entire life with one special person. Not that she believed that would ever happen for her, since her mind had been set forever on becoming a doctor. . .or if that dream proved impossible, a nurse. Marriage might agree with some folks, but she wouldn't settle for only that. Not if she could accomplish something better with her life, something that counted.

Releasing a pent-up breath, she climbed aboard the wagon to check for any other chores needing to be done. Finding none, she settled down with a book instead.

The whole company seemed in joyful spirits as they partook of a wondrous array of food that evening. In Jesse's opinion, the women had outdone themselves. He couldn't remember when he'd last seen such an abundance of delectable fare. Returning to the makeshift tables holding platters of roast antelope, stuffed sage hens, beans, stewed vegetables, biscuits, breads, and a variety of desserts, he filled his plate for the second time.

"Pretty tasty, eh, Reverend?" Ambrose Harris said, his graying mustache twitching into a smile as he helped himself to some browned potatoes.

"Sure is. It's truly amazing what the ladies can do with Dutch ovens, open fires, and deep pits. Seems they get better the farther along we are."

The pharmacist jutted his chin toward one of the baking pans. "Try some of my wife's potpie. It's her specialty."

"Don't mind if I do." Dishing out a generous portion, Jesse sampled it. "Say, that really is good. I'll have to give Mrs. Harris my compliments." As he ate, he turned and let his gaze skim the clusters of chatting travelers seated on the grass or on barrels and crates, while they ate and visited with one another. "I've enjoyed getting to know you and your wife along this route. And those three lively daughters of yours must be great company for the two of you."

His chest puffed out a bit. "That they are. Of course, Emma, our oldest, is as happy with her nose buried in a book as she is talking. She's read about half my library already—and I'm talking pharmaceutical journals and medical texts, for the most part. But the other two keep us hopping. Our little Susie seems to be the daring one, always chasing off after butterflies or baby rabbits."

Jesse gave a half smile. He would have liked to ask a few more pertinent questions about Emma, but thought it prudent to refrain. He easily picked her out in the crowd, standing with her mother and some of the other ladies across the circle. Her sable hair, loosed from the pins and sunbonnet that normally held it captive, hung to her shoulder blades in soft waves, glazed by the setting sun. It was hard to drag his attention away from the fetching sight.

She looked his way just then, and their gazes held for a moment before she smiled shyly and lowered her lashes.

When everyone finished the main courses, interest centered on the sweet treats the women had labored over most of the afternoon. A few ladies tended the desserts, slicing pies and cakes and doling them out. Jesse was more than delighted to discover Emma among them and quickly moved to her line.

"That apple pie looks mighty good, Miss Emma," he said, stepping up when his turn came.

"I hope you enjoy it, Reverend," she said, a reserved smile softening her brown eyes.

"Did you make it?"

"No, it's my mother's. I had other chores today."

"Well, thank you just the same. I'm sure it'll be delicious." A glance over his shoulder revealed no one behind him, so Jesse saw no need to move on. He cleared his throat. "The music and square dancing will start soon. Will you be staying around to join in?"

She shrugged a shoulder and grimaced as her gaze moved beyond him to where the other young people were gravitating toward each other. "I've never been much good at it."

"But it's not all dancing, as you know. You've heard us singing all those favorite songs and hymns, I'm sure."

A doubtful expression appeared, then vanished as quickly, and he plunged bravely onward. "What I'm really hoping is that you might consider coming for a stroll. With me, I mean, if you weren't planning to stay around to sing. It's a wonderful evening."

This time, something entirely different clouded her eyes. He couldn't determine whether it was reluctance or apprehension.

"It's very nice of you to ask," she said softly, "but I'm afraid I'm not much company."

"Why don't you let me be the judge of that?" he countered. "You don't even have to talk, if you don't want to. I can do enough of that for both of us. . .and Barney will tag along, of course."

When her demeanor eased a fraction, he could see he was making a little progress. "I'm a pretty decent guy," he coaxed, with a less-than-serious grin.

It brought an answering smile from Emma. She glanced around at the people still eating. "I'll have to help clean up when everyone's through. But after that I'm free. . .if you don't mind waiting."

"Not at all, Miss Emma," he said. "I'll call back in a while, then." Pie in hand, he headed toward the large campfire that dominated the center of the wagons' circle, where the men with instruments were already gathering and tuning up.

⌒∽⌒

Emma watched the tall, lanky minister stride away, the evening breeze ruffling his unruly curls. She'd admired him since Independence, but since she rarely attended the company get-togethers, the longest she'd seen of him at one time were the occasions he preached the Sunday sermons. For all his lack of wardrobe sense on travel days, no one could fault him when performing his duties in his black suit and fairly crisp white shirt.

And she liked his mind, the way he put his thoughts together when explaining particular scripture passages. Back at home in Philadelphia, her parents had led evening devotions when the family gathered around the supper table, and often Papa would put forth questions that made one think. Sadly, that practice fell by the wayside since taking to the westward trail, because of weariness and other concerns. It might be rather interesting to hear what Jesse Brewster had to say apart from his weekly sermons.

The problem would be making sure he did all the talking. No sense in proving to him what a dolt she was or how little she had to talk about.

On the other hand, it might be better all the way around if he did discover how truly dull she was, Emma rationalized. Then he'd leave her be.

But somehow that thought was not quite as comforting as she'd expected.

All too soon, the last appetite was sated and no one made another trip to the food tables. The leftovers and desserts were collected by the various ladies who'd made them and the makeshift tables taken down and stowed. Then the women drifted over to where folks were dancing to a lively tune.

After carrying the remains of the food belonging to her family back to the wagon, Emma plucked her woolen shawl and went to the front to climb down.

"Allow me," Jesse Brewster offered, reaching up to help her.

Emma tamped down her nervousness and leaned into his hands, pleased when he respectfully set her down as if she weighed no more than a feather.

"I'm glad you agreed to come walking," he said, helping her to adjust the shawl about her shoulders.

She smiled her thanks. "As you said, it's a lovely evening. And, Barnabas," she crooned softly, venturing a friendly pat on the dog's head, "it's nice to have your company."

He licked her hand and plodded along beside them.

"You have a wonderful family," the minister began. "I've grown to respect and admire your father immensely during this trip. He's always the first to volunteer help when someone needs it. And your mother seems to offer great comfort and advice to the mothers with young children. They all speak highly of her."

"Thank you. Mama wasn't exactly eager for this experience, but she made up her mind to make the best of it." She paused. "Did you. . .leave your family behind when you decided to go out West?"

He shook his head. "I've been on my own for five years or so now. My ma died when I was about the same age as your baby sister. My pa passed on ten years later. A cholera outbreak."

"I'm sorry to hear that."

"Thanks. But I'm carrying out his wishes. He always wanted me to be a preacher. Thing was, I think he envisioned me pastoring a great church. But I felt called to go where new churches were needed to be founded, instead of staying in Ohio, where there's already an abundance."

"I'm sure you'll establish a fine church in time."

"That remains to be seen." He paused. "What are your hopes for the future, Miss Emma. . .if you don't mind my asking?"

She thought for a few moments as they strolled the dim perimeter of the camp, the strains of music drifting toward them on the night air. "If I had my dearest wish, it would be to become a doctor and help people. But Papa says women doctors will never be in much demand."

"I'm not too sure I'd agree with that. Times are changing. Why, back in Ohio, women are admitted to the college program at Oberlin College on an equal basis with men. And I seem to recall reading in the newspaper a couple years ago about a woman in New York who earned a medical degree."

Emma couldn't repress a sigh. "But that's just it. Ohio. New York. The medical schools are back East. And where we're heading couldn't be farther away from them. What hope do I have, really, of attending college? My dream will probably always be just that."

He didn't respond immediately. "Did you ever consider the possibility that God might have other plans for you?"

Stopping in her tracks, she eyed him. "So this is why you invited me to go for a stroll? So you could preach to me?"

"No, not at all," he returned. "I'm merely making conversation. I had no ulterior motives."

His kind tone immediately filled her with remorse. "Forgive me," she said miserably. "Too often I jump to the wrong conclusions. I told you I wasn't very good company."

"And I beg to differ. I'm enjoying our walk and getting to know you a little. I'll pray that God will make His perfect will known to you, and that if it's His plan for you to become a part of the medical field in the future, He'll make a way for you to do so."

"Would you really do that?"

"Of course. What are friends for, if not to help each other achieve our dreams?"

She had no answer and was still a little stunned that he hadn't tried to squelch her hopes. Maybe it wouldn't be so. . . lonely. . .traveling these endless miles, knowing he was praying for her happiness. And maybe going to Oregon didn't seem so bleak a prospect now, if he truly intended to become her friend.

Noticing they'd reached her wagon, Emma turned to him with a small smile. "Thank you for the invitation. It was. . .nice talking to you, Pastor Brewster."

"My friends call me Jesse," he said quietly. "I'd be honored to count you among them, if I may."

It was a simple request. One she saw no reason to refuse. "You may. . .but only if you drop the 'miss.'"

He smiled.

"Good night, Jesse."

"Good night, Emma. Sleep well."

She accepted his assistance to climb aboard, then lingered just out of sight to watch as he and Barnabas strode to his rig.

The rest of the family had yet to return from the festivities, and for that she was grateful. There seemed so much to think about. While she gathered the bedrolls and laid them out beneath the wagon in preparation for the night, she pondered the interesting conversation with Jesse Brewster.

She had admired him since the first day she'd seen him. She liked his mind and his sermons. But something told her he was far more than just a handsome young minister and that it was going to be really nice having him for a friend. . .if nothing more.

Chapter 3

After leaving the rough terrain around Scott's Bluff, it pleased Susan and Deborah to no end when the wagons meandered past Kiowa and Horse Creeks, each of which had banks bright with sunflowers and patches of lavender daisies.

"Won't Mama be surprised at our nooning stop today," the younger girl said, while she and her sister darted to and fro adding to the colorful bouquets clutched in their hands.

"I'm sure she will," Emma said. "Please try not to get dirt from the stems on your dresses and pinafores, though. They're wearing out just from being scrubbed clean."

"Yes, Mother," they singsonged in unison. But paying little heed to their older sister, they dashed toward another grouping of wildflowers.

"I saw them first," Susan hollered.

"Oh, pshaw, there's plenty for both of us," Deborah countered, her longer legs easily outdistancing her sibling's. The two were soon joined by Barnabas, who obviously knew a game when he saw one.

Emma smiled despite herself and stepped around a small velvet-gray sage bush while watching the girls romping with Jesse's dog.

The sight brought thoughts of last night's visit with the minister, and she wondered if it had taken him as long to fall asleep as it had her. She glanced ahead, but could not see him for the canvas top of his rig.

Many of the men now walked alongside the wagons, cracking bullwhips as the oxen labored over the sandy, climbing trail, raising more than the usual amount of dust. After a few hours, Emma no longer found sage an oddity. It grew in abundance, seemingly everywhere. Panting from the effort of hiking the uphill grade, she had a deep foreboding that the easy days had come to an end, and the trail would now begin to exact its toll on animals and people alike. This theory proved true when she noticed a weathered trunk half-buried by sand alongside the path and, beyond that, a broken rocking chair lying on the ground at a cockeyed angle, as if someone had tossed it there in passing.

She glanced at her family's wagon and envisioned the cargo inside. . .the ornate wooden chests full of pretty dresses and fancy dishes, Papa's books, equipment from his store. Already the oxen strained against the yokes as they plodded along the incline, tails switching periodically at flies. Would the terrain grow continually steeper until her parents, too, had to begin to discard belongings one by one? And if so, what would be left to start their new life in Oregon? Unable to consider the ominous possibility, she took a small book on herbs and plants from her skirt pocket and tried to focus on a more pleasant subject.

When they finally made camp at the end of the long day, folks seemed more eager to eat and turn in than to spend a time singing. But after supper, strains of quiet music drifted from the various wagons as the women in the company settled young children down for the night and the men examined their conveyances for needed repairs.

"I wonder if we even made fifteen miles today," Papa said on a yawn. "And this place has the poorest grass we've seen so far. Hope the cattle find enough to graze on."

"I'm sure they'll do fine," Mama said optimistically, but her troubled frown did not ease in the slightest.

"We should reach Fort Laramie in a couple days," he continued. "We'll be able to stock up on some supplies there."

"Splendid. Maybe I'll post a letter back home...I mean, to Myrtle Cromwell," she quickly corrected. "She must be wondering how we're faring on the trip."

The reminder of their former next-door neighbor made Emma feel a pang of homesickness for Philadelphia and all its brick houses and conveniences she had taken for granted. Maybe she'd write to her own best friend also. Likely she'd never see Cynthia Gardner again in this lifetime. That heavy thought pressed the air from her lungs as she put the freshly washed plates and utensils away for morning.

Before getting into her bedroll, she sought a moment of privacy behind one of the larger sage bushes, then returned to the wagon, where she found her two younger siblings already sound asleep.

"Another nice evening," Jesse commented, ambling over to her, his hands in his pockets. "Pretty tough walk today, though. You must be tired."

"About the most tired I've been since Independence," Emma admitted.

"How are you at handling a team of oxen?"

"I beg your pardon?"

Jesse shrugged a shoulder self-consciously. "I was just thinking that maybe I could swap with you from time to time. You could drive my rig, and I could walk."

The suggestion rendered Emma speechless for several seconds before she found her voice. "Actually, I've managed our team quite well, the few times Papa's encouraged me to take over. He felt that Mama and I should know what to do in case of sickness or...whatever."

"Well then, what do you think of my idea? After all, it would spell my oxen, too. You're a bit lighter than I am."

"I'll consider it, Jesse. Thank you."

"You're most kindly welcome. Just being a friend. One who won't keep you any longer, since I know you're bone weary. Good night, Emma. Sleep well."

"You, too. Good night." She watched after him as his long strides took him away. This new friendship with the pastor was growing on her quite rapidly. He would make some fortunate woman a thoughtful husband one day...assuming, of course, the gal was partial to ministers.

The company lingered at camp the following morning for their usual Sunday service. Emma casually spread out a blanket a little closer to the makeshift pulpit than she had on previous occasions. She and her family took seats while other folks gathered nearby on crates or logs or quilts.

Jesse, in his black preaching suit, stepped to the front, his frayed Bible tucked under his arm. "Let us bow in prayer," he said, then paused briefly. "Our dear heavenly Father, we do thank Thee for this new day. And we thank Thee most humbly for Thy great kindness in our travels, for keeping us safe, healing our sicknesses, and giving us strength for the daily journey. We ask that we may be conscious of Thy presence every step of the way, that we might serve Thee faithfully. These things we ask in the name of Thy dear Son, Jesus. Amen."

His keen gaze surveyed the little flock of worshipers, then gentled with a smile. "Let's begin our service this Lord's Day by singing 'Rock of Ages.'" He gestured to the men with instruments, who chose a common chord and played a short introduction before the others joined in:

"Rock of ages, cleft for me, let me hide myself in Thee. . . ."

Thankful that nothing horrid had befallen her family thus far, Emma concentrated on the lyrics and sang from her heart, appreciating the harmonious blend of voices through the remaining stanzas of the hymn. She couldn't help but note how pleasantly Jesse's strong, clear tenor fell on her ears.

"This morning," he said, opening his Bible after the final note, "I thought we'd look once again at the life of David—a man whom the Bible describes, in First Samuel chapter thirteen and again in Acts chapter thirteen, as a man after God's own heart. We know him from many angles: shepherd, poet, psalm-writer, killer of giants, king, and lastly, ancestor of our Lord. Yet along with those impressive qualifications, we find that he had obvious flaws as well. Those of liar, betrayer, adulterer, and murderer.

"Strange, isn't it, how those two lists could pertain to one individual? Yet, could it be that David was a picture of all of us? After all, we each have our good points. But we also have our flaws. We might not have made the choices David did, but who among us has not disappointed God and made wrong decisions we later deeply regretted? Fortunately for us, the Lord has not made all of our failures known to the world."

"Amen, Brother," one of the listeners said.

Jesse nodded and continued. "So how can it be that the Bible holds David up as an example to us? Let me refer once again to the passage in Acts where it states, 'I have found David, the son of Jesse, a man after mine own heart, *which shall fulfil all my will.*' The last phrase must certainly be the key. David, though he sometimes failed, was quick to confess his sin and turn back to God, eager to do His will. Perhaps that is why we remember him and respect him for his godliness. He wanted more than anything to honor God, to do His will. Not many of us will achieve the same level of greatness he did, but we all share that weak, prone-to-sin side."

The simple, yet profound way Jesse preached drew Emma right in. She hung on to his every word as he spoke, taking the concepts to heart, thinking of her own weaknesses. All too aware of areas in her own life that did not please God, she determined to be more conscious of her words and actions in the future.

"So let us close in prayer," the pastor said at last, his voice cutting across her musings. "Dear Lord, help us to be more like Christ, to serve and honor Thee with our lives. Be with us for the remainder of this day as we again take up our westward journey. We ask these things in His holy name, amen."

After the midday meal, Jesse encouraged Emma to drive his wagon, while he walked alongside. She noted the rig's lighter feel almost at once. Obviously the minister had fewer belongings to weigh it down, and his oxen didn't appear to be laboring quite as intently as most of the others.

When he lagged behind to chat with the men driving the cattle, she chanced a look inside the conveyance and found it surprisingly neat. Other than the typical barrels of foodstuffs and a few crates holding books, his sleeping pallet occupied most of the floor, and some articles of clothing hung on nails about the frame. Since she'd half expected to find it in total disarray, her appreciation for him went up another notch.

Two days later, the welcome sight of Fort Laramie, in a hollow near the mouth of the Laramie River, elevated everyone's spirits. The women immediately went into a frenzy of brushing dust from their dresses, tidying their hair, and making sure their children looked presentable. Then the wagons forded the swift-flowing river at an easy crossing point north of the fort.

The long, low wooden buildings comprising the bastion stretched out in a large circle, within a hollow surrounded by high bluffs dark with cedar trees. A sentry in the blockhouse above the entrance raised a big wooden gate to allow the train to enter.

Emma swallowed nervously at the sight of Indian teepees scattered about the outer perimeter, especially when some red-skinned individuals rose to their feet watching the wagons approach.

"Girls," Papa said, "you'd best climb aboard, just to be safe. Rawhide says they're harmless enough and will probably only beg for food and other essentials."

One by one, rigs to the front stopped near the Indians, who'd spread colorful blankets on the ground. Emma and her family watched as each family contributed something: coffee, sugar, beads and other trinkets, or beans. When it came their turn, Papa gave them some dried antelope jerky, which seemed to satisfy them.

Then he flicked the reins on the oxen's backs, and the wagon slowly moved into the confines of the fort. The great open area inside teemed with even more Indians in buffalo hides, squaws in bright robes, lean and rough-looking frontiersmen, mules, horses, and oxen. Emma couldn't get over the noise of the place as she took in the long barracks, which housed some of the soldiers, then noticed a store, a warehouse, corrals, and other buildings of assorted sizes and purposes.

"It appears safe enough," her father announced above the din, halting the animals. He hopped down, then assisted Mama while the girls fended for themselves. "While you go see what supplies are available, Nettie, I'll check on the latest news from back East. I'll meet you shortly."

"Susan, Deborah," Mama warned after nodding agreement to him. "Stay right by my side, you hear?"

"Yes, ma'am," they muttered, their eyes bright with excitement.

Before Emma could decide which parent to follow, Jesse came to her side.

"Almost like being back in civilization again, eh? Want to do some exploring?"

She sought approval from her mother, then smiled at him. "Sounds delightful. What all is there to see?"

"Who knows? I've never been here before. We'll make the rounds of the whole place. There are probably too many ladies at the store right now anyway. My supplies can wait until later."

Somehow, with Jesse Brewster beside her, Emma no longer felt apprehensive about the Indians or other odd-looking individuals loitering about, gawking at the travelers. That experience, an entirely new one for her, sent a surge of warmth through her being.

In the evening the women prepared another company feast, which some of the folks living at the fort attended with dishes of their own, and a great time of singing and square dancing followed. Enjoying the festivities with Jesse, Emma knew she'd be a long time forgetting the special night.

The wagon train spent an extra day at Fort Laramie to rest the animals after the long haul. But all too soon, the respite came to an end, and it was time to continue. In the chill morning air, they took their leave.

This time, they acquired a new member, one on horseback. Rather tall and sinewy, with dark hair and green eyes, he spoke in a slow drawl, announcing his name as Bernard Williams. He seemed friendly enough as he introduced himself to everyone, yet he stayed mostly to himself as he observed the travelers with more than a little interest.

The road leading west from the fort marked the beginning of the Black Hills. Emma, walking beside her family's wagon, focused her gaze on the low, ragged summits, which appeared to hold up the sky itself.

Before long they passed more discarded baggage. Strange items like anvils, bellows, and tools of all sorts. Buckets and spades, mirrors and trunks, cast aside as if of no importance whatsoever. She cast a worried glance at her papa's rig, calculating the weight of their earthly belongings. . .and once again, she felt a foreboding that the worst was yet to come.

Chapter 4

Traveling the more rugged climb west from Fort Laramie, Emma became increasingly disheartened at the number of castoff belongings littering the countryside, many of which had been burned beyond recognition. She tried to put them and the occasional skeleton of an ox out of her mind. Then she spied a cookstove and an intricately fashioned mantel clock beside the trail. Neither of them bore a speck of dirt or rain damage, so she could only conclude they had been discarded from wagons farther up front. She wondered which of the families she'd become acquainted with on the trip had been forced to part with such treasures.

Her father no longer rode in the wagon, but tramped beside the oxen, a bull-whip in his hand to prod them along. Finally he shook his head and signaled to the wagons behind before halting the animals altogether.

"What's wrong?" her mother asked, joining him, her fine features drawn with worry.

Emma held her breath, dreading the answer.

He removed his wide-brimmed hat and swiped a sleeve across his forehead. Then he shook his head. "Look at those poor beasts, sides heaving, all but foaming at the mouth. No sense in killing them just for the sake of a couple of trunks, is there?"

She paled. "But Ambrose. We've already discussed this. My dad carved those for each of the girls to be their hope chests one day."

Inside, Emma knew her mother had offered only a futile argument, but she couldn't help hoping it would somehow forestall the inevitable.

Defeat colored his tone as he raised sad eyes to hers. "I'm sorry, love. I was hoping it wouldn't come to this, but it's the only merciful thing to do at this point."

"I'll go empty them," she said in a flat tone, tears shimmering on her lashes. One broke free and rolled down her face, leaving a moist track on her trail-dusted cheek.

"I'll help you, Mama," Emma blurted. Anything to keep from crying herself. What else would this trip cost them? She couldn't watch when her father hefted each beautiful trunk onto his shoulder and set it carefully beside the trail, along with some heavy apothecary jars and other weighty items from his store. She focused her attention ahead, watching Jesse's lighter wagon lumbering ever onward.

A short while later, Susan and Deborah stumbled upon some bushes sporting currants and chokecherries, which other folks in the party had also taken advantage of. Emma grabbed a pail from the wagon and the three girls gathered what they could to be used later in baking. . .a small blessing on an otherwise difficult day.

Their troubles worsened as they now faced a sharp descent down a steeply washed break in the bluffs, known as Mexican Hill. The wagons creaked and groaned, the oxen bawled in protest, and men exerted all their strength to keep each rig from breaking free of the restraints and charging downward out of control. When at last the final one made it successfully, they took a break and nooned at the river.

Mama barely spoke as she served the cold beans and biscuits left over from breakfast. Papa remained silent as well, though he spread a blanket out for her in the shade of the wagon where she could have a short siesta after they finished eating.

Emma took the soiled dishes to the river and stooped down to wash them.

Jesse sauntered toward her, hatless, his wild, sun-bleached curls stirring on the breeze. "I carved our initials in the Register Cliffs," he announced cheerfully.

"Are you serious?" She stood and shook the excess water from the stack.

"Of course," he answered, his blue eyes twinkling. "Someday somebody might be interested to know that J. B. and E. H., whoever we were, passed this way in 1860."

"I can imagine. We were ever so fascinating." Despite her wry tone, Emma felt strangely pleased at his action. . .and thought about it all afternoon as the train continued.

A couple of miles brought them to the most amazing cut in the entire overland road. . .shoulder-deep ruts etched into the solid sandstone, barely wide enough for a wagon. The bullwhackers and other travelers afoot had also worn narrow pathways in the rock over the years, but nowhere as deep as those carved by the wagon wheels. It felt weird, Emma thought, to be walking on higher ground than the rigs through that section.

In the evening, they camped at Warm Spring, in the canyon of a small tributary of the Platte. Emma's gaze drank in the drift of fragile, downy fluff, shed by the ragged foliage of a grove of cottonwood trees. And it didn't take long for her and the other women to make a beeline for the warm pool occupying the middle of the grove.

"Doesn't this feel elegant?" fellow traveler Penny said on a sigh, rinsing soap from her golden hair. "First water in weeks that's been heated for us."

Still sudsing her light brown locks, her sister-in-law, Bethany, giggled. "Do you suppose uppity Lavinia will impose upon poor Katie to draw her a proper bath?"

Megan and Emma chuckled along with the others. "Thanks, Emma," the blond said, handing the soap to her now that it had made the rounds. "That rose scent is wonderful."

"You're welcome. My father used to sell it in the store."

"If we ever get to Oregon," Penny breathed, "I'm going to positively drown myself in cologne and toilet water for a month. Anything to forget the smell of dust."

"I hope that's possible," Emma mused.

"What?" Bethany said teasingly. "Getting to Oregon or forgetting the dust?"

"Both. I don't think we're even halfway there yet."

"Don't remind us!" Megan chimed in, wrapping her long hair in a towel.

Emma squeezed the water from her own, then followed suit, observing her mother as she washed her younger siblings' hair not far away. Oh, but it felt good to be clean again.

When some of the rambunctious boys in the company returned from exploring and reported the source of the pool as a refreshing spring gushing from a nearby hillside, folks gladly went there and filled their water barrels and other containers with the clean, clear water for tomorrow's journey.

Jesse gave the wheels of his wagon close inspection, then liberally greased the hubs with tallow and tar. The miles covered were taking a toll on everything and everyone, and he knew it was only a matter of time before someone broke a wheel or an axle. As it was, one of his oxen had picked up a pebble in his hoof earlier in the day; but as soon as Jesse noticed him favoring that foot, he quickly pulled off to one side and allowed the remaining few wagons to pass him by while he dug the offending stone out. After the noon rest, the animal seemed fine, thank the Lord.

Finished with the nightly chores, he lowered himself to the ground beside Barnabas and reclined against one of the wheels, marveling at the great job Emma had done handling the team. And she hadn't seemed annoyed when he'd mentioned carving their initials in the soft rock of the Register Cliffs. He wondered what her reaction would be if he'd told her about the *other* set he'd carved. . .J. B. and E. B. He had to admit, "Emma Brewster" had a mighty nice ring to it. The more he got to know her, the more convinced he became that God had positioned their wagons the way they'd ended up. . . and he had a fairly good idea why. The problem was persuading Emma of that.

It struck him as ironic how weary of the endless trail so many folks had grown, while he was praying it would be long enough! He knew he had his work cut out for him.

Even as he sat there stroking Barney's stringy fur, he watched his beautiful neighbor return from the pond, her damp, brunette waves splayed about her shoulders. His fingers itched to lace themselves through those glorious tresses. But he maintained a casual expression when she caught his eye.

"You should try that water," she said airily. "It's truly wonderful."

"I'd imagine once all you ladies are through, we fellows will make our way over there. Even Barney's in dire need of a good washing."

She smiled and dropped down beside the two of them. "I'm glad today has ended. The climb, the hill." Then her expression turned serious. "We passed so many belongings. So many graves. It's hard to imagine what people had left—if anything."

"Maybe that's why the Lord encourages us not to set our hearts on earthly treasures," he said gently. "Nothing is forever here."

Emma met his gaze, her own troubled. "Do you think we'll ever really make it to Oregon?"

"Well, I'm sure hoping we will. God's been pretty merciful to us so far. The weather's been mostly pleasant, even now with the cool nights and frosty mornings. And only a few folks have gotten sick. Nobody's had a major breakdown with a wagon, either."

"But there's still such a long road ahead."

"We don't have to travel it all at once, remember. Just a day at a time. Let's just leave the future in God's hands."

Her sable eyes turned to his for an eternal moment, and she smiled. "Somehow, put that way, it doesn't sound quite so hopeless." She paused. "Would you care to have supper with us tonight?"

"Are you sure it's no trouble?"

"Of course."

"Then, I'd be honored."

"And I'd best get busy, in that case. Thanks for the visit." Scrambling to her feet, Emma gave Barney a parting pat, then hurried to her family's wagon.

Even as Emma peeled the young potatoes and carrots they'd acquired at the fort, her mind refused to let go of Jesse Brewster. She'd never known a minister so near her own age before. . .or one so sensitive and thoughtful. Having heard a number of his sermons, she had no doubt that he was a true man of God. And having spent extra time with him aside from his official duties, she felt he had also become a true friend.

She dreaded the thought of his wagon rotating again to the back of the line, knowing that for an entire day, she would have no one to talk to until their wagon joined his once more.

And how sweet, his having carved his and her initials in the rocks for future travelers to see. What an amazing man.

"The meat is browned now," Mama said, lifting the lid on the pot. "You can add those vegetables to the water anytime."

"Yes, ma'am." She shoved the potatoes, onions, and carrots off the cutting board into the pan. "I've invited Jesse to supper this evening. Do you mind?"

"Not at all. He's a fine, personable young man. Certainly an asset to this company." Her mother tipped her head and eyed her. "You've been spending quite a lot of time with the pastor, I've noticed."

"He's nice to talk to, is all," Emma hedged. But even as she answered, she knew deep inside there were a lot of things about Jesse she liked besides his talking. And the list was growing by the day. That realization stunned her. Maybe it wasn't such a good idea to become too attached to someone who'd be setting off for parts unknown soon after reaching Oregon.

On the other hand, if she stayed focused on her own goals, perhaps it wouldn't hurt to enjoy this friendship, however temporary, as long as it lasted. She could deal with the loss when the time came.

Half an hour later, the pastor made his appearance, scrubbed clean, his wild hair damp and slicked back. He'd changed to navy trousers and a green checked shirt, with the sleeves rolled partway up. "Evening," he said simply, and his smile made Emma's heart skip a beat.

"Good evening." She took in his broad shoulders and sun-browned forearms… and decided he looked like anything *but* a minister. In fact, she had to instruct herself to refrain from gaping like a lovesick schoolgirl. Strange, that his presence would suddenly affect her so. This would never do. Never.

"We're so glad you could come to supper, Reverend," she heard her mother say as she stepped forward.

"It's an honor to be invited, Mrs. Harris," he replied. "And I'd prefer being called Jesse." He held out a wedge of cheese. "Thought I might contribute."

"Why, thank you. That's very thoughtful." She turned to Susan and Deborah, standing near the barrel topped by nailed-together planks of wood, which served as their table. "Girls, go tell your papa that supper is ready, will you?"

"Yes, ma'am," they chorused and ran off toward where he chatted with men tending the cattle.

Moments later, everyone took seats on the upended crates they used as chairs. The parents faced each other across the makeshift tabletop, the girls occupied one side, and Emma and Jesse the other. Emma suppressed her silly nervousness and did her best to relax.

Papa's mustache widened into a smile. "Would you do the honors, Jesse?"

"Certainly. Dear Lord, we thank Thee for Thy presence day by day and Thy bountiful goodness to us. Please bless this wonderful meal and the hands that prepared it. May we be faithful to do Thy will. In Christ's name, Amen."

"Amen," the others echoed.

Mama stood, ladled portions of stew into each bowl, and passed them around.

"Mmm. Looks as delicious as it smells," Jesse commented. "Tastes even better," he added after digging in.

Mama beamed. "Thank you."

"So, Jesse," Papa began. "What are your plans once we arrive at Trail's End? Is there a church waiting for you there?" He took a spoonful of the rich stew.

"No, sir," Jesse replied candidly, helping himself to a golden biscuit. "I'm not entirely certain yet what the Lord's plans are. I only know He's called me to go out West, so that's what I'm doing. I figure when I get there, He'll show me the next step."

"But he hopes to build a great church in time," Emma chimed in. Setting her water cup down, her arm accidentally brushed his, and a maddening flush of warmth flooded her neck and slowly rose upward.

He didn't seem to notice her discomfort. "That's true. But only if it's God's will for me."

"From that fine preaching we've heard these past Sunday mornings," Papa said, "that shouldn't be a problem. Good churches are sorely needed now that the West is filling with new families."

"I only hope there's one within traveling distance of where we'll be living," Mama ventured. "I have no idea of what to expect, really."

"That's what makes this such an adventure," Papa said cheerfully. "Everything will be new."

Emma caught her mother's ambiguous expression and related to it completely. If the two of them would have had their preference, they'd still be living in that stately brick house in Philadelphia, within easy traveling distance to church, school, stores, and even a college or two. But it was far too late for looking back now. They could only wait and see what the future held.

"Do try some of Emma's pan cookies, Jesse," Mama offered, once everyone had finished the last drop of stew. "The currants the girls found were just the right touch."

"We picked almost every one that was left on those bushes," Deborah said proudly.

"But we shared some with Granny Willodene, since she said her bones were too old to go chasing off into pickery places," Susan added.

"That was the Christian thing to do," Jesse said. "God is pleased when we share with others. And I don't mind a bit trying one of Emma's creations," he went on, bestowing a warm smile on her.

"I did my best," she said lightly. "Things don't always turn out right when cooking outside."

He took one from the plate and bit off a chunk, chewing slowly, thoughtfully. "They are very good, I must say. Very good, indeed."

Emma smiled her thanks.

"Well," Jesse said after finishing his coffee and another cookie, "I thank you for this wonderful meal, Mr. and Mrs. Harris. It was a real treat not to eat my own cooking."

"We've enjoyed having you," Mama said. "Emma, dear, the girls and I will clean up this time. You two young people go and have a nice walk before it gets chilly out."

Jesse looked rather pleased by her mother's suggestion and offered an arm as he stood to his feet. "Shall we?"

"All right," Emma said hesitantly. She hadn't planned on this, but she did enjoy being with him. Rising, she drew a calming breath and slipped a hand through the crook of his elbow.

The evening truly was pleasant, but without the sun's warmth, the temperature hinted at approaching coolness while they started around the encampment.

"We probably shouldn't stay out long," Emma suggested. "It's been a terribly hard day."

"Yes. Folks always seem to stick close to their wagons after a troublesome time on the road. Not much energy left for singing and frolicking." He paused. "I surely do enjoy your family. It's easy to see where you obtained many of your own fine qualities."

"What a flattering thing to say," Emma breathed, awed at how he could put her at ease.

"I didn't mean it as flattery. You truly do have some fine qualities, Emma," he said quietly, gazing down at her with those soul-searching eyes of his.

She had no idea how to respond. Her awareness of him was too new. Should she encourage him? Not encourage him? End the friendship here and now? "So do you," she finally said. "I'm glad we're. . .friends."

He took the hint and focused ahead once again. "Well," he said as they approached her family's wagon, "sleep well, Emma. Thanks for the invite."

"You're most kindly welcome," she said and clapped a mental hand over her mouth before she said something she might regret later. She had some deep thinking to do. And some praying.

Chapter 5

After contaminated water along the Platte caused a few queasy stomachs and the loss of two oxen, the Black Hills seemed like heaven. Sweet-scented herbs and sage permeated the air of its hills and valleys, and pure water uplifted the spirit and strengthened the weak. Mountain cherries and currants grew in abundance, along with luxuriant tangles of wild roses in sheltered spots; and broad brushstrokes of larkspur, blue flax, and wild tulips streaked the slopes with breathtaking color. Solitary buffalo bulls roaming the ravines provided variety to the sameness of everyone's diet.

The frequent rains that washed through the hills slowed travel considerably, however, increasing wheel breakage and causing tempers to grow short.

Beyond Horseshoe Creek, where the road climbed to the crest of a dividing ridge, the emigrants had an inspiring view of Laramie Peak. They crossed several little mountain streams that day. But the rocks of this section were particularly abrasive and wore the animals' hooves to the quick, laming several. Bickering began among the weary travelers.

When folks assembled for the Sunday service, the sullen expressions that met Jesse's gaze seemed as dark as the clouds churning overhead. He felt the awesome weight of the responsibility he'd taken on as the company preacher and prayed that God would give him the right words to soothe, encourage, and comfort the people he had grown to know and care about.

"This morning's text is taken from Ephesians, the fourth chapter, verse thirty-two," he began. " 'And be ye kind one to another, tenderhearted, forgiving one another, even as God for Christ's sake hath forgiven you.'"

More than a few folks dropped their gazes to the ground, and square-built farmer Homer Green rubbed a sheepish hand over his grizzled face when his wife, Geneva, elbowed him in the ribs.

Nonplussed, Jesse plunged on. "Despite the hardships of this past week—and I know they've been many—it would benefit us to remember we are in God's loving hands. He has led us these many miles and protected us from all sorts of misfortunes commonly endured by people who've gone this way before. We may have lost a few animals, a broken wheel has delayed us now and again, but so far we're all still present and accounted for. That in itself is a blessing, is it not?"

A few grudging nods made the rounds, and he observed a noticeable softening of demeanors in the crowd. Encouraged, he glanced down at his notes to check his next point.

～～

Emma drew her woolen shawl more closely about herself in the cool breeze and glanced up at the sky every few minutes while Jesse preached, wondering if the storm would hold off until he finished. She'd never seen clouds of that peculiar greenish hue before and could tell from other people's expressions that they, too, found the color eerie.

"And so, dear friends," Jesse was saying, "in closing, remember the God to whom we belong. Think about your own personal failures He has so lovingly forgiven, and then endeavor to be patient with each other, just as you were at the beginning of this trip. Do whatever possible to support the neighbor traveling in front and in back of you. Encourage rather than criticize, help rather than ignore, bearing in mind that you, too, may soon find yourself in need of help from your fellow travelers. Showing the love of Christ to one another will smooth the distance yet to be covered. Now, let us pray."

The first sprinkles dotted Emma's faded skirt before Jesse's final amen. And within mere seconds, pelting rain sent folks scattering for shelter.

Emma and her family barely made it to their wagon before the downpour turned to hail. . .dreadful hail larger than oxen eyes. The cruel ice balls lashed at wagons, plummeting through sun-weakened spots in the bowed canvas tops and ricocheting off the hard surface of the seats in a cacophony of unbelievable clatter.

"Everyone down on the floor," Papa hollered above the unearthly racket, and he quickly drew extra canvas coverings from the barrels and positioned himself over them all as they huddled together with their arms around each other.

Chills raced along Emma's spine at the distant sounds of women and children screaming. . .and worse, the animals out in the open, bawling with no way to escape the brutal torture. Once during the onslaught, she even heard Barnabas howl in pain and prayed that Jesse was safe, that his beloved dog hadn't been seriously injured.

After an indeterminate time, the merciless pounding ceased, leaving the breathing of her dear ones as the only sound within the confines of their temporary haven.

Icy balls clunked onto the floor when Papa raised the canvas to peer out from under it, and they stared slack-jawed at the jagged tears in the wagon's bonnet, the accumulated hail near the front already melding together in globs of white.

"I wonder if anything's broken," Mama said, getting up from her cramped position, her voice strained.

"Time will tell," Papa replied. "Is anyone hurt?" At the collective shaking of heads, he gave a resigned nod. "Then I'd best check the oxen, see how they fared."

While Deborah and Susan started collecting chunks of ice and tossing them outside, Emma surveyed the number of torn spots in the canvas top and knew she and her mother would be busy mending and patching for a while.

The two of them looked up at the sound of approaching hoofbeats and saw the trail master's leathery face peer into the wagon. "Anybody hurt here?" Rawhide asked around the wad of tobacco in his leathery cheek.

"No, praise the Lord," Mama replied.

He nodded. "Well, a few of the company suffered a blow or two, and there's a few oxen down. We'd best use the rest of today for repairs, see if we can get on the road again in the morning."

"Fine," she said with a thin smile, then turned to her brood as he rode on.

"Well, girls, looks like we're going to have a busy day. Susan, Deborah, check to see what bedding and clothing need drying out. Emma, let's see if we can remove the wagon's bonnet without your papa's help. Likely he'll have his hands full elsewhere for a while."

⌘

Relieved to find only one small tear in his wagon's top, Jesse checked Barnabas over thoroughly and gave him a hug. "That sore bump will get better pretty quick, old boy. Soon as I get rid of the hail in here, I'd better put this morning's sermon into action."

Hopping down, moments later, he followed his heart to Emma's wagon. Her younger siblings were hard at work draping bedding over the wheels to dry, while she and her mother panted with the effort of removing the canvas top. "Need a hand?" he asked and climbed aboard to give assistance.

Emma's grateful smile did crazy things to his insides. "How's Barney?" she asked, stepping out of his way.

"He got conked on the head once or twice before scrambling out of the fray and has the lumps to prove it, but other than that, he seems okay. Here, Mrs. Harris, I'll get that for you."

"Why, thank you. Did your top stay intact?"

"All except one small spot near the back."

"As soon as Emma and I finish mending this one, we'll see to yours."

"I'd appreciate that. Once I get this off, I'll move my stuff out of your way."

By the end of the day, thanks to a cooperative effort from the menfolk, all major repairs to the wagons were finished, and the nimble-fingered women had set the bowed covers to rights.

An ox belonging to the tall, rawboned carpenter, Zach Sawyer, had suffered mortal wounds and was immediately butchered to feed the camp. But no one displayed the wherewithal for gaiety around the campfire while they ate the tough beef. Jesse decided a special prayer meeting might be more beneficial. At the conclusion of the meal, everyone joined hands in a circle and thanked God for seeing them through the trial, then lifted individual needs to the Lord. . .but with Emma's small hand dwarfed in his, Jesse had all he could do to concentrate on praying.

⌘

Emma felt the warmth and strength of Jesse's grip even after he released her hand. She gazed up at him as he said a few parting words to stragglers who lingered to talk. And even though she had no reason to stay, she couldn't seem to make her feet walk away. She found the calming effect the pastor had on troubled hearts fascinating to observe.

Finally, only the two of them remained. Jesse focused those dark blue eyes on her and smiled. "I do believe the Lord comforted a few souls this day. I, for one, feel more conscious of His presence, His hand."

"You truly have a way with people," Emma said, thinking aloud. "You always seem to know the right words to help them."

His smile relaxed a bit. "I try. Sometimes those who are weary and at the end of themselves just need someone to bolster them again. To keep their hope alive. Oft times it's a soul rather than a body that's sick and in need of a touch, a smile, a helping hand. There is any number of ways for us to do something of worth with our lives. Think about that for a while, will you?"

Not entirely certain where the conversation was leading, Emma had no immediate answer.

Jesse brushed a fingertip along the curve of her cheekbone, his gaze never leaving her face. "You have a wonderful heart, Emma. One God can use in more ways than you can imagine. . . if you'll allow Him to do so."

Her whole being tingled from his touch. "I. . .I'm afraid to let go of my dreams. It's like standing on the edge of a precipice and having no idea where the next step will lead."

"But if your hand is in His, there's no reason to fear. That's where trust comes in. The step is not hidden from Him."

"I don't know if I'm ready to do that," she murmured as he offered an arm and started with her toward her family's wagon.

"Well, God isn't going anywhere, my friend. He'll wait for you to commit your future into His keeping. Sometimes," he added, an impish spark in his eyes, "His plans turn out to be far better than our own."

But it certainly didn't feel that way to Emma. By honoring her parents, she was being taken far away from the possibility of fulfilling her dreams. Yet she couldn't quite relinquish the last ounce of hope of becoming a doctor. Nothing else could hold a candle to that pursuit.

Arriving back at her father's wagon, Emma fully intended to take out another of his books and read for a while. But she saw her mother hurrying toward her, out of breath.

"Emma, have you seen the girls?"

"No, not since the prayer service. Perhaps they went looking for more berries or flowers."

"Well, I hope they come back soon. I worry when they go off without telling me where they're going. It gets dark early here in the mountains."

"I'll go look for them, if it'll make you feel better," Emma suggested.

"And I'll keep your daughter company," Jesse quickly assured her.

"Oh, would you? I'd sorely appreciate it."

After making the rounds of the camp without success, Emma and Jesse headed into the surrounding countryside, searching the rocky contours and outcroppings for any splashes of color that might stand out against the earth's hues.

"How about over there?" Emma asked, looking off into the distance, where two husky young boys were playing leapfrog in a bowl-like meadow.

"No, looks like Homer Green's kids," Jesse told her. "They might know something, though. Let's find out." Taking her hand, he quickened his pace, and they reached the lads a few moments later. "Either of you seen Susan and Deborah Harris?" he asked.

Two freckled faces grew serious as they stopped their play. "Nope," one of them said.

"Well," the other added, "awhile back we was playin' hide-and-go-seek with 'em, but they got tired of it and wanted to do somethin' else."

"Which way did they go?" Emma asked, alarm racing through her.

He pointed farther up the next rise. "They was lookin' for flowers to make a crown or somethin', they said."

"Thanks." Jesse gave the closest boy a pat on his shoulder. "You two should head back to camp now, before your folks decide to come looking for you."

"Yes, sir," they chorused and dashed off.

"Where could my sisters be?" Emma moaned in despair. "What if darkness falls before we find them?"

"It won't. There's light aplenty left, if we hurry. Come on. Deborah!" he hollered. "Susan!"

Emma added her voice to his and called out their names at the same time, hoping the extra volume would help.

Following what appeared to be an Indian trail, they finally heard Deborah's voice answer one of their calls.

Relief flooded through Emma. "When I lay my hands on those two, I'm going to shake them till their teeth chatter," she said and broke into a run.

Jesse easily kept up.

Rounding one of a series of boulders, they caught a glimpse of the girls standing stiff as broomsticks and huddled together.

"Hurry!" Deborah cried. "Please, hurry. Please!"

Panic flooded through Emma. She would have sprinted the rest of the way, but Jesse stayed her with an arm.

"No. Wait. I'll go. I'll holler if I need you."

An uncanny foreboding rooted her to the spot. Her pulse increased as she watched him approach the rocky clearing where the girls stood. She couldn't understand why he was moving so slowly, so cautiously. Hadn't Deborah pleaded for him to hurry?

Very slowly, she saw him pick Deborah up into his arms, then just as slowly set her down again on his other side. The girl immediately darted toward Emma. He then bent to pick up Susan.

The child's piercing scream tore through the air.

Jesse held her tight and bolted up the rise.

"Is she all right?" Emma cried anxiously as Deborah collapsed, sobbing, into her arms with a single word. "S–s–snakes."

"She's fine," Jesse said, an odd expression on his face.

"The snake!" Susan cried. "It struck at me, but Mr. Jesse didn't let it get me. It bit him instead!"

Emma felt the blood leave her face as she watched the pastor turn ashen and sink to his knees.

"No!" she screamed. "No! Please, please, be all right." Then reason seized her. "Girls. Run for help. As fast as you can. Get Doc Rogers. Papa, too. Hurry!"

"I'm. . .okay," Jesse said, not quite managing a smile. But his complexion said otherwise.

"What can I do?" Emma asked, her mind going blank as she knelt down beside him. "Where did you get bitten?"

"My right leg. Just above my boot."

"Tourniquet. We need a tourniquet," she muttered to herself. She had no apron on today; her petticoat would have to do. Tearing a strip from the bottom edge, she tied it tightly below his knee. "Do you have a pocketknife?"

"Usually," he said, his voice strangely weak. "But not today."

Emma searched helplessly about for something—anything—sharp. Nothing. *Please, God, bring help fast. Please, don't let Jesse die. We need him. I need him.* Not knowing what else to do, she put her arms around him and held him close.

Chapter 6

In between frantic, wordless prayers, Emma rocked her friend in her arms. "It'll be all right, Jesse. You'll see. Just hold on. Please, hold on." But already he was drifting in and out of consciousness and moaning, and she didn't like his coloring at all. She finally eased his head down onto her lap and waited for help to arrive.

When her father and dark-haired Josh Rogers came running, the young physician wasted no time in slitting Jesse's pant leg to the knee, while her pa carefully tugged off the pastor's boot, revealing the angry-looking fang marks in Jesse's rapidly swelling limb. The doctor made two slices across the wound, then sucked out as much venom-tainted blood as possible, spitting it off to the side. His expression revealed little as he worked, but Emma could see the concern darkening his blue eyes.

"He'll be okay, won't he?" she had to ask.

Doc Rogers opened a bottle of spirits and doused the injury, then met her eyes. "He belongs to God, Emma. We'll just have to do our best and trust that His will be done."

"I hate it when people say that," she muttered, gazing down at Jesse and stroking his hair. It felt silky and soft, and the tawny curls lay against his face as he slept, making him look especially vulnerable and young. So young.

"I've brought some hartshorn," Papa said, holding out a small vial. "It often helps this kind of thing."

"We'll try everything we've got," the doctor said. After applying some of the ammonia preparation, he took a roll of bandage out of his medical bag and wrapped Jesse's calf. "We'd best get him back to the wagon now and keep him as quiet as possible. I'll stay with him through the night. Longer, if needed. After that, even if he pulls through, he'll need someone at his side all the time for a while."

If he pulls through. Emma dismissed that statement immediately. He'd pull through if she had anything to say about it. "I'll stay with him," she blurted. "I've been driving his wagon for days."

"I don't know if that's such a good idea, sweetheart," her father protested. "Folks might get the wrong idea."

Emma raised her chin. "Folks? We're supposed to care about *other folks* at a time like this? When Jesse might be—" She swallowed the hateful word. "When Jesse has no one to care for him? You and Mama would be right behind me."

He released a slow breath. "I see your point. But first we're going to have our hands full just getting him through the long hours ahead." He turned to the doctor. "I'll assist you, Josh, all during the night if you need me."

"Thanks. But right now we'd best get him back to camp." Stooping over, he slid his arms under Jesse's limp ones and raised his torso, while Papa picked up his legs. "Mind bringing my bag, Emma?" the doctor asked.

Not trusting her voice, she gave a nod and plucked up the medical kit and Jesse's boot. Then she walked beside him throughout the slow trek back to his wagon.

By the time they arrived, the entire camp had heard the news. Emma pictured Deborah spreading the tale of her and Susan's harrowing experience. She looked from one grim face to the next as the company clustered around Jesse's rig.

"How is the dear pastor?" Lavinia Millberg whispered, twisting a silk handkerchief in her hands, her plump face contorted with anxiety. It was the first time Emma had ever seen the pampered brunette concerned for someone besides herself.

"Dr. Rogers has done all that's possible for now. We can only wait. And pray." Even as she spoke the words, Emma straightened her shoulders and faced the crowd. "Earlier this evening," she said in a voice everyone could hear, "the pastor held a special prayer meeting to pray for us. Now we must gather together and pray for him."

"Is that our shy Emma?" she heard her father ask as he and the doctor gently eased Jesse up into his wagon.

But she paid his comment little mind and maintained her focus.

"Of course, dear," her mother said, and others nodded in agreement.

A circle took shape as the folks from the surrounding conveyances joined hands.

"I'll begin," Emma went on, "and any of you who wish to add a prayer of your own, please feel free to do so." She bowed her head. "Our precious heavenly Father, we bring Your loyal servant before You at this time. He suffered a grave wound while bravely saving two defenseless children, and now he needs Your healing touch. Please remember his faithfulness to You, the way he has shared the truth of Your Word with us during our journey. And please, please heal him. We need him so." Her voice broke on the last phrase, and she couldn't hold back her tears.

Others quickly took up the petition, and to a person, everyone pleaded for Jesse's life to be spared, even the lean newcomer, Bernard Williams, who'd joined the company at Fort Laramie. Later, after the final amen died away and they'd sung a hymn of assurance, they drifted back to their own wagons.

Rawhide, however, moved quietly among them, spreading the word that the train would be lying by for at least a day.

In her bedroll, Emma barely slept a wink between praying and all her tossing and turning. At first light, when the men rose to tend the animals, she slipped to Jesse's wagon, which glowed from the lamp Doc Rogers had kept burning through the night. She gave a comforting pat to Barnabas when he raised his head and blinked his sad brown eyes, but it was her father's face she sought.

He looked up with a grave smile. "He's still with us," he said softly. "But it looks pretty bad. His entire leg is horribly swollen, and he's still unconscious and feverish. Doc and I are trying to bring his temperature down with cool cloths.

Maybe you could get us some more water."

"Of course," she whispered. Taking the bucket he held out, she hurried to the river and filled it, praying all the way that the doctor's treatment would work, that God would intervene, that Jesse would make it.

But even though camp activity was subdued out of respect, he showed no improvement at all. Emma called another prayer meeting that night.

Rawhide was leery of holding the train up any longer, so the following morning, the procession of wagons moved out again, with Emma driving her family's wagon, her father taking over Jesse's, and Doc Rogers maintaining his bedside vigil. His bride, Bethany, handled theirs. Emma no longer took any delight in the passing scenery and, in fact, didn't even notice it, concentrating intently on the rig ahead.

At the noon stop, Papa hopped down and came straight to her. "Jesse's fever seems to have broken. He's still pretty sick, and there's a lot of swelling yet, but the doc thinks he's seeing some improvement."

At that news, Emma drew her first real breath since the incident happened. "Thank You, God," she murmured, then opened her eyes once more. "Can I see him?"

"I don't know if he's quite ready to receive visitors just yet, sweetheart. But he mentioned your name quite often in his delirium. Let's give him at least until tomorrow."

Reluctantly, she agreed, but drew hope from knowing that even during such a difficult trial he'd thought of her.

During the noon stop the following day, Doc Rogers finally decided it was safe to leave his patient and return to his pretty wife, whose face lit up at the sight of him as she flew into his open arms. The tender embrace they shared touched Emma deeply, awakening new yearnings in her own heart. She cast an impatient glance toward the pastor's wagon.

Papa beckoned to her from the opening!

Her pulse pounding in her throat, Emma went over and climbed aboard, barely aware that he took his leave at the same moment.

Her eyes adjusted quickly to the dim canvas-covered interior. She caught Jesse's gaze and weak smile from where he sat propped up on his sleeping mat, pillows and rolled blankets behind his back. Noticeably gaunt and pale, he wore a nightshirt, open at the throat. A sheet covered him from the waist down. So much emotion clogged Emma's throat, she didn't dare attempt to speak.

"Well, if it isn't the gal who saved my life," he said, his voice barely half what it normally was.

"Saved your life?" she choked out. "I've done nothing but pray since you got bitten. Pa and Doc Rogers wouldn't let me anywhere near you."

A faint smile lifted a corner of his mouth. "Nothing better than prayer. But I'm talking about the tourniquet." He paused momentarily from the effort of talking and drew a labored breath. "Doc says if not for that, I'd be greeting weary travelers at heaven's gates now."

"Oh, Jesse," she whispered, sinking to her knees at his side. "We—I—don't know what I'd have done if I'd lost you. I once thought I was the one standing on a precipice. . .but that was nothing compared to what you've been through. I see so many things differently now."

He gave a slight nod, but when he blinked, she could see his eyelids growing heavy. She took his hand in hers, shocked at how utterly lifeless it seemed. "I know you need to rest to get your strength back. I'll bring you some broth later. Don't worry about anything. We're looking after Barnabas." *And I'll look after you,* her heart added as he dozed off.

~

"Driver. Driver!" Jesse called out. "Take it easy, will you?"

"What do you mean?" Emma asked ever so innocently over her shoulder.

He snorted. "What good is saving a fellow's life if you're gonna shake his bones to pieces on this rough road, I'd like to know?"

"Complain, complain," she singsonged. "How quickly we forget our blessings."

"Yes, well, I'll tell you a thing or two about blessings when we make camp this eve, Emma-girl."

"Be still, my heart," she countered.

But Jesse knew from her tone she was as thankful as he that the Lord had spared him. She'd devoted herself to helping him regain his strength, bringing nourishing food at every meal, driving the wagon, tending to Barney and the oxen. He could feel life slowly returning to his bones. . .and love for Emma Harris growing ever deeper in his heart.

She sat with her back to him, handling the traces as the oxen plodded along, and his eyes devoured the sight of the shining sable hair trailing from beneath her sunbonnet, her slim form, her determination. He'd purposely avoided expressing his feelings as yet, but once he regained his normal strength, he fully intended to question her about the statement she'd made days ago. Somewhat fuzzy in his brain, he seemed to recall her saying something about seeing things differently. And he glimpsed a most radiant glow in her eyes whenever she looked into his. Jesse hoped it meant what he'd been praying for.

She'd told him about the difficult sections of the trail he'd missed due to his unconscious state. He had a hard time envisioning infamous Rock Avenue, with its hideous stretch of deformed rock strata jutting up from the earth to torture the feet of travelers and animals, or the alkali swamps, steep hills, odorous mineral springs. Now he had even more respect for the pharmacist's stalwart daughter for managing his rig so competently.

Tonight, he allowed Emma and her father to help him off his sleeping pallet so he could enjoy the music around the campfire. For days he'd been staring at the bowed top, just as a prisoner must ogle iron bars, and felt desperate to breathe air that didn't smell like medicine. But the effort required to make his rubbery legs function had him bathed in perspiration before they even got him to the rocking chair someone had thoughtfully provided. Emma brought along a blanket, however, to ward off the chill mountain air and wrapped it about him.

"How's our patient doing this evening?" Doc Rogers asked, strolling toward him with a doting Bethany on his arm.

"Looks like I'll live after all. Thanks to God, Emma and her father, and you. And," he added, including the encampment, "everyone's prayers, of course. I don't think I'll willfully attempt to go face-to-face with a rattlesnake in the near future."

The doctor clamped a hand on his shoulder. "We're just glad you're still with us, Parson. As it is, we've missed one rousing sermon. Hope you're up to preaching again by Sunday."

"I'll do my best. I'm afraid it's a little hard to concentrate just now."

"That's to be expected. That old rattler pumped everything he had into that leg of yours. But it shouldn't take too much longer for the effects of the venom to be out of your system, I'd wager."

"Hey!" someone shouted. "The Reverend's back!" And for the next half hour, a steady stream of fellow travelers came by to greet him and offer wishes for his complete recovery. The strain of that excitement wore him out royally, and he slept until noon the next day, despite the bumping and jarring of the wagon.

∽

"Jesse, come take a look," Emma urged. "That must be Independence Rock in the distance. We'll arrive in time to celebrate the Fourth of July." She moved to one side so he could join her.

"Well, I'll be," he remarked and eased himself onto the wagon seat. "There've sure been some incredible sights along this journey. God didn't spare the beauty when He fashioned this great country."

She nodded, suddenly aware that his gaze centered on her and not on the faraway landmark. She slanted him a gaze and smiled. "Feeling better today?"

"Much. I'm on the verge of being ravenously hungry."

"That's a good sign. I'll see if I can whip up a buffalo for you when we stop."

"You probably would, too." He shook his head in wonder and reached for the reins. "Tomorrow I'll take over this chore so you can get back to your reading. I've imposed upon your good nature far too long."

"I. . .haven't felt drawn to my father's books lately, for some reason," she confessed. "They just don't seem all that important anymore."

"What does seem important, Emma?" he asked quietly.

She didn't answer immediately. Unsure of how to put words to concepts that seemed the direct opposite of the goals she'd clung to for so long, she finally shrugged a shoulder. "Not trying to outguess the Lord, for one thing," she began. "Giving Him the freedom to close old doors and open new ones. Then having the courage to step through them. Being willing to accept His will, even when it differs from mine."

"You haven't given up the desire to make your life count, have you? To help people?"

"Not at all. But now I see that help comes in many forms."

"I think you've proven that these past couple days. I couldn't have managed if you hadn't stepped into the breach. In fact," he added huskily, "I don't know how I'll do without you when you return to your family. I've grown quite used to looking up and seeing you, hearing your voice. . .feeling your touch on my brow when you thought I was sleeping. . . ."

Emma didn't quite suppress the warm blush that flooded her cheeks. "Who says I want to go back?" she whispered, shocked at her own boldness. Surely he'd think her a hussy.

But Jesse's face glowed with heaven's light. A slow smile played across his lips as he covered her hand with his and searched her soul with those heart-stopping eyes. "I might as well tell you, I'm in love with you, Emma Harris. Have been for some time."

Hearing the words she'd never really expected anyone to say, she saw no reason to hedge. Not when the handsome pastor had just laid his very heart at her feet. "I nearly had to lose you before the Lord finally got through to this hard head of mine. But I know now that I love you, too, Jesse."

"Enough to marry a poor preacher when we reach Trail's End? When I've got my strength back again and can court you proper?"

"No," she said in all candor. "Enough to marry you tomorrow. Seeing how very fragile life is, I don't want to waste a day of it. . .not when I can share every moment with you."

His eyebrows hiked high on his forehead and his jaw gaped in pleasant shock. "How do you think your parents will feel about that?"

She smiled. "Let's just say I doubt they'll be surprised."

"Well I am, my sweet Emma. But there's one thing I must do before we break the news."

"And what is that?"

"Just this." He put an arm around her and drew her close; and when she raised her gaze to his, he lowered his head and gave her a kiss so tender, so reverent, it left her breathless.

Chapter 7

At the crack of dawn on the Fourth of July, the men of the encampment fired off small arms and raised the flag. Then everyone circled the flagpole and sang "The Star-Spangled Banner" in honor of the occasion.

"Three cheers for Old Glory!" someone yelled, and the exuberant crowd gave their all.

"Feel up to reading the Declaration of Independence, Reverend?" Emma heard Rawhide ask. "Somehow it seems more fittin' if you'd do the honors."

She looked up at the too-thin man of God standing beside her and smiled.

"I'll do my best." Accepting the sheaf of papers from the trail master, Jesse cleared his throat and began reading:

" 'In Congress, July 4, 1776. The unanimous Declaration of the thirteen united States of America. When in the Course of human events, it becomes necessary for one people to dissolve the political bands which have connected them with another. . .' "

Amazed at how much stronger his voice sounded this morning, Emma's heart swelled with pride and concentrated on the words while he continued.

" 'We hold these truths to be self-evident, that all men are created equal, that they are endowed by their Creator with certain unalienable Rights, that among these are Life, Liberty and the pursuit of Happiness.' "

Noticeably hoarse by the time he reached the end of the historic document, he grinned as another rousing cheer sounded. Then, charges of gunpowder in the cracks of Independence Rock were set off.

"Now listen up," Rawhide hollered. "We'll be restin' here for the day while all able-bodied men go hunting. No doubt the ladies of the company are eager to cook us all up a royal feast for the celebration. But we're thinkin' beyond today. We need as much meat as can be found. There's a hard stretch facin' us ahead. And," he added, casting a peculiar glance toward Emma and Jesse, "I hear tell I'll be performin' a weddin' later today. The preacher's takin' Miss Emma Harris for his bride, and you're all invited."

A chorus of oohs and ahhs sounded, and all the young women flocked to Emma's side with a raft of hugs and suggestions.

"How wonderful," Megan Crawford crooned. "He's a fine man. He'll take good care of you."

"I'd love for you to use my veil," the doctor's wife, Bethany, offered. "To supply the traditional something borrowed."

Not to be left out, thick-waisted Lavinia Millberg edged closer. "I'm sure I have a gown you'd be welcome to wear. Of course, you'd have to tie the sash a bit tighter."

"And I have a bouquet of dried flowers you can carry," Penny Rogers chimed in, "just in case your sisters already picked all the wildflowers in the area yesterday." Emma didn't know which one to answer first. "Thank you. All of you. You're truly sweet. I'd be honored to borrow your veil, Bethany, and to carry Penny's flowers if Susan and Deborah can't find any. But I have a dress of my own to wear. Just be at our wedding, please. Jesse and I would appreciate your support and good wishes, and we want everyone to share in our happiness."

As the group gravitated back to their own wagons, her betrothed came to her side. "How would you feel about taking in the spectacular view they say one can see from up top?"

Emma's mouth gaped. "After just barely surviving being bitten by a snake, you want to attempt climbing a big rock?"

He flashed a sheepish grin. "It's not reported to be a hard climb. . .and we do have all day. We can go slow. Besides, it's a once-in-a-lifetime opportunity. You wouldn't expect me to leave here without carving a very special set of initials for all the world to see. I'm sure no one would expect my beautiful bride-to-be to soil her pretty hands on mundane chores on her wedding day. How about it?"

Emma cast an incredulous glance at the granite mound, which occupied a good twenty-five acres of ground, and another at her husband-to-be. "I suppose this'll be only the first of many challenges I'm going to face, being married to you."

"Spoken like the gal who's stolen my heart."

"Well, let's get to it, then."

Hand in hand, they started up the gray mass, the sun's rays reflecting off particles of red and white feldspar and mica in the granite. They picked their footing as had so many others, ascending slowly enough to read the many names and dates left by previous visitors, along with scores of initials and messages. Some had been carved into the soft surface, others written in buffalo grease or powder. Emma paid close attention to the sound of Jesse's breathing, intending to stop this foolish scheme should it prove too much for him. But he seemed only slightly winded and grinned like a kid, so she relaxed.

A strong wind whipped about their clothing and hair when they gained the top. Jesse tightened his hold on her hand, and they turned a slow circle, devouring the panoramic vista that spanned twenty miles in every direction, truly a sight to remember. They pondered the meandering trail they'd already navigated through the Sweetwater Valley and surveyed the handful of alkali pools below, which some of the men patrolled to make sure the animals didn't drink from them. Then, turning, they observed another grouping of rugged rocks jutting up from the ground a short hike away. And beyond them all, the snowcapped tops of the Rocky Mountains, with its chill winds announcing a preview of what lay ahead.

"Here's the spot we'll record our visit," he said, taking out his pocketknife and kneeling down. "Maybe I'll put our first names, since they're both short."

"As you wish." Amused at his mettle, she dropped down beside him and sat with her arms wrapped around her knees while he painstakingly carved the letters.

"There." Standing, he offered a hand and helped her up. "How's that? Jesse loves Emma, 1860."

He had etched a heart around their names, which she found particularly sentimental. She smiled, wondering what other fascinating things she would discover about the man she loved. "It's beautiful."

"So are you, my love." He cupped her face in his hands and kissed her soundly as the wind cavorted around them.

Going down, they soon found out, presented more difficulty than going up, but they finally succeeded, their slow jaunt having used up a good portion of the afternoon.

"I have one more thing to show you," he said, a mysterious spark in his eye. "In the wagon. A wedding gift for my bride."

"How could you possibly have acquired a present for me?" she asked, completely baffled.

"I have my ways."

Without the slightest inkling of what to expect, Emma allowed him to lead her to the rig she would soon share with him and accepted his assistance aboard.

"It's in the back," he said, his lips quirking into a hopeful grin. He threw aside a heavy canvas cover and stood aside.

"My hope chest!" Emma gasped, her eyes misting with tears. She brushed her fingertips across her name, carved so lovingly by her grandfather in times past. "But how did you ever—I mean, Papa left it beside the trail miles and miles ago!"

"I know. When your sister Deborah bemoaned that sad fact, I pulled off the road and rescued it. I needed to tend the hoof of one of my oxen at the time anyway. I figured it wouldn't be too heavy for my wagon, and I knew you'd want it."

"Thank you, Jesse. Thank you." Emma moved closer and hugged him. When she raised her lashes and met his gaze, she almost drowned in the love she saw there. "You are incredibly special, do you know that?"

"I try," he said with nonchalance.

Her mother rapped on the wagon just then. "Emma? You need to change for your wedding. Everything's in readiness, and we'll be having a grand feast after the ceremony."

"I'm coming." A last lingering glance at her betrothed, and she hurried away.

Getting ready took less than half an hour. She donned one of her Oregon dresses. . .an ivory tulle with a spray of tiny pearls and sequins accenting the bodice. Mama helped pin her hair up into a tumble of soft curls with some loose tendrils along her cheeks and neck. Then she added the exquisite veil provided by Bethany Rogers.

"Oh, you do look lovely, daughter. My baby, a bride. I can't believe it."

"I know, Mama. It was the last thing I expected to have happen on this journey. But I know this is God's will and that Jesse is God's man for me."

She nodded. "If your father and I didn't share that sentiment, we would not let go of you so easily." She smiled and hugged her, then straightened. "Come. Your groom is probably already waiting."

Susan and Deborah, all curled and beribboned in their own pretty Oregon dresses, held out a bouquet of fresh wildflowers as Emma stepped down. "We picked these special ones for you."

"I hope you were careful to watch out for snakes," she said, admiring the prairie roses and other pastel blooms. She gave each of her sisters a hug.

A row of heavily laden tables sat to one side of the grounds within the circled wagons. Emma could smell a delicious assortment of mouthwatering dishes as she and her mother approached, and she surmised there'd be an array of food similar to what they'd enjoyed at Fort Laramie, complete with baked desserts.

She spied Jesse at the front of the company, standing tall and straight in his Sunday preaching suit, his hair slicked back. His eyes softened as she moved into view, and the crowd, seated on blankets and upturned kegs awaiting the ceremony, smiled their approval.

Emma's siblings preceded her to the front one at a time, while Papa blinked moisture from his eyes and proudly escorted her to her groom's side.

Rawhide Rawson, in the one worn and scruffy outfit that made up his wardrobe, harrumphed and stepped to the center, a small black book in his grip, the usual wad of tobacco missing from his cheek. "Dearly beloved," he read in a flat tone, "we are gathered here to join together this man and this woman in holy matrimony. . . ."

Emma scarcely heard the words as she lost her gaze in Jesse's, so very thankful for God's goodness. Rawhide's voice, the people around her, the lovely day, the smells of supper, all faded to a misty blur.

All too soon the vows had been spoken, and the trail master pronounced them husband and wife. "You may kiss your bride, Preacher."

Jesse smiled and drew her into his embrace, then lowered his lips to hers. Twice.

Granny Willodene gave a hoot and a holler. "Supper's on," she announced. "No sense wastin' the rest of daylight, nor all these good vittles, when folks're starvin' to death. Let's allow the newlyweds to head up the line, then the rest of us will traipse by with our good wishes once our plates are dished up. Parson, we'll have you say grace."

He nodded. "Dear Lord, we thank Thee for Thy wondrous faithfulness in guiding and protecting us day by day. We ask Thy blessing upon this food and those who labored so long to prepare it. Make us strong to do Thy will. And Emma and I give special thanks for Your bringing us together and allowing us to share the remainder of our lives together. In Christ's name, amen."

Emma felt him squeeze her hand, and she glanced up to meet his gaze.

"After you, Mrs. Brewster." A most endearing twinkle glinted in his eye.

"Thank you, Reverend," she replied. Somehow she sensed this was but a foretaste of years to come. . .being honored along with God's man and moving to the front of the line, waiting for him to ask the blessing over this feast or that, among this crowd or some future gathering. Being at his side to help him and help others. Laborers together for the Lord.

If she lived to be a hundred, she could ask for nothing more.

Renegade Husband
by DiAnn Mills

Chapter 1

Spring 1885

Mama, I want an adventure. Something real. And something more exciting than the Nebraska prairie." Audra Lenders stood in the doorway of their soddy and gazed out over the flat land to where the earth and sky met. A pretty sunrise in shades of pink and purple blended together until she could not tell where one color ended and another one began. Birds welcomed the day, their song a bit sweeter this morning. "There is so much of this world I want to see."

"Mercy, Audra. Have you been thinkin' about Pastor Windsor's son again?" Her mother's shrill voice pierced Audra's ears. She loved Mama, but when she became exasperated about something, her voice rose like a screech owl.

"A little. After all, I did tell him I'd think about it." Audra studied the worry lines around her mother's eyes as Mama labored over a list of supplies for her and Papa to purchase this morning.

Mama shook her head. "You know Papa and I don't think it's a good idea for you to travel all the way to Colorado by yourself and then possibly be disappointed. Why, you don't even know this man. Look around you. Archerville has fine men who'd be honored to have you for a wife."

"None of the young men from Archerville interest me. I want a love like in the Bible. The men around here treat me fine, but I can't picture myself married to any of them."

"You're asking for the impossible. Take your mama's advice and stay where you are."

"If Pastor Windsor's son isn't right for me, I'll find a job and earn the money to come home." Audra crossed her arms and returned her attention to the peacefulness outside.

"As stubborn as you are?" A lock of Mama's light brown hair with wisps of gray slipped from her bun onto her neck. She laid her pen aside to tuck back the stray lock. "I'm afraid you'd stay in Colorado rather than admit a mistake."

"My stubbornness is exactly why I wouldn't marry a man who wasn't fittin'."

Mama glanced up. "I do hope you'd return to a family who loves you." Her pale blue eyes softened. "But isn't where we live enough of an adventure?"

The hot grueling summers and the winters that delivered whirling snow and freezing temperatures were not Audra's idea of an exciting journey. The only home she'd known was this soddy—dark, damp, and smelly. Oh, for something different! "Remember when you were younger? Didn't you want to do something more than what everyone expected? See more of our country?"

Mama laughed. "That's why I left Kentucky and married your papa."

"See, you *do* understand."

"I loved your papa, and heading into new territory with my husband was quite different from boarding a train and stagecoach. You don't know a soul in Colorado. Strangers, all of them." She held up a finger. "Outlaws roam that territory—horrible, evil men who care about nothing or no one but themselves. I refuse to think about what might happen to you. How will I ever rest knowing you're there? What if Pastor Windsor's son is not kindhearted?"

"Mama, I already told you what I'd do if we didn't suit each other. Besides, all we're talking about are the 'ifs' and not a word about God's plan."

Her mother picked up the pen and dipped it into the ink well. "Are you reading His Word?"

"Of course I am. I want to be in God's will." By now, Audra felt an inkling of doubt, not with her desire to leave or the surety of God wanting her to go but with her parents giving permission. Perhaps they had decided the matter and no amount of talking would persuade them.

"You keep reading," Mama said. "Sometimes we overlook what God is saying, because we seek permission to do something rash."

Audra gasped. "I'd never do such a thing. Why, that's pure selfishness."

Mama tilted her head. "You could be in the middle of sin and not recognize it at all."

Audra bit back a remark. Her thoughts strayed far from respectful, but she understood her mother spoke out of love. Mama and Papa's reservations must stem from the fact she was the youngest of their eight children.

Hours later while Mama and Papa were gone for supplies, Audra reflected on her mother's words. The thought of looking for a passage in the Bible to clear her way to Colorado unnerved her. She had searched the scriptures for an answer and felt confident of God's blessings. In the quiet of her spirit, she sensed her heavenly Father urging her to make the journey and to consider a role as Christopher Windsor's wife. Not one single passage had convinced her but rather several had spoken to her. All gave her strength and reassurance to trust God above all things. She'd read about Abraham and Sarah setting out for the promised land and understood not everything about Colorado would be perfect. She'd read about Isaac and Rebekah, and Jacob and Rachel—and attempted not to dwell on their problems. But Audra sensed the greatest blessing in reading about Ruth. *Whither thou goest, I will go: and where thou lodgest, I will lodge: thy people shall be my people, and thy God my God.*

Those words pressed against her heart. Surely this was Pastor Windsor's bidding—God's bidding—to become a pastor's wife. Christopher Windsor had to be a good man. How could he be any different from his father?

Audra busied herself in the warm sunshine and finished her chores. She relished the fact that winter was now behind them. She always treasured the first gentle snowfall but, as the months plodded along, she grew tired of the endless drifts and biting cold. Promises of spring put those dreary days aside and birthed new ideas for the future.

Her mind drifted back to Pastor Windsor's last visit.

"Audra, consider marrying Christopher. He's a fine man who loves the Lord. His church is growing, and he needs a wife, a pretty one like you to walk beside him." He reached inside his jacket and pulled out a photograph. "Twins." He grinned and handed her the photograph. Indeed they were identical. Pastor Windsor pointed to the young man on the left. "That's Christopher. The other one is Caleb, and he's a rancher."

The young men resembled their father. Thick hair, large eyes, and wide smiles drew her instantly into a dream world. They looked to have dark brown hair like the pastor, maybe his midnight blue eyes, too. Audra never met Mrs. Windsor. She'd died giving birth to the boys.

Having the pastor speak for his son wasn't the kind of proposal she'd always dreamed of. But the idea challenged her. She wanted the opportunity to meet this Christopher Windsor and see if they could learn to love each other.

With a sigh, Audra strode toward the sod barn to gather eggs. Mama had taken several with her to trade for supplies in town, depleting the ones they had for their own use. Audra found a half dozen and took them into the house before heading for the garden. After pulling a few weeds from around sprouting vegetables, she picked up a pail. The thought of fresh, tender greens for tonight's dinner made her mouth water. Glancing about at the pastel-colored wildflowers shooting up from the spring earth and the sight of new calves and colts exploring the world, Audra had to admit she'd miss the prairie's spring beauty. This was all she'd ever known, but a yearning deep inside compelled her to move beyond the familiar boundaries to the western mountains. The idea of green valleys and aspen trees with an abundance of different kinds of animals and birds made her feel giddy. She'd never seen bighorn sheep or water roaring so fast it foamed up white.

"Give me your answer as soon as you can," Pastor Windsor had said during the last evening visit. They'd been sitting at the table after dinner. Papa enjoyed discussing the Bible, but the pastor obviously had other things on his mind. "I'd write Christopher and make all the arrangements for you. In his last letter, he said he was looking for the Lord to give him a wife."

"I can't go without Mama and Papa's blessing," she said.

Papa cleared his throat. "I promised myself my daughter would never marry sight unseen. I want her to be happy."

"I understand, and I agree," the pastor said. "I'd make sure Christopher provided a place for Miss Audra to stay until they got to know each other."

"It's not what I envisioned for my Audra," Papa said.

"Then I'll be praying God reveals His plan to all of us."

O Lord, please let all of us be in agreement about this. And I do so want to go.

Audra's mind continued to replay Pastor Windsor's request. As late evening took on the colors of sunset, she fed the animals and milked the cow. While she prepared dinner, she wished she knew Mama and Papa's decision. Most girls her age were married and had families. At twenty, she saw her dreams of a good husband slipping through her fingers.

Long after dark, Audra heard the wagon creaking across the prairie. She'd been rocking on the front porch when the sun finally rested for the day. The insects serenaded her as the darkness brought on the quiet. She tugged at her shawl. The night had grown chilly. She believed her destiny lay in Colorado. Now she prayed God gave her parents the same revelation.

"Are you waitin' dinner?" Papa said.

"Sure am. It's ready and still hot."

"What are we having?"

Audra laughed. Papa must be powerful hungry. "Smoked ham, fresh greens, corn bread, and a sweet berry cobbler with lots of cream—and fresh coffee."

"You're going to make some man a good wife."

With those words, he caught her attention. If not for the darkened shadows, she would have tried to read his thoughts by the look on his leathery face. Silence leaped between them. Not willing to let a lighthearted moment vanish, Audra scrambled for words. "Me? A wife? Papa, who would have me? I'd rather go hunting or fishing than stay indoors."

"Perhaps Pastor Christopher Windsor can tame your wild spirit."

Audra startled then trembled. Had she heard correctly? "Papa?" Her voice came out barely above a whisper. All she could see of him was his tall lean frame, not the dark hair and bushy eyebrows or the set of his jaw.

Not a word passed between them. She tore her attention to Mama, who appeared to be shivering in the evening breeze.

"What do you say we get these supplies unloaded so we can eat?" Papa made his way to the back of the wagon, and she followed alongside Mama. "While we're enjoying that fine cobbler, we have much to talk about."

Mama sniffed, and Audra knew for certain it had been decided. She'd go to Colorado.

Six weeks later, a letter arrived from Earnest, Colorado, addressed to Mr. Samuel Lenders. While they sat around the fire before bed, Papa read the letter. Audra longed to hear the contents, but she knew Papa needed time to think on what Christopher Windsor had to say. Finally he folded the missive and placed it in his Bible.

"He has an older couple for you to stay with—a Jed and Naomi Masters. They're good folks and are looking forward to having you in their home. You can live with them for as long as you like. The parsonage needs a little repair, and he's already begun work on it."

Audra nodded and refused to look at Mama. The tears had flowed much too frequently during the past weeks. *A home of her own? A real home?*

"One more thing. He sent money for your travel and mine. He thought it only fittin' that I accompany you to Earnest. We'll take the Union Pacific out of Omaha and ride it to Denver. From there we'll take a stagecoach south to Earnest. I do say he must fare well as a preacher to afford this luxury." He eased back in his chair and stared into the fire. Taking a puff from his pipe, he continued. "And. . .he thanks you for considering marriage and me for allowing this unusual courtship. He promises to love you proper like the Bible says."

This time Audra felt her eyes moisten. She quivered at the mere thought of the future. She felt certain of God's hand in this, and now Papa would make the journey with her. What more could she ask?

"I wish Colorado were closer." Mama dabbed her nose with a handkerchief. "The thought of never seeing my little girl again is hard, real hard."

Audra took Mama's hand. "You have all of your other children and grandchildren close by, and with the railroad we can visit."

"The trip would be costly, I'm sure."

Audra forced a smile. She hadn't anticipated the pangs of loss to cut her so. She wished the money was there for Mama to come, too. "I will make sure I have chickens for egg money, so I can come home."

Mama sighed. "Promise me."

"I promise."

Papa took the letter from his Bible and reread it. Audra wished she knew the many thoughts rolling around in his head; even more so, she wondered what Christopher had written. Papa was prone to a serious nature, and she understood her leaving grieved him.

"If something goes wrong out there," he said, "if this man is not what he seems and you don't want to stay there, I'll come after you. I have a bad feeling about this, but I can't seem to discern if it's a papa not wanting his daughter to leave or a warning from God."

A chill swept over Audra, and her stomach twisted. This was God's purpose for her life. She merely sensed excitement.

Chapter 2

Caleb Windsor woke with a start. Sweat streamed down his face. His heart pounded like a trapped rabbit's, and his mind grappled with reality. He rubbed his face and attempted to focus in the utter blackness. The same nightmare plagued him again, the fifth time in the last month. He'd been accused of stealing horses, and someone had swung a rope over a tree limb and around his neck. That someone was his brother, Christopher.

He moaned, not in physical pain but in spiritual anguish. Wanted posters throughout the territory publicized Caleb's picture as the "bad Windsor twin." The brothers shared identical looks but little else. Caleb had always shouldered the blame for Chris's actions. Each time Caleb hoped and prayed his younger brother would change. Each time he was disappointed. But Caleb hadn't given up, although the thought of swinging from the end of a rope left a mighty bitter taste in his mouth.

Folks compared them to Jacob and Esau—with Caleb as the wayward brother who rebelled against God and all their father had taught. He refused to deny the accusations, and each time he took the punishment. Now he wondered if all those years of covering up for Chris was wrong. He'd pleaded with his brother to stop the lawbreaking, but the last time they talked Chris merely laughed. The next Sunday, he preached on forgiveness and gave the example of his outlaw brother, Caleb Windsor. Chris had to be stopped, but how?

Chris could resolve this very minute to start living right and stop hiding behind his title as pastor. Every robbery and cattle rustling report would end if he'd repent and mend his ways.

Caleb knew one of his worst mistakes came in convincing his brother to take a wife. In the beginning he thought the idea might work. He'd always heard a good woman settled down the worst of characters. But now his conscience screamed at him. How stupid to bring an innocent woman into the heat of this ruse.

"Get married," Caleb had said. "Take a wife and settle down. Leave this life behind. Start a family, and stop thinking of ways you can steal from honest folk. I'll even head to Mexico, and you can start over. No one will ever know the truth."

Chris eyed him for several long moments. A wide grin spread over his face. "I think I will. A pastor needs a wife, makes him look good in the community."

Caleb wanted to land a fist up alongside his brother's jaw. "The purpose is to stop this thieving life of yours. I'm giving you a chance to be an honest man."

His brother laughed long and hard, and it further served to feed Caleb's frustration. "You forget. I'm the honest man."

"You mean you'd use our father and a God-fearing young woman to continue what you're doing?"

Chris chuckled, the devious low laugh that had become a part of him since they were little boys.

"I'll find a way to stop you," Caleb said. "You never have enough. It's always one more job—a little more money or cattle or horses to drive south."

"Be careful. I haven't gotten this far by being stupid. I have everything worked out, and getting caught isn't part of the plan."

That was over three months ago.

Caleb rested his head in his hands and stared up at the starless night. How many nights had he slept in the open, on the run for crimes he hadn't committed?

At first he wondered why his brother requested a bride of his father's choosing rather than select one from Earnest, then he realized Chris's method made him look like a saint in the eyes of their father and the townspeople. Chris didn't care for anyone but himself. The woman due to arrive in less than a week didn't stand a chance for happiness, and who would listen to her complaints? No one in town had any knowledge of her—another part of his brother's scheme.

Caleb knew how cruel his brother could be. He'd lived with the treachery for twenty-five years. The only folks who knew the truth were Jed and Naomi Masters, but they were smart enough not to let on to Chris. The older couple kept Caleb informed of the goings-on. Good thing they did, or he'd have swung from a tree a long time ago.

Currently Caleb had two big worries to take before the Lord. One was his brother's rebellion, and the second stemmed from the young woman who was destined to be his brother's bride.

This was his own fault. He'd tried to play God in the name of love and then made things worse. His brother was masking his unlawful practices under the pretense of a pastor. Caleb could be shot tomorrow for something he hadn't done, and his brother would pull the trigger without a hint of remorse.

❧

Audra thought the railroad trip from Omaha to Denver had been somewhat of an adventure, except the less than palatable food in a few of the establishments along the way. She hid the churning in her stomach for fear Papa would insist they return home. When the train filled up with cigar smoke from a few inconsiderate passengers, she lowered the window. Within minutes, black soot covered her face and clothes. Papa didn't mind the coating of black dust. In fact, he claimed to enjoy every minute of the journey, and for that reason she said nothing about her personal distress. The train had continued as if eating every mile of the vast country.

Now she and Papa bounced along side by side on a stagecoach hitting bumps and holes until she felt certain every inch of her was black and blue. An older man seated across from them must not have bathed for six months, and his dirty and ragged clothes had seen better days. Greasy, gray strands of hair clung to his face and neck. Audra held her breath and exhaled out the side opening of the stage door when she sensed she'd surely faint away. Papa laughed and talked to the man as though he'd known him forever. But Papa always had time for folks. He wanted to make sure they knew the Lord. She did, too, but the saying that cleanliness was next to godliness seemed fitting in this case.

The wagon hit a bump just when she chose to take a gasp of air. The jolt lifted her straight up. Her head banged against the top of the door opening.

"Ouch." She pulled her head inside and reached up to touch the crown of her bonnet.

"Are you all right?" Papa said. "Looks like you best keep your head inside."

"I'm fine, thank you." She rested her hands in her lap. "I'm enjoying the countryside, so different from Nebraska." Although she'd avoided the truth, Audra did appreciate the scenic beauty of Colorado. The mountains and rolling terrain along with thick, green grass and wildflowers filled her with anticipation of her new home—and probably a husband.

"We should be in Earnest in a few hours," the bathless gentleman said.

"Good." Papa shifted in his seat. "My daughter plans to make her home there."

The gentleman raised a bushy brow and nodded. "I'd say a gal as pretty as you will be married up real soon."

"She's picky," Papa said. "She won't be marrying the first man who comes courtin'."

Thank you, Papa.

"I've been lookin' for a wife—"

The moment the words left the man's mouth, the sound of rifle fire popped, followed by another. One of the drivers fired. Audra stiffened and grabbed Papa's arm.

"Don't you dare think of looking outside," Papa said just as the stage lunged ahead.

She didn't answer. Fright enveloped every inch of her. Her gazed fixed on the man's greasy-looking beard. She held her breath.

"Best be sheltering your daughter from stray bullets."

Audra swung her attention to Papa's ashen face. If something happened to him, it would be all her fault for wanting to come to Colorado. His arm wrapped around her and pulled her head against his chest. "Pray," he whispered. "We need God's angels to carry us on to safety."

"God doesn't visit these parts much." The man's voice never wavered with the sound of desperate men's weapons exploding around them.

"Who are those men?" Papa said.

"Outlaws. Most likely Caleb Windsor's bunch."

The name of Windsor seized Audra's attention, and Papa gripped her tighter. "I imagine it's not any kin to the preacher in Earnest," he said.

The man chuckled. Thank goodness, Audra found staring at Papa's right boot a little more pleasing than the man's beard. "Caleb is the preacher's twin brother."

Papa moaned. Audra's head throbbed. "The preacher's twin is an outlaw?" Papa said. "I thought he was a rancher."

Why hadn't Christopher Windsor told her about this? Audra wanted to read Papa's gaze, but the commotion wouldn't permit it.

"Yeah. What a sad situation for brothers."

The stage slowed, and at first Audra believed the outlaws had given up, but when she got a glimpse of two men wearing bandannas riding alongside the stage, she realized the truth.

Audra couldn't stop trembling. All Mama's warnings about evil men flooded her mind.

"I won't let any of them hurt you," Papa said.

How could he stop them? He didn't carry a weapon.

The stagecoach stopped. "You folks climb out of there," a man said. "We don't aim to hurt you, just help ourselves to your belongings."

"Same thing," the bearded man said. "The law needs to put this bunch out of their misery. String 'em up."

Neither Audra nor Papa replied. The door swung open, and a masked man grabbed Audra's arm.

"Keep your hands off my daughter." Papa spoke in a tone she'd never heard before.

"Shut up, old man, or I'll give you a taste of this." The masked man lifted his revolver and pointed it at Papa.

"Throw that gun aside, and I'll show you how a real man fights," Papa said in the same low tone she heard the moment before.

"Please." Audra gasped. "I'm coming." She refused to look at Papa and allowed the masked man to pull her from the stage.

"Take it easy on the girl," one of the outlaws, still on horseback, called. "All we want is their money and any gold jewelry or watches."

Another man threw her trunk from the top of the stage to the ground. She glanced at the drivers—one was slumped over the other. She didn't want to think about what had happened.

"What about the driver?" Papa said. "Can I help him?"

"Too late," the other driver said. "He's gone."

Tears filled Audra's eyes, and Papa drew her to him. "It's going to be all right," he said. "Keep praying."

Breathing a simple request for help, Audra watched the outlaws search through her trunk. Her cheeks warmed as the men yanked out personal garments.

"I don't have anything in there for the likes of you," she said.

The outlaw who had requested she not be harmed glared down at her from his horse. "I'm sure you have money hidden in these clothes."

And indeed she did.

In short order, the precious money sewn in the hem of her dresses lay on the ground.

"You lied to me, little lady," the same outlaw said.

She lifted her head, but Papa tugged on her arm. "She was trying to protect her money."

"I think she can speak well enough on her own," the man said. He must have been the leader, for he nodded, and another outlaw searched Papa's pockets.

Audra studied the outlaw who had defended her—lean, muscular, and from under the brim of his dark brown hat she saw a splash of dark hair. He must be Caleb Windsor. And his identity must be why he asked that she be spared, or so she'd like to believe.

"Say something." The outlaw cocked his revolver.

She stiffened. "Yes, I lied, and yes, I'd do it again. So, are you Caleb Windsor?"

"You have a quarrel with that?"

"I only wanted to know who would stoop so low as to kill and rob innocent people."

The other outlaws laughed. Papa told her to hush.

"I bet you're the little lady sent to marry my brother." The man leaned against his saddle horn. He chuckled, and it made her even angrier. If not for the deceased driver and her fright, she'd have said more. "From the looks of your face and that yellow hair, my brother could have done a whole lot worse. Hope he can handle your sassy mouth."

A man of God wouldn't have need to hear my sassy mouth.

"Keep quiet, Audra," Papa said, or rather he growled at her like an angry dog.

"Is that your name?" Caleb Windsor's pewter-colored stallion reared as though the sound of his rider's voice startled him.

"Yes."

Caleb Windsor dismounted and walked toward her. Audra's heart thumped so hard she feared it would burst through her chest.

"Leave her alone." The moment Papa's words left his mouth, Caleb swung his fist into his cheek and sent him sprawling in the dirt.

Audra sank to the ground beside Papa. Blood oozed from the corner of his mouth. She said nothing for fear she'd be next. A gloved hand forced her to her feet. Caleb Windsor stared down at her. Amusement sparkled from his deep blue eyes. Contempt best described her reaction, and she did her best to tell him of his wretched nature through her gaze.

"I'm that bad, huh?" he said.

"I wouldn't know, sir." His nearness frightened her beyond belief. She'd never forget the coldness in his eyes. And she could never forgive him for hitting her father.

"So it's sir now?" He peered closer into her face. "I think I shall steal a kiss from my brother's betrothed."

Audra took a step back, but he grasped her chin, lifted the lower part of his bandanna, and kissed her hard—too hard.

"Tell that to my preacher brother. I kissed his lady before he set eyes on her." He laughed. For a moment she considered the immense pleasure of spitting in his face, but her actions would place her on his level of wickedness.

"God have mercy on you," she said. "How horrible for a godly man like Christopher to have to claim you as a brother. If your poor father only knew what you've become."

"If you only knew." He touched the brooch on the left side of her traveling dress. She cringed, feeling certain his fingers upon the jewelry somehow soiled her. "I think I need this, Miss Audra. It will serve as a lovely memento of our brief time together."

"It belonged to my grandmother."

"Wonderful. Then we'll keep it in the family." He laughed. "Kindly remove it, or I will do it myself."

Audra's fingers shook as she clumsily unclasped the heirloom. Sticking her finger, she winced.

"What a pity." He wiped the blood from her finger with a clean handkerchief. She caught the initials of CWW embroidered on the corner and wondered why a man of such ill repute managed to carry a clean handkerchief. She could have used it to tend to Papa. Caleb stuffed it inside his pocket. "Good job." He turned to the foul-smelling man who had ridden in the stage with them. "Your warning helped us avoid a trap. Grab your horse, and let's get out of here."

Audra glared at the disgusting pair before her. One simply smelled of his evil deeds, the other reeked of treachery to the brother and father who served God and His people.

"We will meet again." Caleb mounted his horse and tucked the brooch into his shirt pocket. Cocking his revolver, he faced the driver. "Stay here for thirty minutes before you pull out. Understand?"

The driver mumbled a yes. Six men disappeared across what Audra had once believed was a beautiful land. Bending to aid Papa, she wished she'd never heard of the Windsor twins.

Chapter 3

Audra viewed the storefronts of Earnest with a mixture of disdain and regret. Nothing of the original adventure met her expectations. The beauty of snowcapped mountains, the lush green countryside, and the gurgling ripple of water now held little attraction. She'd seen a dead man—his chest covered in blood—and she hoped the gruesome sight never crossed her path again. The deceased had a family and friends who loved and cared for him. It all seemed so senseless—the murder, the robbery, the insults thrown by Caleb Windsor and his gang. Combined with Papa's swollen face, her money stolen, Grandmother's brooch gone, and the whole nightmarish experience, she wanted to turn around and head back to Nebraska.

"Come back with me," Papa said. "I don't think you really want to be a part of this. How can I ever tell your mama that you are in a wonderful place? How can I leave you behind to fend for yourself?"

Audra chose to reflect on his words rather than reply. He spoke the truth. She wanted a godly family, not one overcome with strife. How could God want her to have a brother-in-law who was a thief and murderer?

"We don't have any money to go home," she said.

"I have two hands and a strong back."

Leaning her head on his shoulder, she could only sob. "Oh, Papa, I never meant to cause you such trouble."

He kissed her forehead. "None of this is your fault. Don't punish yourself by believing otherwise." He paused. "Look at all this beauty. It reminds me of a piece of heaven, but Satan has a hold here. We just saw his powerful grip. Better to live in a desert with God than in a palace with evil."

"Maybe we haven't met the good folks yet, the ones who love God." Who she was trying to convince?

"I'm waitin'." His voice rang with bitterness. "I'm telling you the gospel truth. I'm not heading back to Nebraska without you or facing your mother with the truth of this uncivilized territory. From what I've seen so far, life here is godless."

At the moment, she agreed with his conviction. She needed only a precious few words to convince her to leave Earnest far behind. But another part of her wanted to give the town a chance.

The stage rolled to a halt and stopped outside the sheriff's office. Already a few men gathered around them, and she felt the whole ordeal was about to be put on display.

"Sheriff, I have a dead man," the driver said. "Caleb Windsor's gang jumped us."

From the stage window, she saw two men from the crowd lift the deceased man's body to the ground.

"Get him to the undertaker and someone fetch Belle and the girls," the sheriff said.

Audra closed her eyes. *Lord, help this poor family with their loss.*

"I have two passengers inside," the driver continued. "Might want to fetch the preacher, too."

"Someone else killed?" the sheriff asked.

"No, Sheriff, a young woman and her father are here on business to see him."

Papa opened the door and stepped down before assisting Audra from the stage. Her shaky legs nearly gave way. The sheriff stepped from the crowd and tipped his hat. "Afternoon, ma'am, sir, I'm Lee Reynolds, the sheriff here in Earnest." He had a mustache that grew from ear to ear.

Papa sized him up quickly. "We could have used you a few miles back."

"Looks that way. I'm real sorry about the holdup. I'll get the doc to take a look at you."

"I'm all right." He stuck out his hand. "Samuel Lenders, and this is my daughter Audra. It would suit us best if we could see Pastor Christopher Windsor."

The sheriff moistened his lips. No doubt he sensed Papa's disapproval of the local law. Audra shared the same sentiments. "I'd take you myself, but I need to get a report from the other driver and tend to the dead man's widow."

"Shouldn't you be sending out a posse?" Papa said.

Silence split the air so loudly that Audra could hear it crackle.

"What do you do for a livin'?" Sheriff Reynolds frowned.

"Farmin'."

"You stick to farming, and I'll stick to upholding the law."

She held her breath. Papa had been riled enough for one day.

"Sheriff Reynolds," a man called.

Audra swung her attention in the direction of the voice, one that sounded vaguely familiar.

"Pastor Windsor." The sheriff grinned widely, or maybe it was his mustache. "These folks are here to see you."

Identical to his picture, dark-haired Christopher Windsor threaded his way through the crowd. He captured Audra's gaze and held it. Compassion etched his face. "Mr. Lenders, Miss Lenders, I just heard what happened. Please accept my apologies." He reached for Papa's hand then turned to her. "This is not at all how I planned our first meeting."

"And it's not what I wanted for my daughter—ever."

Mr. Windsor took in a deep breath. "I should have told you about my brother, but I wanted to spare our father."

"I am a man of my word, Pastor Windsor," Papa said. "The way I look at it, you deceived me and my family, and now you want my daughter to consider a life under these circumstances? Where is God is in all this?"

Audra had never seen Papa this red-faced.

Mr. Windsor smiled as though Papa's drilling was as commonplace as directions to the church. "Let's fetch your trunk and settle you in at the hotel. After you've rested and gotten something to eat"—he paused and studied Papa's face—"and cleaned up those cuts, we'll talk about the problems with my brother."

"I'd rather know when the next stage heads back to Denver."

Papa hadn't mentioned the lack of money. Anger had a way of talking for a person. At least Mama claimed so.

Mr. Windsor stiffened. "I understand how you feel, but if you'll allow me to explain, I'm sure you'll feel differently."

Audra placed her hand on Papa's arm. "Can't we listen to him? *We have come all this way.*"

Papa scowled. The purplish bruise on the side of his face obviously directed his temperament. She remembered a bad tooth on the same side of his face. No doubt it now hurt as well. "It's gonna take a lot of persuading to make me see things different."

Mr. Windsor sought out a young boy to carry the trunk to the boardinghouse. As they moved down the street, Audra glanced at the buildings: the barber and undertaker, general store, sheriff's office, telegraph, doctor's office, and a hotel advertising baths and meals. Farther down, she saw a white church and a small house. She guessed a blacksmith and livery were there somewhere, too. Most towns had them.

Inside the hotel, Papa stopped. "We can't do this. Those thieves took our money."

"Stay with me," Mr. Windsor said to Papa, "and I'll take Miss Lenders to the ranch that I spoke about in my letter."

"How far out of town is it?"

"A few miles. Shouldn't take more than an hour."

Papa glanced at Audra. Every bone in her body cried out for rest, but he had to hurt even more. "Could we drink a cup of water first?" she said.

"I'll do even better." Mr. Windsor's every word soothed her trampled spirit. He may look like his brother, but he had the tone of an angel. "I'll buy us all a good meal, then we can take a wagon to Jed and Naomi Masterses' ranch where I made arrangements for Miss Lenders."

Papa didn't refuse. He eased into a chair in the hotel's restaurant, obviously feeling every bit of the journey and the blow to his face. Mr. Windsor requested soap and water for them, which cleansed Papa's battle-scarred face and lip. Lines deepened in his face.

Audra nearly wept. The events of the day had shattered her dreams—the robbery, the killing, and Papa's beating. When the hotel owner offered a room free of charge, Papa declined. He wouldn't owe any man.

"Pastor Windsor offered a place for me to sleep, and those lodgings suit me just fine."

Once they ate, Mr. Windsor paid the bill and left them to secure his wagon and horse. Papa leaned against the straight-backed chair and dozed. She hated this for him, absolutely hated it. A short while later, Mr. Windsor returned with a short stocky man who looked to be about the same age as Papa.

"Mr. Lenders, Miss Lenders, this is Jed Masters. He drove into town to see if he could be of service." Mr. Windsor clasped the older man's shoulder. "He's been like a father to me."

Jed reached out and shook Papa's hand. "Afternoon, folks. I thought I'd help out the pastor, since tonight's Wednesday and he has services. I can take your daughter to the ranch. You, too, if you're needin' a place to stay."

Papa startled. Audra hadn't thought about Wednesday prayer meeting either.

"I'd wanted to see your place," Papa said. "But I can't ask the pastor to take us out there and return before evening." He glanced at Pastor. Windsor. "Can we visit the Masterses' tomorrow?"

"By all means."

Papa stood. "I'd like to take a few things from the trunk, if you don't mind." He lifted Audra's chin. "Does this suit you, daughter?"

"Yes, Papa, what you need is rest, and we can talk tomorrow."

"May I have a word with Miss Lenders before you leave?" Pastor Windsor said.

Pleased with his request, Audra saw her father nod. The younger man gestured toward the door. "While your father is gathering what he needs, I'd like to show you the church."

Although she felt every mile of the journey, the thought of seeing Christopher's church thrilled her. They walked the short distance to the freshly painted building. Wrapping her shawl about her shoulders, she glanced up at the steeple and the bell intended to call everyone to worship.

"I wanted you to see God's house." He opened the door. "The members are increasing each Sunday. More importantly, we have many fine people turning their lives over to the Lord."

"What a blessing." The dwelling reminded her of Pastor Windsor's church at home, and she told him so.

"Thank you." His midnight blue eyes radiated warmth, so different from the same-colored eyes that had stared at her earlier. "I'm glad you came, so very glad. May I call you Audra? I'd be honored if you would call me Christopher."

"Yes, of course."

"I feel I must apologize to you again about my brother's actions. He is an impetuous, wicked man, but I know God loves him as I do. I've tried everything to convert him to the ways of our Lord, but he refuses. After today, the Wanted posters will add even more crimes."

"How very sad for you." Audra's heart ached for the man before her. She could only imagine the burden he carried for his outlaw brother. "I don't blame you for today, but like Papa, I wish I'd known the circumstances. We could have been prepared, although the warning would not have readied me for the bloodshed today. Do you know the family of the deceased well?"

"Yes, I do. I cannot rest my head tonight until I have ministered to Belle and her two daughters."

"I, too, feel an obligation to offer my sympathy."

"You are truly a rarity." Tears welled up in his eyes. "Father spoke so highly of you, and the thought of a lovely Christian woman to help me in my ministry caused me to omit the truth. I praise Him that you were not hurt. The thought of my brother striking your father grieves me." He paused. "I am so sorry."

Audra believed every word he spoke. She longed to touch his handsome face.

Right then, she knew she could not leave Earnest until she grew to know this humble man.

∽

Caleb paced the kitchen of Jed and Naomi Masters. He had a bad feeling about today and the young lady due in to Earnest. The last time he talked to his brother, Chris had not changed his mind.

"I'm going to push for marriage as soon as she arrives," Chris had said.

"Why? You might not like her?"

"Doesn't matter. Father said she was pretty and a good lady. Those two things are all I need to know."

"Are you going to put an end to your gang?"

Chris grinned. "Haven't decided yet. Maybe I should pray about it."

Caleb clenched his fists. "That's blasphemy. How can you mock God?"

"He knows I'm going to quit someday. Look at all I do for Him now."

At the sound of a wagon approaching, Caleb's thoughts reverted to the present. He watched Naomi lift the checkered curtain to see if her husband had made it back from Earnest.

"Jed's home," she said. "Maybe he has word about the young lady. Oh my, a young lady is with him." Naomi held her breath then patted the bun resting at her nape. "Caleb, hide in our bedroom until it's safe for you to leave."

Chapter 4

Audra instantly liked Naomi and Jed Masters. They looked to be her parents' age and possessed some of their mannerisms. Both were rather short and round—which meant more to love. Naomi's supper tasted better than her own mother's cooking, although Mama didn't have the different foods that were available at the Masterses' ranch. As soon as Naomi opened her arms to her, Audra felt at home. Oddly, when she first met Mr. Masters, he didn't seem nearly as warm and hospitable, as though he were preoccupied. Perhaps he knew the deceased man.

As she lay in her bed at the ranch and glanced about the shadows, she fought exhaustion to pray one more time for the deceased man's family and all those involved in today's events. Should she return home with Papa or give Christopher an opportunity to court her? The handsome pastor did need a wife and, from his kindly ways, she determined he'd be a fine husband. The man had taken her breath away. Papa, on the other hand, regretted ever leaving Nebraska, and it would take some strong persuasion for him to think otherwise. Not that she blamed him. Confusion hammered a wedge between honoring Papa and following what she'd believed was God's will.

With a heavy sigh, she allowed a tear to trickle down her cheek. Then another. The waterfall of anguish washed over her, releasing all the torment and pain of the robbery. Realizing Papa could have been killed, too, caused her to rise from the bed and secure her handkerchief. The moment she held the dainty cloth to her nose, she remembered Caleb wiping the blood from her pricked finger. What a detestable man. She hated him. Those feelings were wrong, and she knew it, but their vehemence assaulted her nevertheless. What kind of life could she have with Christopher when his brother was a murderer and thief? How would they explain a wayward uncle to their children? For that matter, how did the community view the pastor's integrity?

A light rap at the door grasped her attention.

"Audra," Naomi said. "I hear you crying. May I come in?"

Taking a deep breath, Audra opened the door. The moment she saw the tenderness in the older woman's face, she fell into her arms and sobbed. "I'm scared, and I don't know what to do."

Naomi patted her back as though she were a child. "What is God telling you, dear?"

"I don't know. I was so certain at home, but after today I can't think clearly."

In the darkness, Naomi held her tightly, urging Audra to cry out her sorrow and grief. "Some things are not what they always seem," she said.

Audra swallowed and attempted to speak without sobbing. "I know. I thought this land had to be the most beautiful place in the country. Now it's stained with blood."

"You saw things at their worst. Believe me. I know better days are coming."

"You mean when Caleb Windsor and his men are stopped?"

"I mean ending the violence and getting to the truth of the crimes here."

"Do you think it will happen soon?" Audra's heart pounded a little harder. Oh, how she wanted today sealed away in a forgotten memory.

"I think so. In fact, I suggest you mention to Pastor Windsor that you want the violence to end before you marry."

Naomi's words made perfect sense. "Papa might agree for me to stay with those stipulations."

"I understand from Jed that your papa will stay here until he earns the traveling money to go home."

She nodded and dabbed at her nose. "Poor Mama. She will be terribly upset."

"Let's pray about all this," Naomi said. And they did.

⁓

Caleb and Jed stole through the shadows to a grove of oaks behind the corral, avoiding any of the ranch hands roaming about. The reality of Jed's concealing their friendship and sneaking about his own land always hit Caleb hard.

"Miss Audra is pretty shook up," Jed said. "Christopher did a fine job of making sure you're now wanted for murder. I'm sorry. You didn't need me to remind you of how this situation keeps getting worse." The older man lifted his hat to scratch his bald head. "I don't understand your brother at all."

"Who would ever believe you and I branded cattle all day?" Caleb stopped himself from saying things he had no right to say. Chris was his brother. "I don't understand his reason for robbing the stage that he knew Miss Audra and her father rode. And punching Mr. Lenders's face. It's as though he wants Miss Audra to change her mind about staying."

"I don't think she has much to do with it at all. The way I look at it, Chris wants you out of the territory. You've protected him for so long that he's gotten real confident. But he's also clever. He believes you'd never try to expose him."

"He's wrong there. Today convinced me he has to be stopped. Unfortunately, I could get myself strung up before it happens."

"Still having those dreams?"

"Yeah. What I once believed were purely nightmares now I think is God telling me to do something." Caleb saw the outline of his horse by the light of a three-quarter moon. "Brother against brother. Reminds me of the Civil War. At least then both sides believed they were right. This mess is different. Chris can't possibly justify what he's doing."

"You're right, son. Something has to be done soon, and I'm ready to help in any way I can."

"You always have. To make matters worse, my stupidity has Audra Lenders involved. She tried to sound brave this evenin', but I heard the fear in her voice."

"Did you see her?"

"Once. A very pretty young woman. No wonder Father convinced her to travel West. Maybe she'll head back to Nebraska with her father."

Jed reached for the bridle. "You wouldn't say that if you saw the fuss your brother made over Miss Audra and her father. Mark my word, Samuel Lenders will return to Nebraska without his daughter."

Caleb left the Masterses' ranch and rode into the hills—where he'd lived like a criminal for the past year. He knew the way with his eyes closed. The days of sleeping in his own bed on his sprawling ranch had vanished with the accusation of the first robbery. Fortunately Caleb had a good foreman who ran things in his absence—the only other person besides Jed and Naomi who knew the truth.

He'd prayed for God to show him how to stop his brother. Not a pleasant thought at all, but today a man had given his life for Chris's greed. This made one more time Caleb regretted all the years of protecting his selfish brother. The image of Audra Lenders stepping down from the wagon danced across his mind. She reminded him of an angel. The sun color of her hair gave her the innocent look of a child. Yet he sensed she had inner reserves of strength, judging by the little he'd heard while hiding in Jed and Naomi's bedroom.

Caleb stiffened in the saddle. He refused to allow Audra Lenders to marry his brother. The idea of one more innocent victim falling prey to Chris's selfishness caused a surge of anger to swell in him. Naomi might have to take charge of telling her the truth.

~

Audra hadn't intended to sleep the morning away but by the time she opened her eyes, the sun had nearly reached its peak. She stretched and noted sore muscles. Those things promised to fade, but not the anguish from yesterday. The memories would always tear at her heart.

After dressing, she stepped into the kitchen where the smell of fresh coffee and breakfast filled the room. Naomi kneaded bread on the table. "There's bacon and biscuits left from this morning," she said.

"Thank you." Audra smiled. "I planned to rise earlier and help you."

"Nonsense, you needed your rest. How are you this morning?" Flour clothed Naomi's hands, and when she reached to scratch her nose, white dusted her face.

Audra picked up a towel and wiped off the flour from her new friend. "I'll be fine. I appreciate last night more than words can say."

"Glad I could help. Have you decided what to do?"

"Despite yesterday, I still feel like I'm supposed to stay. Papa, on the other hand, will want me to hurry home, and that is tempting."

Naomi gestured toward the stove. "Help yourself to the coffee. Your papa loves you and wants to make sure you're safe."

"I know."

"Jed said Pastor Windsor is bringing your papa today?"

"Yes, ma'am. I'm anxious to see if Papa is all right."

"A good night's sleep always helps." Naomi smiled. "How does a hot bath sound to you?"

"I'd love it." She poured a steaming cup of coffee. "I feel like I have dirt on me all the way from Nebraska."

The bath did wonders for Audra's sore body. The hot water even soothed her weary emotions. She nearly fell asleep again. Her mind repeatedly swept back to her encounter with Caleb. She shivered then focused her attention on his wonderful brother. The sound of Audra Windsor—Mrs. Christopher Windsor— rolled easily off her tongue. She imagined herself making calls with Christopher, playing the piano on Sunday morning, listening to him prepare his sermon. . . Her dream world lingered like a fantasy.

Finally she forced herself from the metal tub, which strongly resembled a watering trough for animals. No sooner had she dressed than she heard dogs barking. From the bedroom window she saw Christopher and Papa seated atop a buckboard. Audra scrambled to pin up her hair, pinch her cheeks, and smooth the skirt of her favorite light blue dress with little pearl buttons lining the bodice. Taking a deep breath, she hurried from the bedroom.

Papa looked so much better. His face no longer held the drawn pallor from yesterday. He actually smiled when he saw her rushing to him.

"You look well, Audra," he said with a quick hug.

"And so do you."

He chuckled. "I fell asleep before the sun went down and woke this morning like a new man. Unfortunately, I missed last night's church services, but the pastor and I have had a fine talk this day."

"I'm glad to hear that." She wondered if he'd changed his mind. A part of her wanted all the things Colorado had to offer. Another part wanted Papa to protect her from the world. But Audra knew her girlhood days were over, and she needed to step out in faith for whatever God planned.

"As soon as I bid Mr. and Mrs. Masters a good day, I'd like to talk." Papa wrapped his arm around her waist. "I believe we have a fine man here," he whispered.

She glanced at Christopher, who captivated her with a boyish smile. She quivered at his gaze. What more could she possibly ever want?

A short while later, Audra and Papa strolled across a green pasture. In the distance several horses fed on fresh grass while colts played tag between their mothers. The sun shone warm and pleasant. She found it easy to forget the ugliness of the day before.

"I believe Christopher Windsor will take good care of you," Papa said. "We've been talking since breakfast, and I like him. He can't do a thing about his wayward brother but hope he realizes his failings." Papa shielded his eyes from the sunlight and paused. "Jed and Naomi Masters are good people, too. So I'm leaving you in their capable hands with my blessings."

Audra flung her arms around his neck. "Thank you, Papa. I won't disappoint you, I promise."

"Daughter, you have never failed to satisfy me with your spirit for adventure. I hope things work out for you and Christopher, but remember you can always come home."

A veil of disillusion crept over her. She had her future, but Papa must now work to earn the money for his return home. If only she could help him. "I want to find work to help pay your way back to Mama."

Papa shook his head. "I won't hear of it. Christopher is loaning me the money, and I plan to sell off some cattle when I get home and repay him."

Audra gasped. However did Christopher manage to convince Papa to borrow money? "Are you sure?"

"God's been good to us, and your mama and I can do this. Besides, the law is after Caleb, and our money could be found any day."

"When will you have to leave?"

"Two days hence."

She blinked back the tears. Love for Papa and Mama overwhelmed her. She would finally be on her own. All that had happened must be the hand of God.

Naomi and Audra worked together cooking dinner, a roast with green onions and potatoes from the previous harvest. Beans simmered on a wood cookstove that Mama would have loved. The blend of smells filled the ranch house with a tantalizing aroma. Bread rose to perfection and baked until golden brown. While Audra stirred together a milk cake, Naomi took fresh lettuce and wilted it with bits of bacon and fat.

Christopher, Papa, and Jed stayed gone while Naomi and Audra busied themselves with supper. What could those men be doing? A twinge of jealousy nipped at her heart. She thought better of it and dwelled on the days ahead.

Supper could not have been more perfect than if the Lord Himself had eaten with them. The food, the conversation, and the laughter made for a glorious evening. Christopher even asked Jed to bless the food and their time together. She discovered Christopher had a sense of humor—a clever wit about him that could take the smallest thing and create laughter. She liked the trait. She liked it a lot. He looked fine tonight, dressed in blue jeans and a light blue chambray shirt. His eyes fairly danced when he looked at her, and she caught him gazing at her more than once. Her cheeks reddened, but the warmth of the attention left her tingly.

Once Naomi and Audra washed the dishes and put everything back in order, Christopher asked if she'd join him for a walk.

"Your father and I need to get started back to Earnest soon, and I'd welcome your company."

Audra untied her apron. Unfathomable glee filled her from head to toe. She hoped her enthusiasm didn't show. The last thing she wanted was Christopher to view her as a flighty schoolgirl. "I'm ready," she said, and he took her arm.

Outside, the moon shed faint light, but a myriad stars lit the way before them. And to think this honorable, godly man wanted to share this beauty with her.

"You are a beautiful young woman, Audra. I noticed right off that the blue in your eyes matches your dress. I will be the envy of every single man in the territory."

Grateful for the night to mask her blush, she rummaged through her mind for the proper words. "I don't know what I've done to warrant such compliments, Christopher, but you are more than welcome."

He laughed lightly. "Your father is a fine man. We had a good day together."

"He said the same about you."

"Then he shared his approval of our courtship?"

She toyed with a pearl button on her dress. She detested feeling this nervous. "Why, yes, he did."

"Wonderful. I think you and I feel a mutual attraction. Don't you agree?"

Dare she speak the truth or play coy?

"Oh, Audra, don't tell me I've seen something in your eyes that isn't so."

The hurt tone in his voice moved her. "You saw correctly. I'm sorry. I simply didn't know how to respond."

"Then shall we marry right away?"

Startled, Audra ceased her stride alongside him. "I thought we were going to get to know each other first."

"Of course we will." He shrugged. "Forgive me. I'm simply anxious."

"And I, as well, but I do want to spend a little time getting to know you before we pledge ourselves for a lifetime."

Christopher gathered her hands into his. "So you are going to leave this poor heart aching each time we are together? How can I enjoy your company when I know we will soon part?"

She couldn't help but smile at the dear man before her. She wanted to memorize his features, remember his words. "I promised Papa I wouldn't rush into marriage. I do hope you understand."

"Ah, I want to please him, too."

Audra recalled her conversation with Naomi the night before. "What I really wish is for your brother to be captured so we would never have to worry ourselves over him."

Christopher said nothing. "I pledge to you, sweet Audra, that I will use all the blessings of God to have Caleb brought into custody." He squeezed her hands lightly. "Now, if the sheriff captures him tomorrow, I will push you to name a wedding day. The members of my congregation will be so very happy." He pulled her to him and leaned his head toward her.

Audra's pulse quickened. She wanted Christopher to kiss her, but it was too soon. She took a step back, but he tightened the grip on her hands and pulled her toward him.

Panic swept through her. "Please, you're hurting me."

Chapter 5

Christopher released her abruptly. "I'm sorry. I don't know what's wrong with me."

Audra took several deep breaths to gain control. The moment reminded her too much of the day before with Caleb—when he kissed her with such cruelty.

"Please forgive me," he said.

She nodded, willing her body to cease trembling.

"I'd better go. This is not how a gentleman behaves toward a lady. I can't remember ever being this inconsiderate of a woman."

"I. . .I feel it's too soon for affection."

He looked up into the night sky. "I know I'm deeply distressed about the funeral tomorrow, especially since my brother killed the man. Perhaps I've become no better than he."

She couldn't bear to hear the pain in his voice. "I have to tell you what your brother did. I can't seem to remove it from my mind." She hesitated. "Yesterday, during the robbery, he. . .kissed me. The things he said were cruel."

"Oh, no." Christopher moved closer then stopped. "I want to comfort you, but I shouldn't. I will never disappoint you again, I promise."

She watched his frame slump back to the house. He looked so dejected. "Christopher, God gives us all a new beginning."

He stopped in his stride and turned to face her. "Does that mean you are giving me another chance to prove myself?"

His words sounded like those of a repentant little boy. "I think this is simply the process of getting to know each other."

"My dear Audra, your words are a song from heaven."

<hr>

Audra raced her horse across the valley to the west of Jed and Naomi's home between their ranch and the Rockies. She marveled at the sun traversing the sky. In a few hours it would dip below the mountains, and the sky would transform from a vivid blue to orange. Her mount was a spirited sorrel mare, and keeping the horse under control took all of her physical strength. But she needed this challenge—a wild attempt to free her mind from the confusion and tragedies of the past few days. The smell of fresh Colorado air and the wind blowing through her tresses ushered in a whisper to trust what she could not see. Her hair eased from the pins at her nape and fell upon her shoulders, and so did the scattered emotions spill from her heart.

Her life had grown out of control in a matter of a few days. The dreams she'd clung to on the journey from Nebraska no longer sustained her. The situation in Earnest begged for deliverance, but what could she do? Pastor Windsor in Nebraska believed his sons pioneered a new country that needed their strength and courage.

This horrible situation was like viewing a wasp land on her arm and not knowing whether to shoo it away or wait for it to fly away on its own accord.

She loathed waiting on anything. Patience was a virtue, and she longed for its attributes. If she lacked wisdom, she should ask God. But this dreadful silence told her to trust God. Audra wanted to scream about the unfairness of it all, but instead she galloped across a beautiful, untamed land hoping to find the answers in the midst of God's creation.

This morning she attended the funeral for the driver Caleb killed. His wife sobbed all the way through the service, and his two young daughters took turns trying to comfort her while their liquid grief spilled over their cheeks. The scene at the burial site intensified when someone asked the sheriff when he planned to string up Caleb Windsor. Poor Christopher, caught between God's command to love his brother and the wickedness of his brother's deeds.

As soon as the man was laid to rest, she accompanied Christopher, Papa, and the Masterses to a midday meal at the widow's home. There tempers flew, and the sheriff finally took a posse and left town in search of the murderer. Audra chastised herself for not congratulating the sheriff on his work, but something about the circumstances between Caleb and Christopher bothered her immensely. It came as a feeling—a torment of sorts—and God's bidding to simply refrain from speaking did not help.

Shortly after the meal, she bid Papa good-bye and tearfully watched the stage depart. She prayed it delivered him safely to Denver where he would board the train back to Mama. Papa had not asked her today if she wanted to return, or she'd have agreed.

All the way back to the ranch with Jed and Naomi, she tried to understand her uneasiness. Brothers. One a man of God, the other an outlaw. She likened the situation to Jacob and Esau, possibly Cain and Abel. How had this happened?

The mare beneath her heaved, and Audra slowed the animal's pace. She'd thought about the differences between the brothers for as long as she intended. She'd prayed until her words repeated, and still her heart ached. Beside a clear, bubbling stream that danced over rocks and pushed its way downstream, she dismounted and walked the horse until its breathing slowed.

A bird sang out and the sound combined with the gurgling water. The solace spread a comforter over her misguided world. Allowing the mare to drink freely and graze, she snatched up a bouquet of white-petaled daisies.

"Miss Audra, you ride well."

She whirled around to see a man identical to Christopher standing not twenty feet from her. Gasping, she calculated the time it would take for her to get to the mare.

"There's no need to be afraid," he said, keeping his stance against the backdrop of brush. "Contrary to the rumors, I'm not the evil brother. I won't hurt you."

"Caleb Windsor." The whisper of his name ushered in terror. Alone, helpless, she refused to make him angry. Mama's warnings about the ways of bad men echoed across her mind.

"That is me, but you, like so many others, believe my clever brother."

She covered her mouth and watched the mare drink deeply.

"I did not kill the driver or rob the stage."

"I was there," she said without thinking. "I saw you. How can you deny it?"

"Because the outlaw in the family is Christopher."

She drew in a breath. Lies, all lies.

"If I wanted to harm you, wouldn't I have crossed the distance between us by now? Out here," he said, gesturing, "no one would hear you scream." He leaned on one leg, his voice barely audible above the rushing stream of water. "If I had murdered a man, wouldn't I be on my way to Mexico?"

"Why are you here? Isn't it enough that you killed a man? Hurt my father? Stole my grandmother's brooch and the money Papa and I needed for the trip?"

Anguish ripped across his face. "I have but one purpose—to warn you that your life will be miserable if you marry my brother. He covers his treachery with a cross."

Fury erupted from a fiery pit deep inside her. "Christopher is good and kind. He's tried to stop you, urge you to turn your life over to the Lord."

Caleb chuckled and shook his head. "Let me tell you about my brother. He's always been the selfish one. Then five years ago he figured out how to please folks and rob them at the same time."

His words continued to anger her. She longed to fling dirt on the man. Caleb must be so wretched that he discarded the truth like ragged clothes.

"I have a few questions for you, Miss Audra. Has he won you over with his smooth talk? How often has he prayed with you? Has he pressed you for a wedding date? Has he kissed you without the proper amount of time to pass? Does he grieve his wayward brother in one breath and pledge his support to have me hanged in the next?"

Audra felt herself grow ashen. Caleb didn't know the truth at all. His questions were merely coincidences. Lifting her chin, she stared into his face. "Have you no respect for a man of God?"

"Why not ask him the same question?"

"I wouldn't insult his beliefs or the work he's done for God."

"Remember the letter he wrote your father? I thought Christopher might settle down if he had a wife. I suggested the whole thing, and I've regretted it ever since. It was my idea for you to stay with Jed and Naomi. They're good people, and they know the truth. I suggested he send the money for travel purposes. How ironic, since he stole it back. God forgive me." He paused. "Go on home with your father to Nebraska—to my father's church. Marrying Chris will only fill you with disappointment and sorrow."

"Why should you care?"

"I love my brother, but I've made a terrible mistake by allowing him to use me as a scapegoat—something that started when we were boys. And soon he'll use you. After the killing yesterday, I have to find a way for folks to learn the truth. Robbing was bad enough, but now he's committed murder."

"I don't believe you." Her lips quivered. This had to be a trick.

Caleb walked over to her horse and gathered up the reins. He held them out to her and patted the mare on the neck. "Time will tell the truth," he said. "Don't let him convince you to stay at the boardinghouse, because there you won't learn the truth until it is too late." He smiled, so much like Christopher that she shuddered. "Best you head on back to Jed and Naomi's before dusk. I wouldn't want the sheriff's men to mistake you for me."

Shaking, she took the reins and lifted herself onto the horse. For a moment she felt a twinge of embarrassment at not riding sidesaddle, but her emotions were already stretched.

"Look at me," Caleb said.

Fearful of disobeying him, she stared into his face. The same face of the man of God who wanted her to be his wife and share in his ministry.

"Study every feature about me, Miss Audra. Remember my eyes and the tone of my voice. I am not the man you think I am. Ask God to show you the truth." With those words, he turned and walked away.

All the way back to the ranch, she pondered Caleb and the strange encounter. As the sun sank lower behind her, so did her spirits. Her mind seemed swollen with questions. His final statement bothered her the most. *Study every feature about me, Miss Audra. Remember my eyes and the tone of my voice. I am not the man you think I am. Ask God to show you the truth.*

Yes, Lord, show me the truth. Do I speak to Jed and Naomi? Or do I make observations on my own?

The Windsor brother who had robbed the stage did not in the least resemble the Caleb Windsor she met today.

Audra decided not to say anything to Jed and Naomi about meeting Caleb. Every word and gesture stayed fixed in her thoughts. She'd always prided herself in being a good judge of character, but confusion over who to trust clouded her every twist and turn. Even considering Christopher might be the real outlaw seemed incredulous—and moved her to ask forgiveness. Caleb wanted to taint his brother's ministry, and she would not fall into his horrible plan.

Certain the man she met on Jed and Naomi's ranch was Satan in disguise, she planned to tell Christopher as soon as he visited again. The following morning while she helped Naomi finish the last of the weekly washing, Christopher rode up on a dark chestnut gelding. He didn't look at all like a pastor, but more like a ranch hand, rugged and appealing, very appealing.

"Morning, Mrs. Masters, Miss Audra." He leaned on the saddle horn and tipped his hat. "How are you ladies this fine day?"

Naomi turned with one of Jed's shirts in hand. "Just working, Pastor. Trying to keep a step ahead of my ornery husband."

"I suspect you've been working on that little project for a lot of years."

Naomi laughed. "I suppose so. What brings you out here? I'm sure it's not to spend the day teasing an old woman."

"To see you, of course, and say hello to Miss Audra."

"More likely the latter." She gestured at Audra. "Watch this man, Audra. Rumor is he's looking for a wife."

Caleb's words stole across her mind like a throbbing headache. She instantly pushed them away. Smoothing a borrowed apron over her black skirt, she caught Christopher's gaze and felt her cheeks warm.

"Maybe I've found one." Christopher grinned and threw his leg over his horse. "When Miss Audra finishes helping you, could she be excused for a walk?"

"We're done now, Pastor. And why don't you ask her?" Naomi placed her hands on her ample hips and nodded at Audra. "Go ahead, dear."

Audra and Christopher strolled in the direction of the corral where a ranch hand attempted to saddle a stallion. The horse jumped and snorted, its ears laid back in obvious rebellion.

"Have you forgiven me?" Christopher said.

"Yes. I haven't given it another thought." Too many other matters had taken over the near kiss—such as his brother.

"Thank you. I've been so angry with myself that I haven't been able to concentrate on this Sunday's sermon."

"Then put your worries aside and concentrate on God's calling."

He watched the stallion throw the ranch hand into the dirt. "Thank you, Audra. Not a moment has passed that I haven't regretted my actions that night. I needed horsewhipped."

She laughed and relaxed slightly. "I think not." She paused. "I would like to tell you something."

He lifted a brow and for a moment she considered the matter with Caleb unimportant, but now was not the time to start keeping things from her husband—or husband to be. "I met Caleb again."

Christopher's features hardened, and his body stiffened. "Did he try to hurt you?"

"No, he was too busy warning me about you." Audra swallowed hard and forced herself to peer into his face.

"Warn you about me? I don't understand."

"He said you were really the outlaw and that he'd always taken the blame for your actions."

He pounded his fist onto the fence rail. "How dare he? He must have gone mad. Audra, I'm afraid for you. Where did you see him?"

"I'd gone riding."

"Riding?"

Why did she feel as though she'd done something wrong? "I needed to get away, to—"

"By yourself?"

"Why are you angry with me?"

"Audra, this is not safe country. Please do not leave the ranch without an escort. It's too dangerous."

"All right. I simply wanted time alone."

"Until Caleb is found, you'll have to forgo such pleasures." His tone grew tender. "I worry about you. Perhaps you should consider taking a room at the boardinghouse where I can watch out for you."

Caleb's words haunted her again. "I'll be careful. I do enjoy staying here with

Jed and Naomi."

"But what if Caleb shows up here. . .harms you or them?" He pressed his lips together as though he wanted to say more but thought better of it. "Please, Audra, if you lived in town, I would know that you were safe."

Lines deepened across his forehead, reminding her of Papa's plowed fields. "I'll think about it." Christopher had enough on his mind without her adding to his problems.

"If you must go riding, then we can ride together." Christopher's face softened. "I promised your father I would take good care of you."

Chapter 6

Caleb waited at the top of a pine-covered ridge where he knew his brother would pass by on his way to town. He'd seen Christopher head toward the Masterses' ranch earlier and figured he went to pay Audra a call. Caleb followed. He crept on foot close enough to observe his brother draw Audra aside to talk. From the look on Chris's face, he was doing his best to convince her of his sincerity. How often had he seen his brother twist an ounce of truth into a wagonload of lies? The thought made him want to stomp up to the corral fence and lay his fist alongside Chris's jaw. A whole lot of good that would do. He could imagine Audra screaming for help and Chris accusing him of every crime this side of the mountains. Any credibility Caleb might have garnered in meeting with Audra would sift through his fingers like fine dirt.

Still the thought gave Caleb immense satisfaction. He continued to watch the two and, from his vantage point, he saw the expressions on Audra's face as well. At first she appeared stubborn, even defiant, but Chris eventually won her over. The peaceful, sweet glances from her told Caleb all he suspected was true.

For a moment he allowed himself to dwell on his first meeting with Audra. Although she'd appeared frightened of him, she'd displayed such courage. And up close she was more beautiful than ever.

Now Caleb sat atop his horse and kept his focus on the road for signs of his no-account brother. One more time he'd attempt to talk some sense into him. A bird flew overhead, and the sun warmed his back. In the distance he saw angry gray clouds gather and move his way. He expelled a heavy sigh. From the looks of nature, he'd be sleeping in Jed's barn again instead of under a star-studded sky. Since the wanted posters went up months ago, he couldn't ride within ten feet of his own place. Some days he wondered if his own men might shoot him for the reward, to say nothing of the sheriff's men or a hungry bounty hunter.

God, when will this end? Chris has to stop robbing from folks, and I need to clear my name.

Silence, always silence. Every word and action from Caleb worked toward justice and truth, and he prayed God rode ahead of him to pave the way. Like the storm brewing in the distance, he feared he'd be caught without shelter when it all came pouring down.

The sound of hoofbeats rhythmically pounding against the road alerted Caleb to a rider. He moved out from the wooded refuge to take a look. Chris rode at breakneck speed, a man in too big a hurry. Caleb planted his horse in the middle of the road. No matter where his brother headed, he was going to listen to reason today.

"Get out of my way," Chris shouted. "I'm late."

"I don't care if you never get to where you're going," Caleb said. "We're going to talk."

Chris slowed his horse when Caleb refused to move. "What's this all about?"

"Murder, robbery, and Audra Lenders."

Chris laughed. "Guilty as charged. What are you going to do about it?"

Caleb fought the rage brewing inside him like the fast-approaching storm. "Stop you, if I die trying."

"And you might do just that." Chris's words stung with the seriousness of the problems between them.

"Has it come to killing your own brother?" Caleb said.

"You're the one who said you would stop me or die trying."

Caleb sized up his twin, identical in looks but never in mind and heart. "I'm talking jail."

"And what do you think the law will do with a man convicted of murder?"

"That's for a court to decide."

Chris cursed. "I need to check on my horses. Move out of my way."

"Not until we get a few things settled." Caleb tried again to control his anger, but it walked two paces ahead of him. He swallowed hard and caught a glimpse of a patch of sunlight not yet covered by the gray clouds. Hope. God always offered His light. "Brother, you think more of your horses than you do people, and I admit you take fine care of them. But I want you to turn yourself in before it gets worse. There are folks who will vouch for me, clear my name."

"And there are a whole lot more who'll string you up."

"Those are my terms. I give you three days to confess to the sheriff. In the meantime, you leave Miss Lenders alone."

Again Chris laughed. "She's too pretty to leave alone. I know you've noticed. And for your information, I have plans to leave Colorado."

"When?"

"Got me just about enough money to head south for Mexico. I plan on cashing in on my hard work in about six weeks," Chris said.

"That's too long. Three days, like I said before."

"Forget it. I'll do as I please." Chris pulled his horse around Caleb. "I will marry Audra as planned then leave her here."

"Haven't you done enough? I can't stand by and not try to stop you."

"I won't let you. I'm faking my death, and you'll still be on the run." With those words, Chris took off toward Earnest.

Only his faith in God stopped Caleb from going after his brother. The truth was he wanted to pound some sense into him, and he'd most likely hurt Chris a whole lot more than he intended.

The law had ways of handling men like Christopher Windsor. Caleb simply hated the thought of his brother serving time in a rat-infested prison—or worse. Caleb had always looked out for his brother. Chris had been sickly when they were little boys, and the woman who took care of him never seemed to give all the love he craved. Maybe a mother's love would have made a difference, and Chris wouldn't have tried so hard to get folks to notice him.

The storm clouds moved faster than Caleb anticipated. He rode toward the Masterses' ranch. He needed to confront Miss Audra about a few things.

Audra helped Naomi put dinner on the table. Mealtimes were a rush of activity until food was delivered to the ranch hands at the bunkhouse. Those men inhaled their food like they'd never eaten before. Nearly made Audra sick. The storm made things worse as rain threatened to ruin the ham and beans and a huge mound of corn bread with butter and honey. Audra, covered in a parka that belonged to Jed, carried the coffeepot in one hand and a crock jug of buttermilk in the other. A flash of lightning and an ear-piercing crack of thunder caused her nearly to drop both. Once inside the bunkhouse and the food delivered to the three hands, Naomi announced her readiness to step back out in the rain.

"Is it wrong to pray for this to ease up?" Audra said as the rain sliced against the window and another bellow of thunder shook the bunkhouse.

"If it is, then I'm guilty." Naomi shook her head. "Let's go, Audra. Never let it be said this old woman was afraid of a little bad weather."

With Naomi's round body swishing ahead of her, Audra followed like an obedient chick after its mama. She imagined the ranch hands were chuckling at the sight of the two women dashing across the mud-ridden path. A flash of lightning that caused her hair to stand on end made her glad she didn't need to visit the outhouse. She half expected the necessary building to go up in flames at any moment.

Once safe inside the house, she realized she'd been holding her breath. The powerful display of nature reminded her of the storms at home in Nebraska. She'd dreaded them, too.

"All that excitement has made me hungry," Naomi said. "As soon as Jed gets in, we'll eat. Don't you know those men were laughing at us?"

Audra laughed. "I thought the same thing." She hung both parkas on pegs and watched them drip onto the floor. She then set two bowls beneath them to catch the water. "Naomi, despite this nasty weather, I enjoy every minute here with you and Jed."

"Well, thank you. We love having you here, too."

She remembered Christopher urging her to move into town. The thought of ever leaving the Masterses saddened her. As soon as supper rested on the table, the door opened, and Jed stepped inside with a man behind him.

"Good to see you, Caleb," Naomi said. "Got plenty of ham and beans here."

Audra gasped. Why, it was as though Caleb often came to see them.

"Thank you, Ma." He kissed the woman's cheek. "I hate my own cooking."

Jed chuckled. "I'd be the size of a fencepost if it weren't for her feeding me so good."

Naomi nodded at Audra. "I need to introduce our guest."

"We...we've met," Audra said. Christopher would be so upset.

Caleb touched the brim of his rain-soaked hat. "Evenin', Miss Lenders."

Audra met his gaze, mostly out of defiance, but warmth stared back at her. Confused, she busied herself in setting another place for the outlaw. A flurry of questions assaulted her. Why were Jed and Naomi so friendly with Caleb? Were they afraid of what he might do? Were they outlaws, too? Didn't they understand this man cared for no one but himself?

"Caleb is a regular visitor," Jed said as though reading her thoughts. "He's a fine man—not what others think."

Audra swallowed hard and failed to comment. Frightened best described her.

"You can sit down now," Naomi said. "We have plenty of time to discuss the Windsor brothers and the horrible mess Christopher has made of things." She bent her head for Jed's blessing of the food, but Audra couldn't concentrate.

The others ate heartily. Rather than make her uneasiness evident, Audra picked at her food and shoved it around on her plate to make it look like she was eating. Meanwhile, Naomi, Jed, and Caleb talked about everything but what screamed through Audra's mind.

"I do have a purpose for being here tonight." Caleb scooped up another slice of corn bread and reached for the pitcher of honey. He glanced up at Audra. "I met with Chris after I saw him talk to Miss Lenders this afternoon."

Audra trembled and placed her fork beside her plate. He'd been spying on them? "Perhaps you should spend more time following what the pastor says."

Jed coughed and reached for his coffee. With a deep breath, he managed to speak. "If we kept better track of the good pastor, we could have avoided a funeral."

"Pardon me, Mr. Masters, but aren't you confused?" Audra said.

Silence permeated the room, interrupted only by the falling rain outside.

Naomi touched Audra's arm. "Honey, there's a lot you don't know, and I've been meaning to tell you. Guess I knew how badly the news would upset you."

"I've told her already," Caleb said. "But she doesn't believe a word of it. Chris has done a fine job."

Naomi placed her napkin in her lap. "What's happened now?"

"I told him today that I intended to stop him and that he had three days to turn himself in to the sheriff." Caleb pushed back his plate. "He didn't take kindly to it and gave me a little advance notice of his plans."

Jed rubbed his face. "It's all I can do to tolerate the sound of his voice on Wednesday nights and Sundays. Pretending to like him don't make me feel any better about myself either. Go ahead and tell us, son. What's he intendin' to do?"

Audra peered into Caleb's face, not sure if she wanted to hear another lie or not. To think her dear new friends had fallen under his spell. She studied his face. He was a good one at deceiving folks. If she didn't know better, she'd swear he knew Jesus.

"He says he has almost enough money to head to Mexico."

"That's a relief," Naomi said.

"Not really. He intends to follow through with courtin' and marrying Miss Lenders then fake his death. That way the law will still be after me."

"Oh, no." Huge tears slid down Naomi's cheeks. "I know I've asked this before, but why, Caleb? From what you've told me about your father, he's a fine man who did his best to raise you boys right."

Caleb nodded. "He loved us and taught us right from wrong. His congregation kept him busy, but he always found time for us. The truth is, if I hadn't covered up for Chris all these years, he might not be the thief and murderer he is today."

"Don't go blaming yourself. He made his own choices." Jed turned to Audra. "I see in your face that you're doubtin' what we're saying, so I'm asking you to take what we say to the Lord. He'll give you the truth."

She intended to do that very thing. "Yes, sir. Christopher took good care of Papa and has been kind to me. I find this very hard to believe."

"He paid for your father's return home, right?" Jed said. When she nodded he continued. "The money Chris used was probably the same that he stole from you. Now how do you feel about his generosity?"

Audra said nothing. *Lord, help me. They sound so convincing, but Christopher couldn't possibly be an outlaw, could he?*

"Do you understand if Chris follows through with what he's planning, he will never face his crimes?" Jed said. "And Caleb will still be a wanted man."

"And you," Naomi sighed and dabbed at her eyes, "might be left with a child to raise by yourself. If you did find another husband, you'd be married to two men at the same time."

Audra stood from the table. Her cheeks flushed hot at Naomi's intimate suggestion. Why ever did Christopher bring her to these people's home?

"Miss Lenders, please sit down," Caleb said. "No one here wants to hurt you. No one has anything to gain by telling you all this. We're warning you, that's all. Do what Jed says. Pray about my brother—and think real hard about going home to Nebraska."

⌇

Caleb lay awake in Jed's barn, bone-tired and worn out from feuding with Chris. Every time he considered what to do about his brother, the plan exploded in his face. The one he had now didn't look much better. Chris had to be caught in a crime while posing as the town's pastor. But how? Tomorrow he'd talk to Jed and Naomi about it. Between the three of them, God would surely give them an answer.

Audra kept stepping into his thoughts. Besides being the prettiest woman he'd ever seen, she had an admirable strength about her. Beneath those pale blue eyes shimmering like the sun on a patch of wildflowers, he saw true inner beauty. At first he hated the fact she didn't believe the truth about Christopher, but when he pondered on it, he found her trait commendable. She wasn't easily persuaded once she had her mind fixed on something. But her determination also meant when she finally realized the true outlaw, she'd be madder than an agitated nest of hornets.

Tonight, he wondered if he'd ever meet a woman like Audra Lenders. He'd given up on having a wife and family, but after being around her tonight, he suddenly yearned for those things again. *Am I being a fool, Lord? I'm actually jealous of my brother. Coveting is a sin, and I know it, but isn't this situation different?*

Tossing and turning on the straw pallet, Caleb listened to the rain and decided he'd best be gone before Audra woke. Seeing her again with another one of her loathing stares would make him feel less than a man.

Chapter 7

"I sn't this glorious?" Audra said. "I love Colorado—everything about it. The fresh air, the green mountains, all these beautiful wildflowers, the blue mountains in the distance with the white peaks, and a place to stay that is not a smelly soddy."

Christopher laughed. They'd stopped their horses to gaze out over the valley where Jed and Naomi's horses and cattle pastured. "Shall I move my church out here?"

She swung her attention his way with a sudden fierce devotion to this man. How handsome he looked sitting erect in the saddle and peering at her with a mixture of humor and admiration. "Could you?" A lopsided grin met her, and she realized the foolishness of her question. "Guess the ride from town might be a problem for some, and this is Jed and Naomi's land."

"Yes, my dear Audra. A church here would not be wise. Its location in Earnest suits God's purpose."

At times she detested practicality. A fantasy world appealed to her today, one with no worries about tomorrow.

"You look so serious," he said. "What has put such a frown on your pretty face?"

She took in a breath and admired the sunlight haloing his head. "Wanting desperately for everything to be perfect, and yet knowing it is impossible."

"I believe every good thing in life is for the taking."

The peculiar remark from a man of God begged for an explanation. "What do you mean? I thought love and obedience brought God's blessings. I'm not sure if we are to take things."

"We are speaking the same. I used the word *taking* instead of blessings or gifts. God wants us to have all the good things of life."

"I think I understand." Audra needed to meditate on his words later when she didn't have his wonderful company to distract her.

"Shall we lead the horses for a while?

"I'd like that." A breeze picked up a few stray tendrils and tickled her neck. They walked in silence. Every sight and sound of nature welcomed the promise of summer.

"Has my brother frightened you anymore?"

She recalled two nights ago and Caleb's presence at supper. "No, he hasn't said or done anything to make me afraid." *Irritated and angry best describes my feelings about your brother's ridiculous claims.*

"Good. I've decided to denounce his activities at tomorrow morning's service and encourage the men to help the sheriff." He paused and managed what looked like a difficult swallow. No doubt his emotions about Caleb cut at his heart. "I'm fearful folks think I know his whereabouts, which is quite the contrary." He sighed. "The incident that happened after I left you at the Masterses' made folks angrier. The sheriff has to find my brother before anyone else is killed." He blinked and glanced away in the distance. "This is so hard, Audra. My own flesh and blood an outlaw."

"What happened?" Had Christopher learned Caleb had been at the ranch? He'd stayed way into the night talking to Jed.

"While folks east of town were eating their supper, Caleb and his men stole thirty head of cattle. One of the ranch hands saw him and his gang."

"East of town?" Impossible. *How could Caleb be rustling cattle and eating with us at the same time?* A shiver snaked up her spine.

"Are you sure?" When Christopher stared at her oddly, she caught her breath. "I mean how could he be so brazen shortly after the stagecoach robbery?"

"I don't think my brother thinks about a proper length of time before he steps out again with his gang. He has a taste for blood and power, and it grows worse." She paled at the impact of his words. Who told the truth? Confusion twisted at her stomach.

"Oh, forgive me for frightening you. You have no idea how Caleb can manipulate people."

Audra bit her tongue to keep from stating what she knew about Caleb's friendship with Jed and Naomi. An inner urging stopped her, and she'd always been sensitive to God curbing her tongue—even if she didn't always listen. "The crimes must end, Christopher, although the cost of losing your brother is a high price."

Sadness swept over his features. "I lost him a long time ago. I have nightmares of conducting his funeral." He wrapped the horse's reins around a tree then took hers and did the same. "I believe I've been blessed with you, Audra. You will be my ray of light in all of this gloom. Let's talk of more pleasant things, like you and me."

"That is much more agreeable," she said.

A moment later the two strolled side by side while their horses grazed on the new tender grass. She thought of Mama and Papa. When she left Nebraska, she didn't think she'd ever pine away for them, but in these turbulent times she missed them sorely.

"What must I do to convince you of my love?" Boyish innocence ushered in a glimpse of Christopher's heart.

"This soon? We barely have grown beyond our given names." Audra noted a strange sensation clawing at her heart.

"I felt you and I were handpicked by God the first time I set eyes on you. I truly felt an angel stepped down from the stage." He gathered her hands into his and bent closer. "Don't you feel the same? I can think of no one else that I'd rather have beside me for the rest of my life than you, Audra Lenders. Together we can do God's work and build a family of our own. I love you more with every passing moment."

Her pulse quickened at his declaration. A flame burned in his eyes, one that unnerved her. "Oh, Christopher, you invite such dreams into my heart. I think if not for this horrible tragedy of your brother, I'd say yes this very minute."

He drew her closer, and she went willingly, but the force of his grip intensified the panic she'd sensed earlier. "I can take care of Caleb. We shouldn't let anything stand in the way of our happiness."

His grip tightened, and she trembled. "Christopher, you frighten me. Please let me go."

"Don't you think a man has the right to hold his future bride and taste her lips?"

She stared into his eyes. The look he offered spoke of matters intended for a husband and wife. "Take me back to the house. I'm uncomfortable."

Christopher's fingers tightened around her wrist. "Did you think that you could tempt me with your presence out here away from everyone and say no to my affections? How cruel for one who proclaims innocence."

Audra struggled. "I had no such idea at all. Please, Christopher."

His head bent lower and his hot breath sent tremors up and down her spine. An unseen hand pulled him away from her. "Leave her alone, Chris."

She gasped. Caleb Windsor had come to her aid?

Christopher released Audra and turned to swing at Caleb, but Caleb stopped the blow and held Christopher back. "I told you before to leave her alone."

"She is none of your business." Christopher shook off Caleb's hold.

"And I told you that I was going to stop what you're doing. I will defend anyone you attempt to abuse."

"You can't be everywhere. I have plans and nobody is getting in my way."

Caleb narrowed his gaze. "Keep going, Chris, and you're going to hang yourself."

"I don't think so. You're the one wanted for murder and robbery."

Audra stared incredulously. The words flying between the two brothers almost sounded as though Caleb had been right.

Caleb grabbed Christopher by the collar. "I gave you three days, and this is day two. Turn yourself in to the sheriff, or I'm handling it."

Christopher laughed. "I'm the respected Windsor in the community, or have you forgotten?"

Caleb glanced at Audra. "She's listening to every word."

"And what does that mean? Audra and I plan to marry as soon as the law catches up to you—possibly sooner. We may have our differences, but misunderstandings have nothing to do with our love."

Caleb stepped back from his brother. "You know about love? Animals are more respectful of each other than you are." He whirled around to her. "Miss Audra, once I asked you to remember everything about me. Now I'm asking you to remember every word that has passed between Chris and me here today. Think on it. And think on what might have happened if I hadn't been here."

Audra chose not to trust the words of either man. Right now she wanted to be in the security of Jed and Naomi's home. "I'm riding back to the house."

"I'll go with you," Christopher said. "I need to explain."

Audra glared at him, fists clenched. "I'd rather be alone."

"I'll escort you," Caleb said. "I have my horse behind those trees."

"I said I'd rather ride alone, thank you."

"I understand, Miss Audra, but I intend to accompany you until you're safely at Jed and Naomi's." Caleb turned to a clump of trees, and she hurried away to her horse.

"Audra, wait," Christopher called. "All right, believe that lawless brother of mine. He's going to swing for all he's done."

She picked up her pace, not once giving a Windsor brother her attention. "I don't believe or trust either of you." Once Audra reached the tree where her horse stood waiting, she swung up into the saddle only to find Caleb riding up beside her. Every muscle and nerve stiffened. He wasn't riding the pewter-colored stallion but a dark brown mare.

They rode in silence. She considered spurring on her horse, but in truth she needed the solace to pray through what had happened. Christopher's harshness when she refused his kiss shook her more than the twister that carried off the roof of the soddy back in Nebraska. And this wasn't the first time. What she'd learned from Mama about men and what she'd observed from the young men back home had no resemblance to her experience with Christopher. It seemed as though he turned into another man when they were alone, one who frightened her.

Feigning interest in the countryside, she cast a sideways glance at Caleb. He'd come to her rescue, as though he suspected Christopher's behavior. She still trembled and fought to gain control. Uncertainty etched her mind, a state she'd felt more than once lately. Why would an outlaw want to help her? What did Caleb and Christopher's conversation mean?

"Why don't you tell me what you're thinking? Might help to sort things out," Caleb said.

Audra wished she could cry, but those sentiments didn't solve a thing. Taking a deep breath, she tightened her fingers around the reins. "Why aren't you riding the pewter-colored stallion?"

He shook his head. "Don't own one. A horse fitting that description belongs to Chris."

A shiver danced up and down her arms. "Do you ever ride it?"

"It's a one-man horse. High-spirited. I have my own." He stopped in the middle of the path and pushed back his hat, a tan color with a short crown. His dark hair fell across his collar, a little longer than Christopher's. "Keep remembering things, Miss Audra. You'll figure out the truth."

She stared at her gloved hands. "The man who held up the stage rode a pewter-colored stallion."

"I know." He urged his horse forward.

"He also wore a dark brown hat with a high crown."

"I'm wearing my only hat." He expelled a heavy sigh. "Chris will have an excuse for today. Probably will tell you he's unworthy of you and beg forgiveness."

"He should say those things. His behavior was uncalled for."

"Always is."

"Are you saying there is nothing good about Christopher?"

Caleb shrugged and took a deep breath. "He loves that horse. We used to have an old dog he liked. He'd do about anything to please our father. Tell you what, Chris is good with horses. Takes care of them like they were his children. He's clean and neat. When he makes up his mind about something, he doesn't give up."

"Even to be a pastor?"

Caleb's gaze didn't waver. "Even to be a pastor."

"What about you? You say you aren't the outlaw, but how did all of this start?"

He pressed his lips together then moistened them as though he tasted something vile. "Chris spent a lot of time sick when we were younger, and I felt sorry for him. He's always been the rebellious one, had a habit of venturing one step farther than what was right. I hated to see him get punished all the time, so as a kid I started admitting to things I didn't do. That way both of us looked like we were headed for big trouble instead of Chris. As we grew up, I covered for him until I looked like the worst one." Caleb stopped to watch a buck and two deer nibble at some grass to the right of them. "We came out here with the idea of leaving the past behind. Both of us wanted to go into ranching. Soon after, Chris got mixed up with bad company. We argued, then he decided he wanted to pastor a church. We argued about that too, 'cause I knew God hadn't called him. Anyway, about two years ago he started rustling cattle and horses. Somebody saw him, and I got the blame. Nothing's changed since we were boys."

"And you're telling me he's done all of these crimes and covered for himself by being a pastor?" Audra had heard children tell bigger tales than this.

"Yes, ma'am. In a way it's my fault. I started the problem a long time ago."

The even tone of his voice rang with confidence. Doubts crept in like slow rising water. Today the roles of the men seemed reversed.

"Why did you help me?" she said.

"I made a decision to stop Chris, right after he shot the driver." He pointed to an eagle soaring overhead, a magnificent creature with its proud white head and golden beak. The regal bird appeared to guard the earth below. "Besides, you're a lovely lady, Audra Lenders. Naomi tells me your heart is pure gold. She cares for you like a daughter, and you love Jesus."

She held her hat and watched the eagle circle above them. *Oh, Lord, I don't understand what is going on.* Her head ached from trying to discern the truth. "If Christopher has stolen all these things, where are they?"

Caleb said nothing for several moments. "I have no idea where he's hidden them. I've searched the area for miles around looking for the cattle and horses, but I imagine they're already wearing another brand and headed south to sell."

"Where is your ranch?"

He pointed northeast. "I have a good foreman who runs things for me. The sheriff has combed every inch of it and inspected my cattle and horses more times than I can count."

Could he be telling the truth? She relived the angry words Christopher and

Caleb threw at each other.

"So now you believe me?" he said.

She turned away. "I didn't say that at all. Honestly, neither of you measures up to your father."

Audra dug her heels into her horse and raced the remaining distance to the ranch, leaving Caleb in a flurry of dust and dirt. What an outlandish story. The two men deserved each other, the outlaw and the demanding pastor.

She caught her breath. Caleb couldn't have been two places at the same time. Could the ranch owner have lied to Christopher about his brother's actions? That didn't make sense.

Why did Caleb have more manners than Christopher?

Why did Christopher behave like a spoiled child?

Why hadn't she listened to Mama and stayed in Nebraska?

∼✺∼

Caleb skirted the hill overlooking the Masterses' ranch. He expected Christopher to ride in there to make amends with Miss Audra, but he hadn't crossed this way. That woman could charm the honey from a nest of bees. Each time he saw her, his insides turned to apple butter. The way he looked at it, any man would be proud to have Audra Lenders as a bride. Why, he'd gladly spend the rest of his life making sure she wore a smile every day. He hoped she learned the truth soon, because he'd like the chance to win her.

Tomorrow was Sunday, the third day of Chris's deadline to turn himself in. One of Chris's men offered to come forward when he'd been cheated out of his share of a robbery. Caleb had arranged to meet him Monday morning at the Masterses' ranch. Then they'd head into town to meet with the sheriff. With Jed and Naomi planning to testify, Chris should be in jail come mid-afternoon.

He hated doing this to their father, but he had no choice. The killings and robberies had to end.

Chapter 8

A udra paced the kitchen floor with the anticipation that Christopher planned to ride out to the ranch and apologize. Her gaze rested on Naomi's largest iron skillet as the older woman stood cleaning it before she fried chicken. He'd best take his sweet talk elsewhere, or she just might use that skillet on him. She didn't want to hear about his remorse or blame his imprudent behavior on her charms. When she stopped to think about it, no young man in Nebraska ever treated her with such disrespect, and he called himself a man of God. Maybe Caleb and the Masterses had spoken the truth—or both of the Windsor twins were a downright disgrace to their father.

She allotted time for the brothers to quarrel, even throw a few punches, but neither man showed his face.

"Just as well," she said louder than she intended.

Naomi dropped the iron skillet, and Audra startled. "What happened out there with Christopher?"

Audra crossed her arms. "Christopher *and* Caleb. The good pastor needs to work on his manners, and Caleb...and Caleb..."

"Caleb what?"

She shook her head and halted in the middle of the floor. "He's supposed to be an outlaw, but he has this habit of rescuing me when Christopher..."

"Christopher what?"

Audra dug her fingernails into her upper arms. "He can be aggressive."

"Most outlaws are."

"Unlike you and Jed, I'm not convinced that Christopher is the outlaw." She sounded too much like a whining toddler. "Whatever happened to the simple life when a person could tell right off who were the law-biding folks and who were not?"

"My dear, you moved to Colorado and met the Windsor twins." Naomi's tone held a frankness guaranteed to pry loose the cobwebs in Audra's mind, the ones that demanded an explanation of what was really happening in Earnest. "Caleb made mistakes by covering up for his brother, but he's long since seen the result of his decisions. Loving someone doesn't mean you shelter them from their own wrongdoing. All of us have to learn right from wrong by facing the consequences of our actions."

Audra sank into a chair. The anger had vanished, but in its place rested more doubts about Pastor Christopher Windsor. She swallowed hard and remembered...

"Some of the things Christopher said didn't sound like a pastor." She paused. "His ambiguous remarks made me angry. I didn't see a reason for it—like he was arguing with Caleb about one thing but wanting me to believe another."

"Tell me more so I can help you." Naomi took a chair beside her.

"He said Caleb stole thirty head of cattle, but he was here when the rustling took place."

"That's not the first time Caleb's been accused of a crime while he was with Jed and me."

"There's more. He said he had plans, and I don't think he meant God's work. Now I wonder if you and Jed have spoken the truth all along."

There, she said it. Her stomach fluttered—not in fear or sickness, but with realization. The certainty of who was the good man and who was the vile one suddenly became as clear as a mountain spring. Only God could touch her with the truth and leave her feeling convinced. She lifted her gaze to Naomi. A tear trickled down the older woman's face.

"I believe you just answered the question tormenting your mind," Naomi said. "Or rather, God revealed whom to believe."

Audra swallowed. "I have to be absolutely sure. I'm sorry. Accusing a pastor of murder?" She paused to gather her wits. "Do you know Christopher and Caleb's middle names?"

Naomi tilted her head. Confusion etched her brow. "Yes. It's Caleb Andrew and Christopher Wesley."

Audra held her breath and covered her mouth. "The man who held up the stagecoach used a folded, clean handkerchief with the initials CWW to wipe blood from my hand." She moistened her lips. "How could one man pose as a man of God and commit those horrible crimes?" She rose from the chair. Understanding sickened her. "Naomi, he shot and killed that man, comforted his widow and daughters, and then preached at his funeral. Is he mad? He even encouraged the men in his congregation to go after Caleb." Whipping her attention to the older woman, Audra felt herself grow pale. "Why am I saying this? You've known the truth all along."

Naomi gathered up Audra's hands. "At times I've wanted to stand up in the middle of church and shake my fist at him. And Jed? Oh my, if he ever unleashes his temper on that young man, there won't be any place where Christopher Windsor can hide."

"What can we do? I know tomorrow is the third day when Caleb said he'd turn over evidence to the sheriff."

"Do you honestly think the sheriff will believe Caleb? Would you, if you hadn't seen for yourself?"

Audra gazed at Naomi solemnly. "Caleb will get himself killed."

"Jed is going to try and talk some sense into him this evening. Caleb's intentions are noble, but if he's killed, Christopher will find another way to continue breaking the law. There must be another way to prove Caleb's innocence."

Audra deliberated the problem. No man should be punished for something he didn't do. And a guilty man shouldn't go free either. Not that she cared much for Caleb. "Mama and Papa were right. I should have stayed in Nebraska," she said. "Then I wouldn't be in this fix."

"But Caleb would still have this problem." Naomi shrugged. "I care for that young man, and I'm probably selfish here, but God may have had a reason for bringing you here—to help him clear his name."

"Me?"

"Yes, my dear. If anyone in these parts can find out information about Christopher, you can."

"He won't tell me a thing after today."

A slow grin spread over Naomi's face. "What if you went to him and said you had made a mistake? Asked him to give you another chance?"

"Lie? I can't do that!"

The older woman cringed. "I don't believe in lying either. When I think about it, Jed and I have been living a lie to protect Caleb."

"I want to help, but I'm not sure how." The seriousness of the situation settled on her like the heavy air before a storm.

"I suggest you pray about what to do. This isn't your battle anyway, and I was wrong in asking you to put yourself in harm's way."

Audra wrapped her arm around Naomi's round shoulder. "This became my battle when I saw a man killed, attended his funeral, and comforted his wife and daughters. When I think of poor Belle raising those little girls by herself, I want to take a switch to Christopher. Who will be next?"

<hr>

Caleb spotted Jed riding his way. He expected him. No doubt his old friend wanted to talk him out of going to the sheriff tomorrow. But he'd made up his mind. He'd rather risk arrest and conviction than allow his brother to break one more law. Having a witness should help, too, even if the man had once ridden with Chris. With the killing and plans to leave the country, no telling what his brother would do next. He hated what the news would do to their father. He'd been so proud of Christopher entering the ministry. Now their father would learn not only how Caleb had taken the blame all these years for Chris but also how he'd written the letter for Miss Audra to come to Earnest.

Jed waved and rode closer. For a stout man, he handled himself well on a horse, and his age hadn't slowed him down on the ranch either. "I've been looking all over for you," Jed said.

Caleb grinned. "Now you found me. Sure glad you're not a lawman."

"Aren't you the lucky one? We need to talk, and Naomi wants you to come for dinner."

"As if I might be stupid enough to refuse her cooking?"

"Then come with me, and we can talk along the way."

Caleb mounted his horse, mentally calculating when Jed would start in about heading to the sheriff tomorrow morning.

"We've had a good bit of rain this month. The grass is growing up thick and green," Jed said.

"Yes, it is." Caleb laughed inwardly.

"The new calves will fatten up just fine. I might even make a little money this year. Wouldn't you like to ride across your own land and not worry about gettin' shot or hanged?"

Caleb inhaled deeply. "That's what I'm taking care of tomorrow."

"Isn't your witness an outlaw?"

"Used to be."

"Correction, he's still wanted by the law. So who's the sheriff going to believe, an outlaw or the town's preacher?"

"I have to try." An icy chill raced up Caleb's arms, despite the warm temperature.

"Then try smart. God love you, son, but when it comes to your brother you haven't a lick of sense. Do you think he's going to confess when he's already approached men in the church to gun you down?"

"I don't think he'd really go through with it."

Jed reined in his horse. "He doesn't have to. Some bounty hunter or lawman will do it for him."

As usual Jed pointed out the logical side of things. The truth be known, Caleb was tired of fighting his brother. He was a prisoner as surely as if he lived behind bars. He didn't want his brother hanged or sentenced to life in prison. He simply wanted him stopped. *I am a fool when it comes to my brother. He has to face a judge and jury for what he's done.*

"Most likely seeing you dead wouldn't put an end to things. He'd find another way to cheat folks." Jed's words spoke Caleb's thoughts.

"Then what do you think I should do?"

"Like I said." Jed lifted his reins and urged his horse to walk. "Come to dinner. The womenfolk have been talking. Told me about it earlier. They have a plan that needs a lot of prayer."

"Miss Audra? She doesn't care much for me."

Jed shrugged. "Maybe not, but she sees the truth about Christopher."

"Well, I don't want her hurt."

Jed chuckled. "That was quick. Anything else on your mind about Audra?"

Caleb set his jaw. He'd listen to them tonight, but hearing them out didn't mean he'd do what they suggested. Not one more person was going to risk their life on account of him.

～～～

Audra inhaled the tantalizing aroma of dinner. Naomi had gone to special preparations for tonight's meal and had simmered a side of beef all day in onions, herbs, and greens. The biscuits looked lighter than foam off a fast-moving stream, and she'd made a rich bread pudding topped with wild strawberries. All the trouble made Audra wonder if tonight's dinner had been planned for a while. Considering what Caleb intended to do the following day and Jed's need to talk him out of it, Naomi must be doing her share.

What about me? I believe God wants me to help, but deceiving Christopher into believing I still want to marry him isn't right either. Even carefully rewording an apology sounded wrong.

I need Your guidance, God. I'm more bewildered than I can ever remember.

As soon as Naomi and Audra made the trek from the bunkhouse to feed the ranch hands, Jed and Caleb strode in. Immediately, Audra noticed a difference in the younger man. He carried himself differently, seemed self-assured. His shoulders looked a bit broader, and his voice sounded a little deeper. Why, when his life was more in danger than ever before?

"You feeling all right, Miss Audra?" Jed said. "You're a bit flushed."

What was wrong with her? "I'm fine. Must be the cook fire. Evenin', Caleb."

"Evenin', Miss Audra."

Naomi laughed. Audra refused to look at Caleb.

"Let's eat," Naomi said a few moments later.

The four gathered around the table, and Audra ended up next to Caleb. Her unexplainable feelings toward him unnerved her. Her stomach fluttered. Perhaps she was ill.

The enticing smells made her stomach growl. Strange how she could lose her appetite and be hungry at the same time. Normally conversation flew in every direction, but tonight no one contributed to a single topic. Once the bread pudding disappeared and hot coffee was poured, Jed cleared his throat.

"We need to figure out what to do about Caleb's predicament, and I believe the best way to begin is with prayer." He lowered his head. "Heavenly Father, we have a heap of trouble here. You've heard me talk about the Windsor brothers before, and I know You can clear Caleb's name and stop Christopher. So now we're asking You to show us the way. Naomi and Audra have an idea, but we need to know if it is fittin' to Your plan. Show us the truth, Mighty God. In Your Son's name, amen."

Audra lifted her gaze to the people seated near her. In such a short time, she'd grown to love Jed and Naomi. And Caleb. . . He was rather peculiar, but she guessed she liked him in a brotherly way.

She took a deep breath. Then another. What did God purpose for her to do? Had she been hearing Him right this afternoon? Going against the Creator of the universe left her cold and empty.

"Caleb, like I said earlier, Naomi and Audra have devised a way to end all this," Jed said.

"Audra should tell it," Naomi said. "She's the one most involved."

Audra sensed Caleb's attention on her. Her palms grew damp. "I suppose if this is against God's will and I upset Him, He's going to let me know. This afternoon I realized Christopher is wrong and must be brought to justice."

"What are you thinking?" Caleb frowned. "If you're planning to do something dangerous, I won't have it."

"What I'm proposing is to deceive Christopher and find the evidence needed to convict him of his crimes."

Caleb stared at her sternly. "You best be telling me real fast, 'cause I suspect trouble."

Lord, show me the right path. "I'll go see Christopher tomorrow and tell him I've reconsidered the situation between us. I've been terribly upset over the robbery and shooting and can't seem to think clearly. That part's true. If he will accept my apology, I'll offer to move into the boardinghouse. I'll tell him by living in Earnest, I won't see you again, and he and I can spend more time together."

"Miss Audra, you know how he can be. . ."

"Persistent?"

"Yes—and a multitude of other things, too. What will you do about that, carry a pistol inside your apron pocket?" Caleb said, but there was no humor in his words.

Jed chuckled, but Naomi hushed him.

Audra stiffened in the chair. "I'm smart enough not to get myself into those kinds of situations. I plan to win him over by talking of marriage—even setting a date. I can earn his trust."

Caleb rubbed his shoulder and neck muscles. "This is beginning to make sense, but I'm not sure it's safe. Go on and let me hear the rest of it."

"Very simple. Since he's gotten away with so many crimes, I imagine he's rather full of himself." She paused and stared at Caleb directly. "I can prod him for information while making him think he's smart. I can also express my pity for the horrible circumstances about his outlaw brother."

"And if that doesn't work?" Caleb said.

"I'll wait until he's gone and search through his things at the parsonage and church."

Caleb's chair scraped across the floor, and he stood. "Whoa, Miss Audra. Now you're stepping into territory that could get you hurt."

"I hadn't heard this part of it either." Jed glanced at Naomi.

"Neither have I," the older woman said. "Sit down, Caleb, and this time I agree with you. Christopher has killed once, and it'll be easier the next time."

The old inclination for adventure wrapped around Audra's spirit. All her life she'd settled for a boring existence while yearning to be a pioneer—a woman of strength and courage.

"I can't agree to any of this unless you promise not to set foot near the parsonage with the idea of searching it." Caleb leaned into the table. "I want to send you home to your folks in one piece, not in a pine box."

"Bravo," Naomi said.

Audra appreciated her friends' interest in her safety. "I understand what you're saying. If a situation frightens me, I'll step back."

"Miss Audra, I don't know why you're trying to help me, but I am grateful. Rest assured, I will be looking out for you. I have my ways."

Audra stared into Caleb's eyes, midnight blue. For the first time she saw something that really did frighten her.

Chapter 9

Audra walked with Jed to the parsonage. No longer did she fear her actions were wrong. Rahab had protected the Israelite spies, and the Bible listed her among the righteous. And early Christians hid Paul from those who sought to harm him. Not that she considered herself noteworthy, but the biblical examples gave her courage to help stop Christopher's unscrupulous ways.

"You're mighty quiet," Jed said. "If you're having second thoughts, I'll be glad to drive you back."

"Not at all. I was thinking about the mysteries of God. I know I'm doing the right thing, although there are folks who'll think otherwise."

"Little lady, if you believe God is guiding your path, then I wouldn't worry about what others think."

Audra smiled and linked her arm into his. "You and my papa are quite a bit alike."

Jed quickened his stride. "He asked me to watch out for you, and that's exactly what I'm doing, although he might question my judgment on this one. I'm wondering if I shouldn't whirl you around and take you back to the ranch."

"And leave Caleb to fend alone?"

He expelled a heavy sigh and said nothing.

They strolled past the church and on toward the parsonage. Her rehearsed lines set upon her lips as well as the forced smile intended for Christopher. Her stomach knotted as a grim reminder of what lay ahead, but an even greater surge reminded her of Christopher's unlawful ways. Naomi, Jed, and Caleb believed she merely planned to prod him for information. Let them believe what they wanted; she had a purpose.

A mockingbird perched on the white picket fence in front of the parsonage. It offered a shrill call. Jed laughed. "Sorta fittin', don't you think?"

"Sure hope that bird is not making fun of us."

She climbed the steps and noted the fresh whitewash and a comfortable rocker. Clean. Homey. A calico cat curled up on a braid rug pulled to its haunches and stretched. Jed bent to stroke the animal, but it hissed and scratched at him.

Taking a deep breath, Audra knocked on the door.

"It's not too late to change your mind," Jed said barely above a whisper.

"No, sir. I'm—"

The door opened. Christopher's shoulders spanned the doorway. His wide grin radiated charm, and the surprise in his eyes was worth the anticipation.

"Audra, Jed, how good of you to stop by." He stepped back from the doorway and gestured a path to the inside. "I needed a break from preparing this week's sermon."

"I certainly don't want to keep you from God's work." Audra offered a shaky smile and gazed into his eyes. "Jed was so good to escort me here, but my purpose is to have a word with you in private."

Christopher nodded. In addition to the surprise, he tilted his head in obvious curiosity. "Would you like to walk over to the church after I pour Jed a cup of coffee?"

"Water's fine," Jed said. "I know Miss Audra's anxious to talk to you."

Christopher nodded in her direction as though immensely pleased with something. Why did a man so handsome have to be so wicked?

"Then let's not keep the lady waiting," Christopher said.

Audra chose not to speak until they reached the church. She wanted him to think she searched for the right words, which held a lot of truth. She'd been confident while talking to Jed, Naomi, and Caleb, but now she felt incredibly alone.

Me and my adventure. Who was she doing this for? The widow and her fatherless daughters? Jed and Naomi? In revenge for Papa's beating? Her grandmother's brooch? Certainly not Caleb. The man did not appeal to her. He'd gotten himself into a lot of trouble by allowing his brother to bully him. She wanted a man of strength. Audra mentally dismissed the troublesome thoughts and turned her attention to Christopher.

"Audra, I was not expecting to see you again. After our last conversation, I assumed our friendship was over." He opened the church door. "Not that I blame you after my irresponsible behavior."

"I've been thinking about what happened."

"I imagine I've become a nightmare." He shook his head. "Are you heading back to Nebraska?"

She smiled and squeezed a tear from her eye. "I hope not, which is why I'm here." She glanced at the floor—spotless, not one speck of dust. "When I think back on our conversation at Jed and Naomi's, I must admit I'm at fault, too."

His eyes softened. "However, sweet Audra? I remember it all quite clearly."

"But I insisted on the ride. Being alone for such a long time invited impropriety. Then your brother upset both of us."

He pressed his lips together. "Yes, when Caleb accused me of treating you badly, I forgot I was a man of God. He angers me so, but his wicked ways are no excuse for my own sin."

She forced another tear. "Pardon my boldness, but if I moved into the boardinghouse we wouldn't have to concern ourselves with Caleb." She shrugged. "I mean the sheriff will find him soon and bring justice to the people of Earnest, but he doesn't have to ruin our relationship." She again stared down at the wooden floor and studied an ant racing across a plank.

"You would do this for me?" Honey oozed from his words.

"I would indeed," she whispered. "I know you're a busy man with working night and day for the Lord, but perhaps I could help with some of your duties—maybe the ladies' meetings or choir."

"You are such a blessing." Christopher reached to touch her but drew back.

I am not as naïve as you think. "I want to begin again," she said. "If you think our friendship can be mended."

"I'd like nothing better." He walked down the aisle, his hands behind his back. A moment later he turned as though he were a military officer about to address his troops. "I will prove my worthiness, Audra. Things will be different, better, and we may find marriage in our future after all."

"I believe we shall." She walked toward him. When they stood within inches of each other, she stood on tiptoe and planted a light kiss on his cheek. "I will do my best to be understanding of the way you must deal with Caleb."

"What have I done to deserve such a godly woman?"

"I believe I am the lucky one. Your father sent me here to possibly help you in your ministry, and I desire to do all I can to fulfill my obligations."

Perhaps she'd gone too far.

❧

Caleb lifted the post-hole digger then thrust it into the ground. Sweat streamed down his face and soaked his bandanna. He'd worked since sunup setting fence posts for Jed. Not that he didn't want to help his friend, but he'd rather be working his own place. His foreman was a loyal man, and the sheriff knew it. The law had deputies planted on every corner of his ranch looking for Caleb Windsor. No point in putting any of his hands in danger. Or in jail.

He peered up and shielded his eyes from the westward slant of the sun. No wonder his stomach growled. Naomi had packed him biscuits and bacon, but he hadn't taken the time to stop for a noonday meal. Frustration pushed him on. First Jed and Naomi had gotten themselves knee-deep in protecting him. Now Audra was involved. She didn't have the Masterses' grit—and a mistake could get her killed. If she hadn't looked up at him with those light blue eyes framed by all that blond hair, then poured pure sugar into every word, he never would have agreed. The truth be known, if Audra had handed him a noose, he'd have tied it around his neck.

Smitten, Jed called it. A plumb fool is what Caleb called it. She'd hit him blind side and knocked out all his good sense. The truth hammered at his heart: Miss Audra still looked at him as though he were an outlaw. He sank the post-hole digger into the moist earth and deliberated the whole thing again. Even if he declared his devotion to her, what did he have to offer but a life on the run? He blew out a heavy sigh and watched his sweat drop into the hole.

The situation with his brother had to change soon, or Caleb would need to leave the country. Jed had been right about the sheriff not believing Chris's old gang member. Caleb knew it, too. He simply wanted an easy solution. *Lord, forgive me for putting good people in danger.*

In the distance a rider approached. He dropped the post-hole digger and headed toward his rifle leaning against an oak tree. He whistled for his horse. Leaving Jed's tools, he swung onto the saddle and headed for the trees. Once he found safety in the thick growth, he watched the rider approach.

Caleb studied him, an older man and a stranger to the territory. His beard looked unkempt, and his clothes showed the marks of days in the saddle. The man dismounted and studied the area where Caleb had been working. A moment later, he bent and examined the boot prints. *He knows those are fresh tracks. Lawman, maybe a bounty hunter.* The man stood and walked a few paces in Caleb's direction. He tipped his hat toward the trail. *He thinks I'm stupid. Mister, I have learned a trick or two in my life.*

While the stranger made his way back to his mount, Caleb nudged his horse's flanks. He knew every place to hide within miles. Somehow he had to get word to Jed. Chris could have set a trap and included the Masterses in it. Troubles kept piling up, reminding Caleb of drifting snow in a mountain pass.

Two hours later, Caleb felt certain he'd shaken the stranger. Hidden behind a rock on a lofty peak, he watched the man circle around, check Caleb's trail, and head off in the opposite direction.

That could be a trap, too.

Lord, I sure could use a little help here. Would You blind my trail to that man for good?

He waited awhile longer, half expecting the stranger to reappear. Caleb led his horse around to the other side of the peak and studied the outline of the horizon. He looked for the man to come riding into view. Shadows crested the area around him and, unless the man could see after dark, Caleb was safe.

Best he head to Jed and Naomi's and see if they'd heard about anything peculiar.

He rode the last few miles to the Masterses' ranch concealed by a cloak of darkness. Good thing he knew the way. Doubts plagued him about the stranger—hard to predict what a desperate man might do, and both the sheriff and Chris were anxious to get rid of him. He hid his horse in a grove of trees behind the corral and waited until he knew the hands were inside the bunkhouse. He stole around the barn to the house, blending with the forces of the night. Fortunately the dogs knew him, or he'd be in trouble. A light shone through the kitchen window. Everything looked normal, but still he waited. Then he caught sight of the stranger drinking coffee with Jed and Naomi. A Winchester lay across his lap. That didn't look like a sociable conversation to Caleb, especially when the man's dirty finger rested on the trigger. He crept to an open window and bent to listen.

"I've been told you folks could tell me where to find Caleb Windsor."

"Reckon you got yourself some bad information," Jed said. "Try talking to the sheriff."

"The sheriff sent me. Said the preacher's woman told him you were hiding Caleb Windsor."

Caleb refused to believe she was capable of such treachery, but he'd misjudged Chris all his life. To consider his brother and Audra working together against him sent an explosion of rage through his body.

"You mean Miss Audra?" Jed said, not an ounce of surprise in his words.

"Didn't hear her name, but I saw her. Yellow hair, pretty, and from Nebrasky."

"Mercy," Naomi said. "I have no idea where she would have gotten that information."

"Sheriff said she came to him last week with the news. He wired for me."

"Last week?" Jed said.

"I recollect the telegram said Tuesday mornin'."

Audra was here then. She didn't leave until Wednesday.

"And who are you?" Jed said.

"Jim Hawk. I'm a bounty hunter."

Smell like one, too. No wonder you tracked me like a mountain cat.

A chair scooted across the wooden floor. "Mr. Hawk, my wife and I don't know anything about what you're talking about, so you best be on your way."

"I plan on staying a spell until Windsor shows up."

Naomi laughed. "You'll be here until the next frost. Want some more coffee?"

"Don't mind if I do. Think I'll take it with me while your husband and me look at the barns and bunkhouse."

"And if I refuse?" Jed's voice rose.

"Then I'll have to shoot you in the name of the law."

"Is that what the sheriff told you?"

"He didn't say one way or the other. It's how I take care of business."

Caleb had heard enough. Between the sound of Hawk's orders and Naomi telling Jed to do what the man said, Caleb put together a plan.

Hawk and Jed headed toward the bunkhouse. Caleb understood the bounty hunter would pump lead into any of them who objected to his search.

"Here I am." Caleb stepped into the path of the two men. He held his rifle behind him for fear the light from the kitchen and bunkhouse might reveal it. "You want me for something?"

Hawk chuckled. "Looks like that gal was right." He lifted his Winchester. "You're going with me."

Caleb lifted his rifle. "I don't think so." Even in the night air, the man smelled like he never bathed.

Jed spun in Hawk's direction and knocked the Winchester from his hand. In the next breath Jed snatched it up. Caleb stepped in and shoved his rifle under Hawk's chin. "Now, you and I are going to talk. I have a heap of questions."

"And if I refuse?"

"You won't." Caleb pointed toward the barn. "That looks like a good place. How about joining us, Jed?" He needed his friend with him.

"Sure."

The three moved inside the barn where Jed lit a lantern.

"Sit down." Caleb pushed Hawk to the floor. He had to find out who sent him. If he let Hawk go, the man would kill him "Who are you working for?"

"The sheriff. I'm a bounty hunter."

"I know the sheriff." Jed held up the lantern. "And he wouldn't hire a two-bit bounty hunter to do a lawman's job."

"You forget the gal told him where to find you."

"Audra Lenders was here last Tuesday," Jed said. "She's been living with us until two days ago."

"So that means Chris Windsor hired you," Caleb said.

"I said I'm a bounty hunter. The sheriff wired me last week just like I told you." Realization nearly strangled him. The sheriff and Chris were working together.

Chapter 10

Five days later, Audra felt the pangs of regret regarding her move into the boardinghouse. Loneliness cast its shroud around her, with Christopher as her only companion. Three women from his church had paid enjoyable visits, but Christopher said they were gossips and not to establish a friendship with them. They hadn't appeared to be busybodies at all, but she expected him to isolate her from the community. Her aloofness would feed into his cause when she attempted to expose him.

She missed Naomi and Jed almost as much as she missed Mama and Papa. Christopher left her at times to call on his congregation, or so he claimed. Her thoughts lingered on which was worse—enduring his company or being alone. She read and took walks, but rain had forced her inside.

When Audra considered her past anger toward Caleb, she faced a truth about herself. His good qualities were what she wanted in Christopher. Maybe some of the anger pointed at her, too. She had her hopes built on being a pastor's wife, and that aspect propelled her into a fairy-tale world. Being deceived by a man who professed to be a leader of God's people didn't help either.

What surprised Audra the most was how she longed for Caleb. In the beginning, she believed the two men looked identical, but their disposition and spiritual commitments distinguished their physical appearance. Every time they'd talked, he'd been a gentleman. He'd come to her rescue and put himself in danger. Caleb treated her like a fragile porcelain doll. He didn't impose his will or push her toward conducting herself in an ungodly manner. More and more she realized how much she had misjudged him.

She did care for him, very much.

Despair paralyzed her emotions. She wanted to see Jed and Naomi and possibly catch a glimpse of Caleb. Determination seized her the following morning when she shared breakfast with Christopher.

"Would you take me to Jed and Naomi's early tomorrow morning?" she said.

He cut a generous slice of ham. "Do you think it's wise with my brother still roaming the countryside?

"If I'm visiting Jed and Naomi, then neither you nor I have a reason to worry."

He lifted his gaze to reach hers then smiled. "I do have some calls to make near the Masterses' ranch. I could tend to them and pick you up before supper."

"Perfect." She hadn't thought he'd agree so quickly, and for his concession she was grateful. "Can we leave before sunup?"

"Why? Has my company bored you?"

She touched his arm and forced a smile. "Not at all, Christopher. Jed and Naomi are like my parents, and you have to admit I haven't made any friends here in Earnest."

He lifted a brow, and she saw the look in his eyes—the same stomach-grinding sneer he gave Papa just before he hit him. At that moment, Audra despised him, more so than at any other time. How long before he unleashed his temper like a caged animal? "Audra, it isn't my fault you are unsociable. There are many good women in the church."

Whom you won't let me near. She didn't dare rile him and lose her opportunity to see Jed and Naomi, or worse yet fail to catch Christopher breaking the law.

"I'm sorry. The ladies who came to see me were pleasant, but you didn't think they were suitable companions for me."

He nodded slowly. "I will look into the matter today. I have a few women in mind who would be good for you." Suddenly his demeanor changed. He reached for her hand. "I don't want my sweet Audra lonely or bored. I'll escort you to the Masterses before sunrise in the morning. I must keep my lady from pining away for Nebraska and womenfolk company."

"Thank you." She kept her tone low and respectful to keep from screaming at him. She understood exactly what he was doing: catering to her until she set a wedding date. His charm might speak for him to the rest of this town, but she'd seen his other side.

The following morning, Christopher drove Audra to the Masterses' ranch.

"I really appreciate this," she said, "and your offer to introduce me to appropriate women. I trust your judgment completely when it comes to guiding me, especially if we are to marry." The thought churned her stomach.

"You honor me, dear Audra. I apologize for the way I spoke to you yesterday morning. It's my fault that you haven't met the proper women of this town. Yesterday I went by the homes of some of our finest families and made introductions for you."

"Thank you. I guess I wanted too much too soon."

"Nonsense. We've waited all our lives to find each other. And we are eager to have a home and fine friends to go with it."

"You understand me very well," Audra said. All the while she'd rather confront him about his outlaw activities. God have mercy on him for killing a man while hiding behind the deception of a pastor.

⬥

"Mercy, Audra, seems like you've been gone forever." Naomi drew her into a hug. "I hope you two are staying for a while."

"I'm leaving to make some calls," Christopher said. "But Audra wants to spend the day."

"If you don't mind," Audra said. "I'll help with whatever you need. This is Tuesday, a baking day like Thursday, as I recall."

"And we will have a splendid time." Naomi smiled. Her round eyes crinkled, reminding Audra of an old Indian woman who lived in Nebraska.

"Then I will leave you ladies to your fun." Christopher tipped his hat to both of them. "I may need to pray for Jed today."

Audra forced a laugh, so glad to be rid of him. "I will see you near evening."

"For supper," Naomi said.

"Thank you, ma'am. I don't want to impose, but your cooking is far superior to the boardinghouse's. I'll look forward to it."

Audra watched him drive the wagon down the road. As soon as he ventured beyond earshot, relief swept over her. "Oh, Naomi, he makes me ill."

The woman wrapped her arm around Audra's waist as they strolled toward the house. "We have much to talk about while making bread."

"But I have so little to tell you." Sadness laced Audra's words. "I wanted to have something important."

"It's only been a few days. These things take time." She sighed. "I know you haven't had breakfast, so let's talk after that." She hesitated. "I have a few things to tell you."

Audra would rather have waited on breakfast and talked first, but she respected her friend's wishes.

After breakfast, Naomi pushed aside her coffee cup. "We had a visitor a few days ago, a bounty hunter by the name of Jim Hawk." Lines deepened in Naomi's face.

Audra listened. This didn't sound good at all.

"He said Sheriff Reynolds hired him to find Caleb hiding out at our ranch. He also said you told the sheriff about Caleb being here."

Audra's eyes widened. "I never did such a thing."

Naomi shook her head. "We know you didn't. I think Jed, Caleb, and I are better judges of character than that. But Hawk claimed you went to the sheriff last Tuesday."

"I was here." Audra's pulse quickened. Realization caused her to shiver. "Then Sheriff Reynolds and Christopher are working together."

"We believe so."

Audra stood and carried her coffee mug out to the front porch. Her mind spun with the hopelessness of helping Caleb. No one would ever believe his innocence with the pastor and the sheriff on the wrong side of the law. How did Satan gather such a foothold in Earnest?

"But we have God on our side," she said.

"And He is all we need," Naomi said behind her. "I admit this is my biggest test of faith. Jed and I have been through a lot together, but trusting God to deliver Caleb is hard, real hard."

Audra nodded. She kept her back turned to hide her tears. A month ago she didn't know Jed, Naomi, Caleb, or Christopher. Her future looked optimistic, and the idea of an adventure in Colorado was filled with romantic notions. Now all the beauty had been marred by evil men. Who else could be involved? "I'm afraid—for you, Jed, and Caleb. I thought once we found the evidence to prove Christopher's guilt, we could go to Sheriff Reynolds. So what is the answer?"

"Prayer. We simply need to pray for guidance," Naomi said. "When we join Jed at noon, we must have a prayer meetin'. He's checking on new calves."

Audra blinked and swiped at the tears glazing her cheeks. She faced Naomi with a trembling smile. "I'm ready to make bread."

"And we'll talk and pray."

Once the bread dough rested in wooden bowls, left covered to rise, Naomi and Audra weeded the vegetable garden with its sprouts of lettuce, tomatoes, onions, and green beans. Audra worked with a vengeance.

"Are those weeds Christopher and the sheriff?" Naomi said.

Audra glanced up and took a look at how deep she'd plunged the hoe into the earth. She laughed for the first time since she'd learned about Jim Hawk's accusation.

Naomi laughed with her.

"I guess those two had better stay clear of my temper," Audra said.

"You could run all three of those rascals out of Colorado all by yourself."

The laughter continued and eased the anger and depression threatening to overtake her. God was the judge of Christopher and the sheriff. An ill temperament didn't solve a thing.

"Looks like I can fry up a chicken to take to Jed." Naomi dabbed the perspiration from her face with her apron. "I had no idea this weeding would go so fast."

"Go ahead, and I'll finish here," Audra said. "I still have some ugliness in me that needs to be dealt with."

While she finished hoeing, her thoughts wandered to Caleb. She'd like to see him, talk to him if possible.

"Where are your dreams?" Naomi said. She held out a cup of water. "I've been talking to you for the past few minutes, and you were far from here.

Startled, Audra took the water. "I'm sorry."

"You're blushing. Maybe I should have asked who was on your mind."

Audra lifted the hoe and glanced over the garden. "Looks like the weeds have headed for someone else's garden, because they are gone from here."

"You're ignoring me." Naomi wagged her finger. "So your thoughts are softening toward Caleb?"

Audra nodded slowly. "How is he?"

"Quiet. Rather sad. This business between him and Christopher has always been difficult, but I think other things are bothering him, too."

Her heart quickened. "Christopher said the sheriff plans to sell Caleb's ranch to pay back some of the money he's stolen."

"We'll see him at noon," Naomi said. "He's giving Jed a hand."

Audra's gaze flew to her friend's face. She dare not utter another word. Caleb had enough problems without adding a woman to them. In a few hours she'd see him. She'd learned some things since living at the boardinghouse. Nothing grand, but at least she wasn't sitting idle.

Soon the noon meal sat in the back of the wagon, and the two women left the ranch. The thought of seeing Caleb made her feel like a skittish cat. She kept telling herself to calm down, but it didn't help.

"Should I have given you a dose of castor oil?" Naomi chuckled.

"Castor oil?"

"At least you'd have something else to think about. Calm yourself, dear. I see Jed and Caleb heading our way."

Audra studied the figures of the two men riding toward them. Caleb sat straight in the saddle. *Don't stare at him. Look at Jed. Remember what you need to tell both of them.*

Naomi should have given her the castor oil.

—

Caleb guessed Audra rode beside Naomi. He searched in every direction to make sure his brother didn't accompany them. Did she ride to the ranch alone? Had something happened? Was she in danger? He attempted to settle his anxious heart. She'd been in his waking and sleeping moments for days—a vision of grace and loveliness. He stumbled over what to say. Best he simply be polite and let her speak her mind.

"Is this our Audra?" Jed said. "I don't want a thing to eat. All I need is to feast my eyes on her pretty face."

"Jed Masters, you're a married man." Naomi shook her finger at him.

Audra laughed and blushed with Jed's compliment. "It's wonderful to see you—both of you."

She appeared to snatch a glimpse of Caleb, and her cheeks reddened a little more.

Jed dismounted and helped his wife down from the wagon. Caleb held his breath and realized he needed to do the same. The moment his hands touched Audra's slender waist, he felt her tremble. Did he do something wrong? She must be afraid of him.

"Thank you," she whispered. He stole a look at her face. No longer did he see the doubt and distrust from the past. In their place rested another emotion, one he didn't know how to interpret.

"Have you learned anything more about Chris?" Jed lifted the basket of food from the wagon.

"Naomi told me a horrible story about him and Sheriff Reynolds. But what I have to report is small. I'm sorry."

"You've been in town for only a few days, and I apologize for asking," Jed said. "Let's eat first, and then we can talk."

"And pray," Naomi added.

Jed asked the blessing and for guidance about the hardships facing Caleb. "Help us to forgive those who intend us harm," he said. "Watch over our Audra, and keep her safe. And, Lord, we can't do a thing about this unless You fight the battle for us."

They ate on the soft grass with the food placed on an old quilt. They talked as though they hadn't seen each other for weeks. No one mentioned Chris or the sheriff. Caleb forced himself to eat Naomi's fried chicken, pinto beans, and hot bread. He loved her cooking and he was hungry, but today his mind wrestled with other things. If he failed to eat with his normal appetite, they all could tell something was wrong.

His heart had been captured by one young woman with sun-colored hair and pale blue eyes, and he couldn't do a thing about it.

"I want to tell you what I've learned." Audra's voice rang like sweet music through his spirit. "It's not as much as I'd like, but it's a beginning."

"I'm wondering again if this isn't too dangerous," Caleb said.

"Too late. I've already made a few plans of my own," Audra said. "As soon as he leaves town, I'm determined to find the evidence we need. Jed is allowing me to take one of his mares back to Earnest."

Jed cleared his throat. "The horse is in case you need to leave town."

"I don't like the idea of you ever needing a horse. Besides, what are we going to do with evidence once we have it?" Caleb said. "No one in town will believe us."

Jed waved his hand. "When we get the evidence, we could make a trip to the governor's office." He rubbed his chin. "Work's caught up here. Think I'll head to Denver and see what I can learn."

"What makes you think Governor Eaton would listen without proof?"

"Because our story is so outlandish he may believe it's true."

Caleb shrugged. "Possibly." He turned to Audra. "What have you learned?"

"That he's quickly losing patience with me. I refuse to be alone with him, and he wants to marry badly. I have to work fast, or I'm going to be wed." She laughed, but he could hear the trepidation in her voice. "He's finding it harder and harder to play the role of a pastor in my presence."

I'm afraid for you. This idea is foolishness. They needed proof, a place where Chris hid the money and the other stolen items—but not at the risk of Audra's safety. "Anything else?"

"One day he had a call to make to the widow of the man who was killed in the stagecoach robbery. When he returned, I questioned him about Belle's welfare and her little girls, and he repeated their conversation. The next day I saw her walking to the cemetery. I joined Belle and asked if Pastor Windsor's visit the day before had been helpful. She said I must have been mistaken, because the pastor hadn't visited since the funeral." Audra peered into Caleb's face as though determined to find the evidence they needed. "The next time he speaks of making a call, I'll follow him."

Chapter 11

Audra silently challenged Caleb to argue with her. The longer she spent time with him, the more she realized her feelings were not a passing fancy, but the kind of love seen in Mama and Papa and her married brothers and sisters. Caleb most likely despised her for some of the accusations she'd spit his way in the beginning, and she couldn't blame him. After all, she'd been convinced he was an outlaw.

"You will not put yourself in danger," Caleb said.

Each of his words shook her will like Papa swinging an axe over a stack of wood. "I most certainly will. Have you forgotten the sheriff is in this? And the bounty hunter and whoever else is after the reward?"

"I'll hang before I risk you being dragged into the middle of this." Not a muscle moved on his face.

"I'm already in the middle. That happened when your brother stopped the stage and I witnessed a murder." Irritation gave her an edge of courage.

"This is my problem."

"And you are the most stubborn man I've ever met."

"Arguing won't solve a thing," Jed said with a wave of a drumstick. "If there's anyone close by looking for Caleb, you two will have them down on us in no time."

"I apologize," Audra said. "I'm a little angry."

"So am I," Caleb said.

Naomi stood and walked to the wagon. "I have a few slices of milk cake here. It might sweeten Audra and Caleb's disposition." She brought the cake to the quilt.

"I know it's delicious, but I'm quite full." Audra sensed the mounting warmth reaching her neck and face and realized her friends could see her discomfort.

"I've had more than enough," Caleb said. "If I stuff one more bite into this body, I'll not be able to do a lick of work."

Jed handed his plate to Naomi. "Pile it high, wife. Know what I think?"

Audra glanced his way, not sure if she wanted to hear Jed's remark to his wife.

"Not sure, tell me," Naomi said.

"I think these two bickering young people should take a walk and settle whatever's ailing them."

"I agree." Naomi sliced a generous piece of the cake for Jed and then herself. "I can't seem to figure out what's wrong with those two. Any idea, Jed?"

He swallowed a mouthful. "Yep, I do. It's—"

"Let's go, Audra." Caleb set his plate on the quilt.

Her heart fluttered against her chest like a hummingbird's wings. *Please, Jed. I'll be humiliated.* "I'm ready, as long as Naomi will wait until we get back to gather up the food."

"Get on out of here. Jed and I have things to discuss." Naomi waved them away like she was scattering feed to chickens.

Audra hurriedly joined Caleb before the Masterses spoke another word. They walked down a hill toward a winding stream. As they ventured closer, the sound of the gurgling stream and the sight of little whitecaps offered the peace she desperately craved.

"What are we supposed to discuss?" Caleb's tone conveyed his frustration.

"Our bickering."

"Well, we wouldn't be fussing if you'd listen to reason."

"Me?" She raised a brow. "I'm trying to help you—keep you from getting killed."

"And I'm doing the same thing for you."

"Lower your voice or the whole state will hear you."

Caleb inhaled then exhaled. "I simply want to make sure you're safe. We both know Chris can't be trusted."

Audra's irritation seeped through to the surface. "Jed and Naomi have been in danger for quite a while. I don't hear you voicing concern about them."

"Jed and Naomi are different." His attention focused on a hawk soaring overhead. He shielded his eyes against the sun and followed the grand bird's flight.

She watched the hawk, too, but her thoughts were on Caleb's insinuation. "How are they different? Are you saying I'm not smart enough to help?"

He whirled around to face her. "Where did you come up with such a stupid idea?"

"There, you said it. You think I'm stupid." She'd been right all along. How could she possibly care for a man who made her this angry?

"I never even thought such a thing." Caleb's eyes flashed.

"Good. Because I don't intend to sit back and read or knit or write long letters to my family in Nebraska while Christopher continues to break the law." She caught herself before saying another word. "I made a commitment to do whatever is necessary to stop your brother. Mercy, Caleb, just because I'm a woman doesn't mean I haven't any sense."

"I told you I didn't say or mean anything of the like."

She crossed her arms. "We are supposed to be settling our differences."

"That's impossible."

"And I agree."

"We could call a truce. That would make Jed and Naomi happy."

Despite her aggravation, she laughed. "All right. Let's walk a bit."

They strolled on, neither saying a word. She searched for a question or comment beyond the topic of lawbreakers. "Tell me about your boyhood."

He shrugged. "Chris and I did everything together. Mostly got into trouble." He paused. "We lived in western Nebraska not far from the Platte River. We loved the river, fishing, swimming—as long as it was wet."

"I'm glad you got along well."

"We did." He sighed and gazed out to the snowcapped mountains. "When I think about how we were then, I see why Chris is so selfish."

"You don't have to talk about this."

"I don't mind. It's my fault. Whatever he wanted to do, I agreed. I looked out for him, protected him. I remember one time when we were thirteen. We'd been playing near the river, trying to catch a mess of fish. The river was swollen, and he fell in. Chris got caught up in the current. Scared me to death. I jumped in and pulled him out. We both near drowned."

Looked like Caleb had always jumped in to save his brother. "You saved his life." Admiration laced her thoughts.

"I guess. Later he asked me why, and I said because we were brothers. I loved him. Chris shook his head and studied me for the longest time before he spoke. He said he didn't know if he would have saved me. He'd been too scared."

Startled, Audra peered up into his face. "What did you say?"

Caleb smiled, but she could tell he hid his sadness. "I told him not to worry. I'd always be there to help him." He chuckled. "And I've been doing it ever since."

Audra thought about the story. Caleb's recollection painted a clear picture of how two people chose two different paths.

"What about you?" he asked. "Brothers and sisters?"

Audra wasn't certain she wanted to talk about herself, especially with her mind focused on two young boys who were incredibly different. "Nothing interesting to tell. I'm the youngest of eight—stubborn, spoiled—and neither Papa nor Mama wanted to let me go."

He smiled. "I've seen your stubborn streak, but that's not bad."

"Should I remind you why we're taking this walk?" She stifled a giggle.

"We called a truce, remember?"

His tone left an unsettling sensation in the pit of her stomach. "But I haven't changed my mind about what I want to do to bring your brother to justice."

"But you will."

Those words washed over her like ice water. "I think not, sir." She whirled around and started up the hill without him.

"Audra."

She stopped but kept her attention straight ahead.

"Why are you determined to help me?"

Clenching her fists, she considered the question. A myriad answers danced across her mind. "You already know I'm angry about Papa's treatment and the poor widow left to raise her daughters alone." *Don't force me to look at you, or my eyes will give away my feelings.*

"Such nobility you have, Audra."

"Thank you." She started walking again and left him far behind. Justice was a noble cause, but the hint of love tore at her sensibilities. Up ahead she saw a man standing by the Masterses' wagon. Fear squeezed her heart, for Christopher had his back to her. Where had he left his wagon unless he hid it from view?

She bent and hurried back down the hill, nearly slipping in the process. Caleb must be warned. Christopher could have men combing the area. Trailing up the path, Caleb stared at the ground, obviously unaware of her descent. She waved her hands at him. *Please don't shout at me.* In the next instant, he looked up. She touched her forefinger to her lips and rushed to him.

"Your brother is with Naomi and Jed," she said. "I neither saw his wagon nor whether others were with him."

He nodded and took her hand. "Let's cross the stream and get out of sight."

She lifted her skirt with one hand and took his hand with the other. They stepped on round, slippery stepping-stones in a shallow area, where she nearly fell into the cold water. He steadied her, and she caught her breath. In the next instant, they disappeared under a canopy of trees. Conscious of the strong hand gripping hers, Audra realized, as she had before, that a life with Caleb would be spent on the run. It really wouldn't be a life at all but a flight from one safe haven to another.

"I think if you pick a few wildflowers and head back to the wagon, Chris might not suspect the truth," he said once they were into the depths of the trees.

"He could count the plates from lunch."

"I imagine Naomi has cleaned up," Caleb said. "She's used to covering up for me."

"I pray so." She glanced about at the pastel watercolor array of wildflowers nodding their heads in the breeze. "I'll gather up the wildflowers." She gasped. "Your horse!"

"Out of sight in the hills."

"Praise God."

He laughed. "This is my life, Audra."

Again the realization of his perilous existence shook her. Not only would this life be a hardship for her, but her presence would also slow him—endanger him. "I'm so sorry, Caleb. I promise I will do everything in my power, with God's help, to free you from this." She swallowed her emotion.

"For the sake of those who've been wronged."

She wondered if his statement was a question, for the look in his eyes spoke of an inquiry—an inquiry of the heart.

"I mustn't tarry," she said. "Christopher will not be pleased."

He squeezed her hand lightly. "Godspeed, Audra. Please, let's not argue anymore. And promise me you will not put yourself in danger."

"I'll do my best." She broke away and snatched up the senseless wildflowers, crossed the stream, and hurried up the hill to where Christopher awaited: the most incorrigible man she'd ever known.

Already she missed the man behind her. *Caleb, I'm only a woman, but a woman who loves you.*

"Audra," Naomi called.

She lifted her gaze to the top of the hill and waved. "I'm coming."

Naomi clutched her skirts and headed downward. "Here she is, Christopher." She shook her head. "Where have you been? Oh, I see, wildflowers."

Christopher stood several feet behind her with Jed.

"I'm sorry. Every step I took there were more flowers, and then I saw these yellow ones on the other side of a stream. I nearly slipped on the rocks getting to them."

The older woman reached her and expelled a heavy sigh. "I didn't know how else to warn you," she whispered.

"I saw him earlier."

"Has my sweet lady been picking flowers?" A grin spread over Christopher's face. "You are so much like a whimsical child, and I'm fortunate to call you mine."

His words clawed at her heart, along with his endless lies and deceit. She forced a smile. "I hope you haven't been waiting long."

"Long enough to be concerned, but the Masterses said you'd gone for a walk."

She laughed. "If I'd brought a pole, I might have followed the water to where I could fish for trout. And I'd be there still."

"Aren't you the youngest in your family?" he said.

She nodded. "And used to getting my own way."

He linked her arm with his. "I don't mind. Beauty like yours needs to be indulged. You must ease this heart soon and tell me when we can marry."

She despised her role in this charade. *Dear Lord, I pray You are leading me in this, for I'm beginning to feel vile.* "I think we can decide on a date. Perhaps on the ride back to Earnest?"

Christopher shouted like an Indian heading into battle. "Did you hear that, Jed? We're deciding on a wedding day this evening."

"Make sure you give her plenty of time to sew her weddin' dress and all those other things women fuss about," Jed said.

"I agree," Naomi said. "Audra will be the prettiest bride Earnest has ever seen."

Christopher laughed. "If it will hurry the big day, I'll get all the women in town to help her."

How long must this all continue?

⌘

Caleb realized the time had come for him to take action and stop allowing his friends to risk their lives in protecting him. A meeting between Jed and Governor Eaton held a lot of merit, but Caleb didn't need a trip to Denver to understand the authorities required hard evidence. Audra had made headway with the widow, and maybe the woman would testify when the time came. Still, the answers always returned to the same problem: Someone needed to locate the money and stolen goods. Chris probably stored the items right under everyone's nose.

He'd been a fool. Why hadn't he seen the sheriff and Chris were in this together? Jim Hawk might be a part of their gang, too. Who else was involved?

Chris had always been the clever one, but desperation had a way of smarting up a man, too. And Caleb had been dodging the law and his outlaw brother for a long time. Now, with the realization that a fine woman had touched his heart, he had even more reasons to bring justice to the surface.

He allowed his thoughts to linger on Audra awhile longer. If Chris wasn't arrested soon, she could get hurt. He saw a willful side of her that worried him and a fearlessness woven with determination. He also saw a spark of caring. The latter could cause her to act without thinking. He should know. All manner of reason left him when he looked into those heaven-sent eyes. The two of them didn't dare be alone again, not until Chris sat behind bars.

In the past, Caleb had eluded those after him. He played a cat-and-mouse game, and the law or his brother did the chasing. With other innocent people involved, he realized the time had come to trail Chris's every move. He'd follow his brother day and night until he found the evidence.

He'd settle for a bullet or a noose before he'd allow those near him to suffer.

Chapter 12

Y ou cannot wander off anymore," Christopher said. Evening snatches of light played through tree branches in shadows that reminded her of giant fingers. Audra thought how romantic a wagon ride could be with the right man. She'd gladly exchange the queasiness in her stomach for a glowing light in her heart—for Caleb.

"I couldn't resist the wildflowers. You remember Nebraska. This is so different, and I wanted to capture a part of Colorado beauty."

"At the risk of my brother capturing you? Sweetheart, he could hold you for ransom—he is capable of a lot of things."

She swallowed an angry retort. She must continue playing naïve. "I'm sorry you were worried. I'm used to living free and enjoying the land."

"And you will soon again. Caleb can't run forever, unless he leaves the territory."

"I dearly wish the outlaws were caught."

He sighed. "I know, and so do I. In the meantime, think about the possible danger. I'm afraid my brother is up to something—and you might be part of it."

She touched her lips. "Has he said so?"

Christopher paused, most likely to conjure up a story. "He said you were much too beautiful for me. And he reminded me that he had kissed you first."

Someday everyone would know the truth. "How cruel."

"He made a few threats, but I refuse to repeat them." He shook his head and took a deep breath. "Just promise me you will take heed."

"I will. I can do no less than to ensure you peace of mind."

He glanced her way and grinned. "You can give me great joy by telling me when we can wed." He chuckled. "Tomorrow?"

Audra detested the tone in his voice, as though he might truly care. She wanted the charade to end soon. This very night if possible. She'd gladly tell him how despicable he was and never see him again, but the problems wouldn't vanish.

Her finances had dwindled to a critical stage. No matter how many times she counted her meager funds, she had barely enough to live at the boardinghouse two weeks longer. She must seek employment and accept the fact that Christopher would be furious with the idea.

"Are you going to make this poor heart beg?" he said, interrupting her musings.

"Of course not. I think perhaps four weeks from this Sunday?"

"No sooner?"

His pitiful begging unnerved her. "Christopher, I want everything to be perfect, and even four weeks gives me little time." She considered touching his arm, but the fear of him stopping the wagon to steal a kiss halted her. "Won't you need to summon a pastor from a neighboring town?"

"We could ride there tomorrow and make arrangements."

"Is he a friend of yours? I mean is he a good pastor?"

"The best. And I want the best for us. We will remember our wedding day for the rest of our lives."

And her wedding day wouldn't be with him. "Now I feel better."

"Shall I kiss you soundly to seal the date?"

She gasped and stiffened. "I think not. I'm saving all of my affections for our wedding night."

He laughed. "Such a surprise you are, Audra. To taste your sweet lips, I'll wait the month's time. I can hardly wait to tell our congregation. They will be pleased."

And I have four weeks to find the evidence to prove you guilty of all the crimes blamed on Caleb. His kiss is the one I crave, and his arms are the ones I long to hold me.

Back in her room, Audra asked God to give her continued guidance and strength. For certain the next time Christopher made calls, she'd keep a short distance behind him.

⌒

Audra dreaded Sunday. To her, announcing the wedding date to the congregation was like standing in front of God and lying. Deceiving God's people on a Sunday morning worship service? Had she stooped to the same level as Christopher? The reality made her stomach churn. She wanted to bathe in the hottest water imaginable and scrub her skin raw.

"You will make a wonderful pastor's wife," a matronly woman said. "Our sweet pastor needs someone to help him with the responsibilities of the church. It appears to me that you are as beautiful on the inside as you are on the outside."

"Thank you." Audra smiled to keep from crying. Were her near-tears a result of misleading these people or the idea of possibly disappointing God? Or both?

"We need to get you involved in Bible study and our other ladies' meetings." The same woman nodded as if to punctuate her words. "But we'll wait until after the weddin'. My husband is one of the elders, so you and I will get to spend lots of time together."

"I appreciate your thinking about me." What else could she say? It was easy to make a fuss over small children and babies, even spend a few hours in the company of godly women. But discussing her wifely duties after exchanging marital vows with Christopher? Heaven forbid!

She hated all of this. Audra took a deep breath to control her emotions. She wanted a home and family someday, but not with Christopher.

A little boy tugged on her yellow and green flowered dress. She lifted the toddler into her arms, glad for the diversion. "Where is your mama?" she said.

He promptly stuck his thumb into his mouth and leaned on her shoulder.

"You have the touch," another woman said. "Edna Sue, come look where your son is."

A young woman with dark hair and eyes stepped up to her. "I hope he hasn't bothered you, Miss Audra. Although when he gets tired he is picky about who he wants to hold him." She held out her arms, and the child reached for her.

"I enjoyed your son for the brief time I held him." Audra patted his back. He closed his eyes and snuggled up to his mother.

The members thinned out from the churchyard until she stood alone. With no sign of Christopher, she climbed the steps to the church. She hoped he'd left to tend to something—anything—but he always waited for her. The cross on the wall behind the pulpit caught her attention. She hadn't considered this church a real house of God since she learned the truth about Christopher. But now, alone and surrounded by the symbols of worship, she felt the presence of the heavenly Father.

God is here, because those folks who worship seek Him with all their hearts.

She smiled and sensed the love and peace she'd come to recognize as the Lord's special gift to her. If only Christopher had listened to God's voice and responded in obedience instead of rebellion.

Glancing about, she noticed a few hymnals hadn't been replaced, a task she normally completed with Christopher. A few moments later, she had everything in order and still no sign of him.

A small room to the right caught her attention. Christopher entered the church sanctuary from this area and made his announcements before beginning the sermon. The offering plate was stored in the small room. Perhaps he and the elder who held the position as treasurer were gathering up today's offering.

Audra moved to the door and listened. Hearing nothing, she saw it wasn't closed completely and pushed it slightly with her finger, just enough to take a peek. Christopher stood counting the money from the collection plate. She started to speak since he didn't note her presence. At that moment, he stuck a handful of the money in his pocket and the rest into the bag that went to the treasurer.

Immediately she stepped back and tiptoed to a pew midway through the church. Trembling, she picked up a hymnal and pretended to read it. Her frenzied emotions refused to calm, and she willed her heart to cease its incessant beating.

Stealing from his own church—not his church but God's church. The alarm racing through her body shouldn't surprise her. If he robbed and killed the people of this town, would he not take their money from the collection plate?

For once she wished she were a lady lawman or a Pinkerton. Why, she'd arrest him this very instant. She'd march into that little room and pronounce him a murderer and a thief.

"Audra, dear, have you been waiting long?" Christopher closed the door of the small room and interrupted her contemplations.

"Not at all." How could he look so innocent? And his voice sounded quiet and calm, like a pastor's. It sickened her.

He held up the familiar leather bag. "This task was left to me today. Do remind me to take this to the bank tomorrow."

She stood. "I can take it for you. It will give me an errand to do."

"Thank you. This is my week to get paid, and I want money there to cover my salary."

His last words burned inside her. All she managed was a smile to keep from screaming at him for dipping his hands into the collection plate.

"You look lovely this morning." He offered her his arm. "We have a dinner invitation. This is a family who gives generously, and we don't want to keep them waiting."

What an incorrigible man.

✥

Caleb punched his fist into his palm. He'd rather punch his fist through the side of Jed's barn, but nothing would come from it but a broken hand. He felt weak, helpless, and frustrated. Jed had ridden to Denver to see the governor and hadn't returned. What had taken him so long? Caleb should have gone, too. After all, he was the man with the questionable reputation. He held little hope that Governor Eaton would believe his story. With all the wanted posters, the truth looked far from Earnest, Colorado.

At this very moment what bothered him the most was Naomi's news from Sunday morning church. Chris had announced his marriage to Audra for Sunday, July 9. He knew Audra would refuse to go through with it, but she was in an uncomfortable, even perilous, position. The whole situation with Audra and his brother's plan to fake his own death and leave her a widow heated his blood to boiling.

So far, Caleb had spent every spare minute with his eyes on Earnest and their pastor. Nothing had happened yet. Chris may have decided he had enough money and to give up robbing folks. That didn't take away from the fact he'd committed crimes against good people.

A figure in the doorway captured his attention. "Naomi, I'm on my way," he said.

"Keeping vigil on your brother?"

He nodded. "I expect his Sunday afternoons are spent at some poor unsuspecting person's house for dinner, but I can't take any chances."

"I figured as such. Do you need anything before you leave?"

"No, ma'am. I do appreciate the news about Chris and Audra."

"She doesn't have much time."

"Why did she give him four weeks?" Caleb said. "It doesn't make sense."

"I imagine she wants him to think the date has something to do with her livelihood. Chris stole her money, except for a little he overlooked, and she doesn't have any income. Now, don't you go thinking she will go through with a wedding so she can survive, 'cause that's not what I'm saying."

"What are you saying?"

"He's going to make life miserable for her when she backs out, and so will every member of his congregation. But that's not the answer. Don't you understand?"

Realization hit him like a bolt of lightning. "She purposely set herself up to find the evidence in four weeks."

Naomi nodded. "If things aren't resolved by the time of the wedding, she'll find herself a job and do just fine. But by that time she will have lost Christopher's confidence and the hope of helping you."

"I'd have given her money." His words sounded angrier than he intended.

"And I never wanted her to help me."

"She's a strong-willed girl, and she's proud. I know she approached the owner of the general store and the boardinghouse for work, but neither of them had a job for her." Naomi sighed. "She told me she had the qualifications to teach school."

"I'd like to see her teaching. I think she'd do a fine job."

Naomi walked to where he stood and handed him the food. "God will triumph over this. He will not let Christopher go free and leave you to suffer."

Caleb pressed his lips together. "I want to believe the same thing, and I understand His ways are best." He leaned against the side of a stall and uncovered the plate. "I'd gladly give my life for my brother, if it were any situation other than this. In fact, I'd die right now if this would bring him to his knees." He paused. "Maybe that is the answer."

"I hope not." A tear slid down Naomi's round cheek.

"I'm not a brave man, Naomi. Not a real smart one either. But I do know God has a perfect plan."

"Do you trust Him to see you through this to the end?"

He straightened. "Yes, Naomi. I know if I'm looking down a hangman's noose or the barrel of a rifle, He's with me."

"With your kind of faith, this will work out for the best."

He wrapped one arm around her and pulled her to his side. "I pray so." The smell of roast pork tugged at his stomach. "Thanks for taking care of me."

"You're welcome. I wonder if you should be having a conversation with Audra."

He raised a brow. "Why?"

"Because you love her, and she loves you."

He hesitated. How much of his heart dare he confess to this woman? "If my name is cleared, I will approach Audra. Until then, I am a wanted man who can offer nothing but a life on the run."

"Surely there is a place where you two could live in peace."

He smiled. "You are talking like a mother. At least I think so, 'cause I never knew mine." He wiped the tears from her cheeks. "The only safe place for a wanted man is a grave. I will not give up on this fight—not now or ever."

"I understand, and I'm being a silly old woman who loves you like a son."

"We're just stuck, aren't we?" With those words he winked and moved to saddle his horse. He meant those endearing words. A minute more and he'd be behaving like a kid instead of a grown man, crying on her shoulder. Odd how feeling alone made a man vulnerable to his feelings.

"Be careful. Jed should be home on Tuesday."

"I will. I'll check in with both of you that evening."

"Watch out. I don't trust one of the ranch hands—Les."

Caleb sighed. "I'll make sure it's late—like an outlaw."

On Tuesday morning at breakfast, Christopher stated he needed to visit a family and would be gone most of the day. "Those folks have a sick mama. She's not doing well at all. I'm afraid she won't make it."

"May I go along? I could visit with the children. Cook and wash clothes. Do whatever needs to be done." Audra sensed he was lying, and this should prove it.

"I don't think so. You might get sick, too." He smiled. "I want my bride to stay healthy."

"But what about you? The town needs a pastor in one piece."

"I'll be fine. I've done this for a while now, and I haven't caught a thing."

She tilted her head and did her best to manage a quivering smile. "How dear of you to think of me. What is the family's name, and I'll pray for them?"

He leaned across the table and lifted her hand into his. "Sweetheart, you don't know these people. They seldom come to church. Never mind their names, but I'm sure they could use your prayers."

"Most certainly." *Why do I think there isn't a sick mother or a needy family? Christopher, you are simply making this up and making things worse for yourself. God knows what you are doing. You can't hide your lies from Him.* Suddenly a little whisper told her she had not been praying for him. He truly needed the Lord's hand to touch his life.

"Don't look so distraught," he said. "We will make plenty of calls together in the years to come."

"I'm being silly, aren't I?"

"I rather enjoy it."

"Do you suppose tomorrow afternoon you could give me a tour of the parsonage? I really want to see what our home looks like." She paused. "I've wanted to ask you all week—it does not look appropriate, does it?"

"Shall I ask one of the women from church to join us?"

"Naomi?" she said.

"If it pleases you. I always enjoy talking to Jed." He leaned in closer. "The sheriff suspects the Masterses may know Caleb's whereabouts."

Audra covered her mouth. "Surely not! I'd. . .I'd have discovered it while living there."

He patted her hand still encased in his. "Do not alarm yourself, Audra. I'm sure Sheriff Reynolds's information came from an unreliable source." He released her hand and pulled out a pocket watch—a fine gold one. Probably stolen.

"What time are you leaving?" She offered a sad smile and hated herself for it.

He replaced the watch and tilted back on his chair. "Are you missing me already?"

"I believe so."

"I'm sorry, but I'm leaving shortly after breakfast. How are you spending your day?"

"I might go riding. Close to town of course."

Christopher frowned then finished his coffee. "Don't let the outlines of the buildings get beyond you."

"Don't worry about me. I've learned to be careful." Every word sounded as twisted as his. She needed for this to be over soon.

As soon as Christopher left her at the boardinghouse, Audra ascended the stairs to her room. All the while she prayed for Christopher. Once in her room, she dropped to her knees.

Forgive me, Lord, for not asking You to lead Christopher from his sin. Pierce his heart with Your sword of truth. Unite the brothers in a bond of love and forgiveness. Oh, how I long for all of this to be over.

She changed into a riding skirt, one Naomi had sewn for her when she stayed with the couple. Audra had no intentions of using a sidesaddle, and the split skirt often worn by ranchers' wives suited her just fine. Slipping her fingers under the curtain, she peered out through the side of the window and watched Christopher stride toward the livery. He spoke to everyone he met. She admitted he did play the part well. No wonder the entire town believed Caleb rode the outlaw trail.

The moment Audra saw him disappear to retrieve his horse and wagon, she rushed down the stairs and out the front door to the general store across the street. Once inside, she feigned interest in a couple of bonnets artfully placed near the store's window. While she gingerly touched a blue and yellow laced one, she saw Christopher drive the wagon toward the parsonage. Moments later she made her way to the livery.

Papa had shown her how to bridle and saddle a horse when she turned ten years old. Thank goodness, for she needed to hurry, and waiting for the stable boy tried her patience. She led the mare that Jed allowed her to borrow from the livery. She walked the horse toward the parsonage and waited a good distance behind until she saw Christopher leave.

She followed Christopher for over two hours. The wagon ambled west toward the hills that led to the Rockies. She had a difficult time believing a family lived in this secluded area. As usual, the sights and sounds of nature were breathtaking, but she dare not let anything divert her from the task at hand. Once the road wound around the hills, she found it easier to keep a safe pace behind him. He veered the wagon to the right. Audra dismounted and led the mare. From the looks of the thick underbrush, the wagon could not go much farther. Up ahead, she saw the wagon and horse—without Christopher.

Audra tied her mare to a sapling and crept closer. Her heart beat so furiously she feared the sound would give her away. Her foot stepped on a stick, and it cracked like rifle fire. She held her breath and anticipated seeing Christopher emerge from the trees, demanding why she'd trailed him.

In the distance he disappeared on foot around a curve. The sensible part of her said to ride back to Earnest. The part of her that cared for Caleb and all those who'd been hurt by Christopher's actions spurred her on. She continued up a winding path, stealing behind brush and trees.

If he discovered her, she had no weapon. Stupid! Even if Caleb had denied ever making such an accusation, she certainly claimed it now. A horse neighed. Audra stole behind a juniper tree. There ahead, Christopher rode a pewter-colored stallion. She clutched her heart and silently begged it not to explode from her chest. He headed down the path straight toward her. If he didn't find her, he'd find Jed's mare. She imagined her death would be blamed on Caleb.

As Christopher grew closer, she saw he'd changed clothes. Audra held her breath. He wore the same clothes he'd worn the day he robbed the stage and shot one of the drivers. About fifty feet away from her, he turned south. Four other men rode alongside him—the same men she'd seen before. One of them was the foul-smelling man who had sat across from her and Papa. Another she recognized from Jed's ranch—Les.

"You're right on time," Christopher said.

"We're always where we need to be," the foul-smelling man said.

"Right, Hawk. Do we need to go over what we're doing?" Christopher said. "That stage is due in thirty minutes, and it's carrying cash from Denver."

"We know what we're doing," another man said.

"Remember this is my last job." Christopher laughed.

"Yeah. I hear you're getting married," Hawk said and spit tobacco juice several feet.

"Not for long. Soon as I say I do, I'm faking the preacher's death and sending half the state after Caleb while I'm taking life easy in Mexico."

The other men laughed.

"You gonna leave the prettiest girl in these parts?" Les said. "She'd sure tempt me."

Audra squeezed her eyes shut to keep from sobbing. Every muscle in her body tightened. Would any of the townsfolk believe what she'd heard and seen? Suddenly an unseen hand gripped her mouth.

Chapter 13

Audra, you're too close. Chris and his men will find you—both of us."
She willed her body to cease its trembling, but every part of her quivered like a fall leaf. She was safe. Caleb held her, not one of Christopher's men. He smelled of leather and the freshness of morning, not the wild desperation of evil men. The violation she feared had not occurred—would not as long as she obeyed Caleb.

"I'm going to release you. Take my hand, and let's get back out of sight." His breath tickled her ear. "Move quietly. Watch where you step."

She nodded, but still her legs felt like soft jelly. His hand lifted from her mouth, and she breathed in and out in an effort to calm herself. Somehow she rested her hand into his and let him lead her farther into the brush. She did her best to walk on the soft earth, but her footsteps broke through the silence like a crack of thunder.

Caleb stopped and turned to her. "Easy," he whispered. "I'm right here."

A chill raced up her arm, and she knew for certain Caleb Windsor cared as much for her as she did for him. How terribly sad for two unlikely people to be denied their affections. Before this horrible experience came to a close, one of the two Windsor brothers might be killed—most likely the man she loved.

A few moments later, Christopher and his men rode by en route to where the stage cleared an open stretch of land. Staring ahead to where she'd stood only a moment ago, Audra saw how easily she could have been discovered. The thought caused her to shudder.

"I am terribly foolish," she said. "If not for you, they would. . .have found me."

He squeezed her hand lightly then grasped her shoulders. His rigid features spoke for him. "Don't you ever do anything like this again. Luckily I saw you before they did."

"I didn't realize—"

"Hush and listen to me. You, little lady, are allowed to keep Chris company with the idea you might hear something that will help us. No following him. Ever. No creeping around like a lawman. Ever. Do you understand every word I've said?"

She nodded, still too frightened to argue.

"Don't think I haven't considered wiring your folks about the danger here."

She cringed and her stubbornness rose to the surface. "You wouldn't dare."

The menacing gaze emitting from his wide eyes didn't require a reply.

"I want to do more. It's important to me," she said.

"Like today? Promise me this idiocy is over, or I will have Jed wire your folks as soon as he can ride into Earnest."

Feeling like a trapped animal she agreed. "I'll do what you say." Maybe.

His arms dropped to his sides. "Good. I imagine you heard the conversation between Chris and his men."

"I did." She took a deep breath. "Everything is true. He actually intends to marry me, fake his death, and blame it on you."

"I'm sorry, Audra."

"Don't be. I know he's wretched, and you told me this before, but each time I learn something new for myself, I get angrier than I thought possible." She gasped and focused her attention on him. "Your poor father. He will be grief-stricken. He always talks about how proud he is of both of you."

Caleb said nothing, only peered back at her. His wrinkled brow told her he didn't need a reminder of his father.

"I treasure Pastor Windsor," Audra said. "He gives more to others than anyone I know." *And you are so much like him.* "He'll be so upset."

"Do you really think he doesn't suspect something? That Chris hasn't told him about my unlawful activities?"

When she paused to consider the question, her heart plummeted. "You mean he may already believe you are an outlaw?"

"Why wouldn't he?"

She nodded slowly. "Are you telling me it wouldn't do any good for you to contact him, have him come out here, and try to convince Chris to abandon his ways?"

"Our father is already hurting—has been for a long time. Why make it any worse until this is settled?" He paused and expelled a labored breath. "Audra, your suggestion may be a good idea. I haven't written him in a few years. He might take notice and listen."

"You're right, and then if he came out here—"

"He could see for himself." Caleb nodded. Lines deepened around his eyes.

She glanced about and drank in a faint fragrance of wildflowers. A soft breeze rustled through the treetops. She stood next to a man she loved and couldn't utter a word about it. If only he'd talk about something other than Christopher or their father. "This is such beautiful country."

"Torn apart by greedy men."

She forced a lump back down her throat. "I can't believe Les is a part of those men, too," she said. "He's spying on everything that goes on at the Masterses' ranch."

"Naomi suspected him and warned me."

"I remembered Hawk from the stage with Papa and me. He reminded me of a pig."

Caleb lifted a brow. "You recognized him? I caught him at Jed and Naomi's posing as a bounty hunter. He's the one who said you'd gone to the sheriff about me hiding out at their ranch."

She tilted her head. "Who else is in on this?"

"I hope no one. Those other two fellas riding with Chris are strangers. No doubt keeping low. Jed's supposed to be back from Denver today. It will be a miracle if Governor Eaton swallows his story—even so, he'll need proof."

"I'll testify." An idea enveloped her, a wonderful idea. "I can go to Denver tomorrow, and I'll tell the governor the whole story."

"Absolutely not."

Heat flooded her face. "Why? I witnessed Chris and his men today. You need my testimony to clear your name."

"Who is going to protect you until then? How are you going to get to Denver without Chris coming after you? And I guarantee my brother won't be alone. What will be your reason for leaving Earnest?" He crossed his arms over his chest. "Without evidence, it's the pastor and the sheriff's word against a young woman who hasn't been in town long enough to make friends—except for the couple who are allegedly hiding out an outlaw."

"You obviously don't have much faith in my persuasive abilities with Christopher or the governor's ability to discern the truth."

"Audra, please. I want this thing ended more than anyone, but my brother is on the winning side unless we find the money and stolen goods."

Her shoulders fell along with her optimism. "I wish I knew what to do."

"You can take the next stage back to Nebraska."

"I can't." She dare not tell him of her love. He'd force her back to Nebraska for sure—just to keep her safe.

"I know Chris stole your money. I'll pay the fare."

"I don't want your money!" She feared her heart would betray her.

Silence settled thickly, like the dead calm before a violent storm.

"Let's not quarrel," Caleb said.

She understood. Angry words solved nothing. "All right."

"Will you go back home?"

"No. Not now or ever." Audra's heart hammered against her chest.

"Why? When there's nothing here for you but a town full of deceit?"

Mama always said what a person didn't say often shouted louder than the words coming from their mouth. At the time, Audra thought her mother spoke in riddles. Now she understood. Loving Caleb Windsor meant more to her than a life of peace and comfort in Nebraska. If he guessed her heart, he'd have one more burden—whether he shared in the feelings or not. She dare not tell him all the reasons why she had to stay. "I made a commitment to begin a new life here."

"A life with my brother, the pastor."

"I understood right from the beginning that a marriage might not be part of my future with Christopher. I came prepared to find work. Why are you anxious to have me gone?"

"So you don't get yourself hurt."

She'd succeeded in irritating him again. "We're bickering."

"And I need to leave."

She peered into his rugged face. "Are you taking out after Chris?"

"I want to see if I can stop the robbery. At least find out where he's taking the money."

"I'd like to—"

His narrowed gaze stopped her. "Can you find your way back to town?"

She nodded, and they walked to her horse. Many things raced through her mind, none of which she could voice. Every time she saw him could be the last. Every time she took a glimpse into his midnight blue eyes and nearly drowned in them could be nothing more than a memory. His deep gentle voice could become a haunting recollection. Oh, to tell Caleb she loved him. Taking a deep breath, she grabbed the reins and allowed him to help her swing up into the saddle.

"If you don't keep your word, I will escort you to Nebraska myself," he said.

And she knew he meant every word. "I understand. I'll remember every word you say. God be with you."

≈

Trying to talk sense into Audra lessened Caleb's chances of making it to the stage before the robbery. If only he could arrive in time to warn the driver, even if it meant posing as Chris and ordering the stage to return to Denver. The thought of another killing spurred him on faster. What a nest of rattlers this had become.

By the time he caught up with his brother, the stage ambled on to Earnest with a little less money, and hopefully no one hurt. Caleb trailed the outlaws until they split up, his brother heading back alone to where he'd left the wagon.

Anger moved through Caleb like a brush fire. He desperately wanted to get the money back and return it to those it belonged to. The truth made him hotter than Naomi's cookstove. Who'd he give it to? The driver, who'd gladly unload his rife on him? The sheriff? The bounty-hunter outlaw?

Lord, I'm wandering like a blind man in a snake pit.

While he lingered behind Chris, an image of Audra refused to let him go. As much as he wanted to shake the stubbornness out of her, he'd rather pull her into his arms and never let her go. How could one little lady drive a man to distraction? He prayed for her protection and for her to get on the next stage back to Nebraska. It no longer mattered that he'd never see her again; she'd be safe from Chris. Each time they were together, he fought telling her how he felt and how he dreamed of the two of them having a life free of the nightmares chasing them. With a shrug he pushed her from his mind and stuck to his brother's trail.

Back at the wagon site, Sheriff Reynolds waited nearby. He took a long drink from his canteen and waved at Chris. "Thought I'd give you an escort back to town." He pushed his hat back on his head.

"You don't trust me?"

"Not when you'd pin a murder on your own brother."

Chris laughed and patted his saddlebags. "Got it all right here. Double-crossing a sheriff doesn't sound smart to me." He swung down from his horse. "Glad you came by. I wouldn't put it past Caleb to stop me along the road and hand out some brotherly advice. Lately he's been real upset at what I've been doing."

"That sure would make it easier for me. Lynch the thief and fill my pockets."

"Save us all some heartache."

The sheriff eyed Chris with a sneer. "Doesn't it bother you what you've done to Caleb?"

"Nah. He's always been a fool. I'm the one with the brains."

"What about acting like a preacher?"

"I learned how all that was done from my old man. You going soft on me?"

"Not in the least. Just wondering. What about Miss Lenders?"

Chris eased back in the saddle. "Haven't decided what to do with her yet. I'm considering taking her with me to Mexico."

So my brother does have a weak spot when it comes to Audra. She should be safe around him.

"You think she'd go?"

"I think she'd do anything I asked her." Chris chuckled. "I have a way with the ladies." He threw the saddlebags over his left shoulder.

"Why don't you leave her here? Just think of those dark-haired gals in Mexico."

"I prefer the one with sun-colored hair."

"Don't tell me you want to take up with the woman?" the sheriff said.

Chris failed to respond. Instead, he dismounted and hitched up the horse and wagon. "I said nothing of the sort. She'd be a sight better company than you are."

"Bad idea if you ask me. She doesn't come across like the type who'd say nothing about the way you get your money."

"Shut up, Reynolds. You take care of covering for me, and I'll take care of my personal business."

Caleb wanted to ride into the open and lay his brother flat on the ground—his usual response to Chris's actions. Odd, Caleb had never struck his brother even as a boy. It didn't matter. Chris had no right talking about Audra as though she were a faithful dog or a good horse.

"So this is the last job we pull together?" the sheriff said.

"I think so. Not unless you get wind of a money shipment."

"Not likely. The governor wired me about the robberies and offered an armed escort. After today, he'll follow through for sure."

Chris nodded. "Guess we're done then. We'll divide this up a few days before the wedding."

"Why wait so long?"

"I don't want to risk those guys waving around extra cash and folks getting suspicious before I'm long gone."

Chapter 14

Caleb trailed Chris and the sheriff back to Earnest. He was furious with the conversation he'd overheard, but as usual what could he do? He rode out toward the Masterses' ranch in hopes Jed had made it home from Denver. Might be some good news there. Long after the sun went down, he rapped on Jed and Naomi's door. Les and the other ranch hands appeared to have settled in for the night. One of them mentioned a card game and figured they'd be busy for a long time.

"Come on in, son," Jed said barely above a whisper. "Been expecting you."

Naomi pulled the curtains shut then uncovered a plate of food on the stove from supper. She pointed to an empty chair at the table and set a hearty helping of stew in front of him. "How was your day?"

Caleb eased into the chair and stretched out his long legs. "All right." Tired best described him: physically and mentally. He'd rather mend fences from sunup to sundown seven days a week than keep an eye out for Chris and worry about what might happen to those he cared about. Lately he felt like David running from King Saul. Unfortunately, Caleb didn't have all of David's fine traits—only the similarity of running from a man who wrongfully pursued him.

"You look plumb worn out, worse than Jed." Naomi poured him a glass of cool buttermilk.

"Why don't you eat before you tell us about the past few days?" Jed said. "I had a fair meeting with the governor, and I'm hoping some good will come of it." He turned to Naomi. "I could use a glass of buttermilk, too, and another piece of that berry pie."

Caleb rested one arm on the table. His stomach complained of not eating since breakfast, and the tantalizing smells nearly did him in. But his mind raced with questions that held no answers, and he desperately craved them. He stuck his fork into a chunk of beef, tender enough for a baby to eat. Once he'd eaten about half of his food, he glanced at Jed. "I trailed Chris this morning and found out he had plans to rob the stage again."

Naomi groaned.

"I didn't get there in time to stop it, nor could I figure out where they hid the money except Chris took it with him into town. Don't believe anyone was hurt." He picked up a biscuit and heaped apple butter between the thick layers. "Good food, Naomi. Thanks." He paused. "Sheriff met him back in the hills, and together they headed to Earnest."

"So he must keep it at the parsonage," Jed said.

"Most likely. But we have another problem, almost as bad."

"Can't imagine things getting worse." Jed took a long drink of the buttermilk and a generous bite of pie.

"I caught Audra trailing after him, too. She nearly got caught before I yanked her out of there. Don't want to think of what Chris and his men might have done to her."

Jed's eyes widened, and he put down his fork. "What in the world was she doing out there? I thought she understood 'nothing dangerous.'"

"Her foolishness is going to get her killed." Caleb swirled the buttermilk in his glass. "I threatened to wire her father about the goings-on here, even told her I'd escort her back to Nebraska if she ever did anything like that again."

"Did she promise to behave herself?" Jed tugged at his mustache, now frosted in white. "She isn't afraid of anything, is she?"

"I'm thankful she's all right, but she's a woman in love, looking for a way to help her man." Naomi nodded in Caleb's direction.

Caleb looked up. "Where did you get such a crazy notion?"

"By looking at her," Naomi said. "Isn't that right, Jed?"

Jed sighed and pointed a finger at Caleb. "Sure is plain to me."

What can I say? I've seen something akin to love in Audra's eyes, too, or maybe I wanted to see it. "Doesn't matter what you saw or thought you saw, nothing can happen between us as long as I'm a wanted man."

"You're right, son." Jed pushed back his empty plate and stood. Sticking his fingers under his suspenders, he paced the room. "This business keeps getting more complicated."

"I think Chris may have found some feelings for her, too."

Naomi wiggled her shoulders as though she'd just tasted something nasty. "He doesn't know how to care for anyone but himself. How could he find feelings for Audra?"

Caleb suddenly lost his appetite. "From what Chris said to the sheriff, I'd say he's having second thoughts about leaving Audra behind."

Jed cleared his throat. "You mean he's talking about staying in Earnest?"

He shook his head. "Considering taking her with him to Mexico."

"Well, she'd never agree." Naomi planted her hands on her hips. "My lands, when will this get settled?"

"Soon." Jed startled him with the conviction in his voice.

"What did Governor Eaton say?" Caleb said. "Best tell me. It's been worrying at me since you left."

Jed eased back into his chair, his round stomach rubbing against the table. "I wouldn't say the news is bad. It simply could be better. I talked to the governor—explained it all. He said we needed evidence to clear you."

"Did you tell him how long we've been looking?" Caleb felt the age-old frustration creep into his bones.

"Yeah. He's sending a man from his office to do a little snooping around. If you get arrested, he'll wire the governor to make sure you get a fair trial."

"You mean a fair hangin'?"

"Hush, Caleb." Naomi's forehead crinkled. "One more person on our side is a welcome thing."

He stretched back his neck. Tired, so tired. "The president himself could be on our side, but without proof of my innocence we have nothing." Silence grated the room. Outside one of the dogs barked. "I need to get inside the parsonage. The money has to be hidden there. In fact, I have an idea since Miss Audra is so eager to help."

"You're not going to ask her to do anything outlandish, are you?" Naomi said.

"Nope." Caleb laughed, despite the circumstances. "I thought you could invite Audra and Chris out here for dinner. Keep them late, insist they stay long after dark. That'll give me plenty of time to search the parsonage."

"Now I'm being left out of the excitement," Jed said and picked up his pipe. "I'd love to find all the stolen money."

"You're too old for excitement," Naomi said. "You can spend your time thinking of things to talk about with Christopher, since he's one of your favorite people."

Jed scowled. "Old woman, you're getting feistier as the years go by."

She kissed the top of his bald head. "You wouldn't have it any other way."

Jed grinned and winked at Caleb. "This is what you have to look forward to."

Sun-kissed hair and wide blue eyes rested in his mind. Life with Audra would be a glimpse of heaven. . .if he lived to court her proper.

⁂

Audra thought if she shared one more miserable meal with Christopher, she'd be sick. And all over him, too. Goodness, she'd gotten surly. He looked up from his fried chicken and smiled. Why was he being exceptionally nice? Every day brought them closer to their wedding day—she planned to stand him up at the altar by riding out of town in the opposite direction.

"Heard from Jed Masters today," Christopher said.

She gave him her full attention. "I wish he'd stopped into the boardinghouse."

"He was in a hurry. They invited us to dinner tomorrow night."

Her smile came naturally. "Wonderful. I miss them."

"We'll have a pleasant evening of it, my dear. Not too late, though. The thought of driving back after dark with my brother on the loose doesn't sit well with me."

She startled. "How horrid of him to stop us on the road. Neither of us has anything of value for him to steal. The thief already took my money."

"Don't put it past him. He's done worse. I'm sure he'd like nothing better than to ruin our wedding day."

She bit her tongue to keep from giving him a piece of her mind. Pleasantries with him were becoming increasingly difficult.

"I wish he'd take all the money he's stolen and leave the state," he said.

"Where do you think he'd go?" she asked.

"South America is my guess. He could live there like a king."

Just like he planned to do. She picked at her food. "What does the sheriff think?"

"We've talked about it. Oh, Audra, I hate to worry your pretty little head with talk of catching a criminal."

Had they planned to trap Caleb—force him into the open?

"I'm sure we will be fine tomorrow night." He wiped his fingers on a napkin. "I'm not concerned about me, only you." He finished the potatoes and corn on his plate. "Are you a good cook?"

Cook? She considered his question. How tempting to tell him no or offer to prepare him a terrible meal. He'd probably want fried rattlesnake. "I'm not sure how good, but Mama and Papa never complained."

"I suspect I'll be looking like Jed in no time at all."

Can't get plump in prison. "Oh my, a portly pastor, but a jolly one." She covered her mouth to suppress a laugh. "What is your favorite?"

"Fried chicken and cobbler. I love a good apple cobbler with a thick crust and sweet cream."

Audra laughed, but not for the reason he suspected. "Hmm, with mounds of sugar sprinkled on top."

"Yes, ma'am." He leaned in closer. "I'm also looking forward to children—lots of little girls who look like their mama." His gaze lingered on her face, the type that made her feel as though she needed to slap him. "All with silky, sun-colored hair and light blue eyes. I'd have a whole household of my Audra."

She blushed scarlet and felt the heat rising from her neck. Did Christopher have to continue lying so? It was a wonder the good Lord didn't throw a bolt of lightning his way. "You embarrass me, Christopher," she whispered. "What would people say if they heard you?"

He gave her an impish grin. "They'd say there's a man in love who's planning his future."

Audra shivered. For a moment she believed him. The impossibility of ever having a relationship with Christopher made her shudder. He was a killer, a liar, a thief. And he cared not to hide his improper thoughts. With all he'd done. With her feelings for Caleb. Did he think she was that naïve? This had to be a game for him, a diversion to pass the time until he left Earnest for Mexico.

"I've made you speechless with my comments," he said. "But I have a surprise."

She lifted her gaze, dreading his next words. "I can hardly wait."

"If you'd still like to see the parsonage Saturday morning, one of the members will be helping me repair the church's roof, so it'd be proper."

"What about your sermon?"

"It's finished."

"I'd love it," she said. "Can I do a little exploring to see where you have things stored and such?"

"Of course. I like my home neat and orderly, so I don't think you will find fault with my housekeeping."

She forced a laugh. She remembered the clean, folded handkerchief he used to wipe the blood from her finger. "I hadn't thought anything of the sort."

"If the parsonage suits you, we could move up the wedding date."

"You are teasing me. Admit it, Christopher. The wedding date will be here before we know it, and probably before I'm completely ready."

"If I had the money, I'd whisk you away to someplace where no one would ever bother us. What do you say? Back East? Europe? To South America like my wayward brother is probably planning?"

"All on a poor pastor's wages?" She leaned closer and pretended to cling to his witty conversation. How she'd relish the opportunity to hear him admit his guilt. "You and I would have to rob all the good people of Earnest to afford such luxury."

Chapter 15

Mid afternoon on Thursday, Audra and Christopher rode the wagon to Jed and Naomi's. She'd slept little the night before thinking about seeing her friends. They hadn't been attending church lately, and she had mixed feelings about it. Audra wanted to tell them about Saturday's plans to explore the parsonage while Christopher busied himself with the church's roof repair. Giddiness swelled in her, the first real source of joy she'd felt since coming to Colorado. She pictured herself telling Caleb she'd found the money. Soon he'd enjoy the freedom of living on his ranch without fear of being arrested—or worse.

"You're happy, aren't you?" Christopher said. "I hope you are finally putting aside the stage robbery."

Startled, Audra scrambled for words. "At the moment, yes. I pray justice will soon rule Earnest and not this cloud of fear."

"I agree, except that means my brother will be suffering the consequences of his actions."

"All evil men need to understand their ways will catch up with them." To keep from displaying her frustration, she chose to discard the subject of Earnest's unrest. "Colorado is so beautiful. I'm glad this is my new home, and I love Naomi and Jed. They are like parents to me."

"Yes, this territory suits you well. Your cheeks have a nice rosy color, and I can see in your eyes how much you appreciate the mountains."

Since she'd moved into the boardinghouse, Christopher had been a perfect gentleman. To her it seemed like Christopher was two men, and the realization frightened her, for at any moment he could change into a man who was capable of hurting her and others.

"I've never told you I love you," he said.

Those were the last words she wanted to hear. She wished he'd pick up the horse's pace. Nervousness pounded at her temples. "Please wait. We are barely more than strangers."

"I think my heart was smitten the first time I saw you."

"Love takes time," she said. "And we are friends, growing closer every day."

His shoulders lifted and fell. "I want us to declare a mutual love on our wedding day."

She smiled. Her pledge to help end his lawlessness contrasted with his tenderness toward her. The momentary kindness nibbled at her conscience. Had she become no better than he by leading him to believe she cared for him? In any event, she refused to tell him what he wanted to hear. Enough lies had passed between them without her adding another.

"Are you shy about matters of the heart?" he said.

"Yes, I imagine so." A reminder of her feelings for Caleb seized her, the devotion she must keep hidden.

"Then I'll wait. Hearing your love for me is worth the wait, for a hundred years if necessary. For you are truly a treasure. My father hand-selected you for me, and he did a fine job."

She breathed the freshness of the afternoon air, anxious to be at Jed and Naomi's. Tonight she could be with friends, and for a few hours she'd be relieved of dealing with Christopher. With an inward sigh, she realized Caleb had borne this load for years. The least she could do was endeavor to help him clear his name.

"I've been thinking about a trip for our honeymoon," he said.

She turned to him, grateful for a reprieve from the previous topic. "Where did you have in mind?"

"Mexico."

Panic gripped her heart. "What about your church?"

"I could get a good man to watch over things until we returned."

"How long would we be gone?"

He grinned. "Maybe forever. I hear Mexico is a beautiful country."

"You mean establish a new church there?"

"Whatever you want, Audra."

≈≈

Caleb spied Christopher and Audra leaving Earnest in the afternoon. Envy twisted his heart, because he wanted to be seated beside her. As he watched his brother turn to Audra, another thought consumed him—a protective one. His brother and Audra would be alone all the way to the Masterses' ranch and all the way back. He had to believe Chris had no intentions of harming her, and the conversation he'd heard between his brother and the sheriff was not another lie. If Chris truly had feelings for Audra, then he'd honor and respect her.

Wrestling with his own need to find proof of his innocence and to keep Audra safe, he decided to follow the wagon then double back to the parsonage. Granted, he'd have to hurry in his search, but he could manage it. As soon as he finished there, he'd race back to the Masterses' ranch and make sure his brother behaved himself in escorting Audra home.

Beneath a starless night, Caleb stole to the rear of the parsonage. He crawled through a bedroom window and pulled the curtains shut. In the dark, he drew a candle from inside his shirt and lit it. Everything in the room looked perfect, but that was Chris. When they were younger, the two boys argued more about Chris's insistence to keep things in order than anything else. Caleb believed the stolen money and other goods were stacked neatly in a spot where no one suspected. His gaze swept around the room. Where did he begin?

Caleb yanked on a dresser drawer. It squeaked and crashed to the floor. The sound shook his resolve. He refused to move, certain the sheriff waited in the next room.

Why am I going through my brother's house like a thief? He bent and picked up the drawer and slid it into place. Standing in the middle of the bedroom, he blew out the candle. He'd become as low as a snake's belly. His friends protected him.

The woman he loved risked being hurt. Why? If he trusted God, then he needed to listen for His direction. Alone in the parsonage, he realized his hurt and angry feelings combined with his desire to see Chris suffer didn't glorify God.

With the curtains shoved back into place, he crawled out through the window, secured his horse, and rode toward the Masterses' ranch. He had plenty of solitude between Earnest and the ranch to seek the Lord's forgiveness for the things he'd thought and planned regarding his brother. High time he followed God's steps instead of expecting God to follow his.

❧

Audra learned from Naomi about the plan to lengthen supper and the after-dinner conversation. Surely Caleb knew where to search in the parsonage. She'd be stumbling around like a blind person.

Later that evening when she and Christopher finally said their good-byes, the lack of a full moon forced them to light the wagon lanterns.

"I know you wanted to leave earlier," Audra said. "I suppose I should apologize."

"Never mind a bit," Christopher said. "We got started a little later in the afternoon than I expected, and I wanted you to have a good visit with the Masterses."

His good-natured mannerisms struck a guilty chord in Audra. The Christopher she met in the middle of the dusty road on the way to Earnest was selfish and cruel. But of late, he hid it well. The mask didn't make up for the horrible crimes he committed. She simply saw his charming side—the sweetness that the members of his church loved and appreciated.

When Audra was a little girl, a neighbor had the most loveable dog. One day it got sick, and the dog's disposition changed. When the neighbor tried to feed the animal, it bit him. Christopher reminded her of that dog. He had the abilities to serve God in the finest capacity. Instead, he maneuvered the innocent to make a profit.

The wagon ambled on as Audra's thoughts floated from the past in Nebraska to today's problems. Always, she lingered on Caleb—dear sweet Caleb who had suffered the most in all of this.

Night sounds lulled her, and she felt her eyelids grow heavy.

"Are you tired?" Christopher said.

"Very."

"We'll be home soon." He chuckled. "In a few weeks, the boardinghouse will be your old home."

She failed to reply.

"Go ahead and put your head on my shoulder. I'll wake you when we get to town."

"We have a few things to discuss, brother." She recognized Caleb's voice. The wagon came to an abrupt stop.

"Have you been following us?" Christopher's tone spit venom.

"Does it matter? What I have to say won't take long."

Christopher shifted on the wagon seat. "Remember there's a lady present."

"I'm not the one who has a habit of breaking the law to offend her."

"All right, Caleb. Say your piece and leave us alone." Anger laced Christopher's words.

"I've given you plenty of chances to turn yourself in, and nothing's ever changed. You're a lone wolf—too mean to keep company with decent folk. You're a disgrace to our father and to God."

Audra heard the confidence in Caleb. In the past he'd sounded bold, but not courageous.

Christopher laughed. "I think you're talking about yourself."

"The folks around here will soon know the truth about their pastor. Governor Eaton knows what's going on here, and he's not a happy man about it."

"Good! I hope he sends someone to investigate. The sheriff will welcome a hand. Earnest needs to be rid of the likes of you."

"Now that's a peculiar statement since the sheriff is in this with you."

Audra saw Chris reach behind him. In the next instant, a revolver flashed in the dim light. "You are a threat to my future wife. I hate the thought of shooting my own brother, but you give me no choice."

"No!" Audra screamed. "Please, Christopher. Don't do this."

"What's the matter with you? He's a thief and a murderer. Didn't you tell me that you wanted him stopped before we were married?"

"Not anymore. Let the law take care of him." Her heart hammered against her chest.

"Why not now?" Christopher said.

"Audra, I can handle this," Caleb said. "No need for you to get involved."

Christopher flashed his attention her way. "Are you seeing Caleb? Are you? Is that what this is all about? Are you in this with him? Trying to betray me? Tell me, or I'll pull the trigger now."

"Leave her out of our quarrel," Caleb said. From the corner of her eye, Audra saw Caleb dismount. She dare not take her gaze from Christopher.

"Stop right now." Christopher waved the revolver. "No one will blame me for this. No one. Answer my question, Audra. Are you in love with my brother?"

"You're angry." She willed her mind to clear. "Put the gun away. You don't want to do this. How can you live with shooting your brother?"

"Answer my question now." Christopher lifted the revolver.

"Yes." Her reply echoed across the night. "I do love Caleb. Please put the gun down. I'll do anything you say, but don't hurt him."

Christopher chuckled. "Anything? Marry me like you promised?"

"Whatever you want." She blinked back the tears. "Just don't pull the trigger."

"Audra," Caleb said. "I'd rather be dead than have you married to him."

Caleb's words cut through her heart. She had no choice. Couldn't he see that?

"Caleb, are you in love with her?"

She waited to hear his answer. Her pulse quickened. She feared Christopher would not wait to shoot him. This was not how she wanted to declare her love for Caleb, or hear if he shared the same feelings.

"Yes, I am," Caleb said.

"Hate to disappoint you, but she's mine."

Audra flung her body against Christopher. The gun fired. Caleb struggled with his brother. Both men fell into the dirt and wrestled with the weapon. Another shot fired. She scrambled down from the wagon.

"Stay back, Audra," Caleb said.

She obeyed, not knowing what else to do. Amid the sounds of Christopher's cursing, Caleb finally stood with the revolver in his hand. She seemed to quiver more in seeing he was safe than she had during the scuffle.

"Head on back to town," Caleb said.

Christopher rubbed his jaw. "I'm not finished with this."

"I wish you were. How do you think our father is going to feel when he finds out the truth? Bad enough he thinks I'm the outlaw. Worse yet is to learn you lied and deceived folks in the name of God."

"Leave me alone. I know what I'm doing."

He isn't denying Caleb's accusations.

Christopher climbed back into the wagon. "You going with me?" he said to Audra. "Or have you made your choice?"

She lifted her chin. "Do you think I'd go anywhere with you?"

"I'm not finished with you either. There will come a time when you will beg me to marry you. There's no future with Caleb—nothing but watching him hang."

"I'll take my chances."

"You could have had a good life with me, Audra. My affections were real."

She watched Christopher pick up the reins and urge the horse toward Earnest. The light shawl wrapped around her shoulders did nothing to stop the chill racing up her arms. She watched until the kerosene lanterns on both sides of the wagon faded into the distance.

"Audra."

She whirled in the direction of Caleb's voice. Without a full moon or stars, she saw only a faint outline of his figure. She despised the conflict between the brothers. Twins were supposed to be closer than regular brothers or sisters. This had to hurt him beyond words. Now he had the burden of a woman in love with him.

"Are you angry with me?" she said.

"How could I be? I am as much to blame as you are. He asked us questions, and we answered."

"I was so afraid for you. Are you hurt?"

"Nothing that Naomi can't bandage up."

She gasped and stumbled in the dark to his side. She wanted to touch him, make sure Christopher had not hurt him badly. "Are you making light of a serious wound? Did I do this when I pushed Christopher? What can I do?"

"This happened in the scuffle. It's not serious."

Tears seeped from her eyes and trickled down her cheeks. "I never meant. . .it to happen. I didn't even like you. . .in the beginning."

"I understand," he said. "I saw the love in your eyes."

"And I saw it in yours." She wanted to step into his arms, but he gave no indication of wanting her there.

"Until my name is cleared, nothing can happen between us." His voice resounded with conviction. "I cannot hold you or talk about what was said here tonight."

She wanted to tell him she loved him without Christopher pointing a gun at him, but she had to respect his stand. "I believe a horrible trick has been played on us." She paused and swiped at her wet cheeks. "We need to see Naomi. I have a feeling you are hurt more than what you are saying."

"Can you ride in front of me?"

Panic seized her. "Where are you shot?"

"My shoulder. Left side."

"Shouldn't I help you on and then crawl up behind you?"

"I can manage."

She feared Christopher had aimed for his heart and missed. *Dear Lord, brother against brother? This sounds too much like Papa speaking about the Civil War. Please touch Christopher's heart. He can be a good man. At times he's treated me properly. Right now, I'm asking You for healing—for Caleb's wound and Christopher's heart.*

Audra tucked her dress between her knees and lifted her foot into the stirrup. Caleb attempted to help, but he appeared too weak.

"Give me your hand," she said.

"I'm fine."

"Please, Caleb. Let me do something for you. How can you swing up onto the saddle with your left arm in pain?" He reached up, and she grasped his hand. The sole of his boot scraped against the wooden stirrup. When she pulled on him he groaned and nearly fell. "You can climb up here," she said and refused to release his hand.

The horse reared slightly, and Caleb fell onto the dirt road. "Go after Jed," he said. "Tell him I need help."

Chapter 16

When Caleb was a kid, a mule kicked him and broke his leg. Nothing had ever hurt him like that since—until tonight when Christopher's revolver fired into his shoulder. Every time his heart beat, a surge of pain nearly took his breath away.

"Lucky for you that bullet went through to the other side," Naomi said. "Instead of cleaning up this hole, I'd be digging out a piece of lead."

"That's comforting." His shoulder throbbed, worse by the minute. He peered up at Naomi. "I know I should be thanking you for this—"

She raised a brow. "Are you complaining about my nursing? Ah, I bet you want Audra to clean and bandage you up. She might be gentler than these rough, callused hands, but those salty tears of hers might sting a bit."

Naomi's teasing reminded him of Audra's confession earlier. And his own. He couldn't bring himself to look at her for fear he'd melt like butter on a hot day. She'd said little since riding after Jed. Perhaps her mind wrestled with the shooting or the understanding that they both loved each other. How easy it would be to take her into his arms, but how selfish of him to take advantage of her tender feelings.

Although Jed and Naomi sat with them in the kitchen, he needed for Audra to understand the stark reality of living a life on the run. He fixed his gaze on his beloved. "See this blood running down my arm, Audra? Do you remember the way you trembled when Christopher held the gun? That is my life. It will not change until my brother is stopped and my name's cleared." He winced as Naomi dabbed the hole in his shoulder with whiskey poured onto a clean cloth. He'd never had any use for the stuff. His father had called it devil's brew, and by the way it burned his shoulder, Caleb agreed. "If we were together, you'd be bandaging me up, not Naomi. You'd be ripping apart your petticoat for bandages and using creek water for medicine. Our home would be anyplace we could hide. Some farmer's barn that smelled of manure. Or under the stars, where we would pray it didn't rain or snow. If we made it to South America, we'd have to stay there till the day we died and hope the law didn't come after us."

Tears welled in her eyes. She bit her lip, no doubt to stop the sobs. "I know it would be a hard life."

He despised the words coming from his mouth. "Hard? Audra, it's a life not fit for a man, least of all a woman." She stood close enough for him to touch her. How he longed to wipe the tears from her cheeks, weave his fingers through her hair.

"Christopher could have shot you today. I won't have it. The best thing you can do for me is to go back to Nebraska."

She shook her head. "Never. I'm staying here. I will not run from what your brother is doing and allow him to gloat over it."

"Tonight you agreed to marry him, if he didn't shoot me."

Her face paled. "And I would have."

"He could do the same thing again. Don't you see that he will try to get me through you?"

"Then I will hide, too."

Caleb tore his attention away from her and fixed his gaze on Naomi. "Can't you reason with her? Make her see I'm afraid she's going to get hurt."

The lines in Naomi's face deepened. "How can I deny Audra her dreams? I'm an old woman. You are a son to me, and I cannot let you fight this alone either."

"Neither can I." Jed handed Naomi another clean bandage. "We're a ragged sort of family here, Caleb. You have our loyalty whether you want it or not." He clasped his hand onto Caleb's good shoulder. "God is on our side. Admittedly so, we have little chance of success. But with God, justice and truth will win."

Caleb nodded. The pain had weakened him, dulled his judgment. His emotions were tossed. He had to stand firm—for his father, Jed, and Naomi, for Audra, and most of all for God.

Moments passed in silence. He watched Naomi thoroughly clean his shoulder. Good thing Chris's aim was tempered by the dark. A few more inches and that bullet would have pierced his heart.

"I do have an idea," Caleb finally said. "Chris and the sheriff are bent on trapping me, but I think we could set one for them." He turned to Audra. "Would you be willing to go back to the boardinghouse?"

She gasped. Her pale skin grew even whiter. "And give up any chance of seeing you?"

"To help me." He gazed at her. "If it appears you have deserted us, and you must find a place to live before returning to Nebraska, Chris and the sheriff will ignore you. You can be our eyes and ears."

She offered a faint smile. "And how will I get the information to you?"

"I've learned a few things about hiding in the shadows. Also, I have money, and I expect you to take it."

"I don't like taking your money, but I can do what you ask—and I can keep an eye on Chris and Sheriff Reynolds. I shall surprise you and not complain." Hope crested in her blue eyes.

He peered up at Jed, the man who knew him better than his own father. "You said Governor Eaton was sending a man?"

"Should be here in two days. Name's Dixon. He'll stop at the ranch first."

"Best you send Les off until he's gone. And once Dixon heads for Earnest, stay clear of him where others might see."

"What are you thinking, son?" Jed said.

Caleb smiled then held his breath sharply as Naomi tightened the bandage. "Another shipment of money en route to Denver, or at least let the sheriff believe money is on the stage. Chris is angry, and the only way to soothe him will be to satisfy his greed. The sheriff was told that the governor would send an escort on the next shipment, but I think Dixon could persuade him otherwise, especially if an empty strongbox is with the stage. When Chris robs it, Dixon and I will be there. It sounds simple, but I believe it has merit."

"It does," Jed said. "You have a fine plan."

Caleb looked at his bandaged shoulder. It hurt powerful bad. He took a deep breath. "Jed, would you commit the plan to God? We all need prayer."

❧

Audra believed she'd not rest a wink that night. So much had happened this evening. The nightmare with Christopher stayed vivid in her mind. Caleb had nearly been killed. The struggle for the revolver and the discovery he'd been injured played back through her thoughts. Tonight he'd spoken the truth. Running from the law was no life at all.

She shuddered as she crawled beneath the quilt at Jed and Naomi's. She had not tried to talk to Caleb privately. It would be too difficult for both of them. Her love could strengthen him or weaken him, and she was determined not to be demanding. Later, they'd have hours to talk, to hold each other. It was enough to know he loved her, and he knew she loved him.

She laid her head upon the pillow. An image of Caleb stayed fixed in her mind—a home, a family, a life of peace. She inhaled deeply as sleep nibbled at her body. Living in Earnest alone without her friends could not be worse than sharing meals and worrisome hours with Christopher. Already she sensed his treachery. He'd talk badly about her to his congregation to make sure no one befriended her. In the darkness, she smiled despite the ugliness of tonight and the days to come. Jesus would be her only friend. She'd not be lonely, and she'd not disappoint Him.

Chapter 17

Caleb saw Jed swing a lantern twice in front of the kitchen window to signal that Dixon had arrived. With Les sent to round up strays for a few days, Caleb was confident in approaching the Masterses' ranch. Governor Eaton must have believed some of what Jed claimed, or he wouldn't have sent Dixon to look into the situation—unless Chris had done the same thing. That being the case, Dixon may have orders to arrest the infamous outlaw. A queasy sensation settled in the pit of Caleb's stomach. With his shoulder healing, he had doubts about his ability to fight his way out of this one.

Rely on God. Caleb took a deep breath.

He waited nearly an hour before he knocked on the door. Uneasiness crept over him. His mouth tasted as dry as an August day without rain. He felt powerless over this stranger who could very well decide his future. The past four years had left him suspicious and afraid to trust anyone. Jed and Naomi smothered him in kindness before he opened up his heart to them. Now they were knee-deep in this mess with him. Shaking his head to dispel the doubts, he knocked on the door.

God possessed the power, not the governor's assigned man or Caleb's ability to fight.

Jed greeted him with a wide grin. "We've been talking about the situation." He ushered Caleb inside. "Dixon is anxious to meet you."

The stranger rose from a chair—tall, thin, confident. Caleb hid his trepidation and gripped the man's hand. "Caleb Windsor here. Pleased to make your acquaintance."

"Just call me Dixon."

The two men locked gazes. *Good eye contact. Tanned face. Callused hands. Not afraid of work.*

"Jed says the wrong man is on the wanted posters." Dixon neither smiled nor moved a muscle. "I need proof."

Caleb paused. "Are you ready to work?"

"Depends on your story," Dixon said.

"Sit down, and I'll give it to you." For the next hour, Caleb told what had happened over the past four years since he and Chris moved to Earnest. All the while he scrutinized the man before him. Dixon's body remained motionless: no tugging at his beard as if doubtful of Caleb's story or lifting of his brow. Intelligence radiated from his eyes.

"Like I said before, we need evidence," Dixon said. "The Masterses' testimony is good, so is Miss Lenders's, but Sheriff Reynolds already filed a report to the governor naming the Masterses as part of the gang."

"I'm not surprised. He has one of his men working here for Jed. We need to find out where he stashed the money and the other stolen goods," Caleb said. "I have a plan."

Dixon nodded. "Go on. I'm listening."

"Chris is greedy, and now he's after revenge because of Audra. If the sheriff learns of a money shipment heading to Denver and tells Chris, he'll have to steal it. We don't need the evidence for you to arrest him as long as you catch him during the robbery. I'd even like to see your men as passengers."

"This will go hard on whoever is convicted. Brothers, huh?"

"Yep. Our father's still alive, and I don't want to think about him finding out about this." Caleb paused. "I'm hoping my brother would tell you where the money is in exchange for a lesser sentence."

"Good thinking." Dixon leaned back in his chair. "Give me more details."

Caleb continued, just as he had outlined the plan on the night Chris shot him.

"This is worth a try." Dixon pointed to Caleb's shoulder. "Who winged you?"

"My brother."

"An accident?"

"Nope. The only accident was he missed my heart."

Dixon pressed his lips together. "How long before you can ride and shoot?"

"Tomorrow. Don't fret over me. I'll hold my own."

For the first time, Dixon smiled. "I'm ready to go to work. This will take time."

<hr>

In the wee hours of the morning, long after Caleb rode with Dixon to the outskirts of town then back to the Masterses' ranch, he took out paper, pen, and ink from Naomi's kitchen. He remembered where she kept it from the last letter he wrote. That one was for Chris to copy and send to his father about requesting a wife. This time, things were different. He'd be a fool not to comprehend that he or Chris faced possible death over this mess. Caleb's conscience refused to allow their father to believe the years of lies. By candlelight, he dipped the pen into the inkwell and began the painful truth to his father.

Dear Father,

I should have written to you long before this, but I didn't know where to begin. I still don't. Shame and guilt have eaten away at me for a long time. I pray God guides my pen, and the accountings I relate will not turn you against me or Chris, for it is out of love for you and my brother that I tell you these things.

As boys, it seemed like Chris and I were always in trouble, as you well remember. I hated seeing my brother punished, so I confessed to many things that I didn't do. Over the years, the practice became a habit until Chris expected me to take the blame. I thought taking care of him was a sign of strength, but I was wrong. So wrong. When we moved to Colorado, I thought his behavior would change.

I was wrong again. Chris met up with some fellows who had no respect for the law. They became his friends. With them, he found a way to have more horses. I don't think he set out to be an outlaw or to blame me. Their ways were just easier for him to get the things he wanted. When someone recognized him during a raid on a man's farm, he claimed I was the thief. I think out of habit. Soon afterward he went into the ministry.

Father, I wrote the letter for Chris requesting a wife, and he did not balk at the idea. I thought if my brother married a godly woman, he'd end his life of crime. I didn't mind leaving the country if it brought about good for my brother.

Audra learned the truth about Chris, and she is living at the boardinghouse in Earnest. Audra and a dear couple, Jed and Naomi Masters, are the only ones who know the truth. Wanted posters with my name are nailed in every town in the area. Chris refuses to stop. I am asking you to come to Earnest and help me convince him to end his ways.

I'm sorry for lying to you all these years, and I understand this is my fault. If I had allowed him to face the consequences of his actions all these years, the situation would not have gotten so bad. I need you, Father. I firmly believe he will listen to you. My prayer is for Chris to see he is not pleasing God. Please send your response to the Masterses. It is no longer safe for me to be seen.

> *Your son,*
> *Caleb*

For the next few days, Caleb watched Chris every moment of the day until the sun went down. Even then he kept a wary eye on the road leading out of town. He used a pair of binoculars from Jed's Civil War years. If his brother left town, Caleb followed. He observed the company he kept and noted the hours in the parsonage. Only God knew why no one caught him spying.

Chris spent a lot of time in Sheriff Reynolds's office. Most likely discussing what they intended to do with the stolen money. One thought amazed Caleb: How could the sheriff trust Chris with the money, unless he also knew where it was hidden?

Dixon stayed at the boardinghouse, and Caleb felt certain he made contact with Audra. Poor girl, she needed a friend.

Everything rested on finding the money. Caleb had no intentions of giving up. Not this time. Too many people had been robbed of peace, and a life with Audra weighed in the balance.

≈≥

If Audra had had any doubt about Christopher's vindictiveness, she had none now. From the way the members of his congregation snubbed her, he must have announced her unwillingness to marry him from the pulpit. The reason must have been scandalous. A pair of ladies from the choir saw her and crossed the street.

"Good afternoon, ladies." Audra bit back her laughter. "Beautiful day, isn't it?"

They kept right on walking.

Sheriff Reynolds treated her like a stranger, but that was a blessing. The man made her want to horsewhip him. Christopher had not set foot inside the boardinghouse lately. Finally she could enjoy her meals, and the tasteless food now had flavor. Finding work was another matter. The idea of Caleb giving her money didn't sit well. Twice she'd talked to the boardinghouse owner and the gentleman who owned the general store, but they had nothing to offer. She approached the head of the school board, but he was a member of Chris's church and stated the town had an excellent teacher. This morning she'd already been to the general store again, the newspaper office, and the livery—the latter had advertised for a stable boy.

The owner, a huge man who more closely resembled a bear, stared at her in surprise. "What does a fine young woman want with a job pitching straw and tending to horses?"

"I need to pay for my room and board," she said. "I can do this." The thought had occurred to her that she could keep her eyes on Christopher by working there. "Sir, I'm a hard worker. I can be here early and stay late."

He crossed his arms across his barreled chest and teetered back on his heels. "As pretty as you are, I don't want all the young men of Earnest filling up my livery."

"Absolutely not," she said. "I'd be here to work."

He nodded. "All right. I need you in the morning at six—and you best be stopping by the general store and finding yourself some suitable clothes. Can't clean out stalls with a skirt trailing in the manure."

"I will, sir. And thank you very much."

The owner's last instruction would take about half the money she had left, but she now had a job to support herself. *Christopher, you can't come and go without me knowing it. Thank You, Lord. This job is truly a gift from You.*

At the general store, she purchased a pair of boy's overalls, a shirt, boots, and two pairs of socks. A hat crossed her mind, until she remembered she'd be inside the livery and the sun wouldn't touch her face. Good thing Mama and Papa weren't nearby to see her mode of dress. She hoped Caleb didn't change his mind about her once he saw her knee-deep in dirty straw.

On the second day of her employ, a stranger walked into the livery and asked for his horse. Audra knew the animal, a high-spirited stallion that left her shaking in her boots.

"I'll give you a hand," the man said. "Are you the only one working today?"

Audra nodded. Suddenly a pang of fear crept through her. After all she was a woman alone in a livery stable. "Yes, sir." In the faint light, he looked very large. Almost as big as the livery owner.

"Can we talk in private, Miss Lenders?"

He knew her name. "What about?"

"Your friends. My name is Dixon—sent by Governor Eaton."

She relaxed with that knowledge. "Are they all right?"

"One of them would like to see you this evening. I could come by the boardinghouse and escort you in a wagon. I'm staying there, too, so I'm hoping this looks like we're courting." He smiled. "As pretty as you are, I can see why Caleb is a little anxious."

She blushed. "I am, too."

He glanced about. "Quite smart of you to obtain employment here."

"Thank you. It's been only a few days, but Christopher can't leave town without me knowing it."

"Caleb and I are following him, too. Although he could have conversations here that only you'd be privy to."

"I want to do whatever I can."

"Be careful. If what I've heard is true, Christopher Windsor is a dangerous man." She nodded.

"All right, Miss Lenders. My horse can be a handful, so I'll saddle him up."

"Thank you. He's fed and groomed."

He chuckled. "Do you always keep company with outlaws and unruly horses?"

She smiled at the thought. *My adventure.* "Goodness, it looks that way."

Mr. Dixon continued to laugh all the while he was in the livery. When he left, her day flew by. All she could think about was seeing Caleb. And he wanted to see her.

Not too long after the noon hour, Christopher came by for his horse and wagon. "What are you doing here?"

"Working," she said.

He sneered. "Too bad I didn't talk to the owner first."

"Must you be so spiteful?" she said. "Why would you want a woman who loves another man?"

"An outlaw? I'm not stupid, Audra. You've been seeing my brother since the stage holdup."

Her stomach churned. Had Christopher convinced himself of his innocence? "I know who you are, and I know what you've done."

He shook his head while lines deepened across his brow. "I could have given you anything you wanted. Instead you betrayed me."

She shivered. Perhaps he *had* cared for her—in the only way he knew. She doubted if he understood the real meaning of love when he had no respect for God.

"I'll get your horse and wagon ready." She turned toward the stalls.

"No, thanks. I'll handle it myself. I can't trust you any more than I can Caleb."

Evening shadows lingered by the time Mr. Dixon called on her. Excitement raced through her veins at the thought of seeing Caleb. She hoped his shoulder had healed nicely. Oh, for the day when he didn't have to hide out like a criminal.

"You look quite lovely, Miss Lenders," Mr. Dixon said. "I have a daughter your age, and the both of you could rival the queens of Europe."

"Thank you. I should like to meet her."

"A pleasant thought, especially if you and your friend can travel about freely." They walked through the door and on to the awaiting wagon. He assisted her onto the seat. "We may be followed, so be prepared if you're not able to see him," he whispered.

The thought devastated her, but she understood. A sideways glance took in Christopher and the sheriff observing them from across the street. "Certainly, Mr.

Dixon," she said with a smile. "This is a pleasant evening for a ride."

Once they traveled north outside of town, Audra sought conversation to soothe her uneasiness. "I'm glad we're headed opposite of the Masterses' ranch. Perhaps Christopher and the sheriff will think we aren't worth the trouble."

"I'd like to agree with you but, until Caleb rides into view, we'll continue alone."

For the next hour while dusk rested night upon them, Audra and Dixon ambled north. At one point, he stopped to light the kerosene lanterns on both sides. A short while later, he reined in the horse and gestured for her not to speak. The sound of approaching riders met their ears.

"Don't be afraid," he said. "I'm armed, and Caleb is watching." He turned the wagon around as the riders grew nearer. "Hello there," he said. "Who goes there?"

"Sheriff Reynolds and Pastor Windsor."

Audra recognized the sheriff's voice. Now what excuse would they use?

"Is there a problem?" Mr. Dixon asked. By then the two riders came into view and stopped in front of the wagon.

"We were checking on a rumor that Miss Lenders may be in danger." The sheriff cleared his throat. "We've had some problems with a local outlaw and didn't want either of you to face him alone. He's already killed one man and robbed a good many folk."

"Thank you. Appreciate your concern. We haven't had any trouble, and we're on our way back to town." Confidence radiated from Mr. Dixon's voice.

"Miss Lenders, would you like an escort?" the sheriff asked. "Pastor here was concerned."

She stiffened. "I'm fine. We haven't seen anyone to alarm us."

"We're just looking out for our citizens." Sheriff Reynolds tipped his hat.

Mr. Dixon picked up his reins and urged the horse on. A tear slipped down Audra's cheek. She'd wanted to see Caleb. Silence prevailed until they reached Earnest.

"I'm sorry," Mr. Dixon said. "Those two don't trust a move you make—possibly mine, too. The sheriff could have learned who I am."

"You've gone to a great deal of trouble tonight. I can take care of the horse and wagon."

"I think not, Miss Lenders, but to continue our little ruse, you may accompany me to the livery."

The livery was deserted, but Mr. Dixon had already made arrangements to return the horse and wagon late. Audra waited while he unhitched the wagon then led the horse into the stable.

A man stepped from the shadows. She held her breath. Had Christopher or the sheriff decided to do them harm?

Chapter 18

"Audra," Caleb whispered to the slight figure before him. "It's all right." He moved closer and cast aside his resolve not to reveal the intensity of his feelings for her. She looked incredibly small standing there with only the faint light of the lantern coming from the rear of the stable. The halo outlining her body gave her an angelic effect. He pulled her from the entrance back into the blackness and held her close. At first she trembled, but in the next breath she relaxed in his arms. He smelled the faint scent of flowers about her, and his knees weakened. A fierce protective nature seized him.

"I shouldn't be doing this," he said. "Later I'll apologize."

"No, don't. Here in your arms is where I want to be."

"This is where you belong." Perhaps the darkness gave him courage to speak his heart—or made him foolhardy. "I shouldn't be saying this either. I've come for you, Audra."

"What do you mean? Where are we going? Mexico? Canada?"

"Neither of those. I'm taking you to Jed and Naomi. It's not safe here. I've watched Chris and the sheriff follow you. I'm not having you in danger any longer," Caleb said.

She wrapped her arms around his chest. "I thought you wanted me in Earnest."

"I'm afraid he'll hurt you, blame it on me."

She sighed, and he sensed her rebellious streak taking over. "I'm not afraid. My job here at the livery affords me the chance to watch him and the sheriff. Christopher wouldn't dare hurt me and discredit his reputation."

"Evenin', Caleb," Dixon said. Caleb hadn't heard him approach. "In my opinion she's in more danger at the Masterses' place. Listen to me for a moment. He could ride in there and shoot the three of them and cover for it just like he's covered everything else. And you know who'd be held responsible."

Caleb had considered the same, but he could keep a better eye out for them at the ranch.

"If he shot you, don't you think he'd do the same to your friends?" Dixon asked.

"Caleb, please. He's right." Audra stepped back, and he grasped her hand. "I'm safer here. He's been avoiding me until tonight."

"Don't think either of them knows why I'm staying in Earnest," Dixon said. "I prefer not telling them for as long as possible. If he's as suspicious as he appeared tonight, he'll be after me soon. The diversion might cause him to do something stupid—and that's what I need."

"Could buy time," Caleb said. Every day that passed increased the chances of finding the money, but he still believed Audra was safer with the Masterses. "I'd hoped to find what we needed without letting him believe another shipment of money was on its way." He didn't want his brother killed, only stopped.

"You have too much on your mind," Dixon said. "Let's head out of here. Did you say your father was coming?"

Audra gasped. "Pastor Windsor is coming to Earnest?"

"I wrote him, asked him to help me with Chris," Caleb said.

"Do you think he will?" Audra asked.

"Possibly. The letter was a confession about what had been going on. Depends if he believed me or not."

Audra turned to him. "Oh, if he could convince—"

Caleb squeezed her hand. He heard voices, and at this late hour that could only mean trouble. In the time it took to breathe in and out, the voices mingled outside the livery.

"What do you think those two were up to?" Chris said.

"Meetin' up with your brother," Sheriff Reynolds said. "Dixon works for the governor, and he's taken up with Miss Lenders. I'm not stupid. They're working together."

"Dixon believes Caleb?" Chris said.

"I'm saying he's stuck his nose into our business. I'm going to talk to him tomorrow. Ask him if he's found Caleb, like I've known all along who he is."

"Doesn't matter 'cause they don't have any evidence," Chris said. "I'm going home. Had enough for one day."

"You frettin' about Les, too?"

"I'll take care of him. He's gotten greedy. You handle Dixon."

❧

Later Audra recalled every sight and sound of the evening. What started out as a hopeful few stolen moments with Caleb turned into a game of deception. No longer did she doubt that Christopher would hurt her. She believed he'd do anything to save himself—reminding her of Caleb's story of when the two boys played too close to the water's edge.

She prayed Pastor Windsor came to Earnest. This was hope, the possibility of Christopher confessing to what he'd done. But that meant weeks more when she inwardly begged for this to be over now.

Two weeks passed and then a third. Audra watched her once-wedding day come and go. She felt bad about missing church on Wednesday nights and Sundays, but she used those hours to read through the Old Testament. Her days at the livery left her exhausted, and Christopher stayed close to town. Perhaps the chance to catch him with the money had passed.

Not once did she see Caleb. She believed the threat of being caught kept him away. That was like him, staying clear to protect her and the Masterses. Many times she wondered how Dixon and the others planned to ensnare Christopher, and her patience wore thin.

The wife of the boardinghouse owner had started to say hello once in a while, but nothing else. Audra felt like a soiled dove, not good enough to hold a conversation with respectable folks. Dixon, her sole source of communication from Naomi, Jed, and Caleb, often left town early in the morning and didn't return until after she finished at the livery.

One warm afternoon, she recognized Jed's voice asking for her from the livery owner.

"Miss Audra, a couple of gentlemen here to see you." Annoyance rang through his voice.

She stuck her pitchfork into a wet, nasty pile of straw and hurried to the front. Jed caught her attention immediately, but she had to blink a few times in order to see the other man. Her pulse raced with the recognition.

"Audra," a booming voice said.

"Pastor Windsor." She longed to hug him as she used to in Nebraska, but the scent of horses and what she'd been cleaning clung to her.

"Where's my hug?" he said.

She shook her head. "I smell terrible. But it is so good to see you."

"I don't care a lick. You're like a daughter to me."

She wrapped her arms around his thin waist then stepped back. She smelled so bad she couldn't stand herself.

Not knowing who might be listening, she picked through her words. "What brings you to Earnest? Christopher and I did not marry."

"I got word of the news. Right now, I have a few things to clear up." His face dimmed. "Audra, I'm so sorry to have sent you out here to this unfortunate situation." The lines in his face deepened.

"None of this is your fault. I'm sure you're the man to help right things. I feel better knowing you are here."

"Jed is allowing me to stay with him and his wife for a few days. I have to find out the truth."

"I had to learn the hard way," she said.

His face clouded even more than before. It seemed as though he might weep. " 'Tis a sad day when a father is deceived. For many years I thought I understood my sons. Now it appears I've been wrong."

"Do my parents know you are here?"

"I left word with an elder to ride out to their place. I headed here as soon as I received the letter."

"Miss Audra," the livery owner said. "You have work to do."

She glanced at Jed and gave him a big smile. "The situation will be remedied soon. You'll see."

"We're paying a visit at the parsonage before heading to the ranch," Jed said. "We could use a little prayer."

Audra wished them well and rushed back to her task of cleaning out stalls. She shivered, and her stomach churned with what Pastor Windsor needed to do. What if Christopher convinced him that Caleb was the outlaw? But the pastor had come all this way, and for that she was happy and relieved.

Caleb watched the sun crest the horizon. He'd expected his father and Jed over an hour ago. Doubts crept over him. If only he could have heard the conversation going on between Chris and his father. At the very least, he'd liked to have defended himself. At least Jed was there. The thought of his father making the journey to Earnest amazed him. When Jed said he'd received a wire from Nebraska confirming his father's journey to Colorado, Caleb had difficulty believing it. They hadn't really talked in years since he was always in trouble, or so it appeared.

In his solitary position overlooking the Masterses' ranch, Caleb saw smoke rise from the chimney and visualized Naomi cooking supper. He smiled, thinking how she'd been as close to a mother as he'd ever find. And Jed, well, as he'd thought before, the man knew him better than his own father. Caleb wished it all could change among the Windsor men, but the bad communication had been his fault. He understood his failings now, whereas before he believed he'd acted out of love.

As the last bit of sunlight slipped behind the mountains, Caleb's gaze rested on the road leading from Earnest. Jed drove the wagon with Father seated alongside him. He headed toward them. Caleb's heart pounded. He felt like a kid again, afraid of what his father would say about his latest bout of mischief.

"Evenin', Father, Jed." Caleb's horse moved into their path.

Jed stopped the wagon, but Caleb barely noticed. His gaze was fixed on his father, although he couldn't see his face clearly in the near darkness.

"Caleb, it's been a long time." The deep voice resounded around him. How many times had that voice scared him to death? The man had used a switch on Caleb more than a few times—after he'd confessed to something Chris had done.

"Yes, sir. Thank you. I appreciate your coming."

"Son, we have a lot of catching up to do."

Caleb swallowed a lump in his throat. He fought to gain his composure. "I'm sorry about the circumstances bringing you here."

"Caleb, you never asked me for a thing in your life. I'd have traveled across both oceans, if you'd requested it." His voice broke, leaving Caleb longing to wrap his arms around his father's neck. But he couldn't move a muscle to dismount. He was supposed to be a man, not a kid running to Papa for help. "Are you coming with Jed and me?" his father said.

"Not till later when the ranch hands have turned in."

"I see. I'll be spending a few days with these kind folk."

"Good. I'd like to show you what I can of my own ranch."

"I'd like that. I'd like that very much."

Chapter 19

Once Caleb noted that Les had not come from the bunkhouse for the past several minutes, he made his way to the Masterses' door. He'd spent the past two hours mulling over what to say to his father in such a way that Chris appeared less a criminal. Of course, he'd spent most of his life making his brother look good.

Jed must have heard his boots on the front porch for he opened the door and gestured him inside. As usual Naomi had prepared a feast with plenty left over for him.

"Glad to hear you take good care of my boy," his father said to Naomi. "My cooking liked to starve my boys to death. And they had little affection from women."

Caleb met his gaze—no malice, no accusations. In the past, Father spoke the words while he listened. How did a grown man discuss his brother's rebellious behavior with their father?

"I saw Christopher today," his father said. "Naomi, may I trouble you for another cup of your fine coffee?"

She beamed. "Of course. How about a sugar cookie to go with it?"

"Those are my favorite," he said. "What about you, son?"

"Uh, no, thanks." The time to visit grew near. He shook in his boots.

Naomi set the coffee and cookie before Caleb's father. "Jed and I are heading to bed. Pastor, we'll see you in the morning. Caleb, be safe." She kissed his cheek.

Jed scooted his chair back from the braid rug and grabbed a cookie and his mug of coffee. "Caleb, this is what you've prayed for. Let God handle the reins."

Caleb nodded and bid them good night. Once the couple closed their bedroom door, he fought for the appropriate words. God help him. "I don't know how to begin."

"We let too many silent years pass between us."

"I agree." Caleb's coffee tasted bitter. "But it was my fault."

"No, son. I was too busy doing God's work to do anything about the deceit in my own family."

Caleb blinked. "I don't understand."

"I knew you couldn't have done all the things you admitted to, but I left the matter alone. It was easier for me to discipline you than find out why you took the blame. I owe you an apology. I've sought God's forgiveness. Will you forgive me?"

Startled, Caleb allowed his father's words to wash over him. "Yes, sir. I never had any idea that you knew I wasn't at fault."

"I wondered why, but I neglected to seek out the answers. On the way out here, I had plenty of time to reflect on the years you and Christopher were boys. I realized Christopher never had anything good to say about you, and you never had anything bad to say about him. I despise myself for not seeing through what was going on."

Caleb had always sensed the deep responsibility his father possessed in raising his sons and serving God's people. "You had so much work—"

His father waved his hand. "That's not an excuse." He took a deep breath, and for a moment Caleb feared the man would weep. "Would you like to hear about my meeting with Christopher?"

"Very much."

"He was surprised and more than a little upset with me for not writing him about my arrival. He showed me his church and invited me and Jed inside the parsonage. Jed elected to take a walk, leaving us alone. First I asked him about Audra, and he said she'd not proven to be a fit choice for a wife."

Anger simmered in Caleb. "How did you respond?"

"I told him Audra Lenders was a fine young woman, and I didn't appreciate him slandering her fine reputation. Then I asked him about you. He'd written some time ago about your unlawful activities and how you'd damaged his ministry. He said he hated to break the news to me, but you were wanted for murder and robbery. He said you had corrupted Audra and led her astray. He also told me to beware of the Masterses. The law suspected them of hiding you."

Caleb listened to every word. "I swear to you, Father, I have never robbed anyone and never killed a man. Pull out your Bible, and I will swear on the Word of God. I know I shouldn't have said that. My word should be enough." He took a deep breath. "My guilt is covering up for Chris, because now one of us will end up behind bars."

"I don't want to believe either of my sons is capable of murder, but if one is to be punished, I pray it is the guilty one. I told him about your letter and said I was here to learn the truth."

Caleb startled. "You told him about the letter?"

His father nodded. "He called you a liar. I asked him if his words were those of a man of God. He told me to seek out the truth."

"I'd do anything to spare you this heartache," Caleb said. "I'm not expecting you to take sides or choose who is telling the truth tonight. But I am asking you to search for God's wisdom in this, and I promise your decision will never sway the love I have for you."

His father's eyes moistened. "What more could I ask? For now—"

The sound of horses alerted Caleb. He rose to the window and pulled aside the curtain just far enough to view the commotion. "It's Chris and the sheriff."

"They're after you?"

"Yeah, and I need to get out of here."

Jed opened the bedroom door. He was still fully dressed as though he suspected what might happen. "This way, Caleb."

Without hesitation or a glance his father's way, Caleb stepped into the bedroom. Naomi stood with their window open. How miserable for his father to see him running from his own brother like an outlaw.

He climbed through an open window into the warm night air. He heard the sheriff and Chris on the front porch right around the corner from him.

"Evenin', Jed," Sheriff Reynolds said. "We got wind that Caleb was in these parts. Thought we'd stop in and make sure you folks were all right. The pastor here is concerned about his father."

"Thanks, Sheriff. Come on in and sit a spell," Jed said. "We're fine, just talking."

"Go ahead Christopher," the sheriff said. "I'll take a look out here and check with the hands to see if they've seen anything suspicious."

Caleb lit out into the night. If not for his father and Audra, he'd strongly consider riding toward Mexico.

"Caleb."

He whirled around toward the familiar voice near the shed. "Dixon?"

"Yeah. Been watching the house and couldn't get to you fast enough."

Caleb hurried to him. "Those two don't trust anyone, do they?"

Dixon chuckled. "Would you with thousands of dollars at stake?"

"That much?"

"You bet," Dixon said. "If you figure the cattle and horses stolen, gold watches and jewelry and money, it could be even more."

The two ducked behind trees and sheds until they were clear of the house. Dixon had left his horse tied next to Caleb's.

"When can we get the word out about a money shipment to Denver?" Caleb asked. "I've lost my patience with Chris."

"Tomorrow I'll ride to Denver and set it up with the governor. Then I'll make sure the sheriff finds out. Let's hope they take the bait."

"Pray." Caleb said. "I'm afraid this will be my last chance to prove my innocence."

❧

Audra questioned the fact Dixon left Earnest the day after Pastor Windsor arrived. It had been over three days, and still he hadn't returned. She'd grown to depend on him to keep her informed of what happened with Caleb. She remembered when she gave herself four weeks to find the evidence against Christopher. What a foolish idea, thinking a time restraint would aid her. Only God understood her need to help clear Caleb's name.

Like a crack of thunder in the middle of the night, realization took form and seized her senses. All this time, she'd asked God to go with her instead of depending on Him to lead the way. Oh, she'd gone through the ritual of pleading for guidance and deliverance, but when things failed to work out like she wanted, she took it upon herself to take over.

God, I'm so sorry. Everything with Caleb is frightening, and I don't know what to do. Now I see I've been attempting to lead instead of follow You. I thought if I gave myself a limited amount of time to get information from Christopher, You would oblige me. How horribly wrong I've been. From this moment on, I will seek You with my whole heart. I'm trusting You to save Caleb from those who wish to do him harm. I pray Christopher repents of his sins as well as the others who ride with him. Forgive me, God.

She stuck the pitchfork into fresh hay. *And, God, help Caleb unite with his father.*

"Audra," the livery owner said. "Pastor Windsor and Sheriff Reynolds need their horses."

Follow them, a voice said. *Leave the livery and go. You don't need this job.*

⤫

Caleb gestured to the west of where he and his father rode. Lush, variegated green circled his ranch on three sides with a valley of thick pastures for his cattle and horses.

"Beautiful land, son. No wonder you're proud of it."

"Yes, sir. We've added plenty of calves and foals this spring."

"How long since you've been able to live there?" His father's voice rang with sadness.

"About a year. My foreman's a good man. I moved him and his family into my house until this is over."

"What are your plans?"

Caleb studied him. It seemed as though his father believed him, but he didn't want to ask. The past few days with Father had been memorable, no matter what happened. "Not sure. I have my dreams like most men."

"Do they include Audra Lenders?"

Dare he confess his love for her? "I think that dream would come as close to heaven as I could get."

"I want your dreams to be your future." His father sighed. "Christopher has not asked me to stay with him or inquired as to how long I plan to stay."

Caleb thought better of replying. He could see the grief in his father's eyes.

"Is that because he plans to leave the country?" his father continued. When Caleb still didn't respond he stared into the valley. "This grieves us both, and I am helpless to convince him otherwise. How sad it is to know your own son has deceived those he claims to shepherd."

"God will see us through this," Caleb said.

Silence, save for the calls of a crow, surrounded them. Welcoming a diversion, Caleb pointed to a couple of frisky colts racing like the wind. They both laughed.

"What are Dixon's plans?"

"Father, it will grieve you."

His father shook his head. "I'm a grown man. How does Audra feel when you refuse to tell her things?"

Caleb lifted his hat. "I think you know the answer." He chuckled in remembering her independent nature. "She is a stubborn one, but I like her spunk—as long as she doesn't get hurt."

"Is she in the safest place?"

"Since I've done everything but carry her to the stage, I guess so. I used to think living with Jed and Naomi was the best, but Dixon feared Chris might—"

"No need to finish."

"Thanks. I do love her. God has kept me steady company for a long time, and He's given me a glimpse of a woman's love."

"After your mother, I didn't want any other woman."

Caleb understood. "Audra reminds you of her, doesn't she?"

"Not in looks, but in spirit." His father laughed. "You are in for an exciting life."

"I hope so."

"Now tell me what Dixon has planned," his father said.

Caleb hesitated then told him every word. If he couldn't trust his father, who could he trust? "The stage is scheduled to arrive tomorrow late morning."

"Are you seeing Audra tonight?"

"No, I can't. If things go bad, well, it's better this way."

Audra stretched her back and shoulder muscles. She ached all over. Not sleeping had a lot to do with it. Her body craved rest, but when she lay down, her mind spun with thoughts of Caleb. She had no idea what he and Dixon planned or how Pastor Windsor, Jed, and Naomi fared during this.

Trust God. The thought stayed foremost in her mind. She remembered the afternoon she felt the urge to leave the livery and trail after Christopher and the sheriff. She realized the insistence did not come from God, and she willed the voice away. Since then, she continued to pray, although it proved to be the hardest thing she'd ever done.

She walked from the livery, a bit later than usual and headed to the boardinghouse. The owner complained about her ordering a bath every evening, but just because she worked cleaning out horse stables didn't mean she had to smell like one. Her stomach growled. Naomi's cooking sure sounded better than the boardinghouse's.

After her bath, she followed her nose to the dining room. This was chicken soup and corn bread night. Right now it didn't matter what she ate, anything to fill her stomach.

"Miss Lenders."

Audra turned to face Sheriff Reynolds. "Good evening, sir."

"I hate to tell you this, but there's been some trouble."

Her stomach twisted. "What happened?"

"Shooting at the Masterses' place, Miss Lenders." He removed his hat. "I'm real sorry."

"Who's been hurt?" Her voice quivered. Her hands trembled.

"Jed didn't make it." He took a deep breath. "Caleb is hurt bad. He's asking for you."

Chapter 20

S hall we take the wagon or ride to the Masterses' ranch?" Sheriff Reynolds said to Audra.

"The horses are faster." She bit back a sob. All along she understood one of the Windsor twins would be hurt, but she wasn't ready to face it. "Is Christopher hurt?"

"He's tending to his brother. Blood is thicker than the outlaw life."

Oh, God, You can right this. You can comfort Naomi. You can heal Caleb's body. "What about the doctor?"

"He's not home, out on a call."

Once the horses were saddled, she spurred hers toward the Masterses' ranch.

"Slow down, Miss Lenders," the sheriff said.

She matched her mare's pace to his. Confusion etched her mind. They were on a dark road far from town and far from Jed and Naomi's. Another rider joined them, but in the blackness she couldn't tell who he was.

"What is going on?" she asked.

"A trade."

Audra froze at the sound of the voice. "Christopher," she whispered. "I thought you were with Caleb."

He laughed. "You mean my poor wounded brother? I might miss my target once, but not twice. I have no idea where he is. Probably running for the hills."

"And Jed?"

"Most likely sleeping or eating." Christopher laughed.

"You tricked me." Her gaze flew to the sheriff. "You lied to me."

"Afraid so," the sheriff said.

"Why? What do you want me for?"

Christopher laughed again. "You and I, sweet lady, are heading to Mexico."

Was he crazy? "I will not."

"You have no choice. Once we're safe inside the border, you can do whatever you want," Christopher said. "This is your fault. I'd have treated you fine in Mexico, if you hadn't betrayed me with Caleb."

Her heart pounded. "You won't get away with this. Too many people are wise to your treachery."

"Not enough people who amount to anything." Christopher's low, sneering voice shook her resolve.

"A stage is headed this way tomorrow with a sizeable amount of money," the sheriff said. "We're taking it off the driver's hands, and you are our protection. Nobody is going to bother us as long as we have you hostage."

Audra gasped.

"See, we got wind of what Dixon and Caleb planned. Doesn't do them a bit of good to try to catch us robbing the stage when we have you," Christopher said.

"Caleb will come after me." Audra attempted to sound strong.

"Watch us," Christopher said and snatched up her reins. "Tonight you're staying with me, and tomorrow you're going to ride with us."

They broke from the road, and the horses picked their way over a rough path. They made so many twists and turns that she soon became lost. Her comfort rested in God. He knew exactly where she rode with the sheriff and Christopher.

How could Caleb find the evidence they needed when Christopher held her hostage? The situation looked incredibly desperate. Without God's intervention, Christopher once again triumphed.

"Where's the money?" the sheriff said to Christopher.

"In a safe place."

"You don't have it with you?"

"I have everything worked out," Christopher spat at the sheriff like a mad cat.

The sheriff cursed. "You left it all at the parsonage?"

"Think about it. A guilty pastor would not show his face in town. An innocent man returns to his work. I'll get it after we hold up the stage."

"Reckon you make sense," Sheriff Reynolds said. "I'll keep an eye on Miss Audra while you get back to town. Are you sure no one knows about the cave? I don't want Dixon finding me there with her."

"You hadn't been there before, and you've lived here for twenty years."

She clamped her teeth into her lower lip to keep from crying out. Christopher had devised a most clever plan. He admitted storing the stolen money in the parsonage. She could have found it, if not for her stupidity. She could have helped Caleb clear his name. The moment Audra criticized her inability to help the man she loved, she remembered her trust in God. That's all she had left.

The next morning, Jed, Dixon, Caleb, and his father watched the approaching stage far enough from the road so as not to alert Christopher and his men. Dixon used binoculars and Caleb stared in the stage's direction. So much rode on what happened today: his innocence, Chris's capture, the heartache of their father, and Audra. If he dwelt on the gravity of it all for very long, he'd not be able to think past the next minute.

"That's not good." Dixon lowered the binoculars then brought them to his eyes again.

"What's going on?" Caleb asked. Had the stage already been stopped? Two of the governor's men rode inside with an empty strongbox. They were armed, but Chris had more men.

Dixon handed him the binoculars. "Take a look for yourself on that far ridge while I figure out what to do." He gestured north of them.

Caleb peered through the lenses. Chris, Sheriff Reynolds, Les, and two other men sat atop their horses. A woman was with them. Gagged. Fury spiked through Caleb. "They have Audra!"

"Christopher believes he's holding an ace," Dixon said.

"What would you call it?" Caleb roared.

"A challenge."

A rustle in the trees behind them seized their attention. Jim Hawk rode into view. "Gentlemen, you have a problem."

"Let her go," Caleb said. "She has nothing to do with this."

Hawk ignored him and turned to Dixon. "We'll let her go once we get to Mexico. In the meantime, you stay clear of our plans."

"And if we refuse?" Dixon said.

"Caleb loses his lady." Hawk turned his horse toward the brush and trees. "Consider yourself warned. We've watched every move you've made," he said, just before he disappeared.

"Men, we prayed earlier for God to go before us," his father said. "But I implore you to pause with me and pray for Audra's safety and for victory." Without waiting for a response, his low voice echoed around them. "Oh great and mighty God, protect Audra from those who seek to do her harm. Turn my son's heart to You. Let the evil in my household end today, amen."

"The men inside the stage will be killed if we turn our backs on them," Dixon said. "My guess is only one man will stay behind with Audra."

"I'm going after her," Caleb said. "I can get her out of there before the stage comes by."

Jed shielded his eyes and pointed to the road. "The stage is coming now. You don't have enough time."

"Then stop this whole thing." Caleb sensed the desperation roiling through him.

"Impossible," Dixon said.

"You are sending an innocent woman to her death," Caleb said. "At least your men have guns. Dixon, I've got to go after her." He glanced at his father. "I want my name cleared, but not at the expense of Audra. You will see today what I've claimed. Maybe you can talk some sense into Christopher."

Dixon cleared his throat. "Caleb, it doesn't look good for you to disappear just before the stage is robbed."

"It doesn't matter." Caleb dug his heels into the mare's sides and hurried to the ridge. All he could think about was Audra and setting her free from Chris's men. As much as he hated to believe his brother might harm her, he understood Chris would do whatever it took to protect himself.

For the many months Caleb had been on the run, he'd learned the back trails. His horse stepped over familiar rock and climbed up a narrow path to the ridge. He believed Chris put his faith in his plan, not in the God of the innocent.

Today, there will be one more crime blamed on me. Lord, I don't care if I meet You this very hour, but please let me be there in time for Audra.

Hawk's horse stood beside Audra's mare, close enough that a man could not pass between. The others were gone, meaning he simply had Hawk to deal with. A sense of fear danced up and down his spine, as if he were walking into a trap. Caleb refused to consider the eerie sensation. He had a mission.

Peering in every direction, Caleb saw no one. He rode into the clearing behind Hawk and Audra with his rifle in hand. "Hawk, toss your gun onto the ground," Caleb said.

"You don't listen. I told you what would happen if you tried to interfere with our business."

"Looks to me like you and I are the only ones here," Caleb said, reining in his horse. "Drop the gun."

He heard the click of a revolver. "You never were very smart," Chris said. "I set a trap, and you walked right in."

Audra turned and for a moment Caleb caught her gaze. The end had surely come.

<hr />

Audra bit back the stinging tears.

"You never had a lick of sense," Christopher said. "Only a fool cares for people the way you do."

"Then I guess I'm a fool. But I'd rather die a good man than live like an animal."

"Shall I tell you how this is going to happen?" Christopher said. "Not that you have a choice in the matter."

"Why not, since I'm the fool?"

"First of all, we're changing clothes. Then I'm putting a bullet right through your heart. Once we're finished with the stage, I'm heading back to Earnest. Dixon will find you with a bullet and think it's me. After all, you left them to come after Audra. Proves you were the one behind this all along. I'll gather up a few things I need then I'm heading to Mexico."

"What about Audra?"

"She's going with me."

Audra wished she could scream. The sound rose and fell in her throat.

"How low have you gone to murder for money?" Caleb said.

"When I'm living high, I might take the time to contemplate your question."

Pastor Windsor joined them in the clearing. "Christopher, stop this here and now."

Chris paused then stiffened. "I. . .I'm—heading south. You can come along if you like."

"Why would I want to be a part of this? I heard what you plan to do. You'll have to kill your brother *and* your father to get away with this."

Christopher's face clouded. For an instant, remorse etched his features. He shrugged. "Makes no difference to me."

"Yes, it does. You've lived this life long enough to know it leads nowhere. How are you going to sleep? Who will ever trust you? End this today."

"Can't do that." Christopher swung his revolver in Caleb's direction. "Take the shirt off."

Gunfire sounded in the distance, and Audra knew the other men had stopped the stage. Caleb dismounted and unbuttoned his blue chambray shirt. *Help them, God. Turn Christopher's heart.* He tossed it onto the ground. *Dear Jesus, please do something.*

"Why don't we fight it out right here," Caleb said. "Climb down off that horse, coward."

Christopher's face reddened. He threw a bundle of clothes at Caleb's feet. "I don't have time for that. Hawk, wait for me in the trees."

Before Hawk could oblige, Audra kicked her mare, and the horse jumped. A shot whizzed through the air just above Hawk's head. His horse reared, giving Pastor Windsor time to knock Christopher's rifle from his hand. Caleb pulled Hawk from his horse, reached for a rope tied around his saddle, and wrapped it around the big man's hands.

"This is the end of the line." Caleb watched while Pastor Windsor yanked Christopher from his stallion.

Caleb helped Audra from her mare and untied the gag around her mouth. Tears spilled over her cheeks, tears of joy and tears of anguish over the Windsor men.

"It's all over." Caleb pulled her close. "Don't cry."

She snuggled against him and allowed his arms to engulf her. His hands smoothed her hair, causing her to feel like a beloved child.

"Are you hurt?"

She shook her head. "Just relieved." Her gaze turned to Pastor Windsor. Shock registered across his ashen face at how evil Christopher had become.

"Where's the money?" Pastor Windsor said to Christopher. "It will go easier on you if you tell me." He picked up the rifle.

How sad for the pastor to hold his own son at gunpoint.

"If I can't have it, then no one else will either." Christopher sneered.

"For once do something that's good, and tell me where you hid the money." Chris's face tightened. He stared at his father.

"Son, whatever happens, I'm here for you. So is Caleb."

Still not a muscle moved in his face.

"Please," Audra said. "Your father and brother will not desert you. We're all family."

Christopher nodded, and his gaze lingered on her. He did have feelings for her. His glance moved to his father again. "I won't hang if I tell you about the money?"

Pastor Windsor pressed his lips together. "I don't know what will happen in a court of law. Your future in this world is up to a judge and jury. My guess is you'll be in prison for a long time."

"Will you visit me?"

Christopher sounded like a small boy—a frightened little child.

"Yes, son."

Christopher took a deep breath. "It's in the small trapdoor beneath the pulpit."

"Good, now we're going to walk down this ridge and meet Mr. Dixon and his men. Caleb, I have these two where I want them. You go ahead and get Miss Audra back to the Masterses' ranch."

Audra hadn't realized how tightly she'd been clinging to Caleb. He kissed the top of her head. "Come on, sweetheart," he whispered. "Let's go see Naomi. She's probably scared out of her wits."

She nodded. A little while later, the ranch house and buildings came into view.

"Did you mean what you said to Chris?" he said.

Confused, her mind failed to recall what she'd said. Her body still shook. "I don't remember."

"You said that we're all family."

"And we are." Audra could not deny Christopher as a part of her and Caleb's life any more than she could ignore one of her brothers and sisters.

"So you'll marry me?"

"Today if you want."

Caleb grinned and reached across his horse to take her hand. "The road ahead will be rough with Chris's trial and helping my father endure it all, but I do love you, Audra. I will love and protect you for as long as I live."

"And I will love you forever."

He smiled and nodded. "When we get to the ranch, I'm going to kiss you."

"You mean you're not asking permission?" Audra hid her delight.

"I don't want to give you a chance to say no."

"Mr. Windsor, if I'm going to be Mrs. Windsor, then there needs to be a lot of kisses."

Caleb squeezed her hand lightly and winked. A nudging in her spirit told her a new adventure was about to begin—the biggest adventure of all.

Silence in the Sage

by Colleen L. Reece

Chapter 1

With a mighty pull on the reins and an oath, the burly stagecoach driver slowed his team to a trot, finally halting them square in the middle of the dusty West Texas road.

"What's wrong, Pete?" Gideon Carroll Scott roused from his passenger view of the familiar landscape that hadn't changed in the five years he'd been away.

"C'mon, Gideon, you haven't been gone so long you've forgotten what tricks this cursed country can play on a man, now have you?" Pete cocked his grizzled head to one side. "Hear that?"

Gideon strained his ears but heard nothing. A silence unusual to the stage route remained unbroken by even a bird's cry or rustle of a bunchgrass. Even the normally swaying bluebonnets stood still.

For a heartbeat, Gideon again became the seventeen-year-old about to leave for study in New Orleans, who had experienced this peculiar silence on a final ride with his brother. Cyrus, two years older, had yelled, "Take cover! Silence in the sage like this means a terrible storm is coming." He spurred his horse, and Gideon tore after him, but even the fastest horse couldn't outrun the winds that whipped around the Circle S ranch miles out of *El Paso del Norte*, the Pass of the North.

Gideon exulted in the rising wind and the flying sand, yet common sense and training brought fear as well. Too many men had lost their lives because they couldn't beat the elements.

Now the same stillness pervaded. The scent of gray-green sage intensified with the first stirrings of the wind. Lizards had long since fled to shelter. While the world seemed to wait, Gideon's heart pounded.

"We'll try for the rocks," Pete shouted over the dull roar in the distance. "Hang on." He whipped up the horses. "Giddap, you long-legged, no-good beasts!"

Gideon hastily pulled his head back inside the stagecoach. For a long way, he had ridden on top with Pete, but the rare privacy afforded by being the only coach passenger had been too enticing. He smoothed light brown hair, soon to be sun-streaked from riding and ranch chores, and took a deep breath. The reflection of excitement glowed in his Texas blue-sky eyes, and his lean body swayed with the rocking coach. Would they make the huge pile of windswept rocks before the storm hit? he wondered anxiously.

The clear summer sky darkened. Tiny grains of flying sand heralded gusts of sand-laden wind that flattened the sage and raged behind the lumbering coach. Gideon could barely see Pete's hunched shoulders and pulled-down hat, and the driver's yells blended with the growing wind.

"Made it, by the powers!" Pete drove the team behind the frail shelter provided by the rock pile. The next second, he leaped to the ground, grabbed blankets, and adroitly fastened them over the horses' heads to protect them from the blowing sand. Sweating and trembling, the steeds finally stilled beneath his strong and familiar hands.

With a soft scarf over his mouth and nose, Gideon had burrowed back against the innermost rock by the time Pete staggered toward him. "Here," he called and reached out to guide Pete in the ever-increasing storm.

"Worst thing about these storms is they come without warnin'," Pete complained as he slid his scarf over his eyes. He proceeded to lie flat on his stomach and buried his face in his crossed arms. Gideon followed suit. Flying sand still stung the inch of exposed neck between his shirt collar and low-drawn hat. Good thing he'd firmly resisted dressing in his new clerical suit for his return to San Scipio, the closest town to the Circle S. Uncomfortable but inwardly filled with the same defiant attitude toward the weather he'd had as a boy, Gideon longed to laugh at the storm and howl with the wind. Protected somewhat by the rocks, he and Pete would sensibly wait out the storm and be on their way.

"If only my New Orleans friends could see me now," he muttered. "They'd remind me that West Texas is no place for a brand-new minister!"

"Say somethin'?" Pete grunted.

"Not important." Gideon wouldn't have been able to explain if he'd wanted to. Pete's prejudices against anything except what he called a cursed land (but "wouldn't leave for a million pesos") were legendary.

Gideon sighed. All his persuading hadn't changed his friends' ideas—especially Emily Ann's—that he lived in a barren wasteland. Soft, small, and pretty, Emily Ann had tried to dissuade the young seminary student from his vow to serve in a land that needed to know God as more than a curse. Without conceit, he accepted the fact he could have married Emily Ann if he'd consented to remain in New Orleans.

Give up the rugged Guadalupe Mountains, the Pecos and Rio Grande Rivers, the deep draws that hid stray and stolen cattle, even the blazing summers and frigid winters? Life with Emily Ann and her kind offered little in comparison with home. The Circle S sprawled across a thousand acres that included everything from mountains and canyons to level grazing land.

In vain, Gideon tried to picture Emily Ann's reaction to the huge adobe home built around a courtyard in typical Mexican style. Thick walls kept out both heat and cold but kept in comfort and warmth. Bright blankets and dark polished wood, carefully tended flowers, and colorful desert paintings contrasted sharply with the restored homes in New Orleans that had escaped the devastation of the War Between the States. Gideon sometimes wondered if Emily Ann ever thought of the hardship the South had experienced. Her family had spirited her away at the first sign of trouble, and although she plaintively complained of "those cold and uncarin' Yankees," he knew she had reveled in the attention received while staying in the North. Once, she stroked the rich damask of the portieres and said, "To think that *Yankees* came down here and tried to tell us how to live!" Her silvery laughter grated on Gideon's nerves, and he bit his lip to keep from reminding her that few Southerners had been able to rebuild in the way of her wealthy family.

Gideon shook his sand-laden shoulders. San Scipio and the Circle S would seem unbearably crude to a young woman like Emily Ann. He buried his face deeper in his arms, wishing the storm would stop its roaring and go on its way. Yet wasn't this time of waiting exactly what he had felt he needed before reaching home? More than miles lay between the ranch and Louisiana. With each *clip-clop* of the horses' steady gait, Gideon became less the student and more the rangeman he had once been. At times he had to reach into his satchel and feel the reassuring crackle of his rolled diploma, the only tangible evidence that proclaimed he had completed his ministerial studies.

Now his fingers involuntarily crept to his vest pocket. Even his father would find no fault with the record his younger son had made. A clipping from a New Orleans newspaper already had creases from being unfolded and refolded. The late nights and devotion to study that enraged Emily Ann had put Gideon at the top of his class. Surely Elijah Scott would take his love-blind gaze from Cyrus at least long enough to acknowledge his achievement.

Don't count on it, his inner voice counseled. *Lige Scott is a great rancher, a staunch follower of the Almighty—according to what he thinks—but this love for the firstborn son is only rivaled by that of Old Testament patriarchs. In his opinion, Cyrus can do no wrong.*

Once when Gideon was a child, his mother, Naomi, tried to explain his father's feelings. "We were married for so long before we had children, Lige wondered if God were punishing him for something—don't ask me what." Her blue eyes so like Gideon's turned dreamy. "It is hard to be such a strong and powerful man like your father and yet not be able to control his own son."

"I'm his son, too," Gideon had piped in his treble voice.

"I know. So does he, when he stops to remember. We must accept him the way he is, Gideon." Naomi turned and gazed out the window. "It took strength to leave everything we knew and come to Texas after it became a state in 1845. The way was hard. Many in our party didn't make it. Every death diminished Lige, for his enthusiasm had been the driving force that encouraged friends to make the journey with us. Once we got here, he worked hard, harder than any one man should work. He stood by my bedside when Cyrus was born and watched us both nearly die. Is it any wonder he cannot see faults in the son who finally came from God?"

"But, Mother, you went through all that, too," the youthful Gideon protested. "The long trail, the hard work."

"It is different for a woman," Naomi gently said. A light her son would never forget shone in her eyes. "Women are helpmeets, companions, and strengtheners to their men. I pray that one day God will send to you a strong, true wife."

"She must be like you," Gideon sturdily maintained.

His mother ruffled the sun-streaked hair and laughed. "We hope she is much better," she teased. "Now, get about your studies. Even though he says little and expects much, your father is proud of the way you grasp learning. Besides, it will be many years before you need think of taking a wife!"

Gideon coughed against the closeness of the scarf across his face, then chuckled to himself. He could imagine the look on his mother's face if Emily Ann had been willing to visit Texas. The chuckle faded. Perhaps the response from the child that his future wife must be like Naomi had secretly built up resistance to Emily Ann.

Would the storm never end? Who could tell whether minutes had turned to hours in this poorly sheltered spot? Gideon forced himself to look again to the past to avoid the miserable present.

Born in El Paso in May 1852, Gideon was just nine years old when Texas seceded from the Union and joined the Confederate States of America in 1861. Yet those days remained clear in his mind. He had asked Cyrus, "How can part of a country just cut itself off? Isn't that like my fingers saying they won't be part of my body?"

Eleven-year-old Cyrus had ignored the question. "Father doesn't want to talk about it. He says a lot of trouble can come from what's happening." For once the careless, daring boy was cowed. "I heard him talking with Mother. He says there is going to be war."

"You mean people killing each other, like in our books?" Gideon jerked up straight. "But we're going to feel the same way."

The war years hadn't changed life drastically on the Circle S. Season followed season. Stock had to be rounded up and driven to market. Chores kept needing to be done. Yet long after the fighting ended and Congress readmitted Texas to the Union in 1870, two years after the elder Scott's native Louisiana again became part of the Union, Gideon remembered the lines that etched themselves in his father's face and aged him.

During those years, Cyrus and Gideon entered early manhood. Cyrus laughed at the idea of wanting to learn more than he already knew from books. He rode like a burr in the saddle; roped, hunted, and tracked like an Indian; gambled and drank; and yet managed to keep his father unaware of his grosser habits. Gideon sometimes wondered how Lige could fail to see the marks of debauchery when Cyrus returned from a spree with a story of being holed up through a storm or off herding cattle. Bitterly, the younger son reminded himself again and again of his father's well-known blind spot. Years of standing in Cyrus's shadow had produced a certain callousness, but his tender heart still longed for a father's approval.

Gideon's fifteenth birthday seemed a welcome harbinger, as shortly afterward a hardened-to-the-saddle traveling minister arrived in San Scipio. Never had the inhabitants of the little western town heard the Word of God preached with such power and passion. The few services made an indelible mark on a boy who had known about God since the cradle. At fifteen, Gideon came to know God and His plan of salvation through His only Son, Jesus, as the most challenging, exciting story life offers. He said nothing to his family, but the next weeks and months of riding gave him opportunity to let the knowledge of God's goodness sink deep into his soul. On his sixteenth birthday, he dug fingernails into his callused palms, stood square in his worn boots, and told his parents, "I want to be a minister."

The tornado he expected failed to come. To Gideon's amazement, the nearest to an expression of approval Lige had ever given his son came to the seamed face. "Do you feel the Almighty is behind this, or are you just looking for a way to get off the Circle S?" Lige asked quickly but thoughtfully. A flush of pleasure and determination arose in Gideon's anxious heart.

He straightened to his full five-foot, ten-inch height, his keen blue glance never wavering. "I have to tell others what God did for all of us."

"Then go to it, son." Lige's mighty hand crushed his son's in a grip that would have broken the bones of a lesser young man. "I need your help for a time, but I give my word. On your seventeenth birthday, if you still feel this is what God wants of you, we'll send you to New Orleans. There are still some distant relatives there, a few of whom are rebuilding. You'll be welcome." A wry smile crossed his face. "More than welcome. You'll naturally pay your way, and the money will help them."

True to his word, Gideon embarked on his new life the day he turned seventeen. To his amazement, Cyrus traveled with him. Only the night before, he confessed that he hankered to see New Orleans for himself and aimed to find a pretty little filly to bring home, if there was one who had the nerve to tackle Texas and take him on.

After some protest, Lige rolled his big eyes and agreed to the change in plans. "I reckon we can get along without you the rest of this spring and through the summer," he admitted. "Mind you, be back by fall roundup, though." His crisp order couldn't hide the pride he carried for his older son, who stood an inch taller and outweighed the stripling Gideon by fifteen pounds.

While Gideon settled into the studies that would give him the background Lige insisted he have "to be not just a parson, but a *good* one," Cyrus hit New Orleans like a cannonball. In spite of lodging with the same relatives, the brothers seldom saw each other. Spring bloomed into summer, and Cyrus played at being New Orleans's most eligible bachelor. Gideon dove into his books like a man starving for knowledge. The rare occasions when their paths crossed offered little opportunity to share more than greetings.

Suddenly Cyrus grew restless. "Can't stand this heat," he told his brother and mopped his brow. "At least in Texas when it's hot, you aren't so dripping wet all the time. Besides, I'm sick of the scent of oleander." He grinned his devil-may-care grin and added, "I'll take trail dust and the smell of sage anytime."

Instead of staying until fall, Cyrus awakened Gideon one sweltering mid-August night. Eyes red and breath foul with the fumes of brandy, he muttered, "Going home. Nothing worth staying for here," and then he lurched out. By the time Gideon came fully awake to dress and reach his brother's room, Cyrus lay passed out on his bed.

Gideon felt torn between love and disgust. Why couldn't Cyrus see what he was doing to himself? Why didn't he accept Jesus and find excitement in following Him instead of seeking it in gambling halls and who knew what other places? For a moment, he wanted to shake some sense into Cyrus, but he finally went back to bed. He regretted his decision the next morning when he went to

Cyrus's room, now laid bare of all clothing and belongings.

Weeks later, Naomi wrote that Cyrus had come home "without the filly he hoped to rope" and rather quiet. Gideon suspected his brother had tarried along the way to rid himself of the marks of dissipation accumulated during his binge in New Orleans.

"Gideon?" Pete's voice interrupted his companion's reverie. "You still alive in there?" A rough hand shook his shoulder, and sand cascaded off Gideon's hat, shirt, and vest. He sat up and stamped his feet, tingling from the movement after their cramped position during the storm.

"Passed on by, didn't it?" Gideon jerked the scarf off his face and watched Pete busy himself with unmasking the team. "Arghh! Feel like I rolled in a sandbank."

"Better be thankin' that God of yours we ain't plumb smothered." Pete's weather-split lips opened in a grin. He finished with the horses, which stamped much as the men had done, obviously glad to rid themselves of their burden of sand.

Pete tossed a canteen to Gideon, then gave each of the horses water in his big, cupped hand. "Drink up. There's enough to get us to San Scipio, and we'll water down good there."

Curious at the comment about thanking God, Gideon replied, "I'll ride the rest of the way on top."

Pete just grunted, but when they got back on the road and headed through the sage toward San Scipio and home, Gideon asked, "Pete, why'd you say that, I mean, about being thankful?"

"Think preachers are the only ones who know God's ridin' the trails and watchin' over folks?" Pete shot back, then slapped the horses with the reins. "Giddap." He swallowed some choice name for the animals and added, "I know what you're thinkin'. I ain't much, and I don't claim to be nothin' but what I am, an ornery, miserable stagecoach driver. But I reckon it's ungrateful not to be glad the Almighty's on the job."

A thrill went through Gideon. *Could he encourage the seed of faith in Pete's tough old heart?* "You know the Almighty cared enough about *all of us,*" he emphasized the words, "to send His Son to die for us."

"Pretty big of Him." But Pete's voice discouraged further comment, and he gruffly added, "Save your preachin', boy. It ain't goin' to be easy to start out in your home range." He sent a sharp glance at his passenger. "How come you didn't just stay in New Orleans? Plenty of churches there, ain't they?"

"That's why, Pete," Gideon quietly said. "San Scipio doesn't have even one, and the way I figure it, home folks have just as much right to hear the gospel as city folks." He stared unseeingly at the road ahead. "I know lots of them will think I'm just a kid. I guess I am!" He laughed, and some of his melancholy left. "Not that I'm comparing myself, but the Bible tells about a whole lot of people who spoke for the Lord when they were even younger than I. Jesus talked with the priests in the temple when He was only twelve. I'm ten years older than that."

"Didja do some preachin' for practice back there?" Pete asked. "Were you scared?"

"Scareder than the time I tangled with a polecat and had to go home and face my father," Gideon confessed.

Pete threw his head back and roared. "Son, you're gonna be all right. Just keep rememberin' who it is you're doin' this for and don't pay no mind to those who give you, uh, fits." He quickly changed the subject. "Where you goin' to start in preachin'?"

Gideon wondered at the gleam in Pete's eye but only said, "Mother wrote that Father had made some kind of arrangement for a building." His straight brows drew together. "My dream is to have a real church in San Scipio someday."

"Hmm." Pete swung the horses successfully around a bend and motioned with his whip handle. "There it is."

From their vantage point on the hill, they could see into the sleepy town of San Scipio, nestled between the rises. One long, dusty street boasted a few weathered buildings and a hitching rail, where a few lazy horses were tethered. Shade trees offered some protection from the blazing sun, and back from the main thoroughfare, several homes of varying ages and styles stood closed against the afternoon heat.

" 'Pears mighty quiet," Pete mumbled and urged the horses into a trot toward the general store, which served as a stage stop.

Why should the sleepy village cause a sense of foreboding, Gideon wondered. Or was it just the unexpected silence?

Chapter 2

The arrival of the stage seemed to wave a magic wand that brought the drowsy hamlet of San Scipio back to life. Pete threw down the mail sack, and Gideon leaped to the ground.

"Hyar!" A heavy hand fell on his shoulder.

Gideon spun around in obedience to the touch and voice of authority he hadn't known in five years. Except for a few more lines in his weather-beaten face and the glimmer of a smile so rare his younger son could count on his fingers the times he'd seen it, Lige Scott stood tall, strong, and unchanged. "Welcome home, Son."

The young minister's vision blurred. Could the approval in Lige's voice and face really be for him? He glanced around. "Mother? Cyrus?" His keen gaze caught the darkening of Lige's face.

"At the ranch. Your mother's busy killing the fatted calf."

Strange that the same parable that ran through Gideon's mind fell from Lige's lips. "And Cyrus?"

"Rounding up strays." Lige threw his massive head back, and the Scott blue eyes flashed. With a visible effort, he put aside whatever was troubling him. "I brought the wagon. Figured you'd have a lot of things that needed fetching to the Circle S."

Strangely relieved of the tension he didn't understand, Gideon laughed, and its clear, ringing sound brought an answering chuckle from Pete, who had held back from greeting Lige. "Thought for sure we'd sink when we forded the stream," he joshed as he helped the other two transfer trunks and nailed wooden boxes of books from the stage to the wagon. But when Lige and Gideon climbed into the wagon and the older man took the reins, Pete called, "Don't fergit who you're workin' for."

The horses swung into a rhythmic beat before Lige demanded, "What was Pete talking about?" Lige's long years on the range hadn't quite erased his superior feelings toward his less polished neighbors.

"Pete didn't mean anything." Gideon hated himself for his placating tone, but he couldn't help falling back into the same pattern of behavior he'd used as a child to help his mother keep peace in the family. "He was just reminding me that God's my new boss."

"Huh." The grunt could have meant anything.

Gideon glanced from Lige to the road they were taking. "Why, this isn't the way to the ranch."

"Nope." Lige skillfully turned the team to the left at the end of the main street. To Gideon's amazement, he drove toward the road that wound weary miles to El Paso instead of the beaten track toward the Circle S. A quick swing to the left again, and Lige pulled in the horses. "Well, how do you like it?"

Gideon stared, closed his eyes, and blinked and stared again.

"Cat got your tongue? I asked how you like it." Lige flicked a fly off his forehead and pointed with a long, work-worn finger to a brand-new log building sitting back from the road on a little rise. "We hauled logs a lot of miles to build this, so you'd better appreciate it."

His father's grim warning lit a bonfire in Gideon's brain. "It's perfect." He scanned the building that bravely sat in its sagebrush and mesquite surroundings. Large enough to house all of San Scipio and those who ranched around it, the little wilderness church nonetheless remained small enough to be cozy.

"Dad—" Gideon couldn't go on. He barely heard his own voice using the informal name for the first time.

"I said I'd find a place for you to preach, didn't I?" Lige sounded gruffer than ever. "Well, are you going to sit there like a coyote on a rock or get down and go in?"

Gideon jumped from the wagon and walked through a welter of desert flowers someone had lovingly planted on both sides of the wide, dusty track to the door of the church. Sunflowers and bluebonnets were still damp from a recent watering; the hard clay soil around them lay dry and cracked in places. Blue mountains loomed miles away, yet in the clear air, they looked close enough to reach in minutes.

Gideon's heart swelled. He reached for the door and lifted the latch. Late afternoon sun streamed through windows that must have been hauled in from El Paso. The scent of freshly sawed wood crept into his nostrils. Peace and humility filled his soul. The silence inside the simple building bore evidence of his father's love and the devotion of a town that waited for the gospel of Jesus Christ. Young and inexperienced, could he be worthy of that devotion, worthy of his Lord?

"Well?" Lige's impatient reminder that he waited for an answer whirled Gideon around to face his father.

"It's more beautiful than any church or cathedral I saw while I was gone." Words came faster than tumbleweeds before a wind. "All those churches and cathedrals I saw when you had me visit friends instead of coming home for holidays—why—" He choked off, and his eyes stung. "I wouldn't trade this church for all of those others put together! I'm home. *Home.*"

"Good thing." Lige frowned and turned on his heel. "We'll be dedicating this church come Sunday." He looked back over his shoulder. "Better have a rip-snorting sermon. Folks around here don't want mush." He strode out, his footsteps heavy on the hand-smoothed board floor.

Gideon smothered a laugh. Rip-snorting sermons weren't exactly what he had practiced, but if that's what San Scipio wanted, he couldn't find a better source than the Bible! He looked around the silent, waiting church once more. For the second time, a feeling of unease touched him. The church held everything he could have dreamed of and more. Indeed, he'd supposed his first services would be in some abandoned building or barn. There appeared to be no earthly reason that all was not well. Perhaps the new wrinkles in his father's face had disturbed him or the set of his jaw when he said Cyrus had gone to round up strays. Gideon sighed and carefully closed the door of the new church behind him.

The steady *clip-clop* of the horses' hooves ate up the distance between San Scipio and the Circle S. For as long as Gideon could remember, his father had always stopped the horses for a breather on top of the mesa that sloped steeply above the ranch. Today Gideon was off the wagon seat even before the horses completely stopped. A poignant feeling of never having been away assaulted him. Here he had ridden with Cyrus a hundred times. Here he had reined in the horses on the few solitary trips he made to San Scipio for supplies. A lone eagle winged high above in perfect harmony with the vast wilderness. Below, half hidden by cottonwoods planted when Lige and Naomi first acquired the small piece of land that eventually grew into the present spread, the red-tiled roof and foot-thick cream walls of the house invited weary travelers. Gideon couldn't remember a time that cowboys and cattlemen hadn't been welcome at the Circle S.

"Your mother'll be waiting," Lige reminded, and Gideon sprang back to the wagon.

"Too bad your brother isn't here." The corners of Lige's mouth turned down, and he scowled. Again Gideon had the feeling all wasn't right between father and son.

Thoughtfully, Gideon tried to turn away Lige's attention. "Coming home has taught me one thing. I never want to live anywhere else. I'll be satisfied if the good Lord provides me with a wife and kids and the chance to live here until I die."

The rustle of yellowed grass beside the wagon track and the scream of the eagle sent a chill down his spine. He sought the Lord in a silent prayer. *Dear God, when things are as near perfect as they ever will be again, please take away this awful sense that something is going to happen.*

When they descended from the mesa and drove up to the corral, Gideon felt prepared to greet his mother, who flew from the ranch house as if pursued by mountain lions. Her brown hair had streaks of gray that hadn't been there when he left, but Gideon noted her slender body hadn't changed. Neither had the blue of her eyes.

"My son." She clasped him close, then held him off to take measure with one swift glance. Gideon felt on trial for the years he had been gone and actually heaved a sigh of relief when she softly whispered, "It is well. You have kept the faith." With the lightning change of mood he knew so well, she inquired, "And how do you like your father's surprise?"

Gideon thought of the perfect church waiting for his return. "Nothing could have pleased me more." He cautiously turned to make sure Lige had taken the team and wagon on to the barn before adding in a low voice, "For the first time in my whole life, I feel Fa—Dad is proud of me."

"More than you know, especially since—"

Lige's hail stilled any confidences she might have shared. "Is Cyrus back?"

"Just in." Naomi bit her lip, and Gideon saw the familiar pleading in her suddenly serious face. Lige might deny and refuse to accept that his firstborn son fell short of perfection but not Naomi. Still, for her husband's sake, she strove for harmony by cushioning the clashes that periodically came.

"What's all the shouting about?" a lazy voice drawled from the wide, covered roof extension that made a cool porch. Cyrus lounged against one side of an arched support. "Well, little brother, you ready to save everyone's souls?"

Lige growled deep in his throat as Cyrus tossed a half-smoked brown-paper cigarette to the earth and ground it with his boot heel. "Sorry, Dad. Just have to make sure Gideon remembers he's no angel, even if he is going to proclaim the good news."

Gideon hated the sarcasm that had always reduced him to a tongue-tied fool. This time he found his voice. "I never claimed to be an angel. You know that."

"Good thing." Cyrus's eyes gleamed with mischief as he gripped his brother's hand, and Gideon gave back as hearty a squeeze as he received. "Well! This boy's no tenderfoot, even if he has been living soft in the city."

"Did you find any strays?" Lige boomed, his ox-eyed gaze firmly on Cyrus.

"Some. Not as many as I expected." Cyrus shrugged. "My horse threw a shoe, and I had to come back in sooner than I planned."

"Get it fixed, and get back out into the canyons tomorrow," Lige dictated.

A wave of red ran from Cyrus's shirt collar up to his uneven hairline. "Yes, sir!" He saluted smartly, and Gideon held his breath, but before his father could roar, Cyrus threw an arm around his brother. "Rosa and Carmelita have been cooking for days. Let's eat." He grinned at Lige the way Gideon never could do, and a reluctant smile softened their father's features.

"Give us time to wash," the head of the household ordered. "Then bring on the feast."

An hour later, Gideon sat back with a sigh of repletion. The remains of his homecoming dinner lay before him. Tamales, enchiladas, chicken, a half-dozen kinds of fruits and vegetables from the garden, and a glistening chocolate cake had been reduced to crumbs. "I haven't eaten like this since I left," he murmured.

"Temperance in all things, Brother Gideon." Cyrus pulled his face into a sanctimonious smirk. "It won't do for your congregation to know you are a glutton."

In the wave of laughter from family and servants alike, Gideon wondered how he could ever have had qualms about his return to San Scipio and the Circle S.

Not satisfied with his needling, Cyrus continued. "So, what is your text for Sunday, Brother Gideon?"

An unexplainable impulse caused him to retort, "Perhaps I'll use Cain's question, 'Am I my brother's keeper?' Genesis 4:9," he added in the spirit of fun.

A cannonball exploding in the middle of the long table couldn't have produced more devastation. Cyrus leaped to his feet, anger distorting his features. "Just what do you mean?" He glared at his brother much as Cain must have done to the ill-fated Abel. "Don't think that becoming a parson is going to make you anything except what you are, the *younger* brother." Rage tore away every shred of control. "I'll have no mealymouthed, holier-than-thou snob of a brother bossing me around!"

"I didn't mean—" Gideon couldn't believe the ugliness of his brother's discourse.

"Sit down, Cyrus," Lige commanded. He stared at Gideon. "I'll have no such talk at the table or anywhere else on this ranch. As Cyrus says, being a preacher gives you no right to make remarks about your brother."

Gideon started to protest but caught the patient and resigned shake of his mother's head and subsided, feeling the pain of injustice from Lige's remarks. *Nothing had really changed.* It didn't matter that his father had built a church. When it came to taking sides, Lige Scott would never uphold the younger brother over the elder.

So much for coming home. Perhaps Emily Ann and the others had been right when they said he should have accepted a church somewhere other than in San Scipio. Yet, as he'd told Pete, who needed Jesus more than persons like Cyrus? Jesus clearly taught He came to heal the spiritually sick, not those already in His service.

That night when all had retired and Gideon restlessly moved around his rooms, he wondered. Even his pleasure at discovering Mother had enlarged his former bedroom and cleared out rooms on either side to provide a study and sitting room dwindled at the memory of the supper table scene. As he stood for a long time looking at the brilliant, low-hanging stars in the midnight blue Texas sky, he realized there had to be more behind Cyrus's reaction than not being able to accept joking. In the past, he'd delighted in the few times when Gideon managed to get ahead of him.

As if conjured up by thinking about him, a heavy knock brought Gideon to the door.

"May I come in?" Cyrus's bold gaze took in the refurbished rooms. He raised one eyebrow. "Some accommodations. Personally, all I need or want is a place to sleep." His tone abruptly changed from indolence to vigilance. "I want to know why you said what you did at supper." He stood crouched as if posed to spring.

"First thing that popped into my mind," Gideon frankly told him, but a warning went off in his mind. *Cyrus must have some secret to seek me out like this.*

Cyrus relaxed. The smile that could charm a rattlesnake into retreating replaced the watchful gaze. "Sorry." He half closed his eyes again in the habit he had that hid any expression from others. "Like I said, I just don't want you lording it over me." He laughed. "Get it? *Lord*ing over me, although God knows, sometimes I could use a trailmate like Him, if He's everything Dad and Mother and you think He is." He gave Gideon no opportunity to reply. "If He puts up with me long enough, who knows? I might shock Him and everyone—me included—by asking Him to ride with me." The next moment, he crossed the room in long strides, his spurs clinking musically. "I'm off for a night ride. Want to come?"

Gideon's irritation melted. "Give me five minutes," Gideon told him. He threw on riding clothes and stole out after his brother in the starlight. He felt like a kid again, when he and Cyrus were supposed to be sleeping but went riding instead.

The cool night wind and the exhilaration of riding in the open country blew cobwebs from Gideon's brain and doubt from his heart. All of his love for Cyrus returned, along with an even deeper love for his brother's soul. He might have spilled out the first Scripture that came to mind, but how true it was. Ever since he first accepted Jesus, he had longed above all for Cyrus to do the same. He *was* his brother's keeper. But the night sky and the feeling God lingered close opened his heart to an enlarged truth: Every follower of the lowly Nazarene assumes keeper-ship of all others who need to know Him. The same surety that caused him to announce on his sixteenth birthday that he must spread the gospel of Jesus Christ settled into his soul more deeply than ever.

Before they reached home, Cyrus halted his mount. He waited for his brother to pull up beside him, then addressed him in a low voice. "Gideon, no matter what happens, you'd never go back on me, would you?"

The friendly night had turned menacing. "Of course not." Gideon tried to see Cyrus's expression, but shadows and his low-pulled hat effectively camouflaged his face.

"And you'd forgive me? Seventy times seven?"

"What's this all about?" Gideon demanded sharply. His very soul chilled at some hidden meaning.

"Seventy times seven?" Cyrus repeated, then spurred his horse into a magnifi-cent leap. "Never mind, kid. Just testing you. . ." Cyrus's racing figure was swal-lowed up by the darkness.

Gideon slowly followed. Something about Cyrus frightened him. What had his brother been up to? Why should he ask such questions, request such a prom-ise, then ride away before Gideon could answer? He had no more answers when he rubbed down his horse and slipped back into his bed.

The next morning Cyrus had returned to his old teasing self, wanting to know if "the parson" had time to help round up strays or if he planned to sleep all morn-ing and practice his sermon the rest of the day.

Relieved but wary, Gideon rolled out, stowed away an enormous breakfast, and spent the day in the saddle. He came home stiff, sore, and convinced he'd better take it a little easier until he got his old skills back. The next day he settled with a Bible and writing materials and began making notes for the dedication sermon. How could he impress on his neighbors that his youth meant nothing, that the message he bore remained unchanged and unlimited despite the frailties of the messenger who carried it? Time spent on his knees paid off, and over the next several days, Gideon successfully balanced study, preparation, and range riding. Serving his "par-ish" would entail miles of hard riding to obscure dwellings; he rejoiced when he discovered he no longer felt stiff.

On Saturday night, Cyrus headed for town after being turned down by Gideon, who refused to accompany him. "Yeah, I guess it wouldn't look too good for a preacher to be part of a San Scipio Saturday night," Cyrus admitted. But he didn't heed his brother's pleas for him to stay home, either.

"Will you be there tomorrow?" Gideon asked wistfully.

Cyrus swung to the saddle. "Think I'd miss it? It's going to be better than the entertainment Blackie gets for the Missing Spur."

"I hope so." Gideon shuddered. The Missing Spur Saloon had a reputation for the so-called entertainment offered to its patrons. "How can you stand it?" he blurted out. "Why don't you find yourself a nice girl, instead of hanging around those—"

"Mind your own affairs, Parson." Cyrus's blue eyes turned icy. "If Dad asks where I am, tell him I rode into town to get a new bridle. It's true enough." He pointed to the patched-together job he'd done on his bridle and laughed mockingly. "You never would lie for me, so I won't ask you to. Just keep your lip buttoned about what you may or may not know." His horse impatiently danced, and the next instant, the two vanished except for a dust cloud kicked up behind them.

Gideon disconsolately headed for his room. Although his sermon still needed a few touches, once inside, he stood for a long moment by his deep-set window, watching the wagon track toward San Scipio and praying that somehow God would soften Cyrus's heart.

At last he went to his desk and forced himself to put personal troubles aside, losing himself in the truth of the Scriptures. For hours he considered, rejected, and, in spite of his best efforts, listened for the neigh of a horse, the jingle of spurs, or the soft footsteps that would signal Cyrus had returned.

Darkness paled. Dawn stole over the distant mountains. Gideon awakened from the uncomfortable position where he'd fallen asleep with his head on his crossed arms at the desk. Could Cyrus have sneaked in without him hearing?

In stockinged feet so as not to rouse his parents, the young minister slipped across his room, down the hall, and into Cyrus's bedroom. Yet Gideon's fingers trembled as he pushed open the door and stepped inside.

The room lay empty. The bed, neatly made.

Chapter 3

For a long time Gideon stood in the empty room and stared at his brother's unwrinkled bed. Disappointment and the nagging worry something had gone wrong swept over him. Even back in his own rooms, Gideon lay awake, wondering why Cyrus hadn't come home. He had promised not to miss the dedication of the little church and his brother's first sermon in San Scipio.

Gideon found himself defending Cyrus as he had always done. *Maybe when he reached town, his horse went lame and he stayed with friends,* he thought hopefully. Clinging to the thought of what meager comfort it offered, the troubled young minister finally managed to sleep for a few hours. He opened his eyes to a glorious summer Sunday morning and a laugh that sent relief surging through him.

"Cyrus!" Gideon tumbled into his clothes and raced to the courtyard, bright with flowers and shaded by carefully tended trees.

"Well, Parson, is your sermon ready?" Cyrus stood up from teasing a small lizard and turned his brilliant blue gaze toward Gideon.

"Ready as it will ever be." Gideon thought of the hours of prayerful study he had put into that sermon. "Glad to see you made it home. I was beginning to wonder if—"

"Shh." Cyrus furtively looked at the house, then back at his brother. "I'm sorry, but I won't be able to hear your preaching after all."

Gideon's spirits dropped. "Why not?" He stared at his brother, noting the honest regret in Cyrus's face, the misery in his eyes.

"I got word in town that—" Cyrus swallowed and shrugged. "It doesn't matter. I'm riding out as soon as the rest of you leave for church." His fingers crept to his breast pocket. Gideon could see the ragged edge of an opened letter before Cyrus stuffed it deeper in his pocket.

"When will you be back?"

"Maybe never." The somber voice stayed low, barely discernible.

"You can't mean that!" Gideon burst out. "It will kill Father. If you're in trouble, say so. You know we'll stand behind you."

Cyrus's lips twisted, then set in a grim, uncompromising line. "Not this time." He raised his voice and gave Gideon a warning look. "Well, Father, today is a proud day for the Scotts, isn't it?"

Yet Gideon saw the strong face crumple for a moment before Cyrus averted his face from Lige Scott's beaming glance. His heart felt like a cannonball in his chest. *I must find a chance to talk with Cyrus before leaving for San Scipio!*

His brother proved more clever than he. After he finished breakfast, Cyrus looked at the big clock that had traveled west with the older Scotts and then made an announcement. "Instead of riding in the buggy with you, I'll take my horse, and then I can head for El Paso after church. Talk around town is that one of the ranchers there is selling out and going back East. Maybe I can pick up a few head of prime horses."

"Not on the Sabbath," Lige ordered. "Stay in town and see the horses tomorrow."

"I reckon it won't hurt just to look at them on the Sabbath, will it?" Cyrus assumed an air of injured innocence. "The buying part can wait." He strode out without waiting for a reply.

After excusing himself, Gideon followed Cyrus outside. At the corral, Cyrus had already uncoiled his rope to lasso the horse he wanted. "Cyrus, *don't go*," Gideon pleaded, out of breath from chasing him.

"I have to." The rope drooped from his fingers. "I'll ride out of sight, then when you're gone, I'll come back for a few belongings."

"I don't understand," Gideon cried.

"I hope to God you never do." The lariat sang and expertly dropped around a big bay's neck. Before Gideon could think of a way to stop Cyrus, his brother had saddled the bay, mounted, and ridden off with a mocking farewell wave. Shaken, Gideon wondered how he could go ahead and preach just a few hours later. He retraced his steps to the house, but instead of joining his parents, he went to his room, knelt by the bed, and stayed there for a long time, unable to pray.

When the Scotts arrived in a churchyard crowded with horses, buggies, wagons, and people on foot, a most irreverent cheer arose. A startled Gideon observed Lige's broad shoulders held straight and proud and Naomi's shy smile. Now that the day for which she'd waited so long had arrived, it seemed the most natural thing in the world to be helped down from the buggy seat and ushered into a sweet-smelling church. The absence of piano and organ did not discourage the lusty a cappella singing of familiar hymns. In this first service ever held in San Scipio in a church, ranchers and merchants, women and children raised their voices in harmony and song that lifted even Gideon's disturbed heart.

Then it was time. Clutching the pages he'd labored over so long, Gideon Carroll Scott stepped to the hand-hewn pulpit. As he looked at the first carefully written paragraph of his sermon, the words swam before him. Paralyzing fear such as he'd never known constricted his throat. To hide it, he quickly bowed his head and shot upward a frantic, desperate prayer for help. When the rustling of the congregation stilled, his mind stopped reeling. He opened his eyes and looked at the sermon, then deliberately laid it aside.

"Friends." Gideon paused and looked from one side of the packed church to the other, from front to back. Women in their best dresses held children on their laps. Men sat straight and waiting beside them. Young people eyed one another from the protection of their families. Many had grown so much in the time Gideon had been away, he could only place them by their proximity to the families he knew. Unfamiliar faces stood out like whitecaps in the gulf of waiting souls.

"Friends," he said again, "I had prepared a special sermon that seemed to be in keeping with this significant day." He held up the pages. "I can't give this sermon, at least not today. I feel that Almighty God simply wants me to share with you what He and His Son, Jesus Christ, have done for me."

Warming to the subject, Gideon told in the simplest terms possible how as a fifteen-year-old boy he had invited Jesus into his heart. Something in the way he spoke kept the congregation's attention riveted on him. Babies fell asleep in their mothers' arms. Children listened in wonder. Young and old responded to the Holy Spirit that had prompted Gideon to forsake fancy preaching and merely testify.

He went on to say how he came to know the only thing he wanted to do in life was to help others find Christ, as the traveling minister had done for him. He touched lightly on the years in New Orleans of study and preparation amid the Reconstruction efforts. He said nothing of those who wooed him, who predicted obscurity and waste in a life given to a tiny West Texas town. Instead, the great longing for his friends and neighbors to meet, know, and love the Lord rang in every word. Gideon could feel the rush of caring and ended by saying, "Not one of us can save ourselves. God in His goodness offers the only plan of salvation the world ever has known or ever will know. Will you open your hearts to His Son?"

He sat down, drained yet exultant. Here and there, faces made hard from years in a raw land trembled with emotion as tears spilled down weathered cheeks. An untrained but harmonious quartet sang the beautiful hymn "Faith of Our Fathers." A short dedicatory prayer followed, and Gideon's trial by fire ended. Handshakes that ranged from the tentative touch of the elderly to staunch grips by mighty men warmed the new preacher. Yet the knowledge that the one he most longed to bring to Jesus even now rode alone and lonely lay heavily on him. So did the guilt of carrying that knowledge.

Although Lige and Naomi didn't think anything about it when Cyrus failed to come home by Wednesday, Lige grumbled because Cyrus had missed the sermon. "Wouldn't have hurt him, and common courtesy demanded he be there," he boomed in his big voice more than once. His brow furrowed until the lines looked even deeper. "Sometimes I wish Cyrus were more like—" He broke off, as if unwilling to express even hesitant disloyalty to his firstborn.

The younger brother's heart pounded at the implied approval, but when Cyrus hadn't returned by Saturday, Gideon knew a crisis was fast approaching. Should he tell Lige the little he knew? Gideon's troubled mind queried. All he really knew was that a certain letter had reached Cyrus that evidently alarmed him into vanishing. Besides, deep in his heart, Gideon couldn't and wouldn't accept Cyrus's desertion. In spite of his faults, Cyrus loved the Circle S and had been branding calves with the S brand shortly after he learned to ride. Gideon had helped when he got old enough, but never had his heart been in it. Always, books and learning and what lay outside his own way of life lured him away from the range.

At supper Saturday evening, Lige turned to Gideon. "Do you know anything about your brother?"

The analogy of Cain and Abel returned: The Lord had inquired of Cain concerning his brother Abel's whereabouts. Unlike Cain, Gideon did not lie when he said he didn't know. He felt compelled to add, "He seemed, well, strange that Sunday morning when he rode away."

"*Strange?*" Lige's ox eyes looked more pronounced than ever.

Gideon licked suddenly dry lips. "He said he wouldn't be in San Scipio to hear me preach, but he wouldn't say why or where he was going."

Lige's heavy fist crashed to the table, and his face mottled with anger. "Why didn't you tell me this before?"

Gideon forced himself to keep his voice low, his gaze steady. "I hoped that whatever bothered him would disappear and he'd come back."

"Is that all you know?" His father's penetrating glance backed his younger son to the wall.

"Yes." Gideon would say no more; what he suspected might or might not be true. He wouldn't distress his father more by passing on suspicion. In all probability, it would only make Lige rail against him in his blind unwillingness to admit Cyrus capable of anything less than perfection.

~

Gideon's second sermon went more according to what he had prepared. After fasting and prayer, he was able to lay aside the fact of Cyrus's continued absence and concentrate.

At dawn on Monday morning, Lige rose and announced he would ride to El Paso. "Will you come with me?" he asked Gideon.

Used to being ordered and not invited, Gideon hid his astonishment and agreed. During the long ride, the intangible silence between them reminded Gideon of those eerie moments in the sage before the storm. They found the rancher who had horses to sell, and Lige discreetly led the conversation around to what buyers had been there. "One of the men from San Scipio appeared mighty interested," he said. "A little taller than my son here. Heavier, but similar coloring."

The rancher shook his head. "No one like that's been around here. I'd shore have remembered." He brightened. "Long as you're here, d'yu see anything yu like?"

Before Lige could say no, a high-stepping sorrel caught Gideon's attention. "I'd like to look at the mare," he told the rancher.

A close inspection and short ride resulted in the purchase of Dainty Bess, who had won Gideon's heart with her frisky but gentle ways.

"Yu're a good judge of horse flesh," the former owner admitted. "I'da took her back with me 'cept it's too far."

Gideon transferred saddle and bridle, attached a lead line for the horse he had ridden to El Paso, and swung aboard his new mount. "Thanks," he called. When they crossed the first hill and left the ranch behind them, he commented, "Mother will enjoy riding this horse—that is, when I'm not on her!"

"How can you be so all-fired excited over buying a horse when your brother's off God-knows-where?" Lige's criticism effectively doused Gideon's attempts at conversation. Even though he knew his father spoke from the depths of misery and concern, Gideon's old resentment returned in full force.

As much as I can and as often as my duties to the church allow, I'll try to take Cyrus's place, he vowed. He knew it wouldn't be easy. Five years had taken a toll on the range skills he once had. Sometimes he took longer doing chores or his hands proved awkward in roping. Most often Lige said nothing, yet Gideon felt the same second-best feeling he'd experienced through the years. Even if he could ride and rope and brand full-time, he'd never be Cyrus. For that, Lige couldn't forgive him.

He often felt as if the weeks following Cyrus's departure were a stack of dynamite just waiting for a spark to set it off. Once it blew, life would never be the same. To make things worse, Gideon ran into a problem with his ministry. In his naivete, he had thought all God would require of him would be to preach, visit, and comfort. He soon discovered the folly of his thinking. Time after time, he called on God to give him strength and patience with his congregation. Good folk they were, but all too human. Gideon wished he had a peso for every time he had to become a peacemaker; a sermon was sorely needed on the subject of putting aside petty differences and pride and jealousy so the Word of God could be proclaimed.

Naomi Scott proved to be a valuable ally when it came to socializing. "Just don't pay any more attention to one family than another," she quietly advised. "If you call on the Simpsons, then make sure that within a few days you also call on the Blacks, McKenzies, and Porters. Things will settle down in time, but for now everyone wants to make sure they get equal attention from the new minister." Her smile died. "And, Gideon, beware of Lucinda Curtis." Real anxiety puckered her brow. "She's spoiled and bent on getting her own way. More than one cowboy has had to leave town because of her wild tales, which," she added, "I just don't believe. Lucinda isn't that pretty, even with all her specially bought clothes and haughty ways."

Gideon sighed and ran his fingers through his now sun-streaked hair. "Why didn't they warn us in school how silly young women can be?" He laughed ruefully. "I can't physically drink gallons of lemonade or spare the time to spend afternoons in cool courtyards! Yet every unmarried female in San Scipio seems to feel such activities are part of my job. Most of them are nice enough, but sometimes I feel the way a jackrabbit must feel when being chased. As for Lucinda," he said grimacing, "she must have taken a course in tracking her prey. How she knows where I'm going to be and manages to arrive just when I'm leaving is beyond me." He thought of the tall, thin girl with the straw-colored hair and faded gray eyes that could melt with admiration or flash pure steel when crossed. "What can I do about it?"

Naomi thought for a long time, her hands strangely idle, her blue eyes deep and considering. "Perhaps you can do nothing except to be very careful. Time will take care of the problem." A dimple danced in one cheek, and her eyes sparkled. "One of these days, the Lord will send a special person into your life. Not a butterfly who knows little more than how to preen and chase, but a real woman who will love, cherish, and complete your life."

On impulse, Gideon decided to tell her about Emily Ann. "Always the Southern belle, she would have married me if I'd agreed to remain in Louisiana and take over a church. She was sure her father could arrange such a position." He laughed. "Once I saw how shallow she was inside, I dropped off her list of admirers. Wonder how many others have been on it since I left New Orleans?" He took his mother's hand. "A long time ago, I decided that until I met someone like you, I'd go it alone. Not really alone, I have my Lord. But sometime. . ." He couldn't voice the longing he felt to have a companion, one who would support and love him, bear his children, and grow old with him.

Gideon remembered that conversation, and once or twice in the next few weeks, he even hesitantly approached God about it. Although he loved his work, the natural longings for a home of his own stirred him more than at any time before. He had so much time for reflection, especially riding Dainty Bess, a sure-footed mare that needed little guidance. While he rode the range or into canyons to visit isolated ranches or for pleasure, Gideon not only came closer to God but permitted himself to dream.

Now and then he caught qualities in one San Scipio woman or another that he admired but never in Lucinda Curtis. Always courteous, he nevertheless had a hundred valid reasons for turning down the supper invitations at her home unless others would be present. The same held true for lingering after church until everyone had gone except Lucinda, who expected to be walked home. Gideon became adept at making sure a group remained to discuss music or basket dinners. He also used the distance between the Circle S and San Scipio as an excuse until it grew more threadbare than the strip of carpet in the entryway of the town's only boardinghouse.

One afternoon the young minister had just finished posting a notice on the church door about special services he planned to hold when Lucinda appeared. Trapped by his well-bred upbringing, Gideon would only politely greet the pink-gowned maiden.

"Do let us go inside. It's more comfortable."

"Why, don't you think it's nice out here?" Gideon motioned to an inviting bench he had recently placed in a shaded area. Not for a gold mine would he enter the church building and give her an opportunity to start talk as she had done with others. "I only have a little time. What can I do for you, Miss Curtis?"

"Please call me Lucinda." She blushed and looked down, but no modesty appeared in her eyes when she looked up again. "It's so much friendlier." She held out a white, well-cared-for, and obviously useless hand.

Gideon pretended not to see it and ushered her to the bench. "What was it you wanted?" He'd be hanged if he'd call her Lucinda.

"I, we, well, some of your congregation are concerned over your having to ride in from the Circle S." She lowered her lashes in an imitation of Emily Ann when she wanted her own way. "Autumn will come soon, then winter. We'd never forgive ourselves if you lost your strength from overwork."

Thunderstruck at the idea of her interference, Gideon couldn't say a word.

"Papa agrees with me, with us."

He would, Gideon thought sourly. Tom Curtis's spineless demeanor when it came to his only child was the stuff of legend in San Scipio. The storekeeper's pride and blind adoration of his child even outranked Lige Scott's.

"Anyway, when I just up and said it shouldn't happen, Papa said he'd be glad to build a room on our house just for you." She clasped her hands together and laughed, but Gideon saw the gloating triumph she couldn't hide. "You'll be like one of the family."

It took all his Christian charity not to shake her silly shoulders until she rattled like the doll she was. Gideon stood. "I'm in perfect health, Miss Curtis. Thank you for the offer." He couldn't manage to say he appreciated it. "I wouldn't even consider such an arrangement." With the cunning he'd developed against her wiles, he said frankly, "I'm sure you're aware there is already jealousy in the congregation." He forced himself to smile. "Such a move could create problems and charges of favoritism." He lowered his voice confidentially. "A young minister living in a home where there's an unmarried woman. . ." He let his voice drift off. "You can see, it just wouldn't do." Could even Lucinda Curtis swallow that serving of applesauce?

It slid down smoothly. "Oh, Reverend, why, I never once thought of that. What must you think of me?" Crocodile tears swam in her eyes. Fortunately, she didn't give Gideon a chance to reply. "We'll forget the whole thing, shall we?" She rose. "I really mustn't keep you." She gave him an arch smile. "It is so nice when a young man considers a woman's reputation."

For one moment, Gideon thought he would ruin the whole thing by laughing in her face. Instead, he told her, "A woman just can't be too careful."

Lucinda glanced at him sharply, and he wondered if she were remembering the rumors she had started about those cowboys. "Thank you, Reverend. Do you have time to walk me home?"

Not by a long shot, he wanted to tell her. Instead, he said, "No, but thanks again for your, er, concern." She picked her way across the churchyard, then stopped to wave gaily before she turned the corner. Not until he mounted Dainty Bess and got a mile out of town did he vent his anger and disgust by urging the faithful horse into a dead run.

Chapter 4

Judith Butler adjusted the mosquito netting over four-year-old Joel's small bed and swallowed hard. The small blond replica of Millicent lay in a spread-eagle position as usual. Flushed with sleep, his cheeks rosy and curly hair tangled, he tugged at Judith's heartstrings. Terror rose within her. What if she should lose him after all her struggles in the past four years to fulfill the promise she had given her dying half sister?

Judith's knees weakened, and she dropped into a shabby chair next to the sleeping boy. She rested her tired head crowned with its coronet of dark brown braids against a pale, slender hand whose calloused palm told her story of hardship. The dark brown eyes that lit with twin candles when she smiled closed. *Dear God, what am I going to do?* she silently prayed.

Only this morning her landlady had reluctantly told her she couldn't keep Joel and her much longer unless they paid something. The worn woman looked away as if ashamed to see the fear Judith knew sprang to her face.

Judith coughed as she explained, "Just as soon as I'm a little stronger, I'll be able to get work. I appreciate all you've done for us, caring for Joel when I had the fever. Please don't send us away."

The landlady's eyes filled with tears. "My dear, if I had money to buy food, I would never let you go. But with my man helpless ever since the carriage accident, I have to think of him, too. Don't you have something else you can sell?"

Judith thought of the few remaining pieces of jewelry that had brought in but a pittance when the larger pieces had been sold. The barren room she and Joel shared in the ruins of an old New Orleans house had been stripped one by one of the fine, mahogany pieces that once stood in the Butler home. Now only two cheap beds, a cracked bowl and pitcher, and little else remained. Precious Joel had made a game out of seeing their furniture go.

"It's like living in a tepee," he said with his enchanting grin, which showed small even teeth and set his blue eyes sparkling. " 'Sides, we've got you and me."

Judith's slender shoulders convulsed in a shudder. Her long illness had put a sudden end to the needlework that had supplied enough extra money to pay for their room and simple meals. Even now her hands shook so that she couldn't hold the needle. Unwilling to disturb Joel's slumbers with her agitation, Judith quietly rose and crossed the almost-empty room to kneel beside the limp curtain that sifted daylight from the single window. She unfastened the window and swung it open, hoping for a little relief from the early summer heat. A few weeks from now, it would be unbearable. Even if she could afford to stay, how could she and Joel live through another summer in this furnace of an attic? She longingly thought of her parents, both casualties of the war: her father in battle, her mother from worry and illness. The little room faded, replaced by her own merry cry and pattering feet down the steps of the beautiful home that had once been hers. . . .

"Father's come! Millie, he's here." Six-year-old Judith ran to greet him, closely followed by nine-year-old Millicent who, in spite of being older, clung to the more daring Judith and leaned on her for strength. As fair as Judith was dark, she had adored her half sister from the time their father laid the baby carefully in her arms. "A present for you, Millicent, my dear. Your own baby sister."

"I'll need my good older daughter to help me care for her," the second Mrs. Butler, who had never seemed anything but a real mother to Millie, added. She had married Mr. Butler a little over a year after his first wife died, so Millicent never knew any other mother.

Now she laughed and sped after Judith but stopped short on the wide veranda. "Why, Father, you're a *soldier!*"

"Isn't he beautiful?" Judith scampered around the tall, gray-clad man whose grim face relaxed into a smile when he caught her up in his arms. He held out his hand to Millicent.

"You're going to fight the nasty Yankees, aren't you?" Judith slid to the ground and leaned companionably against him with Millicent on his other side.

"Child, just because others don't believe as we do doesn't make them nasty," he protested. Deep lines etched his face. "I pray to God I never have to take a life. God created Northerners and Southerners alike, and He doesn't love us any more than He loves those who see things differently."

His wife joined them, fear and trouble in her pretty face, the features Judith had inherited distorted with care. "If only God would stop this awful happening." Tears sprang to her large brown eyes, but she impatiently dashed them away.

"Girls, I don't know how long I am going to be gone," Gerald Butler said somberly. "I wish I didn't have to go at all, but I must. Always remember this: No matter how far away I am, every night just before the sun goes down and every morning when it rises, I'll be thinking of you and praying for you. Be good soldiers. Take care of your precious mama and each other."

Childish joy in his appearance fled. Judith and Millicent clasped his hands. Their mother took their other hands, and the prayer that followed burned into the children's minds, along with the special look he gave their mother before he mounted and rode off to war, his shoulders proud and square.

For a time their world of gracious living and love continued in much the same way. When the long lists of casualties began arriving, all traces of gentility faded. Gerald Butler's prayer was granted. He fell in his first battle without ever having fired a shot, his commanding officer wrote in a sympathetic letter. As life went ahead in its new order of living under Yankee control, Judith couldn't even remember when things were different. But when at last the fighting ended and troops withdrew, as great a horror as the occupation by Northern forces confronted the Butlers.

Even her great love for her daughter and stepdaughter couldn't rally Mrs. Butler enough to overcome the loss of the only man she had ever loved. Although she held on through the war, shortly afterward, she fell ill with swamp fever. A few weeks later, she died, leaving a bewildered ten- and thirteen-year-old to face life with only God as their protector. Distant relatives offered to take the girls but not together. Older than their actual years because of the tragedies they had faced, Millicent and Judith clung more closely than ever. They unearthed the family treasures their mother had managed to secrete and keep hidden for all the long years and sought lodging with an old friend who welcomed them.

Life's cruel blows continued. When the family friend died, the girls moved on from place to place. Millicent grew thin and pale from kitchen work once done by Negro slaves. Judith sewed long hours until her small fingers sometimes bled from the coarse materials. Yet they could not and would not be separated.

Days and weeks limped into years. At seventeen and fourteen, their contrasting beauty attracted attention. Yet the modest upbringing and Christian principles instilled in them so long ago kept them aloof from the gaiety with which some tried to forget the past. Sometimes they shyly talked of the future.

"How will I know when I'm in love?" Judith demanded and bit off the thread from the seam she had just finished. Her plain dark garb worn from necessity and not choice added little to her beauty, but her fresh face and sparkling eyes needed no enhancement.

Millicent's fair face shone flower-pale against her drab clothing. "I always think that if someday someone looks at me the way Father looked at Mama just before he rode away, I'll know he loves me."

"I remember that!" Judith dropped her sewing. "I don't remember, though. Did Mama look the same way?"

"Yes." A smile curved Millicent's lips upward in the gentle way that made her resemble the Madonna Judith had seen in a painting. Her eyes held dreams and softness. "Dear Judith, how blessed we are to have such memories. God has indeed been good to us all these years." She trembled, and her smile faded. "When I think how we could have been taken away from each other, it frightens me." Her blue eyes grew feverish, and she clutched her arms together across her thin body. "I think I'd rather die than to have that ever happen."

"Silly, no one's going to separate us." Judith deliberately soothed her sister, as she had done since childhood, when she realized her own strength and Millicent's frailty. "Oh, I suppose if we get married, we might not live together, but let's marry gentlemen who will let us stay close."

Twin red spots burned in Millicent's cheeks and provided unusual color. "I'd like to see any man even *try* to separate me from my sister!"

Judith's mouth dropped open. Seldom did Millie exert herself, but she certainly sounded positive now. "Why don't we wait and worry about it when it happens?" she suggested practically. "In the meantime, there's enough light for me to whip in another seam." She bent to her work, but soon the flying needle slowed and stopped. "My idea of heaven is to never, ever have to sew another garment."

"Judith!" Millicent gasped. "Don't be sacrilegious."

She looked up in honest surprise. "God says we're supposed to ask for what we want, and I'm asking that He let me do something else when I get to heaven besides sew." She giggled, and even pious Millie couldn't resist her mirth. "Maybe all the robes of righteousness will be already made by the time I get there."

"My stars, you have funny ideas." Her sister stared at her and shook her head. "When I think of heaven, I think of God and Jesus and Father and Mother and my own mother."

"I do, too," Judith said in a small voice. "I just wish Jesus would come back soon." She threw down her sewing, and tears that had been bottled up for months fell. "Oh, Millie, will we ever really be happy again?"

The older girl knelt beside her and put both arms around her. "Life is hard, but God takes care of us, and we can be happy knowing our family is with Him. Think of all the soldiers and families who don't know Jesus, how much harder it is for them." She comforted Judith, and their mingled tears helped to wash away sad memories.

The summer of 1869 proved to be both disturbing and joyous. Judith learned that Millicent had met a dashing young gentleman who admired her and sought her out at every opportunity. *If Millie is in love, why doesn't she bring the young man to meet me?* she wondered.

"I will," Millicent promised, but she sent a sad glance around their poorly furnished abode. "It's just that we've no place, and—"

"If it's good enough for us, it should be good enough for any gentleman caller," Judith interrupted fiercely.

"Don't you see? We can't *have* gentlemen callers here without a chaperone." Millicent smiled in a way that made her sister lonely for the first time. Hot jealousy against this stranger who had come between them joined forces with the protective instinct she had always displayed toward Millie.

"It's all right, really it is," Millicent assured her. "He's tallish and as blond as I am. When he looks at me, I—" She broke off, unable to express what she felt.

"Do you feel the way Father and Mama did that day?" Judith whispered.

The ecstasy in Millie's face stilled her sister's protests. "Oh, yes. If he doesn't love me, I don't know how I can go on." A dark shadow crossed her sweet face. "There are so many girls. They come and go at the place I work. Why should anyone so wonderful even look at a humble serving maid?"

"Anyone that wonderful would be bound to see past your job," Judith snapped, still troubled. "Hasn't he even asked to meet me?"

"N–no. But I've told him all about you, how clever you are with a needle and how we've stayed together all this time." Doubt crept into the blue eyes. "He just laughs and says there's plenty of time. Since I'm only seventeen and don't have a guardian, I suppose he wants to make sure I know what I want."

Judith's lips formed the question, but she couldn't quite ask, *Do you? Do you, Millie?* Instead, she held her tongue and prayed that God would care for her sister and keep her safely.

A few weeks later, Judith received the shock of her life. She came home dog-weary from hunting new quarters that might be more pleasant than those they now had. Never had she seen Millie more radiant. *"Look!"* Her sister held out her slender hand. A shiny gold ring encircled her finger.

"Millicent, you haven't, you didn't. . . *Where did you get that ring?"* Judith stared in horror, her stomach churning.

"It's my wedding ring." Happiness and regret blended in her voice. "I'm so sorry I couldn't tell you, but we, I knew how opposed you'd be to my marrying so young and especially when you haven't even met him, and—"

Judith cut through her babble. "You actually got married without ever telling me?" Suspicion crystallized. "Was this *his* idea?"

"Please don't feel badly, dear." Even Millicent's contrite apology couldn't dim the shining radiance of her face. "Everything is going to be wonderful. I'll just be gone a few days for a short honeymoon, then we'll have a home together for always. My new husband says he will be glad to have you live with us." The sound of carriage wheels outside the window sent her scurrying to look out. She snatched a valise from the bed. "Come meet him before we go."

Judith hesitated, feeling caught in a moment somewhere between the order that had been their lives and the uncertainty ahead. "I'd rather wait until you come back," she managed.

"I understand." The sweet smile that characterized Millicent showed that she did, but her new allegiance overcame even the bonds of sisterhood. With a warm squeeze of Judith's shoulders, she sped toward the door. Her heels clattered on the staircase, and the lower door banged shut.

"What am I doing?" Judith frantically came out of the shocked trance into which she'd fallen. She raced to the window and leaned out. *"Wait!"* The word couldn't compete with the street noises and laughter of children. Millicent's face turned upward, but Judith knew she didn't look toward the window but into her new husband's face.

I must see what he looks like, she thought quickly. Judith leaned out farther but only glimpsed blond hair and the back of the man's head as he helped Millicent into the carriage.

"Wait!" she called again. "Millicent, I'll be right down!" Even as she called, she knew it was too late. The carriage wheels began to turn, and the harness jingled as her sister rode into a new life, leaving Judith behind.

It's only for a few days, she told herself again and again. She made excuses for Millie's absence, saying she had gone away with friends, yet for three nights Judith cried herself to sleep. There had to be something wrong with a man who would not only hastily marry a seventeen-year-old but who did it furtively and without her only close relative's knowledge. He must have known how Judith would object; perhaps he was afraid she would sway her sister against such an act. In the silence of the evenings, Judith often heard thunder in the distance that warned of a storm waiting to break. Was this small island of silence during Millicent's honeymoon also the prelude to a storm, one that would shatter Judith's world and perhaps Millie's as well?

All through those long, waiting hours beat the question, *What shall I do if she never comes back? I don't even know her husband's name!* Judith sought her Lord as never before in her young life. She stormed the very gates of heaven on Millicent's behalf and her own. She prayed for forgiveness for the hatred in her heart toward the man who had stolen Millie's love. Sometimes she even cried out for God to take her away from an uncaring world that had hurt her so deeply.

Too upset and ill to work, Judith lay on her bed listening for the sound of carriage wheels. A dozen times she leaped up and pelted to the window. When the right carriage finally came and stopped, she had fallen into a fitful sleep, her tear-stained face in the curve of one arm. Millicent found her that way, and compassion filled her. She slipped back downstairs as arranged, but with the word Judith should not be disturbed. "You can meet her tomorrow," she told her husband. "I'll stay with her tonight."

He quickly agreed, and Millie's heart swelled with love and pride in his understanding. She watched the carriage roll out of sight, thrilling that such a man had ever desired her. Then she went back to her sister, her heart filled with happy plans for the future.

"Millie?" Judith roused when Millicent reentered their room. "Is it really you? I dreamed you went off and didn't come back. I felt so alone. I didn't know what to do or where to go." She broke off. "Where is he?"

Millicent hugged her and laughed and removed a charming new hat. "We decided I'd stay here tonight. Tomorrow—" She lowered her voice to a mysterious tone. "Tomorrow we're going to see about finding a proper house. Oh, Judith, I've never been so happy in my whole life!"

Judith had never been more miserable. Yet curiosity pushed aside foreboding. "Where did you go?"

"To a wonderful inn just north of town. Then we shopped, and see?" She whirled, and her light blue summer dress flounced around her. "That's not all." She tore open a large parcel she had carried in with her. "Your favorite colors." A fluffy yellow and white dress tumbled out. "We found a shop where they sold dresses already made. It should fit. I just remembered that you're four inches taller." Millicent held the dress up to her petite five-foot, four-inch frame where it dragged on the floor.

Her troubles momentarily forgotten, Judith tried on the dress. It settled over her young body as if it had been designed exclusively to highlight her dark brown hair and eyes. "It's lovely, the prettiest dress I've had since—"

"I know." Millicent's shine dimmed. "But how glad Father and Mama would be to know we're going to be happy again." She laughed and confessed, "Don't ever tell anyone, but even on my honeymoon, I missed you so much I could hardly wait to get back to tell you how wonderful life is going to be. After tomorrow, we'll never have to worry about a place to live or having enough money to pay our way." Her sapphire eyes sparkled. "We'll wear our new dresses."

Somehow the excited girls managed to sleep a little. Judith found herself so caught up in anticipation that the little worries that pricked her heart like dressmakers' pins lost themselves. By ten o'clock, they had primped and preened until every shining hair lay in place. For the first time, Millicent wound Judith's shining braids around her head in a coronet. "The new dress needs a new hairstyle," she announced. "Besides, fourteen is no longer a child."

Judith found herself blushing up to the high lacy collar of the pretty gown. Could that really be her own image in the mirror? The girl with rosy cheeks and smiling mouth? How different from the way she had felt while Millicent had been gone! "Pooh," she told her reflection. "I worry too much." She turned toward her sister, lovely in the pale blue gown and the serenity Judith knew came from happiness. She wanted to open her heart, to confess all her doubts, yet doing so would only hurt Millie. Perhaps someday when they were both old women, they would laugh together over the younger sister's misgivings. Now they were too silly, too unreal in the clear sunny morning to utter. Not one bitter drip should be allowed to spoil Millicent's perfect day, Judith vowed with all the passion of her years. *She may never again be exactly this eager and happy.*

The thought startled her. Why shouldn't Millicent have hundreds of happy, eager days? How perfectly ridiculous to allow her own trepidation to color her judgment and imagine all kinds of ridiculous impossibilities. She twitched her skirt again and strained for the sound of carriage wheels.

They did not come.

The clock that had been in the Butler family for generations slowly ticked off the seconds, the minutes, the hours. At first Millicent laughed and admitted what a sleepyhead her husband had proven to be. He liked to stay up late and rise at his leisure. The clock ticked on, relentlessly passing noon, one o'clock, two. By three, Judith had lost interest in her pretty dress and changed. "You don't think there's been an accident," she finally said, then wished she'd kept silent.

Millicent's face turned the shade of parchment. "Surely he would have managed to send me word." She slowly rose. "We must go to where he lodges immediately."

"Wait, Millie. A carriage just stopped."

Color flowed back into her sister's face. "Thank God!" She ran to the door and flung it open. "My dear, where have you been?"

Chapter 5

J udith followed her sister to the door and glanced first at the Negro, then at Millicent, whose hand went to her throat. "Who are you, and what do you want?" she demanded.

"I have a message for the other young lady." The man held out a folded paper, turned on his heel, and hurried down the stairs.

Judith glared at his retreating back but turned back to her sister when she heard a low moan. "Millie, what is it? Is your husband hurt? Do we need to go to him?"

Millicent tottered back inside the open door and sank to a shabby settee. Every trace of color had drained from her face. She wordlessly held out the paper, and Judith grabbed it from her.

My dear,
New Orleans just isn't the place for me. I'm leaving for home today. I have wronged you by going through with the marriage ceremony. Forgive me, if you can.

There was no signature.

Judith crumpled the page the way she wished she could crumple the man responsible for the devastation of her beloved sister. "How could anyone be so cruel?" Fury threatened to choke her.

"I thought he loved me." Millicent looked as if she had been stabbed.

"Quick, what is his address?" Judith sprang to the occasion. "Surely he can't have gone yet!"

The pride of her father stiffened Millie's spine. Her blue eyes flashed. "Do you think I want him to come back after this? Never!" New dignity raised her head and dried her tears.

"You don't love him any longer?" Judith's brain spun.

"Loving someone has little to do with honor and respect," Millicent quietly said as her fingers mercilessly wrung a handkerchief. "Even if he came back, this would always be between us." A little color returned to her face. "It isn't even a matter of forgiving, which I could do. I'd have to, according to the Bible. But forcing him to stay when he wants to be elsewhere. . ." Her voice trailed into silence, the same silence that had hovered in the poorly furnished room while she had been away and Judith waited.

"What will we do now?" Judith asked. For the first time in her life, she felt incapable of making decisions.

Millie's lips set in a straight line. "No one knows of our marriage except we three. The family I work for granted me the time off for a rest. Tomorrow I will go back." Never had she appeared stronger. "We will go on as we have." She looked around the room and shuddered with distaste. "As soon as we're able, we will move to another part of the city and leave no address."

"But what if he should come back?" Judith cried, her heart aching at the stony look in Millicent's eyes.

"Dear sister, if he really wants to find me, he will." Long lashes swept down to hide Millie's eyes and made little dark half moons on her white cheeks. "I don't think he will, though." Her lips trembled, and she hastened to the window and looked out as if seeing far beyond the familiar street below.

Through a relentless summer and a welcome fall, there was no sign of the peripatetic bridegroom. Millicent and Judith sold a few more heirlooms and established themselves in new quarters. One autumn day, when leaves whirled before the wind, Millie told her sister she had an announcement to make. She stood by the window as she so often did.

In the silence, Judith's heart pounded for no apparent reason. What could make Millie look like that, exalted, yet despairing.

"I am with child."

At first Judith could but stare. A multitude of feelings rushed over her: shock, disbelief, even admiration that her sister could be so calm.

"You're going to have to help me," Millicent went on. "The baby will be born next spring, late April or early May. Between now and then, we must save every penny we can. No matter how hard it is, I'll never give my baby away for others to raise."

Judith ran to her and hugged her fiercely. "Of course you won't! We'll take care of the baby and—" She broke off. "Millie, don't you think you should let him know? You could send a letter to where he used to live. . . ."

Millie looked full into her sister's eyes. "No, I thought it all out before I told you. This is my child. He forfeited the right to it by leaving, even though he had no way of knowing there would be a baby." Her eyes glowed with feverish intensity. "Don't you see? He comes from a well-to-do family. Suppose he claimed the child? We have no money to fight for my baby." She caught Judith's hand and held it until the younger girl winced. "Promise that no matter what happens, you won't let him take the baby."

A warning flutter inside Judith died before her sister's agony. Making such a promise might be wrong, but Millicent's peace of mind had to be assured. "I promise." She squeezed the clutching hand. Yet another clutching hand, cold and frightening, held her heart in a grip so powerful, she wanted to cry out.

The coming of the child changed everything. They first needed to find a place where neither was known or Millicent's condition would bring shame and speculation. After much searching, they finally relocated in a drab but still respectable boardinghouse. Millie disguised herself with loose clothing and continued her maid's work. Judith sewed until her eyes burned. Babies needed things the sisters could ill afford, but little by little, a pitiful array of tiny garments lay waiting and ready. On the last day of April 1870, a frightened but determined Judith helped

Millie in what fortunately was an easy birth and delivered a squalling but perfectly formed boy.

"We have no money for doctors," Millicent had insisted. "Babies come, and we can manage." All Judith's protests failed to sway her. "I'll be all right, and you're strong, almost fifteen years old."

The first weeks after her son's birth, Millicent's magnificent determination alone kept her going. She named the baby Joel Butler, and the little horde of money the girls had been able to save carried them through. A few times, Judith mentioned contacting the baby's father but found Millicent even more opposed than before. A few months later, a complete reversal occurred. For several days, Judith had been aware of the way Millie's gaze followed her whenever she was in the room. One fall evening, she quietly said, "I'm not sure if God will allow me to stay long enough to raise Joel." Her eyes held sadness but no fear. Judith noticed how frail she looked before she went on.

"All those months ago, I made you promise; now I want you to change your promise." The appeal in the thin face would have melted a heart carved from ice. "I still want you to keep my baby, Judith. But if the time ever comes that you are no longer able to do so, I release you from the promise not to contact Joel's father. There are papers hidden beneath the lining of the old trunk: the marriage lines, names, and addresses." She reached out and clung to Judith's hand. "Never read them or use the information unless you feel you have no choice but to lose Joel."

"I promise." Judith's throat felt thick. She tried to cover it by saying, "Here we are at dusk, talking gloomy thoughts!" She lit a candle, and its flickering light steadied into a glow that dispelled some of the shadows. "There, is that better?"

Millicent roused herself from her private thoughts, and they said no more. Yet the knowledge of the pact between them made Judith feel old beyond her years. Her gaze strayed toward the box they had carefully lined with soft material for a crib. He was so good, like a little golden-haired angel. He seldom cried, and his large, intelligent eyes and well-shaped head made him seem older than his few months on earth.

"Dear God," Judith whispered long after her sister slept that night. "Please, don't take Millicent. You and she and Joel are all I have left." Waves of loneliness washed through her. A few minutes later, the peace of her heavenly Father descended, and the troubled young woman slept.

As if relieved to have talked things out, Millicent rallied. She continued to work, while Judith sewed at home and cared for Joel. November and December passed. During an unusually chilly January, Millicent contracted a bad cold that kept her home. She arranged with her employer to send Judith in her place. The hardest thing was not allowing Joel to come near her lest he also become ill. By February, Millie still could not work, and a cough lingered that frightened Judith, no matter how much her sister tried to assure her. She called a doctor, who silently examined Millicent and shook his head. Judith followed him into the hall.

"I can't do anything. She let it go too long." His keen eyes bored into Judith. "You'd better contact some relatives and make arrangements for yourself and the little boy."

Somehow Judith managed to murmur her thanks and pay him as well, her heart filled with terror. If he took it on himself to let the authorities know if Millicent died, they would come and get Joel.

Millie brought it up when Judith went back into their room. Thin and wasted, she ordered her sister to get everything packed. "You don't have to tell me what the doctor said," she began. "I think I've always known how things would be. Don't cry, Judith. There isn't time. I want you to take the last of Mama's jewelry and sell it now. Sew the money into the bodice of your dress." She took a deep breath and coughed until exhausted, but her spirit permitted no giving up. "The hardest thing you've ever done is what you must do soon. As soon as God takes me to be with Father and Mama, you must flee. Don't wait for anyone to come. When the landlady doesn't hear stirring, she will come up and find me."

"*That's horrible!*" Judith cried. "I can't do it!"

Millicent rose up on one elbow. "You must. If you love me, grant my last wish. What does it matter who buries me or where?" Fever painted red flags in the sunken white cheeks. "Don't you see? Joel will be taken from you if you don't escape with him." She panted, more beautiful in her illness than ever before. "Now go and sell the jewelry. I've remembered the name of an old friend who may take you in and never tell anyone. It's written down in the front of the big Bible." She fell back to the thin pillow, her eyes filled with pity.

"Poor Judith. So young to have all this tragedy. Please don't mourn for me. I'll be with loved ones, and soon you and my little son will come. Even if it isn't for years, it will seem in the twinkling of an eye for me." She coughed again. "Dear little sister, God will give you strength to do what you are required. He will uphold and sustain you. Now, go."

Unable to argue in the face of such courage, Judith got out the last of the jewels, donned a cloak, and hurried to the man who had purchased other items from them. Back with the money, she discovered that Millie had been doing more planning.

"Go right away and see if Mama's friend will take us, but don't say when we're coming," she ordered. "Then tell our landlady that I'm sick and we'll be moving soon. Get a drayman to come for what furniture we have left."

Again the necessity of providing for the future lent strength to the failing young woman. For several days, she kept on in spite of her obvious weakness. Not until every direction had been carried out and only a pallet on her floor remained did Millicent relax.

"It won't be long," she told Judith. "But I am so happy you will keep Joel. Remember your promise." She fell asleep with a smile on her pale lips.

All night Judith kept vigil. The light of a guttering candle showed when Millicent's earthly sleep changed. Not one tear fell. Judith had gone beyond that in the hours and days before her sister's death. She had to be strong for Joel.

After a final survey of the room, Judith left the bit of money she could scarcely afford to repay the landlady for her trouble in contacting the authorities. On a scrap of paper, she wrote, *I'm sorry it isn't more, but I must care for the child.* Once again she was glad that the room had been listed under "M. Greene," Millie's middle name. In the first rays of morning, she quietly took the sleeping child from his nest at the foot of Millicent's pallet and slipped into the mists of dawn.

Judith would never clearly remember how she and Joel existed. She stretched the bit of money in her dress while making her small charge's clothing from the leftover pieces of her sewing jobs. One by one, the familiar childhood furniture pieces vanished. Yet Joel thrived and provided joy to the girl's sad heart. While others her age danced and frolicked, she held her head high and cared for Joel. Still a child at heart in many ways, she played with him and made up games. When time permitted, she took him for walks, and although many times she ached to buy him all the things others had, he never asked for anything.

Once in a while the old friend who now served as her landlady cared for the charming little boy while Judith delivered her work. She didn't care to allow her personal situation and business world to touch by taking him with her.

Weeks, then months, then years passed. Soon Joel would have his fourth birthday; Judith, her nineteenth. She had developed into a tall, slender young woman whose dark brown eyes still lit with twin candles when she played with Joel. Her shining coronet of dark brown braids suited her as no other hairstyle. Even Joel, who liked to brush her hair at night, thought it prettiest when coiled around her shapely head.

Because of Millicent's experience with a faithless lover, Judith almost innately distrusted men. Those she met through business who showed open admiration received instant rebuffs. Millie had been so sure of her happiness, perhaps too sure. Yet Judith could never fully regret the sad circumstances when Joel confidingly tucked his hand in hers and said he loved her.

If only she hadn't allowed herself to grow run down by skimping on meals so she could put away extra for Joel! Suddenly Judith's secure world crashed. Sickness struck and lingered. Panicky, she tried to continue her work and could not. Even when the fever left, she crept through the days like a ghost of her former strong self. During her delirious periods, the thought hammered until she thought she would go mad. *The promise. The promise. I must keep my promise to Millicent.* Part of the time she couldn't remember what it was, and she felt too sick to care. She fought with all her remaining strength and came back from the brink of death. If anything happened to her, no one would know who Joel was! Could it be right for him to be put away and cheated out of his rightful inheritance? Over and over she considered the circumstances. If only God would help her know what to do now that she simply could not care for herself and Joel as she had done these long, hard years. . . .

Joel moved in his sleep, and Judith returned from her long mental journey to the past. She reached beneath the netting and straightened his tangle of sheets, smothering the noble brow. A wave of love stronger than any she had experienced flowed through her. She couldn't care more for Joel if he were her own son. Wasn't he her own, given to her by Millicent?

"I have to decide what to do, heavenly Father." She resumed her post at the window. "It may mean losing him, but I can't take the chance of growing ill again and not being able to provide for him." Her gaze strayed to the old trunk that held their meager supply of clothing and worldly goods. Dread filled her, yet the time had come for action. She resolutely stood and crossed to the trunk. Her hands shook so she could barely open it, but she finally lifted the lid and propped it back.

"Papers beneath the lining," she muttered. She loosened stitches so tiny as to be nearly invisible, her throat tight at the thought of Millie secreting the pages until no one would suspect the trunk contained any item but the obvious.

The few papers crackled as she withdrew them. Such a small witness to the short time Millicent had loved and rejoiced and found happiness to sustain her. Judith had to blink away the tears that persisted in coming between her and the important documents. She barely glanced at the wedding certificate. What she needed was an address, somewhere to send a letter admitting the existence of a four-year-old boy for whom she could no longer provide.

A scrawled page in the same handwriting she'd seen in the note delivered that fateful day almost five years earlier caught her attention. She snatched it up and scanned it in the fading light. "Oh, no!" She desperately pulled aside the screening curtain to get more light. Somehow moisture had seeped into the old trunk and the address was unreadable.

Judith frantically dug behind the lining for other pages but found none. She turned to the marriage lines and gave a soft cry of gladness. Clear and bright, the date of July 29, 1869, proclaimed to a more or less interested world that Millicent Butler and Gideon Carroll Scott had been united in holy matrimony.

Her gladness turned to despair. What good was a name without an address? She had no idea where this Gideon Carroll Scott lived, either while in New Orleans or when he went back to the home he mentioned in the cruel farewell note. Millicent, usually so open, had never talked about him except the times she extracted Judith's promises concerning Joel.

"Dear God, this is a mountain neither Millie nor I expected," she whispered. In spite of the warm evening, her hands felt icy and nerveless. "Now what can I do?"

Should she make inquiries in New Orleans? If so, where would she start? If she went to Millicent's employer with the story of Joel's birth, they would laugh her to scorn. Millie had been proud they had never known. Besides, opening the past might prove disastrous. What did the authorities do to young women who stole away a child, leaving no trace?

Strange that the memory of her father's words when he rode off to war came back to her now. *Every night just before the sun goes down and every morning when it rises, I'll be thinking of you and praying for you.* A passionate longing for her dead father rose within Judith. How distressed he would be to see her in such straits. Yet always he had taught that her heavenly Father loved her even more than he, although to her young heart it had hardly seemed possible.

Too weary to think longer, Judith sought out her bed. She fell asleep with a prayer for direction and guidance on her lips. Morning brought Joel to her bed in his usual whirlwind manner, and for a time she forgot their uncertain future. Yet throughout the day she found herself saying over and over in her heart and mind, *God, I am helpless. It's all up to You.*

With a round-eyed Joel beside her, Judith found the strength to delve into the depths of the old trunk. "What's this?" he asked and pointed to a slight bulge in the side. His eager fingers worked the lining loose. "Why, Judith, it's *money!*"

"It can't be," she argued, but there lay a small pouch with money in it and a paper in Millicent's fine handwriting that read, "Passage money, if ever needed." How had her sister been able to put it away from their scant income? Now if Judith only knew where to go! Or should she just give the money to their landlady and hope for the best? She rejected the idea as soon as it came. Such a temporary solution wouldn't cure their problems.

That afternoon, Judith and Joel walked through the poor neighborhood just to get away from their room. Dirty newspapers swirled in the street under horses' hooves. Perhaps she should rescue one and see if anyone needed a house-keeper, someone who would allow her to bring Joel, too. Judith managed to grab a paper slightly cleaner than the others. She idly turned the pages, pausing at one that showed a small group of men in front of a stately building. If only things had been different! She'd like Joel to go to college one day, but there seemed to be little hope unless God Himself intervened in their lives.

She started to turn the page, then stopped. A frank-faced, smiling young man stared at her from beneath the headline: West Texas Man Leads Class in Academics. Would she ever know a young man like that? Probably not, but Joel could become one. She curiously read the words beneath the picture, wondering why anyone from West Texas would be going to school in New Orleans. The next instant, she stopped breathing, only to start again when her head spun. She closed her eyes and read the caption: Local lads found it impossible to keep up with a young ministerial student from the Wild West. Gideon Carroll Scott returns to San Scipio, Texas, for his first pastorate.

Chapter 6

T he newspaper dropped from Judith's numb fingers. Blood rushed to her head as she bent to retrieve it. Her avid gaze sought out the featured picture. Was this man a scoundrel, an utterly heartless rake who broke Millicent's heart and left behind a world of trouble and misery? Impossible! And yet, how many Gideon Carroll Scotts could there be?

He had been in New Orleans all these years, hiding under the guise of one studying to be a minister! Appalled at the further evidence of his wickedness, a rush of fury sent determination coursing through Judith's veins, bringing strength to overcome the weakness caused by her illness. *Mr. Gideon Carroll Scott has a big surprise coming,* she thought with a small amount of satisfaction. She tore out the article, stuffed it in her reticule, and managed to steady her voice. "Come, Joel. It's time for us to go home."

He trotted obediently beside her, one chubby hand confidingly in hers. Now and then he pointed with the other at some wonder: an especially colorful rose, a dog on a leash, a strutting peacock on a shady lawn. His laugh rang, and his blue eyes shaped like those of the man in the newspaper shone in the sunshine. "Look, Judy."

"Yes, dear." Preoccupation made her answer less interested than usual. When he questioningly looked up, she hastened to add, "Aren't they beautiful?" From the time Joel first walked, he had developed an inner sense that told him when his beloved Judy was troubled. Sometimes it took all her best efforts to hide her feelings so he could be the normal, happy child God had created him to be.

As soon as Joel fell asleep after their simple supper of bread and milk, Judith got out her writing materials. Page after scorching page, she wrote to the missing Gideon Carroll Scott and ended by saying she and Joel would be on their way west by the time he received her letter.

When the white heat of anger faded, reason took over. What if by some strange quirk of fate this wasn't the man who deserted Millie? "Oh, dear God," she whispered. "It must be. I asked You for help and found the newspaper. But I have to be sure. Please guide me." For a long time, she sat there thinking and listening to Joel's even breathing. At last she reluctantly tore the letter to bits. Time enough for recrimination later. Now she must make sure of her ground. She took a clean sheet of paper and wrote a simple message:

If you are Gideon Carroll Scott, who married Millicent Butler who died in early 1871, contact me.
    J. Butler

She added her current address; she must stay until she received an answer. Checking to see that Joel still slept, Judith hurried downstairs and outside to post her letter to San Scipio, Texas. Surely someone there would know Gideon Scott. The paper had named it as his hometown.

She had no choice but to use a little of the designated passage money to stave off eviction until she heard from Texas. Yet, day after sweltering day passed and no message came. Judith forced herself to take up her needle and work, even when the fabric shook in her unsteady hands.

"Why d'you work so hard, Judy?" Concern shone in Joel's eyes as he leaned against her knee.

She roused from her fatigue and smiled. "Can you keep a secret?"

"Oooh, yes." His face lighted up. "Is it a nice one?"

"It's a bi-i-i-ig secret," she solemnly told him, unwilling to label what they must do next as nice. "Don't tell anyone."

"Not even God?" he anxiously asked. "We tell Him ever'thing."

"You dear!" She laid the almost-finished garment aside and pulled him into her lap, noting how worn her dark dress had become. For a moment, a vision of a fluffy yellow and white dress danced before her to be sternly put away, as the dress had been long ago. "God already knows, but we won't tell anyone else. We're going to leave here and go on a long, long trip."

"Like Mama went to heaven?" He snuggled closer to her. "That would be nice. We could see Mama and Jesus. Maybe even God."

Judith hastily corrected the impression she had given. "Not to heaven, Joel. To Texas."

"Is that close to heaven?"

Although the memory of one man's faithlessness colored her reply, Judith felt compelled to explain the situation to Joel as best she could. "I don't think so. Joel, we've never talked much about your father's family. That's because they live in Texas, and now we may get to see them. Would you like that?"

Joel's face looked puzzled, but he nodded his head.

"This is hard for me to say to you. Your mama named you after her family when you were born because your father left New Orleans and went back to Texas. I think it's time for you to know your real name: Joel Scott." Sensing that she had imparted too much information for him to process immediately, Judith returned to the details of their impending trip. "Can you imagine what Texas will look like? Think of all the cows and horses we'll see!" From her limited supply of Texas lore, she painted an exciting picture, wanting only to cry until every tear inside her washed away her misery and the need for this hateful trip.

In spite of the silence from San Scipio, she still clung to the forlorn hope Gideon might write. But as summer relentlessly continued, Judith knew they must go. With another autumn and winter just ahead, she didn't dare chance not being able to work. After a final sleepless night of prayer, she purchased passage and left New Orleans with Joel and the shabby trunk that contained little more than their well-worn clothes, the big Bible, and the precious wedding certificate.

Dust, heat, and coarse food threatened to choke Judith, but the fear of the unknown was more unpalatable. One of few women on the trip, she endured rough men who treated her kindly and palefaced men who eyed her and attempted conversation.

The endless journey sometimes made her wonder if she and Joel had been crossing Texas all their lives. Overheard conversation told her how proud Texans were of their state, and she bitterly wondered why. She spoke little with her fellow travelers and reserved all her energy for Joel, who thrived on the attention after years of being so isolated. A few times she reluctantly relinquished him to a keen-eyed driver who invited "the little feller" to ride up on top with him. Joel returned big-eyed and chattering. Long-eared jackrabbits fascinated him. Tumbleweeds made him laugh with their antics. He sniffed sagebrush and said, "It tickles." Even in her misery, Judith couldn't help seeing how the little boy brought gladness to all around him. *God, may it ever be so* became her constant prayer.

Just when the exhausted young woman felt she couldn't go on another day, their driver, Pete, bellowed out, "San Scipio comin'!"

"Son Sip-yo comin'," Joel echoed.

Judith roused from her listlessness. Torrents of weakness washed through her, but she could not give up now. She instinctively turned to her source of comfort. "Dear God," she murmured so low no one else could hear, "help me to go on in Your strength. Mine is gone."

The horses topped a hill. Interested in spite of herself, Judith looked down at San Scipio, cupped between two rises. Could that be a town, the one long and dusty street with only a few buildings on each side? She leaned forward and glimpsed other buildings back from the so-called thoroughfare. The horses picked up their pace.

"Whoa, you ornery critters!" Pete stopped the stage before the building marked GENERAL STORE in faded letters on a weather-beaten board.

Judith's spirits crashed. In her need to find Joel's father, she never once thought it would be in a place like this or that places like this even existed. "Sir, isn't there a hotel?" Her voice trembled, even though she tried to keep it steady. Pete, who had leaped down and opened the door of the stagecoach, pushed his sombrero back on his head. Trouble loomed large on his unshaven face. "Naw, and the boardin'house ain't much, either."

"Wh–where can we go?"

Pete scratched his cheek. "The Curtises have the biggest place, but yu don't wanta go there." He peered at her, and his face reddened. "Beggin' yure pardon, ma'am. But d'yu an' the little feller have kin here?"

Judith urged Joel off her lap as she considered her answer. "Gideon Scott is a relative of ours," she said somewhat awkwardly.

Glancing from Judith to Joel, enlightenment slowly came to the driver's face. "Well, by the powers, I shoulda. . ." He quickly swallowed, then mopped his face with a trail-dusty kerchief. "Stay right here." He helped them down and to a bench away from a small group of curious onlookers. Down the street Pete went in the clumsy way Judith had come to associate with Texans, who seemed more at home on horses than on foot. She vaguely wished the driver hadn't recognized Joel's lineage, but what did it matter? Before long, San Scipio and the hills and valleys would ring with shock concerning Joel's identity.

A few minutes later, Pete returned, followed by a towheaded lad who looked to be about fifteen perched behind a high-stepping horse pulling a light buggy.

"This here's Ben. He's rarin' to drive yu to the Circle S."

"*The Circle S?*" Judith raised inquiring brows.

"Lige Scott's ranch." Pete swung the trunk expertly aboard the buggy and helped his former passengers up into it. "Good luck, miss. You, too, little feller." He lowered his voice. "Don't pay no mind if Lige raves. It's his way." His smile warmed Judith's heart, and at that moment, she felt as if she were leaving her last friend. Her grizzled guardian angel tousled Joel's curls. "Don't yu fergit yure pardner Pete."

"I won't," the little boy promised.

"Neither will I." The grateful look Judith sent him brought an even deeper red to his windburned, leathery face. "Good-bye, and God bless you."

Ben touched the horse lightly with the reins, and the buggy rolled away. Judith didn't look back, but Joel turned around and waved to their benefactor.

"I'll just drive past the new church," Ben told his passengers. His eyes gleamed at the thought of driving this pale but pretty visitor and little boy all the way out to the Circle S. The coins Pete had given him jingled merrily in his pocket. "We got ourselves the greatest preacher there ever was."

"Oh?" Judith grasped the opportunity to learn something about Gideon.

One word of polite interest was enough to loosen Ben's wagging tongue. A straw-colored lock of hair dangled on his forehead, but it didn't slow his praise. "Gideon went to N'Orleans and studied so he could be the best preacher ever. Don't see why he needed to go, but he did. Anyway, he, oh, here's the church." Ben pulled in their horse. "Door's closed. Preacher don't stick around much; too busy out visiting folks. Here, let me help you down. You can see inside, anyway."

Judith bit back tears when she observed the faithfully cared-for flowers and the obvious love that had gone into the building. Black anger for the perfidy of the minister warred with the hatred she felt for having to expose his sin and shatter the tranquil silence that surrounded the building. Inside, the presence of God hung in the quiet air. Ben nearly burst with pride, showing the careful work put into the San Scipio church.

"We all helped," he said simply. "Sometimes when I hear Gideon preach, it makes me wonder if a feller oughtn't to get right down on his knees and thank the Almighty for bringing Gideon back when he coulda had a big city church."

Judith bit her tongue to keep from shrieking out the truth. The fall of his idol might change boyish devotion to God into bitterness. *What an awful thing Gideon has done, not just to Millicent or his congregation but to himself,* she thought. Her fingers pressed the reticule that held the creased picture of him. How like an angel he looked, how like Joel. Yet hadn't Lucifer been the fairest of all before he turned from God?

Back in the buggy, Joel fell asleep in spite of the changing country through which they passed. Ben rambled on, repeating almost verbatim Gideon's first sermon and the story of his conversation. "Pushed his notes away, he did. Just stood there and talked kinda quietlike, but you coulda heard an owl hoot a mile away, everyone was so still."

Again Judith had the feeling of wrongness. Doubt assailed her. If she had spent the last of her substance to come to San Scipio and it turned out the young minister had nothing to do with Millicent and Joel, what then?

I can always sew, she told herself, but misgivings continued to attack. Not many women in this part of the country would be in need of a dressmaker or seamstress, no matter how skilled. Perhaps that family Pete had mentioned could use her services.

She took advantage of the next time Ben stopped talking to catch his breath. "Do you know the Curtis family?"

"Huh, who doesn't? Old man Curtis is the storekeeper, 'cept his high-toned wife and daughter run him and the store, too." Ben put on a falsetto voice. " 'Oh, Mr. Curtis, you mustn't even *think* of puttin' the nicest goods out for sale! Lucinda's in des'prit need of a new gown for the ball.' "

"*Ball!* You have balls in San Scipio?" Judith forgot her troubles for a moment.

"Huh-uh." Ben grinned a comradely smile. "That's just what Mrs. Curtis called the big re-cep-tion she aimed to give for Gideon." The grin stretched into a guffaw. "Not on your tintype did it come off. Preacher up and said he'd rather just have folks come to church on Sundays, and he'd shake their hands after services."

"What did Mrs. Curtis say?"

"Not much, but Lucinda simpered around and told everyone how noble Gideon was until San Scipio wished she'd keep still."

Judith tried to fit what Ben related to the image of a young man so selfish he would marry a girl and walk out on her. It seemed impossible. Yet hadn't there been belated recognition in Pete's eyes when he glanced at Joel? Too weary to figure it out, she sighed until Ben stopped the winded horse on top of the mesa above the Circle S in the same place Lige and Gideon had rested weeks before.

"The Circle S," Ben said unnecessarily.

Restful. The word came to mind with Judith's first glance below. After the shock of San Scipio, she had feared a shack. Instead, she saw the red-tiled roof and cream adobe walls turned pure gold by the slanting sun. A feeling of coming home tore at Judith. Distant hills gave way to higher mountains. An eagle, twin to the one that winged in the sky to welcome Gideon home, cast its dark shadow over the trail ahead.

"It's so still." Judith automatically lowered her voice.

"Cyrus must not be home, or it wouldn't be."

Something in Ben's guarded voice made her inquire, "Who's Cyrus?"

"Gideon's brother, but they ain't alike." Ben miraculously stopped talking and urged the horse forward down the steep decline to the valley floor. "Circle S's the biggest and prettiest spread around. Dad says if I still want to next year when I'm sixteen, I can hire out here." His hands firm on the reins, Ben slowed the horse for a turn.

"You really love it, don't you?" Judith marveled.

Ben turned an astonished gaze toward her. "Of course I do. I was born and raised here, ma'am." His tone said more than his words, and Judith subsided. She couldn't help but see the difference between the Circle S and other places she'd passed.

"Water and care make the difference," Ben said. Had he read her mind? "The Scotts are a hardworking outfit." He brought the light buggy to a stop in front of the house, and Judith noted the courtyard, bright flowers, and plentiful garden.

"Lige? Gideon? You've got comp'ny." Ben jumped down from the driver's seat and courteously helped Joel, who had awakened flushed and curious, and then Judith.

"Where are we, Judy?" Joel wanted to know. He rubbed the sleep from his eyes.

"We're at the Circle S, dear. It's a big ranch." *That can't be my voice, calm and practical,* Judith thought. *Not when my stomach's going around in circles.*

"Are we going to stay here?" Joel didn't wait for an answer but ran to a nearby rosebush to sniff the flowers. Judith felt reprieved.

"Ben, who is it you've brought us?" A crisp voice with a hint of a Southern accent penetrated Judith's confusion. She turned sharply, and dust sifted from her dress. A woman, whose gray-streaked brown hair shouted middle age but whose slender figure and questioning blue gaze whispered youth, stood near the arched support that held up a wide-roofed porch. Her simple dress of blue calico matched her eyes and fitted her body well. The welcome in her eyes for any stranger reached out to Judith, adrift in a friendless land, unless she counted Pete and Ben.

"I—I am Judith Butler," she began. Her heart pounded. *How can I destroy the peace in this ranch woman's face by informing her of her son's treachery? Or will it all prove to be a terrible case of mistaken identity?* In that moment, Judith fervently hoped so. Better to have made the long trip for nothing than to bring shame to one Judith could have loved as a mother in different circumstances.

"Who are you talking to, Naomi?"

Judith knew she would never forget her first sight of Lige Scott. To her frightened vision, he loomed sky-high and desert-wide. His massive head sat square and proud on strong shoulders. Lige's blue eyes, darkened with some strange and unidentifiable emotion, stared at Judith from a network of lines in a range-hardened face. Brown hair predominantly gray successfully told the story of his hardworking life and the fight to get, hold, and expand the Circle S.

"Ben has fetched us a visitor." Naomi smiled and gracefully walked down the steps. "Her name is Judith Butler, but she hasn't told us where she comes from or why she's here."

Lige followed his wife to where Judith stood frozen. If it had seemed impossible to tell Naomi Scott why she'd come, it was preposterous to imagine accusing Gideon to this heavy-browed father. Judith couldn't move. She could not speak. She swayed from weariness, and Ben, openmouthed, steadied her. If only someone would say something, anything, to break this terrible silence before a storm Judith knew would never end.

"Judy, I like it here." Joel deserted the roses, ran from behind the buggy, and stopped between her and the Scotts. "Do you live here? Are we going to stay with you?" he asked.

Chapter 7

Oh, *God, not like this,* Judith silently prayed, despising herself for not speaking. Now it was too late. Innocent, beautiful Joel stood smiling at Naomi and Lige, repeating his question. "Are Judy and I going to stay with you?" The look in his Scott-blue eyes and rosy face showed his eagerness.

Naomi gave a choked cry. Her face turned whiter than cotton. Lige's mighty frame jerked as if someone had shot him. Disbelief turned into anger, then fear on his face. Finally he burst out, *"Dear God in heaven, who are you, boy?"*

Joel's mouth rounded into a little *o*. He put one finger in his mouth.

Lige fell to his knees before the child and asked again, "Who are you?" Sweat glistened in the furrows of his face.

With the sensitivity of his young years, that strange ability to know when others hurt, Joel's happiness fled. Judith suddenly found her voice. "His name is Joel Scott, sir."

"No. *No!*" Lige stood and backed away as if pursued. But when Joel's eyes filled and he ran to Judith, the stricken man mumbled, "Forgive me, boy." He passed one hand over his forehead. "Naomi, take them inside." Before she could comply with his order, Lige glared at the transfixed Ben. "On your way and not a word of this to anyone, you hear?"

"Yes, sir. I mean, no, sir." Ben almost fell over himself getting back into the buggy and turning the horse. A cloud of dust followed his rapid progress away from the Circle S and the four left behind to sort out the mystery. Someday Ben might speak of this day, but now all he wanted to do was get away as fast as he would from a threatened rattlesnake.

"Miss Butler?" Naomi Scott regained her composure, although to Judith's excited gaze, she appeared to have aged ten years in the past few moments. "Will you come in, please?" She smiled at the wide-eyed little boy who clung to his aunt's skirts, held by a tension he couldn't understand.

Judith followed the woman into a large hall with a polished dark floor and massive dark furniture. The brightness of Mexico relieved the somber mien: Colorful serapes adorned the cream plaster walls, and matching woven rugs made islands on the waxed floor.

"Oooh, pretty." Joel's love of beauty overcame his temporary shyness. He pointed to an open door leading into the flower-laden courtyard with its splashing fountain.

"Perhaps he would like to go out while we talk," Lige said hoarsely, his gaze fixed on the small boy with a strange intensity Judith couldn't translate.

"May I, Judy?"

"Of course." She hugged him and watched him run into the courtyard before turning to the Scotts. "I apologize for intruding this way, but your son—

he—" She swayed and would have fallen if Naomi hadn't caught her arm and led her to a settee. "Child!" The hostess in Naomi rose to the needs of a guest. "Why, you're worn out."

Naomi's kindness threatened to destroy completely what little composure Judith still possessed. "It's such a long way," she faltered. "If I could have a glass of water, please."

Naomi clapped her hands, and a smiling, dark-eyed Spanish woman in a bright, flouncy dress came into the room. "Carmelita, a cool drink for our guest, please."

Before Judith's brain stopped spinning, a tall fruit drink of unknown ingredients, an elixir to restore her spirits, turned the world right side up again.

Aware of Lige's pacing, Judith said, "I didn't want to come here, but I've been sick, and if anything happened to me, there's no one to care for Joel."

"If the boy is really a Scott—and with that face, he can't be otherwise—he will be cared for," Lige interrupted, his anger distorting his features.

Fortified by the drink and spurred by the contemptuous disbelief in Lige's voice, Judith's jaw set and her own anger flared. "Oh, he's a Scott all right."

"You have proof of this?" Naomi asked. Judith had the feeling hope still lived in the woman's heart. "When and where were you married?"

A rush of hot color stained the young woman's smooth cheeks. "Joel is not my son but my half sister's." She then forestalled the inevitable question as to why Millicent hadn't come herself. "Millie died before Joel was even a year old." She fumbled with her reticule. "I've taken care of him since."

"You aren't much more than a child yourself," Naomi observed. "How did you manage?"

"I am nineteen, Mrs. Scott." Her level gaze didn't waver. "One does what one has to do." She glanced at Lige and caught a grudging admiration in his big eyes. A moment later, the papers crackled in her fingers, but a strange reluctance made her add, "Would you like to hear the whole story?"

Naomi nodded, but Lige said nothing. Taking his silence as a consent, Judith began with the death of their parents, the unusual closeness between the sisters, and the advent of Gideon who, according to Millie, was every storybook hero rolled into one. "I couldn't understand why he wouldn't meet me," she said. Tears sparkled on her long lashes just remembering that awful time.

"Looking back, it appears he knew he couldn't get Millie any way except by marriage." She ignored a growl of protest from Lige and rushed on. "Anyway, they went away for a brief honeymoon. I'd never seen Millie so happy as when she came back wearing a pale blue dress. She had brought a beautiful gown for me, and we got ready the next morning and waited for her husband to come." Those agonizing hours returned. "He didn't even have the courage to tell Millie all his talk about making a home where I'd always be welcome was just that, talk. He sent a Negro with a message." Judith fished it out and read the words made faint by the years.

A terrible cry burst from Lige, but Judith knew she must go on. Once told, she never intended to mention that time again. "Your son might as well have put a gun to Millie's heart. Something in her died, perhaps the will to live. A few months later, she knew she was with child, and I believe she forgave everything because of the coming of her son." Judith quickly sketched in the next months, culminating with the death of her half sister.

"She made me promise I would only search for Joel's father if the time came when I could no longer care for him."

"But why?" Naomi cried. Her hands twisted, and the pain in her eyes made Judith look away. "Surely she knew that in such circumstances. . ." She couldn't go on.

"She knew her husband's family was well-to-do and feared Joel might be taken from her," Judith said in a dull voice. Would her lagging strength help her finish this ordeal?

"Did my son know about the boy?" Lige stepped closer. His eyes gleamed.

"I don't see how he could, sir." Judith felt pity stir inside her. A man whose pride had been knifed in the way only a wayward son can do, Lige's big shoulders sagged. "We did everything possible to keep Joel's birth quiet," Judith added.

"Thank God he isn't guilty of more sins," admitted Lige, but his eyes showed that didn't lessen the magnitude of this audacious marriage and desertion. "Did he. . .do you know if he knew of your sister's death?"

Colorless, Judith shook her head. "He had no way of knowing that, I believe, because her death would not have been publicized, and Millie was known to our neighbors as Millicent Greene. When I fell so ill and didn't get my strength back, I knew I had to find him." The same fury assaulted her as when she learned of the effrontery of Millie's cowardly husband by hiding away to become a minister. "It's ironic, but the same means that alerted me to your son's whereabouts elevated him!" She intercepted the blank gaze between the Scotts but continued, "I wrote to him here in San Scipio and told him Millie died in early 1871 and asked him to contact me."

Judith heard the bellow of a terrified bullock that had escaped its master and burst into view not far from where she stood. The rage and pain resembled that in Lige Scott's voice. "Then that's why he—my son, my son!"

"Sir, I can never tell you how sorry I am to come here, but Joel must have someone in case I can't go on." Her low voice echoed in the too-silent room. Spent, Judith leaned back against the cushions of the settee.

"Then our son still doesn't know he has a child?" Naomi inquired. Her face sagged with shame. "Such a beautiful little boy to be fatherless for so many years." She patted Judith's hand. "You were right to come, my dear, although the shock is almost more than can be borne. Elijah, we will open our hearts and home to these orphaned children, both of them."

Before he could reply, two persons simultaneously entered the hall. Joel ran back in from the courtyard, his face lighted with happiness. A tall man with sun-streaked hair and an open face hurried inside. Their paths collided. A last-minute catching of the child in his arms saved Joel from a nasty fall. "Whoa, there, *muchacho.*" The man laughed down into the child's face, then went blank with astonishment. "Why, who are you?" He whirled toward his parents and Judith.

In a sudden motion, Judith sprang to her feet and planted clenched fists on her hips. "You are Gideon Carroll Scott."

He looked amazed and set Joel down. "I don't think I've had the pleasure of meeting you, miss."

"Nor I you." Judith clenched her teeth. "Joel, dear, would you go back into the courtyard for just a few minutes more?" She forced a smile.

He sighed, and she knew he sensed the undercurrents that were turning the placid room into a sea of emotion. His feet dragged, and the joy of discovery he'd shown before now was sadly lacking.

"Is something wrong?" A shadow came into the young man's blue eyes. "That child, he looks so much like—"

"Why shouldn't he look like the Scotts?" Judith cried, her nerves strained to the breaking point. "He's *your* son!"

"*What?*" Gideon stepped toward her. "Are you an escaped lunatic?"

"Gideon!" Lige thundered, and Judith observed the profound change in the man. His shoulders squared. Life flowed back into his face and, with it, the darkest fury she had ever seen in a human's face.

"What's this all about?" Gideon demanded. He planted fingers in her shoulders and held fast. "How dare you come here with such a story!"

"Do you deny it?" Judith tore herself from the cruel grasp.

Gideon's face flamed until he looked like an avenging angel. "Deny it! My dear woman, you must be mad."

She lost control. "Then deny this." She snatched the carefully preserved wedding certificate and thrust it into his face. "Gideon Carroll Scott and Millicent Butler, my half sister, united in holy matrimony, July 29, 1869, in New Orleans. More like unholy matrimony." A sob escaped despite her best efforts. "You married her, carried her off for a few days, then deserted her. Your child was born the following April."

"It's a lie!" Gideon yanked the paper from her hands. His face turned ghastly. "I never even heard of a Millicent Butler, let alone married one. Father, Mother, you don't believe this woman, do you?"

"Do you deny you were in New Orleans at that time?" Judith prodded, while something inside her wished he could.

"Of course not. Cyrus and I were both there. I'd just started studying to be a minister." He looked at the wedding certificate, then started. Color poured into his face, and he squinted and peered again. "This isn't my handwriting, even though it looks like it."

"And I suppose this isn't, either." Judith produced the farewell note in its dilapidated state.

"I don't understand." Gideon went white to the lips. His eyes blazed like twin coals. Then recognition set in. "There's been a terrible mistake."

Why should her heart leap? What was this stranger to her? Judith's nails dug into her palms until they ached.

"What have you done, Gideon?" Lige marched to his son, his face a mask of stone.

"Why are you so willing to believe that I am guilty?" Gideon shouted. "I tell you, I've never seen this woman or heard of her sister." All the longing of years for his father's approval blended into his cry of despair. "If you want the truth, find Cyrus. It would be like him to marry someone using my name, and he's always been able to imitate my writing."

Crack. Lige's mighty open hand struck his younger son with such power that Gideon staggered. Bright red replaced the white of his left cheek. A suspicion of froth ringed Lige's mouth. "How *dare* you accuse your brother of your wickedness? I won't have it, do you hear?"

Gideon didn't give an inch. His eyes blazed. "Can't you even trust me until I can prove you're wrong? I have no son, and I have had no wife."

Something inside Judith turned over. If ever a voice and face proclaimed the truth, Gideon's did. Uncertainty gnawed at her. Could this young man honestly be the victim of a sadistic joke?

"Judy, are you all right?" Joel's eyes looked enormous, and he raced back inside to his sole source of comfort. "Everyone's yelling. Let's go somewhere else."

Where? rang in her brain, yet she kept her voice quiet. "If someone will drive us back to San Scipio, we'll go away. Perhaps I can find work in El Paso." *If we have money enough to get there*, she thought. Suddenly Pete's weathered face came to mind. Surely he'd help her, lend her enough to go on. Besides, God wouldn't let them down, ever.

"The child stays here." Lige, more in control than ever, belligerently stepped between Judith and the door.

"My Judy, too?" Joel rushed in where angels would have hesitated on the doorstep. He looked anxiously up at Lige.

"Of course." With a visible effort, the tall man tempered his voice. "Boy, do you like horses?"

Joel allowed himself to be sidetracked. "P'r'aps. That's what Judy says I must say when I don't know." His enchanting, innocent laugh lightened the atmosphere. He looked around the room, cocked his head at Gideon, and said, "Why do you look at my Judy so? Don't you like her?" He sat down on a stool and put one hand beneath his elbow and his chin on the supported hand. "We came such a long way. But if you don't want us, we have to go."

Naomi gave a little cry and clapped her hands. "We want you very much, child. You're our own—" She bit off the end of the sentence and called to the maid. "Carmelita, take Miss Butler and Joel to the big room with the alcove." She then explained to Judith, "It has a small bed in the alcove for Joel and a large bed for you. I'll send up hot water immediately. Would you like supper trays instead of coming down tonight?"

Her thoughtfulness, coming so close on the cease-fire of hostilities, left Judith unsteady. "If you'd be so kind. I know Joel is exhausted."

"So are you." Naomi put a strong arm around the frail shoulders that had carried such heavy burdens for so many years. "Don't worry about anything. Whatever has happened is done and not the child's or your fault. You are welcome here, and we will talk later when all of us are less upset. Now go with Carmelita."

It seemed a long walk from the big hall to the airy rooms, but Judith rightfully attributed it to her fatigue. Even Joel acted subdued. Unused to scenes and fiercely loyal to his Judy, the little boy clung to her hand and walked sedately instead of skipping as he normally did. "We don't have to stay," he repeated after Carmelita left them. "It's nice, though." He walked to the window and looked out into the courtyard. "The flowers are pretty. Did God make them?"

"Yes, dear." Almost too tired to respond, Judith strove to bring a more normal tone into their conversation. Time enough later to sort everything out. First she must bathe Joel, see that he ate, force food into herself, and put her charge to bed. She hadn't counted on Naomi Scott's graciousness. She herself appeared with the maids bearing hot water and supervised the filling of the tub screened off at one end of the room. She then carried Joel to her own quarters, returning later with a rosy boy in place of a dusty one. Naomi remained with them until Joel fell asleep, then personally tucked Judith into an enormous bed, plumped the pillows, and dropped an impulsive kiss on the young woman's forehead.

"Don't worry about a thing." Her gaze turned toward the worn Bible. "You're a Christian, aren't you?"

"Yes, for all my life."

"I am so glad." Naomi patted Judith's hand, then knelt by the bedside. "Our Father, we thank Thee for the gift of Thy Son. We thank Thee for sending these, Thy precious children, to us. We do not always comprehend Thy ways, but help them to know Thy loving care is around them, and grant them peace and rest. In the name of Thy Son, Jesus. Amen."

When the tears of weakness crowded Judith's eyelids, she simply squeezed Naomi's hand, which rested on hers, and listened for the closing of the massive door. She had thought she would lie awake for hours. Instead, she fell into a deep and dreamless sleep.

Judith awakened at sunrise when a cock crowed. The thick adobe walls shut out the sounds of the house, but through the open window came noises she had come to identify with life in the West. Too tired to care, she gratefully remembered Naomi's admonition to sleep as long as she could. She turned over and closed her eyes again.

"Judy, are you awake?"

She stirred from the fathoms of deep sleep to discover Joel in his nightshirt standing by her bed. Automatically, she scooted over and made room for him. The long rest had done its work well. Today might bring more problems, but at least she had survived the confrontation with Gideon.

Her heart lurched, and again she wondered why she should find it impossible to believe Gideon Carroll Scott's treachery. She considered it with part of her mind while answering Joel's chatter. Connecting such a frank-faced young man, who looked every bit the part of a man who longed to serve his God with his all, with what she knew of Millie's husband and Joel's father took more imagination than she owned. If she hadn't had the marriage certificate, the farewell note, and the young man's face stamped in miniature every time she looked at Joel, Judith could never have believed what had to be true.

"Judy. *Judy!*" Joel shook her arm hard, slid from bed, and ran to the window looking out toward the corral. "Come quick. There's a baby horse looking in our window!"

Almost as excited as the child, Judith dropped her meditations and sped across the large, richly carpeted room. *Dear God,* she prayed, *we've been in some pretty strange places, but this is the first time You've ever led us to one where we wake up and find a horse staring in at us.* Laughing at herself, she hugged Joel and said, "Let's get dressed. Who knows what's next?"

Chapter 8

From that first San Scipio sermon, Gideon loved his chosen work. He rode early and late seeking out isolated families, bringing the kind of ministry they most needed: not always a retelling of the gospel, but a living message of Jesus Christ that permitted and encouraged his participation in whatever the family might be doing. Whether rounding up strays, branding cattle, or even digging postholes, the most hated cowboy chore, Gideon had experienced the tasks on the Circle S and was an able helper.

"I never heerd tell o' no preacher doin' sich things," one grandmother protested. "Jest don't seem fittin'."

"Now, Granny." Gideon gave her the smile her Irish grandmother said warmed the cockles of her heart. "Remember how Jesus worked in the carpenter shop? I'll bet if He were to drop in, He wouldn't command you to leave bawling cows that needed herding. No, He'd take care of the work first, then have words for you of an evening, when the sun's ready to hit the bunk and let the moon have a chance to shine."

"You shore talk purty. Say, Gideon, when're you aimin' to find yourself a gal and git hitched?"

Gideon threw back his head and laughed. Mischief twinkled in his eyes. "Granny, are you proposing to me? Why, I believe you are. You're blushing all over your face."

"Go 'long with you, Gideon Scott. Don't you know a preacher's s'posed to be serious?" she scolded, even though she couldn't help laughing.

Gideon shook his head. "I find a whole lot more places in the Bible where we're told to be glad and rejoice than to go around with a face so long it's in danger of getting stepped on." He warmed to his subject. "When Jesus says He came to bring life and to bring it more abundantly, I believe that included real happiness and laughter. If more folks could see that, more of them would want to follow Christ."

"I plumb agree," the old woman said surprisingly. "There's enough miz'ry in life without it creepin' into religion."

"Good for you, Granny!" Gideon shook her hand, amazed at her hard strength and insight into things eternal. "Tell you what. First time I get to feeling bad, I'll ride back over here and let you preach me a sermon."

"I kin do it, too," she boasted, and her dark eyes sparkled. "How do you think I raised me five fine sons?"

Her question perched on Gideon's saddle horn when he turned the sorrel mare Dainty Bess toward home. Of all the horses on the Circle S, he liked her best, but he saved her for riding and chose heavier stock for working the range. From earliest dawn to last daylight, he rode and roped, talked with his heavenly Father, and prepared down-to-earth, practical sermons suited to the San Scipio area. No lofty sentiments could ease the harshness of life in West Texas in the 1870s. Gideon's prayers that incorporated pleas for today's strength and tomorrow's hope offered his widely scattered and diverse congregation a rope to which they could cling in times of trouble and happiness.

Cyrus's continued absence remained the one thorn in Gideon's side. The young minister had made surreptitious inquiries but so far had run into only dead-end trails. If a tornado had swooped down and clutched Cyrus, his disappearance couldn't have been more complete. Again and again, Gideon prayed for his brother, whose wasted, reckless life lay heavy on Gideon's soul. "Oh, God," he cried a hundred times. "Somehow, make Cyrus see and know how much he needs You." Yet weeks drifted by with no trace of the missing brother.

That one thorn also wedged itself into the new and tenuous relationship Gideon and his father had begun to develop. Gideon spent every spare minute he could find trying in some small way to replace Cyrus. Not in Lige's affections, but merely in working on the Circle S. While he would never be as proficient in range work as the superbly trained Cyrus, the long hours in the saddle plus practicing with rope and gun brought their rewards.

"Seems strange for a preacher to be practicing shooting," he told Lige one late afternoon when he had brought down a hawk threatening the baby chicks Naomi adored.

"God forbid you ever have to use that gun except in times like these." Lige nodded at the downed hawk. His face, which had grown more downcast since Cyrus rode out, turned hard. "You won't always be where you're known and have the backing of friends. Son, when that time comes, remember this: If those who test you know you can shoot and shoot well, chances are you're less likely to have to than if you never packed a gun and relied on being a preacher to protect you."

It was a long speech for his father. Gideon took a deep breath. "Thanks." The word *Dad* hovered on his lips but wouldn't come out. Not since Cyrus left had he felt he could say it, for Lige had returned to the forbidding father figure of childhood.

One morning when Gideon had ridden into San Scipio, Sheriff Collins sought him out. Long and lanky, his soft-spoken way hid iron nerves and sinews. "Heard anything of Cyrus lately?" he asked in his searching drawl.

"Why, no," Gideon said, his heart beating faster. "Have you?"

The sheriff shifted his quid and spat an accurate stream of tobacco juice into the street. "Naw. Just curious as to why he'd ride out so suddenlike." He grinned. "I consider myself a brave man, but I don't plan to ask your daddy about it."

"I don't blame you." A look of understanding passed between them. Gideon decided to lay his cards on the table. "Sheriff, it's half killing my father. You know how he is about Cyrus."

"Huh, everybody knows. Rotten shame how blind a man can be when he sets such store in his son and won't hear a thing against him." A heavy hand came down on Gideon's shoulder. "Is there anything I should know?"

"I've racked my brain over and over. All I know is that Cyrus planned to be at the church dedication. Then he rode into town, got some kind of letter, and said he was riding out." Gideon didn't add the part about Cyrus's strange talk, asking Gideon to promise he wouldn't go back on him, forgiving seventy times seven and the like. "All I could figure is that Cyrus had been gambling and someone threatened to come collect. Father hates any kind of betting. Even Cyrus couldn't get away with that." He wrinkled his forehead. "Except if that's true, why hasn't whoever wrote the letter shown up?"

The sheriff glanced both ways. No one lounged within earshot. "Something you ought to know. I saw the envelope. It came from New Orleans."

A rush of blood flowed to Gideon's head. *New Orleans?* But Cyrus was only there that one time five years ago. He never writes letters, didn't write to me once while I was gone. Who could be trying to contact him after all this time?" The idea troubled Gideon. Surely if Cyrus had been up to his usual tricks, it wouldn't take this long for a cheated or irate gambler to trace him.

Sheriff Collins spat again. "If I were a gambling man, which I ain't, I'd bet that if I could find that letter, some of the mystery might get solved." He grinned companionably at the younger man. "Now, it's none of my affair 'less I get a complaint. Like I said, I'm just interested."

"Thanks, Sheriff." Gideon slowly walked into the general store and made his purchases, absently noting the way Lucinda Curtis bustled around and made a great show of efficiency in waiting on him. He tipped his wide hat politely and backed out, then filled his saddlebags and headed home. *Would it be wrong to search Cyrus's room?* Never had he trespassed on the unwritten law of privacy Lige established between the brothers when they were small. Did the desire to know where Cyrus had gone—and why—warrant breaking this tradition?

Anything that would straighten things out and bring Cyrus back to Lige was justified. Gideon couldn't bear seeing his father turn more and more inward with each passing day. Naomi hadn't expressed her concern verbally, but it showed in her gaze at her husband.

Rejoicing in the thickness of walls that muffled and silenced movement in other parts of the adobe ranch house, long after every light had been extinguished for the night, Gideon crept into his brother's room. Except for the clothing that Rosa and Carmelita had hung up, nothing in the room showed signs of entry. Gideon forced himself to go through each drawer of the tall chiffonier, each pocket of the clothing in the closet. Not a telltale scrap of paper showed itself. But why should it? Gideon remembered as clearly as if it had been only an hour ago how Cyrus's fingers had strayed to his breast pocket that morning in the courtyard.

"Too bad he didn't change clothes," the searcher muttered. He tried to put things together in sequence. Evidently, Cyrus had received bad news from the letter, yet it had been the night before when he demanded loyalty from his brother! Had Cyrus carried a guilty secret, perhaps for a long time, that he knew would be exposed someday but hadn't expected it to happen so soon? It seemed the only explanation. Either that or a premonition of trouble ahead so strong it forced him to ensure Gideon's support.

Gideon carefully replaced everything he had disturbed in his fruitless search.

He also spent a long time praying for Cyrus before he fell asleep.

Several days later, Gideon headed for home in the late afternoon on Dainty Bess. Usually the horse whinnied when he turned her toward the ranch house and corrals, but today she stepped as lightly and smooth gaited as if they had been on the trails for an hour.

"Good girl." Gideon patted her silky mane, then relaxed in the saddle. One of her best qualities was the little guidance she needed, especially on the trail home. Gideon's mind stayed free to pursue his thoughts and dreams. When the mare stopped of her own accord on the mesa above the ranch, Gideon was roused from his comfortable slumped position in the saddle.

"Dust cloud. Wonder who's at the ranch?" Gideon waited to let Bess's heavy breathing from their climb return to normal, then headed down the trail. "It's Ben, from town. He's sure making tracks with that buggy." Gideon raised one eyebrow. The towheaded youngster's driving skill and carefulness beyond his years certainly didn't match the way that horse and carriage pelted away from the Circle S.

Dread filled Gideon. Perhaps someone in town had been hurt or needed him. Or something had happened to Cyrus. . . He touched Dainty Bess with his boot heels, scorning the spurs most cowboys used. "Hi-yi, Ben!" Bess picked up speed and flashed down the winding wagon road toward Ben. Gideon pulled her in short, and Ben stopped his panting horse. "Somebody hurt or dead?" Gideon demanded.

Ben shook his head. "Comp'ny at the ranch."

Why does the boy look so upset? Gideon wondered. A reader of faces, he saw disillusionment, anger, and the desire to get away rise in Ben's eyes. "Is something wrong?"

"Find out for yourself." Ben clucked to the horse and drove off, this time at a pace more fitting for the climb from valley floor to the mesa top.

"Something's sure eating him," Gideon commented and watched the buggy until it turned the bend and slipped out of sight. "First time he hasn't been friendly." He thought of the faithful way Ben and other young people came to church and of the high hopes he held for their salvation. He knew Ben had accepted the Lord in his heart, but so far he hadn't made it public. Gideon knew he would wait until the Holy Spirit did its work, so he didn't push. Besides, boys like Ben—and the way he'd been at fifteen—had to be *led* to the Master, never driven.

In spite of his eagerness to discover who Ben had delivered to the ranch and why it upset the boy, Gideon rubbed Dainty Bess down and watered her before going into the house. He hesitated on the cool porch, held for a moment by the same feeling he'd experienced those times before a storm. Silence, ominous and threatening, filled him with a reluctance to step across the threshold into the big hall.

To make up for his anxiety, he hurried inside, his long steps eating up the polished floor. A small blue and white and gold whirlwind raced in front of him. Unable to stop his momentum, Gideon snatched up the little boy and held him with strong arms. "Whoa there, *muchacho*." First he laughed, but then as he peered into the child's eyes, he felt the blood drain from his face. "Why, who are you?" He turned toward his parents. A strange young woman exploded from a settee and planted clenched fists on her hips. Travel-stained and dusty, with dark brown eyes that matched her coiled, braided hair, she glowed with an unearthly light. "You are Gideon Carroll Scott."

How could five simple words carry so much hatred and reproach? Gideon mumbled something and put down the child, who slowly went into the courtyard at the stranger's bidding. Who was she, and who was the child who looked enough like the Scotts to be one?

Ice water trickled in his veins. "Is something wrong?" Gideon asked. "That child, he looks so much like—"

Then it came. The squall Gideon had known lay waiting behind the closed ranch house door. "Why shouldn't he look like the Scotts?" Beautiful in her scorn, the young woman faced and indicted him. "He's your son."

The room spun. *Is the woman mad?* An eternity of accusations followed, along with a wedding certificate bearing his name. *Dear God, this can't be happening!* Gideon turned to his parents for comfort. *They can't believe this preposterous claim, can they?* His heart turned to a lead ball and sank to his boots. Lige believed the charge. It showed in every terrible twitch of his shaken body.

"This isn't my handwriting." He tried to defend himself. The girl produced a second piece of evidence, and light broke. *Cyrus.* Cyrus, who would stop at nothing to get what he wanted and leave others to bear the blame and shame. A flash of insight solved the strange pleas for seventy times seven forgiveness. *No, God, not this time. Let Father see what his precious older son has done.*

Gideon cried out his defense and received a blow that bruised his face but cut into his heart. Even the flicker of doubt in the woman's eyes when he proclaimed his belief that Cyrus had done this couldn't change a father's loyalty to one son at the expense of another. The temper Gideon had inherited but tried to control blazed. "Can't you even trust me until I can prove you're wrong? I have no son, and I have had no wife!" Again uncertainty showed in the watching dark eyes. Then the child called Joel ran back, frightened, needing reassurance. Gideon couldn't move, not when the stranger said they would go. Not when Lige protested. Not even when Joel asked with childish perception, "Why do you look at my Judy so? Don't you like her?" Only when Carmelita led the visitors away did strength return to Gideon's limbs and free him from the paralysis of shock.

"Father, I have never asked much from you, but I ask you now. Do you honestly believe that I am capable of marrying a woman, then deserting her?" Gideon knew his future hung in the balance. He saw doubt rise in his father's eyes. He saw the massive head begin to shake from side to side and the mouth form the word, "No." Then a transformation killed the final hope struggling for life in the young minister's breast. His mouth tasted the ashes of dishonor placed on an innocent man.

"The child is a Scott." Lige's sonorous voice rolled his verdict into the hall, where it hung in the air.

"I am not the only Scott who lived in New Orleans in the summer of 1869," Gideon said rashly, as if pouring kerosene on the fire of Lige's reactions.

"Only a sniveling coward puts blame on a man who is not here to defend himself," Lige bellowed. He raised his hand to strike again the son who dared accuse his favorite.

"*No, Elijah!*" Naomi planted herself squarely in front of her enraged husband. "We have never known Gideon to lie." Magnificent in her rare opposition to the lord of the household, she held him at bay in defense of her man-child. "There is more to this than we know. I feel that. Until we find the truth, we will keep the child and the young woman here."

"The truth? Woman, what more evidence do you want than a marriage certificate in your son's writing—" Gideon winced at the words *your son*, but Lige went on. "Also a note and the child himself!" Suspicion blackened his face. "Or are you also accusing Cyrus?"

"I am accusing *no one*, despite what you call evidence." Naomi didn't give an inch. Her face the color of parchment, her blue eyes shone with the fire of motherhood roused on behalf of her young. Gideon's cold heart warmed. All the adoration and love the lonely little boy had poured out on Naomi when denied his father's affection paled into insignificance when compared with what he felt for her now.

"Someday I will prove what I say is true," he promised. Before either could reply, Gideon turned on his heel and went out, his steps echoing in the hall. *How? How? How?* they mocked.

By finding Cyrus. The answer came sharp and bright as a lightning flash. He must leave San Scipio, find his brother, and for the first time in his life, force Cyrus to take the consequences of his actions.

Gideon's lips twisted bitterly in sharp contrast to their usual upward tilt. Father would rage and fume, but in the end, he'd be so glad to have his object of adulation back, the anger would dwindle and vanish. The presence of a grandson's softening influence would finish the job. Lige would cling to the boy as a second Cyrus.

"Father will also probably coerce Cyrus into marrying the woman," Gideon whispered into Dainty Bess's mane when she came at his whistle. "God forbid! Any woman who marries Cyrus will be in torment, especially one as untouched and frail as she." Yet what else could she do? Her gown bore mute witness of poverty. Her eyes showed she would never have sought out Joel's father unless she had come to the limits of her strength and ability to care for her nephew. How old was she? Eighteen? Twenty? She had cared for four-year-old Joel when little more than a child herself.

Respect stirred within him. Although he hated what she had done to his life with her false accusation, how could he help but admire a plucky girl who had become a mother by necessity? Gideon thought of the look in her eyes when she first announced him as Joel's father, something she obviously believed. Never before had he seen reflected in anyone's face the belief that he was despicable, beyond contempt.

His jaw squared. "Dear God," he breathed and swung into the saddle for a healing ride, forgetful of the fact he hadn't eaten since breakfast. "Any man who would do what she believes I did to her sister deserves that look." Shame for Cyrus and the passionate wish his brother had been different rose into a crescendo of protest. "Someday, somehow, with Your help, I'm going to prove to Father and to her I am innocent!"

Yet a jeering voice so real it rang in Gideon's ears and beat into his tired brain continued the measured cadence begun by his boot heels in the hall. Over and over the questions *How? How? How?* tormented him until he thought he would go mad.

Chapter 9

In the mysterious way Noami had always used to calm her stubborn, volatile husband, she again prevailed. Lige's first decision to disclaim Gideon as his son fell before her reason. While Gideon and Dainty Bess spent the night outdoors and an emotionally exhausted Judith slept soundly, Naomi's quiet voice and Lige's rumbling continued. Shortly before dawn, Naomi fell into a restless sleep, but Lige addressed Almighty God. Hadn't God put fathers in control of their sons? he reasoned. The Bible offered countless examples of what happened when those fathers allowed wickedness to creep into their homes. Lige therefore told God what he planned to do to straighten out the mess, then fell asleep justified.

For the sake of bright-faced Joel, whose winning ways had already softened Lige's stern outlook on life, all discussion was held in abeyance until Carmelita took the boy to the kitchen, where Rosa welcomed him with a smile and a hug. Lige waved the family into a small sitting room. "I have considered this whole unpleasant matter," he began.

Gideon made a sound of protest that died in his throat when his father glared at him. He glanced at Judith, white-faced and still. *How horrible this must all be for her,* he thought. First the long, tiring trip, then a plunge into confusion. Although she admitted she had slept, dark circles still haunted her eyes.

"Your mother has requested that I wait to pass final judgment on your actions." Lige's stony face showed doing so went against everything he believed. "Very well. You say Cyrus is somehow involved, which of course is impossible, but I will give you one month to see if you can locate and bring him back to the Circle S." A world of longing tinged his words. "Miss Butler, according to your story, you sent a letter to Gideon?"

The accused minister could keep silent no longer. "I never received a letter, but when Cyrus said he was leaving, he had a letter in his pocket." Gideon ignored Naomi's warning look. "Sheriff Collins in town said he saw a letter from New Orleans."

"Sheriff Collins?" Lige's face turned purple. "You dared discuss Cyrus with *him?*"

"Father, he asked where Cyrus had gone and brought up seeing the letter."

Cunning and pride resulted in Lige barking, "And did he say he saw the name of the person the letter was addressed to?"

Gideon's heart sank, knowing which turn the conversation had taken. "No."

"See?" Lige turned triumphantly to his wife. "Miss Butler's letter, if this were it, obviously came to Gideon."

"Then why did Cyrus open it?" Gideon demanded. "You trained us from the cradle that a sealed letter to another family member was not to be tampered with."

Lige shrugged. "Perhaps the seal had been broken."

"Then why didn't Cyrus just give me the message? Why did he ride away and say he might never come back?"

"I am not on trial here," Lige roared. "Neither is your brother. Before God, if it were not for your mother, you'd be sent packing." The veins in his neck became cords, pulsing with angry blood. "Gideon Carroll Scott, I offer you a month, for the sake of Naomi's pleading. If by that time you haven't proved to my satisfaction your innocence in this affair, San Scipio will know of your guilt. That is my promise."

Any chance of ever proving Cyrus guilty to his father seemed slim. Yet a month could change much. "I will leave today." Gideon stood, and his mouth set in a straight, grim line.

"Remember, one month. Not a day longer." The judgment followed Gideon when he stepped into the hall. Yet he was not to leave the ranch without one more disturbing interview. An hour later, he had packed what he needed, saddled Dainty Bess, and bade his mother good-bye. Lige had ridden out after delivering his ultimatum without another word to his son. Torn between what lay ahead and had been, Gideon lightly mounted Bess.

"Wait, oh, please, wait!" Judith ran toward him, casting a furtive glance back at the house. She obviously didn't want to be observed. Her dark eyes caught gleams from the sun, and she looked distraught. "Mr. Scott, I don't see how you can be innocent, but if I have falsely accused you—if indeed this brother has used your name—I hope you find him."

The unexpectedness of her seeking him out left Gideon speechless.

She stepped closer and peered up into his face. "Good-bye, Mr. Scott. May God—" She broke off as if not knowing what to say to him.

"Miss Butler, even if I can never prove it, I am not guilty in spite of the apparent evidence against me. Do you believe me?" Suddenly it seemed imperative that she do so.

"I don't know. It doesn't seem possible that you, a minister of God. . .you seem so honest and yet. . ." Her voice trailed off.

"I thank you for coming out here," he said softly. Then he touched Dainty Bess with his heels and rode away, not looking back but still able to see the troubled girl with her dark eyes that tried to look into his very soul.

Judith's slight change of manner toward him raised his spirits. So did the long, impassioned prayer he made near a big rock off the trail a few miles from the Circle S. "Dear God, You know I am innocent. You know I have no way to prove it. Your power can open doors I don't even know are there. You can uplift me and lead me to Cyrus. Surely this is why he ran away."

Gideon determinedly put aside what could happen if he caught up with his brother. By some means, Cyrus must be made to return to the ranch and clear his brother's name. Yet as the days flew into a week, then another, doubts clouded the searcher's mind. He could not find a trace of Cyrus. What if all these weeks he had lain somewhere in the canyons or over a precipice, the victim of an accident or foul play? The thought whitened Gideon's lips. He hadn't even considered such a thing, but now it seemed highly possible. Cyrus often consorted with evil men who knew he liked to carry money on him. Why hadn't he thought of such a thing before?

"Because of the way he left," Gideon told Dainty Bess. "He planned to go for some unnamed reason. I believe Judith Butler's letter forced his hand."

More days passed. By the end of the third week, Gideon daily stormed heaven. "Dear heavenly Father, ever since I gave my heart to You, I've tried to follow in the footsteps of Your Son. Where are You now? I need to find Cyrus. Only You know where he is. Why aren't You leading me to him?" Always after such a prayer, the young minister experienced pangs of guilt, but low anger also rose. He read the Bible, noted the promises, and prayed again.

Sometimes he wondered if the prayers even got beyond the wide sky above him. Bitterness as acrid as the alkali water he found in distant waterholes seeped into his soul. Was this how the Israelites felt when they wandered in the desert? Forsaken, deserted, and so alone they could barely go on?

Miles from the ranch with a few days left, Gideon turned back. He had considered vanishing the way Cyrus had done, but he rejected it as the coward's way out. Once more he would stand before his father and ask for mercy and trust. If Lige withheld it, Gideon would turn Dainty Bess back to the trails, never to return home.

⌀

From the moment Gideon disappeared from sight, a time of waiting began for the Circle S, especially for Judith. She often wondered what strange impulse had caused her to seek out the young man with the sun-streaked hair and starlight in his blue eyes. At times she prayed for him in a stumbling manner that reflected her troubled mind. On one hand, there was the written evidence; on the other, there was the spirit of a man who looked into her eyes and pledged his innocence. Like a weather vane subject to each change of wind, so Judith veered from disbelief to a wavering acceptance of Gideon, the minister, as compared with Gideon, husband and father. Then again, the very beauty of his face could be what deceived Millie so thoroughly. Judith grew weary thinking of it.

In those waiting days and weeks, Joel, however, thrived as never before. Besides the love Naomi and Lige had for their new grandson, the good food and fresh autumn air bolstered the joyful child. The "baby horse" that had peeked in the window that first morning became Joel's own. In a specially designed saddle Lige proudly said he had fashioned when Cyrus was small, Joel jounced and bounced around the corral pulled by a lead rope and loved every minute. He lost some of his toddler chubbiness and gained a tanned complexion from endless hours outdoors.

"Judy, are we going to stay here f'rever and f'rever?" he anxiously asked one day when they sat together in a porch swing.

"Do you like it here that much?" She held her breath, almost hating to hear the answer she knew would come.

"Oh, yes!" His twin sapphire eyes glowed. "Gramma and Gran'pa and Rosa and Carm'lita's so nice." His joy dimmed, and he scooted closer to her. "Don't you like it, too?"

"I love it." She felt his little wiggle of joy. "I just don't know if the Scotts w— want me." Judith hated herself for the break in her voice.

Joel climbed into her lap. "Don't be sad, Judy." He stroked her now rounded cheek, a result of proper food and freedom from responsibility. "Gran'pa says if you and Gideon get married, everything will be all right."

"What?" She set the child farther out on her knees so she could look directly into his face. "Joel, are you making that up?"

His sensitive lips quivered. "I don't tell stories, Judy. You said God doesn't like it."

She could still scarcely believe his childish gossip. "I know, dear, but think very hard. Did Mr. Scott really say what you told me?"

He nodded vigorously until his blond curls bounced. Anxiety still filled his eyes. "That's 'zackly what Gran'pa said. Don't you want to marry Gideon?"

"I barely know him," she retorted, then hugged Joel hard. "Don't worry about it." But she sensed the resistance in him.

"Judy, you wouldn't ever go away and leave me, would you? Not even here." He slid down from her lap and leaned against her arm. "I heard Gramma say her boy went away and left her. Not Gideon. Another boy."

"I won't leave you," she promised. Yet deep inside, the thought formed, *If this is what Elijah Scott has in mind, how can I stay?* Once the hateful idea had been so carelessly planted, Judith felt on edge. She caught the appraising looks Lige gave her now and then and appreciated the way Negro slaves must have felt on the auction block. *Sold to the highest bidder! Given in marriage to appease a powerful man who thought he could play God!* In her thoughts, Judith bitterly parodied an imaginary auctioneer.

Her turmoil continued. She wanted to ask Naomi about the diabolical plan, but she dared not. There had been no word from Gideon in the days and weeks he had been gone, and such talk would upset her more. If Naomi knew and approved of the plan, the seeds of trust growing between them would be permanently thwarted; if she didn't approve, how long could she hold out against the driving force of her husband? If only Gideon would return with Cyrus! Night after night, Judith prayed for it to happen. Nothing could be worse than this prolonged silence, not knowing what might happen next, now that Joel had innocently betrayed Lige's scheme.

The charming San Scipio area and the Circle S offered as a respite a variety of places to ride. Judith soon outgrew the capabilities of the gentle horse assigned to her and took on a trustworthy but more spirited pinto named Patchwork. By the time Joel and his pony graduated from the corral to short rides near the ranch, Judith had already explored much of the surrounding countryside. Autumn frosts had wielded their paintbrushes and left behind brilliant colors in the hills and valleys, mesas, and the deeper canyons. Joel loved to roll in piles of leaves whipped off the trees by capricious winds, but only after Judith had carefully stirred them to make sure no snakes lurked in their depths. At times, when she could put aside her fear of the future, Judith found herself laughing as she hadn't done since Millie died.

"I like you when you laugh," Joel told her solemnly, and she realized that through the years, even her best efforts to keep cheerful for him hadn't been a complete success. Now, although the strain of Gideon's return remained, the freedom given her by Naomi and Lige and the servants' eagerness to watch Joel had left its mark. Judith's favorite place to ride was the mesa top above the valley because it offered the widest view for miles around. Near the end of the fateful month of Gideon's grace, Judith found she paused there often, looking for the dust clouds that heralded riders. A few times they came, but Gideon didn't.

On the morning of the thirtieth day, Lige laid down his breakfast fork. Judith had long since learned to rise when the Scotts did and earn her keep and Joel's by working as a daughter of the house, although she was gruffly told it wasn't necessary. Joel usually awakened then, too, but this particular day, Judith had left him sleeping in his alcove.

"You know what day it is." Lige's voice sent shivers up Judith's spine that intensified when she saw that same look she had observed before, when he appeared to be measuring her.

"We know, Lige." Naomi smiled and passed freshly made apple butter to Judith for the hot biscuits Carmelita brought in. "It will be nice to have Gideon home again." She calmly ate the scrambled eggs still on her plate. "Folks have been wondering why the business you sent him on is taking so long."

Judith choked and buried her face in her napkin. When she emerged, Carmelita had gone back to the kitchen and Lige sat staring at his wife, then glanced meaningfully at Judith. She murmured a hasty, "Excuse me, please, I think I hear Joel," and escaped.

After she had helped him dress and sent him to Rosa for breakfast, she slipped out, saddled her horse as she had learned to do, and rode slowly away from the ranch. Patchwork danced a bit but settled down to her quiet command, "Steady there, girl." The now-familiar track to the mesa top invited her, and once there, she scanned each direction. Relief filled her. No riders. Yet the day had only begun, and hours would pass before the stroke of midnight.

Twice again that day Judith saddled and rode to the mesa. Once she saw Lige's mighty horse ahead of her, and she rode behind concealing bushes until he had gone. The second time, in early evening, her sporadic vigil paid off. Dust clouds in the early blue dusk hid whoever made them, but Judith's heart thudded. Suddenly afraid of the next minutes and hours, she raced back to the corral, hastily unsaddled, left Patchwork to the ministrations of one of the hands, and ran into the house.

"There are dust clouds on the road from town. I couldn't see who or how many. . . ." She couldn't bear the unreadable expression on Lige's face, the open apprehension that shone in Naomi's eyes. "I must change my clothing." She managed a shaky smile at Joel, who sat on his grandmother's lap holding a picture book.

Why had she ever thought the waiting hard, she marveled while bathing, then donning a clean dress. Naomi had wasted no time in helping her nearly destitute guest sew a few simple house gowns and one dark dress suitable for church. Judith smoothed the pale green folds, then more firmly anchored her coronet of braids. At least the wanderer would return to a well-groomed houseguest instead of a travel-worn visitor. The irrelevant thought brought color to her face.

Before she got to the big hall the family used most often in the evenings, now warmed by logs in the enormous fireplace against the ever-colder nights, Judith peered out a window that overlooked the front of the house. Dainty Bess, a horse more worn than any she had seen, stood with drooping head. Judith then fixed her gaze on the matching figure who slid from the saddle and buried his face in the horse's mane before leading her to the corral. The fruitless journey showed in the sagging shoulders and slow steps. Judith strained her eyes, desperately hoping to see a second horse, a second tired figure, and turned away stunned to realize how disappointed she felt that Gideon had come back alone.

She slipped into the warm room, and Joel ran to her. Together they curled into a massive chair, where Judith's filmy gown made a splash of light against the tapestry. The atmosphere felt thick enough to cut. Dreading the moment when Gideon would come in, she nevertheless wanted to see him. At least the uncertainty would end.

With slow steps dragging from fatigue, Gideon faced his father, his judge. Gone forever was the boyish face Judith remembered. In its place was a strange countenance whose tired body still carried a dignity of its own that could not be denied, except by the one who refused to see it.

"*Well?*" Lige's question snapped like a whip.

"I couldn't find Cyrus."

"The month is up." Relentless, unforgiving, and self-righteous, Lige Scott folded his arms across his mighty chest. "I have done what your mother asked. Now you will do what I command."

Naomi ran to her son and wordlessly embraced him. Judith saw in her a beaten woman, at least for now. Yet she released Gideon, clapped her hands sharply, and waited until Carmelita came in. "Please take Joel to his room."

"Yes, Señora." Joel ran to her, and they disappeared. Childish laughter mixed with Carmelita's natural joy drifted back, but the lines in Lige's face did not soften.

"I have considered what God would have me do," he announced.

Judith wanted to shriek. *God! When have you ever listened to God?* Every prayer she had heard him make since she arrived was telling God how things would be, a kind of after-the-plans-formed courtesy.

"Considering all the circumstances and knowing that even as God condemned Eli for not controlling his sons, so shall he not spare fathers who permit wickedness in their family, I offer you two choices." He hesitated, and the world stood still.

"The first is to confess your sins before your congregation, to repent and seek God's forgiveness, mine, and then the people's. If they will accept it, you may continue shepherding the flock."

"You ask this of *me?*" Gideon threw off all evidence of weariness. "To stand before my people and *lie?* Father, how can you?"

Judith thrilled to his final stand for justice, but Lige's answer cut into her thoughts like a knife through a ripe peach. "It is no lie." His mighty fist crashed down on the table before him. "You had your chance to prove the falsehood against your brother. Will you accept this penance?"

"Never!" Gideon drew himself to full stature. "I have never lied, and I never will to save my reputation or my life."

A curious look of—was it relief?—crept into Lige's eyes. "There is a second way. The child's future must be assured. You will marry Miss Butler, become the father to Joel you should have been for years, and take the place on the Circle S of the brother you so mysteriously drove away." Lige's thundering voice cracked on the last words.

Chapter 10

At first his father's outlandish suggestion of marriage didn't register with Gideon. His brain focused on the shocking accusation that he had been responsible for Cyrus leaving. A coldness that matched West Texas in January blanketed him. The next moment, he went white-hot, grasping the full significance of Lige's decree. But before he could respond, Judith sprang up to confront her host.

"How *dare* you play God and dispose of your son's and my lives like this?" she cried. Gideon thrilled at her courage. "You think forcing us to marry will solve everything?" Her ragged laugh reminded Gideon of a dull saw pulled through hardwood. "I know nothing of this son Cyrus who ran away, but the more I hear of him, the more I believe it's possible he did just what Gideon said, married Millie under an assumed name to cover his wicked—"

"Hold your tongue, Miss Butler. You are in no position to say what will or won't be in this household." The normal timbre of his voice added a deadliness his wildest ragings never achieved. "A grandfather's claim to Joel will outweigh yours, especially when I can give the boy everything and you are obviously penniless and dependent on charity." An unpleasant smile under raised shaggy eyebrows drove home his point more clearly than the threat.

"You couldn't be so cruel as to take Joel." Judith knew she fought against terrible odds. "I wish to God I had never let you know of Joel's birth. Better for us both to have starved in New Orleans or even for him to have been taken from me than to know he must live where every thought is controlled." Her eyes blazed. "And you call yourself a follower of the meek and lowly Jesus!" The rasping laugh came again.

"Elijah Scott, I am ashamed of you." Naomi took Judith in her arms. "If you drive this girl away—and your *second* son—I will also leave and take Joel."

"*Mother!*"

"*Naomi!*"

Gideon and Lige's exclamations blended. Disbelief gave way to knowledge. Naomi Scott meant every word she said. Her set face showed this was no careless thrust meant to hold her husband at bay. She looked at him over Judith's shoulder. "I mean it, Elijah."

"You, too, would desert me?" His face worked, an awful thing for Gideon to behold. Once he had witnessed a beaver dam crack, crumple, and fall before a relentless, flood-swollen stream. Now his father evidenced the same signs.

"First Cyrus, then Gideon, and now Naomi. What have I done to deserve such misery?" Stubborn to the end, it was apparent he could see no wrong in himself.

Gideon couldn't stand any more. His father had been driven to the dust by phantoms real and imagined, by an unreal pride in his elder son and utter faithlessness in his younger. Gideon licked dry lips and with pounding heart said, "Miss Butler, will you do me the honor of becoming my wife?"

He hadn't thought Judith could turn more pale. From the shelter of his mother's arms, Judith whipped around and stared at him. "No, oh, no!"

"Wait," he implored, conscious of Lige's open mouth and the way Naomi's arms dropped from Judith's shoulders. "It will be an empty contract shoved down our throats for Joel's sake. I knew when I came back unable to prove my innocence, I could never stay on the Circle S. God has allowed me to stand guilty in the eyes of the world and of San Scipio when they learn of this affair." He laughed bitterly. "Well, I'm through trying to preach and lead people to a God I can't trust. I'm riding away. Miss Butler, you won't be troubled with the presence of a husband, even one in name only. Don't answer now, just think about it." He turned to Lige. "Will that suit you?"

Stricken dumb by Gideon's shocking capitulation, Lige mumbled, "No need to ride off if you marry."

"There's every need," Gideon contradicted and felt his chest swell. "I wouldn't even consider such a thing if I planned to stay." He glanced at Judith, marble white and still. "Take what time you need before you answer."

"Even if she should agree, how can you accomplish this?" Naomi's eyes reflected all the doubts he felt but shoved back in favor of necessity.

"You three and Joel can go by stage to El Paso. I'll start ahead of you with Dainty Bess. We'll find a justice of the peace, and once the ceremony's over—" He shrugged, and his mouth twisted. "You'll return here, and the happy bridegroom will ride north or west or anywhere on earth that leads away from San Scipio."

Lige's stunned brain came to life. "What's to prevent you riding on and not meeting us in El Paso?"

Gideon couldn't believe what he heard. If he needed further proof his father didn't trust him, he had it in that one sentence. "It's hardly likely I'd suggest marriage if I didn't intend to be there, is it?" He swept aside any chance for an answer. "Miss Butler, just let me know if you'll be willing. I won't interfere with your life. After I'm gone for a time, you'll have no problem providing grounds for an annulment." He threw his shoulders back and walked out, little caring where he went. Had he been *loco* to propose marriage to this stranger? He shrugged. Why not? God wouldn't send a helpmeet for a minister whose faith had gone sour, a God who turned deaf ears to His follower's cries for help and left him to bear the stain of a sin not his own.

For three days and nights, Gideon spent little time at the ranch. He gave Dainty Bess a long rest and rode Circle S horses from early to late. He pilfered food from the kitchen after Rosa and Carmelita had finished for the day and avoided meals with the family. He grieved at the look in his mother's eyes, went out of his way to keep his distance from Lige, and hardened his heart against young Joel, who trotted after him. He observed Judith only from a distance. A few times he caught her dark and troubled gaze on him, but he only tipped his sombrero and walked on.

The fourth morning, early, he noted with satisfaction the toss of Bess's head that showed her eagerness to be out of the corral and back on the trail with her master. She came at his whistle, and he stood with one hand on her mane, his face toward the west. "It won't be long, old girl," he promised. She softly nickered and lipped the oats he held in his hand.

"Mr. Scott?"

Gideon turned. He hadn't heard Judith come up behind him. "Yes?" His muscles tensed. Something in her voice set blood racing through him.

"I–I have thought about your proposal." The rising sun lent color to her smooth cheeks and flicked golden glints into her dark coiled braids. Her hands lay clasped in front of her simple workdress. "For Joel's sake, if you meant what you said about going away and this not being a real marriage, I accept." Color richer than from the sunrise flowed into her face. "I never intended to marry, so it will impose no hardship on me to bear your name." Anguish filled her eyes. "I cannot face life without Joel, and as your father said, I have no way to care for him."

Filled with sudden pity, Gideon dared touch her hand for a moment only. "Look, Miss Butler..."

"Judith."

"Judith." He took a deep breath. "If the idea of this contract is repulsive to you in any way, we won't go through with it. I'll help you fight Father for the right to keep Joel and see that you find work somewhere." He watched the glad surprise that lightened her countenance give way to reality.

"I've gone over and over everything," she said simply. "I can't take the chance of falling ill again. Neither can I stay on the Circle S unless we marry, as your father wishes." Her slim shoulders shook, then squared. "I suppose in his place, I might feel the same." She managed a little smile. "It's too bad, Mr. Scott. In other circumstances, perhaps we could even have been friends."

"Then you believe in me a little?" It suddenly seemed more important than anything else in the world.

"A little."

Something within Gideon released its painful grip on his heart. He caught her hands. "Judith, if the time ever comes that I can prove my innocence, may I come back? I'm not asking any more of you than what we've agreed on," he hastily added when color rose to her hairline. "Since God has forsaken me, I need to have a dream."

"God never forsakes us, Gideon." She looked earnestly into his eyes. "Right now it seems that way to you, but no matter where you ride, remember, He's there."

He started to speak, to protest and deny, but Judith said, "Perhaps one day you will return, absolved of guilt." Her voice dropped to a whisper. "Shall we tell your fath—your parents?"

"Yes." He released her hands and followed her into the house.

Less than a week later, Judith Butler and Gideon Carroll Scott were married in a dusty El Paso office by a justice of the peace who mumbled what should have been beautiful words. Gideon thought he would scream. What a far cry from the joyous weddings he had performed! When he looked at the young woman beside him, however, an excitement he hadn't counted on shook him to his carefully polished boots. How beautiful she looked in a soft yellow and white gown, yet how little he knew of its past. Joel innocently repeated Judith's explanation about the dress.

"Judy said it came with us from New Orleans," Joel marveled. "In the bottom of the trunk. Mama brought it to Judy even before there was me, when she came home from getting married. Isn't it funny?" Pearly white teeth and a laugh like chiming bells made Joel roll with mirth. "Now Judy's getting married in the very same dress."

Had she worn it to test him? Gideon wondered. If he really had married Millicent, surely he would recognize the gown. Curse Cyrus! Not only had Cyrus ruined his opportunity to minister in San Scipio, he had blotted out all chances for a normal life. What would it be like to have Judith as his real wife, to ride and laugh and love and serve with him? The scales dropped from Gideon's inner vision. He stared at Judith and missed some of what the justice of the peace was droning.

He loved her. Of all the girls in the world, how could God allow him to meet and marry Judith Butler, whose best efforts at comforting him only came to trusting and believing in him a little?

"Place the ring on her finger and repeat after me," the official ordered.

Gideon obediently took the slim hand in his and slid on the plain gold ring he had purchased in El Paso. "I, Gideon, take thee, Judith. . ." A sudden longing to take her and ride away to a place where they could build a new life with Joel left him weak with longing, regret, and a renewed anger at Cyrus. He finished his vows, heard her low responses, and felt her hand tremble in his. Caught up in the desire for his marriage to be more than an empty contract, when the justice of the peace said, "You may kiss your bride," Gideon bent and kissed Judith full on the lips.

"Oh!" Reproach crept into her eyes, red to her face.

"Must a man apologize for kissing his wife?" Gideon recklessly whispered. Spurred by the knowledge that he was about to ride away forever, he kissed her a second time, then hurried her away from the curious eyes of the amazed witnesses. Once outside, he swung into the saddle and picked up the reins.

"Gideon, when are you coming home?" Joel called from the circle of Judith's arms.

"I don't know." His heart ached. Somehow he couldn't say the word *never*. "Father, Mother, good-bye."

Naomi's steady gaze never left her son's. "*Vaya con Dios.*" *Go with God.*

Gideon looked at his father, stunned to see him nodding, silently adding his benediction. Last of all, he turned sideways in the saddle and faced Judith. The red lips he had kissed moved in a wordless farewell, and something in her eyes flickered, an expression he could not describe or understand.

In another moment, he would bawl like a heifer stuck in a thicket. To cover the love he knew must be shining from his face, Gideon mockingly called, "Good-bye, Mrs. Scott," and pressing his heels into the horse's sides, rode away.

His added words, "God keep you, my darling," were lost in the clatter of his horse's hooves and died undelivered in the dusty air.

❧

The tumbleweed trail swallowed Gideon as it had swallowed hundreds of pioneers before him. Old, young, wicked, misunderstood, restless, and driven, they thronged west, away from homes and families. They were a breed apart in a land that cared less about a man's past than what he would become.

Into this new world that made West Texas look tame by comparison rode Gideon, tormented by God's failure to help him and his new love for a wife he could never claim. In lonely campfires, he saw her smile; sunrise on the water brought back the dawning day when she said she would marry him. Her dark eyes stared at him from every shady trail, and her spirit rode beside him until he sought out the company of others, no matter how undesirable, to drive away memories. In the wasteland between sleep and waking when no man can control his thoughts, Gideon dreamed of a day when he could go back honorably. He awakened, haunted by the realization he had nothing to offer her even if he proved Cyrus's guilt and cleared his own name. Judith had miraculously retained her deep faith in God through everything life dealt her, whereas he, a minister, had not. His broken faith and corroding soul could never be "equally yoked" with Judith's unswerving faith.

A hundred times he told Dainty Bess, "If only things had been different, what a minister's wife she would be!" He often felt guilty for marrying her, although she had asserted she had no interest in marriage. Suppose she met someone who changed her mind? Would she feel bound by those mumbled vows and give up a chance for happiness? He writhed, jealously cringing at the thought of Judith as another man's wife.

Weeks later, he rode into the mining country of Colorado through snow that clogged the horse's hooves and slowed them until he wondered if they could make it. His present apathy left him caring little for his own life, but he pressed on because of his faithful horse. Bess deserved better than death in a blizzard because her cowardly owner holed up and froze. Now at the bottom of his stores of flour, beans, and rice, and without hope of finding fresh meat, blood rushed into his face when he reached to the very bottom of his saddlebag and found a small sack. "What on earth—" Gideon stared at the contents. *Money.* His cold, bewildered brain couldn't understand. Had some outlaw who crossed his trail and shared his grub left it there, a rude payment for kindness, stolen from some bank?

Suspicion crystallized and became belief. The odd look in Lige's face, especially just before he rode away from El Paso, provided the answer. Had Father carefully hidden the money, knowing Gideon would only find it when he had exhausted his reserves?

From despair to renewed determination, Gideon knew now he would go on. He would search and find Cyrus or somehow make the folks back home proud, the folks and Judith. For the first time in days, he permitted himself to think of her. Strange how after all this time, every meeting with her stood etched against the stormy background of their acquaintance. Most often in his thoughts, he saw her in that yellow and white dress, his unclaimed bride.

Wise in the ways of evil men, Gideon sewed his money into his clothing and kept out only enough to hire rude lodgings for the winter. He couldn't expose Dainty Bess to the freezing days and colder nights. Besides, until spring came and he could travel, it didn't matter where he stayed. Gideon settled down into his new world and became part of it.

For the first time, he patronized the gambling halls, never to bet heavily but enough to feel the deadly hold on men's hearts and souls. Was this how Cyrus had felt, urged on and radiant when winning, desperate when luck smiled on others and turned a cold shoulder on him? In an amazing streak of luck, Gideon won a sum large enough to send a gleam into the eyes of those at the table. Unwilling to become the target of men who thought nothing of killing for gold, he took advantage of an old trapper's offer to accompany him on his lines and get away from town. All winter, he remained with the mountain man but refused to go mining the next spring.

"You've been good to me," he told the bearded miner turned trapper. "Here, take this grubstake. Find yourself a mine."

"If I do, I'll find you and pay it back," the man promised. But Gideon laughed and rode away. The chances of striking it rich always loomed large in the men's minds.

He drifted north through Colorado and Wyoming, then into Montana. Spring, summer, and fall, he hired out on ranches, glad for the riding and roping. Yet in late fall, almost a year from his hasty wedding and departure from Texas, he faced himself in a bunkhouse mirror far from home and sighed. Money, he had. Comrades, as many as he would let be friends. Peace, there was none.

He scowled. *Was there no spot on earth where he could be at peace with the past?* Drifting hadn't been the answer, but neither had ignoring God. He remembered the kindliness of the trapper and the long, companionable tramps on the trap line. The next morning, he quit his job and rode south in search of another quiet winter like the year before. To his amazement, hordes of people had poured into the area.

"What's happening?" he demanded of a red-faced cowhand hitching his horse to a rail before a new saloon.

"Where yu been, mister? Thought everyone knew about the boom." The amiable cowpoke grinned and told Gideon a miner had struck it rich nearby, bought half the town, and was "nee-go-she-ating" for the other half. "If yu want a job, his office is over there." The hand pointed to a new log building across the busy street.

Curious, Gideon ambled over and was met with a bear hug like he'd never had before. The strike-it-rich miner was the same man who had taken Gideon on his line and been grubstaked by the Texas rider. His gratitude knew no limits. He installed Gideon in the best room in the finest hotel that had sprung up and opened an account for him in the new bank that made the young man's eyes pop.

He also gave Gideon some advice. "Son, I don't know where you came from, but if you're as smart as you appear to be, you'll buy yourself a ranch somewhere, maybe Arizona. You've got enough money to stock it and hire good hands. Find yourself a pretty western gal, have some kids, be happy. Wish I'd done that."

Gideon's heart leaped at the idea of owning a ranch, but then his mind intruded. What good would it be without the wife and kids he could never have? A mocking little voice added what his heart could not, *What good without Judith?*

Chapter 11

The second winter Gideon spent in Colorado was nothing like the first. No longer a trapper's helper but a valued friend and guest in Tomkinsville, as the boom town was now called after its new owner, he spent his days playing cards in the saloon. He even picked up the coarse language of his fellow gamblers, drank for the first time in his life, and bitterly blamed God for his past. His one pleasure in his downward slide was that he now used his treacherous brother's name as his own. If anyone had told Tomkinsville that "Cyrus Scott" had once been a preacher, no one would have believed it. The few times he allowed himself to drink too much, he passionately hoped news of his tough reputation would get back to his father. If it did, Lige would admit fault in the son he had felt did no wrong.

Gideon also learned to fight and licked a half dozen cowhands known for their skill with fists. He carried his gun, remembering Lige's words that men would respect him once he'd proven himself.

Ironically, the situation Gideon had avoided like riding through a cactus patch prompted his first gunfight. A young woman named Lily, the newest of those who sang and danced in the saloon, caught his attention. Her dark eyes reminded him of Judith, and she didn't seem to belong. He befriended her, then encouraged her to leave and go elsewhere. If Lily stayed in this ungodly atmosphere, she wouldn't be able to hold out for long.

"I've got plenty of money to get you started," he told her simply. Some of the old goodness that life had erased from his face shone again. "Is Lily your real name?"

She shook her head, and red flags waved in her dusky skin.

"Good. Go to Denver or Colorado Springs or anywhere. How did you ever fall into this miserable life, anyway?"

"My parents died. I had to do something to live." Lily suddenly looked older than her seventeen years.

A pang went through Gideon. *Judith had been desperate, too, trying to earn a living for herself and Joel. What if she were forced into such work?*

Never! his mind shouted. He squared his shoulders. *Neither should this young woman.* He waited while she gave notice to the saloon owner, then escorted her to the first outgoing stage, warmed in spite of the snappy cold weather by her broken, "God bless you."

Gideon's action did not endear himself to the saloon keeper and his friends. A few days after Lily left, Sears, the biggest and meanest of them, drawled, "Too bad the rest of us ain't well heeled like Scott here. We coulda set Lily up right smart an' had us a cozy little—"

A well-placed blow cut off the suggestion. His eyes blazing, Gideon leaped from his chair at the card table and faced the foul-mouthed man. "It's men, no, *animals* like you that ruin women who have nowhere to go. You're a rotten lot!"

"An' you think *yore* better?" The humiliated Sears reached for his gun. Gideon's shot knocked it out of his hand before it ever cleared the holster.

"One more crack like that about any woman, and I'll kill you!" He backed from the saloon into black night, his gun held steady in case one of the others tried anything. Once outside, he dodged behind buildings, more afraid of himself and God than of being followed. What had he come to—Gideon Scott, whose bright and promising career had been cut off?

Revulsion filled him. His stomach heaved, and it took supreme control to keep from retching. Once he could have defended Lily by using God's Word. Now he looked down at the gun he still held. Cold sweat drenched him. Had his threat been valid? Would he have killed another human being?

Somehow he reached his hotel room and barred the door. When he lighted his lamp, the wild-eyed apparition he beheld brought his gun up until he realized he faced the mirror above the bureau.

"Who's there?" Gideon spun. The room lay silent, empty except for himself and his mirrored reflection. "Who spoke?" he demanded, wondering if he were going mad, trying to remember where he had heard those words and when.

"The prodigal son." Gideon dropped heavily onto the bed. "Luke 15. 'A certain man had two sons.'" Uncontrollable laughter shook him. "And all these years I thought the story reversed, that the elder son, Cyrus, was the prodigal!" The rest of the parable on which he had preached a half dozen sermons came back: The younger boy went to a far country, wasted his money in riotous living, and found himself in want, hungry and sick. " 'And when he came to himself, he said—' " Gideon choked. " 'Father, I have sinned against heaven.' Oh, dear God, what am I doing here?" Desolation greater than any he had known swept through him. Tonight he might have killed a man. If he kept on with the way he now lived, he couldn't avoid bloodshed. He had seen it in the eyes of the onlookers when he drew his gun with lightning speed. Every would-be gunslinger jealous of his reputation would be standing in line. Kill or be killed, the law of the frontier.

Yet unlike the repentant sinner in the parable, Gideon could not return to his earthly father. He could always return to his loving heavenly Father and find peace and a measure of comfort that might help to heal his shattered, lonely life. Before he slept, he had poured out his heart in prayer and slept as he hadn't slept since he left the Circle S. Tomorrow he would follow his benefactor's advice and ride out and find a ranch somewhere. Arizona appealed to him: plenty of land for those who were willing to work for it, defend themselves from Apaches, and dig in. Something of the range-loving boy he had been still lived inside Gideon. After a prayer of thanks to God for bringing him to himself, he slept and dreamed of a new, brighter day, one that might sometime lead to exoneration and Judith.

With a thundering knock and crashing of wood, armed, angry men stormed into his room later that night. Gideon bounded from bed, trying to make sense of the confusion. A match flared. Rude hands grabbed him. Oaths fell on his ears like hail. "Git yore pants on," he was ordered while someone lighted the lamp.

With a wrenching effort, he tore free. "I demand to know why you are here." Something in his face halted his attackers but not for long.

"Yu've got yore nerve. First you shoot up Sears in the saloon, then trail him to his shack an' knife him."

The low grumble sent horror into Gideon. He had heard of mobs who hanged accused persons first and asked questions later. "Fools," he cried. "I could have killed him when I shot him, you all know that. Why would I wait and take a chance of him getting me?" He saw uncertainty grow in some of the faces. "Do you think I'm that *loco*? Your friend outweighed me by at least forty pounds."

"What good is that when some jasper sticks a knife in your back?" someone called. The crowd's mood turned ugly again with "Hang him" and "String him up" heard from all corners.

"That will be just about enough of that." The quiet but deadly voice from the doorway stopped the yelling. Tomkins stood cradling a sawed-off shotgun. He patted it significantly. "This gun here's touchy, boys. Used it to stand off claim jumpers, grizzly bears, all kinds of undesirable critters." He looked at Gideon. "What's all this uproar?"

"Sears and I had an argument. He drew on me, but I beat him and shot the gun out of his hand, then came home. I don't know anything more. These, er, gentlemen seem to think I sneaked up on him and knifed him."

"You didn't, did you?" Tomkins's eyes gleamed.

Gideon shook his head, but someone cried, "He lies!"

For a single heartbeat, Gideon once more stood defying his father. The same words he used with Lige fell from his lips in a hotel room hundreds of miles away. "I have never lied, and I never will to save my reputation or to save my life. I know nothing of who stabbed Sears." He tensed, ready to spring if Tomkins didn't believe him. When the big head nodded, Gideon relaxed.

"D'yu have a knife?" an unconvinced man bellowed.

"Of course. Every rider carries a knife."

"Look like this one?" The triumphant man held out a knife, careful to touch only the tip.

Gideon shuddered at the ghastly dark stains on the blade that glinted wickedly in the dimly lit room. "It's ordinary enough to look like mine."

"Where's yore knife?" the questioner demanded.

"In my saddlebag hung on the nail in the livery stable," Gideon told him.

"Who knows it's there?" Tomkins asked with a concerned expression on his lined face.

Gideon shrugged. "Anyone who may have looked in the saddlebags." Alarm triggered inside him.

"How come yu leave yore knife there?" the persistent voice went on.

Gideon put both hands on his hips and glared. "I've never used a knife except for range work. I didn't think I'd need it here in the hotel."

"Best we mosey on down to the stable and have a look-see." Tomkins stood aside to let the others pass, then ordered, "Stop! On second thought, I'll just make sure no one decides to tamper with evidence by removing Scott's knife just as a friendly little joke." His tone left no uncertainty as to the fate of a person who tried it.

Gideon pulled on his clothes and a heavy jacket, glad his bankbook lay carefully hidden inside the jacket lining. If the worst happened, perhaps he could leap to Dainty Bess's back and ride out.

Ten minutes later, Tomkins unwillingly ordered the sheriff to lock up Gideon until the case could be looked into more thoroughly. There had been no knife in the saddlebag, and Sears lay close to death. "If he doesn't make it, you're safer here than at the hotel," Tomkins told the despairing young man. He scratched his grizzled jaw. "Don't worry. We'll get to the bottom of this, but I wish to God you'd taken my advice and got out of this place before getting yourself into trouble."

"So do I," Gideon said soberly. For a moment, he felt tempted to confess who he really was, how he'd taken his brother's name and hours before realized the dead-end trail he'd been riding. Realizing it could do more harm than good, he said nothing.

Strange how many times he had felt the silence before a storm. When Tomkinsville settled down for the rest of the night, not a dog barked. Even the light snow that had fallen earlier in the day ceased. Yet Gideon felt the same eerie sensation that preceded Cyrus's flight and Judith's arrival. Would he have another night of life? Would Tomkins's power in the boomtown be enough to sway the mob if Sears died?

"Well, God, if this is my last time to tell You I'm sorry for everything, especially for not trusting You, so be it." Gideon flung himself on the miserable excuse for a bed and hoped San Scipio would never learn what had befallen the minister they once revered.

Anxious days and high hopes followed black nights and despair for Gideon. Sears began to mend, then suffered a relapse. For three days, Tomkinsville held its breath but not its invective against the coward who had knifed him. Finally, the big man turned toward life and in a couple of weeks regained enough of his strength to respond to questions. Yet he seemed strangely reluctant to talk.

"Don't know what's got into him," Tomkins admitted with a worried frown. "Says he plans to talk when it will do the most good, at the trial." He sent Gideon a keen glance. "I'll be glad when this is all over. If you're cleared, you better skedaddle out of here. This whole thing has left a bad taste with folks. Even if you're innocent, you won't be popular in these parts." He stretched his big body. "Leastways, he didn't die. The most you can be charged with is attempted murder, which is bad enough."

After Tomkins had gone, Gideon met the Lord in prayer. "Dear God, is there a reason behind all this?" He refused to let his friend bail him out. Uncomfortable as it was, the jail offered a certain security in case Sears took a turn for the worse again.

Lulled by a sunny day that promised an early spring but had blizzards lurking up its sleeve, the citizens of Tomkinsville turned out in droves for the trial. Before going to the saloon-turned-courtroom, used because it was the largest building in town, Gideon prayed. "God, I have no defense but the truth. I commit my life into Your hands." He stopped, remembering the shock in Tomkins's face when he handed him the precious bankbook wrapped in brown paper and addressed to *Mrs. G. Scott, c/o Circle S Ranch, San Scipio, Texas.* "If anything happens, mail it."

Tomkins peered at the address. Gideon could see questions trembling on his tongue, but his loyal friend merely pocketed the package. "I'll return it after the trial," he said brusquely.

Colorado justice, often swift even when it wasn't sure, dragged while the prosecutor reached into his bag of tricks to impress the inhabitants of Tomkinsville. He painted a picture of the accused man that would have done Satan himself proud. In awful, rolling tones, he built up a setting in which Gideon, angered by his failure to kill Sears in a fair fight, vindictively followed the other man like a wolf stalking its prey. If Gideon hadn't known better, he would have been swayed by the man's false but vivid reenactment of attempted murder.

Under oath, Gideon admitted his knife had disappeared and the one used on Sears looked like it. However, he maintained that his shot in the saloon had gone exactly where he aimed it. "Sir, I've never killed a man, and I didn't mean to kill Sears."

"Then why did you say, and I quote, 'One more crack like that about any woman, and I'll kill you!' "The prosecutor fairly oozed satisfaction.

"I was angry."

"So angry you followed Sears and tried to finish the job." The prosecutor turned to the judge with a deliberate gesture. "I rest my case."

Tomkins himself had elected to defend Gideon. He grinned when he stated flatly, "I'm no lawyer, but I carry considerable weight around here." Now he leisurely stood and walked to where he could face Gideon yet not block the judge's view of his face. "How long have you known me?"

"About a year and a half."

"Tell the court under what circumstances we met."

Gideon couldn't follow the line of defense in Tomkins's thinking but obediently recited, "I came here a year ago last fall, did some gambling, and won some money. Thought I'd be better off away from town, so I went trapping with you for the winter."

"And you grubstaked me in the spring so I could go back to mining. Me, a trapper and miner who'd never had much more than the clothes on my back."

"Yes."

"Judge, this man is the real reason why Tomkinsville is booming. If he hadn't been good to a broken-down old miner, why, none of our prosperity would have come!" He waved an expansive hand. "I tried to find him and repay him after I struck it rich, but it wasn't 'til he drifted back down from Wyoming and Montana that I could locate him." He stepped closer to Gideon and clapped him on the shoulder. "Scott's no more capable of knifing anyone in the back than, than you are, Judge!"

"Prove it!" shouted the red-faced prosecutor.

"I call as my witness, Eb Sears."

Gideon gasped, as did the judge, the prosecutor, and every man present.

"Now, Mr. Sears, tell us in your own words what happened," Tomkins said, "and tell it straight."

Before he began, Sears shot an unreadable look at Gideon. "Aw, I was drunk and loud. Said some things about Lily I knew weren't true. He hit me. I got mad and drew. So did he." Sears pointed to Gideon, who silently prayed and clenched his hands into fists.

"In your opinion, did Mr. Scott try to kill you and miss, the way the prosecutor said?" Tomkins probed.

"Naw." A reluctant respect and a personal code Gideon wouldn't have expected from Sears straightened the slumping witness. "He's chain lightnin' and could shoot the eye out of a mosquito."

A little ripple of surprise ran through the room, and Gideon felt himself start to sweat. The next few moments could mean the difference between conviction and freedom.

"Mr. Sears, under oath, did Cyrus Scott knife you? You've been strangely silent ever since it happened."

Sears scratched his head. "At first, I thought so. Seemed logical. Then I started wonderin'. If he wanted to kill me, he shore coulda done it in the saloon, with everybody there havin' to testify I drew first. Naw, I don't think he knifed me."

"Do you have any idea who might have?"

Stone-cold, dead silence followed the question.

"Mr. Sears, I repeat, do you have any suspicions? Did anyone hate you enough to do this?"

Sears grunted. "I ain't the best-liked hombre in Tomkinsville." He hesitated, then said, "I've had a lot of time to think. Maybe it wasn't exactly me someone was after."

The ripple grew to a murmur, stilled when the judge banged his gavel on the bar. "Silence!"

"Just what do you mean?" Tomkins leaned forward. So did Gideon.

Sears squirmed. "I don't like accusin' anyone, but certain folks were real upset when Lily up and left."

"How do you know that?" Tomkins's voice cracked like a bullwhip.

"Lily told me." Red crawled into the tanned face. "Said when she quit, the boss ranted and raved and said he'd get even with Scott." The red deepened, but Sears looked square at Tomkins. "Maybe he saw this as a good chance. Besides, we'd had a fallin' out over the girl. I was sweet on her, and so was he, and 'til Scott came, she sorta liked me. I'da married her." He hung his head and stared at the floor. "That's why when I said all that stuff about Lily I knew wasn't true, it was 'cause I was jealous." His head snapped back up. "I shouldn't have been. Lily told me flat out Scott never asked nothin' from her, which is more than some—"

"*Liar!*" The saloon owner stood and clawed for his gun. "Too bad you didn't die when I knifed you."

"Hold it right there." A gun had miraculously sprung to the visiting judge's hand. Tomkins and the sheriff disarmed the raving man, whose tongue had been loosed by too many drinks he had served to his friends and himself, celebrating Gideon's conviction prematurely.

"Best one I ever had here." His eyes blazed hatred for both Sears and Gideon. "Those innocent types bring in customers, but she'd have come around if it hadn't been for you." He spat in their direction. "Can't tell me Scott doesn't have her waiting for him somewheres. Men don't help women like Lily unless there's something in it for them. I fixed him, stole his knife—"

The judge cut into the babbling. "Mr. Scott, you are cleared and free to go. Sheriff, lock up this murderer! He's confessed, and I sentence him to. . ."

Gideon missed the rest amid the wild cheer that shook the rafters. With Tomkins leading him, he walked out, feeling free and dirty. His sin had led to this moment, and he knew it would take a long time to rid himself of the taint of Tomkinsville.

Chapter 12

J ust before Christmas of 1876, Gideon, who had now reverted to using his own name, reined in his horse and surveyed his earthly kingdom. After traveling through much of Arizona, thrilled by its deserts and plateaus, chastened by the expanse of blue sky that make the red-rock canyons and monuments even more torrid, he had found the Double J spread not far from Flagstaff. *The name holds a certain appeal*, he ruefully admitted.

He sobered when he considered what Judith and Joel would think of Double J, surrounded by oak and manzanita, sage and pine. There were cattle enough for a good start, thanks to Tomkins. One thing Gideon had done before leaving Colorado was to seek out those whose money he had won in gambling and repay them. He would not begin his rededicated life with the Lord by building on tainted money nor under a false name. Before he left Tomkinsville, he told the whole story to his benefactor.

"You love the lass, your wife?" Tomkins shot a keen glance into his eyes.

"More than life, second only to God."

"Son, things have a way of working out. Go on out to Arizona. Get settled. Be God-fearing, honest, and work hard." Wistfulness crept into his eyes. "If I were younger, I'd go with you." But Tomkins shook his shaggy head. "Maybe one day you'll see me come riding in if my luck breaks. I've got a lot salted away, but as long as I keep finding more, I suppose I'll stay here."

"You'll always be welcome." A hard grip of hands, and Gideon rode away knowing he'd always have a friend in the man he once so carelessly helped.

Now he sat easily in the saddle and wondered what came next. He'd been from Tucson to the Grand Canyon of the Colorado River, from the White Mountains to the Mogollon Rim and into the Tonto. Yet something about the Flagstaff area held him. He thought of the group of settlers who had camped there not long before. They made a flagstaff from a pine tree and flew the American flag from it. Folks said the incident provided the name for the birth of a town.

The knowledge of men Gideon had gained both from preaching and wandering proved invaluable in selecting cowboys for the Double J. "Don't hire just anyone," Tomkins had warned. "Handpick wranglers who'll give you loyalty, not just a day's work."

Gideon heeded the advice. He never hired a hand who couldn't look him straight in the eye without wavering. He never hired a man who shifted when he spoke. He made it clear there would be no red-eye on the job, and if he heard of any man getting "likkered up" on Saturday night, that hand could pack his gear and ride out.

"Aw, Boss, what're you runnin', a Sunday school?" Gideon's foreman, Fred Aldrich, complained. "How'm I s'posed to keep a wild bunch of cowboys workin' if they can't bust loose on the weekends?"

"When you hire them, tell them what the rules are and remind them we may have a hot enough time if the Apaches hit us," Gideon told him.

Aldrich heaved a sigh clear from his dusty boot tips to the crown of the sweat-stained Stetson that shaded his keen, dark eyes. "We're gonna be the laughin' stock of all Arizony," he muttered, but faithfully carried out his orders. Because Gideon knew his standards would make it hard to get riders, he not only paid top wages but promised that any cowboy who stayed a year or more would get a bonus. The offer, a share in the Double J or a good horse and saddle, hit Arizona like a desert storm. Aldrich stuck his tongue in his cheek and solemnly confirmed the offer, sourly adding, "That's what comes of havin' a boss from Texas. Thinks his way's the only way, and shoot, he might just be right!"

Wide-shouldered, grinning cowboys, some still in their teens, came out of curiosity but stayed because of their new boss. They differed from the Texas cowboys in subtle ways. Arizona demanded more daring men because of its raw newness. It cared little for background, everything for the measure of a man. Gideon's outfit answered to names like Lonesome and Cheyenne, Kansas and Dusty. No one asked where the riders came from, and prying into a rider's past was taboo.

Gideon sometimes found this tolerance maddening, and he blew up to Aldrich one day. "Everyone knows that Stockton, who's planning to run cattle in the Tonto, is a notorious outlaw going respectable."

"Shore, Boss. Arizony's always willin' to give a man a second chance." He shrugged. "This territory's gonna be a state someday, and if it takes reformed crooks to do it, so what? Out here, long as a man's goin' straight, we figger more power to him." He half closed his eyes. "On the other hand, we also keeps our eyes peeled so he don't go back to his takin' ways, takin' other folks' property."

Gideon subsided. Who knew better than he the need for a second chance?

Although the Navajo had been put down, their final defeat coming in a fierce 1864 campaign led by the famed scout Kit Carson, the Apache had not. Small bands terrorized and raided. Cochise and Geronimo were names to respect. They led warriors against forts, towns, and lonely ranches, but the settlers were still determined to find homes. Hunted and forced farther back into the remote and seemingly impenetrable canyons, infuriated by broken treaties, the original Arizona inhabitants fought for their lives.

So far, the Double J hadn't been a target, but the threat was ever present. In some ways, Gideon pitied the Navajo and Apache. How would he feel if a horde of strangers came in and took his land? Even in the short time he had owned the Double J, he had grown to love it. With every sunrise, he looked east and thought of the past. Each sunset brought a feeling of well-being along with gloriously painted skies. He had finally conquered the poignant regret of his sins; if God had forgiven him, he had no right not to forgive himself. A desire to return to the Lord's service haunted him. Yet how could he?

That desire continued to grow. Now and then, he rode into Flagstaff on Sunday, wishing there were a church. His restlessness finally made Aldrich ask,

"What's eatin' you, Boss? Yore jumpier than a fish swimmin' upstream."

Gideon took a deep breath. "Fred, what would the boys say if I invited folks out from town, anyone who cared to come, for Christmas? We could decorate and have candy for the kids and read the Christmas story out of the Bible. Sing songs, too."

Aldrich considered. "Might not be a bad idea. I reckon the boys could stand such goin's-on for once." He cocked his head to one side. " 'Tain't none of my business, but who're you aimin' on havin' read that story?"

"I thought I would," Gideon told him frankly. He looked around the large room. "Think it will hold everyone?"

"All those who'll come," Fred said cryptically. "The boys and me can stay in the kitchen if this room fills up." He grinned. "It'll be pure pleasure for us to do yore decoratin' after all the hard work we've put in this fall. By the way, Boss, now that winter's comin', what about the hands? Are you layin' them off like most of the other ranchers do?"

"Nope. Every day that's nice enough, we'll be busy working. I want this ranch house expanded. We'll add a second story—"

"Whoopee!" Aldrich's face split wide open, and he howled like a banshee. "You must be aimin' to get hitched, huh, Boss?"

Gideon's excitement died. "No."

Red faced, Aldrich broke off his rejoicing. "Sorry, Boss." He hastily stood and mumbled, "I better go see what the boys are up to. Anyhow, they'll be glad to hear they won't be loafin' this winter." He backed out, obviously embarrassed.

Gideon realized the crisp air straight off the San Francisco mountains had worked through his heavy jacket. Late December was no time to dream outdoors. The boys would be waiting for him to give instructions about decorating. They'd ridden out and gathered pungent boughs, laughing and predicting how many would come out from town for "the boss's Christmas." Gideon had overheard Lonesome say, "Bet he's doin' this so we-all won't get to drinkin'. I'd sure like to wet my whistle, but I got my eye on a purty little gal in town. If I stick it out and get to be part owner of this here ranch, she's bound to see what a steady feller I am and slip into harness with me."

A roar of laughter followed Lonesome's confidence, but Gideon knew it was good-natured. The boys wouldn't admit it for a gold mine, but Aldrich had let it slip how proud they were to "help make Christmas for folks, 'specially the little ones."

"Tell them to wear their best," Gideon said. "This is their celebration, too."

Before bedtime on Christmas Eve, the ranch house smelled of fresh greens. Rude benches had been nailed together and lined the walls to give seating space. Gideon's original plan to have a service and treats for the children had met with frowning disapproval from his outfit. Aldrich reminded him, "Folks're comin' from miles around, the way I hear it."

The boys nodded solemnly, and Aldrich went on. "Seems downright un-neighborly not to give 'em dinner."

"*Dinner!* Can we handle it?"

"Hey, Boss, when're you gonna get on to Arizona?" asked Lonesome, always the most talkative of the cowboys. "Just put the word out we'll all be havin' Christmas dinner here, and folks'll be cookin' for days ahead. Wimmenfolk like to shine, and what better place than makin' food for us pore, unfortunate cowboys?"

Gideon sensed a new camaraderie with his men. In a reckless but appreciative mood, he laughed and held up his hands in mock defeat. "All right, but be it on your heads. You'll have to help, and everyone who sticks and helps make this the best Christmas these settlers have seen in many a day gets a ten-dollar Christmas present."

"Yippee!" they chorused, but Lonesome had to have the final word. "I think I just died and went to heav'n, boys. I thought I heard the boss say ten dollars."

"Aw, you've chased so many critters and listened to them beller yore ears are as bad as yore eyesight," Aldrich told him, but the approval in his foreman's dark eyes told Gideon how far he had come with his hands.

Shortly after breakfast on Christmas Day, by buckboard and wagon, on fine horses and half-wild mustangs, the invited guests began coming. Every family brought enough food for a cavalry! Gideon started, dismayed. *What did he know about serving such a bounteous dinner?* As if reading his mind, the women shooed him out of his own kitchen and told him to go "visit the menfolk" and leave them to their work. Although he had thought his bunkhouse cook more than adequate, he revised his opinion when he saw the groaning table laden with Arizona and holiday specialties.

A billowy matron who had taken charge ordered everyone inside, shushed them, and made an announcement to Gideon. "Mr. Scott, this dinner's in honor of the Almighty's Son. It's proper and fittin' for us to give thanks." Without a pause, she bowed her head and prayed, "Lord, on this special day we give thanks for food and friends and Your goodness to us. Amen."

Gideon silently thanked God she hadn't asked him to pray. He found himself suddenly speechless at his overwhelming love for these people, longing for home and thankful. Two Christmases ago, when he had been out on the trapline with Tomkins, they'd celebrated by cooking an extra portion of rice and dried fruit to go with their venison. Last year, to his shame, he had spent Christmas gambling his life away in the saloon at Tomkinsville. His heart felt as though it were bursting. *God, thank You that at least I'm not there.*

When everyone finished eating and even the cowhands admitted that after four or five helpings, things didn't taste so good anymore, the women packed everything away. Round-eyed children sat on blankets on the floor, and Gideon knew the time had come for his "service." He refused to remember other services, the real ones when he openly preached. To do so would leave him unable to continue.

He faced his guests, noting how lone riders who had "dropped by" rubbed elbows with settlers, how former outlaws chatted with the children. In the spirit of Christmas, disagreements and differing viewpoints faded. Gideon smiled. "It's been an honor for my outfit and me to have you come." He saw the boys swell with pride. "We have a little treat for the children, but first, as has been said, it's fitting for us to recognize whose birthday this is. I thought we could sing some carols."

Never had he heard the enthusiasm with which these brave pioneers sang. "Joy to the World" literally shook the ranch house as did "Hark, the Herald Angels Sing" and "O Come, All Ye Faithful." Voices lowered on "Silent Night," and Gideon saw eyelashes blink to hide wavering emotions. When the last note died, Gideon took out his Bible. "I'd like to read from the second chapter of Luke." He steadied his voice.

" 'And it came to pass in those days, that there went out a decree from Caesar Augustus, that all the world should be taxed. . . .' " On and on went the story, unfolding with new meaning as it had for so many years. Gideon read straight through the angels' proclamation to the shepherds, " 'Glory to God in the highest, and on earth peace, good will toward men.' " The shepherds then rose and went to Bethlehem and found Mary and Joseph and the baby Jesus, not in the fine inn, but quartered in humble surroundings such as these Arizona settlers knew so well. " 'And the shepherds returned, glorifying and praising God for all the things that they had heard and seen, as it was told unto them,' " he quoted in closing.

A power greater than his own prompted him to add, "Shall we pray?" He bowed his head, and lamplight shone on his golden hair, for the winter day had been short. "Father, may we, too, glorify and praise You for all these things. In Jesus' name. Amen."

Gideon raised his head. He saw the astonishment in the faces of Aldrich, Lonesome, and many others. *What should he say?*

"Mama, is it time for the treat?" A patient child in her mother's arms broke the silence, and the crowd laughed while memories of the Christmas service retreated to the shadowy corners but remained a vivid part of the day.

"It truly is!" Gideon picked up the little girl and set her on his shoulder the way he used to do with Joel. A pang went through him, but he smiled and went to the carefully prepared little papers of candies he and the boys had painstakingly counted out and wrapped. "Merry Christmas, honey. Come on, all you buckaroos. There's enough for everyone!" A swarm of eager but well-mannered children surrounded him. "Here, Fred, boys, help me," he called.

Five minutes later, every child had found a spot on the floor to enjoy their candy and listen to the grown-ups talk about what a wonderful day it had been. But before the gathering dispersed for home, a little group of men and women approached Gideon. "Mr. Scott, you did fine with the reading and singing and all. The praying, too. Until we can get a church and a regular preacher, would you ride into Flag on Sunday afternoons and hold meetings? Our children need to be raised by the Book, and land sakes, none of us has time during the week."

He didn't hesitate an instant. "I would be proud if you really want me." Yet to accept their genuine offer without a confession would be hypocrisy. He clenched his hands behind his back and added, "There's something you must know first. I left Texas under a black cloud, accused of something I didn't do, but I couldn't prove myself innocent."

The woman who had offered the blessing smiled until her eyes disappeared into rolls of flesh. "If the truth were to be told—which it won't and don't need to be—other folks here are ridin' under some black clouds of their own, and they may not be so innocent, either!"

The crowd laughed, and the spokesman for the impromptu committee pressed, "This is a new land, and what's gone before is gone forever. Will you hold meetings?"

"I will." Gideon straightened to full height. "And I hope every one of you will come." In a wave of laughter and anticipation, the party broke up. The boys lingered in the ranch house as if reluctant to have the day end. Gideon watched their awkward attempts at busying themselves, taking out the crude table and benches, straightening sagging boughs. Finally he said, "Before it's chore time, I want to thank you all." He took a small stack of packages wrapped and tied with string in lieu of ribbon and began to distribute them. "Merry Christmas, boys."

"Aw, Boss, the ten dollars was enough," interjected Lonesome. "Why'd you go and buy us these, anyway?" He spread out warm, lined gloves, his face shining. "I never had no gloves as good as these."

A murmur of assent rose.

To break the emotion he felt crowding him, a straight-faced Gideon told them, "You'll need them when we start building on to the ranch house!"

The outfit groaned, but Aldrich stepped forward. He carried a bulky package. "This is for you, Boss."

Gideon felt like the little girl who had received the first packet of candy. He silently untied the package that Aldrich had set on the floor.

A saddle that must have cost every ranch hand a good share of a month's wages—the saddle every rider covets and seldom owns—glistened in front of him, its silver trim beckoning his touch.

Did good old Lonesome sense Gideon's confusion? "If we'da known a present would cut off yore speech, Boss, why, we'da given it to you a couple of weeks ago when you gave Aldrich orders for us to dig holes for fenceposts!"

They trooped out, devilment clear in their lean faces, leaving Gideon only enough time to call, "Thanks," and weakly sink into a chair, then stare at Aldrich. When the door closed behind the last of the boys, he asked, "Was the saddle your idea?"

"Naw." Aldrich shook his head, and enjoyment of the situation showed plain in his eyes. "Lonesome brought it up, and the rest of the boys wished they had." His grin matched the mischief in the younger hands' faces when he added, "Glad it caught you by surprise. It woulda ruinated everythin' if you'd made some stupid remark about it bein' too much." A warning lay beneath his casual words. He headed for the door and paused with one hand on the knob. Gideon could feel something coming and tensed.

"Folks around here will respect yore mentionin' about Texas and why you left," Aldrich drawled. "Once it's been said, though, no need to talk anymore." He lifted one eyebrow and grinned again. "Merry Christmas, Boss."

"Merry Christmas." Gideon watched his foreman turn up his coat collar against the cold night air before stepping out. The latch clicked, and boot heels thudded across the porch. The silence that follows the emptying of a house when Christmas is over fell, leaving Gideon to wonder, *Surely this silence couldn't herald the coming of another storm.* He had confessed the worst, and these new neighbors cared little.

Yet within an hour, the snow came, enshrouding the Double J and obliterating all trace of the merrymakers who had come, eaten, and worshiped together, then gone back to their own homes, leaving Gideon with his memories.

Chapter 13

Spring in all its glory came to Arizona. Trees greened, budded, and burst into new life, and so did Gideon. The long winter months hadn't been idle, yet he had found time to regain his perspective. He returned to studying his Bible and, when weather permitted, rode or drove into Flagstaff to hold simple Sunday afternoon services composed of hymns, a Scripture reading, and sometimes a short lesson. Gideon always returned home more blessed than his informal congregation. If at times he longed to preach, he restrained himself. Although his bitterness against God had long since fled, he knew the time wasn't right. In the meantime, Aldrich and at least some of the boys usually came to the meetings, often slipping into the last of the benches set up in a cleaned-out barn.

"The Lord began His ministry in a stable. I reckon we can be glad to have a dry place for our meetings," folks said. They bundled in layers upon layers of clothes for the short services and grimly proclaimed that before snow flew the next fall, there'd be a regular church. The stove the barn owner generously put in kept only those in the first few rows warm.

Often while watching the snow fall, listening for the sound of laughter from the bunkhouse, Gideon felt the same uneasiness from the winter silence he'd experienced on Christmas Day. Yet as time passed, the feelings dwindled. The only unusual incident came when two of his outfit slipped the reins and came home from town bright eyed, talky, and smelling of drink.

"You know the rules, boys." Gideon faced his men, heartsick. "I won't stand for drinking."

The cowboys looked at each other, then with mutual appeal at Aldrich. The foreman shook his head, although Gideon saw how much he wanted to speak.

Lonesome took a deep breath. "Boss, we all know the rules, and these two mis'r'ble skunks don't deserve it. But yore always talkin' about how that Jesus feller in the Bible gave folks another chance if they were sorry." His keen eyes challenged Gideon. "Well, it doesn't take much to see how sorry lookin' they are." He pointed to the offenders, who sat on their bunks with heads drooping. Disarranged clothing spoke clearly that their pardners had already administered a certain amount of justice.

Lonesome went on. "We just don't want to have the Double J crew broke up." The memory of shared word and loyalty shone in his eyes and in the eyes of the others.

Gideon had the feeling he was on trial more than his men. With a quick prayer for guidance, he said, "All right. I'll let it go this one time but *never again*. If any of you ever come home drinking, pack and get your time. As for you—" He marched over to the culprits. "The offer's still good about earning a bonus, but you'll have to start your year as of right now, because I'm firing you and rehiring you this minute. Like it or lump it, and don't make me regret it."

"Fair enough." One of the cowboys held out his hand. Remorse for letting down the outfit and gladness for a second chance showed in his mighty grip. The second did the same. There might be grumbling later, but for now a sigh of relief swept through the bunkhouse, and Gideon went out feeling God had lent him for one night the wisdom of Solomon.

The threatened breakup of the Double J wove unbreakable strands that held through temptation. With an outfit so determined to stay together, any cowpoke who even thought of straying found himself promptly rounded up and brought back to the straight and narrow. No one ever mentioned the boss's handling of the winter crisis, but the long hours of spring work and the spirits of his hands told Gideon the whole story.

Spring also brought problems. Aldrich dragged in long faced and angry one sunny afternoon. "Boss, our cattle are disappearin'."

"*Disappearing!* How?"

"Well, it ain't four-footed critters that are responsible," the foreman said sourly. "We found signs they're bein' driven. Rustled. Plumb stole right off the Double J."

"Indians?" A chill went up Gideon's spine.

Aldrich made a rude noise. "Naw. They kill a beef, take what they want, and let the rest lay." His eyes half closed in the way they did when he considered. "How about givin' me a few of the boys to scout out Stockton's place?"

"Take anyone you need. I'll be ready as soon as you are." Gideon jumped up and reached for his hat.

"You stay here, Boss. Me and Lonesome, Dusty, and Kansas can do the job. I'd take Cheyenne, too, but he's sorer than a mule sittin' on a cactus. Toothache."

"I wouldn't think of letting you go without me," Gideon said blandly and caught the gleam in Aldrich's eyes, although he grumbled all the way out the door. Ten minutes later, the little band had mounted and headed toward Stockton's spread.

"I thought you were sick," Gideon told Cheyenne, whose swollen jaw gave mute evidence of pain.

"Not sick enough to miss the fun." He grinned crookedly. "I'm hankerin' to see what that bunch of yahoos does when we ride in."

"Who's *ridin'* in?" Aldrich demanded. His brows drew together over keen eyes. "We're scoutin', remember?"

"Yeah," Cheyenne hastily agreed, but not before Gideon saw the exchange of glances between the cowboys.

"No gunplay," he ordered, remembering the Tomkinsville saloon.

Lonesome, who could look cherubic in feigned indignation, retorted, "Why, Boss, are you *loco*? Us pore old cowpokes can't hardly bear to kill a rattlesnake." His remark dropped into a silence broken only by the rhythmic beat of their horses' hooves.

"I thought Stockton was supposed to be reformed," Gideon mused aloud when they reached the borders of the former outlaw's ranch. "Why do you suspect him?"

"Suspect? We're just curious. Well, what d'you know!" Lonesome spurred his horse, and the others followed. "Funny, I'd swear that's a Double J brand on that steer." He pointed to a small bunch of cattle in a thrown-together corral. "There's another one. Mighty pee-coo-liar how they got in there, huh, Boss?"

Rage at the blatant thievery straightened Gideon's spine. His hot Texas blood boiled. "Stay here!" he ordered. Before his men could protest, he put Dainty Bess into a dead run toward the corral. Three men, none of them Stockton, leaped from their horses and faced him.

"What are you doing with my cattle in there?" Gideon yelled and pulled Bess up in front of them.

The sheer daring of his confrontation paralyzed Stockton's men. "Uh, they must have got mixed in when we brought in—"

"Liar!" Gideon bounded from the saddle. "Does Stockton know about this?" His voice rang in the clear air, and he read the answer in the men's faces. In a flash, Gideon leaped back onto Bess and uncoiled his lariat. Circling it over his head, he snugged it over a poorly set fencepost. "All right, Bess!" *Crash!* The post gave way and dragged behind them. A mixture of Double J stock and other brands poured out to freedom.

"Yippee-i-ay!" Lonesome bellowed, then panic clutched his voice. "Boss, *look out!"*

His warning came seconds too late. Something struck Gideon squarely in the back. He reeled in the saddle, then fell to the ground, conscious of a volley of gunfire before the world went black.

⁂

As Judith Butler Scott in her yellow and white dress watched Gideon ride away from their wedding, something deep inside her begged him not to go. The truth she had begun to accept burst into full bloom: Gideon could not be guilty of the accusations she had made. His kisses confirmed it. Shy and reverent, they lingered on her lips and witnessed to his innocence. Blood pounded in her head. She rested her hands on Joel's shoulders for support. Would she ever see him again, this splendid man who had married her and ridden away for the sake of his family?

Somehow she pulled herself together. For Joel's sake, she must go on. Judith glanced at Lige Scott and shrank back from the naked heartbreak quickly veiled in his eyes. His two sons were both gone. He turned and looked at Joel, and Judith shivered. She must fight, or Lige would take possession of the child in an attempt to create a second Cyrus. Despair filled her and blotted out everything but the need to walk carefully, at least for a time. Yet her heart cried out for help, and the peace of God strengthened her. She could do nothing until she regained her stamina lost through sickness and worry.

The journey to El Paso had seemed endless. The journey back felt even longer. Judith had the sensation of being smothered, imprisoned. Would the Circle S swallow her and Joel?

Naomi stirred beside her, smiled, and patted Judith's hand. Her low assurance, "Things won't seem so bewildering when we get home," did much to comfort the distraught bride. As long as Naomi remained her friend, Judith could survive.

To her surprise, once they reached the ranch, Lige helped her down and said gruffly, "You're our daughter now. Naomi will see you have what you need."

His rude attempt at kindness threatened the shaky control Judith struggled to maintain. "Thank you." She blinked hard. "Come, Joel." Tired from the long journey and excitement, he trotted after her, and after a hasty wash, they both fell asleep. They didn't waken until Carmelita tapped on their door and announced supper would be ready soon.

Although for a time Judith remained on guard, as early winter came, then blizzards beyond anything she and Joel had imagined, she learned to relax. She often felt as if they'd been on the Circle S forever. Lige gave an expurgated version of Gideon's absence, merely stating he had gone away for a time. Whether he believed Gideon would return was a matter between Lige and his God. He continued to treat Judith as the daughter he had called her and frankly idolized Joel. She worried, yet perhaps someday she could... Every time she got that far, she put it out of her mind. Her somedays were in God's hands.

The first spring after Gideon rode away brought Joel's fifth birthday and a beautiful collie pup from his grandfather. He promptly named it Millie after asking Judith, "Would Mama like it?"

"I'm sure she would." Judith hugged him to keep her tears from showing. Yet Joel owned a more priceless possession than earthly parents. His Friend Jesus was real to the boy, an ever-present comrade of the trail. Judith often marveled at the depth of his faith and prayed it would never be tarnished.

Summer, fall, winter, and a second spring elapsed, and nothing had been heard of either Gideon or Cyrus. New patches of white marred Lige's hair. A shadow lurked in Naomi's eyes even when she smiled and played with Joel, who adored her. Because of the distance to town, Naomi and Judith continued the child's education. Lige's sad eyes brightened when he saw how quickly Joel grasped the things he learned and put them into practice. He sent away for books to fill a library, and Joel discovered new worlds beyond the borders of Texas. Best of all, he loved the Bible stories Judith read to him.

A new minister had been installed in the San Scipio church, an older man with a kindly face and a great love of the Lord. He could not preach as Gideon had, but he taught the Word of God and people liked him. Only Lucinda Curtis openly mourned "the untimely and unexplained departure of Brother Scott."

Judith never knew how Lige managed it, but her marriage to Gideon remained unknown to San Scipio. Possessed of great power because of his large holdings, he didn't hesitate to wield it in his own interests. In any event, she gladly accepted the secrecy. Most of the fold in San Scipio would have exclaimed for a day or two, then continued to welcome her, except for Lucinda. Judith dreaded the other woman's bold attempts at companionship and pleaded Joel as an excuse to avoid the elaborate affairs given by Lucinda and her mother. Something in the washed-out gray eyes warned of a serpent's venom.

Joel's uncanny resemblance to the Scotts fed the gossip mill for a time until a drunken cowboy shot up San Scipio and turned attention toward himself. For the most part, Judith existed in a state of waiting, happy when she forgot she was Mrs. Scott, restless at other times.

Joel's growth and joy in everyone and everything on the Circle S helped her develop patience. She couldn't say what it was she waited for. Yet, how often in the evening her gaze turned west! Was Gideon somewhere beyond the horizon, struggling to patch up his life as best he could? Did he remember the woman he had married and renounced? If bright dewdrops sparkled in her lashes, no one knew but God. The love she held for her absent husband secretly warmed her. If they never met again in this life, they would in the next. She believed it with all her heart.

The summer of 1876 brought startling news to the Circle S in the form of a visitor. Tired, dusty, and determined, a big man rode in one early evening and asked to see Mrs. Scott. Rosa led him to the large room where the family gathered evenings before going to bed. The visitor looked around, noted each person present, and then strode directly toward Judith. "Mrs. Scott?"

"I am Mrs. Scott." Naomi stood, dignity in every line of her body.

"And you?" Keen eyes pierced Judith's confusion.

"I am Mrs. Gideon Scott."

"Ahh." A sigh of satisfaction lit the worn face.

"Who are you, and what do you want?" Lige put Joel off his knee and approached the man.

"I have news of your son. When have you heard from him?" The stranger's gaze bored into Lige, then turned back to Judith, ignoring Lige's strangled cry. Suddenly a great hand on his shoulder whipped him around, and Lige demanded, "What is your business here?"

"May I sit down? I've come a long way." The man didn't wait for permission but brushed dust from his pants and seated himself. "You have two sons, Cyrus and Gideon." He looked as if he were enjoying himself.

"Who are you?" Lige towered over him, but his hands shook.

"Tomkins is the name. In early winter of '74, I was running a trapline in Colorado. I'm a miner, but I was down on my luck and needed money for grub. A young feller rode in, took to gambling, and made a pile of money. He was smart enough to know it didn't make him popular, so he joined me trapping for the winter. In the spring, he grubstaked me."

"What was his name?" Lige's hands formed claws.

Judith held her breath, but let it out in a disappointed sigh when Tomkins spoke. "He called himself Cyrus Scott."

"Called himself! Wasn't that his name?" The great light of joy and hope dimmed in Lige's face.

"Turned out it wasn't. Anyway, he rode north. Said he aimed to work in Wyoming, maybe Montana." Tomkins grinned and rubbed his unshaven chin. "That summer I struck it big. Can't tell you how grateful I was to the young feller. Tried to find him and couldn't. Then just before snow flew, he came back to

Tomkinsville, the boomtown that sprang up after the strike."

"Did you find out who he was?" Lige said hoarsely.

"Not then. I set him up in a hotel, put enough in the bank for him to buy a ranch, and told him to leave town." A dark cloud blackened Tomkins's face. "He hung around, though, befriended a saloon girl, nothin' more," he added when a little moan escaped Naomi's white lips. "Felt sorry for her, ma'am. She was just a kid, so he gave her money to go away. Well, one of the bullies got likkered up, said some nasty things, and drew on my friend. Scott yanked out his gun quicker than lightning and shot the gun out of the scoundrel's hand."

He quickly sketched in the cowardly knife attack, the lynch mob, and the trial while his listeners sat wide-eyed and tense.

"Once cleared, Scott came to me and told me his story." Tomkins's gaze raked Lige. "How he got accused of something he didn't do on account of his brother."

"Gideon!" Judith's glad cry brought a smile to the leathery face.

"He rode out on the prettiest little sorrel mare I ever saw. Said he thought he'd take my advice and buy a ranch in Arizona. Oh, he gave back all the money he got gambling. Tomkinsville's still talking about it." He scratched his head. "Didn't need it, anyway. He helped me, and I saw to it he had enough for that ranch and to get it stocked. I had business down this way and thought I'd stop by. Gideon's a proud man, and he never once lied. You might keep that in mind if you're still judging him." Tomkins got up, and in spite of the Scotts' offer of hospitality, he said he'd better mosey on. He walked out, spurs clinking.

Judith roused from the shock of all she'd learned and ran after him for a private word. "Mr. Tomkins, do you know where in Arizona my husband, er, Gideon might be?"

"No, ma'am." He shook his head. "If I did, I'd be tempted to hunt him up. Fact is, I've been considering it ever since I left Colorado. Once I get done with my business, I might just head west instead of back home."

"Take me with you," she cried.

"You love him, lass?"

"With all my heart, more than anything except God."

"Then it's all right." Tomkins smiled at her. "When I asked him that question, he said the same thing. 'More than life, second only to God.' I told him things had a way of working out."

"Bless you!" Judith impulsively stretched and kissed the grizzled cheek. "Will you take me to find him?"

"I reckon." Dull red suffused his face, but doubt crept into his eyes. "It might be better for us to wait and see if we can smoke out where he is. Can you be patient awhile longer, lass?"

Torn between wanting to leave immediately and the common sense of his suggestion, she reluctantly nodded.

Tomkins promised, "I'll get my transacting done, see what I can learn, and stop back in a few weeks. A big company in Houston's been pestering me to sell out my holdings. I'm considering letting them have the whole shebang. I haven't had half the fun spending my gold as I did looking for it." His eyes twinkled. "Maybe I'll retire in Arizona and see if I can find a likely partner who'll sell me half ownership in a ranch."

"Don't say anything to the Scotts," Judith warned, hating herself but knowing it had to be said. "Lige won't let Joel go easily, especially when Gideon's involved." She proudly raised her head. "I won't sneak out when the time comes, but until it does, we have to live here."

Tomkins nodded. A few minutes later, he rode away, carrying Judith's hopes and dreams in his calloused hands. When Lige threw her a questioning look as she entered the big room, she simply said, "Gideon sends his love." Blushing, she fled before he had time to respond.

Judith expected to hear from Tomkins soon. Each time Lige picked up mail in town, she anticipated a letter. None came until just before Christmas. Tomkins had fallen ill in Houston and hadn't been able to do anything about locating Gideon. He then had to hurry back to Colorado to close a deal and get the mines sold. Now winter must pass before he could do more. He regretted it but was sending out letters to different parts of Arizona where Gideon might be. He promised that even if they came to naught, he'd come and get Judith in the spring. They'd follow the sagebrush trail and find her husband if it meant visiting every ranch in Arizona!

Resigned but impatient, again Judith settled down to wait.

Chapter 14

The shooting of Gideon was followed by a burst of gunfire from the enraged Double J riders that crippled two of the rustlers and sent the third fleeing for his life. Enraged by the incident, the worthy citizens of Flagstaff, led by Aldrich, rose in mighty protest, stormed in a body to Stockton, and tersely told him to move on. "We can't prove for certain yore in on it," the foreman snapped, "but with our boss lyin' gunshot and the doc sayin' he ain't sure if he can pull him through, the Double J boys are a mite edgy."

Stockton's face showed his guilt, but he sneered and told the volunteer posse, "I've been planning to go, anyway."

"You'll stay healthier," Aldrich agreed. His fingers crept suggestively to his pistol butt. "I hear other parts of Arizony are more con-doo-sive to a long life and better for rattlesnakes."

A week later, Stockton vanished with his herd, after a few interesting riders and Aldrich, in his words, "just moseyed by to make sure none of the Double J stock took it into their heads and follered."

Gideon lay bandaged and broken. The doctor who had been summoned from Phoenix shook his head when he saw the location of the bullet. Rolling up his sleeves, he promptly called for cauldrons of boiling water and set to work. Aldrich, in a brave effort to do anything to help, followed the doctor's barked commands as if he'd studied surgery for years. When the bullet had been extracted from its dangerously close position to Gideon's spine, the foreman stumbled from the room into the waiting group of cowboys.

"Well?" Lonesome's question and haggard face bore witness to the outfit's love for the boss.

Aldrich wiped great beads of sweat from his forehead. "How the deuce do I know? Doc says he won't be able to tell for at least twenty-four hours, if then."

"How bad is it?" Dusty demanded, his face dark.

"If it had been a half inch closer to his spine, he'd have never walked again. As it is..." The foreman shrugged and mopped his face again.

"We should've killed them galoots outright!" Cheyenne stared at his friends.

"Naw, the boss hates killin'," Lonesome reminded. He turned back to Aldrich. "Anythin' we can do?"

"Just pray." Silence fell on the motley group, broken only when someone coughed and another shuffled a worn boot. One by one, the hands slipped out. If they followed the foreman's advice, only they and "the boss's God" would know.

For a week, Gideon's life hung in the balance. The Phoenix doctor stayed on, enlisting the help of Aldrich or one of the boys to watch while he snatched fragments of sleep. Gideon mumbled, cried out, and whispered, but loyal punchers who sat for hours by his bedside and gave him sips of water kept their mouths shut.

Not even with one another would they discuss what they heard. More than once, whoever rode herd on Gideon came out of his room with a thoughtful expression on his face. The relationship between the boss and God became clearer than ever during his delirious state.

"If he dies, I'm goin' after Stockton," Lonesome told Aldrich.

The old warhorse of a foreman, aged by years of worry and danger, shook his head. "Gideon wouldn't want that." If Lonesome noticed the change of address from *the boss* to *Gideon,* he didn't let on. Instead, he reluctantly admitted, "Yeah, too bad."

Slowly the dreaded fever cooled. On the eighth day, Gideon opened his eyes, unsure of where he was. Aldrich stood bent over him. "Don't try and talk. Yore better, and I'll get the doc."

Reassured, the injured man relaxed and slept. The second time he woke, his stomach felt hollow as a log and the dizziness in his head had settled down. But not until days later, when Aldrich and Lonesome got him up and he took a few shaky steps, did he see any of them grin.

"Whoopee!" The outfit yelped and beat their hats against their jeans. "Can't keep our Texas boss down." Leaning heavily on his supporters, Gideon dropped into a chair with obvious relief, an effort almost ignored by his friends.

"Vamoose, cowpokes, and let him rest," Aldrich ordered, and the laughing bunch roared outside to let off all the steam they'd stored up during Gideon's danger.

"Your face is blacker than a midnight storm," Gideon accused his foreman. "What's eating you?"

Aldrich slowly sat down opposite him and fiddled with his hat. "I've got a kinda confession to make."

Gideon stretched and winced when the still-healing muscles pulled. How good it felt to be alive and able to walk! "Shoot."

"The night the doc said he didn't know if you'd pull through, he said we oughta notify yore next of kin. I snooped around and put some of yore mumblings together and—"

Gideon froze. "You did *what?*"

Aldrich's plaintive tone told how much he hated his confession. "I wrote to yore—to Mrs. Judith Scott at San Scipio, and told her you were lyin' here shot up."

Every nerve in Gideon's body tingled. He stared, openmouthed, unsure whether to whoop with joy or bawl out Aldrich for interfering in what didn't concern him.

The foreman stood and regained his usual cool manner. "Just thought I'd mention it in case, uh, we get unexpected vis'tors." He clinked out before Gideon could speak.

Visitors! What if Judith and Joel should one day walk through the door of his Arizona ranch house? For the first time, he admitted the building he and his men had done that winter represented the dream they would come. He lost himself in reverie for a time, then sternly put his memories aside. Nothing had changed, except he'd gotten himself shot up, and the doc said he might never ride straight again and might walk with a limp. "Lucky at that," Doc added sourly, but Gideon just smiled. He knew the doc pretty well now, and the dedicated man would be the first to give credit to the Great Physician who pulled Gideon back from death.

He wished Aldrich hadn't told him about the letter as weeks passed and no answer came. His final hope of someday clearing himself and returning home at least for a visit flickered and went out. "Well, God, it's just us again. I'll do the best I can and trust You," he said one dusky evening when the sun's passing left trails of red and purple in the western sky. Yet he wistfully turned east and added, "But please, be with the boy—and her—and make them happy."

Hundreds of miles east of the Double J, life on the Circle S splintered with the arrival of a scrawled note. Unsigned and dirty, as if carried and passed hand to hand for weeks, the smudged name ELIJAH SCOTT with the address following was almost illegible. "What's this?" Lige demanded when Carmelita brought it to him at the supper table in early spring. He opened it, stared, and jerked as if shot. "Carmelita, where did this come from?"

Her liquid brown eyes held no guile as she said, "A man threw it from a horse and rode away, even though I called, 'Señor, do you not want to water your horse?' "

With a loud cry, Lige pushed his chair back from the table with such a mighty thrust, it overturned and crashed to the floor. He rushed to the door, yanked it open, and disappeared, leaving the door swinging. Naomi, Judith, Carmelita, and a wide-eyed Joel stared after him, then Judith came to her senses. Vaguely aware of boots pounding toward the corral, she snatched the grimy missive and read aloud.

Tell G I'm sorry. Maybe someday I'll come back. Dad, forgive. . .

The rest of the sentence was blotted, and only a sprawling *C* served as a signature. The steady beat of hooves and a stentorian voice shouting, "Cyrus, son, come back!" faded into eerie stillness. Naomi's lips trembled, and Judith burst out, "Thank God!" but the older woman finally cried, "God, have mercy on Elijah!"

Her own joy forgotten, Judith realized what this would mean to the stern father who had sacrificed his younger son to blind worship of the elder. Pity engulfed her and wiped away forever her anger at her father-in-law. The torment he had created for himself was punishment far beyond the laws of retribution.

Hours later, Lige returned alone. Joel lay asleep upstairs, but Naomi and Judith waited, huddled close to a blazing fire that seemed to offer little warmth.

"Was it Cyrus?" Naomi whispered.

"I don't know." Lige looked beaten, and Judith could not bear to gaze at him. The glazed eyes and the massive drooping shoulders showed more clearly than any cry of remorse the awful truth that lay ahead.

"Elijah, we must give thanks." Naomi stood and crossed to her tall husband. Judith could scarcely believe her eyes and ears. The woman who had sat crushed for hours grew in strength to meet the need. "Cyrus is alive. *Alive*, Elijah! All these months and years—" She faltered, then hope filled her face. "Don't you see? Our prayers have been answered!"

A ray of light penetrated Lige's despair, then died. "It is my fault," he said brokenly. "If I had been the kind of father I should have, Cyrus would have confessed openly." Misery returned to quench the hope. He crushed Naomi to him as if needing her physical presence, as if needing something to cling to while the world crashed around him. "And you, Judith, daughter, your life ruined because of me. Oh, God, what have I done? Where are the sons You gave me? Cyrus, Gideon, forgive me!" He buried his face in Naomi's lap.

Judith's heart pounded. She ran to the man whose self-righteousness had caused such tragedy. "Lige, Naomi, Gideon is somewhere in Arizona. When Tomkins came last summer, he told me." She could feel bright color creeping into her face. "My life isn't ruined. *I love Gideon.* I realized it on our wedding day. Tomkins is coming back soon, and we're going west to find Gideon."

Lige raised his head. A trace of his old arrogance reared up. *"You aren't taking Joel!"*

"Yes, Lige, I am. He needs a father." Soft color mounted almost up to her coronet of braids. "I—I am sure Gideon loves me, and he will raise Joel as his own."

Lige's body went rigid, then he threw back his head and took a deep breath. "You are right, child." He freed himself from Naomi's arms and shook himself as if coming out of a daze. "I drove my sons away. God won't allow me to destroy Joel."

Judith walked to him, took his heavy hand in her own, and gazed into his face. "Our God is a God of forgiveness. Gideon will only be glad you know the truth; I know that. You will be welcome in his home, with or without me, and Joel will always love you."

A little of the pain left Lige's eyes, but he left the room with the shambling steps of an old man who has outlived joy. Naomi ran after him and left Judith alone with the love she had openly confessed for the first time singing in her heart and in the still, spring air.

⌘

A few weeks later, Tomkins arrived. Lige Scott whitened but valiantly pulled himself together and welcomed the man who would be taking Judith and Joel with him.

"I haven't been able to find Gideon," Tomkins admitted, "but that's not surprising. Most of the messages I sent may never have reached Arizona. A man can't depend on riders who like as not take it in their heads to stop in Utah or New Mexico. We'll find him, and when we do, he's going to be one happy rancher." The miner's sally brought a blush to Judith's smooth cheeks. Yet her greatest joy came when Lige frankly told Gideon's faithful friend how he'd misjudged his son and pleaded for Tomkins to convince Gideon to forgive his father.

"Sho', he's already done that." Tomkins's hearty respect for a man who admitted his shortcomings showed in his lined face and relieved some of the suffering evident in Lige's brow. "That boy of yours is too big, or maybe it's his God that's too big, for him to hold a grudge. Better consider selling out here and heading for Arizona, Scott. Plenty of room there to leave behind troubles."

Judith saw the war that waged in Lige's heart, the leap of hope grounded by other considerations. "No, I need to stay here in case my older son comes back." The poignant admission brought tears to Judith's eyes, especially when Lige added, "Maybe someday."

"Gideon won't know me, will he, Judy?" Joel asked when she told him they were going to Arizona. "See how big I am?" He flexed his almost seven-year-old arm, and she pretended to find a muscle. "Can I take Millie? And my pony? Are Grandpa and Grandma going?" He hadn't lost his ability to ask questions.

"No, dear. Millie needs to stay and take care of the Circle S. It's hundreds of miles, and we don't have a way to take her."

"Begging your pardon, Mrs. Scott, but there's no reason Millie can't ride along." Tomkins plunged into the conversation and received a gleeful hug from Joel. "The pony's getting too small for you, young feller. Besides, Gideon will have a real horse you can ride. I found some other folks who are heading west, so I up and bought a couple of covered wagons. We'll join with the band and be real pioneers." He cocked his head to one side. "You can take that pretty little pinto Patchwork if it's all right with the Scotts."

"Absolutely." Lige acted eager to cooperate. Judith could see the memory of his and Naomi's trek west long ago color his face and bring back life. "There's a trunk of Gideon's he might as well have, too, and my daughter will want to carry bolts of goods for clothing. Probably hard to get out there."

Judith's last sight of him was at the top of the mesa with Naomi, where she had dreamed so often. To her amazement, Tomkins had discovered that her tow-headed friend Ben, who had first delivered her to the Circle S nearly three years before, longed passionately to go west and find Gideon. Now eighteen, strapping and cheery, he would drive Tomkins's second wagon.

Each day brought her closer to Arizona, closer to Gideon. If at times the thought crossed her mind he might have ridden on, she squashed it. God had worked in such incredible ways to bring them together, surely He wouldn't stop now. The dust and discomfort, storms, and threat of hostile Indians all became things she must endure.

Joel loved every minute of the long trip. He followed Ben around, rolled with Millie, and romped with others his age on the wagon train.

Some wagons turned off before the train went into Arizona. Other families saw places in New Mexico that attracted them. But Tomkins and his charges faced west, bound by a love for a young man who had captured their hearts with his sincerity and dedication. Always they asked if anyone knew of Gideon Scott. No one had heard of him until they reached Arizona.

"Gideon Scott. Hmm, name sounds famil'r," a frontiersman told them at Phoenix. He thought for a moment, his face in a dreadful scowl. Then it cleared. "Yup, he's the young feller that's set Arizony on its ear with his newfangled idees. Won't 'low no drinkin' and ree-wards his cowpunchers by makin' them part owner of the Double J. Up near Flagstaff, he is." Dismay swept across his face. " 'Fraid I got bad news for you. He got shot up bad a few weeks ago. Can't say whether he made it. You kinfolk?"

"I'm his wife." Judith felt proud to say it out loud, and she managed to smile in spite of her stricken heart. They'd come so far. *Please, God, let Gideon be all right.*

That night Joel echoed her prayer at their nightly worship they held regardless of where they camped. "God, take care of Gideon," the child prayed, his hand warm in Judith's, and together they finished with, "For Jesus' sake. Amen."

The new and strange country they traveled between Phoenix and Flagstaff brought wondering exclamations from Joel, whose gaze riveted on strangely formed cactus, red cliffs and canyons, and a host of other exciting things. Judith barely saw them. She resented the slow, steady pace of the mules that pulled the wagon, and her mind raced ahead of them, longing for the moment they would reach the Double J. The significance of the ranch's name beat into her brain and steadied her wildly beating heart when she wondered if Gideon would truly be glad she had come. As they passed through the huddle of buildings that made up Flagstaff and forged on, Tomkins muttered that they couldn't be that far from the Double J. Judith's pale face and haunted eyes urged him on, and Ben and Joel fell strangely silent. If their beloved Gideon had died, better to find it out at the ranch than from some wagging tongue in town. The hands would allow them to camp there, regardless.

⁂

Why hasn't Judith answered Aldrich's letter?

The unanswered question pounded Gideon night and day. Yet days had limped into weeks that dragged by until spring slipped into the past and summer came. The doctor had been right. Gideon would always walk with a limp, and when he rode too long or too hard, his back hurt. A dream that had begun some time before of one day retracing his wild journey from El Paso to the Double J dimmed. He didn't know if he would ever be able to ride that far, even to carry the message of his Lord as he longed to do, then return to San Scipio and stay until he found Cyrus.

Sometimes he cried out to God, wondering if his father had intercepted the letter. Even though Lige believed him guilty of despicable behavior, he'd said Gideon could stay on the ranch. Surely he would respond if he knew his son lay dying.

Hope dwindled as time relentlessly rode on. More and more, Gideon relied on his heavenly Father for comfort. He would never be alone as long as the Lord traveled with him. There had to be a reason why no word came from Texas. Gideon's part was simply to trust God in all things, even when he didn't understand.

One afternoon Gideon sat astride Dainty Bess on a rise above the ranch house. Something white moved in the distance, dipped with the contour of the hills, reappeared, and was followed by a second large white shape.

"Well, I'll be. Covered wagons!" Gideon curiously watched them, then said, "Giddap, Bess. Looks like we have company." He rode to meet the wagons, idly wondering where these settlers planned to go. When, within good seeing distance, he discerned the face of the first wagon's driver, gladness filled his soul. *"Tomkins?"* Dainty Bess raced toward the billowing white wagon sail. She slid to a stop, and Gideon exploded from the saddle onto the ground to meet his old friend.

"You're a sight for sore eyes," Tomkins greeted and pounded him on the shoulder. "We heard you might be dead, and—"

A soft patter of feet interrupted him. "Gideon, you're alive." Judith ran straight to him, heedless of Tomkins's loud guffaw.

"You came." He stared at the white-faced girl clinging to his arm. "When you didn't answer Aldrich's letter. . ." He blinked to make sure she really stood there, travel stained as he had seen her so long ago, but beautiful and with a look in her dark eyes that repaid every heartache Gideon had experienced.

"I received no letter. Cyrus wrote and asked for forgiveness, but we were coming, anyway." Tears blotted out her incoherent explanation. "Oh, Gideon, God is so good." She raised her face to his.

He kissed the trembling lips and tasted salt. His arms circled her, never to let her go. "Judith, my wife." His heart overflowed. *"Thank God!"*

A second pair of arms surrounded him. He looked down. Joel's bright head rested against his jeans.

Later, there would be time to share the last weary years, Lige's remorse and repentance, and all that had separated them for so long. The silence in the sage had been broken. When storms threatened and howled above them, Judith and Gideon would face them together, united in love and blessed by faith in their heavenly Father.

Kimberley Comeaux gets her inspiration from all sorts of places: travel, history, dreams, and once overhearing (okay. . .eavesdropping on) a conversation between a couple arguing in the grocery store line. She not only is the author of thirteen inspirational romance books but also writes and produces church musicals. She has been married for twenty-eight years to her best friend, Brian, and has one son, Tyler, and a daughter-in-law, Kellie! Kimberley resides with her family near New Orleans.

Kristy Dykes—wife to Reverend Milton Dykes, mother to two beautiful women, grandmother, and native Floridian—was author of hundreds of articles, a weekly cooking column, short stories, and novels. She was also a public speaker whose favorite topic was on "How to Love Your Husband." Her goal in writing was to "make them laugh, make them cry, and make them wait" (a Charles Dickens's quote). She passed away from this life in 2008.

Award-winning author and speaker Darlene Franklin recently returned to cowboy country—Oklahoma. The move was prompted by her desire to be close to her son's family; her daughter Jolene has preceded her into glory. Darlene loves music, needlework, reading, and reality TV. Talia, a Lynx point Siamese cat, proudly claims Darlene as her person. Darlene has published several titles with Barbour Publishing.

Sally Laity considers it a joy to know that the Lord can touch other hearts through her stories. She has written both historical and contemporary novels, including a coauthored series for Tyndale House and another for Barbour Publishing, nine Heartsong Romances, and twelve Barbour novellas. Her favorite pastimes include quilting for her church's Prayer Quilt Ministry and scrapbooking. She makes her home in the beautiful Tehachapi Mountains of Southern California with her husband of fifty years and enjoys being a grandma and great-grandma.

DiAnn Mills is a bestselling author who believes her readers should expect an adventure. She weaves memorable characters with unpredictable plots to create action-packed, suspense-filled novels.

Her titles have appeared on the CBA and ECPA bestseller lists; won two Christy Awards; and been finalists for the RITA, Daphne Du Maurier, Inspirational Readers' Choice, and Carol award contests.

DiAnn is a founding board member of the American Christian Fiction Writers, a member of Advanced Writers and Speakers Association, Mystery Writers of America, Sisters in Crime, and International Thriller Writers. She is co-director of The Blue Ridge Mountain Christian Writers Conference, Mountainside Marketing Conference, and the Blue Ridge Novelist Retreat with social media specialist Edie Melson where she continues her passion of helping other writers be successful. She speaks to various groups and teaches writing workshops around the country. DiAnn and her husband live in sunny Houston, Texas.

DiAnn is very active online and would love to connect with readers on: Facebook, Twitter, or any of the social media platforms listed at diannmills.com.

Colleen L. Reece was born and raised in a small western Washington logging town. She learned to read by kerosene lamplight and dreamed of someday writing a book. God has multiplied Colleen's "someday" book into more than 140 titles that have sold six million copies. Colleen was twice voted Heartsong Presents' Favorite Author and later inducted into Heartsong's Hall of Fame. Several of her books have appeared on the CBA Bestseller list.

More Romance Collections from Barbour. . .

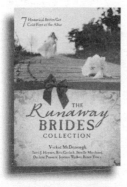

The Runaway Brides Collection

What is a woman of the 1800s to do when she feels pressured to marry without love to protect her family, to gain wealth, to fulfill an obligation, or to bend under an evil plan? *Run!* Seven women facing the marriage altar make the decision to flee, but who can they now trust?

Paperback / 978-1-68322-817-2 / $14.99

The MISSadventure Brides Collection

Seven daring damsels don't let the norms of their eras hold them back. They embrace adventure whether at home working what is considered a man's job, or leaving the city for a rural assignment, or by completely crossing the country in pursuit of a dream. And while chasing adventure, romances overtake them.

Paperback / 978-1-68322-775-5 / $14.99

Find These and More from Barbour Publishing
at Your Favorite Bookstore
www.barbourbooks.com

BARBOUR
PUBLISHING

JOIN US ONLINE!

Christian Fiction for Women

Christian Fiction for Women is your online home for the latest in Christian fiction.

Check us out online for:

- Giveaways
- Recipes
- Info about Upcoming Releases
- Book Trailers
- News and More!

Find Christian Fiction for Women at Your Favorite Social Media Site:

Search "Christian Fiction for Women"

@fictionforwomen